The -30- Press Quarterly
Issue Two

Annual Edition
2016

Cover artwork by Grim. Follow him over at www.grimstories.tv *or on Instagram* @grim.stories

Interior design by Ashley Franz Holzmann

Edited by Amber Whelpley and Ashley Franz Holzmann

30press.com

To the writers who make us us.

Table of Contents

Introduction From The Editors

This is more than just a Quarterly issue this time. This issue will include the annual best of the year from the NoSleep monthly writing competition on Reddit. Not only does this book contain the normally collected works from the winners of the October, November, and December contests, it also includes the year's best as voted by the community.

This bad boy is much heftier than last quarter. It also took us quite some time compiling and sprucing up this anthology. Hopefully you enjoy the efforts!

This eBook is a portal to a plane of existence that's just slightly out of phase with our own. At first blush, it appears the same: the people, their concerns, the look and feel of the world around them. As you delve deeper, though, you'll begin to notice that death stalks everyone from the shadows, breathing down shirt collars and running its bony hands through their hair.

Peril is the natural state of this dimension, fear a price to be paid for merely existing. If fright overcomes you—if you decide you can't live with half your body clutched in the salivating maw of madness and despair, always inching closer to grinding you away into oblivion—and you try to return home, you may find yourself stranded with no way back. Enter at your own risk.

-30- Press is a publishing company that is owned and operated by independent authors. We're an author-centric publishing house/marketing firm that believes in integrity over profits, corporate ethics, and publishing the best damn product possible. Connect with us at 30press.com.

The contest associated with this publication is run each month over at

NoSleep. Our winners and runners up receive a place in this publication as well as YouTube narrations and Reddit Gold. Donating a prize to the contest is a great way to drive traffic to your site or build a base for your product. If you'd like to donate a prize, contact /u/EtTuTortilla on Reddit.

If you find yourself completing this book and having enjoyed the experience, we ask that you please take a few minutes to leave us a review. Every review truly helps. Also, please feel free to stalk and follow the authors. They're amazing and deserve all of the non-harassing harassment you can give them..

Ashley Franz Holzmann
Chief Operations Officer
-30- Press
March, 2017
30Press.com

October
—2016—

The Summer I Met David

By K. Oresnik, Reddit User /u/*TheLovelyFreja*

Winner—October, 2016

When I was young, we lived in an old farmhouse. I remember my father telling me that it was more than one hundred years old, and that its age was the cause for the strange noises in the middle of the night. I never believed him. I was convinced that the noises were just David messing around downstairs. But in those early weeks of our friendship, no one in my family believed it was him. I never bothered to question why.

My father had inherited a sixty-five-acre pig farm that he and his father had built from the ground up. I can't remember how many pigs we had, but it was enough to warrant two barns.

I lived on this farm, with my family (three older brothers and one younger brother), until I was eight. We moved quite suddenly after a bad accident involving Joey, my younger brother, leaving him paralyzed. I didn't understand then why my father sold his farm at the time, but I do now.

We had no neighbors to speak of. To our left, you'd have to go down more than five miles of road and cross a highway before you happened upon the next home. To the right, if you followed the large hill up and went around the bend, eventually you'd come across Mr. Carlin's house. I didn't know much about him other than he owned the cornfield that sat on the other side of the street right across from our house. And that he always waved at me when he was on his tractor. My mother, at one point, had informed me that Mr. Carlin had once had children and a wife, but a house fire had killed them all, and left him alone. That was back when his house was right across the street from ours, before he'd planted the cornfield over it.

Now, it's important to note that Mr. Carlin was nearing eighty, and my mother told me that this had all happened when he was a young man. I suspect a good fifty years had passed from the time his home burned to the ground, snuffing out the lives of his family, to the summer that I met David.

It was the first Monday afternoon of summer; I was especially happy because I hadn't had to go to school, and at the time the first Monday was something of a commodity. I'd taken my pink bike with pretty red ribbons on the handlebars for a ride in the long driveway. But being the spunky six-year-old I was, I'd grown tired of doing circles just outside of my house. I craved adventure. Or at the very least, a chance to poke and prod spiders at the bridge.

I knew there was no chance of my mom or dad allowing me to go down to the bridge by myself, but what they didn't know couldn't hurt them. My dad was off on the farm, doing whatever it was he did, but my mom was still inside, which meant I couldn't go. Not yet.

I bided my time, doing circles in the driveway until I watched my mom drive away, heading toward her church group. I saw my chance, and I took it. It was late afternoon and the sun was high in the sky, beating down unforgivingly upon me. Jack, my oldest brother, was shirtless and tossing large bales of hay onto a wagon. I rode up to him, and sweetly as I could muster, I begged for permission to go, reminding him that the bridge was still in his sight and barely fifty yards from our home. Jack's lips pressed together in a thin line, like they usually did when he was thinking. His eyes narrowed and he looked back toward the barn. "Dad doesn't like you goin' off on your own, you know that. He'll want one of us to go with you."

My lower lip folded out into a pout, and I gave him the sad eyes I'd spent weeks perfecting in the mirror. "I know," I whined. "But you're busy, and Jim is with dad, and I don't even know where Johnny is. Please? I've been in the house all day helping mom with cleaning. I even scrubbed the walls, Jack! The walls!" I was acting as if I'd been done a grave injustice, when in all reality, mom and I scrubbed the walls once a month. Between a toddler brother and three older siblings, the walls were always getting filthy.

But Jack didn't know that.

My oldest brother's gaze fell upon me. And I looked up into his green eyes, giving him the most pathetic whimper. He looked over his shoulder one more time, in search of our father, who was nowhere to be seen.

I knew I had him in the palm of my hand. The thing about being an only sister in a house full of boys is that they developed this weird need to keep me safe, and also happy. And sometimes that extended to them letting me do things I knew I shouldn't have done.

"Alright, Jazzy," he said, using the nickname I despised so much. It made me sound like a baby. I wasn't a baby anymore. "But just this once, and if you get caught, don't tell Dad that I was the one to tell you it was okay. Alright?"

I jumped up excitedly. "Yes!" I cried happily, before hopping on my bike and peddling as fast I could down the gravel driveway. My plan was to get the hell out of there before Jack came to his senses and realized my dad would have murdered him for letting me go off on my own. We lived under strict rules; no one younger than Jim (at age ten) was allowed to go anywhere on their own. Even if it was just down the road. My father was a strong believer in the buddy system. His worries didn't stem from an area riddled with crime, but instead, the simple fact that it was summer. Summer meant migrant workers, and migrant workers meant a bunch of people around Mr. Carlin's house that no one in the family knew.

I managed to get my little butt all the way down to the bridge without Jack calling me back or Dad coming out of the barn and throwing a tantrum.

Once there, I spent my few precious moments of freedom twirling thin sticks into the sticky spider webs. At the first few nudges, the spiders would get excited. They'd glide across their webs in a graceful display that I can only describe as beautiful. Their small, shiny front legs poked and prodded at the stick, as it tried to decide what was invading its space and ruining its home.

After several seconds of trying to decide what it was, the spiders would often climb off their web and explore the stick, giving me a chance to put my palm below them and wait patiently for them to descend down and tickle my skin with their tiny prodding legs.

My mother was terrified of spiders. My brothers, not wanting me to inherit her debilitating fear, had taught me that they were nothing more than hairy bugs. I thought them to be endearing, which was admittedly strange for a small girl.

I was about to let my fifth spider of the day go in the weeds beside the metal posts of the bridge when a small voice drew me out of my own musings. "Is that a spider?" it asked incredulously. I stood up and turned around only to find a boy, probably a year or two older than myself, standing just a few feet away from me. His eyes were locked onto the spider that was now dangling from my fingertip. He gave me a toothy grin as I stared up to him.

"Yep," I answered, very used to people being overly critical of a weird girl who liked arachnids.

"That's cool. I love bugs," he admitted.

My eyes lit up. "I do too!" I gushed happily. "My name's Jasmine. What's yours?" I asked, using the same old introduction they'd taught us in kindergarten and first grade.

"David," he answered, pronouncing the word funny. He said it Dah-Veed. It took me a full minute to put together that he was Mexican. Which made sense given his dark hair and skin, something not often seen in the area I lived in.

"Wanna play?" I asked, handing the boy a stick. He said he did, and there we stood, shoulder to shoulder, disrupting webs and talking about the pretty designs on the backs of the spiders.

Soon enough we'd run out of the large, black-furred arachnids to play with, but that didn't stop David. He went wandering over to the other side of the bridge and found a sleek, bulbous, fat spider to poke at. "Come here, Jasmine!" he called, laughter in his voice. "Look at how pretty this one is! You should hold it! I'll pretend to take pictures!"

I was filled with a sudden, tingling sort of fear that started at the base of my spine and moved up to my limbs. My tiny hand reached out and slapped the stick away from David's hand. "Ow!" he shouted, glaring at me.

"You can't touch those, David," I explained, trying to keep my sudden fear and anger in check. I did what I could to explain this to him like my father explained everything to me: calmly, quietly, without anger or judgement. "You see that red dot on its back? If you look at its belly, it'll have a red hourglass on it. That means it's poisonous. It's a black widow," I explained. "You can't touch them. If you get bit, you could die."

David only laughed, shaking his head. "Who told you that?" he asked. "Whoever it was is lying. My dad and I catch these all the time," he insisted. He spoke with such conviction and such surety that I remember thinking that perhaps I'd remembered wrong. Maybe it was the spiders with the yellow dots on their backs that I shouldn't play with.

I looked over to him. "Are you sure?" I asked. I waited for a nod before I picked up my stick and began the slow process of twirling it along the web.

The spider had just started poking at the twig when a familiar voice called for me. I spun around, eyes on my house, where Jack stood waving his arms. "Come inside! It's time for dinner!"

"Can I bring my friend?" I shouted back.

Jack paused for a long time, eyes on David and me before he nodded. "Sure. Why not?" he asked. "I'll ask Mom to set another place."

I threw the stick to the ground, abandoning the spider. I turned back to David, who for one reason or another looked a little angry. I brushed it off, not knowing or really caring why he might be upset. "Do you want to come inside for dinner?" I asked.

David's features slowly began to melt into the same pleasant look he'd worn since we'd met. He gave a nod. "Sure. Thanks."

"Do you need to ask your mom or dad?" I asked as I lifted my bike from the ground.

David shook his head. "No. My dad won't worry unless I'm out past dark," he promised. At only five pm, there was still plenty of summer sun left in the sky.

Together, we walked down the road and across the driveway. I left my bike in the garage, and then the two of us went inside. "Hey mom!" I shouted as I entered the home. I pointed over to David. "This is Dah-Veed," I said, using his pronunciation of the word. "I met him by the bridge," I explained. "His dad won't care if he's here as long as he's home by dark. Can he stay for dinner?"

My mom turned to us, her eyes sparkling with amusement and happiness, probably because for the first time in forever I'd brought home a friend. I knew from experience that because David was a boy, the whole house was going to be making jokes about us dating or getting married, but I didn't think I cared. "Sure he can stay," Mom answered with a nod.

"Thanks!" I chirped.

"Thank you, ma'am." David said, a smile on his lips, using the title that most kids used when speaking to an adult.

"You're welcome!" my mom sang back as she grabbed up a heaping glass bowl of potatoes from the counter and walked them into the dining room. Everyone else was already sitting, expectant eyes on David and me as we walked through the threshold.

Confusion washed over the faces of my older family members, while Johnny—who was only two years older than myself—laughed and mumbled something under his breath about me not being able to find a real friend.

I looked over to David, who, to my dismay, looked entirely ashamed. I had never been so livid in my whole life. Johnny's friends were all terribly racist, and while my mom and dad did what they could to stop the behavior, a racist comment, much like this one, occasionally slipped out. I glared at him, but my father was the one to speak. "Johnny!" he snapped. "That isn't nice! Apologize!"

Johnny looked back at us with irritation written across his features. "Sorry," he sneered. He didn't mean the apology, that much was positively certain, but no one else bothered to tell him off so David and I simply took our seats quietly, right beside one another. David glared at Johnny for several seconds, but Johnny made a point of completely ignoring him.

"So, David, where are you from?" my mother asked.

"Mexico," David answered. "My dad and I come here every year in the summer so my dad can work. Sometimes I help too."

"Oh, that's very interesting!" my mother chirped before looking over to meet my eyes. "How did you and David meet?"

I knew exactly where this was going, and I wasn't having any of it. "Mom! We aren't dating!" I insisted.

My mother raised her arms in surrender. "No one said you were. I just asked where you met."

"By the bridge," David answered. I glanced over to him, my mouth filled with my mother's famous herb-and-garlic mashed potatoes. David was sitting politely with his hands folded in his lap. For one reason or another, he hadn't touched his food. In fact, his eyes were still locked on Johnny, who only now seemed to even notice us. His brows furrowed in response, his lips pressed into a thin line.

"Yeah, by the bridge," I answered, once my mouth was no longer filled with potatoes. I watched slow anger rise up in my dad's face and Jack shift uncomfortably in his seat. My father opened his mouth, probably to ask why I thought it was a good idea to go out to the bridge by myself. Suddenly I remembered the spider, and while I hadn't intended to cut him off, I also hadn't grown enough to develop the patience needed to wait for someone else to speak while something so pressing was searing into my brain. "Hey, what spiders are the black widows? Are they the ones with the yellow dot? Or the red dot?" I asked.

My father's brows shot up. I watched Jack visibly relax into his seat. He tossed me a grateful look. "Red dot," Dad answered, his voice leaving no room for argument or uncertainty. I could tell in that moment that he'd entirely forgotten the bridge, his mind now on spiders and keeping me away from the more dangerous ones. "Why? Did you see one?" he asked.

"Yeah, David thought we could play with it, but I told him we couldn't." I left out the part where I decided to do it anyway. I hadn't touched it, after all.

There was no chance it had somehow bitten and poisoned me.

"You and David stay away from those," Dad said, his eyes narrowed at the two of us.

"Yes, sir," we echoed. My father didn't often look angry, so in the rare occasions like this one I was sure to listen to him.

Dinner passed quickly, and David and I were told to go outside and play but to stay clear of spiders. David was acting really weird that night, almost angry. I wondered if it was because Dad had yelled at us. I put the thought out of my mind and played until the sun touched the horizon, when David said he needed to go, and my mother called me inside.

The next several weeks passed without incident. David started coming over every day, becoming a regular fixture in the house. We' played outside, we went with Jim and Jack a few times to go fishing, we even accompanied Mom into town once to go shopping. Mom was nice enough to buy us both an ice cream. Unfortunately, the moment we got outside, David dropped his. He looked so crushed and so embarrassed about the whole thing that I quickly offered to share my own. He took me up on the offer, and my mom was sure to tell me how nice I was being.

I started drawing pictures of David and me together. I was a rather talented artist at my meager six years of age. What I mean by this is that my stick figures had both the proper color of skin and hair. And we were both clothed.

David had quickly become my best friend. It wasn't odd for him to come over and stay from daybreak to sundown. Sometimes he'd be waiting for me outside when I woke up. I'd run to the door, fling it open, and tell him to come in. He always helped with chores, even though Mom said he didn't have to.

We'd been friends for nearly two full months when he first breached the subject of a sleepover with me. I agreed, and hastily ran inside to ask my mom and dad, who were sitting at the table discussing bills. They agreed, but on the condition that he slept downstairs on the couch, and that he and I cleaned up after ourselves.

That evening, after dinner and a few more snarky remarks from Johnny (who was good at making David feel bad about himself—something that pissed me off to no end), we got to work on making David's bed. We made a veritable fort that we decided we'd play in before we went to bed. We'd decided we were in the ocean. David and I were pirates, looking for buried treasure. We searched high and low, crash landing on no less than five islands before our fun was cut short at around nine pm, nearly a full hour after my normal bedtime.

I fell asleep with thoughts of our adventures dancing through my mind. We'd done so much in the past two months. I felt so lucky to have met David. I wouldn't admit it at the time, but I will now. I had quite a crush on him.

I was woken from my slumber in the middle of the night by a large crash and a howling scream. Fear, the likes of which I'd never experienced before, coursed through my body as I threw my blankets off myself and joined the ranks of my parents and older siblings as we rushed down the hall. Joey, my only younger brother, could be heard crying from his bedroom. Jim was quick to rush to him; his soothing voice could be heard through the hallway as he assured the three-year-old that everything was okay.

I remember Jack stopping me just as I'd hit the banister. "Whoa there, Jazzy," he said. His voice was too quiet, too calm. Everyone else sounded frantic and someone downstairs was crying. I was terrified that David had gotten hurt.

"What's wrong?" I demanded.

Jack paused, his eyes moving back to the staircase before looking back at me. "Johnny just fell down the stairs. He'll be okay," he promised.

I watched him carefully. If he was okay, and nothing was wrong, then why couldn't I go see? It didn't make any sense. And then one shouted sentence made everything clear. "I CAN SEE MY BONE!" Johnny wailed from the base of the stairs.

Jack winced, and my heart skipped a beat. "Liar!" I hissed. "He's not okay!" Unshed tears began to well up in my eyes as Jack tried to direct me back to my bedroom. I wasn't having any of it. I tried to push my way back toward the stairwell, but I was barely forty pounds, standing several inches shorter than most of my peers. Jack had taken after my father. He was more than six feet tall, and weighed at least 150 pounds. After several long seconds of squirming and struggling against his vice-like grip I took to screaming. "I wanna make sure Johnny's okay!"

"What if I come with you?" a very groggy David asked from the staircase as he walked up, dodging body after body of worried family members..

I looked up to Jack. "Is that okay?" I asked, wiping new tears away from my eyes with the sleeve of my pajamas. "Can I go to my room with David?"

Jack swiped black hair back with his hand and gave a nod. He leaned down and kissed my forehead. "Sure, Jazzy. Sure," he answered. "Dad and Mom are gonna take Johnny to the hospital. If you or David need anything, you can come and get me. Okay?"

David and I nodded before heading back to my bedroom. We laid down in my bed, head to foot, and talked. We talked about how Johnny's arm looked. David had seen it on his way up; he said the bone was jutting out of the wrist and looked whiter than anything he'd ever seen. He told me my mom put his arm on the pink pillow that we all hated, then she and my dad ushered him outside. We stayed up until sunrise touched the dark sky. David talked all the while, trying to make me feel better. He assured me that Johnny was fine. He'd be okay. He just needed a cast and probably some stitches.

David had a really funny way of always making me feel better.

Over the course of the next few days, Johnny went on and on and on about how he'd been pushed down the stairs. He blamed Jim, but he and Jack shared a room, and Jack assured him that he'd been sleeping the whole time. He'd only woken seconds after Jack did. All the same, Johnny was certain it had been Jim, because he said he saw someone just a little shorter than himself right behind him when it happened. Despite Jim being a full two years older than Johnny, Jim, like me, was short for his age. While Johnny and Jack were both giants.

Johnny and Jim fought for days after that. Always arguing. Always shouting at each other. At one point, Johnny actually took a swing at him. Jim managed to dodge the blow, but Dad had to intervene. He took them both to the kitchen to talk. No one was supposed to listen in when someone got in trouble, but I was a curious kid and decided that I needed to know what was being said. David and I stood in the long weeds that had once been part of the flower garden. The beautiful bursts of violet, red, and pink had eventually been taken over, and drowned out, by chickweeds and dandelions after Joey was born, and Mom suddenly didn't have time to tend to flowers. Our backs were against the front paneling, just below the opened window. We made no noise as we listened intently to what was being said.

Dad questioned Jim over and over about what had happened, but Jim insisted he had been asleep. Johnny called him a liar a few times, and eventually Jim broke down. I'd never heard Jim cry before. It was heartbreaking. He asked over and over why no one believed him, reminding Dad that Jack had vouched for him.

Dad apologized, but Jim wasn't having any of it. He asked to go to his room. I could tell Dad felt bad, just by the way he fell silent, likely nodding his head in response. The squeak of the chair against linoleum was suddenly the only sound in the kitchen. After a solid minute of silence, Johnny's voice rang out. "Someone shorter than me pushed me," he insisted. "It had to be either Jim or Jasmine." I'd heard enough at that point. Looking back, I wish I would have paid more attention to what was being said. But as it was I began to step away. I stopped when I caught sight of something moving in front of me.

Suddenly, the world ceased to exist. Every noise, except the rush of my own blood behind my eardrums, faded away. I was hyper aware of my own heartbeat and the rapid, ragged breaths that tore through my chest.

I've always loved the way snakes move. It's so pretty. So graceful. They have a quiet elegance about them. But this snake made that dizzying, heart-pounding sort of fear creep up on me. My hands went numb, my breath hitched, and I let out a small, distinctly feminine squeak. David looked down, a wide, genuine smile brushed across his lips. "Hey! Look! A kingsnake!" he said happily.

"That's not a kingsnake," I whispered, keeping myself as still as possible. "It's red, yellow, and black. It's a coral snake. They're poisonous!" My voice was tight and pinched. I felt as though I'd been punched in the gut. I kept imagining it rearing up and striking, biting me down to the bone and stopping my heart with its poison.

"No it isn't," David insisted as he reached down to grab it by the back of the neck. Aside from becoming very still, it didn't react. It acted as though it hadn't even noticed his presence. "See? They're nice. I catch these all the time back home in Mexico. You can pick it up. It won't hurt you."

I looked at him with hesitance in my eyes. He'd been wrong about the spider. Why wouldn't he be wrong about this? David rolled his eyes and began to pet it with his free hand. "See? It's fine. Just pick it up. I'll keep its head steady," he promised.

I should have listened to my gut. I should have walked away right then and there. But I didn't. My six-year-old brain was insisting that if David could touch it, so could I. Slowly, so as not to scare it and make it wiggle free of David's grasp, I bent down, my arm outstretched.

"Jasmine!" came a frantic shout from my left. David and I both jumped up. The snake bolted free, heading straight toward me. I shrieked, looking from the snake to my now terrified brother. Jack grabbed a nearby shovel and sprinted toward me. "Stay still! Stay still!" he shouted.

David was halfway across the driveway. "Run!" he shouted. "Run! Before it bites you!" Had I been thinking clearly, alarms would have been going off in my head. If it was a kingsnake, if David knew this, then why did I have to run?

But I wasn't thinking rationally. I was caught in the moment. My heart was in my throat. My hands were clammy and shaking. I felt like I was going to puke. Jack was too far away to help. The snake rose up on its belly, bobbing back and forth as most snakes will before they strike. "RUN!" came David's command again.

I did.

I got two steps away when I felt something hit the back of my shoe. I let out a howl of terror.

THWACK

Before the snake had a chance to strike a second time, Jack's shovel buried its head into the ground. The snake's body writhed and struggled beneath the heavy metal. Its tail whipped the ground beneath it and flattened out chickweed. Jack stomped on the metal part of the shovel over and over, causing the crunch of breaking bones to echo into the pseudo-silence.

The familiar sound of the screen door slamming caused me to jump and spin to face the front of the house. My dad rounded the corner, trailed by my mother, both demanding to know what the noise was about. Jack lifted the shovel and hit the snake a few times just to be certain before he scooped up the corpse and showed my father. "Dummy nearly got herself killed. She tried to pick this thing up," he answered.

All the color leaked from my parents' faces as they stared down at the three-foot behemoth. "Jasmine!" my mom shouted, her eyes alive with fear as she stared over to David and me. "You know what a coral snake looks like!"

My bottom lip quivered and tears spilled down my cheeks. "I thought it was a kingsnake," I insisted. "I really did."

"Jasmine, we don't have kingsnakes around here," my father explained. The fear had been replaced by a quiet sort of anger. I knew I was in for it, and as shameful as it is to admit, I didn't want to go down alone.

"David told me it was!" I shouted. David's eyes widened, and he glared death at me as I confessed to everything. "He told me it was kingsnake! He told me to pick it up! He told me to run!"

"Enough!" my dad shouted. "If David is going to get you hurt, then he can't come over anymore!" he boomed. It was the sort of angry shouting that seemed to shake the whole world. I'd never heard my father yell before. To say I was terrified is an understatement. "You hear that, David?" my father asked, glaring daggers at the two of us. "You aren't welcome here anymore!"

David grabbed my hand, tears in his eyes. He pulled me toward the end of the driveway. "Let's go!" he shouted. I tried to stop, but David was strong. So much stronger than I remembered him being. He pulled me across gravel, forcing me to go.

"Get your ass back here, Jasmine!" my father roared. He'd never sworn before that point. Suddenly, I stopped struggling and began sprinting right beside David. I'd never been spanked. Not once. But I knew, from the stories Jack had told me about when he was little that that's what was about to happen.

"Where are we going?" I asked, as our shoes bounced against the pavement of the road. My heart was clawing at my chest, begging to be freed. My whole body thrummed with excitement and fear. I felt like I couldn't breathe. Tears streamed down my face.

"Into the cornfield!" David shouted back. "We'll go find my dad! He won't let your dad hurt us!"

Looking back now, I know that under normal circumstances, I'd never run from my father. I'd never been abused, and had no reason to fear him. But in that moment, I was terrified. Heavy footfalls exploded from behind us, but I never looked back. I slipped into the cornfield behind David. We dodged large stalks of corn, running this way and that, trying to put as much distance between us and the footfalls as we could.

I shrieked when something hard grabbed my shoulder. Whoever it was forced me to stop. David continued to pull at my arm. It felt as though he was going to rip it from its socket. I howled in agony, my limbs swinging wildly as I tried to prevent myself from being stolen away from my best friend and the promised safety of his father.

"Holy fuck!" Jack breathed. With those words, sudden clarity settled over me. Something was very wrong. Jack didn't swear. My father forbade it. Jack's arms suddenly wrapped around my waist. "Holy fuck!" he repeated. Dread filled my small body. Jack wouldn't have sworn unless something was terribly wrong.

I stopped thrashing. I looked up to Jack. I'll never forget what I saw in that moment. Jack's eyes were wide with fear. His mouth was agape. His hands were shaking. Sweat glistened upon his brow. I'd never seen my older brother afraid of anything. In my eyes, Jack was just as superhuman and invincible as my father was. They were both massive men, more than six feet tall. Both rippling with muscles. Both with beards and calloused hands.

Something had frightened Jack, and as far as I was concerned, if it was enough to frighten him, we were all in trouble. I scanned the field around us, but saw absolutely nothing. My eyes landed on David, who must have seen the same thing Jack did, because he let me go and ran away. "NO!" I shouted. "David! Come ba—"

Jack clamped a hand over my mouth, stifling my urgent cries. If there was something in the cornfield with us, David shouldn't have gone off alone. I considered biting Jack's hand just so I could call out to my friend. But just as I managed to get a small piece of flesh between my teeth, Jack began to swear again. "Shit!" he squeaked, tightening his grip on me. The absolute fear in his voice stopped me from my endeavor. I wanted to ask what was wrong, but his hand was still firmly clamped against my mouth. "DAD!" he shouted as he sprinted toward the road.

"What? Did you find her?" Dad shouted back. I was being jostled back and forth, the motion of it all making me sick to my stomach. I tried to reach the ground so I could run beside Jack instead of being carried. But Jack had me pressed against his chest, my feet dangling helplessly above the dirt.

"DAD!" he shouted again. "DAD!" His voice broke, and I looked up. A fresh wave of nausea washed over me when I realized he was crying. "DAD!"

My dad's voice became frantic as the two of them searched for one another. Finally we broke free of the cornfield just as my dad took a step in. "DON'T GO IN THERE!" Jack shouted, tears streaming down his face. My dad's face paled for the second time that morning. I don't think he'd ever seen his adult son cry. My mother was in a panic behind him, demanding to know what had happened. Jack shouted again that Dad needed to get out of the cornfield. My father eventually stepped away, humoring my brother. My parents flanked him as we all sprinted back toward the house.

Jack practically dropped me onto the kitchen floor, but I didn't really notice. I was too busy watching him cry, and shake, and try to stutter out things that just weren't making sense. Eventually, my eldest brother, that I'd come to think of more as a god than a man, collapsed onto the ground. He cried into himself. Curled up in a ball like a scorned toddler. That image is forever burned into my brain. The utter helplessness that radiated off him. The agony that was etched into each of his features. It's maddening to think of, even now.

After what felt like hours of my brother sobbing on the ground, my mother rubbing his back and cooing soft words, he composed himself enough to speak. "Look at her arm! Look at her arm!" he shouted. His hand shot out to grab my own. He pulled me toward himself. My father stepped toward us. I shrank away, unsure of what to expect from him. But the look of worry in his eyes quelled any fears I had of physical punishment.

"What happened?" he asked, staring down at the handprint-shaped bruise that David had left on my arm. I hadn't noticed it until that moment. Once pointed out to me, I remember feeling more confused than frightened or angry. I eyed it curiously. I'd never bruised so easily before. What's more, I'd never gotten a bruise that large before. "Jasmine?" my dad asked, cupping my chin in his hand. He forced my head up and stared down at me with green eyes. "What happened?"

I gazed back at him, dumbfounded. Why was he concerned with a bruise? Odd as it may have been, it wasn't important. Jack and David had seen something terrible in the cornfield. Why weren't they storming outside, guns in tow? Why weren't they shooting whatever had my brother so frightened? Mountain lions were prevalent in the area; I assumed he'd seen one of them stalking us. Or perhaps he'd seen a raccoon, wobbling with the telltale signs of rabies. My dad had shot one of those once in the backyard. My mother had cried for hours afterward. It seemed logical that if it brought her to tears, it would do the same to Jack.

Despite the utter confusion that plagued my young mind, I answered him. I just assumed we'd get to whatever it was that had happened as soon as he knew I was okay. "David tried to pull me—" I had intended to tell him the whole story about how David and Jack had treated me like a ragdoll and played a quick game of tug of war before whatever it was that was in the cornfield had scared him away.

"No! Jasmine, tell me what really happened!" Dad shouted again. I jumped, pulling my arm back, not really understanding why I was in trouble.

"That is what happened!" Jack said, his voice obtund and distant. He sounded distraught, broken, and a little angry.

"What do you mean, 'that's what happened'?" my father demanded. My mind was spinning. Why were we talking about David? Why did anyone care about what happened between me and David? Why was this what we were talking about?

"I MEAN WHAT I SAID!" Jack shouted, burying his face in hands. I jumped, letting out a small squeak as I put a few feet between myself and the cluster of family members. No one yelled at Dad. No one. That was suicide.

But Dad didn't get angry. He didn't shout. He didn't threaten to kick Jack out. Instead, his features crumpled and he looked back to me. "Jasmine, tell me what happened." There was something about his voice that made my stomach hurt again.

"I JUST TOLD YOU!" Jack shouted, standing up suddenly from his place on the kitchen floor. He stabbed a hand at the refrigerator, to the picture of David and me holding hands. "He looked just like her fucking drawings!" My heart leapt. Jack swore again. But as my eyes went over to my dad, I realized he wasn't angry. He acted as though he hadn't even heard the word. His features were pale and his hands shook at his sides. "Skinny kid, brown skin, black hair, jeans, red shirt."

It was in that moment that something struck me. I'd never thought much about it before, but the way Jack shouted about David's clothes made me realize I'd never seen him outside of his red t-shirt and dirty jeans. "But…" Jack's voice drew me out of my thoughts. "But…" His voice broke, and he buried his face in his hands again, tears streaming down his face.

"What?" my mother asked. "Jack! What!"

Jack looked up to them, his face white as a sheet. Tears stained his cheeks and ran into his beard. His voice trembled. "He didn't have any eyes."

***

The couple days after my ordeal with Jack and David in the cornfield left me

21

feeling broken and hollow. I had a million questions, but as it turned out, no one was willing to even speak of my friend. My mother acted as though it hadn't happened at all. I'd ask her some question about how she'd spoken to him if she'd never seen him, and she'd shush me. It was the single most frustrating experience of my life.

Dad got really quiet; he hardly talked to anyone unless he absolutely had to. He always looked tired. Always raggedy and worn out. I found out about a week after our escape from the field that Dad was sleeping on the porch with a loaded shotgun at his side. He didn't buy Jack's story of David's missing eyes. He'd come up with his own theory. Someone was hiding the cornfield, and had tried to kidnap me. He wanted to make sure they didn't come back.

It was a weak theory. One formed on little grounds. But he was a religious man, grasping at straws, trying not to believe in the monster under the bed.

I think Jack's reaction was the worst, though. He went from being an outgoing, loving, wonderful older brother to a complete stranger. He was a jittery, anxious mess. He mumbled, constantly, about empty eyes. He was plagued with nightmares so intense that he'd wake screaming in the middle of the night. Most of those nights, he would flail about. Twice he knocked his lamp off the side table. Each time, it caused a thunderous, ear-splitting noise that made my heart jump into my throat. Both times, my parents ran into his room to make sure he was okay.

By the third time a loud noise came from his room, neither of my parents checked on him. While they weren't angry with him, and while they wanted to help, none of us knew how. So we ignored it. It probably wasn't the best approach, and I know Jack felt disconnected with the family. Looking back, I wish I'd found a way to reach out to him in his time of need.

Johnny and Jim became distant, though not in the same way as Jack. They did it on purpose, never staying in the room with anyone but each other for very long. They grew unbelievably close and began to watch movies with each other almost every night. Usually they were superhero themed, their favorites being Superman and Batman. While they weren't thrilled with being around the rest of the family, they made it very clear that they'd rather die than be in the same room as me.

But in the end, I'd finally gotten the answers I'd craved from the two of them. They'd been in the living room watching *Superman II* when I climbed up on the couch. Johnny scowled at me, but I pretended not to notice.

My six-year-old frame fidgeted on the couch as I waited for a good point on the movie to speak. After what seemed like years, there was a lull in the action. Seizing the moment, I turned to my brothers. My stomach flipped with nervousness but I pressed on anyway. How else was I going to get answers if not through them? Mom and Dad weren't going to tell me anything, and asking Jack anything right now seemed cruel. "How'd Mom talk to David if he wasn't there?" I asked, proud of myself for keeping my voice steady.

Johnny glared over to me, his lip curled up in a sneer. I shrank back, suddenly very worried that my question might result in physical repercussions. I'd been hit, once, by Johnny, and wasn't eager for a repeat. "She didn't talk to him, stupid," he hissed, his voice flat and cold. It made my heart speed up. "You were playing a game. She just played along. Don't you remember when Jim had an imaginary friend and Mom and Dad talked to it too?"

"Yeah," Jim sneered. "At least mine was normal. It was just a dog. And I knew it was fake."

I lifted my arm in protest, brandishing the massive bruise along my forearm. "Does this look fake?" I demanded, my eyes narrowed in absolute hate.

Johnny's face twisted into a hateful glare. His teeth gritted tightly together. My heart fell. I tried to scramble away, but I wasn't fast enough. Something hard collided against my back, sending me crashing against the pale living room carpet. Pain bloomed along my side and arms. I turned around. My brothers wobbled and became distorted as I watched them through tears. "Get out of here, freak!" Johnny hissed.

I picked myself up and did as I was told, wiping tears away from my eyes with the sleeve of my shirt. I cried that night, like most nights after David's disappearance. Despite knowing it was wrong, because of all the pain he'd caused my family, I missed him. He'd been my best friend. He'd made me feel better when Johnny broke his arm, and I knew he'd make me feel better about Johnny pushing me.

My six-year-old mind wasn't capable of understanding what was going on. I couldn't believe that David, who had seemed so very real to me, was imaginary. I couldn't accept that no one else could see him. I couldn't understand why Jack was so sad and frightened.

My loyalty to my best friend hadn't faltered. I was positively convinced at the time that David hadn't meant any harm. I fully believed that he'd only pulled me into the cornfield because he was frightened of my dad—an understandable reaction. My father was scary when he was angry (something that, admittedly, didn't happen often).

At the time, it never crossed my mind that he'd actually tried to kill me twice. I never pieced together that he had known both the black widow and the coral snake were venomous.

The days dragged on. I fell into a deep depression. Eating and sleeping became hard. I was no longer in love with the outdoors. I was actually looking forward to the start of the school year. It was a welcomed change from being stuck at home all day with siblings who were either broken or completely hated me. The only person that had remained unchanged by the events was Joey, and he was simply too young to have developed resentful feelings toward me.

Our family seemed entirely broken, and I felt that I was to blame. I tried to fix us twice. My first attempt happened at dinner time, exactly one week after my escape from the cornfield. I'd waited for everyone to sit down and begin eating before I announced that everything was okay, because David did have eyes. Everyone fell silent. Johnny and Jim glowered at me. My mother told me that David wasn't appropriate dinner conversation. Jack broke down and left. My dad announced he wasn't hungry and retreated to the back porch. I excused myself and went to my room, where I continued to brood, feeling worse for having broken us further.

My second and last attempt came the following day. It was Sunday; we were on our way to church and I suggested, in all my six-year-old wisdom, that we take our concerns to the priest. My father locked on the brakes so hard I thought I might fly clear to the front seat. My mother glared down at me. I thought Johnny was going to skin me alive, the way he glared. Jack cried again. I was told that I should never tell anyone outside of the family what had happened.

I decided in that moment that the only way to save our family from this odd sort of destruction was to completely ignore the subject of David entirely. After all, that seemed to be what everyone else wanted.

Days bled away, and eventually I had my first nightmare regarding my old friend. In the dream, I was asleep, until I felt a light, slick prodding at my cheek. I opened my eyes, only to see an eyeless David standing above me. I woke screaming and crying. When my mother rushed in to see what was wrong, I lied. I told her I'd had a nightmare about being chased by a massive dog. It had been a reccurring dream for me just last year, and was the sole reason my father had yet to get the German Shepherd he so desperately wanted.

She believed me. She gave me a kiss, a hug, and told me to curl back up. She reminded me that there weren't any dogs around.

I didn't sleep for the rest of that night.

The next day, I was greeted with terrible news. Mittens, the barn cat who had just had a litter of kittens less than two months prior, had gone missing, along with all seven of her babies. My brothers and I spent hours looking for them. We even set traps, arming them with fresh meat and wet cat food. It took a solid three days for Jack to decide that a coyote or fox must have gotten to them. I was devastated, but I kept my sadness to myself, not wanting to burden anyone in the family with it. I'd learned over the course of the last week and a half that no one was interested in my problems. It was the sort of despondent revelation that filled me with a sudden sense of haplessness. My world, once so small and safe, had been shattered, leaving in its wake something ugly and raw.

The next few days went on as normal. I took the pictures I'd drawn of David and me, and I threw them away. Without my chatter, and the reminders that used to hang from the refrigerator, the family began to feel normal again.

Dad started sleeping in bed. Mom stopped walking around with that wide, delusional smile on her face. Jack had a few good days in which he didn't cry… and he even laughed. Johnny and Jim were still distant, but they stopped trying to push me around so much. Joey never changed. He remained the sweet toddler he was, too young to understand much of anything. It was nearly a full two weeks after David had disappeared that our family started to mend. Saturday morning had started as it usually did. Jack, Dad, Jim, and Johnny were out on the farm, doing whatever it was they did. Mom and I were inside. She was washing dishes in the kitchen. Joey was playing on the floor beneath the kitchen table, reciting the colors of his toys to himself. I was in the living room, dusting—my least favorite job.

The front door slammed and rapid footfalls echoed in the hallway. I assumed it was Jim, who often sprinted through the hallway, rounding the corner and sliding to a halt in front of Mom as she stood at the sink. He'd usually ask her for water or lemonade to bring out to the boys while they worked. I peeked around the corner, bored and looking for a reason to abandon my post. I hoped Mom would ask me to get Jim whatever it was he wanted. Mom must have thought it was Jim too, because she'd dried her hands and was waiting, leaning against the counter. She stood, looking dumbfounded as the footfalls stopped but no one entered the room. Curiously, she stepped over to the hallway to look. I watched as she paled, blue eyes widening. She wiped her hands nervously on her apron and moved back to the sink. Curious, I stepped into view. "Who is it, Mom?" I asked.

"Jim must have run back outside," she answered.

"The door only opened once, and I never heard footsteps back to it," I countered, the words out of my lips before I could stop them.

Mom's lips pressed into a thin line. Her eyes shone with an odd mixture of fear and anger. "What are you supposed to be doing right now?" she demanded.

I shrank away. "Cleaning," I answered, my voice defeated.

"Then I suggest you get to it," she snapped as she submerged her hands once more into the soapy water. I spun around, intent upon going back to my work before I was yelled at. But a sharp cry of pain caught my attention. My mother pulled her hand back; blood trickled down her hand and into the soapy water, staining it red. My eyes widened. "Son of a bitch!" she shouted. I gasped. I'd never heard her swear before. She was such a soft-spoken, sweet woman. It sounds stupid, but I didn't know she knew how to swear. "I thought I put all the knives up!"

Quickly, keeping pressure on the deep cut along her pointer finger, she rushed out of the kitchen and toward the downstairs bathroom. I could hear her fumble with the medicine cabinet as I walked closer to the sink. The large knife block that my mother kept just to the left of the sink had toppled over and three knives had fallen into the soapy water. I pulled them each out, careful not to cut myself, rinsed them off, and placed them back in the block.

"Jasmine!" my mother called from the other room. "Come in here! I need help getting this Band-Aid open!"

I glanced over to Joey, deciding whether or not I should take him with me. I stared at him as he walked from toy to toy. It was too risky to leave him alone. I walked toward him, arms out, trying to get him to come to me. "NOW!" my mother shouted from the bathroom. I jumped and scurried down the hallway, deciding that he couldn't get into much trouble in the few seconds it would take to open a bandage for my mother.

I pulled the paper apart and took the protective layer of plastic off before handing the massive bandage to my mother. She took it and placed it over the top of the huge gash before wrapping it all in what my father referred to as 'people tape.' It was some sort of medical tape used to keep water away from bandages and to keep gauze in place. We used it frequently on the farm.

I dashed back into the kitchen, my heart beating out of my chest as images of my brother getting past child locks—and under the sink to where we kept the bleach—danced through my head. But as I rounded the corner, my eyes landed on the toddler who sat under the table, playing with a small blue block. He repeated the word blue over and over. I smiled, feeling stupid for having been worried.

I scolded myself inwardly for being so silly. I'd allowed myself to get sucked in to Jack's delusions. I'd somehow convinced myself that something nefarious was happening, when in all reality, Jim had likely come in and run back out, and the knives had probably just fallen over.

It wasn't until I made it all the way back to the sink that I saw the glowing red dot on the stove. My heart sank. I made my way, slowly, over to it. All the burners had been turned up as high as they could go. Joey was too short to reach it. None of my brothers would have done that. Neither I nor my mother had done it.

Nausea swept over me as I crossed the room and turned each of them off. I should have told my mother, but she was visibly shaken from the recent happenings and I didn't want to worry her. Besides, she was only going to ignore it, the same way she had ignored everything else. When she came back into the kitchen, I only gave her a small smile. "I'll finish the dishes," I offered.

Her features softened. "Thank you, Jazzy," she answered.

I spent the next several hours on edge and jumpy. Suddenly I was unsure of everything. I couldn't convince myself that David wasn't the entity Jack thought he was. I felt like my eldest brother, constantly looking over my shoulder, waiting for something bad to happen.

But hours passed and nothing happened. Eventually I managed to put the thoughts out of my mind. Lunch came and went, the boys showered and changed into regular clothes. Joey sat on the kitchen floor with Dad while the two pushed toy cars to one another. Jim, Johnny, Jack, and I sat in the living room. Jack was reading something while the boys and I watched a movie. Johnny had tried to kick me out, but Jack had snapped at him and assured me I could stay.

Mom was tending to the garden, happy to have a break from being indoors.

"Jim!" my dad snapped from around the corner.

"What?" Jim asked, from his place beside Johnny.

My father went silent for a long time. The sound of cars sliding against linoleum had entirely ceased. Nearly a full minute of silence passed before my father responded in a small, careful voice. "Are you in the living room?" he asked.

"Yeah," Jim answered as he stood up and went to stand in the doorway. He leaned against the frame as he spoke to my dad, who was just out of sight. "What?" he asked again. Silence.

Jim stared into the room expectantly before understanding washed over his features. He stiffened, his eyes widening. "Is Mom in the bathroom?" he asked.

Johnny clicked the pause button and the familiar streaks of static molded to the screen, interrupting the fight scene between Batman and a villain I didn't recognize. We all fell silent, straining our ears, trying to listen for whatever it was that had frightened Jim and apparently my father. Finally, I heard it: the sound of the shower running. Jim was infamous for taking too long of showers, which explained why my father had barked at him for it.

"Maybe it's your mother," Dad reasoned.

I turned around, looking out the window only to find my mother, stooped onto the ground, just her hair visible in the glass. My breath hitched.

The shower immediately shut off. The door creaked open. I watched as Jack winced away, trying his best to ignore the exchange and submerge himself into his book. It quaked in his hands. He bit his lower lip. "Stay with your brother," my father commanded. I heard him move down the hall, toward the bathroom. "Jane?" he called for my mother. "Honey?"

I looked back again, only to find my mother's hair bobbing slowly up and down as she weeded the garden. I knew he wouldn't get a response.

The footfalls ended. "Who is it, Dad?" Jim asked.

Silence that seemed to last forever filled the home.

"No one," Dad answered. I jumped with the sound of his voice. Goosebumps rose along my arms. I stood up and made my way to the bathroom, shaking off Johnny's protests and squirming past Jim as he tried to physically stop me. I scurried down the hall, skidding to a halt beside my father and peeking into the bathroom. The mirror was steamed. The walls were slick with fresh water. The shower curtain had been drawn. My father was looking inside of it; the color had leaked from his face.

He took a step back and shooed me out of the room. He closed the door. The shower started again.

My father squeezed his eyes shut. I tried to turn around, but he grabbed both of my shoulders and pushed me forward with such force that I couldn't have stopped if I tried. We spilled into the kitchen. Dad immediately let me go and barked my brother's names.

The toilet flushed.

He picked up Joey and informed everyone that we were all going to town to grab ice cream. Joey clapped and shouted celebratory words.

The bathroom door opened.

Footfalls padded down the hallway.

Jack pushed Jim and Johnny out the door, his whole body trembling as he hurried them along. My father grabbed me by the arm and pulled me outside. His grip never faltered as he dragged me forward; the whole while I craned my neck around, trying to get a glimpse of whatever it was. Somehow I'd convinced myself that it couldn't have been David, that David was definitely a real person. Whatever this had been was different.

Dad pulled me outside. The warm air and the stench of the pigs outside hit me. Dad slammed the door and urgently pulled me over to the driveway. Gravel crunched beneath my feet. The door swung open. It slammed against the wall with a deafening bang. Jack screamed and immediately grabbed both the boys' arms. He pulled them along as he sprinted toward the car. Ear-shattering crashes erupted into the pseudo-silence. Over and over the door swung wildly, slamming shut and bouncing against the wall. "Jane!" my father shouted as my mother rounded the corner, heading toward the front door. "No one's inside!" His voice shook as he screamed the words.

My mother's eyes widened. She dropped her spade on the ground and headed toward us, her gait swift and clipped.

I opened the car door and was immediately hit with the smoldering heat. My father almost always let the air conditioning run for at least ten minutes before putting Joey in the car, but today was different. He buckled him into his car seat, despite his wails as the hot metal of the buckle touched his sensitive skin. "It's too hot! I'm thirsty!" he cried.

"We'll buy you a drink when we get to the store," Dad said, a wide, fake smile plastered upon his lips. I could see the fear and anger just below the surface. He looked a lot like Jack always looked. Except Jack wasn't keeping himself together nearly as well as Dad was at the moment. He was sitting in the very back of the old station wagon, his features crumpled, crying silently as he stared at the house. The door could still be heard slamming furiously.

I don't remember being scared in that moment. I could see the fear on everyone else, but my mind couldn't process what was happening. I sat quietly, stunned, unable to function or speak or even move. I simply receded into myself.

My dad peeled out of the driveway, leaving the home behind us. I think he hoped the few hours we'd be out would see everything returned to normal.

We got ice cream first; as promised, my father bought Joey something to drink as well as a small vanilla cone. Then, despite the fact that we really couldn't afford it (my father had just purchased a new work truck that same month), we went out to eat. We spent nearly three hours out before we began the long drive home.

The sun was just touching the horizon as we pulled into the driveway. Joey was nodding off. Jack was still a mess in the back. Jim was trying his hardest to comfort him. Johnny was pissed, brooding quietly to himself while glaring death to me. I was busy watching the home for any sign of a moving door.

I saw it before it hit the car.

BANG

My window cracked with the force of the heavy metal. My father swerved and nearly hit the light post. My mother shrieked. Jack burst into tears, and so did Joey. I stayed motionless. The spade my mother had been using to garden earlier had come hurtling toward me. Had my window been down, like it usually was, it would have likely driven itself straight through my skull.

"Dad, Dad, can we please, please stay at a motel? Or… or… can we grab the tent? Can we sleep anywhere but here?" Johnny begged from the backseat. I turned around to meet his gaze. He looked like he'd aged ten years in those few moments. His eyes were puffy and red from crying. His skin was blotchy. I didn't recognize him as my brother in those moments of terror.

"I… don't have any money…" I could hear the defeat in my father's voice as he spoke.

"Then the tent?" Jack begged. "Please, Dad, please, can we get the tent?" There was a certain urgency to his words that I had never heard before. A kind of fear that I hadn't known existed in adults swept over him. "Dad? Please?"

"Yeah, yeah," my dad answered, nodding his head. "Yeah, Jackie, yeah, we can camp for the night. I'll call up Steve while we get our stuff together. See if he isn't willing to drop by and do chores for the next few days. Everyone go inside, pack up your clothes, and get together the coolers. Pack food that won't go bad. Grab all the bottles we have for water, and fill them." His instructions were given in a way that left no room for arguments. His eyes landed on Joey. "Jack, you stay out here with Joey," he instructed. "Jazzy, Johnny, Jimmy, you guys all go upstairs, and stay together for the love of all things holy." He locked eyes with Johnny. "I mean it. Don't any of you go anywhere else without the others. You understand me? Mom and I will go to the basement and get the camping gear." Everyone nodded.

I could see the shame on Jack's face. Not only had Dad called him by his old nickname, but he'd given him the task of looking over Joey. Everyone knew it was just so he didn't have to go inside. He was so broken already, I don't think anyone trusted him to keep himself together long enough to do anything.

We piled out of the car. Jack grabbed Joey and set him atop the car while we all filed inside. We didn't notice the water until we got to the far end of the hallway connecting to the kitchen. There was what I thought to be a large puddle in the middle of the floor. It took until I heard the faucet to understand what had happened.

The sink was on.

Judging by the flooded kitchen, it had likely been on the entire time we were gone. Our shoes slipped and slid as we walked through the kitchen, looking around, entirely dumbfounded. My father turned the sink off, but it didn't stop the noise. Jim was the one to peek down the side hall to the bathroom. "The bathroom's flooded too," he announced.

My mother burst into tears.

"This doesn't change anything. Get upstairs. Get your stuff together," Dad insisted. We fled upstairs, only to find fresh puddles leading into the bathroom. Someone had plugged the drains in the sink and the tub and turned them both on. The bathroom and part of the hallway was flooded. It would be a miracle if the living room—the room directly below the upstairs bathroom—wasn't soaked.

While we gathered our things, and my father gathered the tent and camping equipment in the basement, my mother mopped. She cried the whole time.

Finally, we had gathered everything and headed outside. The last noise we heard before closing the door and locking it behind us was the sound of the kitchen sink turning on.

Our drive to the woods, just a few miles away, was entirely silent. We lost something that day. Something so much more than a good night's sleep or the convenience of having a refrigerator and microwave at our disposal. We lost our will to fight. We lost the upper hand we'd once had. We'd lost the battle, and whatever was in our home knew it.

It was for this reason that the next few days passed in a haze. We went to bed. We got up. We ate. We got dressed. We sat around in the woods. We didn't speak. We ate again. We sat around, silently. We ate again. We slept.

This went on for three days before my dad decided he couldn't take it anymore. His fear had melted away, leaving only anger and aggression in its wake.

Despite my mother's tears, Jack's pleas, and Johnny's refusal, we went back on the third night. My father insisted that we wouldn't be driven from our own home.

I wish we'd just left the whole fucking place behind.

The house was flooded, yet again, and the wood flooring had become waterlogged and swollen. The sinks had been shut off and drained. Somehow that was more frightening than anything. We all helped my mother mop up the mess. She still cried.

I wanted to sleep downstairs, or in the room with Jack and Jim, but my father refused. He insisted that if we ignored this presence, if we prayed, if we acted as though nothing was wrong, it would go away. Jack didn't believe him, and he made this very evident. For the first time in my life, the night ended with screams. But it was all for naught; my father won the argument. Eventually, I was sent off to bed.

I don't know how, but eventually sweet oblivion pulled me down.

Something slick and wet touched my cheek. "…Jasmine…" came the whispered call. My dream world shattered, giving way to the darkness that had encompassed my room. The sun had long since died along the horizon and the timed nightlight I had on my desk had turned off. The moon and stars were hidden behind clouds. The room was completely dark.

And then it wasn't.

For no discernible reason, the floor lamp across the room clicked on. Light flooded the room, instantly causing me to cringe away. As I slowly blinked away the pain and tried to focus, I became very aware that something was wrong. There were small puddles in the middle of the room. At first, while I studied them, my brain wouldn't allow me to fully comprehend why this was significant.

Water.

Puddles.

Footprints.

Suddenly I couldn't catch my breath. Understanding hit me all at once. The familiar urge to vomit filled me. I opened my mouth, intent upon screaming, but I couldn't force any noise to leave me. My hands shook and my bladder emptied. Hot liquid spilled down my legs and puddled beneath me, soaking into sheets. The pungent odor immediately stung my nose, causing me to gag. It was the first time I'd had an accident in years.

BANG!

I had no idea what the noise was, only that it sounded like a gun shot and had happened just inches to the left of my bed. Fear gripped me tightly, forcing the breath from my lungs and filling me with the sudden need to puke. I screamed and leapt off the bed. My legs wobbled as I sped toward the doorway.

BANG!

The door slammed

Click

The room went dark.

I spun around, my body pressed tightly against the wood of the door. I was hyperventilating, unable to take a full breath. My hands shook as I searched blindly for the light switch.

I stopped dead as a new sound penetrated the pseudo-silence.

Breathing.

I could distinctly make out someone else breathing.

With trembling hands and a new reserve to get the door open, I clicked the light on and screamed. "DAD!" I shrieked as loudly as I could. My voice was panicked. My heart clawed at my chest, trying to free itself from the cavity. Before me stood the person I'd managed to half-convince myself had just been some sort of dream, the person I couldn't believe was responsible for the horrors that had filled the home the last few days.

There David stood.

Red shirt soaked and clinging to brown skin. Black hair flattened against his scalp. But the most terrifying part, the reason for the desperate screams, the reason I couldn't breathe, or think, or even manage to cry, was his eyes.

They were gone.

Just empty sockets in their place.

"DAD!" I shrieked a second time. My hand went to the doorknob as I tried desperately to open it. It was locked! Except my door didn't have a lock.

"DAD!" Tears were streaming down my face and I suddenly realized why Jack spent his time crying. "DADDY!"

Frantic footfalls exploded from my parents' room. "Jasmine!" my dad called back, his voice wild with fear. "Jasmine!"

"DAD!" I shrieked.

I physically shook as my dad hit the door with all his might. "Open the door, baby!" he shouted, banging against it and jiggling the doorknob.

"What's wrong?" Jack's voice came out of nowhere.

David took a few slow, dangerous steps toward me, rounding the bed. His bare feet hit the ground with a sickeningly wet noise. He left puddles with each of his steps. I sucked in a sharp breath. "No, no, no, no, no!" I whimpered as I stumbled further away from him, to the corner of my room. I curled into myself. "Please leave, please go away, David," I begged through ragged sobs.

David cocked his head, slowly, staring at me with empty sockets. A wicked smile spread along his lips. He took another step forward.

"DADDY!" I choked out through desperate sobs.

"Unlock the door!" my dad shouted from the other side.

"There's no lock!" Jack's words were quietly hissed. I knew they weren't meant for my ears, but I heard them all the same. There was a pause, a full two seconds of absolute silence. David took another step.

My dad's furious pounding became frantic. I could practically hear the panic behind each of the blows he dealt to the door.

I molded myself against the wall, convinced I was going to die. "Back up," came Jack's voice.

BANG

Splintered wood showered the room as Jack's foot collided with the door, forcing it open. A figure dashed into the dark room and scooped me up, pressing me against his muscular frame. I let out a quivering breath and wrapped shaking arms around my father's neck. My small face buried into his shoulder as I cried away the fear and pain that racked my six-year-old body. "Daddy!" I said the word over and over; each time it brought with it a sense of peace and safety.

My father's hand rubbed my back, and he allowed me a few minutes of quiet as I sobbed.

"Can we leave?" I choked out. "Please? Can we go camping? Please?" I craved the boring serenity of the forest. I needed the safety the trees offered me. I couldn't stay here anymore.

"No," came my father's response. My heart sank. I began to wail. Tears streamed down my face as I loudly begged my father to allow me to leave, but he refused. "We have to ride this out, Jazzy. We can't let this thing drive us away. We can't let this ruin us." He continued to talk, but I'd stopped listening. Despair and desperation filled me to the very brim, until I thought for sure I'd burst.

"Would you like to sleep downstairs on the couch, Princess?" Jack asked, his voice soft and his features strong. He wasn't crying. He wasn't sad or frightened. He looked… determined. "I'm going to sleep down there. I'll stay with you through the night," he swore.

My father tossed him a glare but stayed quiet as I nodded my head rapidly.

Jack pulled me into his arms and a sense of safety washed over me. Despite his many breakdowns over the course of the last few weeks, I still thought of the man as invincible. I melted into his arms and allowed him to carry me down the stairs. He pulled extra blankets from the closet with one arm, because I refused to be put down.

Jack made his bed on the couch, while I curled up on the chair. I'd initially wanted to sleep beside him, but the couch wasn't large enough.

We turned on the TV and put in *Aladdin*. It was my favorite movie at the time (mostly because my name was in it). Jack, who usually wouldn't have agreed to watch it, seemed happy about it, saying he needed something light to calm his nerves.

Despite the fear that still racked me, I hadn't slept decently in nearly four days. Soon enough, exhaustion took over and I found myself fighting heavy eyelids. I dozed off around the time Genie started singing about being the best kind of friend.

When I woke up, the TV was making a high-pitched, whiny noise, a blue screen illuminating the room. The rest of the house was quiet. I nearly sank back into sleep. Had I not heard the sharp intake of breath from the left side of the room, where Jack had fallen asleep, I might have.

Jack was curled up at the edge of the couch. His whole body trembled. His eyes were wide and shiny with fresh tears. He was staring straight at me. I remember, in that moment, being confused, not knowing why he'd be looking at me as though I'd grown a second head.

"You're in my spot, Jack." The words were sharp and venomous, heavy with the promise of violence. My body stiffened. I felt as though my lungs had been deflated. My stomach lurched. Fear gripped me tightly, wrapping withering fingers around me and sucking everything but ugliness and despair away from my small body.

Slowly, I turned, only for my eyes to land on the same wet, eyeless version of the boy I'd once known. He turned to me, his lips twisting upward. "Are we having a sleepover?" he purred. David reached toward me and the world seemed to slow. I willed my body to move, but it refused to obey.

"NO!" Jack's voice boomed from my left. A massive hand wrapped around my arm and tugged me out of the chair. David's face twisted with anger, but I was safely in Jack's arms. He sprinted up the stairs, me pressed tightly against his chest, much like I had been when we'd first run from David, back when he'd been my friend instead of my monster.

Jack threw open the doors to the boys' rooms. "Up!" he shouted. "Get up! We're leaving! We're fucking leaving!" Both the boys sat up, looking rather groggy and confused, but they did as they were told.

A small shriek from the other side of the hall sent me crashing to the ground. It took me several dizzying seconds to realize that Jack had dropped me before sprinting toward Joey's room. He threw open the door. It bounced off the wall with a loud thump, causing Joey to scream louder. Jack scooped him up in his arms and headed down the hallway. The toddler never stopped screaming. "Let's go!" Jack shouted again.

"What the hell is going on?" my father shouted above the noise and confusion as he stormed out of his room.

"You want to stay in this hellhole?" Jack spat back, eyes narrowed in absolute disgust. "You fucking do it, but I'm not staying, and I'm sure as hell not leaving them," he shouted, stabbing a finger at my brothers and me. "Get your shit, and come with us, or fucking stay here. I don't give a good damn!"

My dad narrowed his eyes in anger. He opened his mouth, probably to shout back, but before he could, Jack's fist shot out. It connected with my father's jaw, sending him staggering back.

My breath caught in my throat.

I couldn't believe what I'd just seen.

Before my father could react, Jack shoved us forward. We all fled, rushing down the stairs and tearing through the hallway. My father bounded after us, roaring angrily, shouting something about kicking Jack's ass. But as we spilled outside and the cool air hit us, we stopped in our tracks.

Johnny vomited.

"Fuck!" my dad shouted.

"Fuck me!" Jack hissed.

Jim cried for the first time since my father had blamed him for breaking Johnny's arm. I didn't understand what everyone was so upset about. I followed Jim's line of sight as he sobbed and wailed. There were things hanging from the trees. They swayed as the summer breeze bade them to dance. I turned my head this way and that trying to understand what they were. At first I thought them to be hummingbirds hovering in the trees.

It took until Jim choked out the word "Mittens!" for the shapes to make any sense to me. There, in the tree, against the light of the moon, hung our cat and all seven of her kittens. Strung up like fucking Christmas decorations, their small bodies limp and lifeless. It was the single most lurid, grotesque thing I'd ever witnessed. My stomach churned. My mind went numb. I collapsed onto the ground. I couldn't catch my breath. I puked. It splattered along my legs and nightshirt.

I was a fucking mess. Covered in vomit and piss, I sobbed away the feelings of absolute terror. "Get to the car!" my father shouted, but he sounded distant, as though I was hearing him from under water. Something pushed me to my feet and pulled me toward the car. I curled into myself and sobbed the second I hit the seat.

Mom and Dad filed into the car soon afterward and we sped away from that godforsaken house. There was a lot of shouting happening, but I couldn't focus long enough to understand any of it. I tried to piece together everything I knew about the situation.

Mittens and the kittens were dead.

David had done it.

David was dangerous. I knew this because he scared Jack and Dad, the two strongest and bravest people I knew.

David was haunting us. David wasn't human.

David was going to kill me.

These thoughts ran through my mind long after my father had parked the car just outside of the woods we'd escaped to prior. They ran through my mind as the family tried without success to sleep in the cramped vehicle.

They ran through my mind until a single word, spoken in a terrifyingly familiar voice, broke through the silence. "Jasmine?"

We had been huddled in the car, holding tightly to one another as we tried to cling to thoughts of safety.

David shattered all that.

A sense of cataclysmic doom settled over us as we stared back at the sopping wet boy. I felt as though the ground had been pulled out from under me. As though the world were no longer real or solid. I felt wronged. Destroyed. Violated.

It was an odd sensation.

But one well deserved, I thought.

We'd found a haven, a place of safety. A home in the forest where we thought the monster that had systematically demolished our lives couldn't reach us.

And yet... here he was. Standing just inches away from my window. Hand on the cracked glass. Empty sockets staring out at us.

***

A scream, so loud that I felt myself vibrate with it, sliced through the silence. I still don't know who it belonged to. More panicked voices joined in before my father sped away from mouth of the forest, heading toward town.

I remember that drive being the most frightening of my life. Not because David was somewhere behind us, or because I thought he might follow us, but because of the erratic way the station wagon zigged and zagged on the empty country road. I couldn't think of anything other than the question of what might happen to our souls if we were to die in that moment. Would David capture them? Hide them away in some den, where we'd be at his mercy for the rest of eternity? Would our Heavenly Father search for us if he did?

I tried not to think about it.

My father did eighty the whole way there, never slowing down until we were on Maple Road. It was a familiar stretch of pavement adjacent to our church, dotted with small middle-class homes armed with manicured lawns and flawless gardens. The tires squealed, staining the cement with black rubber as we came to a screeching halt. My father's eyes were wide and frantic as he turned around, staring at the lot of us. "Stay right here," he commanded, before jumping out of the car and running up the cement steps to the small, blue home that we'd parked in front of.

Confusion swept over me. Aside from our church, which peeked over the tops of the trees, I didn't recognize anything. "Where are we?" I asked, looking around at the obtund faces of my family members. Joey was still wailing, snot was running down his face, and his cheeks and forehead had turned bright red. Mom was trying to calm him, but nothing was working.

"Father Brown's house," Jack answered from the back, his voice hoarse and defeated. I glanced back to him curiously. Father Brown taught at our church. We went every week, and Mom went to church group twice a week.

I wanted to know why we'd chosen to come to Father Brown's house. Despite the fact that he was our priest, we never saw him outside of church. He wasn't like any of my dad's friends, who came by on the weekend to play cards. He was practically a stranger. But another question was prodding at my small mind, one I couldn't possibly ignore. "How do you know?" I asked as I watched my father ring the doorbell time and time again.

"We went to his house for dinner once, when you were really little. It was before Joey was born. You were too little to remember," Jack explained as he leaned against the seat. His head was resting on the soft cushion. He looked exhausted, great bags perched just below his eyes. The color had gone away from his cheeks. But his eyes were open, seemingly without any difficulty. I had my doubts that he would ever sleep again.

The door swung open, pulling my attention from my brother and back to my dad. Out stepped a very disheveled-looking Father Brown. The two men spoke to one another, but even in the silence of the car, I couldn't hear what was being said. It seemed like forever before my father turned around and waved us toward himself.

Father Brown's eyes settled on each of us separately as we walked up the sidewalk. Pain washed over his features and he made a small noise of pity. "Come on inside, guys. Jasmine, Johnny, I don't have any clothes that will fit you, but you can wear one of my t-shirts for the night, and we'll see about getting your clothes washed," he informed us.

Walking into the house made me feel light. There was a certain peace, a calm sort of serenity that settled over the home. It was a welcome change from the thick, heavy feeling at our own home. Father Brown allowed us to shower. He fed us. He gave us new clothes and washed those soiled with vomit and urine.

We were sent to bed at midnight. I didn't think it possible that I would sleep, but I was proven wrong in mere minutes. I sank into sweet oblivion while curled up in Jack's arms, my face pressed into his chest. For the first time in weeks, I felt safe.

The sun was just touching the horizon when I woke up. The green numbers on the clock across the room proclaimed it to be just after five am. My throat was on fire. I hadn't realized until just then that I hadn't drank any water at all that day, and I was beginning to feel the repercussions. I laid entirely still as I toyed with the idea of getting up. I was warm and comfortable, wearing only the t-shirt Father Brown had given me. While massive, and fitting more like a dress, it still meant I was going to be cold the second I stood up. I sucked in a deep breath, deciding it was best that I just stand up and do it—if I didn't get something to drink, I'd never be able to get back to sleep. Just as I began to lift Jack's arm up off me, a voice from the other room penetrated the silence.

"Ghosts are entirely fictional. They simply don't exist. When your soul parts with this world, you cross over immediately. God doesn't allow souls to slip through the cracks," Father Brown said, his voice sounding entirely certain.

"You don't understand," my father interjected. "You didn't *see* what—"

"Hold on, hold on," Father Brown cut him off. "I'm not invalidating your experiences here, Joshua; what I'm telling you is that it is absolutely not a ghost. Now, while ghosts don't exist, *demons* are very, *very* real."

My heart leapt. Had I made friends with a demon? Was that possible? Did that mean I was bad? Would I go to Hell for talking to him? Would God be angry with me for not recognizing him for what he was? My stomach churned as I imagined all the things demons were supposed to do to good Christian families. I'd heard the stories in church. I didn't understand them entirely, but I knew they found joy in tormenting those that followed the word of the Lord.

"What can we do?" my mother asked.

"An exorcism. Unfortunately, it isn't as easy as me just coming in and reciting the rite," he informed my parents. "There is a very strict set of rules. There will have to be an investigation. We'll have to collect—"

"What?" came a shout from behind me. I screamed. Joey began to cry. Jack jumped up from his place, using his body to shield as many of us as he could. "Jasmine brought a *demon* to our house?" Johnny snarled. He glared down to me. "Good job, idiot!" My features crumpled. I hadn't been the only one listening.

Now everyone would know that I was to blame. Jack would hate me the same way Jim and Johnny did. Tears streamed down my cheeks and I curled into myself. "I'm sorry," I cried. "I'm sorry! I didn't mean to! I'm sorry!"

I'd expected angry words from my oldest brother. I'd expected him to turn on me. Instead, he kicked Johnny, making him cry out in pain. "Stop being so mean to her!" Jack snarled. "It's not as if any of us knew any better either!"

I stared up to Jack, warmth spreading through my chest as I realized I hadn't made him into an enemy as well.

"ENOUGH!" my father roared. "GO BACK TO BED!" Immediately I flattened myself down onto the ground, afraid of what might be done if we didn't listen.

Father Brown and Dad went somewhere else, probably to finish the discussion, while my mother picked up Joey and rocked him in the chair. The whole while, she glared at Johnny and me, likely blaming the two of us for having woken the baby.

I never got back to sleep that night.

The next morning, Father Brown offered to do the farm chores for us. My dad agreed that the boys shouldn't be there, but he was sure to insist that he would accompany the priest. For two days we stayed, my father absolutely adamant that no one but he and my mother were allowed to leave the safety of the home.

On the third day, everything changed. My mother and father spent every waking hour away from Father Brown's house. Despite our many prying questions, they refused to tell any of us where they were going.

School started that Monday, day six into our stay with the priest. Mom and Dad were gone, something that had become very normal for us. My two older brothers and I had gotten dressed and packed lunches, but Father Brown informed us that we wouldn't be attending school that week. We'd go the following Monday, instead. It should have been the most exciting news ever. But it felt wrong, and made me feel sick. It made the whole situation seem worse. Not only had David driven us from our home, but he'd put a stop to our daily activities. The boys had stopped helping Dad with chores. Instead, he and Father Brown did them. Mom and I didn't clean the house anymore. Now we weren't even going to school.

Everything was wrong.

I hated it.

None of us voiced our concerns; instead, we helped Father Brown with chores. We watched television, we cared for Joey, we played cards and games, and we kept our fighting to a minimum. For days this went on, until Thursday.

We woke up to find our parents still home, sitting at the table, sipping coffee with the priest as though it were entirely normal. I threw myself at both of them, showering them with love and affection. Mom was smiling. Dad seemed happy. I didn't know the reason behind their joy, but I remember feeling as though everything was going to be okay.

We were instructed to pack up our things and get to the car. Father Brown gave us each a hug or a handshake and told us we were always welcome back if ever we needed it. I remember being sad that we were leaving, but grateful at the same time. I missed my home, and while I didn't plan on ever sleeping in my room on my own again (I much preferred curling up beside Jack), I did want to go back.

When we pulled up to the home, there was a sleek, red Geo Metro waiting for us. My siblings and I tossed questioning gazes to it, but Mom and Dad didn't seem concerned. Dad parked, got out, and shook hands with a very tall, very wide man. He was dressed in black slacks and a green t-shirt. Red hair clung to his scalp and chin. Over his shoulder, he slung a green backpack with an odd, white, swirly symbol on it. He and Dad spoke for what seemed like forever before Dad motioned for us to get out.

"…feels heavy here. I don't think I've ever experienced anything like it." A light accent played along the words the new man spoke. It had a bouncy, rolling lilt to it, reminding me of leprechauns. It took me an embarrassingly long time to realize he was Irish.

"Can you do anything about it?" my dad asked, his voice trembling with concern. He was practically wringing his hands in front of himself. I looked behind me to find the rest of my family. They shifted uncomfortably, eyes darting around the farm as though they expected David to walk out of the house or barn at any moment. My mother clutched Joey to her chest, despite his protests and flailing arms. She positively refused to put him down, which only served to piss him off. He used tiny hands to push away from her, shouting something about being a big boy and needing to walk.

"Oh, absolutely!" the man answered, drawing my attention away from my brother. I watched the tension melt away from my father's shoulders as he exhaled with sudden relief.

"Why don't you show me inside, and we'll get started?" the man asked, before tossing a gaze our way. With a wide, toothy grin, he introduced himself as Brett and extended a hand to me. Jack pulled me closer to himself, although I couldn't for the life of me figure out why.

Walking up to the old, wooden porch had my skin crawling. The house looked awful. Once proud and pristine, almost every window was cracked. The paint on the siding had begun to chip. The plants my mother worked so hard on had withered and died.

Dad opened the door and we stepped inside. Goosebumps rose along my arms. The air was thick, hot, and heavy. It was hard to breathe. I suddenly felt as though ants were crawling along my skin. I reached up, taking Jack's hand in my own and molding against him. It felt so wrong here. Suddenly, I couldn't get the image of David's eyeless face from my mind.

The man placed his bag on the table and began to pull out a small white pamphlet, as well as a glass bowl and four bottles of water. Pathetic little sticky notes labeled them as 'holy water.' I hadn't known it was wrong then, but the older members of my family did. I watched as disbelief washed over my parent's faces. Jack actually laughed, a terrible, bitter sort of noise that sent a shiver down my spine.

I craned my head upward and opened my mouth to ask what was funny (or perhaps, not funny?). Before I could get a single syllable out, static erupted into the silence. I jumped. Jack pulled me up into his arms. Johnny and Jim screamed.

...*Making love until the break of dawn.* H-Town's "Knocking Boots" blared through the radio. Static. *And I will always love you! I will always love you. My darl—* Static again. *Whoot! There it is!* The radio whined, a loud, terrible screeching noise, and began to shake. It vibrated down the counter until it slid off, stretching the cord tight and dangling as it blared the words to various songs.

I screamed and buried my face in Jack's shoulder.

Brett laughed. "It's okay, dear," he assured me. "You can't let it bother you." It didn't make any sense to me. Why wasn't Brett terrified? Why didn't he jump like Johnny did? Or cry like Jack did? I sniffed away tears, and nodded. But try as I might, I couldn't make my body stop trembling. I didn't want to see David again, and I had a feeling that that was exactly what was about to happen.

I peeled myself away from Jack's chest, craning my neck so I could watch Brett while still managing to stay in my brother's arms. "Throw your little fit while you can," Brett taunted. He pulled the plug away from the outlet and allowed the radio to drop to the ground. With a smug sort of smile and a few more reassuring words, he opened a bottle of holy water.

Brett's hand hovered over the bowl. He tilted the bottle. Not a single drop poured from the open mouth before it was knocked from his hand. Holy water rained down upon the room, splattering the walls and soaking the floor. The bottle rolled, stopping only when it hit the far wall. It made a slow glugging noise as the liquid poured out onto the already-destroyed wooden flooring. Brett's eyes narrowed. He seemed genuinely confused for several long seconds before he reached for a second bottle.

SLAM

All three bottles on the table were suddenly careening across the room. They hit windows, they slammed against cabinets. One cracked the glass of the oven.

Brett swallowed hard, eyes wide with unmistakable fear.

He pulled one final bottle from the backpack. With a shaky hand, he unscrewed the top, his eyes darting around him nervously. I held my breath, waiting for David to send it hurtling across the room.

Brett poured the water.

It sloshed against the glass sides of the bowl.

With bated breath, we watched in horror and fascination as he lifted the pamphlet up off the counter and opened to the first page. He spoke in a quivering voice, without any conviction, much the way Johnny spoke to Mom and Dad when he was lying.

Brett dipped his fingers in the holy water and allowed it to drip onto the floor. "Most glorious Prince of the Heavenly Armies. Saint Michael the

Archangel; defend us—"

A small pitter-patter sliced through the silence. My fists tightened against Jack's shirt as I spun around, searching for the source of the noise.

Joey's favorite blue ball bounced into the room. We watched in utter silence and awe as it rolled to a stop at my mother's feet. Joey squirmed to get free, shouting about his ball. My mother held him tightly and moved away from it as though it might bite her.

Jack kicked the ball away from us. It spun and fled down the hallway.

It rolled back, only to stop at my mother's feet for a second time.

My heart was thrumming so quickly I thought it might actually leap from my chest. My hands were wet with sweat. Tears were streaming down my cheeks.

Brett licked his lips. The pamphlet shook in his hand. He began the prayer over, getting no further when a slow creak interrupted him.

With wide eyes I watched the cupboard just above my father's head open. He leapt away. His massive hands grabbed the shoulders of both my brothers and pulled them back, away from it.

There was no warning.

No puff of smoke, like in the movies.

No ominous music.

It just happened.

It was like an explosion. Streaks of white and blue and pink and green careened to the ground. An ear-splitting crash shook me to my very core. Before I could process what had actually happened, the shattered glass of every plate, bowl, dish, and cup my mother owned was splayed at our feet.

Every cabinet was open and emptied.

Joey was screaming. I didn't realize until Jack placed a hand on my back that I was too.

My mother had burst into tears.

My father suggested we leave.

Brett insisted he could do this, and started the prayer over.

The burners turned on. I could feel the heat from where I was. A bright light sparked to life behind the cracked glass of the oven. At first, I thought there was some sort of fire inside of it. But as it grew brighter, I recognized the shape as that of the heating coil inside of it.

BANG

The coil exploded. My mother shrieked. She turned to dart out the front door.

Something touched my foot.

At first I thought it was Jack, but it was too cold… and it was wet.

I looked down to find nothing at all. But I felt the invisible fingers tighten around my ankle.

I shrieked.

An unseen force jerked me out of my brother's arms. I hit the ground with all the force of a freight train. White bursts of light exploded into my vision. My eyes rolled aimlessly in my head as I tried to get my bearing again.

"What the fuck happened?" my dad shouted.

"Something pulled her!" Jack shouted back.

My dad's eyes widened and he leapt forward, my name on his lips. Heavy footfalls exploded just inches away from my feet, and terrifyingly enough, I found myself being dragged. My father gave chase, but he wasn't nearly as fast.

"DAD!" I shouted. **"JACK!"**

I slid along the hard, wet floor, heading for the stairs.

My heart sank.

In that moment, I knew I was going to die.

There was absolutely no doubt about it. David had me now, and he was going to kill me. I clawed the ground, leaving long claw marks along the soft wood. I made a desperate grab for anything at all as I flailed and kicked, trying my best to get away. Heavy sobs tore through my body. I managed to stop myself as I latched onto the doorframe.

My father was just feet away from me.

My heart was racing. Tears streamed down my face. I feared the worst: That they wouldn't get to me in time. That David would pull me upstairs, lock me behind a door.

"Dad!" I shrieked again.

Brett lunged forward, throwing the entirety of the bowl at me. Cold water splashed against my skin, soaking me to the bone and stunning me enough to cause me to let go of the wall. Pain bloomed along my ankle where David had grabbed me. I wailed in agony. It felt as though my leg had caught fire. I thrashed, my hands going to it immediately as nails dug into the flesh around it.

An angry half-growl, half-hiss shook the very foundation of the home.

Jack grabbed my arm and pulled me up. I clung to him, wrapping arms and legs around him as tightly as I could. "I wanna leave!" I shouted. "I wanna leave!"

BANG

All at once, the doors and windows slammed shut. There is no more menacing and terrifying a sound than the simultaneous clicks of a dozen locks.

I buried my face in Jack's shoulder and cried. David had no intentions of letting us leave. "Don't let him take me again, Jack! Don't let him take me!" I pleaded through heavy sobs.

Jack rubbed my back. His lips touched my forehead. "You aren't goin' anywhere," he swore.

The faucet turned on.

Static filled the air. My eyes landed on the now- unplugged radio that lay on the ground beside Brett. "Jasmine, Jasmine, Jazzy, Jasmine. JASMINE!" The familiar voice oozed from the static. "Jaaaasmiiiiiiineeee!" he called my name wickedly.

My father's heavy boot crashed down upon the radio. It shattered, but the static, and my name, never stopped. Instead it became distorted and drawn out. Somehow, that made it so much worse. Panic was taking over. Joey and I wailed. Johnny had curled up, shaking in the corner as he sobbed. Jim was clinging to my mother, his face buried in her shoulder. Even my father was crying.

DING DONG DING DONG DING DONG DING DONG DING DONG DING DONG

The doorbell rang again and again.

The faucet turned itself on and off.

Jack peeled me away from himself. I clawed at him, grabbing handfuls of his plaid shirt. "NO! NO! NO!" I shouted desperately. "I WANNA STAY WITH YOU!"

Despite my sobs and protests, he handed me over to my father. "HOLD HER!" he shouted. Dad's muscular arms wrapped around me. Jack pulled his shirt up over his head, wrapped his hand with it, and dashed to the largest of the kitchen windows. He drew an arm back, and with an ear-splitting crash, the glass shattered around him.

With curses on his lips, he was quick to knock out any remaining glass.

Click

The windows and doors unlocked.

Creak

The door swung open.

Jim ran toward it, but just as he stepped across the threshold my mother pulled him back. The door slammed shut and locked again.

A laugh trickled through the broken radio. "ALLLMMMMOOOOSSSSTTT!" it teased. I couldn't breathe.

Every door in the house swung open and slammed shut. I could hear them from upstairs, from the basement, down the hall. We were surrounded by the sound. Jack knocked the screen out and began to wriggle his way out of the window.

I heard the crunch of his feet against gravel, and then he called out. "Get out here!" My mother shoved Joey into Jack's arms first. Then I slid through to the outside. I'd never been so happy to see the outdoors in my life. Johnny and Jim were next. Last were my parents and Brett.

Brett tore through the driveway, leapt into his car, and peeled away without ever looking back. Jack whispered a few mumbled curses under his breath as we rushed to our own car. My father sped away. He swore to us, in that moment, that we'd stay with Father Brown until we could get a real priest in to exorcise the home.

"Do we have to go back?" Jim demanded. "Can't we just sell it, and leave?"

There was a long pause. "Who's going to buy a haunted house?" Johnny asked.

Another long pause settled over us as the reality of the situation set in. We were fucked. Entirely and completely fucked. We had no means of finding a new place to live. We could only invade Father Brown's home for so long. We couldn't sell, because who would buy? We had no money to buy or rent something else.

We were stuck.

"What if it's not the house that's haunted?" Jim asked, shattering the somber silence that had settled over us. He stared over to me.

I felt like I'd been punched in the stomach.

Jack hit Jim, but the damage had been done.

What if? What if *I* was haunted? I couldn't get that thought out of my mind.

The rest of the drive to the house passed in a haze. Once there, we practically ran into poor Father Brown's home, never bothering to knock. Luckily enough, he didn't seem upset about it. Together, through sobs, we recounted the terrifying events of the day.

Father Brown asked to see my ankle. The perfect shape of a handprint had been burned into my skin. It wasn't blistered, although it was a bright shade of red and peeling along the sides. He made small noises of discontent and mumbled something about it being first degree. He turned it this way and that, his eyes looking more worried the longer he stared at it. Finally, he looked up to me, a wide, fake smile plastered upon his lips. It was the same sort of smile Jack had worn the night Johnny had broken his arm.

"You'll be okay, Jazzy. Why don't we spread some aloe on that? It'll heal up," he swore.

I didn't argue. I just followed him into the bathroom, where he asked me to sit on the side of the bathtub. I sat down, the cold porcelain biting into my skin and making me squirm. Father Brown swung the medicine cabinet open. The mirror glided past him.

Had I not looked up at that very moment, I might have missed it.

Father Brown's kind smile and soft eyes stared back at me from the mirror.

As much as I wanted to ignore it, as much as I wanted to trust Father Brown, I couldn't. I'd seen David in the mirror. There was a point in my life that I might have dismissed it as what my mother called an overactive imagination. There was a time where I would have moved on with my life, and mentioned it to Jack or my mom later.

But that time of innocence was long gone. The child I'd once been was dead. She'd died when David had broken into her room. When he'd threatened her life with a flying spade. When he'd called her name through a broken radio.

I no longer had the luxury of assuming the best in people. I had been thrown into a world composed entirely of uncertainty and insecurity, only to emerge jaded.

In that moment, I didn't know what it meant that I had seen David in the mirror. I only knew that it made the man who had given us shelter, who had offered us his home and his love, dangerous.

The sinking feeling in the pit of my stomach returned. No longer were Father Brown's soft-spoken, gentle ways calming. Instead they hearkened to a time in which I'd been naive enough to trust David.

"Jasmine, I need you to breathe, sweetheart." Father Brown's voice broke through my thoughts. I tried to pull away, fresh waves of fear washing over me. My fists shot out, desperately trying to connect with anything solid. Over and over I hit his arms, but his vice-like grip never wavered. He went to his knees, leveling with me. His eyes met mine as I screamed, wordlessly, in absolute horror. "What happened, honey? What just happened? Why are you so scared?"

I was frantically trying to get away. Desperately searching for a way out of his grasp. "What's going on?" My mother's voice rang through the hall. I jumped. Father Brown's grip never loosened. The points where his fingers dug into my arms were starting to ache. I was going to bruise. "Is everything okay?"

Father Brown looked at her, concern etched into his brow. "I don't know." He sounded distraught, as though he were genuinely worried about what was happening. I wanted to believe that he was, but I couldn't let myself think he was anything more than the monster that had been terrorizing my family for weeks. His eyes met mine. "Jasmine, baby, I need you to breathe. Tell me what happened."

My gut quivered with anxiety and terror. I knew what I'd seen. I knew I had seen David in that mirror. I also knew I couldn't get away from him on my own. He was three times my size. My only hope was the aid of a family member. Now was my chance, but my frightened mind couldn't compose the words I needed. Instead, I offered only a shouted, vague explanation. "He's not Father Brown!" I watched my mother with wide, tear-filled eyes. I willed her to believe me. I silently begged her to understand what I was saying, because my young, terror-riddled mind couldn't formulate much else of a response.

"What?" Father Brown asked. Confusion swept over his features. His fingers loosened and he released me. I fell back, landing on my butt. Quickly, I rose to my feet and scurried to my mother, where I latched onto her leg.

Finally out of Father Brown's grasp, my mind and my mouth began to work in tandem again. "It's David!" I shrieked. "It's David! I saw him in the mirror! I saw him!"

Father Brown watched me with curious eyes. He cocked his head, his eyes softening. "Jasmine, did you see David in the mirror while we were in the bathroom?" he asked. I wanted to hit him. I wanted to hit him for being stupid. Why was he asking me that? I had **just** said that, hadn't I? Instead, I simply scowled at him and nodded. "Are you absolutely certain? I need you to be positive about this."

I molded to my mother's side, watching him with cautious, careful eyes. I wouldn't fall prey to David again. I wouldn't find myself locked in a room with his eyeless, soulless self again. "I'm sure," I growled, my lip curling up in disgust as I spoke. I was doing what I could to make it clear that I had no interest in talking with him any further.

Father Brown's face turned to stone. His features became hard and almost angry. "Excuse me," he said as he stood and crossed the room, heading toward his office. "I have to make a few phone calls."

My mother pulled me into the bathroom and applied the aloe ointment to my burned skin. She asked me to tell her what had happened. I recounted the events to her, only for her to purse her lips and fall silent. I was so used to her ignoring the happenings, so used to her trying to explain it all away, that when she didn't, I got nervous. I think her quiet acceptance of it was the most unsettling things I'd ever experienced. It seemed that she'd given up on ignoring David.

For one reason or another, the very idea of her giving up hurt.

I pushed the thoughts away, because there was something much more pressing to focus on.

The mirror.

I kept my eyes on it the entire time.

David never appeared.

For the next several days, I kept my distance from Father Brown. He, my parents, and Jack spent their time whispering among one another. I didn't get an opportunity to hear much, just bits and pieces.

I'd managed to piece together that Brett had been a psychic. I didn't know what that meant at the time, and resorted to asking Jack, who told me they were people who could see ghosts.

I reasoned that I must have been a psychic too, since I could see David before anyone else could. This new information concerned me, because Father Brown kept calling Brett a charlatan. Another thing I didn't understand. When I asked Jack about that word, he informed me that they were bad. That made my stomach hurt. I wondered if it meant I was one too.

The last thing I gathered from listening in was that someone very important was going to go to our house. They planned to bless it. I didn't know what that meant either, but I didn't want to ask Jack, afraid he'd figure out I'd been eavesdropping.

The weeks dragged by. We stayed with Father Brown throughout the month, leading into the next. Strict rules were set in place, for reasons I didn't understand. We weren't allowed to leave the home for any reason. Every morning, noon, and night, we had to pray with Father Brown. He would say a bunch of words I didn't understand at the time. I'd never heard Latin. Looking back, it was likely some sort of exorcism ritual. While we repeated these words, Father Brown would pour water over our heads. I remember being annoyed that my hair was always damp.

We slept in what I had affectionately begun to call 'the dog pile' on the living room floor. I could usually be found curled up in Jack's arms, while Jim and Johnny slept just to our right. Mom and Dad slept on the floor in Father Brown's basement, because there was no room upstairs for them.

We never went school.

Dad would run to the office once every Monday to get our school work and textbooks. We'd complete the homework in the safety of Father Brown's house and Dad would return the work the next Monday, only to get more.

It was a boring cycle that made my head hurt and my stomach churn every time I thought about it, but I kept a smile on my face and reminded myself that it was so much better than the nights we'd spent huddled around one another in terror.

It was mid-October when Mom and Dad sat us down and told us that David was gone. We were informed that we were leaving that same night. With uncertainty in my eyes and questions on my lips, I packed up my belongings. We said goodbye to Father Brown. I cried. He'd become a rather familiar and comforting person in my life. I didn't really want to give that up.

The drive home was silent. I think each of us had our doubts about the home being safe, but none of us vocalized them. My father parked in the same place he always had. I remember touching the cracked glass of my window as he put the car in park. I half expected something sharp and metal to crash into it. But nothing happened, and soon I found myself walking up the wooden stairs and into the home.

When once it had felt hot, clammy, and heavy, now the air was thin and pure. Just as it always was at Father Brown's home. I tread through the kitchen, trying not to think of why the big window was missing. I looked around the floor for any signs of the broken dishes, but found none. Whoever had been here to do whatever it was they did, must have cleaned it up. They'd also replaced our stove with a new, shiny black one. It didn't match the rest of our kitchen, but it was nice. I continued toward the staircase. My eyes darted to the hallway, my stomach churning as I listened for the sound of the shower.

Nothing.

Just as I rounded the corner, heading up the stairs to my room, I noticed the scratch marks on the floor. No amount of scrubbing could erase away the evidence of my struggle with David. I felt as though I couldn't catch my breath, but for the sake of everyone else, I pushed away the tears that threatened to spring to life and ran up the stairs.

We packed our stuff back into our rooms, although I made it clear that I wasn't going to mine alone. Jack offered to come with me. He let me sit on my bed while he hung my clothes up and chattered to me about things that didn't matter. My eyes stayed glued to the tree. The one that stood just outside my window. The one Mittens and her kittens had been hung from.

I swallowed hard and stood up, trying to find anything at all to take my mind off David. Unfortunately, the first thing to catch my attention was my broken door. I ran a hand along the sharp, jagged edge. Splinters bit at my fingertips.

I couldn't stop my mind from wandering to that night. The first night David had shown me who he really was. Goosebumps rose along my flesh, and a shiver that had nothing to do with the temperature danced down my spine.

I felt stupid, and used. I felt wronged, and misled. I wanted to know why David would have done such a thing to me.

"Jazzy?" I jumped at the sound of my name. Flashes of an eyeless David sprang to life in my mind. I spun around, my hand over my heart. My eyes were wide with panic. A small squeak fled my lips. Jack stood on the other side of the room, his hands raised in surrender. "Jazzy, it's okay," he promised. "Just me, baby. You're okay."

I struggled to catch my breath and nodded. "Yeah," I answered, my eyes darting around the room in search of my own personal monster. He was nowhere to be found.

"Jack?" I asked, my head craned upward as I stared into my brother. It was the first time I realized how very much he looked like Dad. His beard was reddish-brown instead of dark and gray, but he had the same strong cheekbones and masculine features my father did. He had the same sharp eyes that said he was smarter than he let on. They shared the same hairline and the same build. Jack really did look like a younger version of my father.

"Why's it safe now?" I asked, concerned that Mom and Dad were wrong. "Everyone is so sure David isn't going to come back, but I saw him in the mirror that one time," I insisted, biting my lower lip. "I don't think anyone believes me though."

Jack's eyes softened and his hand went up to his chin, brushing at his beard as he regarded me with uncertain eyes. Finally he sighed, and motioned for me to come to him. He sat on my bed and pulled me up on his lap. "Jazzy, I don't understand any of this nearly as well as Father Brown does, but I'll tell you what I know. David is a demon. He's from Hell. Just like other demons, he wanders the Earth and looks for innocent people, like you, to mess with." His words made me feel like I was going to vomit. I squirmed uncomfortably, but all the same, I knew I needed to know what had happened. Jack swallowed hard and paused for a long time. I placed a hand on his, trying to make him feel better.

Jack smiled, a small, sad laugh trickling from between his lips. He rubbed my back and took a deep breath. "Demons can attach themselves to places, or people. David attached himself to you. It's why he followed us to the woods, and why you saw him at Father Brown's house."

My breath caught in my throat. I was haunted. I felt sick. My skin crawled.

"Father Brown and some of the higher-ups at the church got together. They decided upon the best way to handle this, and they came to the house. Every day, they prayed here. They blessed it. They asked the people from the church to come out and pray. Father Brown didn't tell me much about what happened, all I know is that at first, David was acting out. He knocked things over. He broke things. He pushed people, and even locked the doors so the priests and church-goers couldn't get inside."

Jack's hand landed on my own. He squeezed it tightly. "But in the end, God won. Because God is bigger than any demon," he swore. "And now, we're safe. Thanks to Father Brown and all the men and women who helped him." He smiled, a wide, genuine smile.

I couldn't decide in that moment how I felt. There was a strange cocktail of emotions running through me. Guilt. Love. Hatred. Gratitude. They swirled around inside of me, mingling with one another and leaving me shrouded in confusion. I simply gave a half-hearted nod and fell silent. I leaned into Jack, curling up on his lap. His body heat reminded me that I wasn't alone. Listening to the beat of his heart and the slow intake and exhale of breath calmed me. I wrapped my arms tightly around him and molded to him.

I don't know how long I stayed like that, holding onto Jack as though he were the last solid thing on the planet. But eventually, one thought screamed so loudly in my mind I couldn't ignore it. It penetrated the haze of confusion that had shrouded me and spilled from my lips. "I'm not sleeping in here alone," I announced, leaving absolutely no room for argument. I'd sleep outside if I had to, but under no circumstances was I ever sleeping in that godforsaken room again. "Johnny and Jim are sleeping in their room, and I don't think they'll let me sleep with them. Can I sleep with you?"

Jack gave a nod. "Sure thing," he answered. "But I'm sleeping in the living room right now." He offered no explanation, although I thought it was probably because we'd become rather accustomed to falling asleep with a movie playing on the television. Father Brown had suggested it the first few nights. It had caught on, and stuck. No one had tried to put a stop to it, so it simply never ended.

I crinkled my nose in disgust and stuck out my tongue. "No thanks," I answered, shaking my head. I had absolutely no interest in sleeping down there. I could barely even look in that room without seeing David standing behind that chair like he had the night we'd fled the home for Father Brown's.

Jack looked down to me thoughtfully. "Why don't you see if you can sleep in Mom and Dad's room with them?" he asked.

I hopped off his lap and did just that. My parents agreed without much thought, before asking me if I was done putting my things away. I proudly announced that I was, leaving out the fact that Jack had actually done everything. My pride was instantly dashed when I was immediately put to work. My mother and I spent the day trying to scrub down and repair what we could. The boys got to work repairing the flooring and repainting the entire house.

For the first two weeks, I refused to enter any room by myself, which made the chores incredibly difficult. I'd be scrubbing the counters or doing dishes when my mother would announce that she had to go to the bathroom and would be right back.

I wasn't having any of that.

I'd pick Joey up and stand just outside the door while my mom did whatever it was she needed to do.

Other aspects of my life changed just as drastically. Whereas the bridge had once been my favorite place to go, I wouldn't go near it at all. I went as far as to absolutely insist that if we were driving somewhere, we took the long way, going over to the highway and crossing over a different bridge seven miles down the road. I panicked when a family member left for too long. I covered all the mirrors in the house with sheets and pillowcases, and had a meltdown any time any of them were removed. At night, I insisted upon sleeping in my parents' bed. I would wake my father or mother every time I needed to use the restroom, and demand that they come with me and stand just outside the door.

This became our reality, and it stuck for a long time. So long, in fact, that at one point my mother wanted to send me to therapy. My father refused, reminding her that I'd likely be regarded as insane if I ever told a mental health professional what had happened in our home. My mother gave up that idea almost instantly.

While the first month or two was clunky and filled with a certain kind of unease that put me on edge, it eventually did get better. Slowly, I started to accept that David had indeed left. The realization allowed me to stop following my mother everywhere, and while I wouldn't be on a separate floor from everyone else, I would go into separate rooms from time to time.

As the weeks passed and my fears began to melt away, I began to fall in love with our home and our property again. Slowly, I became more adventurous. I began exploring the property on my own (although I still kept my distance from the bridge). At first, I started going just past the barn and back, but eventually I craved more. I wanted to explore. I wanted to find bugs and snakes. I wanted to count what wildlife I could see. I wanted more from life than being stuck in a home, afraid of the rooms that surrounded me.

One day, I laced up tall hiking boots, packed two bottles of water, and headed out into the vast expanse of the back fields. My father had never planted anything, insisting every year that we'd be fencing it in and getting cows. I was always thrilled with the prospect, but somehow it never happened. I found myself incredibly thankful for my father's procrastination. The massively overgrown brush provided a fantastic hiking trail.

As I got further and further away from my home and the fear I had of David shed itself entirely, I began to see the beauty in the nature around me. Grassy hills rolled over the horizon. Colorful trees dotted the landscape. A creek sliced through the earth like a vein, babbling as it rushed over stones. It was like something straight out of a painting. I found myself wondering how I'd never noticed how very beautiful our backyard was. Or how I'd ever managed to be bored a day in my life.

This became my new ritual: instead of finding ways to get to the bridge, I'd hike out into the field until my home was just a small dot, and then I'd hike back. It seemed like every time I did it, I found a new bug that I'd never seen before. I began making friends with arachnids again. For the first time in months, I felt normal.

With the realization that we were free, and safe, came the start of school (until then, my father was still bringing home our work and turning it in to the office on Mondays). My grades soared. I made friends for the first time in my life.

Life couldn't have possibly have been better.

We had nearly four solid months of pure bliss. We'd managed to repair everything in the home, from the peeling paint, to the wilted garden, to the flooring and doors; everything was back the way it should have been. Johnny and I were even on decent speaking terms, something that hadn't happened since I'd first started talking to David.

In fact, the only sign that anything had ever been wrong at all was the simple fact that I refused to sleep in my own bed. I still curled up directly in between my mother and father.

The school weeks came and went. Johnny, Jim, and I were doing exceptionally well, and so, one Friday night, Jack gathered us together and told us he'd take us to a movie as a reward. I was so excited. We hadn't decided which one yet, but I didn't really care. I would have sat through just about anything to get my hands on a bag of popcorn and a cherry Icee.

It was well past midnight, and I was still tossing and turning, trying to force myself to sleep. But I couldn't lie still with all the excitement. I'd turned over for the millionth time when the baby monitor buzzed with a sudden burst of static.

My body went rigid. I wanted to reach out and shake my dad awake, but I was filled with a sudden dread that made me believe that if I moved, something terrible would happen.

So I stayed as still as I could. Taking small breaths. Trying to make myself invisible. I waited for another noise for what seemed liked hours.

I'd nearly managed to convince myself that the old monitor had just glitched when a hoarse, menacing voice began to half-sing, half-talk into the radio. "...*Hush li-ttle...ba-by...*" it sang in a low growl. Its words were slow and mildly distorted. "...*Don't...say...a...word...*"

My father was up and out of the bed before I had time to scream. My mother shrieked something about her baby and leapt out of bed, tearing down the hallway, out of sight.

"NO! NO! NO!" my father shouted over the pounding of his fists against the wood. "There's no fucking locks on the doors! How is it locked!"

My stomach dropped. I couldn't catch my breath. It was happening again! It was happening again! A wheezing breath rattled from the monitor. "...

Mama's gonna…buy you…" The voice cut out as heavy fists pounded against the door again. *"…A…mock-ing…bird…"* It groaned and wheezed, sounding like death incarnate. Joey began to whine, a small, pathetic sort of sound that rippled through the silence of the bedroom and tore at my heart. I felt useless. Why was I just lying here while David terrorized my brother?

Because I was a chicken.

The whining began to build to small fussing. A slow hiss, not unlike that of a snake, echoed through the monitor. *"…I said hush…"* the gruff voice reminded him.

"Please don't cry," I begged through tears, as I wrapped myself in the blanket. I couldn't even imagine what David might do to Joey if he cried.

But my pleas fell on deaf ears, and soon Joey's desperate wails echoed through the halls.

"What's going on?" Jack's groggy voice called from the other side of the hallway.

"It's happening again!" my mother screamed.

Someone, probably Jack, dashed through the hall and hit the door so hard I felt it shake from my place in the bed. I could hear it begin to give way from the monitor. The monitor cut out for three entire seconds. Those were the longest moments of my life. I strained my ears, trying to listen for Joey's cries from down the hall, but hearing nothing. My mind wandered into dark places. Had David killed him? Had he killed my brother?

Finally, the static returned, and mercifully the only thing that could be heard was Joey's desperate crying.

I held my breath, listening intently, waiting for the sound of David's wheezing. Joey was still screaming from the monitor. I could hear my frantic parents as they shouted from just on the other side of the door. Again and again someone hit the heavy wood, but Joey's door was heavier than mine had been. It was harder to break down. I had my doubts that they'd reach him time. I prayed that he wasn't being hurt.

"Fuck! This isn't going to work!" Jack shouted. I could hear the panic in his voice. Tears streamed down my cheeks. I was so sure in that moment that

Joey was going to die. I was so sure that nothing in the world could be worse or more frightening.

I was wrong.

Creak

THUMP

Creak

THUMP

The sound went on and on. It was close. So close that I was sure it was coming from inside the bedroom. My hands and feet tingled. My body went cold. A deep ache began in my stomach. I could feel the thuds vibrate through the wall that the bed was pushed up against. My heart caught in my throat. I tried to convince myself that the noise was coming from the monitor. But I knew that was bullshit.

It was distinct. Very different from the frantic thudding of fists against the door to my little brother's room. Separate from the desperate screams of my parents as they tried to rescue their youngest child from the clutches of the demon. They were systematic. Almost as if timed. There was something about the calm, languid way they happened that was absolutely maddening.

It took me a solid minute to get up the courage to peek out from under the blankets. Even as I did it, I moved as slowly as I could, so as not to draw attention to myself.

My breath hitched.

I tried to scream, or gasp, but my lungs were deflated. They pleaded for oxygen that I couldn't give them. A cold sweat began to bead along my brow. Ice ran through my veins. I could have sworn my heart stopped.

Sitting upon my mother's rocker, hands folded neatly in his lap, was David. He swung his feet sweetly, just inches above the wooden floor. The chair creaked as it rocked, and thumped against the wall, time and time again. Had his eyes not been missing, he might have actually looked sweet, sitting there upon a too-big chair.

His attention snapped to me. Empty sockets locked onto my form. His brows pulled down into a scowl. His lips turned down into a deep frown. His tongue darted out of his lips, forked, like that of a snake.

I nearly vomited.

"Bye—oh ba-by…bunkin…" The words leaked from him like a sickness, sounding sinister and dangerous. "…David's…goin'…huntin'…" he hissed. The tongue, long, flat, and forked, snaked from between his lips.

David slid off the chair. He moved like a liquid, as though he had muscles and bones in places that I did not. He dropped to his knees and began to crawl toward me. There was something about seeing him—on the ground, eyeless but staring through my soul all the same, forked tongue darting from between his lips—that left me breathless. I was entirely unable to speak or even scream. Never had I been more frightened. Not when the house had been flooded, or when he'd trapped me in my room. Not when he'd hung our cats from the tree. Something about how he moved reduced me to nothing more than a sobbing mess.

I pleaded with God to make him go away. I silently begged for Him to stop the monster that had made it his life's work to fuck with me. But it was no use. David crawled across the floor, until he was so close to the edge of the bed that I could hear his breathing and smell the putrid scent that rolled off him.

A gnarled, ashen hand gripped the side of the bed. He pulled himself up. I was just inches away from him, staring into empty sockets framed by skin that looked too aged to be his. I couldn't think. I couldn't move. I couldn't scream.

BANG

An ear-splitting noise reverberated from the monitor. It was all I needed to break whatever hold David had on me. I scrambled away, intending to leap off the bed and run to my parents. "JACK! DAD! MOM!" I screamed, hoping one of them would hear me.

I got to the edge of the bed and came to a screeching halt. My hands shot out as if I could ward away the beasts that wriggled below me. On the floor, dozens of snakes slithered along. One rose up; I recognized it only by the hood around its head.

Cobra.

We didn't have cobras where we lived. For the life of me, I couldn't figure out how they'd all gotten into the room.

From behind me, David laughed. It was a bitter, angry sort of growled noise that turned my stomach. "You gonna run again?" he whispered, but the voice was not his own. It was deep, growly, and scratchy. Tears sprang to life in my eyes. The world blurred, becoming hazy and distorted. "Run. Run. Run," he hissed. I turned back to see him crawling along my parent's bed. He was getting closer. His teeth were sharpened to a point. The flat tongue shot out again, flicking at the air. "You gotta run," he taunted. "Gotta run from the monsters. Gotta run from us. Run. Run. Run."

"JOEY!" my mother's voice rang from the monitor. "Joshua! Come help me get Joey down! How the hell did he get up on the shelf?" she asked. Joey only had one shelf in his room. It was useless, because it was too high. It hung just a foot away from the ceiling. Even Dad couldn't reach it without a stepladder. I imagined my poor little brother perched seven feet in the air, crying for his parents.

The bed shook, pulling me from my thoughts. I glanced back.

David was getting closer. He was right on top of me, moving with slow, exaggerated steps as though he were drawing this out.

I inched toward the edge of the bed. The cobra bobbed back and forth, not unlike the coral snake had right before it had struck the back of my shoe so many months ago. "Go ahead, Jasmine," David taunted. "Jump. It won't bite." I turned back. His lips were twisted up into a wicked smile.

"JASMINE!" Jack shouted from the hallway. He balked at the doorway, his eyes wide as he gaped at the beasts on the ground and the monster beside me. His fingers found the switch and the room flooded with yellow light.

David hissed from beside me, forked tongue darting from his mouth. "Come and play, Jack," he taunted.

Jack grabbed something large and silver from his neck and held it up. It wasn't until it gleamed against the light that I could make out its shape. It was a large cross. He must have been sleeping with it around his neck. "And Jesus healed many who were ill with various diseases," Jack shouted the words with conviction, holding the cross up to point it at David.

David's nose crinkled in absolute disgust. He cringed with every word. His hands went to his ears. He began to thrash upon the bed. His legs flailed, causing blankets to bunch up around them. "SHUT UP!" he screamed, but Jack pressed on.

"And cast out many demons; and He was not permitting the demons to speak, because they knew who He was." The snakes below me began to smoke and sizzle. They writhed in pain, twisting and contorting. I saw my chance and I took it. I pulled myself to my feet and darted across the bed. As my feet hit the edge of the bed, I catapulted off. At first, I was certain I wasn't going to clear the snakes, but by some miracle I landed hard upon the ground, with a massive thud, right beside Jack.

David let out a roar and leapt to his feet. His features were twisted with unimaginable hate. His hands curled into fists at his side.

He screamed.

It rattled the walls and sent a chill down my spine. I'd never heard anything so terrible in all my life.

I clung to my brother, who continued to shout holy words.

David's body tensed. He crouched down, as though to jump toward us. Jack's hand pushed me behind him, shielding me with his body as he continued to shout bible verses at the demon. David jumped, propelling himself forward, and with a massive thump he hit the wall.

At first, I thought he'd missed. I thought that perhaps the words Jack was reciting had fucked his focus up so badly that he'd actually missed. I knew how wrong I was when he scurried over the wall, crawling along it like a spider might.

My eyes widened. Jack clutched the cross to himself and grabbed me.

We ran.

David took chase. Just behind us, I could hear him running on all fours along the wall. He hissed and seethed, cursing Jack. He threw out threats and promised a fate worse than death. Jack shouted the words louder.

Panic filled me as I realized we'd run directly past the staircase and to the end of the hall. David was directly behind us. I was sure that all he had to do was reach out, and he could pull me away from my brother.

Jack darted left and pulled me to his bedroom at the end of the hall. He slammed the door and pulled me into his lap. Together, we cowered in the corner beside his bed. Outside the locked door, we could hear the pitter-patter of David's hands and feet as he scaled the walls. Something hit the door, causing it to shake. David screeched.

"LET ME IN!" he roared. "LET ME IN! LET ME IN! I'LL KILL YOU! I'LL RIP YOU APART! I'LL HANG YOU FROM THE FUCKING TREE! I'LL EAT YOUR FUCKING HEARTS!" I didn't know it at the time, but Jack had coated his door in holy water.

David continued to rage just outside the door. The sounds of breaking glass and furniture being tossed around echoed through the hallway.

And then it stopped.

For a long while it was silent.

The creak of a door opening sliced through the stillness.

BANG

The door slammed.

Johnny screamed.

Cold worry knotted in my chest. My fingertips drummed on my legs nervously as I looked up to Jack. His eyes were wide. All the color had leaked out of his face. I recognized fear when I saw it. I felt as though I'd been punched squarely in the gut. If Jack was afraid, then I should be afraid.

Another desperate, panicked shriek cut through the air. My mind crawled into dark places. A small voice in the back of my head asked if Johnny's bed was surrounded by snakes. If David's serpent-like tongue flicked at the air just inches away from him. If David was singing fucked up versions of nursery rhymes to him, just as he had to Joey and me.

Jack's hands trembled as they tightened around me. The terror was practically radiating off him. My mouth gaped. My eyes were wide and filled with tears that streamed down my cheeks. I pleaded with God to save my brothers. To do something. Anything at all, so they wouldn't die in their rooms.

I don't know if it was the prayer or if Jack had simply come back to his senses. Either way, hot anger rolled through his eyes. I'd only ever seen him truly angry one time prior. It had been early last summer. Jim and Johnny had been out in the back field playing. Dad had been in the barn with the pigs. Mom had been at church group with Joey. Jack had come inside just long enough to grab something to drink. When the desperate and terrified screams of my brothers tore through the silence, he'd shouted at me to stay inside and had darted through the front door. I watched and listened through the open kitchen window. Johnny and Jim were screaming about a coyote that foamed at the mouth, wobbled, and chased them. They pointed behind them, to the barn, declaring that it was just on the other side.

I'd watched as Jack stomped back into the home, anger rolling off him. He pushed open the door and stormed toward the stairs. He'd gone to the gun cabinet and left with a loaded rifle. Less than ten minutes later, an ear-splitting bang sliced through the summer air. Jack returned, promising the boys that they were safe.

Now that same sort of anger oozed from him, and I knew, without a doubt, that Jack would do everything in his power to rid the world of the monster, the same way he had when he'd put down the coyote. He moved me over and pulled himself to his feet. The sound of my father's footsteps and desperate cries for Johnny to open the door nearly drowned out Jack's commands. "I'm going to close the door. Do not open it under any circumstances," he instructed.

I nodded in response and watched with ever-growing terror as my older brother—the man who had acted as my savior for these past several months—opened the door. He was stepping out into the unknown, abandoning the safety we'd found in his room. I peeked around him, out into the hallway. The end table and the vase that had been sitting upon it had been tossed across the room. Shiny green glass glistened atop the dark wood. My father stood before the door, shoeless, both socks soaked in blood as he banged against the door, desperately calling the names of his sons.

Jack slammed the door closed.

Suddenly, I was very alone.

I don't know what happened in those moments that Jack was away. Only that he never shouted any more bible verses. The only voices that penetrated the heavy bedroom door were muffled and quiet. I couldn't make any of them out. I couldn't even tell who was speaking. Frustration washed over me, and I thought about crawling closer to the door and pressing an ear against the wood, but I was too frightened to move.

The minutes ticked by. Finally, the door creaked open, my heart thrumming in response. I imagined David peeking around the corner, forked tongue flicking at the air.

Instead, Jack stood in the hallway. He offered me a small, sad smile. "All clear, chica," he informed me. I stayed firmly planted in my spot, looking past him to the hallway. The floor was smeared with blood, likely from the unprotected feet of family members as they navigated the hallway. Jack crouched down and opened his arms. "C'mon, honey," he coaxed. "It's all okay. No more monsters."

That sentence felt wrong to me. It sent a shiver down my spine.

Jack was acknowledging the existence of monsters.

And why shouldn't he?

Wasn't that exactly what David was?

A monster?

For the life of me, I couldn't figure out why that word bothered me so much more than the word demon. Looking back now, I suspect it's because my family had spent my entire life up until that point telling me that there was no such things as monsters. We were a Christian family, which meant that demons were something I heard a lot about. That concept was easier to grasp.

With my stomach still churning, I was quick to pull myself to my feet and run toward him. I practically threw myself at him. Muscular arms wrapped around me and pulled me up onto his shoulders. Slowly and carefully he began the long trek downstairs. Twice he let out a small hiss of pain, cursed, and stopped to pull out a sharp piece of glass that had buried itself in his soft flesh.

Both times I offered to walk, and both times Jack teasingly told me to shut my little mouth.

Jack brought me into the living room, where he placed me safely upon the floor. Everyone, save for my father, was already gathered there. My mother held Joey in her arms. He sniffed pathetically, still hiccupping softly, a few stray tears streaming down his cheeks. Johnny was curled into a ball, sitting on the couch, rocking back and forth slowly. His eyes were haunted and his features were stony. I remember thinking he looked more angry than frightened. Jim was curled into his own ball on the couch, but fast asleep. I nearly laughed. Mom always joked that Jim could sleep through anything.

Jack placed me on the free chair, his lips touched my forehead, and a massive hand swiped my curly hair back away from my face. "Listen, honey, I have to help Dad with some stuff, I'll be right back, okay?" he asked. I simply gave a nod and leaned back into the chair. "That's my brave little soldier. I'll put a movie on for you, you won't even notice that I'm gone." That was a lie. Jack was one of the very few people in the world that made me feel safe. He was the only one I could always count on being there. Mom and Dad were so worried about Joey, Jim, and Johnny that they didn't have very much time for me. Looking back, I can't help but wonder if they resented me for bringing David to the home. I have to wonder if they secretly hoped that David would just take me and leave the rest of their family alone to heal. "Mommy and the boys are right here if you need anything. Call me if you need me." I nodded one more time. Pleas for him to stay danced on the tip of my tongue, but I bit them back, reasoning that if Jack said he'd be back… then he would. So I sat quietly in the chair as Jack put a movie in, started it up, and handed the remote off to me. "I'll be right back," he swore again.

I watched the previews instead of fast-forwarding through them. Eventually *Oliver and Company* began to quietly play. I allowed the music and voices to fill the silence without ever actually paying any attention to it. My mind, and my eyes, were on Jack and my father. I was nervous that David might come back and tear them away from me.

I listened, keeping a close watch on where they were. I had developed a plan. If either of them screamed, I would grab the flask of holy water perched upon the counter in the kitchen and I'd douse them in it, just like Brett had done with me when David had tried to steal me away.

No screams came.

In fact, I could hear the muffled sound of the two of them talking quietly in the kitchen. It eased my mind a little, and allowed for me to relax. I waited patiently for Jack to return, watching him and my father every time they came into the room to hang something up or douse a wall with holy water. The two of them built a veritable fort of holy items in order to keep us safe from David. The movie was nearing the end when Jack and Dad were finally finished.

Jack wandered into the room, a wide smile that never reached his eyes spread along his cracked lips. He looked old, older than he had the night before. He looked sad.

I hated David for what he'd done to my brother.

Jack lifted me up and sat down upon the chair, setting me down on his lap. I leaned against him, resting my head on his chest and wrapping my arms around him.

My father sat down on the floor and leaned against the couch in front of where Jim lay sleeping. Together, we sat in silence, allowing the movie to play out without ever really watching it. When the movie ended, I hopped off Jack's lap and grabbed two more. I showed them to him, and he picked his favorite of them.

We continued this cycle four times before strangled rays of light touched the horizon. The sun peeked over the hills and splashed the sky with brilliant colors. It greeted the world through bare trees, casting elongated shadows. They looked like long, withered fingers that blindly groped at the world around them. I might have thought it beautiful had my mind not been on David.

My father stood, having never gotten to sleep again, just like the rest of us —save for Joey and Jim. He used the kitchen phone to make a call; I figured out halfway through that he was talking to Father Brown. I gathered that the priest would be visiting us sometime that afternoon. I couldn't deny that I found relief in the thought.

The morning was somber.

No one talked.

We ate in silence.

We began chores in silence.

In fact, the only thing to break the quiet was a deep, rattling sort of cough that plagued Jim. He insisted he was okay, just feeling under the weather. But true to form, my worrywart of a mother cornered him, armed with a thermometer. Mild concern turned to deep worry as she watched the numbers on the thermometer go up and up and up. When it finally beeped, it was up over 104. My mother immediately announced that she and Joey would be taking Jim to the doctor.

Because my mom was gone and everyone else had to do chores, I was stuck going out to the barn with everyone. My dad firmly believed in the buddy system when David was around. Unfortunately for me, Jack was with Dad, which left me with Johnny.

We were tasked with feeding the pigs, which meant endless trips of buckets filled with feed. Jack had mixed a bunch up for us in a large, black container and handed us scoopers and a bucket each. My body was already sore and achy from lack of sleep. My mind was cloudy, both with the events of last night and with tiredness. I had been so frightened earlier in the day that I couldn't sleep. Now all I wanted was to curl up on the couch, where Jim had been sleeping, and rest.

But that wasn't an option.

So I filled my bucket with the yellow and brown feed and began the long trek to the last pan. I struggled, my whole body tipped to the side as I half-carried, half-dragged the bucket beside me. Sweat beaded along my brow. I grunted with each heft. I tried to assure myself that I could do this, but the bucket weighed half as much as I did. My arms, weak and thin, weren't up to the task. They shook and wobbled with every step I took. Twice I had to stop and catch my breath.

I was three quarters of the way there when I heard Johnny's footfalls quicken behind me. He was rapidly gaining on me. He never slowed until he was directly to my right, walking in tandem with me. I looked over to him, curious; he could be moving so much faster than me. Why would he keep my pathetic pace?

His eyes widened and he turned toward the pigs to my left. "Hey, what's that?" he asked.

I craned my neck and searched the pens, but I didn't see anything out of the ordinary. Just small, noisy piglets gathering near the bars, eager to be fed.

I didn't see his foot as he slid it in front of me. I tripped, falling to the ground. The bucket hit the cement with a loud, metallic clank. Feed spilled everywhere. Johnny gave a bitter snort and mumbled something about me being a loser. Pain bloomed along my knee. I pulled myself up, watching as Johnny struggled with his bucket to get it to the end of the line of pig pens. My hands clenched at my sides. Johnny had never been mean to me before last summer. I didn't understand why he'd changed. Or perhaps, I didn't want to think about why he had.

Throbbing, sharp pain stung my knee. I winced as I rolled my pant leg up, careful not to brush against the tender area. My knee was scratched. Blood trickled down from the two small cuts. It stung like a bitch, but it wasn't anything that looked too bad. I rolled my pant leg down and silently wished Johnny would trip and fall too.

He didn't.

But he managed to push me to the ground three more times before chores were complete. By the end of it all, my legs and arms were bruised and my self-worth had suffered dramatically.

When all the pigs had been fed, Johnny and I went inside where I silently went to the sink to begin dishes. Johnny pulled a comic book out from one of the drawers in the living room and sat at the table. Every now and then he'd look up, glare at me, then, as though nothing had happened, he'd go back to reading.

I did what I could to ignore him. But eventually, that was no longer an option. I couldn't reach the line of glasses at the end of the counter. I could have pulled a chair over, and reached them then, but I worried that Johnny would just push me off it. I huffed and glanced back to my older brother. "Can you help me?" I asked, trying to keep the anger out of my voice. "I can't reach the cups." I pointed upward to the line of tall, slender glasses. They were fancier than the ones David had destroyed. They'd come from a woman at the church who said that giving us her old dishware just gave her an excuse to buy new ones. She seemed excited about the prospect. My father wasn't thrilled with accepting them, but he had little choice in the matter.

Johnny clenched his jaw tightly and placed the comic book down upon the table. He met my eyes, glaring straight through me. "Go eat dirt," he spat.

I pursed my lips and pulled the stepstool out from the closet. I kept a good eye on Johnny, who never moved his place. Instead of pushing me down, he resorted to tossing angry, berating words at me.

I wanted to cry by the time Jack and Dad wandered back inside. Dad went directly upstairs to clean the glass off the floor and then to shower, while Jack stayed downstairs. Jack looked like hell. Big bags rested under his eyes. He kept stretching and yawning. But all the same, he showered, and returned to the kitchen clothed in something clean. He pulled the refrigerator open and turned to look at me with brilliantly green eyes. Despite being tired, and probably just as scared as the rest of us, the smile on his lips never faltered. Looking back, I understand now why his eyes were puffy and red. He'd been crying. I suppose he'd decided, sometime between the time we left the house for Father Brown's and then, that he wouldn't let us see him cry anymore.

"Hey sweetie," he chirped. I completely missed the sad undertone if there was one. "You hungry?" he asked, pulling piles things out of the refrigerator. "I'm thinking of making scrambled eggs, or maybe a BLT. I haven't decided. Either of those sound good?"

I shook my head, not trusting my voice to stay level if I answered him. Despite my best efforts at acting normal, Jack saw straight through it. "What's wrong, Jazzy?" he asked, concern carved deep into his features.

I broke down.

I cried and told him about how Johnny had pushed me down. How he'd mumbled under his breath, every time, something mean and terrible about me.

How he'd spent most of our time in the kitchen hurling insults at me.

Irritation swept over Jack. He placed everything back in the refrigerator and walked over to me. Right there, in the middle of the kitchen, he sat down and pulled me into his lap. His giant hands swept my curly hair away from my face, a thumb wiping away the few traitorous tears that streamed down my cheeks. It took him a long while to speak, but when he did, he offered me the best bit of advice I'd ever received. "Listen here, Jazzy-pants," he began playfully, his tired eyes sparkling with something close to mischief. "Johnny's only mean because he's jealous. He's a pansy. He cried when David went into his room. He hid under his blankets. I know, because that's where I found him, curled up in a ball, hiding under all four of his blankets. He didn't run. He didn't call for help, like you did. He just hid and cried. He's just jealous that his little sister is braver than he is," he said with a wink. "Just remember, love, when people are mean to you, that's about them, not you. Okay?"

I nodded, using my palm to wipe my eyes. Suddenly, Johnny didn't seem so big, and he didn't seem so scary. I hugged Jack, thanked him for being so nice, and scurried off to the living room where I sat in front of the television again, waiting for Jack to join me. The two of us curled up on the couch together. He had brought with him a BLT that he desperately tried to get me to try, but I refused. I had very little interest in food at the time. It didn't take long for him to give up and eat the sandwich himself. I leaned into his side, watching *The Fox and The Hound* until my eyelids grew too heavy and I could no longer fight off sleep. I slipped into sweet oblivion.

My eyes opened reluctantly against the burning light outside. A loud, barking, hoarse sort of noise cut the through the silence, making me jump up and latch onto Jack. "Jack!" I whispered, my voice urgent and frightened. "Jack! Wake up! I think he's back!"

Jack's eyes flew open and he jumped up. At first, he looked dazed, but ready for a fight. The sound cut through the silence again, and I watched as the tension in his shoulders melted away. "It's just Jim," he assured me before pulling me up from my place. We walked into the kitchen, where my curious eyes landed on Jim, who sat at the table, coughing into his hand. A horrible, deep, rattling noise shook from deep within him. He winced in pain and rubbed his chest.

"Hey, dude," Jack said, a feigned smile perched upon his lips. "You sound like crap."

"Thanks," Jim answered, his voice slightly annoyed. "That makes me feel all kinds of better."

Jack's smile widened. "That's my job," he teased.

Jim rolled his eyes and pulled his sweater tighter around himself. His thin arms wrapped around his frame, trying to conserve his heat. His cheeks were pink and his eyes were glossy. It had been a long while since I'd seen anyone this sick. In fact, I thought the last time had been when Johnny had gotten pneumonia. "What'd the doctor say?" Jack asked, hiding the worry in his eyes and his voice. I was too young to pick it up at the time, but looking back, it was definitely there.

"It's a viral infection," Mom answered with a sigh. "Nothing they can do as far as medicine goes. We just have to keep him on Tylenol to keep the fever at bay, and go back in two days if it doesn't break."

Jack nodded. "Probably just a cold," he decided, but all the same he placed a hand atop Jim's head, ruffling his hair. Jim swatted his arm away. "How's the throat? Feel like you can choke down some orange juice? The vitamin C will do you good," he reminded him. Jim simply shook his head, moaned, and leaned down to rest his head on his folded arms.

"Don't be such a drama queen," Johnny said from across the room. "It's not like you have pneumonia."

Jack shot daggers back to Johnny. "You," he said, stabbing a finger in his direction, "you leave Jim alone. He doesn't feel well. And if I ever hear about you shoving Jazzy around like that again, I'll kick your ass. You understand me?"

Johnny rolled his eyes, mumbled something that sounded a lot like 'go fuck yourself' under his breath, and headed back into the living room where he collapsed onto the couch, reading his comics. Mom and I got to work making homemade chicken-and-noodle soup for Jim. She prodded me throughout the process, asking me more and more about what Johnny had done. I was honest, but while she seemed annoyed, she never said anything to him.

Lunch came and went. Jim picked at the soup, never actually eating anything. Instead, he stirred it, lifting some in the spoon only to let it dribble back into the bowl. He waited, head balancing on the palm of his hand, elbow planted firmly upon the table, until everyone else was done. "Can I go lay down?" he asked, eyes on my mother.

"Yeah, honey," Mom answered with a nod. "Just go to the living room."

Irritation swept over his features. Anger flashed through his eyes for a split second before he wiped it away, replacing it with a pained expression. "My bed's a lot more comfortable. Can I sleep up there instead?" he asked.

Dad shook his head. "Not alone, buddy," he answered.

I watched as his hands curled into fists. His teeth gritted and his nostrils flared. "Then can someone come with me?" he pressed on, voice far less friendly. "Please? I'm so tired, and I'm achy all over, and I just wanna sleep. The couch is so uncomfortable. There's no way I'll get to sleep in there."

Johnny leapt up from his seat, his comic books clutched in his hand. "I'll go," he said, glancing back to Mom and Dad. We all knew he just wanted to lounge around and read, but no one felt like arguing. Jim was a grump when he was sick, and Johnny had been a pain in the neck all day. My parents agreed, and if I were being honest, I was glad to be rid of the both of them.

Mom and I spent the next few hours working on chores around the house. Mom functioned best if she could rely on a routine of some sort. Jack had once explained this to me, so I did what I could to keep her happy by going along with it. Even if I did think it was stupid that we were scrubbing baseboards despite the fact that David had sprung up out of nowhere last night. The day bled on. Father Brown came to the house. He placed holy items in every room of the home, save for Johnny and Jim's (he gave the item to my father, to place in there after Jim woke up). He walked around the house sprinkling holy water on the ground as he chanted in some language I didn't understand. He had us gather and hold hands. Together we said several prayers. Finally we were done, and Father Brown said, with a certain level of confidence, that if David were around he would have reacted.

Soon enough, he announced that he had to go. Mom offered him dinner, but he declined, explaining that he had an appointment he had to make. He asked that we contact him if anything more happened, and offered to allow us to stay with him if need be. My parents thanked him, but my father assured him that, at least for now, we would stay where we were.

My father was—and still is—a very stubborn man. A man who, as it would seem, would rather put himself in harm's way than accept kindness and charity.

The days dragged on, and Jim got worse. He never came out of his room, but Johnny reported that he would lie on the bed, shiver, and moan in pain. My heart ached for him. Jack and I would routinely bring him food and juice, but he never touched any of it.

He started howling in the middle of the night, screaming in agony and writhing against the pain. Mom and Dad would get up and sit beside him. Twice Mom took him into the ER late at night, but despite his cries of pain and the sweat that poured from him, the doctors said they couldn't find anything wrong with him. According to them, it was just a viral infection.

But we didn't believe them.

Things got worse and worse.

His fever refused to go down for more than a few hours at once. He'd spent entire hours screaming in pain. Nothing seemed to bring him any sort of peace. It was on the third day that the fever had spiked to nearly 105. Despite having no luck with doctors prior, my mother informed us that she'd be taking him back that afternoon. She swore she wouldn't leave this time until they gave him some sort of medication.

My father thought that was a good idea. She headed upstairs, and we waited, but she didn't come back down. For nearly an hour she stayed up there, my father checking on her occasionally. Jim was absolutely refusing to get up out of bed. He was complaining of pain, saying it would *hurt to leave his bed*. He complained that his skin felt like there were millions of needles poking him all at once, and his head felt like it might explode from the pressure. Eventually, Mom grew tired of arguing and pulled the blankets up off him.

That's when she screamed.

Jack, Dad, and I ran up the stairs. I'll never forget the sight of my older brother, lying on a sheetless bed, atop hundreds of dead bugs. Spiders, centipedes, flies, and other small insects lay motionless in piles all around him. They toppled over as he shifted. His hand smeared piles of them into the mattress as he squirmed. They broke into pieces, crumbling like dust and leaving streaks of black behind.

"What the hell is all this?" my mother screamed. "What the hell are all these bugs doing in your bed?" The look of horror in my mother's eyes set me on edge. She was the queen of denial, always looking for a way to explain the unexplainable. Always grasping at straws when something truly terrible happened. Ever since David had returned, she'd stopped.

Jim only growled in response. His lips curled up into a snarl. His back bowed and his head craned in an odd direction. He contorted and twisted. His eyes rolled back in his head. His whole body trembled. He let out a terrible, growling sort of scream that shook me to the very core.

"GET OUT!" he cried. The top of his head and his feet touched the bed, but suddenly the rest of him bowed, lifting off the mattress entirely. "GET OUT!"

My father tore a silver cross from its place on the wall just outside of Jim's bedroom and dashed toward him. With a sizzle and a hiss, he pressed the metal against Jim's skin. Jim shrieked, thrashing in pain and swinging wildly in the air. His fist hit my father, sending him staggering across the room. Suddenly, Jim was up and out of the bed.

He dashed across the room and tore past us, running down the hall and taking the stairs three at a time. When he reached the bottom, he turned back to stare at us. His eyes were dark, sunken, and hollow. A twisted, terrible smile was plastered upon his lips. "Run. Run. Run," he hissed from the bottom of the stairs. "Better catch me. Catch me. Catch me. Catch me." With that, he sprinted into the kitchen where we'd left Joey in his Pack 'n Play.

A bitter, angry laugh trickled from his lips as Jack and my father raced down the hall. Above the stomping of their feet against the stairs as they chased after Jim, I heard the wail of my brother and a half-growled shout. "HUSH LITTLE BABY!"

"JIM! YOU PUT HIM DOWN!" Jack roared, as he turned the corner. "Don't you dare hurt him! You put him down!" I'd never heard my brother so angry. Tears streamed down my face and I looked around, desperate for someone to turn to for comfort.

There was no one.

I was alone.

I didn't remember seeing my mother go downstairs, but I realize now that she must have. I didn't know where Johnny had gone, but he wasn't in his bed.

I was at the top of the stairs, sobbing uncontrollably as I listened to my family scream at Jim, pleading with him to put his youngest brother down. Joey wailed, sobbing desperately. He screamed for my mother and Jim screamed back at him to shut up, which only made Joey's wailing worse. I pressed myself against the wall, unable to catch my breath. My hands shook at my sides. My shoulders shook with heavy sobs. I slid down the wall, trying to make myself as small as possible. I covered my ears and pulled my legs up. Slowly, I rocked back and forth, trying not to think of what Jim might do to my little brother.

I didn't understand what possession was at the time. I didn't understand that David was controlling Jim's every move.

I didn't understand that my brother was no longer my brother.

As far as I was concerned, Jim had become a monster.

CRASH

Joey shrieked, his desperate cries filling the house for three terrible, uninterrupted seconds. And then… silence.

My heart dropped.

I was sure he'd died.

"Drop the knife!" my father roared. The house shook with another loud thump. I could hear something, perhaps boots, knocking against the floor time and time again.

And then, another scream. This one deeper, filled with a sort of rage that was palpable, even from upstairs.

I yipped and pulled myself into a tiny ball. My heart thrummed, my mind raced. Tears streamed down my cheeks, and I prayed. I begged God to stop Jim before he killed anyone else. I begged Him not to let my family be torn apart any more than it already had been.

BANG

The walls shook, and the windows rattled.

Joey shrieked.

Relief the likes of which I'd never known flooded me. My little brother was alive! Possibly injured, but alive all the same!

"SON OF A BITCH!" Jack shouted. "HE FUCKING STABBED ME!"

CRASH

The familiar sound of glass shattering and hitting the ground sliced through the silence.

THUMP

There was a series of loud yells and bangs. It sounded as though someone were throwing furniture around downstairs. It sounded like it had the night David had been unable to get into Jack's room.

"LET ME GO! LET ME GO! LET ME GO!" Jim shouted, though his voice wasn't his own. It was scratchy and growling, and sounded more like David than Jim. "GET OFF ME! I'LL KILL YOU! I'LL GUT THAT LITTLE BRAT! I'LL STRING YOU ALL UP FROM THE TREES! I'LL DECORATE THIS HOUSE WITH YOUR FUCKING BLOOD! I'LL MAKE YOU BEG ME FOR DEATH!"

"Don't kill him, Josh! Don't kill him!" my mom shouted.

BANG

"We aren't gonna kill him," Jack growled. I'd never heard him so angry. I'd never thought my brother could sound like a monster. "Take Joey, and get the hell out of here!"

"Where's Johnny and Jasmine?" my mother yelped, her voice nearly entirely drowned out by the growling screams and the loud bangs.

"Do I look like I fuckin' know?" my father barked.

"Get the fuck out of here! Find the k—" Jack cried out in pain. It was the sort of noise that nightmares are made of. "Son of a bitch!" The sound of flesh pounding against flesh filled the air.

"Don't hurt him!" my mother shouted.

"FUCK OFF!" Jim screamed. "GET OFF ME! GET OFF ME!"

Rapid footfalls exploded, getting closer and closer. I curled tighter into my ball and sank into the corner. I imagined David scaling the walls, coming for me at full speed. "JASMINE!" my mother screamed. "JOHNNY!"

It took everything in me to peel my eyes open and search for my mother. I found her desperately running toward the stairs. "I'm here," I tried to shout, but the words died as soon as they left me. I sucked in a deep breath and uncurled from myself. "I'm here!" I said louder. "I'm here!"

Relief washed over her features when she spotted me. I kept my eyes locked on my mother as she rushed up the stairs. Joey clung to her, looking shaken up but unharmed. My spine tingled in anticipation and anxiety. I was waiting for Jim or David to jump out of nowhere and snatch her away.

It never happened. She came to a stop safely at my side. I hadn't noticed until that very moment that I was shaking, and sobbing, almost uncontrollably. "Where's Johnny?" she demanded.

I shook my head. My body and my mind were numb. I opened my mouth to answer, but no noise came out. I tried again with the same result. It wasn't until the third attempt that I managed a small, choked, "I don't know."

"I'm right here," Johnny's voice rang out from the bedroom behind me. I jumped and let out a shriek of horror. With images of empty eyes and pointed teeth dancing in my mind, I spun around, eyes urgently searching for the source of the noise, only to find a shaking, crying Johnny retreating from the closet.

Mom immediately spun around, heading toward the stairs. She waved for us to follow her. "Let's go! Let's go! We're going out to the car! Let's go!" she shouted rapidly, giving us no time at all to think before she barked her next identical command.

My mind was moving slowly, and as a result, it got stuck on one detail. "Why are we going to car?" I demanded. "What about Jack and Dad?" There were very few things I considered certainties. Most of the ones I'd once clung to had been ripped out from under me when David had arrived. But among the very few left was the knowledge that under no circumstances would Jack or Dad ever leave us anywhere. *Ever.*

"Don't argue with me!" my mother snapped. "Get your ass up! Let's go!"

BANG

"NO! Hold him down!" my dad shouted. "No, no, no! The knife! Don't let him get the knife!"

A metallic clank hit the ground, and both Jack and Jim shouted. The downstairs was flooded with loud, growled sorts of noises. "Hold him still! Hold him still!" my father shouted.

"I'm trying!" Jack snapped.

I stayed in my place, shaking, tears streaming down my face. My mother stomped toward me, her eyes filled with sudden fiery ire. She grabbed my arm and wrenched me upright. I cried out, hot pain blooming along my shoulder. "SHUT UP!" my mother screamed, her face just inches from my own. "SHUT THE HELL UP, AND GET DOWNSTAIRS!"

I didn't argue.

The sound of feet stomping against the floor and the bang and clatter of a chair falling to the ground sliced through the air. Jim wailed, his voice deep and angry. I walked slowly, following my mother, but dreading going anywhere near my brother. I didn't want to see him. I didn't want to see what had happened to him.

But there were only small, muffled words from my father and Jack.

I felt like I was walking to death row as my foot hit every wooden step individually, getting me closer and closer to the source of the noise. Dread bubbled up inside of me. My feet hit the last step too soon.

I found myself following my mother and Johnny through the living room and past the kitchen. I managed to keep my eyes away from the kitchen entirely for nearly five whole seconds before curiosity got the best of me.

Johnny and Dad looked exhausted. Their clothing was ripped in places, and stretched, giving it an all-over sort of disheveled look. Their hair stuck out in every direction.

Jack was bent over, huffing, trying to catch his breath. Sweat and blood gleamed along his brow. Crimson oozed through the fingers of the hand that clamped down upon his left arm just below the shoulder. It dripped onto the floor with a slow sort of pitter-patter.

Jim was shouting and growling, sounding more like an injured animal than a human. He was rocking the chair back and forth, causing the wooden legs to crash against the floor. His hands were firmly bound behind him. Duct tape circled his chest and connected him to the chair. The gray tape did the same for each of his legs. He shrieked furiously.

His eyes moved to me as I stared.

He stopped. His whole body went still. He glared up at me from behind sunken eyes.

A sinister laugh trickled from between his lips.

Dad stood up and crossed the room to stop at Jack's side. "Let's see." His words drew me away from my thoughts, allowing me to pull my eyes away from Jim. I watched with worry etched into my brow. Jack winced as he pulled his shirt up over his torso. His arm retreated from the sleeve. A large gash stared back at the world, perched just below his shoulder. Blood trickled down his bronze skin, leaving streaks of crimson behind.

My dad turned the arm this way and that to get a better look, his brows furrowed, his lips pressed together into a thin line. It was the look he got when he was deep in thought. "You need stitches," he decided, looking back to my mother. "Take Jack to go to the hospital."

"Not a chance in hell," Jack answered. He pulled away from my father's grasp stubbornly. "I'm not about to leave you and the kids here alone with him. I'll be fine. We've got gauze in the medicine cabinet. I've gotten deeper cuts while fuckin' around in the barn, and I've never gone in for those. You remember the nail I shoved through my foot while jumping off the back of your truck?" he asked, trying to smile through the pain.

He was doing a fantastic job of ignoring Jim, who raged just behind him.

I, however, was not. I couldn't peel my eyes away from him for more than just a minute or two at a time.

"You remember the hospital visit afterwards?" Dad pressed on.

Jim stared me down, his tongue running over his teeth. In a sing-song sort of voice he began to chant something I couldn't understand.

The lights flickered.

"You gonna call Father Brown?" Jack asked. Dad gave a nod. "Then I'll go in after he gets here. You're gonna need help if he gets loose," Jack said, motioning to Jim.

Jack's eyes softened the moment they hit Jim. Demon dwelling within him or not, the outside form belonged to our brother, and I could see from the look in his eyes that this hurt. It hurt more than it had hurt those times David had terrorized us in his own form. It hurt in a different sort of way. One that, even now, I'm not sure I fully understand. "I'm sorry, Jimmy," Jack said, his voice sounding hollow and defeated. "This will all be over soon."

Jim's features soured. His lips pulled back, revealing teeth. His nose crinkled. His eyes went hard and dark. "Oh no it won't," he hissed angrily. "We're just getting started, Jackie."

No one tried to talk to Jim after that.

Dad called Father Brown and asked that he come down right away. I didn't hear the whole conversation, but I gathered that Jim was possessed by David, something that I think, to some degree, I had already known.

Jim spent the next twenty minutes struggling in his place, grunting and screaming. He made low, angry noises that sounded more animalistic than human. He fought against the ropes. He growled, he hissed, and he tossed out insults to each and every one of us. He laughed, a high-pitched, uncontrolled sort of laugh. He whispered words I couldn't understand, in languages I knew he didn't know, under his breath. He screamed wordlessly at the air.

Twice he toppled over his chair. Both times he tried to bite my father as he righted him.

Seeing Jim in the state he was in was hard, but there wasn't much of a choice. Mom had to be there to help. She was the only one of us that had any medical training at all (she'd worked briefly in a hospital as a Nursing

Assistant). If Mom was inside to help with medical stuff, and Jack and Dad were inside to restrain Jim in case he got loose, then what choice did we have? We were stuck.

So we stayed in the kitchen. We cried. We watched our older brother as he struggled with the demon that wreaked havoc on his body. My mother tried, time and time again, to place cold washcloths on his forehead or on his neck. Each time, he would buck, or turn suddenly and try to bite at her fingers.

Slowly, the family began to break down. My father was angry; I could see it all over his face. I watched him seethe, likely pissed that there was nothing he could do to end his son's suffering.

I watched my mother cry and plea with it to release her baby.

I watched as the demon laughed at her pain.

At some point while I sat against the wall, Joey in my lap, trying to ignore the screams and sobs, Johnny had gotten up to stare out the window. His shoulder slumped, his body stood with a sort of tilt to it, his head hung. He looked entirely broken. I couldn't help but feel bad for him. As much of an ass as he'd been to me earlier, I knew on some level I'd deserved it. I had brought this hell to us. I deserved his anger, and he deserved an outlet to release it. Perhaps I didn't rationalize it like that at the time. But I remember feeling at peace with the idea that Johnny would likely never forgive me.

I was okay with that, because I'd never forgive myself.

I stood up, picking Joey up, and wandered over to the window as well. Needing a change, wanting not to have to focus on Jim any more. We watched the familiar silver car slow at the front of our driveway. "Dad, Father Brown is here," Johnny called, his voice obtund.

The Sable pulled into the driveway and parked directly beside my father's station wagon. Father Brown and two men I didn't recognize stepped out, stretching and pulling bags out of the trunk. Not more than ten feet away from me, Jim began to laugh, a deep, angry, sour sort of noise that caused my stomach to flip and turn. His eyes widened and his mouth opened. He shouted something to the heavens that I didn't understand. His body began to sway as he repeated the words over and over again.

There was a loud click that drew my attention back outside.

The barn door opened.

Boars and sows rushed out.

"DAD! THE PIGS ARE OUT!" I shrieked. The boars were dangerous, I knew that much. Dad had a very strict rule about us not going anywhere near their pen. He always warned us that if they tasted blood, they'd frenzy and maul anything in their way.

I watched terror wash over the faces of the men in our driveway. They were too far away to be able to run to the home quickly enough to avoid being mauled.

They began to scramble for the still-opened doors of the car, seeking safety within its confines.

The doors slammed.

My heart sank as I watched them pull desperately at them. Father Brown fumbled with his keys, looking back at the pigs who rushed them with fear dancing in his eyes.

Heavy footsteps tore past me.

I looked up. At some point, Dad had gone to get his gun. He threw the door open. It slammed against the side of the house with a sharp bang. "GET INSIDE!" he shouted.

He raised his gun.

BANG! BANG! BANG!

Three boars went down. They thrashed and screamed on the ground. Blood poured out of their skulls, staining the once pale-colored gravel.

My dad was one hell of a shot. I'd never seen him miss anything. He and Jack routinely had contests. My father always bragged that if he could see it, he could shoot it. I'd never been more thankful for how often he practiced.

I watched in absolute horror as the group of men stumbled all over themselves to get inside. They tripped and stuttered up the stairs, but the boars never faltered. One particularly large black boar charged forward, mouth gaping. It was less than two feet from Father Brown's legs as he surged forward.

The pig began to close the distance.

Father Brown changed course, opening my father up for the shot.

BANG!

The pig went down. It shrieked in pain, but died quickly.

The men climbed up the steps, bursting through the door and spilling into the living room. My father slammed the door. The sound of hooves on the wooden porch echoed through the home.

Father Brown panted, anger washing over his features. "We nearly died! Why were the pigs o—"

Jim screamed and rocked back and forth in the chair. "GET OUT!" he ordered angrily. His voice was deep, but sounded split, as though there were two voices talking in unison, harmonized completely. It made me want to vomit.

Father Brown's eyes widened with something akin to fear. His attention snapped to Jim. The color leaked from his face. "Dear God," he whispered, hand on his chest.

Father Brown stepped into the kitchen, flanked by his two companions. Jim huffed and growled. Spittle flew out of his mouth. His back arched. His nose crinkled. His lips curled. "STAY BACK!" he barked. "STAY BACK!" His head jerked back and he let out a deafening roar. "GET OUT! GEEEEET OOOOOOUUUUUUT!" he growled. "GET OUT!"

SLAM

The kitchen door swung wildly, hitting the wall behind it before slamming closed. Over and over again it went on, just as it had the day we'd left for the forest. The kitchen windows slid up before slamming back down. Long cracks spidered along them, but still they continued. The glass began to chip and fall away, hitting the ground, but they never slowed. "GET OUT!" he shrieked. "GET AWAY!"

Father Brown swallowed hard. With shaking hands, he placed his bag on the table and pulled from it a bible and an odd metal thing with holes on the top. I didn't know it at the time, but it was designed to sprinkle holy water.

The two other men also pulled items from their own bags. The shorter, balding man with thick glasses and a limp brandished a large metal cross and a bible. The taller, thinner man with wispy brown hair took from his pouch a few small coins, a bible, and some medical supplies.

"We are about to begin," Father Brown said solemnly, looking to us. "Usually I wouldn't allow the children to be present, but I'd say here is the safest place for them." Looking back, I know now that he was worried that David would find a way to kill us, just as he'd tried to kill the priest and the others. His eyes returned to Johnny and me. They were hard and cold. When he spoke, he did so in a way that left no room for arguments. "Listen carefully, do exactly as I tell you. You understand? When we begin, it will say and do things that your brother, Jim, would never do. You must forgive him what's about to happen. It isn't him we're dealing with tonight. When it speaks, do not speak back to it. Do not listen to anything it says. Don't even look at it." The priest's words shook me to the very core. I gave him nothing more than a weak nod of my head. "Hopefully this will all be over soon."

Jim laughed, a low, growling sort of noise. It oozed from his lips and tumbled through the air, broken and jagged. The sickly noise slithered up my spine and made my heart thrum out of control. Suddenly the air around us felt heavy and too warm. Jim's neck craned around to stare out the window. He hissed a few broken words that made no sense to me.

"Shit!" Johnny breathed as he nudged my side. I spun around and followed my shaking brother's line of sight. There, surrounded by puddles of their own blood, the pigs that my father had shot down began to stir.

It was small at first. Just a kick of the leg or a twitch of the head. But soon, they began to struggle to their feet. They stumbled, back and forth, their hooves clip-clopping on the blood-stained gravel. I looked on in horror, watching bits of blood, skull, and things far too dark and thick to be blood fall from their heads.

To this day, I'm convinced David raised four pigs from the dead. My lungs emptied. I vomited as I watched their once-lifeless bodies roam the outside. Tears streamed down my face. I would have nightmares about that for years to come.

Father Brown turned to me as I whimpered, following my line of sight. "Come away from there," he called. I looked back to see his eyes filled with fear and the color gone from his cheeks. He looked as though he'd aged twenty years. I don't think he'd ever seen anything like the lurid scene that unfolded outside.

I didn't have to be told twice. I shuffled across the floor, keeping my eyes low and away from Jim. I found a place in the corner, as far away from Jim as I could get without actually leaving the room. With Joey on my lap, I sat with my arms wrapped tightly around him. I hadn't noticed Johnny leave the window, but soon enough he sat beside me, tears streaming down his cheeks.

The three of us huddled together and sobbed.

Father Brown began to speak. "In the name and authority of the Lord Jesus Christ, we renounce all the power of darkness which may exist in this area or in the life of Jeremy Isaac for any reason. We bind all evil spirits assigned to Jeremy Isaac and forbid you to operate in any way, in the name of Jesus Christ."

Jim began to laugh.

His head shook back and forth, slowly at first, and then more rapidly. His movements became jerky and unpredictable. Saliva and foam began to spill from his parted lips. He rocked his chair back and forth. A loud buzz hummed, and bees, flies, wasps, and a dozen other insects began to pour slowly into the room. Try as she might, my mother couldn't find where they were coming from. It was as though he were materializing them.

His choked laughing never ceased.

The priest repeated the prayer over and over. Jim laughed each time.

It wasn't until the ninth time the three men chanted it together that disgust and anger washed over Jim's features. His laughter ended. Fire burned just beneath the surface. He raged, screaming and cursing as the men spoke.

There was a terrible squealing noise from outside. The pigs began to drop back to the ground. The bugs, too, fell to the ground.

Father Brown shook the metal container, splashing holy water along Jim as he spoke, this time with more conviction. "I command you, oh devils, give me your name and the time of your departure."

"FUCK YOU!" Jim shouted. His whole body went rigid. Languages I'd never heard, and couldn't identify, spilled from his mouth in a voice that didn't belong to him. Father Brown regarded him with cautious eyes. The tall, skinny man went to his side, placing a finger on his bound wrist and throwing out numbers. At the time, I didn't know they represented his pulse, only that the numbers fluctuated from very high to very low.

"I command you, oh devils, give me your name and the time of your departure!" Father Brown shouted.

"**NNNNNNNN…NNNNNNN….NNNNNNN… NNNNOOOOOOOOOOOOOOO!**" Jim growled, his voice more animal than human. Spit flew from his mouth as he shouted. He rocked in his chair back and forth; his eyes were dead and cold. The house began to quake. "NNNNNOOOOO!" he shouted again.

"I command you, oh devils, give me your name and the time of your departure!" The three men chanted the words over and over again.

Jim's neck craned back. He tried to buck, he tried everything in his power to get out of the chair, but to no avail. "NAAAAAMMMMMEEEEEEEES!" he shouted. "NAMES! NAMES! NAMES! YOU WANT MY NAAAAAMMMMMEEEEEES!"

"In the name of the Father, Son, and Holy Spirit I rebuke you, oh evil thing! I command you, oh devil, give me your name and the time of your departure!" Father Brown shouted. Sweat poured down his face, but he repeated the words time and time again.

Jim began to shake, his eyes rolled back into his head. His whole body shook. Foam spilled from his mouth. His body tensed and became rigid. "He's seizing! He's seizing!" the taller, skinny man shouted. "Someone help me!" He was busying himself, trying to push Jim's rigid, bowed body back into a sitting position.

The world seemed to slow.

It was as if I had all the time in the world to shout a warning to the second priest.

But I couldn't make my voice work.

Jim's head snapped up. His eyes gleamed in the dim light, looking almost as though they were glowing. Heavy with the promise of violence, they were no longer his eyes. They belonged to David. A twisted, evil smile played along his lips, curling upward in an almost unreal fashion.

Jim lunged.

He bit down on the man's cheek.

The priest screamed in pain.

Suddenly every adult in the room was on him. They tried to pull him away, but to no avail. Jim's teeth sunk in further and further. The wails of agony became more desperate. The priest flailed and shrieked. He gripped Jim's shoulders, trying to gain enough leverage to push himself away.

Beneath the panic of the moment, I could hear a slow, joyous sort of laugh that trickled from Jim's chest. His eyes gleamed with amusement and satisfaction.

Finally, Jim released the man.

He stumbled back. Blood poured from the perfect circular wound left behind.

Boisterous laughter flooded the room as blood and mirth poured from Jim's lips. "No names," he hissed. "No names."

***

The sun was dying, strangled rays of light touched the horizon, colors splashed along the evening sky as the moon began to peek into view. Sunlight danced off the pointed edges of the glass that jutted from the windowsills and lay discarded upon the floor.

The discontented grunts of the pigs outside filtered through the broken windows and echoed through the home. A cool breeze carried with it the smell of hogs and straw. Hooves clip-clopped on the wood of the porch.

I focused on each of these details separately as I tried to ignore the withering screams of my brother as he thrashed in the chair. I looked away as the tall, skinny man dashed out of the room, my mother on his heels, mumbling something about likely needing stitches. I kept my eyes off Jack as he silently cried. He crouched down, his hands buried in his hair as he watched his baby brother fight the demon inside him.

If I kept my eyes on the window, if I focused on the pigs and the breeze and the dying light, then I didn't have to think about what was happening.

Father Brown began to scream something, but I was doing everything in my power to ignore it. My fingers absently trailed through Joey's thin hair as I tried desperately to quell his despondent wails. He squirmed in my grasp, throwing his body this way and that. He kicked the ground and demanded that I left him go. My arms held steadfast, but to this day, I don't know how.

As I was jostled from side to side with my brother's struggle, I felt distant, detached, almost as though I weren't there at all. As if every piece of me that wasn't my physical body was somewhere else.

I stayed in that wonderfully murky place of peace for as long as I could. It wasn't until the ground beneath me began to quake and the things on the shelves began to fall and shatter upon the ground that I returned—kicking and screaming—to the present. Father Brown was standing over my screaming brother with a cross in his hand. Jim, who had once been as bronze as Jack, was now ashen and gray. His skin had turned a sickly sort of pasty color. His lips were blue. His eyes shone with a deep rage that set my teeth on edge.

"...give me your name and the time of your departure!" the priest shouted, one hand firmly grasping Jim's shoulder. The other held the cross, like a weapon, in front of his face.

Jim threw his head back. A low, choked, ragged laugh trickled from between his parted lips. The priest's hand shot out, taking Jim by the chin, and he pulled his head back down so Jim was forced to look at him. He shoved the cross into his face. "LOOK AT ME!" Father Brown shouted.

Jim only laughed, his eyes diverted, and landed squarely on me. My stomach dropped, ice rolled through my veins. "Me, me, me, me..." Jim repeated, the voice no longer his own, it was deep, sounding almost as though it had been slowed.

Father Brown's grip tightened. He wrenched Jim's head back so he had no choice but to look at him. "Your name, devil! Give me your name! It is God who commands you! Give me your name!"

Jim's smile disappeared, leaving only hostile revulsion in its wake. His nose crinkled, his lip curled, his eyes grew cold. He huffed through gritted teeth, spittle flying out of his mouth and onto Father Brown. "I've burned down a dozen homes," he warned, the stove burners beginning to glow. Heat radiated off them. "I'll burn this one to the ground too. I'll watch the skin melt from your bones, and I'll relish in the fact that it will be *nothing* compared to hellfire." The doors slammed shut, and the locks clicked.

My father rushed over to the stove, turning them off one by one.

And one by one, they' turned themselves back on.

Father Brown leaned further in as he hissed the words into the ear of the demon. "I command you, unclean spirit, whoever you are, along with all your minions now attacking this servant of God." Jim began to twitch, his eyes slamming shut in agony as he writhed, trying to get away. "By the mysteries of the incarnation, passion, resurrection and ascension of our Lord Jesus Christ, by the descent of the Holy Spirit, by the coming of our Lord for judgment, that you tell me by some sign your name,"

"No names!" Jim hissed, his eyes bleeding to black. "No names."

Father Brown continued, his grip growing tighter as he leaned into my brother. The house vibrated as Jim cried out and fought against the restraints. "And the day and hour of your departure. I command you, moreover, to obey me to the letter." Jim began to snap wildly at the air, trying to catch Father Brown's flesh between his teeth, but to no avail. He screamed away the pain, his muscles tensed, his back bowed. "I who am a minister of God despite my unworthiness; nor shall you be emboldened to harm in any way this creature of God, or the bystanders, or any of their possessions."

Jack stumbled, jerking weirdly and nearly falling to the ground. His hand went to his neck, which was now bare. The silver cross necklace he'd been wearing had been torn from his person by an invisible force. The cross, upside down, stuck to the wall. The pigs outside began to squeal.

Father Brown took a handful of Jim's hair and wrenched his head backward. His face lingered just inches away from Jim's. "Depart, then, transgressor. Depart, seducer, full of lies and cunning, foe of virtue, persecutor of the innocent. Give place, abominable creature, give way, you monster, give way to Christ, in whom you found none of your works. For he has already stripped you of your powers and laid waste your kingdom, bound you prisoner and plundered your weapons. He has cast you forth into the outer darkness, where everlasting ruin awaits you and your abettors. Your name! Tell me your name! God commands you! Tell me your name!"

Jim screamed, but instead of the dark, growling voice I'd come to expect from his body, it was sharp and nasally. It tugged at my heart, making me want to run to him.

It was Jim's voice.

He shrieked over and over again. Tears began to pour down his cheeks. His eyes widened, moving rapidly in search of anyone but the priest who lingered just above him. His body began to quake. "I'm sorry! I'm sorry! Please stop!" he pleaded with the priest. "Please! Please stop! Please!" He began to sob. His eyes were filled with both confusion and horror as he realized the man above him wasn't about to let him go. Jim's chest began to fall and rise at an alarming rate. Sweat beaded along his brow. "MAKE IT STOP!" he pleaded. "PLEASE, PLEASE, DAD!" He tried to writhe out of Father Brown's grasp to search for our father, but the priest held on too tightly. "Dad! Where are you? Daddy! Please help!" He winced in pain as Father Brown tightened his grip and forced him, again, to look at him. "MAKE HIM STOP! IT HURTS!" he sobbed pathetically. "IT HURTS! MAKE HIM STOP!"

My father had managed to turn all the burners off and was now looking at his son in absolute horror. He rushed to his side, as his child pleaded with him to make the pain go away. Father Brown's arm shot out, though his eyes never left my brother. "Stay back!" he commanded. "Stay back! It's not Jim!"

My father's features crumbled, confusion and sadness played in his eyes. "What do you mean?" my father asked, his voice sounding hollow and distant. "He's my son. That's my son you're torturing!"

Jim's features were caked with terror, his jaw trembled, his body shook. Wide eyes darted from the priest above him to his father. "I-it's me!" he swore. "It's me! I'm Jim! Please, Father, please let me go!"

"No!" Father Brown shouted, cold eyes staring into the face of the child below him. He motioned to the wall, where the cross still hung, upside down. "It isn't."

A rage-filled roar stirred within Jim's chest. The pigs outside began to squeal and stomp. "USELESS!" he growled. "FUCKING USELESS! FAILURE OF A FATHER! LET ME GO! LET MY GO!"

My father stumbled back, his eyes wide and his hands trembling. He took three steps back before bending over and sucking in a deep breath. Jack clasped a hand against his shoulder and bent down to whisper something to him that I couldn't hear.

The priest pressed his cross against Jim's temple. The beast writhed and screamed, hurled insults and berated everyone in the room, but Father Brown shouted a prayer above his words nonetheless. At the end of it all, he opened the shiny vial and dumped its contents atop Jim's head. "YOUR NAME!" Father Brown shouted. "GIVE ME YOUR NAME!"

Jim threw his head back, his eyes rolled into his head, his body trembled and shook. Foam poured from between his lips. "ELIGOS!" he shouted, a strangled sort of noise. "ELIGOS! ELIGOS! ELIGOS! ELIGOS!"

"Eligos," Father Brown seethed, his hands finding Jim's face as he pulled him down and stared into the face of the beast. "I see you, Eligos. God sees you! I command you, in the name of the almighty Father, in the name of His son, and our savior, Jesus Christ, that you depart this servant of God. I command you to leave Jeremy Isaac. I command you to depart! LEAVE!" he shouted.

With all the deafening noise around, I had hardly noticed Joey's desperate cries as he buried his face into my shoulder. But suddenly, with the last word of the priest's prayer, everything went silent. The pigs ceased their cries and their movement. Jim no longer shouted or growled. His body went very still, back still bowed against the tape that kept him in place. Jim's features went slack, his chin rested against his chest. He was contorted in an odd sort of way that burned holes in my memory. His eyes had rolled back into his head; only the whites were showing.

The seconds ticked by, and for a long time, Joey's crying and the hard breathing of Father Brown were the only noises in the room.

The necklace fell to the ground with a metallic clank.

A deafening shriek tore from Jim's chest. He shook. He thrashed. He contorted.

And then he fell, slumping in the chair, entirely motionless. Father Brown bent down, his forehead touching Jim's as he prayed for him.

With shaking hands and tears in their eyes, my father and Jack freed Jim. My father carried him, as though he were only a toddler, as we hurried through the front door and waded through a sea of pigs to the car. My mother sat beside Jim the whole ride to the hospital, keeping a close eye on his heart rate and making sure he was still breathing.

Jack was given stitches and sent on his way, while Jim was admitted into the hospital and kept for nearly a week. The prolonged fever, combined with the physical strain of the exorcism, had left him weak and ill. Concerns of brain damage were expressed.

I'd never been so relieved when all his cognitive and physical tests came back normal.

For the next six weeks we stayed with Father Brown. Jim joined us at the second week. Despite him not suffering any long-term physical repercussions from the event, he didn't escape unscathed. It would seem that the psychological damage done was unending. Night terrors became his new reality; they were frequent, nearly every day, sometimes multiple times a day. He began to wet his bed. He refused to be alone, even for just a moment or two. He'd jump at every small sound and disturbance. He hardly did anything but sit in front of the television, but even then what he viewed was very limited. Anything more mature than Disney movies and *I Love Lucy* reruns was too much for him to handle. He'd begin to shake and rock in his place, mumbling something about not wanted to be invaded again.

It was near the end of the third week that my father began going back to the home to fix things. Each night he'd return, telling us that it had been quiet, that there had been no sign of David anywhere. Father Brown assured us that we'd never face Eligos again. That he'd been cast down into the depths of Hell.

We believed him, and nearly two months after the exorcism, we moved back into the home.

Things were clunky, and hard at first. We all slept in the living room, each of us too frightened to sleep anywhere else. The upstairs went entirely unused by everyone but Joey, who frequently played in his room. We didn't allow it at first, but as we slowly began to accept that David was gone, we started allowing him to go up and play with his toys.

Jim hated even being near the staircase, and often set up blockades when Joey wasn't up there. All of us knew that a simple wall made of end tables, pillows, and blankets would never keep David at bay (hell, it hardly kept Joey out), but none of us pointed this out. We let him cope in whatever way he could.

My father and mother started making preparations to sell the home. The housing market had tanked. Our real estate agent tried to convince my parents to put the move on hold for a few years, until the market bounced back. She warned that even with the massive amount of land we were offering with the home, it was likely we'd get less than three quarters of our asking price.

My parents didn't care.

They wanted out.

We all did.

We showed the home to several prospective buyers. Three times we thought we'd sold it, and all three times the buyer backed out. Two of them said they had a sinking feeling about it. Another said the property itself made him feel nervous.

This did nothing to calm our nerves.

The months dragged on. The hot, sticky months were behind us as we headed into winter. The trees were bare, and the grass was a dead brown sort of color. We hadn't gotten snow in nearly a decade, but my father swore that we might that year. I couldn't deny that I was excited. I'd never seen snow before. At least, not in real life, anyway.

My parents hoped that perhaps the cool weather would stifle some of the smell from the pigs and encourage buyers.

We had no such luck.

It was three days before Christmas, the morning crisp and cold. I started my day the same way I had for the past six weeks. I pulled on high-top, pink swampers and followed my father, Jack, Jim, and Johnny outside.

I had started helping the boys on the farm, and I was quite proud of myself for it.

With me gone from the home in the mornings, Mom was left to do the indoor chores with Joey. But he was little help, and often lost interest within the first few minutes. My mother never pushed him, the way she had the rest of us, to stay on task. Looking back, I'm sure she was driven by guilt. So, while she scrubbed away at dishes or wiped down walls, Joey could often be found playing in his room by himself. Sometimes, I'd hear him laugh from the window upstairs as he threw a ball against his wall or rolled his trucks across his floor. He was good at occupying himself, a trait that my mother rather appreciated, since none of us had had it as children.

I followed behind my line of siblings and waited for my father to tell me what I would be doing. Most of the time I was paired with Jim, since Johnny still had a nasty habit of knocking me down or trying to make me cry every chance he got. Today was no different. Dad told Jim and I to feed the pigs, so Jack mixed together feed and we retrieved the buckets.

I'd gained a good amount of muscle in the past several weeks. I no longer struggled with the filled bucket as I carried it down to the last pen and emptied it into a large feeder. Jim and I silently passed one another time and time again as we slowly filled every feeder in the barn.

Soon enough, we were done, and ready to head off to the second barn, where nursing sows and piglets were kept. My swampers, caked with brown mud, kicked up dirt as Jim and I made our way down the driveway, a little ways further from the home. This was my favorite part of the day, partly because I got to see the cows, and partly because Joey's window faced the barn. He'd always slap the glass and call cheerfully to me as we passed. I thought it was the cutest thing. Most mornings, I would spend several minutes waving back to him and making silly faces.

I'd just reached the barn door, my fingers grasping the cool metal, when the sound of a window opening drew my attention away. Joey was notorious for opening the window to shout hellos down to us, but it was mid-winter, and positively freezing. The heat was on in the house, and I knew damn well that Dad or Mom would swat him for doing it. I turned around just as he called a cheerful, "Hi, Jasmine!"

"Joseph Lucas! You close tha—" My voice died out, caught in my throat. My eyes widened, and for a moment I thought my heart had stopped. I wanted to scream. Or cry. Or point. Or do something to get Jim's attention, and show him what was happening.

But I was frozen in my place, unable to move.

Jim paused, concern etched along his brow as he stared at me. "Jazz?" Jim asked, waving a hand in front of my face. I wanted to react. I wanted to tell him to turn around. Internally I was screaming for him to look up, but my lips refused to obey. So instead I stared, my mouth agape and fear scrawled across my features. "Earth to Jasmine. You okay?" he asked, narrowing his eyes. Finally, he turned to follow my line of sight.

His body stiffened. The familiar sour smell of urine flooded my senses. The putrid liquid splashed along Jim's pants and trailed down his pant leg. I could hear it puddle in his boot.

He was the first of us to manage to speak. It was just a choked sort of noise that I think was supposed to be *no*.

Standing right behind Joey, eyeless, dressed in a red shirt and jeans, was David.

His lips turned up into a terrible smile.

Joey's features crumbled as he watched us in complete confusion. I couldn't peel my eyes away from the window as my baby brother spun around. I could see fear radiate off him, even with his back to me. He shrank away from the beast, trying to make himself as small as possible.

David pushed him, sending him through the screen of the window and hurtling toward the earth.

Jim and I ran, but we weren't nearly fast enough. Joey tumbled through the sky and landed on his back with a sickening thud. As we sprinted closer to him, I watched his eyes peel open and shut and his head wobble from side to side as he opened his mouth time and time again to try to scream. No sound came out, but tears streamed down his face all the same. I don't think I'll ever get that image out of my head.

I knelt down beside Joey, trying to remember what to do, but I was drawing a blank. Did I move him? Or keep him still? I didn't know. My heart pounded against my chest, and finally I found my voice. I shrieked, time and time again, through heavy sobs. Joey jumped with each of my wails, his tiny eyes opening only to shut again.

Jack and my father were at my side in an instant. They shouted questions, but I couldn't answer. All I could manage were the same ear-piercing screams.

Jim pointed upward.

Jack's head tilted, eyes stationed upon the window. Anger rolled over him as he caught sight of David, who stood in the window, a smug smile plastered on his lips.

"MOM!" Jim shrieked. I wasn't sure if he was calling her out to help with Joey, or if he was shouting for her because he was afraid of what David might do.

The rest of the details are all a little blurry. Joey wasn't moving. Everyone was hysterical. Jack dialed 911. I don't remember what happened in the nearly half an hour it took for 911 to get to us. Only that my father sat next to my brother the whole time, his massive hand covering Joey's. My mother cried and kept a hand on his chest, making sure that he was still breathing.

The men came and lifted him upon a stretcher. Mom and Dad rode in the ambulance while Jack drove us to the hospital to meet them. I remember the car being filled with silence, occasionally shattered by a heavy sob. I remember Jim looking out the window with that thousand-yard stare of a child who had seen too much. I remember feeling entirely responsible, and Johnny's piercing glares only confirming that for me.

Joey underwent nine surgeries and stayed in the hospital for nearly a solid month. Several internal organs had ruptured, and he'd shattered multiple bones. He never walked again. His spine had been broken in four places.

We never returned to the home.

We stayed with Father Brown for six months while we closed on the house. My father said he informed the new owners of the strange happenings, and they assured him they weren't superstitious. To this day, I don't know if that's true or not. I also know I'll never go back there to find out.

We left, moving north, putting as much of the country between us and the home as we could. For the next twelve years, I lived with my parents in the small home they'd bought with the money we'd made off the house.

Twenty-one years later, our family had recovered from our experience with David. Jack went to school and became a preacher. He married a lovely woman, and together they had two children. This winter, they'll be welcoming their first grandchild into the world.

Jim moved to California in his early twenties. He spent two years doing a lot of nothing before he went to school. He got a degree in religious studies and has spent a good portion of his adult life studying demons.

Johnny left home to move in with a group of friends at the age of eighteen and never looked back. He never had any interest in college, and instead opted to get a job at a local factory. He's managed to make supervisor.

I never forgave myself for inviting David into our home. I moved out at eighteen to live with a friend of mine while we went to school. I managed to earn a degree and moved out of state for my first real job. I met my husband there, through a friend. We've been happily together for nearly six years now. I've never seen David again.

Joey didn't let his disability stop him. He graduated high school and is currently pursuing a degree in teaching.

My parents never recovered from their guilt. My father turned to drinking, and my mother receded into her shell. All of us, save for Joey, live out of state, so we really only see them twice a year during family get-togethers. They like to act happy, but I think we can all see past the facade.

My relationship with Johnny was never repaired. He's made it clear that he'll never forgive me for bringing David into our lives. Oddly enough, neither Jim nor Joey blame me. Jack insists that it could have happened to anyone, and blaming anyone other than Lucifer himself is pointless. My parents have never spoken about who they blame. It's a topic they both avoid entirely.

An Email From My Daughter's Killer

By Henry Galley, Reddit User /u/*DoubleDoorBastard*

Runner Up—October, 2016

———————

Do you believe in coincidences?

Seems like a funny question, doesn't it? I've never paid it much thought before now, either. Perhaps I have some explaining to do.

As of yesterday, it's been a year since my daughter went missing. There was never any ransom note, no remains discovered, and not an iota of evidence to support the standard theories of foul play and kidnapping. Aside from her absence itself, the whole situation seemed freakishly clean.

At only fourteen years old, she'd gone missing without a trace.

Her name was Emily. I can say that dreaded "was" with confidence now. It's a bitter blessing; one that's come at great cost to all of us.

When Emily disappeared, she left myself, her father, and her older brother, Joseph, in a state of perpetual anxiety. The limbo of monstrous uncertainty. Every phone call was a needle pressed into our skin, and every newscast that aired about that poor girl "still missing, presumed dead" felt like having boiling water poured down our throats.

Not knowing: that's the real torture. Until yesterday, I truly believed that.

Until yesterday, when I got an email from an unknown source. An email claiming to have the truth of what happened to Emily on that terrible day.

The following is the content of that email.

***

From: imsosorry1234@gmail.com

Subject: An Apology For What I've Done

Hello Mrs. Stanfield.

I won't tell you my name. That's not important right now. What's important is what I've done, and how sorry I am for doing it.

I'll be quick and honest. Emily is dead, and I killed her. I would love to tell you it was quick, and merciful, but it was neither. She died slowly and terribly. I can't imagine that my initial enjoyment of that fact will serve as any kind of consolation.

I've loved Emily for a very long time, in what you might call an improper way. The hardest part was knowing she could never love me back, at least not in the way I loved her—though this wasn't for lack of trying. I'd made passes before, just silly attempts really, but she was never receptive to my affection. She was disgusted by me, and that made me feel small, and angry. Though I can be thankful of the fact that she never told you about any of it.

I guess it would have been terribly embarrassing for her if you knew. Not that she'll care now.

Do you know how hard it is to cope with fantasy, Mrs. Stanfield? I've had such ugly dreams about Emily, and I know that they're ugly, but I still can't help but find them so exciting. I've wondered many times over the past year whether it was the ugliness of it all that made me so passionate.

When all you've got is a fantasy, a fantasy that you think is unattainable, you spend a lot of time refining it, like a sculptor chipping away at a statue, hoping to find perfection hidden in the granite. It doesn't matter how many times you secretly loosen the valves with your hands, that just keeps the fantasy down—it doesn't destroy it, can't destroy it. It just gains another component. Maybe it's another fifteen minutes of torture, another scream. Maybe it's a different tool added to the kit.

By the time the fantasy comes to boil, it's too complex to be satisfying on the basis of thought alone. You have to make it into flesh. Warm, satisfying flesh. And I did, Mrs. Stanfield, I really did.

I have to be honest with you, it wasn't so much about wanting to live my fantasy as it was about wanting to know whether I had it in me to carry it out. There was no dignity in pleasuring myself to the thoughts of violence, only in being able to say that I had the courage to do the one thing that'd been giving my life any sort of meaning.

And, a year ago today, I proved that I did have that courage.

My little indiscretions were in the past. I was patient, like a crocodile, I played the long game. I got Emily to trust me again with time, I let her be comfortable around me, let her drop her guard.

She was on her way home from school when I finally took a chance and made my move. I'd picked out an old, beat-up shack in the woods in advance. I threw down a woolen tarp and prepared some shackles, I even lit a few candles for romantic effect. More for myself than her, admittedly.

Emily was apprehensive at first, but I managed to talk her into visiting the little cabin with me. The door was shut and bolted behind us before she ever even saw the gun I was holding, but when she did she was a good girl and didn't scream. Though I must say, I was a little disappointed at that.

I'm not a pornographer, so I won't be lurid with the details of what I did. I'm aware that it's perverse, but the wind outside hardly matters when you're a hurricane. My whole life was perversity, hidden and locked away, Emily was the outlet for that perversity. Part of me thinks I only ever loved her because she was convenient, because she was accessible.

I used a hammer, a knife, a pair of pliers, and a power drill. It all got messier than I expected, so much blood, so much… other things. All in all it took a few hours before she finally died, which was admirable, she never did let me have my fun. Emily was such a strong girl, you should be proud of her, Mrs. Stanfield.

For my own pride, I'd like to state that I didn't fuck her before she died. I couldn't bring myself to cross that barrier, knowing her eyes would be on me while it was happening, the thought of it disgusted me. She died, to the best of my knowledge, a virgin.

Once I was fully done with her, and the euphoria of it all had passed, it dawned on me what a terrible thing I'd done. My pleasure turned to disgust, and all the sweetness that was inside of me while I was killing her turned sour. I realized that I was not meant to be a murderer, that it didn't suit me, that beyond the temporary pleasure of the act the thought of taking someone's life repulsed me.

I was a fantasist who made a terrible, terrible mistake, one that cost the life of a promising young girl. If there is a grand plan out there that we're all a part of, I could feel that what I had done was a deviation from that natural law. I was disgusted at the act, and at myself. This little experiment had backfired on me entirely. I was so out of my depth.

Once I'd gotten over the initial wave of fear and panic, I cut up Emily's body into smaller pieces that were easier to carry. I took all the pieces, wrapped them up in the woolen tarp, and burned them with lighter fluid in the woods. After that, I buried the bundle of charred bones and ashes, wishing I could have just forgotten all of it.

Killing Emily and doing the things I did to her body were not acts of courage, I've realized that over the past year. They were acts of obsession and cowardice, of a person not strong enough to overcome their darker urges. I've been wracked by guilt, surrounded by reminders of the life I've taken and can never give back.

That's why I've decided to do the courteous thing and let you know that I've decided to take another life: mine. All I can ever be is a danger to the people around me, a time-bomb destined to blow up and hurt another innocent. The only altruistic thing for a person in my position to do is take myself out of the picture.

I'm sorry for what I did to Emily. I don't expect for you to forgive me, nor do I think I deserve it. I just hope this gives you some sense of closure and allows you to move on.

My sincerest apologies.

***

After I read that terrible email, I cried for hours. I didn't have that violent reaction because I believed I'd been contacted by my daughter's killer, but just because I felt like someone was playing a horrific joke on my family after we'd been through so much. And on the anniversary of our Emily's disappearance, no less.

I didn't show my husband, or my son. I couldn't bear to. I just bore the cross myself and wore a brave face for them, knowing the anniversary was hard on all of us. I wouldn't let the monster on the other end of that email tear up my family.

But this morning, I heard two almighty bangs ring out from Joseph's bedroom. By the time his father and I had forced open the door, it was too late. He'd somehow gotten his hands on a gun and fired two shots: one through his laptop, and another through his forehead.

So, with this in mind, I'll ask you all again: Do you believe in coincidences?

November
—2016—

My Dad Finally Told Me What Happened That Day

By Jared Roberts, Reddit User /u/_nazisharks_

Winner—November, 2016

Annual Runner Up—Best Series, 2016

———————

I went to visit my dad not too long ago. We have a good relationship, we just don't talk all that much. His health is starting to decline. He was a little wistful. We were each just having a beer not saying much, when he said he had something he needed to tell me.

"You're old enough, you may as well know."

I didn't know what he was talking about, so I asked him.

"Remember that time I got home from work real upset and I wouldn't tell you what happened?"

I did remember. It wasn't something I would ever forget. He wasn't just upset. He was scared of something. I'd never seen Dad scared in my life until then. He was the kind of guy whose bar fights are town legends. I also remember he told me to never ask him about it, so I never had.

What he told me disturbed me profoundly. I've been bothered by it ever since. I hope writing it out will help me deal. First, a little background.

First Incident

When I was really young, like four or five, my dad and I lived in a cheap apartment building on the ground floor. I don't remember much about it. I know I didn't like it there. The kids weren't nice to play with. They'd steal my toys. And it was just a grimy area. But we were having tough times and it's what he could afford.

Probably what I remember most about the place was how I would be woken up from sleep every once in a while by flashing lights. I don't remember being too worried about it at first. I just assumed there was a lot of lightning in that area. I was five. I didn't know jack about meteorology.

One night, my dad had my uncle and his wife over for a crab leg dinner. I remember it distinctly because it was the first time I'd ever eaten crab. While they were talking, I casually mentioned the lightning from the previous night. Dad said, "There wasn't no lightning last night."

I thought he was just clowning around, so I laughed and told him how the flashing lights woke me up. He and my uncle got serious. That freaked me out. Because they were always silly when they got together. They asked me more questions about the lights, nothing I recall exactly. But they decided I was probably seeing headlights from cars driving by, shining on the curtains.

I guess I believed them. But after that, I'd always get nervous when the flashing lights would wake me up. Because I knew it wasn't lightning anymore. A few times I called for Dad when it happened, but when he'd get to my room there was nothing to see. He started telling me it was all in my head.

We moved out of that apartment after a year or so when Dad's handyman business picked up. The flashing stopped when we left. So I came to believe it was a combination of passing cars and my imagination. It wasn't something I ever gave much thought to again until recently.

Second Incident

One time I was helping my dad out on a job. This was a bigger job, kind of rebuilding a whole house, so he had a few other guys working with us. Some of them I knew and some I'd never seen before. I was used to it. It's what he always did on bigger jobs.

I was sitting off on my own eating my lunch and listening to my CD Walkman. Dad generally didn't eat lunch. He'd just get too into the work. So he was still busy on site. Suddenly I notice a guy walking toward me from the general direction of the site. I didn't remember seeing this guy before. But he was making a beeline straight for me. He was an oldish guy. His head was shaved. And he was wearing a Ramones t-shirt.

He sat down beside me—way too close—and didn't say a word. I took off my headphones, because I didn't want to be rude, and said, "Hi." He told me my dad was looking for me and I should head back as soon as I'd finished my sandwich. That was the plan anyway, but I said that was fine. To make things less awkward, I said I liked the Ramones. He didn't seem to even know who they were.

After sitting with me for a few moments longer, while I ate my sandwich uncomfortably, he got up and started walking away. I was relieved. I started to put the headphones back on when he stopped suddenly. I don't know why, but it freaked me out. I froze. He turned around and fixed me with the most hateful stare I'd ever seen. I didn't know what it felt like to be hated until then. It was like he wanted me dead.

I remember wondering what I should do when he attacked me. But he didn't attack. He just shouted, "Someone's been sleeping in your bed and I don't like it!"

He stalked off, leaving me puzzled and terrified. It was probably eighty-five degrees out, but I was shivering. I put the rest of my sandwich away and went back to work. I asked my dad who that guy was a little later. He said he had no idea what I was talking about. I described the guy. Dad said nobody like that even worked on the site!

At the time, I figured it was just some weird drunk. But now it has a whole new meaning. Things I didn't catch before stand out. Like my sandwich was still in my box when that guy talked to me. How'd he know what I brought for lunch?

Dad's Story

When I was fifteen, Dad was called out on a job at some house way on the other side of the bay. In the town I grew up in, you have two sides. One side of the bay has all the beaches and the mall; the other side has downtown and a lot of woods. The old apartment was on the beachy side. The house he was called to was a quarter of the way to the next town on the woodsy side.

So he showed up in his van with all his tools. The front yard was really overgrown. No vehicles in the driveway, except a rusting husk of what used to be a '70s model Chevy. The house was in pretty bad shape. But he went up to the front door. Before he could knock, he saw a note telling him to come right in and they'd be back soon.

He didn't like going into someone's home without them there, because he didn't want to be accused of anything. But he'd driven far, so he went ahead. He got to work on repairing some wood rot around the window frames. He'd been there for nearly an hour when he thought he heard someone. He went to check. There was still no car in the driveway, except for his van.

"Hello?" he called.

He heard what sounded like a door slam. Dad was not the kind of guy to get nervous. He was a local legend for his bar fights. But he told me he was starting to get creeped out. And that just pissed him off. So he started stomping around the house. He saw the back door was wide open, leading into the overgrown backyard. He wondered if it was just the wind moving the door. He closed it and was going back in to work when he decided to just look the place over. Just in case.

He looked around downstairs. There was nothing much to see. The house was in bad shape, but it was furnished. The place was kept fairly clean and tidy. The electricity still worked. Someone was definitely living there, just not able to keep the place up.

He'd pretty much satisfied his concerns, but he went upstairs to look around anyway. Upstairs was much the same as down. Clean and tidy, just in need of repairs. Something didn't feel right about the place to him. Dad's never been much of an intuitive kind of guy, so those must have been some bad vibes.

The last room at the end of the upstairs hall was closed. It was the only door that was closed. It was jammed in the frame somehow, but he got it open. It was just a bedroom. All painted yellow with yellow furniture. He spotted some wood rot around a window frame upstairs, too. He had been told there'd only be three windows to do and this one made four. But he checked it out. When he did, the sill just lifted right off and there were papers and things stuffed between the walls. He'd seen it all. It didn't surprise him.

He pulled the papers out because he planned to go ahead and do this window too, 'cause he's like that. He wouldn't ask for more money. He just wanted the whole job done.

When he pulled the papers out, he saw it was mostly photographs. Dad's big on privacy. He just happened to see the photographs and he knew he was looking at something bad. He started flipping through them. They were all pretty much the same. The back of each picture was dated. But every one of them was a picture of a little boy sleeping. Dad recognized me and that ground floor bedroom right away. He remembered my stories about the flashing lights. It hadn't been in my head at all. Someone had been taking pictures of me sleeping for almost a year.

He told me there weren't any pictures of other boys either. Whoever took the photos was only taking pictures of me.

He called the police, of course. The listed owner for the house was an elderly couple living in Vancouver. They used to summer in the home, but just hadn't gotten around to it in years. They didn't even notice they were still paying the electric bill. They had no idea about the pictures or hiring my dad. It was a dead end. I had so many questions after he told me this. For one, why would someone who was so far away from our apartment make a thirty-minute drive at night just to take pictures of me? How'd they even know me? How'd they fixate on that one apartment or kid? And why call my dad out to find the stash of pictures after a decade of leaving us alone?

Dad actually had an answer for one of those questions. In a way, I find this creepier. Turns out he went out to the wrong address. He wrote it down wrong. When the police checked his answering machine tape for clues, he had actually been called to a much closer home by a completely innocent guy. He stumbled on this house and stash of pictures completely by a random misunderstanding. So who left the note on the front door?

***

I got a lot of really insightful comments and questions from the last post I made. You guys saw things from perspectives I just didn't think of and that got me thinking. There are things I really need to know. So here's an update on what I was able to learn in the last few days. I feel more confused now than I did before. Maybe you'll all see more in it than I do.

First, I tried talking to my dad, but he wasn't in the mood. Shut it right down. I pressed him a little on the flashing lights and he told me I should ask my Uncle Matt. So I did. Uncle Matt and my dad get along great. Never seen them fight in my life. But they're very different. Matt's easygoing, jokey, always has a kind word for everyone. That's why I was shocked when he actually got mad. He told me to never ask him about it again and to leave him alone.

That would've been the end right there, but my biweekly phone call to my mom was due and I didn't really have anything else to talk to her about. So I told her what Dad had told me, what I remembered, and what happened with Uncle Matt.

"What the hell were you thinking?" she scolded, pretty typical of her. "He still feels it was his fault."

The hushed way she said it, like someone might overhear, chilled me. I didn't even know what she was talking about. There were some odd things in my family that I kind of knew, but no one really talked about them. This is the version my mom gave me.

What Mom Said

My Dad and Uncle Matt had a younger sister named Flora. I never knew her as 'Aunt Flora' because she was gone before I was born. When Flora was eight or nine, weird things started happening to her. My dad only talked about them when he'd been drinking gin, Mom said. Gin made him brood. She used to hide his gin because it'd freak her out when he talked about these things.

Like this one time my dad woke up because he heard noises in the kitchen. He came out to see what was up. Flora was making a peanut butter and sugar sandwich in the middle of the night. He asked her what she was doing, because if their mom caught them in the kitchen at that hour, they'd have their butts reddened.

Flora told him she had to make a sandwich and a picture for "Mr. Chawed Froy." Mom said Dad would shudder when he said that part of the story. His voice got real low when he'd say the name. So my dad got mad at Flora, because he thought she was being dumb or half-dreaming. Then she showed him the picture she had drawn. It was a drawing of a boy sleeping with "Matt" written above it.

My dad, being the oldest child, was very protective of Matt and Flora. He immediately felt that something was wrong. He took the picture and tore it up. And he told Flora she had to get back to bed right away.

She told him Mr. Chawed Froy would be mad, because she promised him. Dad asked her who this person was and what he looked like, because he meant to tell their mom. She said she didn't know what he looked like, but he talked to her from the drain in the bathroom sink. He told her all sorts of things and she'd been talking to him every night for a month.

At this point, my mom said she didn't want to talk about it anymore. It was giving her the willies. She didn't even like saying the name. Mom was always kind of superstitious about things. Like she would be afraid to say the names of certain diseases. She'd never say 'cancer,' as if saying it causes it. She said just saying the name 'Chawed Froy' made her feel like she was being watched. But I asked her more questions and she kept going.

She said my dad didn't believe Flora. She must have been dreaming or just imagined the whole thing. He took the sandwich and ate it himself after sending Flora back to bed, so his mom wouldn't find it. He remembered the sandwich well because peanut butter and sugar was not something they ever made in the household. He had no idea where she'd heard of it.

He forgot all about what happened for a few days or weeks. Until one night he woke up to pee and could hear funny noises as he got near the bathroom. The light wasn't on, but Flora was in there alone. He stopped outside the door to listen. She was whispering a whole conversation in there. He figured she was half asleep and didn't know what she was doing. He went into the bathroom to get her. Then he heard it himself. There really was a voice coming from the drain.

Mom said he would get a distant look when he talked about this and just set the gin down, like he couldn't drink anymore (and my dad can always drink more). The voice he heard sounded cold and metallic. Probably from coming through the pipes, he figured, but it scared the crap out of him. What it was actually saying was even worse.

Mom said he'd try to imitate the metallic voice, saying, "Come outside, Flora, come on outside, no one has to sleep out here." Flora whispered into the sink that she couldn't, because her brother might catch her. And the strange voice told her, "He never should have et my sandwich."

Hearing it made my dad's hairs stand on end. My Mom said it's the most scared he'd ever been. Not one to freeze, my dad pulled Flora out of the bathroom and slammed the door. He warned her never to talk to Mr. Chawed Froy again, because he was bad.

He ended up telling his mom and they found where some pipes had been messed with under the house. They also found some drawings of my dad and Uncle Matt sleeping. They were all burned right away and their mom forbade them to talk about it. They didn't handle scandals like that too well at the time. But my dad saw some of the drawings before they were burned. And they weren't drawn by Flora.

I had never heard anything about any of this before. Dad and Uncle Matt almost never talked about Flora anyway and when they did, it was always cryptic. I didn't know what this had to do with me, but my hand was shaking holding the phone.

I thought she was done, but she said that was just the beginning. My mom usually gets tired of talking after ten minutes or so. I was surprised. Maybe she needed to get it out of her system.

She said that after that, Flora used to complain about flashing lights in her bedroom. Everyone just figured she was seeing the light from the lighthouse, because it was still active back then. She complained about it for nearly two years, saying she had trouble sleeping. Her mom got sick of it and put thicker curtains in her bedroom and she kept complaining. They ended up getting her a sleeping mask. Problem solved.

Not long after that, Dad, Matt, and Flora went to a friend's house to hang out, because he had a record player and his parents would get him any records he wanted. They'd all just listen to music together. Flora left to go home before Dad and Matt did. But she never made it home. They never found her body. In theory, she could still be alive, but nobody really believes that. Mom thinks Dad and Uncle Matt always felt personally responsible for it, because if they'd just left with her, she might still be alive.

My mom figures that's why the flashing lights thing upset Dad and Uncle Matt so much. And I guess I was opening old wounds by asking about it. At the same time, I find it really spooky that the same thing would happen to both me and Flora. And upsetting that it hadn't been taken more seriously when it happened to me. I also felt really bad about hurting Uncle Matt. I visited him the next day to apologize. I told him my mom explained everything and I really had no idea. He wasn't mad anymore. Actually, he apologized to me too, because he said I deserved to know.

What Uncle Matt Said

He said there was a little bit more to it than what my mom described. A week before she disappeared, Flora had started complaining about the flashing lights again. They figured either she was forgetting to put on her mask or it had been in her head the whole time. Then a day or two before she disappeared—he couldn't remember—she woke up and the mask was gone. She couldn't find it anywhere. They figured she just didn't want to wear it anymore. But now he wasn't so sure.

Another weird thing, around the same time, was that they found footprints in the snow outside the house. It had snowed almost three feet overnight. These footprints led out of the woods behind the house and went straight to Flora's window. The thing that Uncle Matt said creeped him out the most was that the footprints at the window didn't face into the window. They faced back toward the woods where there was nothing but trees. For the footprints to not have been covered by snow, someone had to have walked to Flora's bedroom window sometime after midnight and stood there staring into the woods in a blizzard.

Strangely, he said they never really worried about it much. Everyone knew everyone there. It just stands out in hindsight.

The day she disappeared, they got a call from Timmy Jean, the boy with the records, telling them he just got a new one. Uncle Matt said Timmy was an only child. He thought the records were how Timmy's parents got him off their hands and made him some friends. So he was normally really excited when he got a record to share. This day he sounded flat, emotionless. Matt had to ask if he was even speaking to Timmy. And the whole time, Uncle Matt felt like someone was listening in. He could hear a sound in the background that wasn't quite breathing. It was like someone saying 'yeah' really softly.

Around this time, where my dad and Uncle Matt grew up, the phone lines were all what they called 'party' lines. Each home's phone would have a different ring so they knew who should answer. But anyone could answer or listen in on anyone else's phone call. So having someone else on the line wasn't unheard of, just impolite.

They went to Timmy's, but when they arrived, Timmy said he hadn't called them and he didn't even have a new album. Uncle Matt and Dad decided to hang out with Timmy and listen to some old albums anyway. But Flora was really disappointed and wanted to go home. So she left alone. He remembered thinking it was too bad she had left, because they found her sleep mask in

Timmy's room.

That was the last time they ever saw her, Uncle Matt said. He was trying hard not to tear up. He said he remembered it like it was yesterday. Her little brown shoes, bows in her hair, and, he said, the oversized Ramones t-shirt they'd found during a trip to the city. It had been her favorite band.

I felt an awful pit in my stomach when he said that. I don't think I'd ever mentioned the detail about the Ramones t-shirt before. Not that Uncle Matt would pull my leg on something like this. I guess it could be a coincidence. A lot of people like the Ramones. But I've never felt so unsettled in all my life. I told him about the guy in the Ramones shirt. He told me to just drop it, because "it was a long time ago." That was all he had to say.

There's a lot of what Uncle Matt said that I find strange. Like how unconcerned he seemed that Timmy hadn't made the phone call. Or the sleep mask.

I'm visiting my dad for Thanksgiving tomorrow. I'm going to bring two bottles of DeKuyper gin. Have a happy Thanksgiving. I'll let you know if I find out anything more. Or if I don't.

***

I just want to thank everyone again for your interest in my personal journey and for sharing your views. I might have walked away from it by now if it weren't for your support. Because the more I learn, the less I seem to understand. But I did learn more from my dad over Thanksgiving. I had to mull it over for a few days. Now that I have, I feel comfortable sharing it.

When I first unloaded the bottles of gin, Dad looked at me like I was setting a trap. In a way, I guess I was. I wonder if he knew what I was up to? I know at least he hadn't talked to Mom. They still hate each other. But Dad's a man's man and doesn't turn down a drink.

I kept waiting for the opportunity to start asking questions. But it never felt right. Turns out I didn't have to. Dad asked me if Uncle Matt talked. I told him he had, but that there was a lot that didn't make sense to me. "Get used to it," was his answer.

I was starting to get upset with all the secrecy. We'd always been a family of straight talkers. Or that's how we thought of ourselves. I didn't see why this was suddenly changing. So I asked him, why he wasn't more alarmed by the flashing lights in my room when the same thing happened to his little sister? Or why he didn't immediately think I was in danger when he found those pictures of me? Why didn't he do anything?

He told me he did more than I'll ever know. That I was typical of my "video game generation." And to go ahead and have another drink, 'cause it's Thanksgiving. I did, but I wasn't feeling very thankful.

After sitting in silence for a while, which is pretty typical for us actually, he said, "Never liked that little rat." I just waited for him to elaborate. Dad talks at his own pace. "Timmy Jean, I mean," he said.

I hadn't expected him to say anything about Timmy. He was about as peripheral to what had happened as I could imagine. But Dad had a lot to say about him.

About Timmy

Dad said Timmy wasn't really a bad kid, he was just strange and pale and weak. Most other kids didn't like him. His parents didn't seem to like him. Even the kids who did like him didn't really like him.

The general opinion was that Timmy's parents were always gone, although it was hard to tell whether they were home or not. They kept to themselves. Rumors went around that they were brother and sister. One thing that was certain was that they'd inherited money. Unlike everyone else, they didn't keep any livestock. They just bought everything from the general store for Timmy and disappeared. Dad said today it'd be called 'neglect,' but people watched out for each other back then.

One thing that always struck Dad as peculiar was how whenever they wanted Timmy to do something other than listen to records, like go play kick-the-can, he'd say he was going to ask his parents. None of them had seen or heard his parents in the house, so they were surprised. But Timmy would go into this one room, close the door behind him, and they'd hear him talking to someone in there. He'd come out and tell them he had to stay put.

This happened a few times, he said. Not that they invited Timmy Jean out all that much.

Another thing he didn't like about Timmy was that he'd just do strange things. Sometimes he seemed pretty normal. Then he'd change, just like that.

This one time they were listening to some new record he had. He turned it off and told them he'd learned a new song and dance. Dad wasn't interested, thinking it would be childish. But Flora and Matt wanted to see. Timmy started walking backward in a circle, shaking like he was freezing, and making shrieking sounds. It was annoying the hell out of Dad, so he told Timmy to cut it out. But Timmy kept doing it.

Dad had never seen Timmy show any emotion other than excitement over his records. When he was doing this 'dance,' he looked downright hateful. Flora started crying and Matt looked pretty scared too. Dad never had patience for stupidity. He grabbed Timmy by the shoulders. He said he remembered how Timmy felt—his skin was cold and jelly-like and he could feel his small shoulder bones like they weren't covered at all. He shook Timmy until he stopped and was back to normal.

Timmy started playing the record again like nothing had happened. Dad said they left, because Flora was too upset.

It was after that, Dad said, that he went to get Timmy for something—he couldn't remember what—and Timmy wasn't home. That was weird in itself. But Dad went inside to look for him just in case. He couldn't find him. So he decided he'd just ask Timmy's parents where Timmy had gone.

He opened the door to the room Timmy always went into. The room was kept really dark. They could never see anything when Timmy slipped in. Now he knew why. It wasn't a bedroom at all. It was just a closet. There was a cushion thrown on the floor, some bread crusts, and pieces of paper. Dad said he'd seen enough. He closed the door and got out, and never went back to Timmy's again. Because when Timmy would go in that room, they wouldn't just hear Timmy talking. They'd hear someone talking to him.

I'd already drunk more gin than I should have, but that still sent shivers through me. But I thought of something. I asked Dad if this happened after Flora disappeared. He said 'no.' So I asked, how was it he was at Timmy's the day Flora disappeared?

"Your Uncle Matt doesn't always remember things right," he said. He gave me a stern stare when he said this, like it was something I should keep in mind to the end of my days. I know Dad's looks very well.

About Uncle Matt

He said Matt came up to him that day and said they had a call from Timmy to come over and listen to the new record. He'd heard the call come in and that was nothing strange. But he never went with them to Timmy's. He went to the general store to pick up a present for Betty Coffin, a girl he fancied, and Matt and Flora went to Timmy's by themselves.

When he was at the general store, he remembered being surprised to see Timmy in there just picking up some food with a big wad of bills. He'd never seen that much money in one place in his whole life, so he wasn't likely to forget it. He told Timmy 'Hello,' but Timmy just paid for his food and walked out with his food and his bills. And Flora never came home from Timmy's that day.

"And that's all I know about it," he said.

I told him Uncle Matt said he was listening to music with him and Timmy when Flora left on her own. Who was he listening to music with, then?

"Wasn't Timmy," was all Dad said. It was so eerily matter-of-fact.

I took another shot of gin right there. I hoped it'd stop me from shaking. When I looked at Dad, he was staring down with a sad resignation I'd never seen in him before.

My dad could drink me under the table ten times over. So after that last shot, he had to put me to bed on his couch. That was the end of our talk.

Lying there on the couch, I suddenly remembered something from way back, when my family would go down to the beach. We'd all sit around the fire, the adults would drink and tell stories about growing up in that hamlet, and the kids would roast marshmallows and shiver listening to these stories. There were true stories and ghost stories all mixed together.

These were the only occasions where I'd ever heard them talk about Flora before. After what my Dad said, I remembered a story Uncle Matt had told.

He said that he and Flora would go for these long walks in the woods together. My Dad used to go with them, since he was expected to watch them. But once he hit his teenage years, he got more interested in girls than babysitting.

They'd decided to go back into the woods behind Hyman's general store. There are no trails or anything. They just picked a spot and went into the woods. You can go back for miles and miles into just pure woods. It's all national parkland today. Normally they'd walk about thirty minutes or an hour. Dad would have them walk parallel to the edge of the woods. Without Dad there, they just kept going deeper.

They'd been walking into the woods for well over an hour. Or at least he thinks it was. Flora wanted to turn back by this time, but Matt wanted to keep going deeper. She followed him because she was scared to go off alone. But she got upset and said she was going back on her own. He told her that was fine and not to get lost.

Uncle Matt said she wasn't gone thirty seconds when he felt her tugging at his arm. He got mad, because he thought she was bugging him to go with her again. But when he looked, she was pointing at something behind him. He said really seriously that he'd never forget how wide and scared her eyes were. He turned and saw a man standing out in the woods. It scared him, too. The man didn't really look scary. He was just a man. But there was no reason for anyone to be out so far in the woods. They shouldn't even have been there.

The man had his back to them, looking deeper into the woods. He wasn't moving at all. They crouched down as quietly as they could to watch him. But he didn't do anything but stand there.

Matt said he didn't like it one bit. He felt there was something really wrong about what was going on. He took Flora by the hand—something he never did—and they walked away, making as little sound as possible.

He kept glancing over his shoulder as they walked. After a few minutes, he was satisfied that they were well away from the man. He was long out of sight and probably hearing range.

After a few minutes more walking, Matt heard a thudding sound. Flora squeezed his hand tighter, so he knew she heard it too. But they didn't say anything to each other. They were too scared. The thudding kept getting louder. Then he heard this scream, at the top of someone's lungs, like they'd been hurt. Matt looked back and saw the man they'd seen earlier running right at them full speed through the woods, screaming the whole time. No words.

Matt said he and Flora were so scared they couldn't even run. They backed up against a tree and crouched down. Matt thought the man was going to kill them or hurt them and he didn't know what to do about it.

When the man caught up to them, he stopped short only a few feet away. He took in a deep breath and shouted in their faces, "GET OUT!" They were too scared to move. So the man kept shouting it at them. "GET OUT! GET OUT!"

Finally Matt tugged at Flora and they ran and ran back the way they came. When they were almost out, they heard Dad calling for them somewhere back in the woods. They were about to go running back to Dad so he'd protect them. But then they saw him at the tree line and ran to him. He took them home and that was that. He said they never told their mom because they figured they were just trespassing.

After Uncle Matt finished his story, everyone was quiet for a good long time. The story seemed to bother Dad more than anyone else. I remember being especially upset by it, just because it bothered Dad.

Then Dad said he remembered that when he first went to get them, he couldn't find them. He figured they'd just gone home. But he couldn't find them at home either. He looked in the general store and down on the fishing wharf, but they weren't there either. So he went back to the woods. Just as he got there, he saw them running out of the woods screaming and crying. He asked them what was going on, thinking they'd just seen a bear or something, and they just kept bawling. So he brought them home and questioned them to get the whole story. He said he never told Uncle Matt at the time, but he saw them coming out of the woods as soon as he got there. He never did call out for them.

I don't know why I suddenly remembered that story. It's just another weird thing that happened to my family. Just an hour away from where Dad grew up, in the nearest bigger town, there's a huge sanatorium up on a hill, looking over the whole town. The guy in the woods could just be some guy who got out of there and they had the misfortune of startling him. Could be completely unrelated to everything else.

So that gave me a lot to think about. I don't feel any more secure or confident after what Dad told me. If anything, I'm more confused and unsettled than ever. The last several days have been a strange ride. But I know there's no way I can let it go now. I'll try to find out more and I'll continue sharing what I can.

***

I managed to find out more about Timmy. I had to hit up people I haven't spoken to in a long time or barely know at all, but eventually I hit a few relatives who knew more than I ever expected to find out.

Before I share what I learned about Timmy, though, I've been asked in the comments how I can keep such a level head while I keep uncovering these weird incidents. I guess because it's distant. I shake and shiver and feel dread when I'm hearing about or remembering these events. But it's still way back there. Even my dad finding the pictures in that house happened years ago. That's been changing lately. Little things have been happening that have been making me uneasy.

For one, my mom has called me twice since Thanksgiving. I know this isn't overtly creepy. But we normally only talk once every two weeks. On top of that, she hasn't been herself. She's been trailing off, going silent for long periods, and sometimes it's like there's an echo when she speaks. I started wondering if someone's tapping into our conversations—like with a baby monitor, or something.

And she's been saying strange things. For instance, after being quiet for a while, she said, "It's lonely down here." I asked her what she meant by "down here," since she didn't live any farther south than me. She just said, in a tone so flat she could've been reading it, "You should come. It's wonderful down below." She changed the subject right after and seemed normal after that. My first instinct was to worry she was depressed or something. But I don't know. The last thing she said was if I hear anything strange about her to not believe it.

I've also been receiving other phone calls. They started a little before Thanksgiving. First call was an instant hang-up. The next time just silence. Each time after that, I'd hear sounds. Cars going by, walking, wind blowing. The kind of sounds you'd hear from a butt-call. But they were distorted, almost like someone was imitating the sounds with their mouth.

Last night it changed. There was a voice. The voice had a tinny, metallic tone and that same echo as when Mom called. The combination made the voice sound inhuman and evil. The words weren't sinister at all, but the way they were said made me feel like I was in danger for the first time since I started this investigation.

The first time, all he said was, "I'm on my way." I tried to say, "Wrong number" back, but whoever it was had already hung up. I got a call a little later and the same voice said, "I'll be there soon." This time he didn't hang up right away, so I said he had the wrong number. A moment after I said this, he hung up.

On the third call, he said, "I can see your house now." And, again, hung up immediately. I kept waiting for another call any minute, but after a few hours, I relaxed. I figure it really was a wrong number and they figured it out. I mean, given the last two weeks, I have every reason to be a little jumpy.

I got about halfway through an episode of *Gotham* on the DVR before the phone rang again. I didn't say anything immediately. Neither did he. After a minute or so, he said, "I'm right outside."

As soon as he said that, I heard a noise at the front door. I don't know if I've ever been so scared before. I don't have any firearms, but I do have a machete. So I grabbed it and went to the front door. I opened it, ready for that hateful face from the building site. Or worse. But my dad was there, actually.

He asked what the machete was for. And I asked him what brought him out to my house so late. It's a long enough drive and Dad rarely visits anyway. He got pretty irritated about that. He opened his flip phone (yep), and showed me a text apparently from me. In the text, I asked him to come out immediately: "It's an emergency." I told Dad I hadn't send him that text. I hadn't send him any texts. I've never lied to Dad before, and that carries weight. He believed me.

To be honest, though, I was glad he was there at just that moment. We had a drink together and then he said he was going to get back home. I asked him a few questions about Timmy before he left. He didn't much want to talk about it, but I'll add what he told me into the account of what I learned.

After Flora disappeared, Dad and Matt were expressly forbidden to have anything to do with Timmy. For Dad, that suited him just fine. Dad nevertheless told his mom that Timmy couldn't have been responsible, since he'd just seen him at Hyman's general store. His mom said there had always been something wrong with that boy and she felt if Flora hadn't gone to his home that day she'd still be alive. While Dad and Matt hoped she was still alive, their mom never really believed she was. She said she saw a dove fly into the house the day after Flora disappeared, but when she chased after it she couldn't find it anywhere. Dad said it was just grief and these kinds of supernatural beliefs were common then. I tend to agree.

Timmy made no efforts to reach out to Dad or Matt either. He started keeping to himself after Flora disappeared. They'd sometimes see him by himself at Hyman's, buying a lot of food, way more than one boy should require. They never talked.

Suspicions about Timmy and concerns about his missing parents grew. The police had looked around Timmy's house a little, since it was where Flora had last been seen, and found nothing. But now they were asked to search the house. They wouldn't say what was wrong or what they found in there. The rumor was that Timmy's parents hadn't been there in a long time and that the police had come out of the house pale and upset. Small towns always have rumors. Hard to say if they're true or false.

Timmy was placed with some distant relatives in the larger town an hour away. They said he was strange and they didn't like him. He was always up and walking around at night. Sometimes he'd stop over the vents in the floor and just stare into them.

After he'd been there for a bit, they started to hear him talking to himself in the middle of the night. They'd come up to him to see what he was doing and there would be no one else around. They started watching him. They noticed he only did this when he was standing over the air vents. They even found him crouching down over one once.

This girl, a third cousin of his, said it still creeped her out. Because she knows she heard someone answering him one time. Those vents couldn't have been more than a foot and a half wide, she said, but she heard a man's voice coming up with the air. She couldn't make out what was being said, but she heard laughter that made her run and hide under her covers.

She said she thinks this part may have been a dream, but she always swore she saw a finger poking up from the vent, too. She told her parents, but they said to stop making up stories and that he'd been through a lot.

Her sister said sometimes Timmy would walk out to the woods and just stand there, staring into them. They asked him why he did that. He said he was waiting to be taken. He went farther into the woods when she tried to talk to him more.

One time, the same girl said, she heard him talking into the air vents like usual. She was tired and it was upsetting her, so she went to get her parents and have him sent to bed. On her way, she noticed Timmy was still sound asleep in his room. The talking had to be coming up from the vent all on its own.

They said Timmy would sometimes steal food from the house and take it out into the woods. When he was caught, he said he had a treehouse. But they never saw it if it existed. They'd sometimes wake up and find him staring at them in the middle of the night. They had to start locking their doors.

They would whine to their parents to send him away all the time. But they were careful not to do it when Timmy was around because, despite everything, they didn't want to be mean. One time he asked them why they wanted him sent away. They couldn't figure out how he'd heard.

He had been living with them for nearly six months when something happened that changed him. They didn't know what it was. But he stopped all of the weird behavior all at once. He wouldn't talk to anyone. He hardly ate. Then one day he just ran away.

He's been a missing person ever since. His parents never turned up to look for him. There was no evidence either way. So the case went nowhere.

They also said that years later, when his house burned down, pictures of the fire appeared in the local newspaper. People talked about it for weeks, because in the picture, the smoke looked just like the devil. Horns and everything. They tried to find the newspaper in their closets, but neither of them could find it.

I include that part not because I believe in a horned devil that manifests itself in smoke patterns. I think it's interesting that his cousins thought he was so creepy that the devil would be in the smoke particles coming off his burning house.

That's what I know about Timmy. He hasn't been seen or heard from since, from all I can find out. Same for his parents. Where his home was is just a lush field of rhododendrons.

One last thing. After Dad left last night, I noticed my mailbox lid was up. I knew I'd closed it earlier when I checked the mail. So I looked inside. I found an envelope with a Polaroid photo inside. An old one, too. It was of me, Mom, and Dad all at the park together. This park is actually the same place where Dad grew up. The houses are mostly gone. Hyman's general store is still there as a museum. I had to be only four or five in the picture. I don't even remember Mom going to the park with us.

I wondered if Dad had found it and stuck it in my mailbox. But Dad wouldn't bother to bring it to me if he had found it. He wouldn't see the value in it. I kept looking at it, wondering what it was doing there. It took me a surprisingly long time to see it. In the background, in the thick Johnson grass, there was a man crouched down and watching us. He was barely visible. I couldn't discern his face or any expression in his eyes. I just had a vague but real feeling he meant to do us harm.

I don't want to be too alarmist. The "strange things" happening to me may all have innocent explanations and I'm just jumpy. And I still want to get to the bottom of things. My investigation's hit a bit of a dead end. But I'll keep you all posted.

Confessions

Again, I have to thank you all for your input. I realize I've been stupid and glib. I've always been passive and I don't like getting too excited about things. Thinking about it, maybe it all goes back to when I'd freak out over those flashing lights and my dad would tell me it was in my head. He downplayed everything… so now I just kind of do the same. But still, it's my character flaw, not his. I have to take responsibility.

So I went ahead and called in a wellness check on my mom. And I went ahead and called the police about the photograph and strange text. I called Dad over, since I knew they'd want to see his phone. This is where things got perplexing.

The police officer who responded seemed to know Dad pretty well. He was an older man, about Dad's age, maybe a little older. I'd never met him before. Dad introduced him as "Kirby" and said they used to live a few houses from each other, back where they grew up. Kirby did most of what I expected from the police. He looked at the photograph. He checked out the text. He took my statement. He decided to hold onto the photograph, just in case. But he said it wasn't likely there was anything the police could do about it.

Once he was done with me, he gestured for my dad to come outside with him for a talk. I don't think he realized I saw. Dad told me to wait inside and he'd be back in a moment. There have just been so many secrets lately. So I listened in at the door.

"Does he know anything about it?" Kirby asked.

If Dad answered, I couldn't hear it.

"That's what this is, isn't it? Sure looks like it."

Again, no audible answer.

"What we did back then—" he was saying, but Dad interrupted him to say, "It was a long time ago. This here's just a dumb prank."

"Quit being stubborn and stupid, Francis!" he said. Nobody ever called Dad by "Francis." It was always "Frank" or "Frankie." Calling him Francis was a good way to break your jaw. So was calling him stupid. But Dad didn't say anything back.

"What the hell else could this mean?"

"Smarten up," Dad said. "We did the right thing, anyhow. You know it."

"Says you. Says me, too. Someone might not agree. Watch yourself, Francis."

Kirby got in his car and left right after that. Assuming the "he" in the first question was me, I can say I don't know anything about what they were saying. I asked Dad when he came back in. He didn't get mad. He said it was just something that happened a long time ago and to mind my own business. I told him this had become my business. I reminded him that he told me about the pictures he found in that old house because he thought I was old enough to hear it now. He said, "I guess I was wrong." That was that.

I tried calling Mom to see if she had any insight, but there was no answer. Not unusual, though I'm still glad I called that wellness check on her.

I called Uncle Matt next. To my surprise, he said he had something he wanted to show me and that he'd be over later. When he did come, what he showed me really shook me up. And it made things make a little more sense. Maybe that's why it shook me.

Uncle Matt's Confessions

Uncle Matt told me that a lot more things happened when they were children than I'd ever hear about. Not that he wouldn't talk about them, but he didn't think he even could. Some of those things stuck with him, he said, and they'd bother him all the time. What he used to have fun doing started to make him feel sick. He thought about killing himself a few times. He even took himself to the sanatorium for a day. I had no idea about any of this! Neither did Dad, he said. He didn't want anyone to know.

He started seeing a therapist after this. Something Dad would've made fun of. I don't know if that's true. But it's what Uncle Matt thought. The therapist insisted he try hypnosis sessions, because he was just holding back too much. He agreed. What he'd brought with him was an old cassette tape the therapist let him keep of one of those sessions. We put it in my CD/cassette/record player and listened.

On the recording, Uncle Matt was talking about the day Flora disappeared. He said he remembered getting a call from someone asking him to come to Timmy's. He knew the person talking to him wasn't Timmy. The person sounded weird and frantic. He tried to tell the person 'no,' but this man kept saying that he really was Timmy and he was really lonely down here and he needed them to come listen to "the music records" with him. Especially the new one.

On the recording, Uncle Matt said that he figured Timmy had to be there, at least, and he wanted to hear the new record. So he got Flora and Dad. He didn't bother giving them any details about the phone call.

On the way there, Dad left to go meet a girlfriend or something, so Matt and Flora went alone. When they got to the house, the front door had been left open and they could hear the song "Love Hurts" playing from upstairs. They'd heard the song before, so they knew it wasn't the new album. That was good, because they wanted to listen to it for the first time all together.

When they got upstairs, Timmy wasn't there. He remembered that the room smelled like burning tires. It had never smelled like that before. Uncle Matt took the needle off the record. Then he noticed Flora backed up into a corner and whimpering. Uncle Matt looked where she was looking, because she was looking right at something. He hadn't seen it at all. But there was a man lying down under the bed. His face poked out of the dark just enough for them to see his blank stare and huge smile. His smile just didn't look right. There was no happiness in it at all.

He started coming out from under the bed. The man was looking straight at Flora and shouted, "I don't see you in the dark anymore!" Uncle Matt stood between Flora and the man, because he was scared for Flora. The burning smell was stronger the closer the man got. He thought he'd seen the man before, a few years ago. The man put "Love Hurts" back on and laughed. The laugh sounded fake, like an animal imitating a human. He danced around them, laughing sometimes and then screaming like he was in pain. He kept putting the needle to the beginning of the track and dancing.

One time, when the man went to move the needle back to the beginning of "Love Hurts," Uncle Matt told Flora to get out. She ran, but the man put his hand on Matt's shoulder. "I like you when you sleep," he said. He held Matt around the neck and they danced backward around the room, over and over. Sometimes he made sounds like a wounded creature.

After a while, he let go and crawled back under the bed. He was lying on his back, looking up at the mattress. Uncle Matt figured he could leave. He was scared to try because he thought the man might stop him. But he started out the room to the stairs anyway. He looked back, just in case. The man wasn't under the bed anymore. He'd already gotten up and was just a few feet behind Uncle Matt. He froze when Uncle Matt looked at him and didn't move a muscle. Uncle Matt walked backward the rest of the way, down the stairs and out of the house. The man never moved.

"If I just listened to my gut, we never would've gone there. If I kept Flora with me, she might've been okay. If I'd been smarter and gone with her right away, she'd be okay. All the time I know it's my fault she's gone and she ain't coming back."

That's where the tape ended. Uncle Matt listened to the whole tape with me with his head down. He told me he really doesn't remember it happening that way at all. He said he was sure he'd told me the truth. But he wanted me to hear this.

I think Uncle Matt was so traumatized by what happened, he isn't able to remember it. I don't blame him. What's on the tape matches up with the story my dad told me. So it's probably right. Uncle Matt didn't know who that guy was or what had happened to him, but if he was with Matt and Timmy was with Dad, that guy couldn't have been involved in what happened to Flora any more than Timmy had been. Or, at least, it's not very probable.

Dad's Confessions

Another bit of information just fell into my lap. It's funny the way things all happen at once. Like you'll never have heard an old song, then suddenly you'll hear it three times in one day. Mom called later that same night. She wanted to know what I'd called for. I told her about what I'd overheard Dad and Kirby saying. She said she never wanted to believe it, but it must be true. I told her she had to tell me and she agreed. What she told me isn't what I'd expected at all.

She said a long time ago, a sad, lonely man was placed in the sanatorium when they found him living in the walls of the hospital. He had no family and no friends. After they determined he was harmless, they released him. He wandered through the woods for days. He wandered so far back he got lost and was thirsty and hungry. Then he found a house. He thought it was strange for a house to be in the middle of the woods. But he needed food and water. An old man came to the door and let him in. He had no idea how long he was in there. Something bad happened in that house, so he ran and ran away from the house as fast as he could go.

He ran until he came to a little one-store town, Dad's hometown. Some of the children in the town would talk to him and bring him sandwiches, because he made them think he was a good ghost. One lonely boy in particular gave him a place to stay. Timmy showed him music and got him all the food he wanted. He taught Timmy all the tricks he'd learned in his life. Hiding and listening and crawling. And the things he'd learned from the house in the woods. He got so used to the boy, he would get mad if Timmy left the home or did anything but spend time with him.

He tried to hide himself as much as possible, but when Flora disappeared, people noticed him. They figured out he'd been staying with Timmy. And they figured he did something to Flora. My dad remembered what Flora had said about seeing a man in the woods. And he remembered the voice in the bathroom sink. He riled everyone up against the man. So the man hid even more. He hid well enough that everyone thought he was just gone.

When he thought they'd forgotten about it, he figured he could go back to normal. But they hadn't forgotten. Dad saw him. He got some people in town together. They chased him all the way to Dad's house. Dad followed him under the house. When he thought he'd cornered him, he followed him up through a hole in the floor. It took him right under Dad's bed. Dad saw there were trinkets and bedding under there, like the man had been sleeping right under him all along.

Dad was so mad he dragged the man out. They beat him up. When they were done beating him, they burned him up. And when they were done burning him, they buried him. They never talked about it since. They agreed they had just done what they had to do. But what they had done was murder.

That's how Mom told it. It was such a weird story. It wasn't like her to talk like that. I asked her where she'd even heard the story. She just said it was another one of those things Dad would say when he'd been in the gin. She said that one took a lot of gin. It bothered him more than anything else.

I didn't know whether to believe it or not. I changed the subject. I told her I had called a wellness check on her, because I was worried. She told me I shouldn't have done that. Why? She said I was wasting police time. She wasn't even at her home. She was on a business trip.

I guess this whole thing has made me bolder. The next day I confronted Dad about what Mom told me. I asked him if it was true. He just asked, "Where did you hear that?" I told him Mom had told me. I'll never forget this for the rest of my life. He placed his hands on my shoulders like he's only done once before, when he gave me the "life advice" I'd need after graduating high school. And he said, "Son, I never told your mother that. And she's not from our town."

The way he said it, like he knew something was horribly wrong, scared the life out of me. This mystery is upsetting my life and family in the worst way, because it's in my ideas. He brushed it off as Mom being a major B. I think there was something more. I still don't know if the story was true or false. He won't give me a straight answer. He won't deny it, either.

Lastly, I did get a response on the wellness check. They were let into Mom's home by a house sitter. The sitter said she'd been in the home for a week and that there was nothing to worry about. The officer called Mom and she backed up everything the sitter said. Looks like Mom's story checks out. The officer who called me said he was running a trace on her cellphone anyway, because something wasn't "sitting right."

I'm not sure where to go with this investigation next. I'm a little scared to keep going, to be honest, even if I knew what to do next. If I find out anything more, as always, I'll share.

***

It's been a rough week. I haven't been able to reply to comments. You'll understand why after reading. But I still needed to write this. Get it out. I don't think you know what a support you all have been.

After my last update, I did something I haven't done since Mom left. I broke down. I called Mom up and told her everything that's been going on and how it's been affecting me. I told her I couldn't take it anymore. I have a regular life I should be leading. I have a job and friends. But I'm trapped in this maze of lies and secrets (yes, I can get very dramatic). She said she would book a flight immediately. Then we'd get with my Dad and talk things over, all three of us.

I told her she didn't have to do that. I know she's busy. Plus she and Dad still hate each other. She told me she still loves Dad and always has, they just had too many differences. He couldn't accept her for who she was. But she always thought it was their destiny to be together. Her happiness in life was the hope that we'd all be a family, like we should be.

I don't know if she was just saying this to make me feel better. It did make me feel better. It also felt weird hearing Mom talk like this. She had never been the most emotional person. I thought that's why she was a good fit for Dad—you have to be thick-skinned to be around him.

She said she'd see me soon to put an end to this. And she said, "I hope your Dad makes the right choice." I wondered what she was referring to, but she was gone before I could ask.

I called Dad up right away to let him know, because her flight wouldn't take longer than four or five hours. She'd be arriving in time for dinner. As I expected, this wasn't welcome news to him. But not for the reasons I expected.

Turns out he's been getting reacquainted with Betty Coffin. I said that seemed like a strange coincidence. But not at all. Telling the story reminded him of her. "Curves, son," is how he described her. She'd sent him a message a while back telling him she'd gotten back into town. He'd just been too busy to write her back and then he forgot. It just so happened they'd made dinner plans that evening, and he'd be going to her place (!).

Dad hadn't really bothered much with relationships after he and Mom divorced. He'd tried. Every so often he'd meet a woman he really liked and seemed to like him. Well enough to introduce her to me. Something would always happen that scared them away. He used to joke that he was cursed. I think he probably internalized that. It was pretty much never his fault, though.

Sonya accused him of calling her in the middle of the night and telling her weird things. I overheard the fight. I remember one of the things was, "You'd be so much better without bones," and that he kept calling her "Jellyfish." I know Dad wouldn't do that. He would never think of something so surreal in a million years. But she believed it was him.

Andrea said she started to notice that things in her house would move while she was asleep and it only started when she started seeing Dad. Her CD collection, in particular. She also said that one night she woke up because she heard Dad get up and go to the kitchen. She looked out into the kitchen and saw him staring into the fridge. She started drifting back to sleep again when she heard more noise. The fridge door was still open, but she couldn't see him anymore. This got her mad, so she shouted for him to keep it down and close the fridge door. That's when Dad said, "What's the hell's going on?" He was still lying in bed right beside her. She wouldn't have anything to do with him after that.

Parker was my favorite of all Dad's girlfriends. She was a tomboy type. She loved camping and she'd traveled a lot, so I'd hear all about different countries from her. She also talked about strange things happening while with Dad. Like hearing him talk to her when he wasn't in the house. But she didn't let it get to her. They were together for a while. One night she had an accident while driving out into a remote stretch that leads to a dinky copper-mining town nearby. She died a day later in the hospital from complications. It didn't seem important at the time, but now I remember Dad wondering why she'd been driving out that way, anyway. And her sister yelling at Dad that he'd told Parker to meet him out there.

There were other incidents. I probably don't know about them all. But this one time, back when I got Dad set up on ICQ in like 2000 or so, he started talking to this chick. He said she hit him up. He was a two-finger typer, so I imagine it took a while to bang out messages. After he got interested enough to ask for pictures, she sent him a zip file full of them. All pictures of himself with a black silhouette (MS Painted into the shot). I traced the account as best I could and it got me to an address: the general store out in the national park. He just wanted to drop it and we did.

Anyway, with so much bad luck in love, I guess I was happy for him. He shouldn't be alone forever. It was just awful timing. I even wondered if he was putting her in danger by dating her. But I couldn't tell him that. I told him I'd deal with Mom and he could have his date.

While I waited around for Mom to call and let me know she'd arrived, I decided to search my house for holes, bedding and such. I don't think that's paranoia at this point. But there were no holes under the bed. No nests in the closet. The plumbing seemed secure; the vents blew air smoothly. Then I noticed the fridge didn't look straight. I actually thought I was being ridiculous, so I tried to distract myself. I ended up pulling it out anyway. I never believed anything would be there. But there it was: a little hole, sizeable enough for a little boy to squeeze into.

I got a flashlight and my machete. I was sure someone's hand would grab me the moment I put my head in. No one was in there, though. The space was only wide enough for a very slim man to stand very stiffly. And I didn't see any holes in the wall where he could look into the next room (my bedroom). He would've just been standing there staring into the darkness behind my fridge. What would be the point? I kept wondering. Then I saw the doll. It was made of twigs and had my face on it. Just looking made me feel uncomfortable. I refused to touch it. Call me superstitious, but it felt unnatural. I'd only just made that discovery when I saw another doll behind it, bigger and seeming to watch the smaller doll. Its face was a picture of someone who just looked evil. I don't know what evil should really look like. I just know this face made me feel like evil was there.

I've learned my lesson. I immediately called the police and requested Detective Kirby. When he got on the line, before I had a chance to speak, he asked me if I was okay and if I was alone. I answered yes to both questions, "as far as I know," but I wanted to know why. He said he'd been about to call me.

He said they'd just gotten word from the police department in my Mom's town. He hesitated. I figured they'd found someone breaking into her house or a creepy letter. But what he had to say was a lot worse than that. They'd found what they believed to be her body deep in a wooded area. It was so remote, it was pure chance a camper had found her.

I assured him that whoever they found was not my mother. I had just spoken to her. She was on her way. The line went silent. I insisted that I be allowed to make an identification so they can drop this nonsense. Kirby said the body was past identifying. She'd been dead for over a year. Dental records confirmed it was her. The only identifiable thing was her Ramones t-shirt.

I hung up on him. I had no idea how to process this information. If someone tells you the sky is brown and salt is sweet, do you accept it immediately? I had been speaking to my mom every two weeks for the last several years and never noticed a change in her behavior or personality—until the last few days. If she was dead, who had I been speaking to all this time? It had to have been her. I know my own mother's voice, her mannerisms. She had known everything my mom should know.

So I started to wonder about this Detective Kirby character. Maybe he wasn't on the level. He seemed to have a strange hold over my dad, calling him "Francis" like that. So I called up the police department in Mom's town. When I identified myself, I was immediately transferred to a detective. He told me the trace on the phone had come back. All calls from that phone were coming from my own town. Moreover, the phone is even registered to a local address.

I felt an emptiness inside. I still feel it. It's only gotten worse. I didn't even have to ask about Detective Kirby anymore. I asked anyway and it was confirmed. But I already knew. It couldn't have been my mother I'd been talking to. She was dead.

I needed to let Dad know right away. I tried calling him. It went straight to voicemail. I hoped this meant he was already with Betty and was safe. I decided to look up Betty Coffin, so I could call her and reach him that way. I found her number with an online phone lookup. It was a landline. I called it just in case. Maybe someone in her household knew her cell number.

A young-sounding woman answered the phone. She sounded a little overexcited to get a call, like she'd been waiting. I introduced myself and explained that I really need to get through to Betty and it was an emergency. "Is this some kind of joke?" she asked. I almost lost my temper, but she explained first. "My mother has been missing for a week, sir."

I called Detective Kirby back. I told him he had to get to Dad's right away, because he was in trouble. In as succinct a manner as possible, I told him what I knew. I was hyperventilating. I don't know how he understood half of it. I'm so glad he listened and believed me, though.

I couldn't stand just waiting at home. I got in my car and rushed to Dad's. The lights were on when I arrived. That was a good sign, I thought. The front door was unlocked. When I walked in, I heard music. I recognized the song, actually. It was Bobby Darin's "Dream Lover." I'd never heard Dad listen to anything but country. But maybe he was trying to impress the girl. Maybe she had come to his place instead.

I called out for him. But he didn't answer. Dad's always had such amazing hearing. Even at his age, he could hear way better than me. And he was a great dad. I haven't always made him sound great. But he's my hero, y'know?

I knew something was wrong when he didn't answer. I searched everywhere downstairs. The damn song kept playing on a loop. It wasn't even coming from Dad's stereo. I went upstairs next. The song started over just as I got to the top. When I got to Dad's bedroom, I saw where the music was coming from. A record player was on his bed. I stared at it, not really comprehending why I was so afraid to go near it. I wasn't thinking straight. It took me too long to realize it. But the song couldn't be on loop. Someone had to be hand-looping it.

I backed into a corner involuntarily. I felt control of my bladder near slipping. I even screamed when I heard something downstairs. But I heard them say, "Police," and I almost cried with relief.

The whole time, he was watching me. All I saw was an eye at first. Looking at me through a hole in Dad's box spring. I started to panic again. The officers —one was Detective Kirby—drew their guns. I pointed to the box spring as a hand reached out and set the needle back to the beginning of the song.

They demanded the man get out. He started to make awful sounds. I'd never heard anything like it. Inhuman screams. And one intelligible thing in all the screams: "Sleep in me!" Cold chills swept over me like only once before.

They finally dug him out. It was the man I'd seen at the building site. The weirdo that shouted at me. The same one that gave me chills before. He was wearing a dress and a wig, with some smeared makeup and a bloodied nose, but it was the same man.

I could barely stand to look at the creature. But he wouldn't stop staring at me. I asked where Dad was and he said, in my mother's voice, "Giving birth to you was the happiest day of my life." I felt nauseous.

Then, in a perfectly normal voice, in the most reasonable and yet most sinister tone I'll ever hear, he said, "He made me so, so lonely. But you don't know. And I'll never say another word as long as I live."

They took him away. So fast it felt like a dream. Detective Kirby took me with him. I was left to go home and rest. Rest only came when I passed out. And while I slept, they found Dad. The address my mom's cellphone was registered to was the same house where Dad found the photos. "Betty" must've called him out there. He'd been stabbed in the neck multiple times. He's the toughest guy ever, so he was still alive when police found him. But it was too much. He didn't make it.

That's really all I can say now. This was almost impossible to write. I think I must still be in shock to have written it at all. There's a little more I need to say. But it's going to have to wait a few days.

Loose Ends

I really wanted to just drop this. Crawl up in a ball and forget everything. But I have to put all the pieces together. What I have of them, anyway. I owe it to Mom, Dad, and myself. And to all of you for standing with me during this nightmare.

After arresting that thing in my dad's house, police combed the old house, my house, my dad's. They found material that's helped to shed some light on the events I described in the previous updates. Scraps of paper, a journal of sorts, and photographs, combined with additional information from others who grew up with Dad.

What I want to do here is not to give you each little piece of information. We've all had enough mystery. I want to give you the whole story. And by the "whole story," I mean how I think it all fits together. It may not be 100% correct, but I wouldn't be sharing it if I didn't think it was pretty close.

So, let's start at the beginning. A schizophrenic was released from the sanatorium (really an asylum). He wandered the woods until he had some kind of episode back there. He came out in the little town of Grand Greve. "Chawed Froy," since I have no other name for him, went around convincing children to bring him food, like the peanut butter and sugar sandwiches. When he met Timmy, he even got a place to stay.

Chawed and Timmy skulked around together. He got sandwiches. Timmy was interested in other things. In particular, the family that lived a few houses down. They were the only kids around that would hang out with him. He particularly liked Dad. Dad was handsome, tall, and athletic. So he got Chawed to ask Flora for more than just sandwiches. He wanted to see Dad and Matt sleeping.

When Timmy's parents found out he'd allowed a hobo to squat in their home, though, they got mad. They never beat Timmy. They just yelled at him. Then they tried to kick Chawed out. So Chawed and Timmy killed his parents. Police first found the bloodstains in the house and then the bodies beneath it.

With his parents' camera, Timmy started snapping photos of Dad, Matt, and Flora while they slept. Flora noticed the light. She was just a lighter sleeper, apparently. This didn't stop Timmy. He kept taking pictures for over a year. Finally, one night, Flora caught him. She told him she'd tell her mom and that he was going to be in big trouble.

The next day, Chawed called them over to listen to records. I would guess at Timmy's request, but who knows. When Timmy was coming back from buying food, he saw Flora walking away from the house. He didn't want her to tell on him for taking the pictures. So he grabbed her and dragged her into the woods.

He didn't kill her right away. In all the photos they found hidden in that house, there was one faded photo of a teen girl. It was Flora. I'm sure of it. In the photo, she was in some sort of a cabin. She wasn't tied up. But she looked so, so unhappy. The whole cabin seemed tinged with unhappiness. It was an awful-looking place. She was twelve when she disappeared.

So she was kept somewhere after her kidnapping. Somewhere no one ever thought to look for her. Only Timmy and Chawed knew where she was. Probably where Chawed hid while police looked for him. After Timmy thought it was safe for Chawed to come out, my dad was first in finding him and was involved in the man's murder. That much was confirmed for me by

Detective Kirby.

Timmy was already at his cousins' home by this time. He'd been taken as soon as his parents were found. So wherever Flora was being kept, she was left alone once Chawed died.

While he was at his cousins', I think Timmy had a psychotic break. Chawed really was his whole world. He'd drawn Timmy into his delusions. Timmy talked to what he thought was Chawed in the vents and in the woods, but I don't think anyone was there. No fingers poked out of the vent. Because, if it wasn't all in Timmy's head, who had that been?

After some time with his cousins, who didn't even like him, he ran away. He probably had money stashed somewhere. Or maybe he just became a beggar.

My dad, on the other hand, grew up and moved on. He met a beautiful gymnast and married her. That's where I come in. We were a reasonably happy family, from what I understand. Until something happened that made Mom and Dad resent each other. They divorced. Dad fought like hell for custody and Mom went back west where she'd originally come from.

Not long after Mom was out of the picture, I started seeing the flashing lights. When I told Dad and Uncle Matt, it terrified them. The possibility that I could end up disappearing like Flora is just about the only thing that could terrify my dad.

What I never knew is that after I told them about the lights, they went out to the park together while I stayed with Uncle Matt's wife. They spent all day looking for the place they'd buried Chawed, but they found it. And they dug him up to make sure he was really dead.

That's why Dad was so insistent that the lights were just in my head or passing cars. Because the guy they believed was behind Flora's abduction was dead and buried. And they had to believe it was him behind it, because if they didn't, they'd murdered an innocent man. Since this man probably murdered Timmy's parents, he wasn't that innocent. But they didn't know that.

Years later, when Dad found the pictures of me in that house, he knew he'd been wrong. Whoever it was, he figured, was the same person who had taken pictures of Flora. They'd murdered the wrong person and I was in danger. He went out looking for anyone suspicious. Roughed up a few guys. But nothing came of it.

What I think happened is that Timmy was still obsessed with Dad. He did something to sabotage Mom and Dad's relationship. Then, when Mom was out of the picture, he inserted himself into the family in the only way he knew how. By sneaking pictures of me while I slept.

I believe Timmy must've had our phones and homes bugged. He'd adapted to being a shadow in our lives. Maybe he imagined he was something more. After a while, this wasn't enough to satisfy him anymore. He murdered my mother and pretended to be her for a year. I think this gave him what he really wanted: to be Dad's wife and my mother.

His obsession with my dad wasn't just admiration. He was in love with him. He resented my mom, hated her even, for taking what he believed was his. He wasn't taking my picture because he wanted to scare me or abduct me. He thought he was being motherly. He drew pictures of himself nursing me and Dad smiling behind him. And whenever Dad found a new girl he was interested in, Timmy had to take her out of the picture, like a jealous wife. He believed his delusion sometimes.

When I let him/Mom know that I was investigating these events, I think it made him feel more important in our lives. I think it also threatened him. Becoming aware of him was ruining his illusion that he wasn't really my mom. That's when he started acting out.

When he talked to me as Mom, telling me Dad had to make a choice, I think he expected Dad to see him as Mom and fall in love. Betty Coffin's body was found. He had killed her just to seduce my dad into meeting him. The choice was between Betty and Mom. Because Dad chose Betty, Timmy killed him. He ran back to Dad's house and into the box spring, where he'd been living for a few weeks. The music, the makeup, and the dress were all supposed to be for Dad's reunion with "Mom," if he'd chosen her.

I wish I hadn't encouraged Dad to go on that date. If I hadn't, he might still be alive. The whole thing is so stupid. Insanity, obsession, and loneliness, all unprovoked by us. I hate Timmy and I want him to rot, but then I don't even know why. He really was just crazy...

Kicker

I wrote all of this feeling real sure of myself last night. It was therapeutic, at least. I needed to put it all into some sort of order. This morning, I got news that just shakes it all up. You all remember the Etch-a-Sketch, right? Like that. While everything I said is, in a way, still true, there's one very important part that's wrong. A part that makes a lot of it make no sense at all. Detective Kirby told me they were unable to identify the man they caught at Dad's home. However, they could positively state who he wasn't. This man was not Timmy Jean. Timmy is a resident at a group home over three hundred miles away, where he's been for the past four years. He's practically a shut-in, Kirby says. He never goes anywhere. Ever. The man they arrested has no identification, his prints aren't in the system, no dental records, nothing. And so far he's stuck to his promise: he hasn't spoken since that night. Other prisoners avoid him like they're afraid. They won't say why, just that there's "something wrong." And they're right.

One Last Thing

The last thing I want to leave you all with is a strange story I heard from an old friend of Dad's. Dad's friend is a ranger at the national park where Dad's town used to be. He said over the years he'd heard odd stories about things deep in the woods. But one from not too long ago stands out. And he felt the urge to tell it to me. I have no idea why. And I can't say it connects to anything else. It has nothing to do with my family or Timmy. It just feels like it fits, somehow.

A couple from out of town was in the area to do some hiking. The park connects to the Appalachian Trail, so a lot of experienced hikers come through. They decided to do a little off-trail hiking. As I mentioned before, there are miles of untouched woods back there. So they had plenty of room for exploring.

After hours in the woods, the realized that their compass wasn't working at all. Their phones had no signal, of course. They were lost. That deep in, the woods were pretty dense and the sun was starting to set. They were experienced enough to have adequate water, rations, and camping gear, so they didn't panic. But they kept walking, hoping to make it to a road or ranger's camp.

When it got too dark to see, they started to set up camp. That's when the girl told her boyfriend she could see a light. He looked and saw it too. It looked like artificial light. They weren't sure if they were still deep in the woods or not, but it felt eerie. They walked carefully toward it, using an emergency flashlight.

They couldn't hear any traffic as they got near and saw no other lights. But the light seemed to be coming from a real house. A little aged, but no cabin or shack. There was a clearing around the house, large enough for two people to walk side by side.

The guy insisted they examine the perimeter first. His girlfriend thought he was being ridiculous, but he told her he had a bad feeling about the place. She thought the woods at night were just making him jumpy. Still, she went along.

Shingled roof, wood-sided walls, curtained windows, and even a front porch. What they couldn't find was a road. Or even a path or trail. Nothing but woods. The woods surrounded the whole circumference as densely as any other part of the woods. That didn't sit right at all.

But they needed help. They knocked on the only door. An older man answered the door pretty quickly. He looked well groomed, dressed in a nice shirt and pull-over sweater. "Evening, strangers," he said, like it was no big deal.

The boyfriend apologized for bothering him, and explained how they'd been wandering the woods all day and his house was the first they had found. The man was understanding. He invited them inside and seated them in his living room. It was nicely decorated and toasty inside.

They didn't even notice her at first, but there was a woman seated in the corner of the room. She didn't say anything, but nodded politely to them when noticed. The guy and girl exchanged glances. They felt horribly uncomfortable.

The man returned to the living room with a tray of tea. He set it in front of them, then sat across from them. They each poured themselves a cup.

The man watched them very carefully. They didn't like the way he scrutinized them. The fire crackled and popped—sinisterly, it seemed to them —behind him. The tension of the silence kept mounting, so the guy decided to say something. He noted that he hadn't seen any roads or paths around the house. "Nope," the man agreed. So he asked how the man came and went. To this, the man said he stayed put. How about supplies? The man leaned back in his chair and looked at the guy suspiciously. "You're awful curious," he said.

They heard a strange, wet thudding noise somewhere else inside the house right then. The man didn't react, so they pretended to ignore it. But they were both starting to get nervous being in the place.

The guy asked the man how far from the nearest road they were. He was calculating in his head whether they had enough battery to get them to it in the dark. The man answered that they were very far from any road on all sides.

The girlfriend said it was weird to her that it the place was so hidden. Unless someone knew it was there or stumbled on it by pure chance, no one would ever find it.

The man asked which they were. And then said, "How do I know you didn't come here to kill me?"

They didn't know what to say to that. They figured it was a joke and laughed uncomfortably. But he just smirked at them. He excused himself then and vanished around the corner into a dark hallway.

While they were alone, they looked around the room. There was a painting hanging over the fireplace that kept catching the guy's attention. He didn't know why. He hated art. It was a scene of a couple walking through a clearing. There were thick shrubs around. Now that he looked at the painting more closely, he saw something that he swore hadn't been there before. Staring out from one of the shrubs was a man's face, watching the couple with a look of pure hate. The guy was really creeped out, but he didn't want his girlfriend to see it.

They drank more of the tea, because it was warm. They'd taken a few gulps when they noticed the girl in the corner again. They only noticed her this time because she was shaking her head, almost imperceptibly. But she kept doing it. Shaking her head and looking at the teacups. She became perfectly still again when the man returned.

The guy tried to explain to the man that they must be going. He didn't feel well and there had been way too many red flags to keep ignoring them. But the words that came out of his mouth were slurred and ineffectual. He passed out.

When he woke up, he had an awful headache. He shook his girlfriend awake as well. They realized they'd slept for some time. The guy suspected they'd been drugged, but couldn't be certain. The man was nowhere to be seen. Neither was the woman. And the couple's gear was missing.

They wanted to leave right away, but needed their supplies. They had no idea how far from any roads they were. So they went searching the rooms of the house. There were three doors down the hall. All led to bedrooms. The first two were empty. So was the last, but it had their gear on the middle of a child's bed.

They grabbed their stuff and prepared to leave. But the guy saw a curtain covering an opening at the very end of the hall and he had to know. He pulled it open. It was just a closet. The man and woman must've left the house, he thought. Then he noticed his girlfriend's face. She was terrified of something, so much that she was backing away and tugging at him. He looked back in the closet. It was the man, crouched down naked in the bottom of the closet and looking up at them with a smile that crossed most of his face. But his eyes fixed them with the most unmistakably intense rage. He started crawling out of the closet toward them on all fours and making sounds like they'd never heard any living thing make before.

They ran out the house and straight into the woods. They moved as fast as possible, cutting themselves and tripping several times. Something in their guts kept telling them that the man was right behind them, like the man in the bushes in that horrible painting. And he was going to kill them.

151

They finally came out of the woods onto a dirt road and from there slowly followed it to a real road and found their way back to town. They told the park rangers about it and were advised to keep the story to themselves.

Later, they looked the area up on Google Earth. It took them a while, but they spotted the clearing in the woods. It was even deeper in than they'd thought. As they zoomed in, the guy saw something weird in front of the house. He cleaned up the image as best he could. Still a little blurry, but the couple knew what it was. The man was standing in front of the house and looking straight up. Like he knew they were watching. They sent the image to the rangers as proof.

I know there are still so many questions. What really happened to Flora? Was Timmy dealing with someone else? How'd he know so much about Mom? Who was that guy who got arrested? Why was the Ramones t-shirt on my Mom's body? I just don't know…

So for now, that'll just have to be

THE END.

The Mugwump That Came to Thanksgiving

By Marshall Banana, Reddit User /u/*demons dance alone*

Runner Up—November, 2016

For starters, this story is much less whimsical than the title might lead you to believe.

What is a mugwump? The answer is "fuck if I know." Nor do I know where my aunt found one.

My grandfather had always kind of spoiled Aunt Carol. She was the first girl born into the family, and was a diva from day one. When my grandfather's cancer metastasized, it was like the martyr jackpot. She would call us at all hours of the day with some sob story about how poorly Dad was doing (and by implication, her). Meanwhile the bulk of the actual care went to my uncle Bob and aunt Amy. Carol used her dying dad as an excuse to monopolize every conceivable holiday. When Grandpa passed, the sigh of relief from the whole family could have caused a typhoon. We had hoped this would put an end to the holiday shenanigans.

Apparently not.

We were just in the doorway—my wife hadn't even gotten my youngest's coat off—when Carol bustled over.

"Oh, it's so good you're finally here!" We were an hour early for dinner. "I wanted to make sure seating wasn't a problem. I need to sit by Clarence, you know; he can't eat on his own."

The name "Clarence" did not belong to any cousin I knew, and I could see from her face it was a baited hook to get me to ask who Clarence was. I ignored it and dealt with my kids before walking into the dining room and stopping short.

What sat strapped to a booster seat was pink and fleshy and… wet. It was the size of a toddler, completely hairless, with an oval opening for a mouth. Its bulging frog eyes had no visible whites. And not once did it stop wheezing through the whole night.

"What the fuck is that?" I said, forgetting my rule against swearing in front of kids.

Aunt Carol smiled smugly and fluffed the pillow behind it. "I found Clarence all alone. My poor little mugwump needs me. It's so nice to finally have something I can really care for."

Meanwhile her adult son Kevin just looked downcast behind her. I'd never felt so much for the poor guy before.

"What is that? Why is it at the table?" My wife wouldn't let it go. "I don't want it around my kids, it looks unsanitary."

My aunt's smug expression didn't waver. "Clarence needs special care. He's a special boy," she cooed at the pink lump.

I almost threw up right then and there. I don't even know how I made it to dinner.

The thing about dysfunctional families is you get adjusted to weird shit really quickly. Something really fucked up is sprung on you, and you have a moment where you look at it and think "this is normal now."

So my aunt had a mugwump. And it was sitting at the dinner table.

Carol hadn't actually done any of the cooking at the house. My cousin

Kevin's much-beleaguered girlfriend had done the side dishes; Aunt Amy had done the turkey. Carol's contribution was some shitty centerpieces she'd picked up at Dollar General.

And the horrible, pink nightmare seated at the table, of course.

No one was in the mood for dinner when all was said and done. It was an utter tragedy. We had a show-perfect golden-brown turkey, my wife's patented bacon beans, and my oldest daughter had even baked a loaf of French bread.

And we couldn't touch a bite of it because Carol decided "Clarence" had to be served first.

She fetched the baby-food mill and immediately began gouging pieces out of the turkey to put in it. She chose all the wrong bits, too—the crispy ones that resisted being ground up. All the time that damn thing was wheezing. It was like a dentist drill in each ear.

My eldest was pale. I gave her her first glass of wine and told her it was okay.

We tried to ignore the spectacle as we served plates, but the thing about Aunt Carol is that if you ignore her, she just gets louder.

She talked about how the mugwump didn't have a "bathroom hole" (her words, not mine) and so she'd just put a diaper on for appearance's sake. She had to keep baby talking to it in a near shout as she shoved spoonful after spoonful of candied yams and stuffing bits down its oval maw.

I don't know if that thing had a tongue, or if it could even swallow. Half of whatever she put in it just slid out its mouth anyway. The skin at its neck kept bulging like a frog's. Aunt Amy made the mistake of looking over mid-chew and had to spit it out into her napkin. Uncle Bob, the oldest sibling, carved the turkey with murder in his eyes.

When the mugwump took too much mashed potatoes and started choking, that's the point when my youngest daughter threw up. The stupid pink thing just started hacking, patches of the skin on its head pulsing in time with the coughs. My little Katie bent to the side and just unleashed a torrent from her stomach.

In retrospect, I'm surprised it took that long for someone to toss it.

After that, though, all bets were off.

When Carol used her finger to fish a bacon bit off the mugwump's cheek and popped it in her mouth, Aunt Amy gave up and ran to the kitchen sink. Uncle Craig made it through two gut-churning dishes, but when Carol grabbed the giblets to put in the grinder he darted outside.

My oldest gave a wine-heavy burp. I hadn't been watching her and she'd had three glasses. I used that excuse to get my family away from the table. My wife was close behind, desperately covering her mouth.

The girls shared the toilet bowl. I spit a little into the sink, but managed to regain my composure. My wife said, "fuck it," and puked in the bathtub. I think she specifically aimed for the girly soaps Aunt Carol left in the corner of the tub.

We all just took a moment to breathe and concoct our excuse to get away. Because when someone like Carol is acting like that, a rational explanation like "you and your pink tumor-child are disgusting" isn't going to make an impact.

When we made it back to the dining room, the only two people left in there were Aunt Carol and Kevin.

Kevin was watching Carol coo over the food she was shoving into the thing's mouth with angry tears in his eyes.

"This is why dad divorced you, you know," he said.

Carol didn't react. She gasped at how clever "Clarence" was when he made a noise very close to a burp.

We formed a war party in the kitchen. We were past disgust and had arrived at anger. Fuck that thing. Fuck Caroline, for that matter. We had to get her out of the house. But how?

Kevin's girlfriend hit the million-dollar idea.

With coaching from all of us, she crept out to the dining room with a fake smile on her face.

"Hey, Carol? Do you know where the whipped topping is? I've got two pumpkin pies ready to go out."

Carol was incensed. She slammed the spoon down. "That's absurd! There's no way two pumpkin pies will last this whole family!"

Grumbling, she gathered her purse and ran out to the store. While she was gone we took care of business.

We got some towels to pick the mugwump up (no one wanted to touch it) and brought it to the backyard. That's when we found out that whatever a mugwump is, it's effectively immortal. Stomping on its head just led to it reinflating after a minute. Axes couldn't cut it. We even threw salt on it, to no avail.

Finally, we just stuck it back in the house and burned it down. The house had been Grandpa's, but at this point every fond memory we had built there was gone. Aunt Amy stuck a towel on the burner and turned it up to high. We put the thing on the kitchen counter and left. Carol's highly efficient shopping ways meant that she didn't get back for almost three hours. The firemen had to restrain her from running in after "Clarence." We had already told them that Carol was crazy and there were no children left in the house.

I don't know what's worse: the fact that burning down my grandfather's house was the high point of the evening, or the fact that it was only the second-worst Thanksgiving we'd ever had.

***

Well, you've all heard the tale of my second-worst Thanksgiving. To tell you the tale of my absolute worst, you'll need to know some things.

First: Aunt Amy is Uncle Bob's wife. They were together for a long time before that, but they only just married recently.

The reason why?

My aunt Carol.

My uncle Bob is the oldest child in their family. It goes Bob, Carol, Uncle Craig, Uncle Tim, my mom. As such, he got held accountable for a lot more than the rest of the family. So when Bob went to his father saying he was going to ask for Amy's hand, Carol threw a fit.

Why?

Are you ready for this?

Because, as the oldest girl, she had the right to marry first out of all the siblings.

And Grandpa went with it.

My grandfather was a lovely man in many ways, but his single blind spot was the mold spore that was his oldest daughter. You know why my mom wasn't present in the last story? She hates Carol with a fiery, molten hate and takes every opportunity to ditch holidays around her.

So Grandpa vetoed the proposal. And Uncle Bob waited. And waited.

I would have just said "fuck it" and gone ahead with the marriage, but Bob was conditioned to accept his father's word as law. Finally, Carol married my cousin Kevin's father. You'd think that would be the end of it, but no. When Bob asked about money for the marriage, Carol always had some excuse. They were expanding the house (never did). They needed emergency medical funds (Kevin was covered under his father's policy).

When Bob suggested a simple courthouse wedding, Carol lit into him about the indignity of depriving his father of a real, big family wedding.

Well, say this much for her: Aunt Amy stuck around. She's always been an aunt everywhere except on paper, and I love her dearly. We all do.

So the worst Thanksgiving happened in my grandfather's last year of life. As I've said before, Bob and Amy had been doing most of Grandfather's care while Carol mostly whined about how difficult it was. She actually had the nerve to try and ban Amy from Thanksgiving, seeing as they weren't married and Amy therefore wasn't "really" family.

Uncle Bob retrieved his balls from storage and told her that Amy had been working harder in one year than Carol had in her entire life, and if she so much as mentioned this again he would kick her out.

She pouted, of course. It's what she does. But Bob thought that was all. I don't think I would have made that mistake.

My mom actually came to this, her father's last Thanksgiving. My dad stayed home, pled the flu. Really, he was just watching football, the lucky bastard.

We all had fun saying hello to Aunt Amy, complimenting her on how hard she had worked and how good the food smelled. You could practically see steam rise from Aunt Carol's scalp. She tried to steal attention by making loud, tragic announcements, such as: "I just realized this may be our last Thanksgiving as a [big, tragic sniff] family!" We ignored her as best we could.

I popped up to see my grandad. He'd been a big, broad man and the cancer had gutted him into a scarecrow. The light was gone from his eyes at this point; the machines were doing everything. I held his clammy hand in my own and tried to remember good times.

Of course, Carol had to ruin it by bustling in, rearranging pillows and asking "Dad" a bunch of rhetorical questions. I gave it about five minutes before I left, trembling with anger. Come to find out later that it had happened to everyone; Carol butted in on their private moments with her dying father to grasp for attention. None of us suspected she might have had an ulterior motive.

Well, as you can see from my last post, Carol is not much of a cook. She thinks she is. She is not. The bitch could burn water.

Aunt Amy, after months of dealing with her bullshit, had become an expert Carol wrangler. Carol could manage one dish. *One*. It could not be oven-cooked (so she wouldn't interfere with the turkey), nor was she allowed to make a dish that someone was already bringing. Carol made a face, but obeyed. Aunt Amy, to give her credit, was at least a little more suspicious of her than Bob. But the whole day was a frenzy of cooking and so she lost track of Carol.

Carol was making some sort of individualized meat pie and confiscated the turkey giblets. Bob usually uses them to make mouthwatering gravy, but let them go for the greater good. She used Pillsbury biscuit dough for the crust. How did she make meat pies when she was banned from the oven? Our dear friend, the microwave. It made the house smell like dogfood, a smell that makes me anxious to this day.

Uncle Tim was down from the Air Force that day. He actually kicked Carol out of the room so he could have personal time with the father he hadn't seen in years. After taking his time, Tim emerged with a disturbed look on his face and held a whispered conversation with Uncle Bob. It came out later that the surgery stitches on Grandpa's chest had been disturbed. They were bleeding and bruised, like someone had reopened them and then drawn the sutures back up too tightly. Bob figured Aunt Carol had messed with them for sympathy and filed it away for later, wanting to spare us the big screaming fight that would ensue.

Hahaha. Spare us.

Carol plopped a little individual pie down on every plate, not asking any of us if we even wanted one. My older girl Jill was just starting in on her vegetarian kick and made a face. My little Katie almost shoved it in her mouth, but I took it away from her (thank God).

True to form, Carol had to stop the whole dinner to make a long, self-indulgent toast.

"As you know, my father is reaching his last, wretched moments." Carol dabbed away a tear.

Mom, who hadn't missed the possessive singular "my," gripped her knife tightly.

"I want everyone to know that he was a great man. That he suffered so much but always provided for his family."

The veins on Bob's neck were standing out. Aunt Amy was gripping his hand so tight her knuckles were white.

"That's why I've put on this dinner tonight. So that we might give thanks for my father giving us each—"

Uncle Bob broke. He pushed the chair back so hard it fell over. "Shut up. Shut the hell up about giving. You don't know a single goddamn thing about giving. Your own father is dying, and you're still taking from him!" He pointed at her. "Don't deny it. Cut this bullshit about giving, Carol."

Carol was never one to realize when someone was angry with her. She drew herself up, indignant.

"That's exactly what I was doing," she said, "I was making sure to give a piece of Dad to everyone."

As one, we looked down at our meat pies.

"Oh dear god," Aunt Amy said.

The ER is crowded on holidays. Family brawls, kitchen accidents, everything terrible under the surface comes bubbling out. Getting a doctor to look at Grandpa was a nightmare. While the uncles took him to the hospital, where he underwent emergency surgery, my mom and Aunt Amy took turns disposing of what we later confirmed to be pastries filled with my grandfather's tumorous flesh.

***

* * *

To everyone asking why we didn't cut Carol off after the first incident, well, you've severely underestimated how dysfunctional my family is. Over time we found that it was just easier to deal with Carol in person because she could throw some wicked tantrums.

Case in point:

When my little Jillybean was six and her sister was still just a gleam in my eye, we planned a family getaway to the beach. I invited my cousin Ellie (visiting from out of state with her kids), her brother Ty, and my cousin Kevin, who had to work.

On my way to Uncle Craig's house, where we had planned to meet up, I got a text from Kevin that I didn't read until I was pulling into the driveway.

Kevin: *i'm sorry im so fuckin sorry i don't know how she found out.*

At that exact moment, Carol stepped out of the house in a robe and a big, floppy sunhat.

"There you are, dear! You can help me load my bag on the luggage rack," she said, which is how I found out she expected to come with us. Just like that. No invitation; no one even told her we were going.

I coolly explained to her that there was only enough room in two cars for the people we had invited out, but logic bounces off her head like a bird flying into a window. She said I could just drive and hold Jill on my lap, it's how they did it back in the day. I said that was unsafe. She said it was fine. I said it wasn't fine. She told me not to be difficult. Finally I snapped and told her she wasn't invited, wasn't wanted, and could fuck off for all I cared. She made what is colloquially known as a catbutt face but didn't throw the loud tantrum I'd been fearing. No, what she did was much worse.

Ty and I decided to get some last-minute sunblock and took Ellie's husband along to show him around. When we got back I was pulled from the car and handcuffed on the hood while my terrified daughter watched.

Carol had told the cops I was a drug addict who had stolen her niece, and that the other two men in the car were my accomplices. While that was sorted out (it took hours), Carol took Jill for a ride in her car and told her all about how she'd be living with Carol now, that her daddy was in jail and her mommy was going to leave because of that. Jill was crying to the point of hyperventilating when they pulled back into the driveway and met my wife, who Kevin had summoned knowing his mother's tendency for bullshit. I don't know what kept my wife from murdering Carol right then and there, but she grabbed Jill and went to work getting us free. When I got out I just hugged the both of them, kissing them over and over and promising Jill she'd never have to live with Aunt Carol ever.

And Carol... Carol didn't see that she did anything wrong. I mean, you've seen how she reacts to things. She genuinely thought she deserved to go with us, and that making a false police report was a proportionate reaction. What can you even do with someone like that? Grandpa (still kicking at the time) apologized to me for Carol's behavior but told me to forgive my aunt in the interest of family.

But enough about that.

You want to hear how we got rid of her, don't you?

Well, you can tell from these stories and my use of present tense that Carol is still alive. We as a family hope so, at least.

To start things off, Uncle Bob and Aunt Amy got married. It was a blast. Bob wore sunglasses, we did the hustle, the reception was shoes-optional. Carol just sat seething through the whole thing because she couldn't successfully steal attention in such a big shindig. She tried her best, though. She wore a white dress (to a wedding!) and had numerous fake fainting spells. Tragically, she had no date and no mugwump to feed.

Well, the wedding could have gone on for days, but it wrapped up at eleven. We were all staying at this B&B in town, and as such decided to carpool because there weren't enough designated drivers to go around.

I plopped into the front seat, my wife piled into the back with my girls. We were merry with good food and drink.

And Carol opened the driver's side door.

Few things will sober your ass up faster than fear. Carol was a terrible driver. To the point where she no longer had a license. Well, the drink slowed my response time, and I was unable to snatch the keys from the ignition before Carol shut the door and started the car.

"Ugh. Glad that's over." Carol rolled her eyes and screeched into reverse. I winced as I heard the crunch of my tail light hitting someone's back bumper. My wife squeezed our girls in the backseat, all huddled together like frightened rabbits.

The thing about being in a dysfunctional family is that it messes with your reactions. A normal person might respond to someone just getting into their car and driving off by saying, "Pull over or I'll call the cops and tell them you're abducting us."

We stayed quiet, hoping Carol would just take us to the B&B without too many incidents. I was in no state to drive anyway, and it was such a short way. How much damage could she do?

God, the mental gymnastics I went through.

Well, we missed the first turnoff to the town. Katie piped up, "Auntie Carol, we were supposed to turn back there."

"Hush sweetie. Don't talk, it distracts the driver."

I let that one go. There was another turnoff coming up, she could make that one.

"All right, just up here, you see that sign? We turn here. You see that sign? YOU SEE THAT—"

She cruised right by it, squinting. "What sign?"

I gave a growl of frustration. My wife's face was white in the rearview mirror.

"Carol, stop the car. I want to get out."

"Nonsense, dear! We're in the middle of the country! No reason you should have to walk!"

Carol drove on. The road was dark because there were no streetlights out here in the countryside.

I thought of so many things. Engaging the e-brake, grabbing the wheel. But I wasn't alone in the car, and was afraid of what a panicked Carol could do to my family.

"Oh, there it is!" There was a turnoff coming up, almost invisible from the amount of overgrown weeds. Carol put on her signal.

"Carol, this isn't the bed and breakfast."

"Of course it is, dear!" Carol turned too fast, making my stomach lurch. "I was just here this afternoon."

You'd think a minute into our drive up the long, winding path would clue her into the fact that this was not the restored colonial building that sat on a busy street between an antique shop and a wine bar. But no.

The driveway finally ended at a large, white house that had "bad news" written all over it. The windows had sheets tacked over them on the outside. The yard was so overgrown Katie could have walked into it and disappeared.

There were men—silent, staring men in white clothes—that walked up as the car rolled to a stop.

You'd think that Carol, squinting over the dash, would finally realize that this was not our destination.

Instead, she turned off the car, took the keys from the ignition, and opened the door.

"Excuse me, which one of you is the valet?"

A man stepped forward, hand out.

"Carol—goddammit—no!"

Before I could even get my seatbelt off, she handed the keys off to this gentleman in white.

Someone opened my door. The men were at the front and back doors, gesturing for us to come out. Katie was wide-eyed with fear. Jill looked like she'd bite the first hand that came near. Well, I decided I wasn't getting my keys back just by sitting in the car and got out.

The men were looking at Carol's white dress.

"What a lovely thing," one said.

Carol, whose biggest weakness was vanity, blushed. "Aren't you nice young men?"

"Carol." I tried to keep my voice steady. "This isn't our hotel. I want the keys back, and then we can drive out of here and pretend we never saw any of you. No harm, no foul."

"Oh, pooh! You don't know how to be nice!" She turned to the men. "I'm so sorry for my nephew's manners. Do you have any coffee?"

My girls pressed into my back. My wife had her arm tightly around me, ready to go down swinging.

The man who took our keys tilted his head. Then he turned and started walking to the house.

"No!" I pressed forward as much as I dared. "She doesn't speak for my family, I do! Give me those goddamn car keys and let us go."

The man didn't move.

Carol smirked at me. "You see what being rude gets you? Lila raised you with no manners, no manners at all."

She tossed her head and walked after the man.

So, picture this: it's dark, in the middle of fuck-knows-where. I've got no car keys and my family clinging to my back. We're surrounded by a bunch of creepy, no-expression dudes dressed entirely in white. What the hell do you do?

Well, when you figure it out, go back in time and tell me. I was a complete blank. All we did was sit there and shiver until the men started moving. They bunched up behind us, until I felt compelled to walk forward.

One of them drew up beside Katie. "I'll take that," he said, reaching for her hand.

Katie screamed and flinched back. Jill bared her teeth and pulled Katie further into her.

The man looked down at Jill's plum-colored dress. "That is not a pure color."

I let that go without comment. I was coiling up for a big strike, ready to cave someone's head in.

The man looked up at me. "Is she not pure?"

It took a minute for that phrase to trickle in. "Is she... are you asking if she's a virgin?"

"Yes."

We were being led out to the yard. There were large hedges, styled into weird, abstract shapes. White sheets fluttered between them.

"No," Jill said, "I fuck tons of guys. And girls."

"And the little one?"

Rather than deck him for implying my youngest daughter was a slut, I shook my head. Katie trembled in her pretty pink dress.

"And her?"

My wife laughed out loud. "Take a guess for that one, Sherlock."

The men stopped. It was very unnerving. They were completely silent; the only sounds in that yard were our frightened breath and the wind flapping through the sheets. Through the leaves of one hedge, I saw a branch so smooth and pale it looked like an arm.

"Then the woman. Carol. She is the only one?"

"Sure," I snapped.

The man who had been speaking nodded. We were grabbed from all directions, all at once. The girls screamed.

"Then you must come with us until we can persuade you to part with her."

"Wait!" I screamed. "Wait, wait, wait, you can have her!"

The men paused. Katie was sobbing. Jill was twisting in their grip, so was my wife.

"I'll give you Carol," I said, "and all it will cost you is my car keys."

The men turned as one to the house, like they were listening.

Finally, one of them said, "It is good."

As we were escorted out, I saw one of the hedges swaying in the breeze. At least, I think there was a breeze.

One of the men met us at the car, keys in his palm. I swiped them before they had a chance to change their minds.

It's a funny thing, terror. My family just shuffled into the car like we were leaving church. I think we were all kind of numb from shock as the car bounced down the long, winding drive. It wasn't until we hit the road again that I woke up, stepping on the gas so that the tires screeched.

I drove with one hand on the wheel, the other holding my wife's, as we pulled into town. The girls looked shell-shocked. When we finally parked and got out, I gave each of them a nice long hug. We couldn't sleep properly so we piled onto the suite's bed, the girls sandwiched between us, and sat up talking.

It's very telling that no one missed Carol until weeks after the wedding.

Kevin called us up, saying he'd received a notice from his mother's kennel service. Her Yorkie had only been paid through two weeks, and now they were demanding more money. Carol was first and foremost a dog lover, so this was actually out of character for her.

No one at the wedding knew where Carol had gone. She wasn't actually on the designated drivers list (I guess getting into our car was just a whim—that or Kevin's girlfriend had kicked her out for one too many passive-aggressive jabs) and no one had paid much attention to her after the reception. We had come in kind of late, had we dropped her off?

I maintained eye contact with my wife and spoke calmly and slowly. I had gotten us lost after recklessly deciding to drive tipsy. I hadn't seen Carol. None of us had.

My wife gave me a small, approving nod.

They never found Carol, but they never looked very hard for her either. The family healed over it, like a tree heals around a chopped off branch.

And Carol? Yeah, I hope she's still alive. I hope those spooky assholes never figured out that she wasn't "pure," that she was just vain enough not to deny it. I hope she lives a long, full life with both feet planted firmly in the ground.

***

Well, just because Carol's with her nice friends in white doesn't mean I've run out of stories for you. Today's tale comes from my mother, who hated Carol possibly more than anyone in the family.

See, Carol had already sucked all the air out of the house by the time my mom was born. I think it was a combination of Grandpa's old-school leanings and the fact that there was no other female in the family until my mom was born (from what I hear, Gramma just kind of stewed in depression most of their lives). Carol was given free run of the house, which probably set the precedent early on. After Gramma died, Carol would forcibly try to mother her family, and by family I mean my mom. Carol not having a maternal bone in her body meant that it was mostly just controlling behavior, holding her to some bizarre standard of what a "lady" did (a standard that did not apply to Carol, mind you).

All this culminated in the event that led to my mother moving out before she'd even finished high school. Grandpa never stopped her, and gave her some money because he felt guilty about not being there for her more (money that Carol immediately called and tried to get back).

High school prom. My mom had a dress that looked like an organza wedding cake. Her hair was crimped. Her eyeshadow was powder blue. She was ready.

…except.

Except she needed an escort. An escort, like she was a debutante going to a royal ball.

And who to escort her?

Why, her older sister, of course!

My mom is a fighter. She fought. I mean she physically fought. Uncle Bob is the only reason Carol has two eyes left in her head—my mom was going for broke. Finally he was able to talk her down from her blind rage by begging her to do this "for Dad." Mom finally relented that Carol could come, but she would have none of the privileges she'd been demanding. No veto power over her dates, no "helping" mom with her hair, no coming into the prom itself.

Not that that stopped Carol from trying to interfere. She took a bunch of jabs at Mom's date. The guy had terrible hair, he was a nerd, his family was poor, he wasn't good enough for Mom, yada yada… well, not to get too corny, but that nerd is my father. So Mom won on that count.

Well, no one was having something Carol couldn't have. So she needed a date too. Said date was a complete mystery until the night of the prom, so Mom just figured she had made someone up out of jealousy and was planning to throw a fit when he didn't show.

Oh, how wrong she was.

My nerdfather showed up in his dad's ill-fitting tux with a corsage he made out of origami. Supposedly having a date didn't stop Aunt Carol from hitting on him. My dad gets the cold horrors to this day when reminded about it. Carol was bizarrely inappropriate, "accidentally" brushing against his naughty bits and making comments about preferring mature women. You'd think my mom would be furious, but actually she was fighting really hard to hold in her laughter.

She wasn't laughing when Carol's date showed up. To get you ready for this hunk of manhood, I'll inform you that he introduced himself as "Slim."

We have no idea where Carol found this guy. Carol was like a dowsing rod for the bizarre, as you've seen. He was clearly in his forties, leather fringe vest, Hulk Hogan mustache, cheap tats, and one white, milky eye. I wouldn't have believed my mom about this walking, talking stereotype, but she showed me the picture Uncle Tim had snapped at Carol's insistence. My dad has a deer-in-the-headlights look, my mom looks both distressed and angry, and Slim towers over Carol, who is doing this faux-demure smile.

Carol has some really old-fashioned ideas of men and women. Like, medieval old. It was best when the man was older than the woman and ordered her around. Men should pay for everything (yet Slim kept bumming money off her and my mom, wrap your head around that one). Women couldn't so much as burp without apologizing a million times, but men could be as raunchy as they wanted because "that's just how it is." Men could never control their urges, so being alone with a man was an open invitation.

And of course, her all-important edict against being "rude."

Mom couldn't refuse to let a fortysomething stranger on her prom date; it would be rude. She couldn't turn down his chivalrous offer to sit in the backseat with him (Dad fell on that grenade and said he got carsick riding shotgun, so Mom got to ride up front). No asking Slim about his eye, his employment status, or who the hell he was. Personal questions were the rudest of all, don'tcha know?

So my mom had two choices. One was to stay at home, miss prom, and probably still have to deal with Slim. The other was to brave the car ride, go to prom, and possibly ditch Carol.

She went with door number two.

Slim spent the whole ride making gross jokes about high school girls. Carol spent it drilling my dad for info. I think she still had her heart set on "stealing" my dad from her sister, and Dad was not used to her brand of crazy so he was deferentially polite. My mom was heartbroken by the time they actually got into the school; she thought Dad had been put off by her crazy family. She said when they got their tickets, they had a moment where they each looked at each other and just laughed. Then they went to drink punch and dance.

I'm happy to say that portion of the night went well for them. They had a real connection (otherwise I wouldn't be here, would I?) and enjoyed bonding over how crazy Carol was. Sadly, that good portion ended when my mom couldn't fight her bladder anymore and went to the ladies' room.

Carol came in (blatantly breaking rule number three) calling mom's name. My mom contemplated just not answering for a minute before responding.

Carol said her little prom date was waiting for her by the rear entrance; she shouldn't be rude and keep him waiting.

Mom thought it was weird that my dad would be out there, which is where people ducked out to smoke. But okay. He probably wanted to ditch the prom and Carol.

There were no lights back there, so my mom was waiting for her eyes to adjust as the one-way door closed behind her. When her night vision kicked in, she saw not the dorky silhouette of my father but the glow of a cigarette reflected in one milky eye.

Around this time, Carol approached my dad, who was waiting with two slices of cake like the gentleman he was. After some nauseating flirtation, Carol said that my mom had ditched him for some other guy, she was so so sorry and would he like to dance?

My dad knew exactly two things in that moment: one was that he didn't and would never trust Carol. The other was that wherever my mom was, she was probably in peril. So that nerd turned his back on Carol and summoned his nerd pack to spread out and search for her.

My mom, meanwhile, was waffling between fight and flight. Slim stood in the middle of her escape route, and she was in heels for the first time in her life.

Slim killed his cigarette. "Yer sister wants to go now."

"That's not what she told me. She said my date was looking for me."

Slim laughed. "We oughta go anyway. Gettin' close to your bedtime, little girl."

Slim picked up a cup he'd had sitting on the ground next to him. "Here. Finish your punch and we'll go."

My grandpa, being old-fashioned, had not educated my mother on the finer points of date rape. My mother smelled the punch for liquor and found none, so she took a drink. She hoped it would put Slim off his guard; maybe she could charge past him to freedom. Screaming for help never occurred to her, because good ol' Grandpa had ingrained in her the need to never make a fuss about anything.

Mom said that when her legs started to go, that was the scariest moment of her life. Slim had watched her drink, then he held his arms out like he was going to catch her.

One of Dad's friends, acting on a whim, pushed open the back door. Mom flopped over to him, fighting her suddenly clumsy tongue to beg him to bring her inside. Dad said his friend took one look at Slim and knew the score.

"Hang on now, I'm her uncle." Slim was walking to them with his hand out. "It's alright."

Dad's friend grabbed my mom under the armpits and yanked her back inside.

Well, in my mom's impaired state, she realized she had been poisoned. And the best way to get it out would be to vomit. So she had him drag her to the bathroom where she was in good hurling company. My dad, having heard through the grapevine what was going on, went into the bathroom and held Mom's hair while she tossed it. That's when she knew he was a keeper.

Dad and his friends took charge of my mom that night, whisking her away to an all-night diner and giving her a lot of coffee until she could talk without slurring. Then she slept on the floor of his den in the middle of a protective nerd field. Never felt so loved, she said. In the morning, Dad's mom made her eggs and waffles and gave her a nice hug.

All the good feelings of that morning promptly dissipated when she arrived home and saw Carol waiting at the front door with her arms crossed, radiating disapproval.

How dare she ditch her chaperone! How dare she be so rude to Slim (who disappeared, probably due to her rudeness)! How dare she spend the night at a boy's like a common slut!

Mom stepped out of her heels, walked up to the porch, and calmly punched Carol right the fuck out. Then she turned around, got back in the car, and went to live with my father's family.

Uncle Bob was responsible for getting my mom's stuff to her. Even so, quite a few of her clothes disappeared before they could be accounted for, along with some of her jewelry and the pillow Gramma had sewn for her. Mom ate the loss, because it was a small price to pay for her freedom. My dad's family were lovely people who helped them out a lot, and so my mother had a non-dysfunctional family to model after when I came along.

And Slim? Why, he was best man at their wedding!

…I kid, I kid. He kept showing up to the school and then the waitress job my mom got, so my dad's dad threatened him with the cops if he didn't cut the shit. He would still pop up from time to time, shooting her a wink with that milky eye from across the grocery store or on the street. Every time she was tempted to forgive Carol, Mom said, that guy would remind her why she shouldn't.

***

Today I'd like to tell you about Aunt Carol's divorce. Kevin was a little over eight when she split from her husband Leland, and instead of celebrating sweet, sweet freedom he went through unimaginable torment via his mother.

So with all I've said about Carol, you'd probably think her husband, Leland, was a better person.

You'd be wrong. Carol would only ever have married two kinds of people: a deaf-blind-bedbound saint with a bottomless bank account, or someone as scummy as her. Leland was the latter. Wasn't much of a dad, wasn't much of a husband, his only saving grace was his mother who did the bulk of Kevin's care. He was rich, so none of us thought Carol would ever leave him. We underestimated her.

Carol randomly decided one day that Leland wasn't deferential enough to her and threatened divorce. This was over his office phone in the middle of the day. By the time he got home that night, Leland had divorce papers to throw on the coffee table right in front of her.

Carol tried backpedaling, offering counseling or a second honeymoon instead. But I guess even guys like Leland get tired of throwing money down the black pit that is Aunt Carol, so he pressed for a separation.

Leland brought a lot of assets to the marriage. He had money, property, stock options, the works.

Carol had exactly one asset. And no, I'm not talking about her crazy.

Kevin.

I've said before, Carol wasn't much of a mother. Well, as soon as it looked like she might not have her son anymore, Carol decided she wanted him. Unfortunately for her, Kevin was with his grandmother that day. Carol showed up and demanded her son, saying that they were moving to Mexico right this minute. And yes, that's exactly what she said to Kevin's grandmother. She was actually dumbfounded when the old woman slammed the door in her face.

Of course, it didn't end there. This is Carol we're talking about here.

Leland decided to keep Kevin around. Not to protect him from Carol, oh no, but because he wanted to establish residency prior to the custody hearing so he wouldn't have to give his wife so much money. While Carol dropped off the radar for a while, Leland kept Kevin under tight surveillance.

Which is why it came as such a shock when Kevin was kidnapped from school right in broad daylight.

Kevin was under strict orders to wait for his grandmother's car before he even thought about stepping outside. He was walking across the schoolyard, maybe fifty feet from her car, when some random burly dude ran past and scooped him up. They got into a blue van with taped-up plates that was idling at the corner with its side door already open. The whole thing, from grab to getaway, lasted about fifteen seconds. Totally planned.

Kevin's grandmother made a police report, but without the license plate there wasn't a whole lot to go on.

That's where our family comes in.

You may have noticed this from previous stories, but there's a real strong "deal with it yourself" mentality running through us. Sometimes it's harmful, like when you've decided to euthanize a mugwump. But sometimes it's good, like in this instance.

Uncle Bob couldn't just let his nephew disappear without doing anything, so he enlisted Uncle Craig and my dad to drive over and grill Granny for details. The old lady was taken aback at how not-crazy they were compared to Carol, and gave them all the info she could remember. Bob got the idea to drive around just to see if anything matched that description. Well, he must have pleased some deity that day, because they spotted a blue van outside this car shop. They weren't sure it was the right one until a guy came out, toweling the grease off his hands. Granny confirmed it was the kidnapper.

After they dropped her off back home, they went back to the shop to confront the guy. My dad said it was his idea—to ask the guy about getting a quote—that got him close enough to the car that my uncles could jump him. They grabbed either arm and slammed him up against the car, screaming about their nephew.

At the first question about Kevin, the guy blew up. They could all fuck off or he'd call the cops. Drug dealer thugs weren't about to intimidate him.

Ah yes, that old chestnut.

Bob said they weren't drug dealers, they were the kid's uncles and if he didn't fess up he would be eating his own teeth. I can imagine the guy's face in that moment, when that light switch first flipped.

They weren't drug dealers?

No.

They weren't sent to kidnap Carol and bury her in a shallow grave?

The only one who wanted to see Carol at that point was a divorce lawyer.

Dad said the guy just got pale and started babbling. Carol had told him that her ex-con hubby had gotten out of prison and wanted to take the son she had raised by herself, just so he could use him to run drugs. I think they didn't report the guy to the cops because they felt sorry for him. Carol had fed him this long line of bullshit and he'd scarfed it down like a Thanksgiving turkey.

Dad promised not to turn him in if he just told them where he had taken the kid.

The guy stammered that he'd dropped him off in an empty field outside of town. Carol hadn't been there, but a withered old guy in camo gear was. As per Carol's instruction, he gave Kevin over to the old man.

The guy apologized. He hadn't wanted to do it, Kevin was a nice kid and had actually talked to his captors like they were human beings, but Carol had promised she'd be along shortly to take Kevin with her.

Of course, that never happened.

Bob told Leland about the field; Leland got the cops to organize a search party. The field turned up completely empty, not even a breadcrumb to be found. Uncle Craig speculated that she'd given Kevin to some crazy survivalist who probably knew how to hide someone away really well.

Of course the person who could have enlightened everyone, Carol, was nowhere to be found until she called Leland and requested a custody meeting. Anyone else in any other family would have been met with cuffs as soon as she walked in the door. But a combination of Leland's apathy and my family's closed-off nature meant that the only ones in the room that day were Carol, Leland, and Leland's lawyer.

Carol was smirking when she came in. Leland's lawyer (former lawyer, I should say) told me that she didn't even look mildly upset about her son. She wanted to talk terms first.

Leland said okay, sure, you can have *this much* alimony.

He probably low-balled her, but Carol snapped up the amount.

And Kevin would see her—

No. Carol cut in. She got Kevin. She got full custody *and* the money.

At this point, both men were gaping at her. And Carol just sat there smirking.

Did Carol know anything about her son's whereabouts?

Smirk. Shrug.

Because if she did and didn't turn it over, she would be legally barred from custody.

Well then, maybe Kevin would just stay lost then, wouldn't he?

The lawyer said he had never seen anything like it in all his years of mediation. A woman so emotionally removed from her offspring that she would abandon him to a stranger out of greed.

Leland caved. It wasn't the money, really, or his son. He just couldn't stand Carol getting so much over on him. Carol smiled and took the terms, saying she'd be in touch… and right as she stepped out of that office, she was confronted by her brothers and brother-in-law.

They were picking up Kevin. Right now.

Carol frowned for the first time that day. Couldn't it wait? She had an appointment.

Bob got right in her face and told her that if they didn't get Kevin, he would tell Dad that she sold her own son. Carol whined against it, but they physically pulled her into the car and went driving.

They went out to that field. When asked how they'd get Kevin back, Carol smirked. Who knew where he was? Maybe they'd look and get lucky? Dad said he had to try very hard not to hit her then.

Carol got out of the car and walked off into the field. Dad said they tried to watch where she went, but somehow she just vanished as she walked away.

They waited for half an hour. Finally, when they were contemplating sending one of them back in the car to get cops, Carol came out of the field (from a completely different direction than the one she'd been traveling), walking like she was casually strolling to the store.

Completely alone.

Dad said she opened the passenger door, offhandedly said that they'd probably want to look in *that* part of the field, and then got in.

The men spread out and searched the field. They found Kevin lying on a tarp in the middle of a stand of mullein.

The poor kid was shirtless and shivering. He had tree branches strapped to his hands and feet, and three lines of deer blood painted down his face. Dad said when they reached him, Kevin flinched back like he didn't even know who they were. Bob took his coat off and wrapped him in it, then picked Kevin up.

Carol was right in the car where they'd left her, looking irked at the wait. They could just drop her off at the law offices, then she could pick up her car.

No, my dad said, Kevin needed to go to a hospital.

Carol made her patented catbutt face. But she was *laaaaaate*. Kevin could sleep it off at *hoooooome*.

Bob said Kevin was staying with them that night, and possibly indefinitely.

Carol got a sly look and said he'd probably get lost again if he didn't live with her. She had custody! She had rights!

The men exchanged a look. Literally the last thing this kid needed was to stay with Carol. But, well… she had them between a rock and a hard place. No one knew better than they did how badly Carol could fuck up their lives. They weren't going to win this battle, but they might win the war.

They argued her down to dropping her off to get her car while they took Kevin to the hospital. They checked him for all the usual things, even sexual assault (which came up negative, thank god).

Kevin was slightly malnourished and had suffered from exposure at one point. In addition to the deer blood on his face, fat mixed with ash had been smeared on his body in a few places. The reason he hadn't talked to any of them so far was discovered when they opened his mouth and found a series of knife cuts on his tongue.

Once they made sure that Kevin was (mostly) okay, they made the long drive back to Carol's. The whole time, Bob kept apologizing to Kevin for making him go back to his mother, telling him he could call anyone in the family at any time for help. My dad said his heart broke when Kevin went up that walk and Carol just yelled for him to come in, she didn't want to get up and open the door.

Carol was floating on clouds of smug. She had her money, she had her son, she had everything.

Until about two months later, when she got bored and dropped Kevin off with his grandmother again. Granny could have called the cops, raised a stink, but I think she knew in her heart that it would only end badly. Carol kept getting "child support" and Kevin ended up in a mostly stable household. It was win-win all around.

I was only a kid when this happened, so most of this is secondhand. Kevin never talked about what happened to him during that time, where he was. Whenever someone asked him about it, he just froze up with a terrified look on his face. So we stopped asking.

To be honest, I would have embraced the chance to have nothing to do with my mother after a fiasco like that. But Kevin's been reeling in the wake of Carol's disappearance, kind of seesawing between grief and anger. I think the poor guy misses the relationship he should have had with his mother rather than the woman herself.

As for me? I say ding dong, the witch is gone.

**

Carol ruined every fucking Christmas she was a part of. Whether it was "accidentally" spilling scalding-hot coffee into my wife's lap so we spent the rest of the day in the ER, or setting the goddamn tree on actual fire, the woman had a talent for it. But there was one Christmas where her evil just permeated the entire day, so that we couldn't get one enjoyable memory out of it.

That ruined Christmas was the first holiday I brought my girlfriend (now wife) Sarah to meet everyone. She had already met my parents and my dad's parents. Now she was ready for the other half.

I warned her. I told her going in that it was crazy. Not "ha ha ha we are soo quirky kooky and zany" crazy, but "homeless dude disemboweling squirrels to wear them like socks" crazy.

She didn't believe me.

Well we got there, we went through the rounds of coat-taking and cheek-kissing, and everything seemed pretty normal. They seemed to like my girlfriend, and she liked them.

Our first taste of Carol was when she tottered over, all fake-nice and cozying up to my girlfriend like they were old friends. She promptly ruined it by making a racist comment (she assumed Sarah was Puerto Rican; she very clearly isn't) and then stepping on Sarah's little toe when she went in for a hug.

Sarah gave me a look when they disengaged. I lifted my eyebrows at her. It wasn't even the tip of the crazy iceberg.

I can tell you what Carol does, but that doesn't get across the utter hell of just being *around* Carol. Having her butt into several conversations at once, demanding hugs so she can leave White Shoulders perfume on your clothes that won't come off after fifty washes, making backhanded compliments, giving unwanted advice, invading your personal space, poking, pinching, prodding every inch of unprotected skin until you want to backhand her, a thousand and one little things that build up like midge bites. Sarah doesn't have the most functional of families, but she was still shooting me astonished looks throughout the night. She was about ready to strangle Carol when the gift giving finally started.

Let me tell you something about Carol and presents. Carol likes to get, and doesn't really care for the "give" part. Big shocker, I know. So we would give her the tacky, glittery baubles we knew she would like, and she would give us any old thing she picked up. I swear to God that is the literal truth. She gave us a towel she found on the road one year. I know this because I saw it on our drive up.

For some reason, this year she decided to give us actual gift-y things. They were all more effort than her usual presents, but the effort was grossly misapplied. Aunt Amy got a saddle and tack when she has never owned a horse or ridden one. My girlfriend got expensive weight loss stuff (Carol had never met my girlfriend prior to this, nor did she need to lose weight). Kevin got a shirt many sizes too large for him, which didn't matter because it was missing all its buttons. My mom got this antique silver brush set with rotting bristles. Bob got his own toolbox—as in, she gave him his own toolbox after taking it at some unspecified point in the past. It even had his initials scratched in the lid.

And Uncle Tim…

I don't know how much of Carol's actions are calculated malice and how much are just plain stupidity. Either way, when Tim unwrapped a lovely picture frame bearing a photo of himself and the wife that had left him not two months prior, it came to the same result.

Tim is not the easiest guy to get along with, but he really loved his wife. He just looked crushed when he unwrapped it, while Carol chirped on about how expensive the frame was. He excused himself out to the car and then we had to pretend we didn't hear him crying for the next twenty minutes.

Ohhhh, but the capper to the evening was Uncle Craig's present. Carol had parked around the corner from the house and was acting all sneaky about it. Right in the middle of the gift giving, she makes a big announcement that we all had to go outside, right now!

We took our mugs of eggnog and prepared for letdown. Instead we came face to face with a boat hitched up behind Carol's car. We were expecting her to brag about how it was a Christmas present to herself, but to our shock she up and handed the keys to Uncle Craig. She had bought him a boat!

Craig had this look on his face like he couldn't quite figure it out. He hadn't helped Carol out at all that year; what was the occasion? Maybe she had just bought a boat on a whim, decided she didn't want it, and gave it to the sibling that had earned the least wrath over the past year?

I can see you right now. You're reading this and shaking your head. That's the proper response.

Well, Carol only stuck around a little while after that. I think she was expecting a bigger response from all of us, but we were way too wise to assume she was doing it out of the goodness of her heart. She made some comment about picking up more coffee and left and didn't come back.

We were cautiously cheerful. Only half a day with Carol? It really *was* Christmas!

Close to dark, Uncle Bob looked outside and saw a handful of guys on Uncle Craig's boat. They were standing on the bumper, patting the keel, touching it all over. He wanted to call the cops, but no. Tim had something to prove after that afternoon, and went outside to confront them.

A little while later he came back in, white-faced, and told us to lock the doors and not even look outside. There was a terrible smell that had rolled in with him, a combination of rotting citrus and bad meat, and it permeated everything until we couldn't even smell dinner in the oven. We tried to soldier on through it but there was just no way. After night fell and the guys (and the boat) seemed to have vanished, we decided to go out to a restaurant.

We came back to the front door hanging open and all the presents missing.

Well, I turned to Sarah and said, "I told you. Crazy, right?"

She laughed instead of crying and we're still together almost twenty years later.

That would be a cute little end to the story, except I got a chance to ask Uncle Tim about what happened in the yard. The guy was a little into his cups when I did this, so he was a lot freer with the information that he might normally be.

He said he went out to confront the guys, shouting to them that they were on private property.

The guys just looked at him. They all looked pretty tough, like they could go from talking to fighting in a second. Tim was pretty hot-blooded, but something about their tense silence made him try diplomacy first.

Tim said that this was his brother's boat.

The guys said no no, it's their friend's boat. Whoever had sold it to him had clearly been a criminal.

Tim said he didn't buy it, his sister did. And she hadn't mentioned the seller.

The guys took a huddle, whispering really harshly in a language Tim couldn't quite place, and then turned around to face Tim again.

What he got out of them is this: they had a friend. Friend got into (not elaborated-upon) trouble and picked up house and ran. Took his wife with him and set sail for the tropics. His boat wound up adrift in a marina miles away from his last reported whereabouts.

Tim said that was quite a story, but what the hell did they want?

They asked him to wait a minute.

They searched over every inch of that boat. They patted every surface and fished a pen knife into every crack. Finally, one of them found a panel that they pried open with the knife. Tim said the smell rolling out of that space made him want to vomit, but the men stayed stoic like it wasn't even there.

The compartment held this fish, about five feet long, that looked a bit like a lion fish but blue. Tim said they didn't even pause, they pulled that sucker out and took turns kicking it in the stomach. Finally, after one of them stomped on it, the lips opened and vomited out a human hand. One of the guys bent down and, without hesitating even a second, started sucking on the fingers.

Tim said that's when he went back inside. Screw the boat, Craig wasn't really attached to it anyway. He knew he was dealing with shit well above his pay grade. He theorized that some of the things Carol had given us had been on the boat, and that the men had stolen all of the presents because they weren't sure which ones.

I think he knew more about the guys than he let on, but I left it there. So Carol didn't give us all tumor-pies or make us watch her feed the horrible thing she found by the side of the road, but she managed to ruin a holiday just by being her. What kills me about this is, in her mind, it was a genuine attempt at being generous. So even when she wasn't intentionally being evil, she was still evil.

***

Carol snatched kids. Yes, plural. Kids. She's done it more than once, and always managed to wriggle out of it like the hagfish she is. I'm only telling you about three of them today, because these are the ones I have the most information on.

I'll start with my friend Trish's tale because it's the least terrible. I had told Trish about my crazy aunt, and she'd kind of laughed it off. No one could be that extreme, right?

Trish is a photographer's assistant and she was helping out at an Easter celebration at a church the day she finally saw my aunt in the flesh. I don't know how anyone can come face to face with Carol and ignore the stench of brimstone clogging their nostrils, but Trish just saw her as a normal (if weird) older woman at first. It was only later that she connected the dots.

Carol had the hand of a little girl who was tugging away from her and saying stuff like, "But I don't *want* to, let me *go*."

Carol dragged the little girl over to Trish. "Can we get a photo now? I'm sure nobody will mind if you let me go first."

Trish stammered, "A-actually, we're working on a ticket system, so you go in the order of the number on your stub. Maybe you and your daughter can talk it over with someone who has a closer number?"

The little girl said, "She's not my mom. I don't know her."

Carol has always wanted a little girl. Scratch that, she wants a mini-me with no thoughts or opinions to show off how great she is. Kevin was an eternal disappointment to her. So rather than go through (yuck!) childbirth again, she would co-opt other people's children. She tried to come after my little Jillian, as demonstrated by her fun little car ride, but my wife and I put a stop to that pretty quick.

Trish, possessing none of this vital information, froze. There was no training for this sort of situation and her brain kind of skipped a beat.

"You're not her mother?"

Carol let out one of her patented fake laughs. "Of course not. But we're just so *photogenic* together, don't you think?"

The little girl looked nothing like Carol, in that she was actually not a buttertroll. Carol posed next to her like they were going to be in a magazine spread. The little girl just looked irritated and bored.

Luckily, Trish was saved from having to make a hard decision by the girl's mother running up.

"Jessica? I've been looking for you everywhere!"

Carol dropped her hand and pouted. The girl's mother, eye on Carol, escorted her away while holding a whisper conversation.

The family only knew Carol as a fellow congregant, and not very well at that. Word spread, and everyone started avoiding her. This only sped up Carol's usual cycle of join-infiltrate-abandon that she went through with each new church. When Trish told me the story, I'll admit I laughed a little bit. This was quite possibly the best case scenario with Carol; she didn't get a chance to do something criminally negligent.

Yet.

The second incident was pieced together by Uncle Craig after the fact.

As it happened, there was a family at a mall. The mom wanted to go in a store, the two kids didn't.

Mom sat younger kid down on a bench, told older kid to watch him just a second, and went in.

Carol came strolling along.

The younger kid was clearly with someone, but Carol still insisted on speaking to him like he was alone. Her conversation was captured on the mall's CCTV. You could even see her purse her mouth as she used that stupid baby voice she thinks little kids love.

She asked the kid if he had been left all by himself.

Older kid butted in that no, there were two of them.

Younger kid didn't answer.

Carol asked him if he wanted anything.

The younger kid said he needed to go potty.

The older kid said no, their mom would be out in a minute.

Carol put her hand out to the kid and insisted she take him potty. The older kid said no, she can't.

Younger kid, taught to obey adults over siblings, hopped off the bench.

Older kid ran inside to get mother. Carol walked off with younger kid.

Of course, they didn't go right to the bathrooms. They stopped off at toy stores and See's Candies, because Carol is a massive tease that likes to psych kids up so she can more effectively disappoint them.

Meanwhile, kid's mother was going apeshit. I admit, making your kid watch your other kid in a crowded mall is not the wisest parenting decision. But that woman in no way deserved to have to deal with Carol.

Security caught up with Carol around Sports Authority. No one had looked twice at a cranky kid trying to wrench away from an older woman. When the guard came up and demanded she turn over the kid, Carol burst into tears. She was only gone a little while! She was going to bring him right back! This was so rude!

Like an octopus shoots ink to escape predators, Carol leaves a cloud of befuddlement in her wake. Somehow the guy ended up letting Carol off with a warning, which hopefully earned him a dope slap from the firm that employed him. It fell to Uncle Craig to sort everything out because... he was home when she called? I don't know, there's a lot of sunk cost fallacy when it comes to Carol's siblings. I think one of the reasons Carol didn't go to jail was that the mother was also considered at fault for leaving her kids alone in a crowded mall.

And then there's the time she abandoned me.

Carol is not a mother, as I've stated. But she makes a point of trying to mother other people's kids. She was always correcting my mom about the way she was raising me, and the corrections were anything but correct. My mom tried to prepare me against her crazy just in case she tried to give me whiskey for a toothache or something like that when she wasn't around. But I don't think any amount of preparation would have prevented this.

For good reason, Mom hated Carol. So she made sure to drop me off at Grandpa's when Carol wasn't there.

You know, I just can't do justice to how cool Grandpa was. He hand-made wooden toys every Christmas, he had the coolest house full of neat junk, and he just loved his children and grandchildren to bits.

It's just that one of those children happened to be Carol, and Carol happened to drop by about an hour after my mother left to run errands.

I was building a train track with Grandpa when Carol came in, all fake sweetness and love bombing. I think kids have an innate sense of when someone is pretending to be nice; they can smell it like bloodhounds. My kids and I do, anyway. I think it was when she started low-key insulting my mom ("Lila *never* brings you over often enough, why don't I see my lovely nephew more," etc.) that I first saw the cracks in her facade.

It was getting close to lunchtime and Grandpa was laying me out some graham crackers spread with peanut butter.

Oh no, no, no, that would never do for a growing boy! Carol would take me out to get a burger, fries, any kind of treat I wanted!

Grandpa pondered. Mom had given explicit instructions not to let me go anywhere around Carol unassisted, but in his mind all his children's problems were the same and they just needed to get over it.

I wasn't eager to go anywhere with Carol, but Grandpa (a beloved and trusted adult) told me it was okay. As I put on my seatbelt, Carol babbled about all the nice things she was going to get me. I wanted a burger? I'd get a deluxe! Mom didn't let me have a whole thing of fries? I'd get the jumbo! And a shake! And a toy!

I've mentioned Carol's tendency to build you up only to disappoint you. I was with her up until she started talking about dessert, saying I wasn't really that hungry. Well that just made Carol determined to spite my mother. I probably just wasn't used to eating normal portions, poor baby!

I will say this, she held to her word that she'd get me food. Nowhere near the feast she'd been promising, but food. She even got me a toy, which I didn't even want or ask for (and it was the girl toy to boot), and waited there in the drive-thru, horns honking behind us, so she could watch me take my first bite.

She made a lot of exaggerated yummy noises at me and drove off.

As soon as she got me fed she was going to take me to the store and buy me a nice toy and then we'd go get some clothes so I stopped looking so shabby—

This was my first glimpse into the depths I was currently adrift in. I said I didn't want new clothes, I liked the clothes I was wearing.

Of course I needed new clothes! My mother couldn't afford nice things, that's why she was always begrudging Carol's nice gifts! I just didn't know what nice things looked like, after all.

I swallowed a fry, appetite completely lost and over half a burger to go. "Aunt Carol, I don't want to go shopping."

"Yes you do, don't be rude," she said, running a stale yellow light.

"No. I want to go back to Grandpa and finish the railroad."

Carol mouthed my words, waving her head back and forth as she did, mocking me. "You're spoiled, you know that? You don't know the value of anything."

I had only one card left in my hand. My mother had told me to play it any time I needed to get away from Carol.

"I need to go to the bathroom."

Carol frowned and slammed on the brakes. My neck still remembers that moment.

"Fine," she snapped, "go right here."

We were (not really) close to a public restroom outside a little park. I remember dingy gray walls and metal toilets with no seat. I took care of business and went back outside.

Carol waited like a responsible adult and made sure I got belted in before driving off and we had a lovely time—*ahahaha no, she fucking drove off and left me.*

I wasn't even scared for a minute. I naively thought that Carol had probably parked and soon she would come around the corner and berate me for taking so long.

I don't know how long I waited, but it felt like forever. I was stuck between staying where I was in case she came back or risking going to look for a phone.

A guy drove up. A bit pudgy, baby face, glasses. He looked like your typical cubicle drone. He just stayed in the car, watching me with a benign smile on his face.

After a while, he got out of his car.

"Are you lost, little guy?" he said.

I was really nervous, and I didn't like being called little. "No, just… waiting on my aunt."

The guy smiled bigger. "Oh, good. She sent me to come get you." He opened the passenger door. "Go ahead and get in, we'll be there before you know it."

More than the mall kid, I'd had stranger danger drilled into my head. I wasn't sure what this guy had planned for me, but it wasn't good.

"No thanks."

His smile grew wider. "Come on. I've got a G.I. Joe in the back, I promise I won't tell anyone if you want to come play with it."

"Sure, I just gotta… get my skateboard." I turned and marched stiff-legged through the park. I turned back twice. Once halfway, I saw the guy watching me go, shading his eyes with his hand. When I got to the other side, I turned around and the guy was gone.

I had my telephone number memorized, but no one was home (Mom still happily running errands, thinking I was safe with my grandfather). I waited in a little shop while the storekeeper phoned the cops. They took me home and waited with me. I'll bet my mom had a heart attack when she saw the cruiser in the driveway, and another when they told her what had happened to me. She called Grandpa, and the old guy thought I was still out with Carol. My mom told him no, the police brought me home. I don't know how she kept her calm telling Grandpa the whole story, but ended up convincing him of the truth (he was still making excuses for Carol right up until she drove off and left me).

Carol must have seen that I'd gone from the spot and, rather than face her father, must've gone straight home. Or she just went straight home without bothering to check on me. Equally likely.

Mom called her house. Her voice was pure, sharp ice as she asked if Carol had seen me.

Carol lied and said she thought I was with Grandpa.

Mom said it was funny, because Grandpa hadn't seen me since Carol took me out.

Carol changed her story and said she had dropped me off at home since I wanted to go.

Mom said that I hadn't been at home.

Carol changed again and said I'd whined about getting a toy in a store and then ran off when she refused.

It was amazing. I'd never seen my mother do this. She was like a spider passing down loops of silk until Carol had woven her own noose. Finally, my mother cut the bullshit and told her cops brought me home, and that if she ever tried doing something like this again, Mom would string her up by her goddamn intestines.

Carol started into her whole *you can't tell me what to do, Dad says*—

Mom replied that she'd already told Dad what happened and her bullshit wasn't going to fly today.

Carol went silent. Then she hung up.

I'm sure she bawled about how unfair it was to her father over the phone, but for the first time in my life Grandpa held firm. And Carol gave Mom a hefty prize: an apology wrenched from her pursed lips. A small victory in the long run, but still satisfying.

Why does she do it? The same reason she dropped Kevin off with a *Duck Dynasty*-looking asshole: because she sees children as things and has zero empathy for anything other than herself. I'm sure if that pudgy dude had ended up molesting and murdering me, she would have found a way to make it all about herself.

***

Well, I've been talking (and drinking) with my uncle Bob, and boy oh boy oh boy do I have a treat for you.

Since Bob is the oldest sibling, he's had more contact with Carol than anyone else living. Even better, he remembers Gramma when she was alive. I struck quite the goldmine with him, learning some very enlightening (and disturbing) things.

I'll start with this anecdote, as it's probably the most lighthearted of all.

So Uncle Bob is one of those DIY guys. If he's not at work, he's in his garage. He was planing some wood with the garage door wide open when Carol rolled up, so he couldn't very well kill the lights and pretend not to be home. He assumed Carol was there to hit him up for money when she popped out of the car, all smiles.

She got a dog!

I've mentioned that Carol is a dog person. She usually takes better care of them than she does of children (in that she actually pays other, more competent people to take care of dogs) and Bob thought sure, this would just be a semi-normal visit. Carol would suck up some narcissistic supply and leave.

A dog, huh? What breed?

Carol shrugged. Some kind of hound? She just went and picked him up.

Bob knew instantly he had to tread with caution. This was probably some kind of theft or illegal trade that she'd partaken in without second thought.

She'd just gone and picked him up?

That's what you did with puppies in the wild, didn't you?

Bob had a brain ache from that one. Not just because Carol was ignorant enough to believe dogs just roamed free for the taking in the United States, but that it automatically fell to him to sort it out.

He asked to see the puppy.

Carol gladly obliged, opening the car's rear passenger door and frightening the bear cub huddled between the seats.

Bob said he had an epiphany that moment. That no matter what low he estimated for her behavior, Carol would always manage to outdo him.

Bob told her it was a goddamn bear cub.

Carol laughed and said no it wasn't, it was a cute little puppy! He'd come right up to her and licked her hands, so she'd decided to take him home! Wasn't that nicer than that scary old park?

Bob was looking at the backseat. The cub had been sick all over and was currently shivering. Bob was no vet, but he thought the cub was in some kind of shock. And that Carol was potentially in a lot of trouble.

And he knew who she'd try to drag down with her.

Bob said she had to put it back.

Carol made a face. Why? It would probably just die! She would take it home and feed it more candy bars because it liked them so much.

Bob restrained himself from pointing out that her behavior would probably have killed a real puppy already and just told her that taking an animal from a federal park was illegal and carried a hefty fine.

Carol got sly and said she wouldn't tell if he wouldn't.

Bob said it probably had a tracker in it and the park rangers could probably tell it had gone off the grid. Massive bluff on his part, but it worked. Carol's eyes got wide and she asked if they could just cut the tracker out. Bob said no, it's probably in its digestive system or something, they should probably just put it back in the park and the rangers would write it off as a blip in the system.

Using Carol's own ignorance on her is probably the most satisfying method of dealing with her bullshit but, my uncle warned me, it can bite you in the ass if you're not careful.

Carol decided to return the cub (Bob drove, because Carol is a menace on wheels) and directed them to the spot where she'd found the cub. It was so far off the beaten path that Bob was surprised she hadn't taken out the tires driving to it. When asked what the hell she'd been doing so far out, Carol said she'd been looking for a pretty place to have a picnic.

Yeah.

Well, they rolled up on the little field where she'd first found the cub. Bob said he felt so sad when he picked that little body up and felt it shivering. He knew it might die, and if it lived it would probably grow up to be a problem bear. But he also knew if he brought it to the ranger station that Carol would throw him under the bus, somehow wriggling out of it like she always did. No, he planned to call in an anonymous tip that he'd seen some tourist messing with a bear cub when Carol was safely out of his hair.

Carol stayed in the car while he picked the cub out of the back. He tried to hold it gently and make reassuring noises as he carried it out into the open, looking for a safe little hollow to put it in.

That's when he noticed the cub's mother on the far side of the clearing. Five feet of shaggy ursine rage, looking right at him. It broke into a gallop.

Bob said his life flashed before his eyes in that moment. He dropped the cub (not his proudest moment) and just ran.

The sound of the bear lumbering after him awoke all sorts of ancestral fears in his muscles. He ran, faster than he's probably ever run, to the car—*where his sister had locked all the doors.*

Bob, operating on some kind of ultra-autopilot, just fell flat and rolled under the car. The bear ran into the car so hard it rocked on its springs. Carol just kept screaming uselessly.

The bear fished under the car for Bob. It had the longest claws he'd ever seen in his life. They looked like they could rip open human flesh like wrapping paper. They left deep furrows in the ground as it scratched after him. Bob joked that he regretted not shitting himself in that moment; the smell would probably have convinced the bear he was dead. He scooted over to the far side so that its claws couldn't reach him. Carol continued to do nothing useful.

The bear swiped at the passenger door, prompting Carol to shift to the driver's side. It lumbered around to the other side of the car, sniffing. Bob moved out of range again.

Carol did the first useful thing she'd done that day and laid on the horn. The bear was startled.

Carol leaned on that horn like there was someone going the speed limit in front of her. The bear lingered for a bit, and then ambled off to the tree line.

Bob waited for a few minutes after it vanished from sight (going deaf from all the honking) before wriggling out from under the car.

He told Carol to unlock the door.

Carol said no, what if the bear came back?

Bob took one look at that tree line, then told Carol if she didn't unlock the door he would use a rock to smash the window in.

Well, that got her to comply in a hurry.

As Bob got in, he asked her why she'd locked all the doors before he could get to safety. Carol confusedly replied that she thought the tracker would stop the bear from attacking humans.

And that, Bob said, is why you don't rely on Carol's ignorance as a failsafe.

As he stopped at his house and got out, Carol actually had the nerve to ask him about paying for the damage to her car. Bob told her to tell the auto shop that the government was responsible and she'd probably get it for free.

Carol drove off happy, and Bob went in and took some aspirin.

Bob said he heard about a problem bear in the park not too long after. It kept attacking tourists in the area until finally the rangers had to euthanize it. Bob said he felt really guilty about that, certain that it was the mother bear they had screwed over.

When Carol got a new Airedale puppy around the same time, Bob snuck into her house while she was out, grabbed it, and took it to a no-kill shelter five counties over. It didn't help with the guilt, he said, but it was cathartic.

***

Carol has burned through many a church in her day. How any right-thinking congregation doesn't take one look and come after her with crosses a-blazing is beyond me. I've mentioned the nice folks who cottoned onto her child-snatching tendencies, but there are more. So many more.

The first ones in my memory are the Catholics. No, our family is not Catholic at all and yes, she totally lied that she had been baptized into the church. She really went for all the pomp and ceremony. She's a big one for ceremony because it's oppression with fancy decorations. So she started saying grace at every family meal and Grandpa just thought it was great that his daughter was getting more spiritual and we should all go along with it.

Let me tell you how Carol said grace: each time it was a long, rambling speech about how we were all wicked and owed the lord fealty and if you so much as sneezed she would make a face and start all over, droning on and on while your stomach turned into a painful vortex of hunger. It was during a Fourth of July barbecue, right after Carol had started over for the ninth time, that Uncle Bob broke. He started shoving handfuls of food into his mouth, chewing noisily and making faces so all the kids burst out giggling. Carol made catbutt face, but her spell was broken and she was powerless to do anything.

That's probably what led to Aunt Amy arriving home one evening to find Carol and the priest sitting in her living room.

The priest said her whole family (read: Carol) were concerned about her living in sin with a man she wasn't married to, and he'd like to talk to her about her (nonexistent) drinking problem to boot.

Amy took one look at them and said she hadn't invited them, and if they didn't get out right now she was calling the cops. The priest immediately knew he'd gone out of his depth, but Carol jumped up and started screaming about how Amy's sin was bleeding into the family and tarnishing it. Amy got a glass of (lukewarm) tap water and tossed it at Carol. Carol fell to the floor screaming like it had been scalding hot.

The priest shot Amy a look like a man who had stepped into a shark tank thinking it was full of dolphins. Amy ignored him and went in the kitchen, loudly counting to twenty. By the time she got to fifteen, she heard car doors.

Bob called the priest and lit into him when he got home that night, sending the final nail into Carol's Catholic coffin.

The next lucky stiffs to get Carol were the Jehovah's Witnesses and let me tell you, that was quite a romp. Carol not only stopped celebrating holidays, she decided we shouldn't celebrate them either. She broke in and trashed our Christmas tree (we couldn't prove it was her, but come on) but the real fun was my cousin Ellie's birthday. Now, JW's are allowed to celebrate anniversaries and birthdays, but Carol decided it was too fancy and "accidentally" fell on the cake Uncle Craig's wife had spent hours making. She chased Carol around with the piñata stick and we let her, because we figured she needed to blow off some steam.

We weren't the ones who got her kicked out of the JW's though, that one was all Carol.

She was chomping at the bit to go and witness to people, and I'll give you two guesses why. The person they sent to go door-to-door with her (not sure what they call it) was alarmed at her car-salesman tactics and general manipulation. She would barge into people's houses and threaten to have a heart attack unless they heard her. The last straw was when she threatened a single mother with CPS unless she let them in. Carol was called into a meeting with an elder, and ended up threatening the elder with reporting him. This brilliant tactic did not endear her to them at all, and Carol was kicked out.

She hopped to the Unitarians next. Lasted a grand total of three months before she accused a girl in the church of having a drug habit. The poor girl had allergies… and was the minister's daughter. Awkward.

This is where it goes from funny to sad and horrible.

At the Episcopalian church Carol joined next, there was this guy. Wife was separating from him and the church. Daughter was straying from the path. Black clothes, heavy metal, Tim Burton movies. You know, typical teenager stuff. The guy was seeking help from the pastor, who told him the usual things you would hear in a case like this: stay strong, every kid goes through something like this, keep the faith, etc.

Then along comes Carol.

Carol cannot go without butting into everyone's business, so she knew all about the guy's divorce. How awful! His wife was an ungodly whore! She was rooking his daughter from the path of light!

The pastor had recommended counseling. Carol said that his daughter was in too serious of spiritual danger for that.

She needed an exorcism.

I don't know how big exorcism is in the Episcopalian church, but if it exists at all I don't think it's anything like the fiasco my aunt planned. She didn't need no fancy priest or holy water. They just needed five strong guys to hold a tiny fourteen-year-old down while they screamed at her.

I can't imagine what was running through this guy's head to let Carol talk him into this. Maybe he was just really grief-stricken about his family and struggling to put it into terms of his faith. Maybe he was a domineering tyrant who sensed his control slipping. Either way, he made the worst decision of his life when he listened to my aunt. I can't even imagine what they told the five guys to get them to help; apparently they were all otherwise upstanding members of the church.

The girl arrived for her three-day stay at her father's house. She left it on a stretcher.

Carol instructed the five men to hold the girl down to a bare mattress in the cold basement while she went through the exorcism rite she had concocted out of sheer bullshit. She pushed verses on the girl (like, actually tore pages from the bible and pressed them against her), spoke in tongues, doused the girl from a water bottle, all the while everyone was screaming at her to let the devil out of her.

The girl kept begging to be let go, she was thirsty and had to go to the bathroom. Carol told the men that if they gave her anything, the ritual would be void and they'd have to start over.

It went on for over a day, a grueling ordeal for everyone involved. When the girl passed out, they thought they had made progress.

Actually no. What really happened was the girl had undiagnosed type 2 diabetes and had just slipped into a coma. When they couldn't wake her up, one of the five men went to call an ambulance. Carol stopped him and said no, if they told someone they would be seen as responsible. She told them to carry the girl upstairs and place her on her own bed, and they would call the wife after a few hours and accuse her of poisoning the girl.

Well, the dad had a limit, and that one was it. He charged upstairs and called an ambulance. They got the girl to a hospital and managed to save her life. The dad lost both custody and the respect of his daughter indefinitely.

And Carol? She spun it around so that most of the fault lay with the father. He's the one who wanted the exorcism; she really requested the five other guys because she wanted to protect the girl from her father! Well, in that horrible convolution that only happens around my aunt, everyone involved wound up excommunicated from that church.

These are just some of the many, many religions tried out by my aunt over the years. The only denominations she skipped over were Judaism and anything involving brown people (because she is also fantastically racist). The only common thread between them is that she used them as a tool to pick at other people, much like holidays or her own son. Right around Bob and Amy's wedding, I think she was trying for the Evangelical megachurch downtown, but as we all know her only religion now is the nice men in white.

***

The last two anecdotes have been (relatively) lighthearted. Today's anecdote is very… not.

You may get the impression that the whole family presents a united front against Carol. That's a little south of the truth. My mom and Uncle Tim resent Carol, resent being told to deal with her, and are generally combative. Bob is basically the pit prop for the family and hates it; he just tries to smooth things over because it's what his dad did. And Uncle Craig just wants to have a life to himself. Can't say I blame him. In dysfunctional families, there's this kind of false closeness brought on not by love but by obligation. What would bring other people together only serves to smother us.

This story occurred when Tim was on wife number two. He was in relatively good spirits, and as such he was much more open to spending time with (certain) members of his family. He, Craig, and Bob all met at Craig's house to have a go at the pool table, drink some beers, basically just do nothing. Craig's wife and daughter were gone for a girls' day out, and so when Craig heard a car door he jokingly said, "here comes trouble."

And in stepped Carol.

Bob said every muscle in Tim tensed up. Tim and my mother sort of compete as to who hates Carol more. Tim has had more time to get sick of her, but then again, Carol never facilitated his near-date rape.

Carol seemed unusually quiet. Craig tried to play the polite but distant host, asking what Carol wanted.

"I, um, think I hit something with my car," she said.

And instantly, they all knew it was bullshit. She'd hit something, and she knew it. She was just starting off small in hopes that it would soften them up.

That might seem like a lot to get out of one sentence, but this is Carol we're talking about here.

"You *think*," Tim said flatly.

Carol nodded. They could see she was waiting for someone to ask about it, so she could foist the responsibility of checking it out on them.

Tim shrugged, took a gulp of beer. "Tell the cops."

Carol pouted a little. "I'm sure it's nothing. Probably just a dog."

Uncle Craig made a horrible connection. "You don't know what it was? Didn't you have your headlights on?"

Carol made a sour face. "Why should I? The other cars use their lights, I can see plenty fine."

The three brothers stared at her. Carol's <u>incompetent driving</u> was legend at this point, but this was a new low.

Bob sighed, set his beer down, and got up.

Tim grabbed at his sleeve, shaking his head.

Bob wearily brushed him off. Uncle Craig rose too, and Tim made an angry noise as he gulped more beer. He declined to join them outside.

"It probably cracked the windshield, I might have to get a new one, but you should just install it because it's too much trouble to go to a shop…" Carol babbled as Uncle Bob snapped on the garage light.

The flood lamp illuminated Carol's car and the poor bastard currently sitting half-in, half-out of her smashed windshield.

Bob shouted "Jesus" and dropped his beer.

Uncle Craig gaped at the car.

And Carol…

When Bob told me this, it sent chills down my spine. He said Carol was looking at them, watching them, reading their reactions. He could see all the cogs in her head working, parsing out how she was going to play this. It disturbed him, but what disturbed him more was that he knew he would be helpless to stop whatever it was.

Tim came out after hearing Bob shout. He took one look at the car and whistled.

"Carol, you asshole," he said.

Carol frowned. "It's not my fault. I didn't see him. Who crosses the road in the dark?"

I'm disappointed that no one asked, "Well who the fuck drives without lights at night?"

Bob shook his head. "We have to call the cops."

Carol made an angry noise through her nose. "Well, that's too much trouble. Can't you just take care of it?"

"Take care of a fucking body? No I goddamn can't."

Craig went down the steps and started looking the guy over. The poor bastard had punched through the safety glass with his head; his face was barely recognizable under all the blood. Craig wriggled him out a little ways, trying to turn him over and get identifying information.

"He's probably just a hobo." Carol crossed her arms like a bitchy prom date. "No one's going to miss him."

"That doesn't matter. Carol, you're looking at a charge of vehicular manslaughter. That's a very serious charge. You can't just—"

The guy in the windshield let out a groan.

They all jumped.

The sound didn't repeat. Craig bravely put his hand to the guy's wrist. "…there's a pulse."

Bob clapped his hands. "Okay. Look, we'll call the cops, an ambulance. If the guy lives, you're looking at a lesser charge. Maybe a suspension, some community service. Let's get him out of there."

Together, the brothers pulled the guy out. He was definitely breathing, faintly, and he let out another groan as they turned him over. Tim theorized that the guy had severe neck trauma from hitting the glass, and that they shouldn't move him too much.

Carol…

Carol had this blank look on her face, arms still crossed. Bob said he thought she was coming to terms with what she'd done, finally facing up to the future she'd laid down.

Bob went inside to call 911. Craig followed to get a blanket for the poor guy. Tim went to fetch the first aid kit.

Bob said that there was this moment, while they were busy in all their little activities, where they all turned to each other and made a realization at the same time. The realization was that they had made a terrible mistake by coming inside.

Tim burst out of the house first. Carol was sitting with her arms crossed, just looking at the car.

"I don't think you need to call anyone," she said indifferently, "he's not making noise anymore."

The guy's head was sitting sideways on his neck, very decidedly not where it was when they went inside.

Bob hung up the phone.

He said that in that moment, he realized that this woman was not his sister. This woman had no relatives, no other person in her universe but herself.

Tim didn't mince words. "You fucking killed him."

"No I didn't!" Typical brilliant defense.

"Tough shit, I'm still calling the cops."

Carol smirked. "I'll just say you did it."

Tim flushed red and charged at her. Sadly, Craig and Tim grabbed him and prevented him from killing Carol.

Carol just shrugged and stood up. "Well… you deal with it." She walked off.

Bob wrestled Tim down, no easy feat. He tried to tell Tim they were stuck, they needed to deal with it, but Tim just kept growling, "Why? Why?"

And… Bob didn't have an answer for him. It was so ingrained into him to excuse everything Carol did, but he had no idea why. In this dysfunctional logic, upsetting the status quo would be worse than covering up Carol's murder of a homeless man.

Craig looked sick, but he didn't object. He helped hold Tim while Bob explained the course the evening would take. They'd smash in the windshield, collect all the glass, and throw it away. They'd take the body and throw it into the river. They'd clean the car, inside and out. No one would go to jail.

Tim, stuck under their weight, eventually agreed.

The dynamic between them changed then, and it changed forever. They didn't talk as they loaded the poor guy's body up, along with the garbage bag of glass, and took it out before Craig's wife and child came back.

When it was all over, Bob dropped Tim off at his hotel. Before the door closed, he said, "Tim—"

"Don't fucking talk to me," Tim snapped, and slammed the door.

Carol got a new windshield courtesy of Leland, who didn't even question her bullshit anymore. Bob considered telling their father what had happened, what he had created by supporting Carol at the cost of his other children.

And Bob knew at that moment if he told their father, there were two possibilities.

One: things wouldn't change.

Two: things would change. Horribly.

He kept it inside him all these years, and to the best of his knowledge, so did his brothers. Bob begged me not to tell his wife.

I said I wouldn't... if he would. Lack of communication is one of Carol's most effective weapons, it's what lets her go on hurting people because no one knows what to expect. Bob agreed that if Amy hadn't left him yet, she probably wouldn't now.

It may sound odd, but that wasn't the most shocking revelation from my uncle. No, that would be the next one, the one from Carol's childhood.

***

Uncle Bob told me this last. It's Carol's origin story, so to speak, and no, she didn't become Carol by falling into a vat of radioactive bitchanium. Bob said Carol has always been... well, Carol. He said as a toddler she would look around sometimes and, finding no one paying attention to her, would fall to the ground screaming. If she couldn't get a toy, she would break it. She would fly into these rages and the only way they'd stop was if Grandpa placated her with a toy or treat.

Gramma wasn't mean to Carol but she was... cool to her. Like, Carol would throw a tantrum and Gramma would just shut off and walk out of the room. I think she recognized, even back then, that there was something bad in Carol, something cruel and greedy.

Carol did not improve as the other children were born. If Uncle Craig started crying and no grown-up was around, Carol (now old enough to walk) would drag him to the closet and shut him in there. Bob said Grandpa would tell that story like a funny joke, and Gramma would get thin-lipped and silent.

There are a lot of things, a lot of little things Bob isn't quite sure of. Like how Tim once got a bunch of "ant bites" in the yard that had no anthills before or since. Or how toys would disappear and turn up in a cache, or never turn up at all. Or the time they all got food poisoning after Carol demanded pork chops and Gramma made meatloaf instead. All things that look suspicious in hindsight, but that no one could really prove at the time.

But one thing he is sure of, one thing that Grandpa told him and then immediately made him swear not to tell anyone else, is this:

Carol was a little under ten at the time of this story. Gramma had become increasingly intolerant of her behavior, and Grandpa as always was trying to "make peace," but as he worked nine to five he wasn't around enough to make much difference.

On this fateful day, Grandpa arrived home to find Bob alone in the living room with the younger kids. Grandpa asked where his girls were; Bob pointed outside.

The house they lived in was kind of out in the sticks. The yard was just a mown patch of scrub that transitioned into trees with no clear line. Grandpa went out to look for them.

Now, there's this sawmill in the area. It's historical (meaning water-driven and rusted to shit), but it's still in semi-operation. Grandpa checked pretty much every conceivable area before he went there, because what possible reason would the girls have had to go there?

Within seconds of him setting foot in the mill yard, Carol skipped up to her daddy.

'She was babbling excitedly, like a kid recounting a day at the beach, as she described Gramma taking her up to see the logs come in, putting Carol's head on the track, and holding it there as a log came sluicing down. Carol said Gramma had pulled her back at the last second, but even so, Grandpa was disturbed. He gathered Carol up and took her home, gave her a popsicle.

Gramma came home not long after. She' had a very weary look on her face. Grandpa decided that she was probably just tired and didn't press about the incident. He just vowed to himself to take more care of Carol from then on. He told Bob this as if he had done Gramma a favor by not discussing her attempt on their offspring's life or getting her psychiatric help. They never spoke of the incident, not once.

Bob said his dad told him that that's what a man's job was: being responsible for your family by shouldering all the burden.

Then I had to tell him that that part of the mill isn't accessible to the public, and that if it had been in operation it sure as shit would have had loggers who would have immediately called the cops over a mother trying to commit filicide. I had to tell him that there was really no way they could have stood by the sluice either, as it's an elevated track. I had to watch his face as one of the cornerstones of the foundation of his life crumbled away.

"Really," he said quietly, "really?"

"Yep." I nodded. "We took a field trip there for Jill's sixth grade class."

Bob said quietly, "god dammit."

I don't know if it was just hammered into him never to question what his father said, or if he subconsciously realized Carol might be lying but chose to believe in it because he needed to justify his father's behavior. He needed there to be a reason Carol was so messed up, and why they kept enabling her.

"I'm sorry," I said. "For a lot of things."

Bob looked down, so I finally told him what we'd done on the day of his wedding. He started out pretty grim, but by the end he was smiling.

"Hell, kid," he said, slapping me on the arm, "you go and do what I never had the guts to."

"Well, it wasn't just me. If it had been… I don't know what I would have done. But it was my girls. When she put them in danger, that was it."

I took a sip of my beer, which had warmed up the whole time Bob was telling the story. Bob looked a bit unsteady, and not just from the 7.6% ale we'd been guzzling.

"I know I let your mom down," he said, "I let Amy down, I let Tim down, I let a lot of people down over the years. And for what?"

I shrugged. "You loved your dad. Plain and simple. If Grandpa had been the one to die, instead of your mom, we wouldn't be here." I pointed at him. "And may I say? He let you down first."

Bob gave me a very small smile.

"You talk too much sense, kid," he said. "'Where'd you come from?"

"My mom had me out of pure spite," I said, which made him choke on his next sip.

I slapped him on the back, finished my longneck, and called it a night when Aunt Amy came home. I made a point of looking at her and raising my eyebrows, and Bob made a "fine, fine" gesture with his hand.

I called my wife to come get my worthless ass. She agreed to after she was caught up on Walking Dead. I pretended to be freezing to death over the phone, and she told me to stick a carrot out of my zipper so she'd know which snowman I was.

God, I love that woman.

I walked around a bit, just mulling over all the things Bob had told me. I don't believe Gramma was ever going to kill Carol. I really think she took Carol aside to try, once and for all, to read her the riot act. And it probably went as well as any time we tried to confront Carol on her behavior.

I don't know much about Gramma. Mom was really little when she died, and whenever she would try to talk about a memory, maybe Gramma in the kitchen or tucking her in at night, Carol would butt in and say something like, "Oh yeah, then you cried soooo loud!" so that my mom basically has no recollections of her own mother untainted by Carol's bullshit. But from what I've been able to gather, Gramma was not the type of woman to murder her own offspring, even if it was Carol. Also, Carol goes apoplectic if you throw a glass of water on her—she would not be cheerful and chatty after an attempt on her own life.

So Carol lied. Pretty flagrantly. And with that lie she bought a lifetime pardon. I can't condone Gramma's alcoholism, but if I was stuck in a marriage where my spouse would believe my attention-gobbling dumpster fire of a kid over me, I'd drink too.

I think I'm going to tell my mom the story Bob told me today. And Tim. And Craig. And I'll tell the wedding story, too. I'll keep on talking and talking, because not talking is what got us all into this mess in the first place.

***

I don't know what I was doing down in my kitchen a little after midnight. I may never know. What I ended up doing was taking a slug of milk straight from the carton as I looked out into the dark of my backyard. Maybe it was my lizard brain rattling through ten thousand years of development to slap my frontal lobe: *there is something moving in your yard.*

My eyes had caught a bit of movement in the far corner of the yard. My tired brain pushed it off as a bit of someone's laundry on a line. It took me way too long to realize it wasn't just a bit of cloth.

It was Carol.

I bent and spit my mouthful of milk into the sink, and then hit the deck. The fridge was still ajar behind me. I shut it and left the milk on the counter.

I only saw a flash of her, but my brain had picked out a surprising amount of detail. Carol was draped in a white sheet that (barf) didn't leave much to the imagination. Her limbs were... odd. Her left leg turned in so she struggled to walk. Her hands were curved into claws, possibly stuck that way. Her head tilted oddly on her neck. I tried not to think of the homeless guy she'd run over and instead formulate a plan.

I crab-crawled out of the kitchen and then ran upstairs to my wife. Sarah was asleep, the TV's pale light dancing on her closed lids.

I shook her arm. She was not happy that I woke her and made a noise like "bluh?"

"Carol's back," I hissed.

Almost instantly, she was awake.

"God dammit," she said, "that bitch does not do us any favors, does she?"

"I guess her friends found out she wasn't all that pure."

My wife rolled out of bed and hopped into her jeans. "I'm taking an ax to her, I don't care—"

I shushed her. I told her about the state Carol was in, about the bushes I saw at that mansion. Sarah's eyes widened.

"If she's immortal or some shit like that, I'm gonna be *so* pissed."

I nodded. "Look, I might be wrong. But just in case I'm right, I don't want the girls here."

Sarah's gaze dipped. I could tell she was thinking about how possessive Carol was about other people's children.

"Also," I said, "I want to check on Kevin. I don't know if she came after us first, but if she did, she'll probably go after him next."

Sarah frowned. "So what do we do?"

"Right now? I propose we get the girls and get the hell out of here."

"I do," Sarah said, kissing my hand. We let ourselves laugh a little.

Katie was still asleep. She made a little murmuring noise as I picked her up.

"Dad, what?" Jillian, in her bed across the room, sat up.

"Carol's back," I said, "get your shoes, we're doing a runner."

Jill blinked and rubbed the hair out of her eyes. "Goddamn. Just call the cops." She turned over and laid back down.

Sarah walked in, tucking her pajama shirt into her waistband. "We're going, young lady. Carol's turned into some weird half-tree and I don't want either of you around her."

Jill rolled over. "Is she serious?"

"You want me to take pictures?" I was wrapping Katie in a big fleece throw. "Yes. We're going to uncle Kev's house and we'll reconnoiter there."

Jill must've realized how serious it was, because she slipped on the Uggs she never wears out of the house.

Katie stirred in my arms as we went downstairs. "Daddy?"

"It's okay sweetie, just be quiet for a minute, okay?"

The deadbolt clicked way too loudly under my wife's hand. We shared a tense look as we gathered behind the front door. What if she was already out there? Jill had grabbed up the poker; Sarah held a hatchet in her free hand.

The door swung wide.

Our front lawn was free and clear.

We wasted no time in surrounding the car. I unlocked the door and then hit the switch to unlock the rest, as the fob would have made the car beep. I settled Katie in and told Jill to help her buckle. My wife got in the passenger seat. I skipped around to get in the driver's side, waiting to put the key in until everyone was settled.

Half asleep, Katie slammed her door.

We all jumped. A thick, heavy thudding came from behind the house.

Carol's gruesome mug floated over the backyard fence. She was so much worse in close-up. Her eyes had retreated back in her head so that you couldn't see the whites, just dark iris surrounded by baggy flesh. Twigs stuck out of her hair. Her mouth was the worst, though. It looked like it had healed over and then been ripped open again. She had no lips, just jagged flesh as she yelled:

"David! David Benjamin Wilson, you get back here right now!"

I started the ignition and slammed into reverse. I turned until we were parallel with the house, and with my free hand I flipped Carol the bird.

"You naughty boy!" She was still struggling with the gate latch. Her hands weren't just crooked, they looked like tree roots. "You naughty, naughty boy!"

Something about that phrasing, about how she wouldn't swear even at a time like this, just made it more disturbing than anything else she could have said.

Hooting, I sped out of our cul-de-sac and onto the open road.

Katie had buckled around her blanket. "Where are we going, Dad?"

"We're going to warn Kevin that his mom's back, maybe plan what to do after that. I might drop you off with Gramma for a while."

Jill crossed her arms. "How did she get back?"

"Hard to say. They might have let her go, or she might have broken out on

214

her own. Either way, I don't like it."

"She was scary." Katie was shivering. I put my hand on the seat back.

"Don't worry, honey. Whatever she is, I won't let her get you."

Jill was silent, watching out the car window. The streets were nearly deserted.

"I want her to die," she blurted out. "I don't care how bad that sounds. I thought she was going to die when we left her."

"Me too, sweetie." My wife was rapidly texting Kevin. "But we'll handle it. Don't worry."

"But you always say that! And then nothing gets done!"

Sarah and I exchanged a look.

I raised my hand. "I promise, on my honor as a father, that we will take care of her. Tonight. If we don't, you get free pick of any family of equal or lesser value."

Jill tried not to smile and punched my headrest.

It took us twenty minutes to get to Kevin's house. He was waiting outside in his robe. As we got out of the car, he talked to my daughters.

"Okay, girls? You're going to go with Tanya," he said, pointing to where his girlfriend sat in her idling car. Tanya gave us a friendly wave. "You're going to go over to her mom's place. I made sure they'll have enough space for you while we talk it over. You'll be safe with her, okay?"

Jill looked from them to me. My wife stepped forward and gave them each a hug.

"You girls be good," she said, "and we'll bring donuts in the morning."

I looked at Kevin. "Actually I was going to suggest my mom's place."

Kevin shook his head. "New orders came in. We'll talk inside."

I waved the girls off. Jill didn't look thrilled to be cut out of the excitement, but I knew they'd be safer away from us at the moment.

Once we were seated around Kevin's table, coffee in hand, we started talking.

"I told your mom what you told me," Kevin began, "and she wants to deal with it. All of it. She said as soon as I got off the phone, she would call the uncles. Maybe Ellie and Ty, if it comes to that."

"I was kind of hoping to deal with this… I dunno, legally?"

"She'll make it disappear!" Kevin sipped his coffee agitatedly. "I don't know where she's been, but she would only come back for one reason: to make us all miserable."

"Kevin…"

"No," he said, "you don't know her like I do. It's all she lives for. It's like she literally can't ever be happy. I'm sure she just disappeared to spite us somehow."

Sarah and I exchanged a look.

Then I did something I should have done a long time ago.

I told him what we'd done.

Kevin looked down at the table, not at us. When we got to the mansion, he got up from the table. By the time we let the men in white take Carol, he was pacing.

"…and by the time we got back, we were in shock," I said, "and after a while it just seemed… better not to say anything. Someone might have felt obligated to look for her then."

"You're damn right." Kevin was breathing heavy.

"Kevin, I'm not—"

"No!" Kevin pointed at me. "No, you should have told me. I would have looked for her! I would have found that place and I would have shot her. *I*

216

would have made sure she could never come back!"

We let that sink in.

"Kev," I said, "not only would I not want you alone with her ever again, killing her isn't worth potentially losing you."

Kevin let out a laugh that sounded like a sob.

"It's true." Sarah stood up and touched his arm. "I know you want to kill your mom. We all do. But there's no reason we have to be isolated on this."

I told Kevin Bob's anecdote.

"You see where not talking got us? We have to move as a unit now, if we want her to go down once and for all."

Kevin's eyes were wet. He rubbed them. "Well good, because your mom called a war party. Her words, not mine. We're all supposed to meet at Uncle Bob's house."

"You'll come with us, right?" Sarah tugged on his hand. "Ride in our car."

Kevin blinked. "If I stay here, I could distract her—"

"Don't even," I said. "You try that cliché bullshit, I'll tell your girlfriend you died choking on mugwump."

Kevin laughed, which sounded weird with his snotty nose. He gave us each a hug, we grabbed up some tools, and away we went.

***

We barely spoke on the drive up to Uncle Bob's. I think we were all mentally fortifying ourselves for what had to come next. The one bit of conversation came from Kevin:

"You know, I always thought it was somehow all my fault," he said quietly from the backseat. "Like, there was something I did that made her treat me like this, and I was stupid or lazy for not figuring it out."

"Amazing how she fucks your mind, right?" I changed lanes. "Look, just because someone donates a chromosome, doesn't make them a parent. It's not your fault she can't act like a human being. She was doing that long before you came around."

Kevin gave a little shrug. He had leaned forward so he draped over the seat back with his elbows. Sarah touched his arm.

"Hey. I've got a tip. That guilt you're feeling? Turn it into anger. Get angry and stay angry. It'll keep you going. It's what got me through my scumbag uncle's parole hearing."

Kevin shrugged. "But I feel like... I feel like if I do that, she wins somehow. Like she brought me down to her level."

"No, man, she wins by making you feel too guilty to act, and then more guilty for not acting." I turned off to the county road where Bob lived. "Who cares about being on her level? You ever kidnapped a kid?"

Kevin shook his head.

"Ever tried to feed your dying father's flesh to his unsuspecting family?"

Kevin, now smiling a bit grimly, shook his head.

"See? There you go. No matter what she says, no matter what head trip she tries to lay on us, actions speak louder than words. Remember that."

Kevin squeezed my shoulder. We were never as close as we probably could have been, but I've always kind of thought of him as the brother I never had.

As we pulled into Bob's driveway, my headlights outlined Uncle Tim. Tim looked relatively jolly, longneck in hand. He gave me a rib-cracking hug when we got out of the car.

"Always knew you were my favorite nephew," he growled in my ear.

Mom was at the door in a festive Christmas sweater, all smiles.

"Hey baby." She pressed a kiss to the sides of our heads. "War party's in effect. Grab some cider and let's get started."

"When I broke the news about Carol, I wasn't expecting this."

"The truth never does what you expect, sweetie." Mom pinched my arm through my coat sleeve. "Deal with it."

I stopped in my tracks when I came to the living room. When Kevin said she'd called everyone, she'd meant *everyone*. There was Ellie and Ty, there was Tim's current wife, all the uncles, my dad, Aunt Amy passing around a tray of crackers and cheese. Even Kevin's girlfriend Tanya had snuck in, shooting us a cheeky grin.

I'll admit, I was kind of overwhelmed as I looked around the room. It hadn't occurred to me how big our family really was, and how many of us had been screwed over by Carol.

My mom took up a fireplace poker and rapped it on the coffee table.

"The war party is now in session," she said. "Now, I'd like to cede the floor to my son, who is going to bring us all up to speed."

I cleared my throat. Public speaking always made me nervous. I started with the wedding story, just in case someone had missed it. Then I segued into what had happened earlier in the night (and already felt like another lifetime). I could see Tim's face seesaw between disgust and anger. Aunt Amy glowered. My mom set her jaw and played with the cheese knife from the snack tray, digging it into the arm of her chair.

"…and so that's where we are," I finished. "I figured she'd go after Kevin next, so we brought him here. As to where she'd go after that—"

"Here," Uncle Bob interrupted.

We all looked to him. Bob was looking down at his hands. Aunt Amy leaned into his back.

"She pushed everything off on me," he said, "especially after Dad died. She'll come after me, to make me fix everything, or punish me. Or both."

I sighed. "Shall I tell them, or do you want to?"

Bob, still looking down, launched into the tale of Carol's hit-and-run. Tim's jaw tightened. Uncle Craig's wife looked at him, shocked. I don't think he had ever told anyone about it. Tim either.

When Uncle Bob finished, Mom shook her head.

"So she just used you as a fixer since Dad died. And you went right along with it."

Tim took an angry swig from his beer.

"Look, I know I fucked up, Lila. And I want to fix that. Tonight." Bob ran a hand through his hair.

Mom looked a little bit appeased. "How do you propose to do that, Robert?"

Tim cut in: "Kill her."

A ripple went through the whole room. Certainly, we'd all been thinking it, but the people who weren't in so deep (Tim and Craig's wives, for starters) looked a little disturbed at the statement.

"But isn't that a little extreme?" Uncle Craig, always the voice of reason. "I mean, we can't do that… can we?"

And I am so glad he phrased it like that. Because that was just the opening I needed.

I stood up to get everyone's attention. I was shaking a little from adrenaline and anxiety.

"I know your dad taught you that family's first, before anything else," I said, "but… Sarah and the girls? They *are* my family. I'm going to protect them, no matter the cost. *Should* I do this? I don't have a lot of other options. But *can* I do this? Oh hell yes I can."

My mom was giving me an "I knew I raised you right" grin. My dad nudged my knee fondly.

Kevin stood up.

"I know I'm responsible for at least part of this—"

Bob's face fell. "Oh no, son, no—"

"—because you didn't want to fuck up my life along with hers," Kevin continued, speaking louder over the protest of his uncles. "But I've been thinking tonight. A lot. And I realized that this is what she does. She uses how much we care against us. She holds us ransom against each other." His voice shook a little. I knew everyone was thinking about the custody battle. "She uses us like weapons. Well, I'm going to turn those weapons against her tonight. You don't have to join me if you don't want to, I'm just asking you nicely: please don't stop me."

Of course no one was going to speak against that. The man was a genius.

Tanya stood up and hugged Kevin. My mom was next. Bob wrapped them both in his big bear arms. Tim just gave them a one-handed back pat. Craig stood and put his hand on Kevin's shoulder.

No one spoke for a long time.

"So what do we do? Ellie blurted out. She seemed flustered. I could sympathize. She'd had to leave her three young kids with a babysitter too. I have to wonder how much Craig kept from her, protecting her in his own way.

"She'll come here," Bob said after disengaging from the hug. "I don't know how long it'll take her, but we'll meet her here. End her here."

Craig spoke up. "What if someone stops her along the way?"

"We've never been that lucky," Tim said. "Why start now?"

"It might take a while. Do we... do we make weapons?" Tanya frowned.

"I've got an idea." I took my wife's hand. "Why don't we tell some stories?"

We all looked at each other.

"Sounds like an idea," my mom said with a smile. "Who wants another

221

cider?"

We exchanged Carol stories, some well-known, some making their first appearance in company. It kept us alert and awake until we heard that heavy wooden thud on Bob's driveway.

***

We killed the lights and crouched down in Uncle Bob's living room. We could all hear the *thump-drag* of something making its way up to the house. I risked a look outside.

Carol was painfully making her way up to the house, her left leg digging a long furrow in the gravel of Bob's driveway.

Uncle Tim poked his head out beside me. He hissed over his teeth.

"Jesus. I expected bad, but I didn't expect that bad."

"*Bobbyyyy!*" Carol's voice rose in an eerie wail up to the house. I think the worst part of it all was that she still sounded like herself. The whiny, nasal screech hit you in the spine like nails on a chalkboard. "*Bobbyyyy! Get out here, I need you!*"

My mom joined us at the window. "Shit."

Suddenly everyone wanted to cluster at the windows. Cousin Ellie turned white. Kevin gagged and had to put a hand in front of his mouth.

"*Hey! I know you're in there!*"

Everyone automatically fell away from the window.

"*If you don't come out here, I'm calling the police!*"

The good mood from earlier had evaporated. It's easier to say you're going to kill someone when they're far away. When they come up to your house looking like a half-Ent nightmare, that's another story.

Uncle Bob stood up at the fireplace. He was listening to Carol call and call, one meaty hand gripping a splitting maul.

"Well," he said calmly, "we can't keep her waiting, can we?"

He nodded to all of us, picked up the maul, and walked out of the room. We followed him.

I've mentioned before that Bob is a DIY kind of guy. His place is kind of like a candy store for makeshift weapons. If there's ever a zombie apocalypse, I'm running to Bob's place.

"Are we actually doing this?" Ellie murmured as she contemplated a drawer full of chisels. I picked up a brick hammer and gave it a quick toss to feel it out.

"Well," I said, "if it helps, don't think of it as murder. Think of it as clearing deadwood."

We gathered at the garage door. Bob hit the switch. The door made a painful grinding noise as it rose to reveal Carol taking her last steps up the gravel before she hit lawn.

Carol stopped, peering around. She didn't look like she could see too well, like she was tracking us through sound.

"Bobby?" she said. "Are you done hiding?"

"Oh yeah," Bob said casually.

We fanned out in a circle around her, giving her a nice wide berth. Carol kept cocking her head back and forth, searching with those pissholes-in-snow eyes. Her mouth hole showed signs of healing together and then being ripped apart again; her words came out a pulpy mess like she had ill-fitting dentures.

"Who's that? Bobby, is David here? He needs to be punished!"

"Well spank my ass and call me spoiled," I said, making her shuffle around to find the source of my voice, "I do believe I *am* present and accounted for."

Carol snapped her head back to look at me. The white sheet she wore wrinkled oddly on her body, like it was made from something other than fabric.

"Bobb*yyyyy*," she wailed, turning back to him, "look what David did to *meeeee*."

She held up her gnarled branch-hands. They looked painfully twisted and swollen, her pinky bent at an unnatural angle to her hand.

"Actually, she did that to herself," I said, "I heard her. She said, 'I'm going with these nice young men to turn into a tree. Don't wait up!'"

"Liar!" Carol hissed at me. "Dirty, dirty liar! You did this and now you're going to prison!"

"For what?" my wife called. "Getting back into his own car after you stole the keys?"

Carol whipped her head around. "Sally? I knew you two were in cahoots! I'm going to get your children taken away and raised right!"

My wife's voice was dark and cold as she said, "It's Sarah, tree bitch."

No one had broken the circle. I knew we were all willing, but I don't think that anyone wanted to be the one to land the first blow.

Kevin sighed. "Why couldn't you have just stayed where you were?"

"Kevvy?" Carol turned to him. She moved oddly because of her stiffness —it gave her a touch of the uncanny valley. She tried to purse her ripped mouth as she spoke in her baby voice. "Kevvy, baby, you need to help Mommy."

Kevin cleared his throat, making a production out of it.

"Why?" he said.

Carol's face twisted. Her bratty tantrum-face was made terrifying by her makeover.

"Don't fun me around," she hissed, "you help your mother. You help me or I'll have to punish you too."

"Don't you fucking threaten him," Tim snarled, hefting a ball-peen hammer.

Carol twitched. "Timmy?"

"It's Tim to you, bitch." My mom stepped forward. "And it's Robert. Or Bob. Not Bobby. Fuck's sake, he's three years older than you."

"Lila?" Carol lifted her branch hand to point accusingly at her. "You raised your boy wrong. I'll see you sent away too."

"Why?" Craig stepped forward. "What are you going to tell the cops? How are you going to spin this, Carol? You look like a wide-awake nightmare."

Carol, now sensing the depth of the shit she was in, tried her other tactic. She folded in on herself, making herself look smaller.

"You're all picking on *meee*," she whined. "I've done so much for you—"

"Like break up my marriage?"

We all looked at Tim. He was seething. If we were taking bets, my money would have been on him to strike first.

"You told my first wife I was cheating," he said, white-knuckling the handle of his hammer. "You told a bald-faced lie because you wanted Mom's ring. You had five of her goddamn rings, what was one more?"

Carol got indignant. "That never happened. You're imagining things."

"You called the cops and told them I was molesting my children," Craig said, "just because I didn't want you to come on vacation with us. Do you have any idea what it's like to have your kids taken from you? Oh wait, you don't. You gave yours up."

"I didn't—"

"And you almost got my kid molested." Mom had a linoleum knife; she pointed it at Carol. "Remember that? The prom thing I could almost write off as an accident, but what you did to David was unforgivable."

"He would have deserved it," Carol exploded. "He was being rude! You're all being rude! If Dad were—"

"Don't." Bob pointed the splitting maul at her. "Don't you dare invoke him, don't even speak his name. He wouldn't have spent so much time protecting you if you hadn't lied to him about Mom."

Carol made a pitiful face. "It's not a lie. It's true! She really did try to drown me."

There was a brief moment of silence, and then it was broken by a sharp, pointed sound.

Kevin had put his ax down to lean against his leg, now slow-clapping so hard it echoed off the house.

"And that," he said, picking up his ax again, "is the punchline. You can't even keep your story straight."

Carol kept opening and closing her mouth like a fish gasping for air.

"Kevvy, I'm your mother," she simpered.

Kevin's face hardened. "You sold me for the price of a facial and a new car once a year. Fuck. You."

Carol's face twisted. She didn't really look human anymore.

"You can't do this to me!" she hissed. "If I'm so bad, you're all worse than me! You let it happen! You can't just blame every problem you have on me!"

"No, but we can blame the problems you caused on you," I said, "like deliberately bringing my family into harm's way."

"That's your fault!" She jabbed her bony claw at me. "You could've taken the keys away, but you didn't!"

"Okay. Well, then you could've turned around and walked back to the car and not been turned into a tree, but you didn't. So that's on you."

Carol growled. "I know people! I'll make you sorry! You can't do this to me! People will—"

"No one will do anything," my mom cut in. "No one even noticed you were missing."

Carol's face fell. And in that moment, I could almost feel pity for her. The monster who never learned she was a monster. Maybe if Grandpa hadn't protected her from the world, she might have done something more straightforward, like become a serial killer. Or a torturer. But instead, she was only just now realizing that she had never fit in this human skin at all.

Kevin's ax struck her in the collarbone, making a hollow sound. And just like that, it began.

One of the first things we learned hacking away at Carol is that the sheet on her body wasn't a sheet, it was her skin—which put those hedges at the mansion in a new, disturbing light.

The second was that whatever had happened to Carol, it made her body really tough. I hammered her bent knee with all my force and still didn't break it. The people with knives were struggling to cut her. Carol bellowed and tossed my wife away with one thorny hand. I stepped on her wrist and pounded on one of her fingers until it finally broke away.

It grew back almost immediately.

I didn't waste time gaping, I just kept hammering away. Kevin gave up on her body and took the ax to her face, just trying to shut her up. The whole time we were doing this, she kept trilling how naughty we were and how we were dirty, dirty liars and my god this woman was annoying even unto death.

Bob spit on his hands, hefted the splitting maul, and buried it in her throat. Carol finally went silent, jaw flapping. Uncle Craig took his pickax dead-center to her torso, opening up the white expanse for the first time. Now my wife, rubbing angrily at her bruise, made the hole bigger with her knife.

Carol was… wrong inside. It was more like a collection of vines and roots, no organs I could see.

We kept chopping bits away from Carol, but they would regrow. We kept at it. Eventually the regeneration started to slow down. We didn't.

We took Carol to pieces on the lawn. There was no blood, not even sap, and some of the pieces still writhed. And this may sound a touch cliché on my part, but we never saw any sign of a heart.

My wife touched my arm, looking alarmed out toward the driveway. I followed her direction and saw a van drifting up, white and silent as a ghost.

I ran to meet it. I had a feeling I knew who it was.

The windows all had limo tint, but as I drew near the driver's side rolled down to reveal a young man with eyes colorless and clear as the moon.

"You let her go?" were the words I panted out.

The young man made a small shrug. "She was not pure like you said."

I rubbed my aching shoulder. "Brother, you said a mouthful."

He peered past me, to where my puzzled family stood on the lawn.

"You have no one left? None of you are pure?"

"Nope." I took a breath. "But we're kind of okay with that."

The young man blinked. He turned to the other men in the van, which was packed full. After some silent discourse, he turned back to me.

"She is resilient now. If left alone, she will come back."

"Thanks for the hot tip. Why are you telling me this?"

Instead of answering, the young man gazed at the mess on the lawn.

"She talked," he said, "exorbitantly. Even after she started her becoming." He put the van into reverse. "We leave her to your care."

I waved bye-bye as the van backed down the driveway. My wife walked up beside me. Neither of us said anything. I just put my arm around her and held her.

***

I write this now after everything has wrapped up. We parted ways peacefully that night, as a family. The four of us—me, Sarah, Kevin, and Tanya—crashed on the floor at her mother's place until morning. Jill was crabby the next day about missing the fun, but a box of crullers helped ease her mood. When we got back to the house, I had to laugh over the carton of milk on the counter. The girls looked at me like I was crazy, cackling over spoiled milk, but I was laughing too hard to explain. My wife called me a murderer. I called her treehands. This time we both laughed. I think it was exhaustion mixed with relief. That, or we really are crazy.

Is our family magically better? No. There're trust issues, infighting, the same crap that every family deals with to some degree. There always will be. But we're talking, and you don't know how good that feels until you've gone without for a lifetime.

We're not the best people. We can live with that. But since Carol's not around, we've been better. Because that's what she really did, when she was around: kept us operating at our worst.

In a way, Carol went home with all of us that night after we had one more round of hot cider to chase away the cold and then went back to our cars. She'll stay with us as a reminder of what not to allow, where to draw the line.

And I think of her almost fondly as I write this beside a fire of merrily burning white twigs.

Goodnight.

Childhood Home Movies

By M.J. Pack, Reddit User /u/*mjpack*

Runner Up—November, 2016

The first DVD arrived in my mailbox on Thursday, April 11, 2013. I remember because it had been rainy, one of those gross, squishy spring days where your shoes stick in the mud that seems to be everywhere. My mailbox had leaked, making most of the mail inside soggy and damp—but not the slim, clear plastic DVD case stuck between weekly pennysavers and credit card offers.

It wasn't in an envelope. It didn't have a postmark or a stamp or even an address. It must've just been…left there.

In bold, Sharpie-black letters, the disc read: **BALLET RECITAL 1992**

My first thought, naive as it was, was that Mom had probably dropped it off. Like, maybe she'd been converting some old home movies and wanted to surprise me. Seems so stupid now. I should've just thrown it away. Instead, I dumped the rest of the wet mail into the trash and slipped the burned DVD into my MacBook.

It was Thursday, April 11, 2013, that everything changed.

The footage started normal enough. Living up to the title written so neatly on the disc, I found myself watching a tiny version of me—little Amanda Schneider in ballet flats and a puffy pink tutu, twirling aimlessly around a stage with other six-year-olds who twirled with the same childish aimlessness. Those white lines that used to come up on VHS videos with bad tracking crept in and out of the recital. They brought back a strange sense of nostalgia.

I was just picking up my phone to call Mom and thank her for my gift when the footage suddenly cut out.

In a dark room, face lit ruthlessly by some off-screen source, sat a woman. She was wearing a ballet outfit, tutu and all—not unlike the one I had been wearing in my recital video. On top of her head was a mussed ballerina bun, sadly askew. Her cheeks were covered in almost equal measure by third-degree burn scars and streaky, smudged mascara. Over her mouth was a thick strip of duct tape.

Had it not been for the burn scars I might not have recognized her. But I did. That, and her eye—the one that was squinched almost closed, swollen from the burns—I could never have forgotten that eye.

It was my childhood best friend, Gretchen. Gretchen Hartman.

"Oh my god," I said to no one in particular. It had been years, probably nine or ten, since I'd seen her. Probably nearly that long since she'd even crossed my mind.

Tears leaked from Gretchen's eyes, the normal one and the disfigured one. She kept shaking her head, looking off-camera at someone. Or something.

Have you ever seen something so unbelievable, so unexpected, that it doesn't seem real? One time, when I was a kid, I saw a terrible accident. It happened right in front of me and I couldn't look away but I couldn't do anything to help, either. This felt like that.

Gretchen let out a wail from behind the duct tape and squeezed her eyes closed. She shook her head harder. Her shoulders strained helplessly against what could only be very tight bonds. I heard my heartbeat pounding thick in my ears.

Suddenly, Gretchen's eyes popped wide open—like maybe she was in pain or something—and the footage cut off her following scream, going immediately to black.

I sat there for a long moment, dumbstruck. Then, across the screen in tall white letters standing out against the black like bones in tar:

INVOLVE THE POLICE AND SHE DIES

These hovered before me, then:

WAIT FOR MORE

And then it was over.

I stared at my MacBook. The video player stared back. With shaking fingers I clicked the play icon. I watched as the footage started over again: me in my innocent little ballerina outfit, Gretchen's burned skin, the bun askew on her head, the duct tape over her mouth. The squinted, squashed eye. The warning at the end: involve the police and she dies.

Of everything I'd seen in the video, that was the easiest to understand.

My hand hovered over my iPhone anyway. How would whoever had sent the DVD know whether I had called the police? Well, that was simple enough: they knew where I lived. That was obvious. The DVD hadn't been mailed to my house; it had been placed in the mailbox, like a horrible little present.

Why me? And why, of all people, Gretchen?

While I sat there, MacBook glowing in the low light of that dreary April day, I found myself doing something I hadn't done in a long time: thinking about my childhood. There's a good reason for that, too. I avoided thinking about my childhood because we tend to avoid things with teeth, and my memories of growing up had just that—dark spots, black places, and gleaming in those shadows, long sharp teeth.

***

* * *

I met Gretchen when I was six years old, about three months after the ballet recital on the DVD. Dad had lingered in the hospital choking on his own blood for as long as I could remember; when he died, we couldn't afford payments on the nice little brick house in suburbia so a few days after the funeral Mom packed us up and off we went. I was pretty young but I remember thinking, why so fast? Why now? Why did I have to lose my dad AND my house, my school, my friends—all in the same summer?

When you're an adult you can put some perspective on the situation. Mom was always a proud lady, our funds had been drained with Dad in ICU for so long and she couldn't bear a foreclosure on top of everything else.

I still think it was a shitty thing to do to a kid.

We took what Mom hadn't sold and moved into low-income housing in what I'd heard called "The Bad Part Of Town," all ominous and worthy of capital letters. We pulled up in front of it, a squat little yellow tinderbox half the size of our pretty gingerbread house with the sturdy columns and stained glass windows. Two square windows on either side of a door that seemed to me like eyes and a mouth, calling out, "Come inside, Amanda. I'm hungry. I want to eat you up just like cancer ate your daddy up from the inside."

The first day we were there, I couldn't stop crying. I tried, I really did, but I couldn't. Mom yelled that I was useless but I knew she was just upset about Dad so I went to sit on the crumbly cement step out front to let her unpack the kitchen in peace.

I rubbed at my eyes with the heels of my hands until I saw stars exploding in the darkness. It hurt, but also felt kind of good too, so I kept doing it even though Mom had said before that I shouldn't.

"My mommy says that's bad for your eyes," said someone behind the exploding stars.

I stopped and looked up to see another girl, a girl my age with kinky red hair and thick coke-bottle glasses. They had pink rims and I remember that the color looked weird with her hair.

"Why?" I sniffled, trying not to let on that I was crying even though it was obvious I had been. "Is that what happened to you?"

The girl shrugged, but said, "No. I woke up one day and couldn't see *Tom and Jerry* very good on the TV and my mommy took me to the doctor and they said I gots near-sights."

"Oh," I said, assuming that meant she had almost-sight and accepting it as fact.

"Why you cryin'?" Gretchen squinted at me. She didn't have the burn scars yet or the scrunched-up eye, just lots and lots of freckles.

I didn't really want to tell this red-haired girl with glasses that my life as I knew it was over, but for some reason I found myself saying, "My dad died," wiping tears from my cheeks. I'd finally stopped crying. "He was sick for a long time and now we're poor so we live here."

An adult might've taken that as an insult but Gretchen's face lit up.

"I'm poor too!" she exclaimed brightly, clasping her hands together. "Most everyone 'round here is! But not a lot of kids. 'Specially not girls. We could be friends!"

I sniffed again. Looked her over with the frank, unbiased consideration only children are afforded. Seemed to come up with one answer: all my friends were gone, Mom was mad all the time, and even though Gretchen wasn't much, this one would have to do.

"Okay," I said, with less enthusiasm than I think she'd expected. Her face clouded over a little, eyes growing dark behind those thick glasses. Eager to get her good mood back—I'd had enough bad moods with Mom, as it were—I added, "I have a Lisa Frank friendship bracelet kit inside. You want me to go get it?"

Her smile returned, brighter than ever.

"Yep yep yep!" Gretchen chirped, reminding me of Ducky from *The Land Before Time*. Ducky was my favorite, so suddenly I felt a little better. Better than I had in a while.

"Can I call you Ducky?" I asked shyly, unsure if this was reaching too far for a new friend. Gretchen flushed pink under her freckles, matching the rims of her glasses, and gave me a hard, brief hug.

"I never had a nickname before," she said. "Yep yep yep, I'll be your Ducky, let's make bracelets!"

And we did.

***

I heeded the DVD's warning and didn't call the cops. After a night of sleep, I still wasn't sure what I was supposed to do. Gretchen and I hadn't spoken in years; I wasn't even friends with her on Facebook and didn't have her family's contact information. I considered calling Mom but I didn't really want her involved in this either.

I was holding my iPhone in one sweaty palm, going over my options the way my grandmother used to worry over a small, smooth stone with an imprint for her thumb, when it occurred to me.

WAIT FOR MORE.

I ran out to the mailbox even though I knew the chain-smoking mailman wouldn't be around for another few hours and was less than surprised to see another slim, clear plastic case resting inside—docile yet dangerous, like a coiled cobra with poison fangs.

I pulled it out and cringed when I read what was printed on it, the same blocky permanent-marker print:

SOFTBALL GAME 1995

Shit.

This was only going to get worse.

***

SOFTBALL GAME 1995

The permanent-marker words taunted me from the shiny surface of the DVD. I'd been staring at it for half an hour, chewing at my acrylic thumbnail, too scared to put it in my MacBook but unwilling to throw it away. What was on this DVD was bound to be worse than the last one. I had three options: 1) throw the DVD away and leave Gretchen to her fate, 2) call the cops and possibly be responsible for her death, 3) watch the DVD and go from there.

I sighed. Put the DVD in my laptop. Held my breath.

The opening footage was shaky, focused on nine-year-old me, growing girl Amanda Schneider at bat during a sweaty summer baseball game. Knobby knees, awkward elbows. My favorite beat-up Dodgers hat on my head. I watched as I looked over my shoulder, unsure, toward the camera in the stands.

"Don't look at me, Mandy, look at the pitcher!" a deep, masculine voice boomed. I covered my face with my hands, knowing what was coming, but peeked through my fingers.

Nine-year-old me glanced back toward the mound just a hair too late; the baseball zoomed past without a swing.

"Oh, Jesus H. Christ," the voice came again.

Shut up, I thought bitterly. Shut up, shut up. I'm just a kid.

"Strike one," called the umpire.

"Get your goddamn head in the game, Mandy," the man yelled. Nine-year-old me's shoulders slumped but I didn't turn around.

It was useless, I remember thinking. That girl was an incredible pitcher. There was a rumor that her dad iced her arm every night.

The next pitch was a fireball; I swung hard but the ball hit the catcher's mitt with a crack. Strike two.

"What did we practice for all week, Mandy?"

I hated those practices. I hated baseball, too, after a while.

The pitcher wound up, rocketed another screamer across the plate. I swung, tipped off the ball. The catcher caught it, no sweat.

"Fuckin' typical," said my stepdad, and lowered the camera just as it cut to Gretchen again.

She was in the same dark room, same harsh light on her pale face. Freckles and scar tissue stuck out in brilliant contrast. Cockeyed on her head was a faded blue hat with the iconic interconnected L and A—I was shocked to realize it was the hat, the same hat from the video, the favorite hat I thought I lost when I moved out of that awful yellow house for good.

She was weeping, mouth still covered with duct tape. It looked fresh. Her hair, once bright red and kinky, hung limp in her face. It was the color of old rust.

Gretchen leaned forward, sagging against her bonds. She looked exhausted. My hat teetered on her head but didn't fall.

The next two minutes were just of her sobbing quietly into the duct tape.

Then, cut to black:

JOGGING ANY MEMORIES?

A pause, then:

FIGURE IT OUT. WAIT FOR MORE. NO COPS.

Then:

OR SHE DIES.

I didn't bother to watch the video a second time. I was already thinking about that summer of 1995, the one where I told Gretchen about my stepdad and how he was making my life a living hell.

***

"He yells at my baseball games," I said glumly, picking at a loose thread on my comforter.

"A lot of parents do that." Gretchen was thumbing through one of my *Tiger Beat*s, pausing to take a closer look at Mario Lopez shirtless. "It's supposed to hype you up."

"Yeah, but that's not what he's doing. Clay doesn't yell nice things, he yells mean stuff." I pulled on the thread and watched as it unraveled. I wondered how I was going to get out of next week's game.

"Like what?" she asked, only half-interested. Mario Lopez's abs were more appealing than my problems for the moment.

"He makes fun of me. Tells me I should be doing better. We practice all week, Gretchen, the whole stupid week but as soon as I get up to bat I get all… watery."

Gretchen lowered the magazine and regarded me from behind her thick lenses. She'd gotten new frames, silver wire instead of pink. They suited her, made her look kind of like a librarian. A smart one, not a mean one.

"Watery?"

"Yeah," I said, seeing how far I could pull the loose thread before it broke. "Like, in my legs. I don't know how to stand or when to swing even though I really do. I can just feel him up in the stands with that goddamn camera, watching me."

She ignored my rare use of a curse word and set the magazine down.

"I'm sorry. That really sucks."

"It does," I agreed. My fingers plucked at the string for another moment, then I let it go and looked at Gretchen. "I don't know what my mom sees in him. He's gross. And mean. And not like…" I trailed off, unwilling to say it, but Gretchen knew what I meant.

"He's nothing like your dad," she said gently, putting a hand on my knee. "From what you told me, I can tell that right off."

I forced a smile and rested my hand on hers.

"Thanks, Ducky. It's hard to explain but I knew you'd get it."

Gretchen squeezed my knee twice—one of our codes for 'everything's going to be okay'—then let it go and began leafing through *Tiger Beat* again in search of more cute boys.

"Why'd your mom marry Clay in the first place?"

"Nuts if I know," I muttered, reaching past her for another issue. "She says he's nice to her but I don't see it. Maybe it's just because he makes money."

"He doesn't make a lot or you wouldn't still be stuck here." Gretchen said this breezily but I could tell there was tension in her voice. We'd been best friends for three years; I knew when she was getting upset.

"I'm not stuck here, dummy. I'm glad I get to live near you."

There was a moment where Gretchen seemed to be staring not at the magazine but through it. Then she said, "One day, you won't be."

Before I could ask what she meant Gretchen was tossing the magazine aside, swinging her freckled legs over the side of my bed and hopping down.

"C'mon. Let's go make some Jiffy Pop. I'm starved."

"Clay's out there," I said wearily, knowing he'd be two or three beers deep by this time of night.

"What's he gonna do?" She put her hands on her hips and jutted out her lower lip in that way she did when she got sassy. "I'll knock his teeth out if he says anything to you. Besides, you're not exactly at bat right now. You're just going to make your best friend in the world some popcorn. Let's see him heckle you at THAT."

That made me laugh. Gretchen could always make me laugh. So we did as she said and made some popcorn and wouldn't you know it, Clay didn't even look in our direction once.

***

There were no new clues in the footage to tell me where Gretchen was being held or if there was anything I could do, other than my Dodgers cap. And what did that mean? For all I knew, Mom had donated it to Goodwill when I left for college. I was left with nothing.

I couldn't do this alone.

After a few hours of thinking, I picked up my iPhone and jabbed out a text message to my best friend Erin:

Can you come over? I need your help with something. Don't tell anyone. It's super urgent.

I hesitated, then before I could talk myself out of it, hit send.

While I stared at my phone, waiting for Erin to reply, I thought about how I'd quit baseball two weeks after that video had been shot. Clay had been furious; Mom was the only reason I wasn't forced to go back. For the rest of the summer, I hid in my room and tried to imagine what life would've been like if my Dad hadn't gotten sick all those years ago.

Erin typed back:

Sure babe, on my way

I responded:

Thanks. Can you do me a favor and check the mailbox on your way in?

***

I ran to the door, nearly slipping on the hardwood in my socked feet. I opened it to see Erin. She was holding a new DVD case.

"Is this what you were looking for?" she asked, puzzled, and held it up toward me.

SCHOOL PLAY 1998

"Fuck," I said, and let her in.

***

It took me about an hour to explain everything to Erin. Well, not everything, if I'm being honest. I didn't tell her much about Gretchen, just that she had been a friend of mine when we were kids. I also didn't go into detail about Clay—just said he was a shitty stepdad and moved on.

At first she thought I was fucking with her. She had this look on her face like she was waiting for me to burst out laughing and say "Just kidding!" but that look went away when I played her the first DVD.

"Jesus Christ," Erin said, putting a hand over her mouth. She glanced from me, to the screen, back to me.

"Yeah," I agreed grimly.

She was silent, staring at the video until the final warning message flashed across the screen: INVOLVE THE POLICE AND SHE DIES.

"You have to do something, Amanda," Erin said at last. She'd gone pale; her skin was the color of rotten milk.

"I know. That's why I called you. I'm too scared to call the cops, even though that's all I can think of. Here, there's another one."

"There's ANOTHER one?" she echoed incredulously, and watched it play with the same stunned silence as the first.

When Clay began heckling me, she gave me this side-eyed glance that told me she felt sorry for me but didn't know what to say. I've seen that look enough to know exactly what it means.

When the second one was over, Erin held up the DVD she'd brought from the mailbox.

"So that means…"

"Yeah." I rubbed my hands over my face, not caring whether I smeared my winged eyeliner or not. "I'm scared to watch it, Erin."

"Me too," she said, but took it out of the case anyway. "We have to, though. You know that, right?"

"Yeah," I said again.

"Here." Erin handed me the disc that read **SCHOOL PLAY 1998** and I slipped it into my MacBook. "You know what, you called me for help so I'm going to do whatever I can. Let's play Nancy Drew this time and really watch it for clues."

"Clues?" I asked, making the video player full screen. "Like what?"

"I don't know, something. Anything. Maybe there's some detail in here that will tell us where she is." She paused, then snapped her fingers like a detective in an old noir movie who's just realized his hunch. "The last one said figure it out! They WANT you to know… I don't know, but there's something they want you to 'figure out.' Right?"

"Okay, yeah, that makes sense." As much sense as this could make, anyway. I smiled and knuckle-bumped her on the shoulder. "That's why I called you, I knew you'd see this from a better angle than I could."

Erin grinned. "Not a better one, just a different one. Come on, play this bitch."

I clicked play.

I already knew what to expect—I remembered what play I'd been in the year of 1998. That's why I didn't let out a shocked burst of laughter like Erin did.

Don't think she's mean or anything—I would've laughed, too, if I hadn't known what was coming.

The opening footage showed a small stage set up in a middle school cafeteria. Beyond it, you could see the shuttered kitchen full of supplies, pots, pans. This did little to help the forced environment onstage. A sadly decorated Christmas tree flanked either side and between them were a motley crew of characters—tweens dressed up in bright colors, some wearing wings—but at stage center stood a short guy who'd clearly not hit puberty yet, covered from head to toe in black fur. He wore floppy dog ears and a bright red collar. At his left was a girl who looked like Dolly Parton carrying a magic wand.

And there I was: blue-checked dress, curled hair in pigtails, glittery red shoes, wide ingenue eyes. In a cheerily false, projected voice twelve-year-old me said, "That's right Toto, back to Kansas! Because there's no place like home for the spirit of Christmas."

No place like home. What a joke.

"It's *Christmas in the Land of Oz*," I told Erin, feeling my cheeks burn.

"It's cute," she offered.

"It's fucking stupid is what it is."

The cast gathered together in an awkward, messy excuse for a group hug, then straightened out again for curtain call. That was it—that was the big finale for the cheap, cheesy excuse of a play. A tacked-on line from the classic film mashed together with some drivel about Christmas spirit. Bullshit.

If you hadn't seen this before, you would've missed the part where my real smile faltered and nearly disappeared when I spotted the camera in the audience. It was only a moment, a brief flicker across my face, but twelve-year-old-me corrected quickly and went back to soaking up the applause with grace.

The footage cut to Gretchen like I knew it would. She was dressed up like Dorothy—like me. Her rust-red hair had been pathetically put into pigtails decorated with little blue ribbons. She was wearing a blue-checked dress, a cheap one that looked like it came from a Halloween shop. If I had to guess, she was probably wearing ruby slippers too, but I couldn't see her feet.

Another strip of fresh duct tape. I wondered briefly where her glasses had gone; she hadn't been wearing them in any of the videos. Did her kidnapper take them from her? Did she wear contacts now? Was this a clue, like Erin had said?

The video stopped, freezing Gretchen in a pose where she was staring miserably at whoever was behind the camera.

I began to panic, wondering if the footage had been corrupted, and saw that Erin had paused it.

"What are you doing?" I demanded frantically.

She held up one manicured hand. Erin was staring hard at the screen.

"Just look for a minute. Study everything. We can't see much, but there might be something here."

I had this crawly feeling, like I just wanted to watch the video and get it over with, but I leaned forward and looked too.

It was just a dark room, a stupid dark room with nothing in it, only the light and the chair and Gretchen. And, of course, the camera.

"I don't see—" I began, then stopped.

Behind her, barely visible, was wallpaper. That was it, it had to be wallpaper—it was this dirty gold color with splotches of brown and pea-soup green.

"What—" Erin said, but I waved a hand at her to shush. I leaned closer to the screen.

When I squinted, the splotches turned into flowers. Flowers being choked by winding, leafy plants that were probably vines but... but...

"They looked like weeds," I whispered, and all at once my breakfast was in my throat.

I knocked over my office chair getting to the bathroom. I barely made it to the sink before the contents of my stomach burst out of me in a hot, vile rush.

I could hear Erin in the other room, calling my name and coming after me, but she sounded a million miles away. I had forgotten. I had forgotten about the wallpaper and now I remembered, but only pieces, jagged little shards of memories that didn't fit together quite right.

***

Clay drove me home after the play. Mom was working but she saw the first half and that was okay because the play was pretty dumb anyway.

"You did a good job up there, Mandy," he said, not taking his eyes off the road. It was the first nice thing he'd said to me since... since I couldn't remember when.

"Thanks," I said, staring out the window glumly. I was back in my school clothes and parka but I'd kept the curled pigtails because they made me feel pretty, like Judy Garland in the real movie about Oz. I traced mindless patterns in the frost on the car window.

"I… I know I give you a hard time." Clay still wouldn't look at me but his voice had gotten softer somehow so I chanced a glance at him out of the corner of my eye. "I was mad when you quit baseball because I knew you could do better, that's all."

I didn't say anything. Waited for him to go on.

"But tonight, up there…" He let out a low whistle between his teeth. "You were great, Mandy, you really were. You…" Clay drifted off again, then looked at me and favored me with a rare smile. "You shone."

My chest felt hot and tight. I offered a small smile back.

"Thanks, Clay," I said shyly. His good nature was so unfamiliar to me I wasn't quite sure what to do; I sort of expected it to be like when a cat rolls on its back, offering you its tummy to pet, then scratches the shit out of you.

But he didn't say anything else. Just went through the Dairy Queen drive-thru and ordered me a cherry slushie, my favorite. I hadn't even known he knew it was my favorite.

When we got home, Clay stayed silent. He took the video camera in its bulky carrying case inside and I followed, wondering if it would be out of line to ask if I could watch the footage of the play tonight. I decided against it. Christmas vacation was almost here and I could watch it when Mom and Clay were at work.

He was settled in his armchair watching *Married with Children* reruns, a freshly opened beer in his hand, when I poked my head into the living room.

"I'm gonna take a shower and go to bed," I said quietly, trying not to drown out Al Bundy. "I'll see you tomorrow."

Clay grunted, noncommittal.

I paused, then added, "Thanks for coming to my play, Clay. It was nice of you."

He didn't respond. I took that as a win and padded my way to the bathroom, locking the door behind me.

The girl in the mirror stared back like she wasn't sure who I was. I suppose I wasn't sure who she was, either. Our director Mrs. Derst had applied all of our makeup before the show and, me being the lead, taken the most time on mine. I hadn't worn makeup before, not for real, just when Gretchen and I were playing around with those fake sets we got for our birthdays. This was how makeup was supposed to look—how ladies looked on the covers of Mom's *Cosmopolitan*s.

I turned my head to the side, admiring how mascara lengthened my lashes. I pursed my lips together. Red, like Dorothy wore in the movie. It looked nice but also kind of dirty, like mouths weren't supposed to look this vibrant, this showy. It was suddenly evident how much baby fat I'd lost in the last year or so.

As I tugged off my school clothes I thought about how I hoped I'd be pretty when I grew up. I knew Gretchen probably wouldn't be, as much as I loved her—she just had all those freckles and frizzy red hair and glasses that made her eyes look tiny in her head. I wished that Gretchen would turn out pretty too but little girls are selfish and most of all I wished it for me.

If I hadn't been so deep in thought, maybe I would've heard the click at the doorknob. The sound of the lock being disengaged. The quiet *woosh* of the door opening.

"I told you that you shine," Clay said softly.

I turned, covering my private areas with my hands, trying to shield my budding breasts from his view.

"You… you can't be in here!" I yelped.

He took another step toward me. Closed the door behind him.

Locked it.

I backed against the wall next to the toilet. I had nowhere else to go.

"You can't be in here," I said again, weakly, but he was moving toward me and all I could do was turn away, press my face against the vine-and-flower wallpaper, and in the last moments of my innocence I realized that the vines entwined around the flowers weren't vines at all… they just looked like weeds.

***

Erin was holding my hair back as I bent over the sink, retching. Saying soothing words into my ear. I was sweating.

I didn't speak for a long time. But when I did, I said through a mouth that tasted like vomit, "I know where she is."

Erin stared at me, wide-eyed, still holding my hair back.

"You know where Gretchen is?" she said. I nodded and wiped my lips with the back of my hand. My mouth was full of that acidic sour-sick taste.

"Yeah." I turned the tap of the sink and ran cold water. Sipped delicately at it, rinsed, spit.

"Okay, I know you're clearly going through a thing right now but you can't leave me hanging like this," Erin said, sounding panicked.

I rinsed and spit again before turning to her.

"She's in my old house. The one on Turner Street. They've been filming in the bathroom."

"Is that what you saw?" she asked.

"Yeah. I recognized the wallpaper." Sure I did, I'd had my face pressed against it enough that I should've recognized it sooner. It was in that bathroom that Clay had raped me when I was twelve, the first time after my school's Christmas play. How could I have forgotten? Dressed up like Dorothy, hair curled in perfect pigtails, smearing my grown-up mascara on the flowers and vines.

I never wore my hair in pigtails again but that hadn't stopped him.

"So let's go get her!" Erin exclaimed. I didn't respond right away; I chewed absently on one of my acrylic nails. "Amanda? Let's go get her, right?"

"We need to finish the video," I said, deciding not to tell her about Clay and the bathroom and why I recognized it.

"What?! Gretchen could be in serious trouble, we need to go get her and you know where she is so let's GO!" She gestured violently toward the door.

"You said it yourself," I said as I leaned away from the sink and headed back to the dining room where my MacBook waited on the table. "There's something they want us to figure out. I've got a piece but not all of it. We need to finish the video."

Erin stared at me like I was a crazy person then gave up, throwing her hands in the air.

"Okay, fine, but then we gotta go!"

We gathered around the screen. I wasn't sure if I could watch without getting sick again now that I knew where the videos were set but I had to try. I clicked play.

Gretchen jerked back to life, still watching whoever was behind the camera through miserable tears. She shook her head once, weakly. Her bad eye sagged, her burn marks lit in ruthless clarity.

Her irises flicked back and forth like her captor was pacing. Then it cut to black again:

YOU'RE ALMOST THERE

A beat, then:

DON'T GIVE UP YET

Then:

ONE MORE

And that was all.

"One more?" Erin said, puzzled.

"One more DVD." I swallowed against my sickly lurching stomach. "We can't do anything until that one shows up."

"Amanda, this is crazy!" She rewound the footage, found Gretchen's face again, then paused it and jabbed an accusing manicured finger at her. "Your friend is in serious trouble! If you really think we can't go to the cops but you know where she is—I mean, this could be a trick! What if they're just trying to stall you? By the time you finally show up after waiting for their last DVD—if there even is one—Gretchen could be dead!"

"That's not the game they're playing," I said softly. Something about this felt undeniable; there was a method to their madness. I was meant to remember something. I was meant to learn something.

Erin wouldn't understand. She hadn't been there.

We let a long, tense pause pass between us before I finally said, "Twenty-four hours. Okay? If I don't have anything in twenty-four hours, I'll just go to the house."

"Twenty-four hours—" Erin covered her face with her hands, overcome, then looked back at me. "Amanda, this isn't some Fox drama starring Kiefer Sutherland. It's not going to be wrapped up nice and pretty by the time the credits roll. This is a real person, a person you knew and cared about, and she could die."

"What the fuck am I supposed to do, Erin?" I demanded. "The video said to wait for one more! If I show up there before I see it, they might just kill her anyway! Or me! There's something here, something I'm missing, I need to find it! And it's on that last DVD!"

There was another moment of silence.

"What did you remember, Amanda?" she asked quietly. "You saw something. Whatever it was, it was so bad it made you sick. It's about that, isn't it?"

I didn't answer. She nodded.

"Yeah. It is. And you can't tell me?"

"I'm sorry," I said, but I didn't really mean it.

"I'm your friend, Amanda. That's why I'm here, getting involved in this insane mess. Because we're friends. If you're not telling me something—"

"I can't." I'd never told anyone. I couldn't start with Erin. I couldn't bear it. I'd already had so many of those side-eyed looks of pity just from people who even met my stepdad, heard how he talked to me—how could I tell a single person that he had a key to the bathroom, one of those slim little metal things you slid into the hole on the doorknob to disengage the lock? That I couldn't avoid that room but I was never safe in it—in fact, that it was the least safe place for me in the whole world? That all he had to do was catch me there when Mom wasn't home and for the next half hour I had to leave my body in order to stay sane?

That it was so horrible I'd somehow pushed it from my mind for the last fourteen years?

I couldn't. That was the simple answer.

Erin let out a long breath.

"Okay. Fine." She pursed her lips, then locked eyes with me. "I need to go home, I have to work early. Take your twenty-four hours to figure shit out without me. But if I haven't heard from you by—" Erin checked the screen of her phone. "—nine pm tomorrow, I'm calling the cops. That's that. Okay?"

"Okay," I agreed. It was the best I could do; the DVDs had been coming pretty quickly so I figured it would be enough time. I hoped it would be… for Gretchen's sake.

"Okay," Erin said again, grabbing her purse and her shoes. She headed for the front door, then stopped and turned to me. "Why did you and Gretchen stop being friends?"

I told her the truth: "I can't remember."

Erin nodded slowly, mouth set in a grim line. "That says a lot, Amanda," she said, and left.

***

I didn't sleep well that night. I spent most of it in broken, shuddery nightmares where I relived what happened in that bathroom over and over again. Sometimes I was a kid, sometimes I was older. In one particularly nasty one I was my twenty-six-year-old self and god help me I actually liked it, the nightmare turned into some lurid, guilty sex dream and I woke from it with a scream in my throat. I was drenched in sweat and had to run to the bathroom to vomit again.

I called in sick to work and sat backward on my couch, staring out the window at the mailbox all morning.

No one came.

By noon I was really feeling the lack of sleep. My eyes were drifting closed; my head throbbed. Before I knew it I was jerking awake, startled and disoriented. I checked my phone: 2:32 pm.

I only had until nine. I forced myself off the couch and went to check the mailbox and wouldn't you know it, the mail hadn't arrived yet but a slim clear plastic DVD case had. It read:

ACCIDENT 1999

My stomach lurched. Accident? What accident?

I brought it inside. Stuck it in my MacBook. I thought about calling Erin first then decided 'fuck it' and clicked play.

The opening footage was of a car. Clay's car, the beaten-up teal Camaro he took so much pride in. I didn't recognize this video.

The camera zoomed in on the gas tank, which was open with the cap popped off. A hand was thrust in view, clutching a dirty rag. A small, pale, freckled hand.

Wait.

Wait.

Something was coming back to me.

"Gretchen?" I said, and at the same time the camera swung around to show twelve-year-old Gretchen with her wire-frame glasses and a brightly colored ski cap over her kinky red hair. She was grinning like she was proud of herself, pointing the camera at her own face.

"We're gonna get him back, Amanda," she said firmly. "We're gonna fuck up his car, ka-blooey, blow it to bits. He can't get away with what he did to you."

Wait...

"I'm doing this for you," Gretchen said, and suddenly there were tears in her eyes made so small by her thick lenses. "Because you're my best friend. That fucker deserves worse. I wish I could blow it up with him inside, but this will have to do."

Wait—

"I love you, Amanda," she said, and suddenly the footage cut away to the same dark bathroom from the other DVDs and my nightmares, but this time it was—

Oh god.

It was Erin.

She was wearing the same ski cap from the video. Her mouth was covered with duct tape and she was thrashing violently in a way Gretchen hadn't in the other DVDs.

I'd done this. I'd put her in danger; how could I have been so stupid? Of course whoever was behind this could see Erin coming and going, they'd been delivering the DVDs so why didn't I think about whether they were watching my house?

I watched her struggle for almost a minute before the video cut to black, and then:

REMEMBER NOW?

Then:

IF YOU'VE FIGURED IT OUT

And:

COME

I left my MacBook open, grabbed my keys, and ran to my car. The old house was twenty minutes away. I hoped I could get there in time.

***

I ran three red lights on my way to the old house on Turner Street where I grew up. How I wasn't pulled over is some kind of miracle because I was doing easily fifteen over the speed limit but the important part is that I wasn't pulled over—I didn't pass a single cop the whole time. Good thing, too, because the very first DVD had laid out the rules: no cops.

The old neighborhood was just as I remembered it: small, dirty, and depressing as hell. Low-income housing seemed to have sunk even lower in the ten years since I'd moved away.

My car screamed into the driveway of the little yellow tinderbox. There weren't any other cars parked outside; a sadly sagging FOR SALE sign was jammed into the badly tended lawn, faded to almost white by the sun.

Now that I was here it occurred to me I'd have to actually go inside. My stomach lurched violently.

I was going to have to go into that house, into that bathroom where Clay stole my innocence over and over again. I was going to have to face whoever was sending the DVDs. My only comfort was that I knew it couldn't be Clay; he'd passed away in 2010. Brain aneurysm. Dropped dead in the middle of Home Depot while shopping for a new power drill.

I attended his funeral because he was my stepdad and Mom needed me there. She didn't know what he'd done and I couldn't remember, but the next day I went back to the graveyard alone. I stared at his grave for a very long time before gathering all the phlegm I had in my throat and spitting on the fresh dirt.

I hadn't known why I did that. Now I do.

I took a deep breath, steeled my nerves, and went inside.

The front door was unlocked; it was late afternoon but dreary-gray outside. No power, so the house was dark and every shadow felt ominous. I repressed the urge to call out "Hello?" like the dumb girl in a horror movie.

I crept quietly up to the bathroom and found I was wrong—there was power. A sliver of light shone from the crack at the bottom of the door. That made sense; Gretchen and Erin had been lit in each of the videos. It also meant she was in there.

I tried the doorknob. Locked.

Since when had the bathroom door being locked ever mattered?

I felt along the top of the doorframe for the slim metal key. Wouldn't you know it, there it was, just where Clay always left it. When I found his hiding spot I started throwing the key away but it didn't matter because they kept appearing, like he had a stash of them or something.

Fucker.

I slid the key into the hole on the metal doorknob and heard the familiar click of the lock disengaging. Slowly, carefully, I opened the door.

Behind a MacBook propped on some old plastic crates and a strategically placed floodlight sat Erin. The ski cap was gone but she was wearing Gretchen's old glasses, the wireframe ones; they made her eyes look like pinpricks. Erin has perfect vision so I knew she probably couldn't see a thing and I was right—she started thrashing violently against the chair, mistaking me for her captor.

"It's me, Erin, it's Amanda," I whispered, unsure where said captor was. I moved toward her and noticed that iMovie was pulled up on the screen of the MacBook. Must've been how they were making the DVDs.

Hearing my voice made Erin stop, then shake her head violently. She tried to speak but the duct tape kept her voice muffled. I couldn't understand a word she was saying.

Her wrists were tied behind her with that yellow plastic-y rope you buy when you tie stuff down in a moving van. The skin beneath it was rubbed raw, red and chafing.

"I'm gonna get you out of here," I said in a hushed voice, but before I could look for something to cut through the rope I heard a voice.

"Well, aren't you a good friend."

I turned around and for a moment I couldn't see anything but a dark shape in the doorway; the floodlight was too bright. Then it went out and as my eyes adjusted I saw her.

Gretchen.

She was dressed normally now, just a plain pink t-shirt and jeans—no glasses or duct tape. Her bad eye sagged beneath the destroyed scar tissue of her face; she was smiling, holding the unplugged cord of the floodlight.

"Gretchen?" I said, because I could think of nothing else to say.

"Oh, so you DO recognize me," she said, sticking out her lower lip. "I'm shocked. I mean, I've been sending these DVDs for a few days now but you never showed up so I was starting to suspect you didn't even remember who I was."

"Of course I recognize you," I said, stunned.

"Really? Because I think I put on a pretty good show but you didn't show up like Prince Fucking Charming to save ME." Gretchen gestured vaguely toward Erin with the end of the cord. "I had to up the ante and bring this one out here to get any sort of action out of you."

"I didn't know where you were." I stepped closer to her, wanting to put distance between Gretchen and Erin. Gretchen made a clucking noise with her tongue and produced a small black handgun from the back pocket of her jeans.

"Don't move," she said, pointing it at me. "Not another step."

Have you ever had a gun pointed at you? Your stomach goes all cold. It feels like the bottom has dropped out of your world and you're stuck in a freefall. But I didn't have time to be scared because it was Gretchen, Gretchen who'd been sending the DVDs and had never been in any danger at all and was clearly out of her goddamn mind.

"I'm sorry I didn't come sooner," I said, trying to make my voice soothing, placating. "I didn't recognize the bathroom until yesterday and then you told me to wait for one more, remember?"

"You expect me to believe that?" she scoffed. "This bathroom was your fucking nightmare, Amanda, come on. Don't fuck around with me. I know you better than that."

"I'm telling you the truth." I kept my eyes on her face and tried not to look at the gun. "I repressed it, blocked it or something. I didn't even remember—remember what had happened here."

Her face softened a little but she didn't put the gun down.

"Do you remember what you did to me?" Gretchen asked quietly. "Do you remember this?" She touched the burn scars, the skin near the corner of her sagging eye.

"Not until you sent today's DVD," I said, and it was the truth.

***

Gretchen stayed overnight for New Year's Eve 1998. Clay and Mom had some stupid office party to go to so we were left home alone with popcorn and some movies from Blockbuster. He had the nerve to say he "trusted" us because we were such "big girls" now. Fucker even winked at me like the secret we shared was a tasty one.

That's probably the only reason I told her.

"If I tell you something, do you promise not to tell anyone else?" I asked hesitantly. We were watching *Balto*, one of my favorites, but I could hardly pay attention.

"You can tell me anything," Gretchen said, squinting at the screen. "You know, I think that goose is the fat detective from *Roger Rabbit*."

I paused the movie. She glanced at me, about to protest, then saw that I was chewing on my thumbnail. It was one of my tells when I was upset; that winter, I had chewed both of them down to the quick.

"What's wrong?"

I waited a moment, my throat working as I tried to get the words out, then suddenly I was crying, great heaving sobs bursting out of me like gunfire.

Gretchen put her arms around me and stroked my hair and soon enough I told her everything.

The next morning, I woke up much earlier than usual to find Gretchen missing. Clay and Mom were sleeping off the New Year's festivities so I snuck quietly around the house trying to see where she'd went. Her ski cap was missing and so were her shoes.

Puzzled, I looked out the living room window to see if she was playing outside or something and there she was, standing next to Clay's Camaro. She was holding Clay's video camera, too, the big bulky one that recorded straight to VHS tapes. It was pointed at her face; she was saying something to it.

I slipped my parka over my nightgown and hurried outside. If she broke that thing I'd be in some serious shit.

"Gretchen, what are you doing?" I called from the steps. She glanced up, eyes wide behind her glasses.

"Oh dang, you weren't supposed to see this yet!" she complained.

"It was gonna be a surprise!"

"What are you doing?" I repeated as I hurried across the cold pavement to meet her in the driveway. Gretchen turned the camera off and set it gingerly in the frosty grass.

"I'm blowing up Clay's car," she said, face beaming.

"You're—you're WHAT?" I looked at the rag in her hand and for the first time noticed the can of gasoline at her feet; it was the one Clay used to fuel up the lawn mower.

"With this," she said, waving the damp rag in my face. It reeked of gas. "I saw it in a movie. You soak some cloth in gasoline, stick it in the gas tank, light it, then—ka-blooey!"

"Gretchen, that's crazy," I said, shocked. I wasn't sure what I'd expected after telling her but not... this.

"He deserves it," Gretchen said firmly. "You told me what he's been doing to you, and we're just kids, no one will believe us over him. He'll win. This way, he loses SOMETHING."

She paused, thinking, then handed me the rag.

"You should do it. You should light it, you should be the one who does it."

"I don't want to do it," I insisted, trying to give the rag back, but Gretchen wouldn't take it.

"You have to. You'll feel better."

It was something about the way she said that, I still don't know what it was but I felt a vital part inside myself snap.

"Don't you get it, you dummy?" I cried, throwing the rag back at her. I threw it hard, harder than I should've, and it hit her in the face, covering one of her eyes. "I'm not going to feel better! I'm never going to feel better, I'm going to be broken for the rest of my life and nothing can change that and this is a STUPID FUCKING IDEA!"

Gretchen took the rag off her face and stared at me, hurt. "I'm doing this for you," she said, sounding confused.

"I don't WANT you to do ANYTHING for me!" I screamed. It was coming out, all the anger and fear and self-loathing and it was directed at Gretchen which wasn't fair but it's what was happening. "We're only friends because I had to move to this shithole neighborhood and someday I'm going to go somewhere else and I'm never going to think about you ever again!"

She looked at me for a long time, like she was waiting for me to take it all back.

I didn't.

"Fine," Gretchen said at last, turning a light shade of pink beneath her freckles. "Fine." She looked down at the rag in her hand and seemed to make a decision. She fished one of Clay's cigarette lighters from her pocket and clicked it to life, intending to set the rag on fire. I guess she meant to throw it at me.

"Wait!" I cried, but it was too late.

The rag caught quickly but so did Gretchen. Her skin erupted in flames where I'd thrown the rag at her, most of the left side of her face. She began screaming. I've never heard a sound like that, before or after.

It didn't take long for her hair to go up, too, and she was just standing there, flailing, so I did the only thing I could do once my panic-stricken body decided to listen to me: I threw her down in the frosty grass of my front lawn, face first, and started slapping madly at her smoldering hair.

It just happened so fast. Mom heard us screaming and came running outside; after a brief moment of shock she reemerged with a wet towel which she threw over Gretchen, putting out the flames at once. Clay followed shortly after her and stomped out the burning rag where Gretchen had dropped it on the driveway. He looked at the rag, at Gretchen, at the open gas tank of his car. Looked at me. Then he went inside and called the police.

***

"You let them take me away," Gretchen said now in the bathroom of my old house. She was still pointing the gun at me but had lowered it slightly. "I went to the hospital and then they sent me to a different hospital, a crazy person hospital, and you let them take me."

"I was just a kid," I said weakly.

"And what the fuck was I?" she demanded, raising the gun again. "I was a kid too, for god's sake, I was just trying to help you and you could've told them about Clay but you DIDN'T, Amanda, you just let them take me!"

I didn't say anything. What was there to say? She was right.

"And the worst part is," Gretchen said grimly, "that you visited me twice. TWICE. In six fucking years."

"Clay wouldn't let me," I said in a small voice.

"Yeah right. You just didn't want to. Admit it. You said what you really thought that day in the driveway, say it now. You didn't want to see me because we weren't ever really friends."

"That's not true." My throat felt like it was closing up; tears stung hot in my eyes. "I didn't mean what I said, I was just upset and—and fucked up—of course you were my friend, Ducky, you were my best friend."

"Don't fucking call me that!" she screamed.

I winced but went on.

"I visited you the first week in the hospital because Clay was at work and I had bus fare but that was all I could do," I explained, trying not to cry. "He was watching me like a hawk, said I shouldn't hang out with the girl who tried to kill him and Mom backed him up and there was nothing I could do!"

Gretchen didn't say anything. She waited for me to go on.

"And then high school happened and I had to get a job to help out with the house and I just—I just got so—and then it got to where it was easier not to think about it, you know? Because he'd finally stopped, you scared him enough that I think he knew you knew and he STOPPED and eventually it was like it didn't happen and—" I drifted off, helpless.

"And when you moved out?" she asked, gun still pointed at me.

"I just wanted to get away from here," I said weakly. "I had to. I had to get away from this house."

"Like I said you would." Gretchen's mouth was a thin, grim line.

"I did come," I said. "I came to the hospital on my way out of town but you were so out of it, Gretchen, you wouldn't even look at me. You don't even remember. So I left, yeah, you're right. But it wasn't to get away from you. It was never that."

Gretchen let out a bark of humorless laughter. "Seriously? You think I'm going to buy that bullshit? Please. You know what I think?" she said. "I think you didn't want to see me because you couldn't bear to look at what you did." She didn't gesture to her face but I knew that's what she meant, the destroyed flesh and drooping eye.

"I didn't get that gasoline out, Gretchen," I explained softly. "I'll take the blame for a lot of this but let's be fair: YOU did that. And you could've killed all of us, you know, that car could've taken out half the block."

"Now you sound like my fucking therapist," she said, and let out another humorless laugh. There was a pause; Gretchen looked at me, then Erin, then raised the gun higher, leveling it at my face. "How about I make us even? Wreck all that prettiness with a nice big hole through one of your cheeks?"

I froze, unwilling to say anything that might anger her more.

"Fourteen years, gone," she spat. "Fourteen. More than half of my life. And all I've got to show for any of it is this awful fucking face."

Gretchen cocked the gun. I felt my limbs go watery.

She paused, then looked past me at Erin. And then she did the worst thing yet: she smiled.

"You can have her," Gretchen said, then put the barrel in her mouth and pulled the trigger.

***

That was three years ago. Three years since Gretchen sprayed her blood and brains across the flower-and-vine wallpaper in the room where my stepdad used to rape me but I still see it in my nightmares. Sometimes they're both there, Clay and Gretchen, laughing at me. She holds the gun while Clay does what he does. It always ends the same way: she eats the bullet and I wake up screaming.

Erin and I don't speak anymore—well, no more than the polite "hey how are you" on Facebook or an occasional "like" on one of our pictures. It's the twenty-first century way of ending a friendship, I guess.

I try not to think about it but my therapist says that's not right, it's what caused me to repress all these memories in the first place. I tried to explain to him the thing about avoiding sharp teeth but I'm supposed to work through it. So this is me, I suppose, working through it.

He also says it's not my fault. None of it—Clay, Gretchen, it wasn't my fault. I didn't ask to be raped. I didn't put the lighter in Gretchen's hand. Or the gun, for that matter.

I don't believe him.

They found a box of home movies in my old bedroom. I think Mom must've left them behind when she and Clay moved out in 2007. Gretchen found them after being released from the mental hospital—I guess she just went straight to the house on Turner Street—and that's how the whole thing started. They've been sitting in my hall closet ever since.

For some reason, tonight, I've decided to watch them. All of them.

Who knows how many sharp teeth I'll find. How many times I'll get bitten by the barbs of my past. But it's something I have to do. Friendship bracelets and baseball games and teen magazines and flowers being choked by weeds… I need to live it all again. It's the only way to leave my poisonous childhood behind.

The only thing I'm really afraid of—really, truly terrified of—is what else I'm going to remember.

I Was Born on a Child Farm

By Howard Moxley, Reddit User /u/*IamHowardMoxley*

Runner Up—November, 2016

———————

"There is no free will."

Those are the first words I ever read. I woke to them every day for many years. They were written on a sign. The sign was hung above the opposite row of bunks in the Sleeping Barn. I have no memories from before the farm; I assumed I was born there.

***

None of the children there knew why we were there or where we had come from… nobody even knew how *long* we had been at the farm. Some children aged. Some didn't. I can't remember much, but that's what happens when you are not given too much to remember.

I remember always being deliriously hungry. We would be fed three small meals a day, but before each one Headmaster Ranon Xinon would make us watch him sprinkle a few drops of clear liquid from an unlabeled brown bottle onto the food. Then he would serve behind a steel door and slide out each meal through a window so you never knew if your meal was poisoned. Most of us danced around the edges of their food. Nobody was eager to dive in, not when we had seen a dozen kids turn blue and die in front of us after picking the wrong meal. Several of us rarely ate the food; I NEVER ate from my plate. I would scavenge what little clean scraps there were in the garbage. I ate four crows (they are just as disgusting as the saying implies) and I would go full Renfield and eat flies, ants, dandelions, cockroaches, clovers, pillbugs... anything living and somewhat edible. I would keep the spiders. I had a special place for those.

Twenty boys and thirty-odd girls worked the fields that provided all the food to "the farm," a crumbling wood compound fenced by tall barbed wire and the surrounding woods. Past that, the wilderness. Even though there weren't spotlights or guards, the farm was much more inescapable than a prison.

Every few weeks Headmaster Xinon would take the near-100 of us to the edge of his farm, where he would blow a strange brass whistle; bloodshot German Shepherds would spring from the underbrush as if they had been waiting for his call, mouths foaming as they gnashed their teeth on the rusted barbed wire, threatening to break in and chew us alive as the headmaster coldly smiled and spoke with a voice that sounded like gunshots fired far away:

"They're old guard dogs gone rabid. I have learned—through one of you! —how to train them so they only obey me, and if you run, they will kill you... or make you wish you stayed here with ME."

***

The farm never had answers. Very few people came—the rare delivery trucks, a prison bus, a black tinted-window Thunderbird that made a powerful turbine roar, as if rocket engines were installed under the hood—and they only dealt with the headmaster. The only person to leave was the driver of the

Thunderbird.

There was a rumor that we were not real kids at all, that Headmaster Xinon was a demon who crafted us all from blood and ash. We never dared speak to the headmaster and asking a question was ludicrous, as a question would mean a touch from his hard, cruel hand, a hand that made the surrounding air a pincushion of pain that would sting your skin if his hand even grazed yours.

But above the poisonings, backbreaking labor and cleaning, scavenging for food and never knowing a single day what was going on, we feared the nights worst of all. Being exhausted from working in the fields all day wasn't enough to overcome the fear of sleep. When it was darkest and the air had fallen still, we would hear the headmaster's creaking footsteps just… appear in the center of the drafty barn without any kind of warning. Sometimes we would hear him walk on the roof. Up the walls. On the ceiling. I can still hear his breathing if I close my eyes, that sick pig's wheezing, agonized breath that sucked air in and out in a guttural exhaust. The breathing and the footsteps would circle and circle until he heard someone cry. That's when the taken would give one last cry before they were gone, along with the headmaster. The missing child would return to their beds in the morning bearing new marks—a glancing finger left a nasty red and purple smear on one's side, sometimes black fingertips dotted their bodies. We would never say anything about these marks to anyone; we were always afraid the headmaster would hear and give us matching marks to boot.

Sometimes he would touch you with his entire palm, leaving a wrinkled imprint as raw and painful as a hot iron brand. I had a few marks as well, but I considered myself lucky that I only had a few marks, as far as I could tell.

I was one of four boys and five girls who cleaned the headmaster's home, the farmhouse. I cleaned the bathrooms and emptied out the shit cisterns by slop bucket and rope. I cleaned the bathrooms and eventually I found a few loose ceiling boards above the toilet when I was scrubbing for mildew,

The -30- Press Quarterly

standing on the windowsill. They were right above his toilet. I began thinking.

***

This was my life for what felt like many years—I swore I could have named twenty-five separate times the frost came, but we had no way to keeping track of time, not even by our ages. I swore sometimes we would see a kid go from looking thirteen or fourteen back down to looking half that. Time made no sense at the farm, and I knew that I wasn't going to get out by waiting. When I woke one morning to find the searing red-hot handprint of Headmaster Ranon Xinon on my upper arm, a hazy, starvation-induced plan emerged from the fog of my brain.

I went to the "special place" by the cisterns where I had kept every black widow spider I had come across. I kept them behind a false brick on the side of the farmhouse, where I had once collected eight of them and discovered that black widows were cannibalistic when grouped together. Only the strongest survived. I kept hosting "tournaments" until 108 black widow spiders were reduced to twenty-six of the most toxic, twitchy, and bite-crazy widows you never want to meet. I was bitten only twice, and came very close to an agonizing death both times. I knew one bite wouldn't do a monster like Xinon in. I was set—I was ready to enact the last stage of my plan when everything changed on a cold day in early December when a helicopter as black as the Thunderbird made a couple of low circles over the farm.

Ranon Xinon went insane. He poisoned half of the meals the day after the helicopter came, and after breakfast, he took us all outside to form a queue next to the chicken slaughterhouse. When he began leading us in one by one, a few joined me and ran. Judging from the screams, he caught most of the runners, but he didn't catch me. I'd spent many nights fantasizing about this moment, when I wasn't listening to his footsteps or sick breathing.

I put the black widows inside an old compartmentalized chocolate box scavenged out of a wood pile, perfect for keeping each one locked away. I went up through the floorboards and hid in the space in the bathroom. The headmaster may not sleep through this paranoia, but everyone's gotta go eventually, even monsters. Those cisterns didn't shit themselves.

It was dark by the time that he arrived with his candle. The sound of him pulling down his trousers and his simultaneous grunt masked the sound of me moving the planks above him aside and pulling the lid off the box of twenty-six nightmares, showering the headmaster with ravenous, crazed gladiators. My beauties began biting the headmaster as soon as they landed. The terror of the child farm, the demon named Ranon Xinon lay curled around his toilet, eyes swelling shut, mouth locked in a disgusted, surprised, outrageous gurgle of horror as spams racked his whole body. Before his eyes swelled completely shut, he saw my small seven-year-old face peering down the hole in the darkness. The missing child. The headmaster began to cackle.

"I knew this could happen. There is no free will. It's fine. I lived ten thousand years already. I lived YOUR happy summers, wonderful marriages, fruitful successes. Your life was beautiful beyond compare. That's why I—" he smashed a few spiders scuttling around his face but I could tell he was fading fast. "You and I are ghosts now," were his last intelligible words before the headmaster's breathing stopped.

I hid for four hours before carefully making my way to the window, the safest place in the room. The spiders were done and gone.

The chopper returned with a convoy of armed men right before sunrise. I was the only survivor of the farm. The captain of the operation was a man named Clinton Moxley, Chief Field Investigator for the Hermetical Office. He adopted me, and I took his last name. He was the one who named me Howard.

I told my father what little I knew. He corrected me on a few things—the headmaster's name wasn't Xinon, he was a man named Clark P. Ganes, an "anomalous individual." The office he worked for tracked the headmaster down here... my father had been the one in the Thunderbird.

Elder Moxley had told me about the time the office had captured the headmaster for study within one of their field labs. The subject grabbed the wrist of Frank Bernwiest, one of the team's eldest members. They saw Frank's seventy-nine-year-old face twist and contort until the wrinkles disappeared and the flesh had lifted up on his face; in a few seconds of agony, Frank was a middle-aged man again.

My father said that he personally stopped the other agents from interacting, as they were gathering film evidence of the unique phenomenon associated with Clark P. Ganes. Frank was known to be a formidable fighter but was helpless to the touch of Ganes. Every time Ganes' hand would land on Frank's bare flesh, Frank would scream, turning more pubescent every second. Clark only let go when Frank was a child again, squirming in old man's clothes.

"He chooses victims who had good lives," my father would explain as he would tuck me in. "His existence is the greatest evidence that time is a physical dimension, something that exists, and has always existed. He lives YOUR years in just a few seconds. Frank was left with nine bad years out of seventy-nine. You would think being young again is great, but remember that he was left with the mind of a nine-year-old, without care of friends or family... you know that pain well, Howard. The office didn't have the resources to care for Frank... we believe Clark Ganes is responsible for over a hundred thousand homeless children across the world. Frank was just one of them, another human with a used-up timeline..."

I asked the only father I knew why he adopted me. He brought me to the master bathroom's dual mirrors and told me to take off my shirt.

"Because I owe you. You were an old man once, Howard. You were my mentor and my partner within the office. You went into the farm by yourself to try to shut it down. I had hoped that you would remember... anything about your past, but... I see the headmaster got to you too."

I looked behind me, using the set of mirrors to see my own back for the first time, and seeing it covered in handprints.

* * *

***

That was many years ago. True to Headmaster's words, I have been a ghost among the living since then. It's been hard even sleeping, especially now.

For the past few nights, I have heard both the headmaster's footsteps and rasping breath next to my old-man bed. My father never said they found the headmaster's body. I know he wants his farm back. He wants me back—he wants ALL his children back.

December
—2016—

There's No Such Thing as Area 51

By Felix Blackwell, Reddit User /u/*Blue Keycard*

Runner Up—December, 2016

For several years I've been an avid reader of NoSleep, but because of my profession, I was never permitted to submit content to it (or to anywhere). Occasionally an Area 51 story pops up. "I used to work at Area 51," or "I snuck into Area 51," etc. These stories always made me want so badly to finally jump in here, but I always held my tongue until now.

Using a series of proxies and all kinds of networking jibber jabber, I *think* I'm in the clear making this post. I won't bore you with the details.

I came here to NoSleep after years of lurking to correct a lot of the misapprehensions and legends about the most infamous military installation in the world. I'm doing this now because even if I get caught, I have a really useful insurance policy: I'm seriously ill and not likely to recover, and I've got no family that I'm in contact with that could be retaliated against. There's nothing anybody can do (I think).

***

There is *no such thing as Area 51*. Sorry! And the fact that it's the golden egg of conspiracy theories worldwide is exactly what the US government wants. I'm writing this in a bit of a rush and I don't have any of my thoughts organized, so I'm just going to break it down as follows:

Groom Lake / Paradise Ranch / Edwards AF Extension / Restricted Training Facility UX104

These are a few names for the place you know as Area 51. I don't know much about its history, but essentially it *was* intended by the US Air Force to be a secret weapons-testing facility during the Cold War. It had a few on-site extensions: one of them was for developing experimental rocket and jet engines, one was for training contingents of troops for nuclear warfare and post-apocalyptic survival, etc. But much like the third *Star Wars* movie, the site and its purpose got out around the time of the Roswell incident, and a media frenzy popularized the base. The government tried at first to quell speculation about it, but then adopted another strategy: feed into the hype, and simply move the base a few dozen miles away.

Today, Groom Lake (Area 51) is a small but functional military airport and base. It's got a bunch of bunkers mostly housing low-security servers, and some munitions tests are performed there. Staff are regularly moved in and out, mostly folks who are low on the totem pole and trying to climb up the ladder to the real facility. There are some very outdated nuclear fallout shelters that are still maintained and used for storage. The facility consumes an enormous amount of power, and everything possible is done to make it *look* like a well-guarded military base that is engaged in some huge, secret operations.

The employees really do fly there every day from Las Vegas on conspicuously inconspicuous jets marked as "JANET," sometimes referred to as "Just Another Non-Existent Terminal." And they want you to notice. And wonder. They want you to wonder where those jets are going.

And they never want you to spend one second thinking about where they came from.

The real "Area 51"

This is the most exciting part, because as far as I can tell in my limited and clandestine researching, nobody has ever divulged the real secret before. It's pretty highly guarded, and they straight up murder people who are stupid enough to share it. Murder isn't even the right word. They *erase* people from existence. Sometimes entire families. That's why the government freaks out when they find that one of their employees is terminal and has nothing left to lose. It's why if you're an employee there, you only see *their* doctors, so that they know about your health before you do. They want you to die real quick of a sudden heart attack, so that you never have a moment to think about how you might do a public service and air their dirty laundry. And sometimes they induce those heart attacks when they determine you to be an HMT, or "health-motivated threat."

But I didn't need to see a doctor to know that I am suffering from the same malignant tumor that killed my father: glioblastoma multiforme. Every three months we get a health evaluation, and every six months we get a CAT scan. I simply didn't report the very damning symptoms this past eval, and I'll probably be gone before they scan me next. I really wanted to do this instead. Maybe just to be the first, I guess. The only other thing I've ever done with my life is fix computers.

The *real* secret military base is McCarran International Airport in Las Vegas.

The history of the airport has always been bound up in military involvement. Before and during WWII, the Army Corps of Engineers and the Air Force were building, storing, training, and doing all sorts of things there. Basically the government (and its corporate benefactors in the military-industrial complex, of course) acquired full ownership of the airport around the time Area 51/Groom Lake exploded in the public eye. It was a rush job, and a simple solution.

For all intents and purposes, McCarran is an airport. It moves civilians in and out and all over the world just like any other airport on earth, but its subterranean operations are really something else entirely.

***

First of all, you have to understand the structure of this military base.

Because it serves ostensibly as a business of public transportation, every single aspect of the base has dual functions. This is called "masking," and it is deployed with remarkable effectiveness at McCarran. To name a few examples, the constant take-off and landing of airplanes provides sound camouflage for cutting-edge engine tests. The public completely ignores these sounds and dismisses them as the standard cacophony of airports. Some of the jets themselves are even equipped with technology under test, while others are used to transport hundreds of government employees dressed as vacationing civilians. At any given time in McCarran, up to six of the gates are filled with employees of the highest echelons of the US military and government. They sit around on their iPhones, dressed as college kids in their pajamas or weary businessmen. And they're paid to look the part.

The entire base is heavily guarded by plainclothes soldiers. Military police, tactical specialists, counter-terrorism forces, and all kinds of soldiers scurry about the airport dressed like cops, airport security, and desk attendants. Their weapons are usually concealed sidearms; the real firepower is packed by the boys waiting around underground. Assault rifles and armor-piercing weaponry are stored around the airport's public spaces in various places. It's not hard to do, because nobody's looking for it. And of course they hire a good number of civilians to work the TSA and other positions; this is called "mixing" and it's necessary. What kind of airport would never post any job listings?

Have you ever watched the mechanics ducking in and out of the planes outside, or seen your luggage loaded onto the plane as you board? Well, all of that cargo transport activity acts as a cover for the mass movement of Special Forces, lab equipment, military hardware, exotic building materials, etc. It's not hard to do. They drive one of those rigs by with all the luggage spilling out of it, and then you instinctively don't question what's on the **other** four rigs behind it. We even have mix-ups and spills occasionally, and nobody bats an eye.

You're always exposed to some level of radiation while flying (and McCarran, by the way, is why the standard of safe exposure is set where it's at), but excess radiation from weapons testing is vented into the earth and out of the nearby desert. Having an airport to explain the radiation is an effective means of ridding the base of nosy folks with Geiger counters. But the true genius of this top-secret military installation is at the largest scale: the base was built under an airport because of the enormity of its power consumption. But it consumes a lot more power than a regular airport, so it was built in a city that consumes a tremendous amount of power—Las Vegas. So the base is hidden from view, even on the electric power grid. Area 51? Not so much. And that's on purpose.

Inside the base

So if Area 51 is the distraction, what do we call the real one? It has many names, but it's usually referred to as the "NEXUS." That's an acronym, but not many people know what it means. Not even me. Everything about the Nexus, from its operations to its structure, is compartmentalized. That means everything is need-to-know, and virtually nobody knows anything more than their own specific task. You could work in an office in the Nexus doing something like accounting, and never have one single clue what the woman next to you does. Or the guy down the hall. They say not even the president knows exactly what's going on there, just a few generals and some dudes in the CIA.

The business culture here is insane. It's like North Korea. Everyone is smiling, everyone is fine, and everyone is happy to say just a few phrases about what it is they do (when we're allowed to socialize, which is not often). Every line is bugged, every room has a camera in it, and nobody knows who's watching/listening or when. So that makes you think, *nobody here is telling me the truth about anything. Not even the guy I share an office with. I wonder if any of us know why we are here.* People you've worked with for a long time will suddenly get "reassigned" or have a "medical emergency" and you'll never see them again. And nobody will remember that person, no matter how many people you ask.

I actually got hired to do some programming for the Navy when I was in my early twenties out of college, and then got sent to Groom Lake to do server tests. They liked my IT/networking skills, so after a series of strange psychological tests and mountains of non-disclosure agreements and background searches, I got offered a job "at a facility near Las Vegas proper." Here are a few stipulations of that job, by the way: it's a $1,500,000 after-tax lump sum plus a $220,000/year stipend, housing/car/medical paid for—but psychological breakdowns, anxiety attacks, grave health conditions, and family issues void the contract. I also sign approximately two new non-disclosure agreements *per week*, most of which read "under penalty of death" somewhere. Employees aren't allowed to leave the grounds for five years, and we all live underground. Term of service is five years, then four in debriefing, wherein we get to live in Vegas but report to another facility four days a week. We are then discharged and observed for the rest of their lives. Our passports are permanently void; we cannot ever leave the continental US. I heard a statistic that twenty percent of former employees commit suicide. I don't know if that's true, but if it is, I bet it's actually "suicide."

The base is underground. It's a network of large structures called hives, which form what is called the "Colony" or the "Nexus." We make a lot of

Resident Evil jokes, by the way. Except unlike in that movie, the government doesn't try to make its employees feel comfortable with fake forests and windows overlooking digital cityscapes. It is a dark, dreary, Soviet-style labyrinth of halls and bunkers, replete with all sorts of submarine-like features: water- and air-tight hatches, trap doors, reinforced blast doors, etc. The only exception are the office 'buildings' inside where chair-moisteners like me work. They look just like the office you work in. Except for the men with guns standing guard 24/7 everywhere, looking over your shoulder. Oh, and the beautiful, almost surreal glow of the cutting-edge laboratories that pock the lower levels of each building. I've never been in them, but I've passed by a few times.

*****

There are **four hives** to my knowledge (although I wouldn't be surprised if there were more). I work in Hive 1. I run some of the servers with a few other guys on one particular floor (there are sixteen floors in our hive), but we monitor and maintain all of the servers in Hive 1 so we move around a bit. I've gotten to skim some of the data that passes through, and from what I can tell, we're the most boring hive. I've compiled the following list based on the things I've intercepted on our network and also from hearsay from other coworkers. The Nexus has multiple networks and they're all decentralized, but there are some ways in which they communicate, and it is via those lines of communication that I am privy to *some* sensitive information. Here's what I know:

Hive 1: Finance, accounting, operations/organization divisions, troop training/housing, and some small-scale weapons testing.

Hive 2: Chemical engineering, some nanotech research, and "advanced psychological fitness," whatever that means, for elite military forces. Probably black ops stuff and how to survive thirty years in solitary confinement at a

Siberian prison. I also have reason to believe this is the hive where the bigwigs meet and live.

Hive 3: Upper levels = bioweapon and disease research/testing. If the government has zombies, they've got to be here. I've wanted to make so fucking many zombie jokes over the years, but I never know which of my coworkers is a rat. Lower levels = advanced space-travel and space-warfare technologies. Particle engines and gravitational beams and the like (guessing, no real evidence). Science fiction stuff. I once saw an email with all sorts of coded language, marked "A-B," which is widely believed to refer to "astrobiology." That's alien life. Maybe it's just some single-celled organisms or fossilized plants from some meteor, or maybe it's something much more advanced. Whatever it is, there must be some reason it's not on the upper levels with all the biologists.

Hive 4: Total informational blackout. There are encryptions and firewalls and network security features protecting this hive that I've never seen before, not even on top-secret Navy projects I worked in the past. I'm being very nonspecific in the language I use to describe our server clusters and networks because I don't want to tell them exactly who I am. They'll eventually find out anyway. But there's a widely whispered rumor about Hive 4: allegedly, the most terrifying thing in the world is in that structure on Floor 15.

There are a few unusual things about Hive 4. First of all, none of the top brass has clearance to get in there. They access it remotely via video feed in their conference rooms, and materials are often transported from 4 to 2 for physical review. I don't know why our bigwigs won't go into 4, but maybe it's because it's too dangerous? There was one guy who worked in 4 a few years ago when I first started, and he caused the first Nexus-wide lockdown I'd ever seen. He was being escorted through 1 thumpers (what we call the squads of black-booted soldiers that grant access to different hives), and he started shrieking about IDAs. I didn't hear his screams, but I heard the gunshot while I was eating lunch. They put a bullet in the back of his head before he could finish his sentence. IDAs, by the way, are interdimensional anomalies. I have no further information on what those are.

Another thing I've read minimally about are "the twins." I don't know who or what these are, but they're the "above-top-secret" gem of Hive 4. It is treasonous to even correspond about them on our secure networks unless you are cleared to do so, and only four employees are. I've only seen a few things about them. One was a medical record. No vitals, unusual vocalizations that manifest hallucinations and psychosis in nearby employees, and skin that produces violent nausea when touched. The document was basically speculation that the skin functions much like the Australian stinging tree or a jellyfish.

I read documents about people who worked with them as well. In 4, a woman was remanded to the psychological ward after being in the same room with them, and a soldier who stood outside of the laboratory where they are kept basically killed himself. Specifically, he peeked inside during a routine access, then began bashing his own brains out with the butt of a pistol while singing an Irish folksong. The woman who was remanded to psych was even weirder: during breakfast with her colleagues, she grabbed a fork, stood up, walked out of the mess hall, stripped all of her clothes off, blinded herself in both eyes, then somehow managed to make her way all the way up to Floor 1 where the access corridor to Hive 3 is located. How she managed to operate the dozens of keycard readers, passcode boxes, and retinal scanners is still under review. Last email regarding her was sent in 2012 about how she sits in the dark of solitary on Floor 11's psych ward with a permanent and blissful grin on her face.

One of my colleagues whom I trust told me that he saw the twins once through hacked access to a video feed. He said they are woman-like, about twice as tall as a full-grown man, with unidentifiable black growths dangling from their heads (like hair but thicker), and they basically float a few inches off the ground and drag their toes lightly as they move. They're utterly pale. He never saw the faces, but he claims that they appear to distort reality (or at least the video feed) in such a way that space looks bent around them. Perhaps these are the IDAs that the earlier dude was screaming about.

***

This is all I have for now. But hopefully the world will know the truth someday about what goes on down here. We are all basically prisoners. We have very limited and supervised access to the internet, so if you don't hear from me again, assume they figured me out.

My Roommate and His Cat in the Hat Costume

By Paul Ross, Reddit User /u/*pross40745*

Runner Up—December, 2016

It was the 1st of November and he was still wearing it. Our party had been on the 29th of October and it was funny then, hell, even on the 30th it still made me laugh when I saw him occasionally creep out of his room to stock up on snacks from the kitchen. When I left the house for my nine am class on the 31st and he was sitting in the kitchen with his Cat in the Hat costume still on… well, then I began to worry.

John was quiet at the best of times, not too many friends, and I wasn't a stranger to sitting in silence at meal times. This was different though, his unnerving smile was all I could really see of his face beneath the prosthetics and makeup. It didn't help that it was a shitty homemade costume either, visible stitching and discolored tufts of fur made it all the creepier. Our other flatmate had dropped out at the start of the semester, so it had been just John and me for a long time. He wasn't an inherently weird guy before this either, quiet yes, but friendly enough.

"Don't you have classes to go to?" I asked as I left for work on the 2nd. He silently shook his head, not looking up from the book he was reading. "Starting to get real fucking creepy round here, man," I muttered loudly enough for him to hear as I shut the door behind me.

285

"I like it," I heard John bark with venom from the driveway.

It was the night of the 3rd when I finally cracked and phoned his sister. The white patches of the suit were beginning to yellow and there was an awful stench permeating around the house. She thought I was kidding at first, but after I explained in detail what had been going on the last few days she went quiet. She assured me that he had been texting her regularly as he usually did but had never mentioned the costume. I'd known the guy for a little over a year by that point, but I really didn't know that much about him.

His sister told me that he'd been obsessed with the *Cat in the Hat* movie after he'd seen it in the cinema when he was eight or nine, but had grown out of that phase pretty quickly. She assured me that she'd phone him and get to the bottom of whatever the hell was going on.

It was the smell that woke me up, that's how pungent it was.

"Don't meddle with my affairs," John said, standing in the doorway with a dim light behind him which partially illuminated that fucking costume.

"What the hell, get out of here you freak!" I shouted in a panicked daze.

"Don't meddle with my affairs," he said again. His tone was calm but there was a definite aggression behind it. He lingered there for a few more seconds, a silent tension between us. It was one of the few times in my life I'd ever felt genuine terror as I gazed at that horrendous cat costume and my roommate beneath it.

The next day in class I was going through my options in my head. My other friends had recommended calling the cops and thought that John was in need of some serious help. I didn't want to get him into some kind of trouble though, maybe even sectioned. My choice was made for me when two police detectives pulled me out of the lecture. They sat me down in the cafeteria with stern looks upon their faces. My first thought was that John had killed himself, I don't know why but that made the most sense to me. I was dead wrong.

"Why didn't you report that he was missing? Did you not find it odd for him not to come home?" one quizzed me.

"He… he isn't missing? He's should be there right now, probably still wearing that stupid costume."

A dog-walker had discovered John's naked body in the bushes not far from my house. The police reckoned he'd been dead since the night of the 29th.

They never found anyone in the house during their search, only that tattered costume which had been neatly folded on top of my bed.

-30- Press Annual
—2016—

Best Monthly Contest Winner
—2016—

I Dared My Best Friend to Ruin My Life; He's Succeeding

By Harrison Prince, Reddit User /u/*Zandsand90*

Annual Winner—Best Monthly Contest Winner, 2016

Winner—July, 2016

———————

My name is Zander, and my best friend is trying to ruin my life. It started out very small, but has quickly grown out of control.

I'm currently sitting inside a church, using their wifi to post this story and taking advantage of their air conditioning. I'm posting this story in case… Well, in case he finds me and kills me soon. It's only a matter of time now, and I want someone to know what happened before I die.

Two years ago, my friend David and I were sitting on the couch at my house, thoroughly bored. It wasn't a temporary boredom either. It was a resounding boredom with life. We both worked full time at the local movie theater making minimum wage and cleaning up after idiots who couldn't keep popcorn and soda in their mouths. We had graduated high school two years prior and had no plans to attend college.

Life looked bleak for us. College didn't sound appealing, work was annoying, and the little free time we had was blown on video games and YouTube. We both still lived with our parents too, which made dating somewhat embarrassing. Looking back, I'm sure we were suffering from mild depression on top of everything else.

These life circumstances blended together to create the perfect storm for what I now have to call my reality.

As we sat on the couch at my parents' house, channel surfing the TV, David asked me if I was bored with life. I responded in the positive, and he sighed.

"High school was so easy because we knew our purpose and our goals were set for us. Outline the English essay. Finish the math homework. Get decent grades. Pass the driving exam. Be home by curfew. Find a girlfriend. Now that we're out of high school, there's no structure. Our lives have become meaningless and we are just floating through space with no aim or purpose."

"Would you go back to high school then?" I asked. He shook his head.

"In the moment, high school was annoying. It's only after looking back that I see how much better it was than I realized."

"What's the solution, then?" I asked.

"Either go somewhere that has structure and can deliver what high school gave us, or create our own structure," David replied.

"Well I don't want to go to college or the military," I said. "And I can't think of anywhere else that provides the same structure. Guess I have to make my own, but I have no idea where to start."

"The thing about high school was that it required a minimum effort. If you didn't give that minimum effort, you would face the consequences. The consequences were bad enough that you and I would put effort into school. When high school ended, that minimum effort level decreased. Now our minimum effort is not enough to improve ourselves. Whatever structure we build has to have those consequences built in and a minimum effort that forces us to improve constantly."

David was, and is, a very intellectual person. He thinks about everything, if you can't already tell. I was pretty dumb compared to him, but I stuck around because he always had interesting things to say. This conversation definitely counted as interesting.

I won't bore you with the entire conversation that we had, but it lasted an hour where we discussed how to build structure into our lives.

I want to emphasize here that boredom is dangerous. Well, it's not dangerous by itself, but it can quickly lead to dangerous things. Boredom can lead to pain, accidental children, technology that disrupts a monopoly, and even death.

Our boredom led to a dare.

"I dare you to try and ruin my life," David said.

"What does that mean?" I asked.

"It's a way to build structure into my life. If I know that you are always trying to ruin my life and actively trying to make me fail, then I am driven to fight back and act on initiative."

"But how could I ruin your life?" I asked.

"You could ruin anyone's life if you gave it enough thought, planning, and action," David said with a smirk. "I'm not going to give you any ideas. I just want you to try and ruin my life."

I remember sitting back and thinking about what he meant. The first thoughts that came to mind were about tripping him occasionally, or hiding his toothbrush every time I went to his house. My young mind didn't fully understand how serious David was being. His mind was running three tracks above mine, so I didn't know what I was getting into when I said, "Okay, I'll try to ruin your life. But I dare you to try and ruin my life as well."

He smiled with a newfound enthusiasm, and I smiled back. I had hoped it would be a great way to relieve my boredom with life. David stood up and punched me in the leg as hard as he could. I shouted at him, mostly out of surprise. He just laughed.

"The dare starts now," he said, grabbing his shoes. "We are no longer friends, we are nemeses." He opened my front door and looked over his shoulder. "Good luck. I hope you'll work half as hard as I will."

Once he left, I just sat there rubbing my sore thigh. Okay, I thought, if he wants a war, he'll get a war.

That night, I laid awake trying to think of ways to make his life harder for him. My ideas were all so childish and useless compared to what he would later throw at me. I'm too embarrassed to list my ideas from back then.

I wish I could say I remembered the day David turned against me for real. But it was so subtle that I didn't notice right away. To my face, David acted completely normal.

While we were at work, I would sprinkle popcorn over a section he had just cleaned and point it out to him. He would just laugh and say, "Is that supposed to ruin my life?" Then he would clean it up. I expected him to do the same to me, but he didn't. His lack of visible retaliation made me bored again so I stopped. Looking back, I suspect that behind my back he was sabotaging my image with our other coworkers and our boss.

Out of the blue, my boss called me into his office and told me that I was fired because I wasn't doing a good enough job. David acted sorry I was leaving and we promised to hang out again soon.

I left, thinking I could make this something good and get a real job. That dream died, and I ended up at McDonald's instead.

After I had been at McDonald's for a month or so, my parents confronted me. They asked me if I had been stealing cash from their wallets. I had never stolen a cent from them, and told them so. They backed off, but only for a week until my mom's debit card went missing.

They confronted me again, this time very angry. They accused me of withdrawing several hundred dollars using my mom's debit card. I have no siblings, so it couldn't have been anyone else in the house. It turned into a screaming match and they demanded that I move out as quickly as possible. With my small cache of savings, I found an apartment near the local community college that housed college students. The rent was affordable enough for me, so I moved out within the month.

I moved in and became instant friends with two of my roommates, Clark and Ivan. Our other roommate, Isaac, kept to himself and stayed in his room playing video games 24/7. Life got good again because I hung out with Clark and Ivan frequently.

David and I had stopped hanging out after I was fired from the movie theater. I hadn't forgotten about him, but I had forgotten about the dare. Every once in a while, I would message him on Facebook or shoot him a text to ask if he wanted to hang out, but my messages were always ignored. Eventually I gave up.

Within six months, I had a great life going. I was dating a girl named Katie, I had been promoted to crew trainer at McDonald's, which paid better, and my bank account was slowly growing.

I only recognize this as David's doing when I look back, but an obscene amount of junk mail showed up with my name on it every single day. Magazines, credit card offers, vacation ads, and even physical letters from real people who claimed to be excited to be my new pen pal. I sorted through them every day trying to find some pattern. Clark and Ivan thought it was hilarious. When I came home late from work, they would sometimes toss the junk mail in the air like confetti as I walked through the door, cheering that the Mail King was home.

One day, I remember feeling sick of getting all this junk mail and deciding to sit down, call every subscription to cancel. I recruited Clark and Ivan to help me, and we sat down with snacks one afternoon and started to crank through phone calls.

In a few days, the tide of junk mail subsided and we celebrated our efforts. That only lasted a week.

The next week, it started coming back in full force. There was twice as much as before, and even some pornographic magazines in the mix. Not only did my physical junk mail increase, but my email became unnavigable through all the new spam messages. Google moved a lot of it to the spam filter, but there were still hundreds of emails that made it through. My email had been subscribed to websites I'd never even heard of.

Clark and Ivan were blown away by the new tide of junk mail. The event was dubbed "Return of the Junk" and became a great icebreaker for Clark and Ivan to introduce me to other people at parties.

One day I was browsing Facebook's "People You May Know" section when I came across someone's profile that had my picture, but a different name. The account was open for anyone to view and had a lot of porn posts, status updates full of swearing, and praises to Hitler. I frowned when I clicked on their pictures. Most of the pictures were the same ones from my Facebook account, but there were some pictures of me that weren't on my account or anywhere else online. Keep in mind, I didn't remember my dare to David, so I was feeling pretty creeped out.

I hit the report button and let Facebook know that the account was a fake and went on my way.

I think three months or so later is when more stuff started to happen. Katie and I were getting very serious and discussed moving in together. The junk mail still rolled in and I'd started to just throw it away. Ivan had moved out to go to an actual university, so a new roommate, Jackson, had moved in. Clark and I attempted to befriend Jackson, but he was similar to Isaac and locked himself in his room most of the time.

A new game became available for pre-order, so I submitted my email to reserve a copy. When I tried to log into my email to make sure the reserve code was there, I couldn't log in. I hit "Forgot Password" and it asked if I wanted to use my phone number to reset the password. I pressed yes and waited for my phone to light up. It never did. I pressed the button three more times, but no text ever came. I tried old passwords I used to use, but none of them worked. I frowned, but eventually just walked away from my computer. I'd try again a different day.

I sat down on the couch and pulled up Facebook on my phone. A popup appeared. "You've been signed out," it said. Then it jumped to the login screen. I thought I'd hit the logout button on accident, so I just typed in my email and password. It didn't work. I tried again, but it still told me the password was incorrect.

My phone buzzed in my hand. Katie was calling me. I answered it and immediately became concerned. She was sobbing.

"Katie?" I said.

"You coward," she spat. "You don't get to just Facebook me that shit, no, you have to talk to me and tell me with your voice."

"Katie, what are you talking about?" I asked.

"Don't play stupid, asshole. Say it."

"Say… what?"

"You Facebook me and say we are through, but when I call, you deny everything? What the hell are you trying to pull, Zander?" Katie hissed.

"Katie, my Facebook got hacked! I was literally just trying to log in when you called. Are you at home? I'm coming over. We are not done, we are far from done, sweetheart."

It took me some time to convince Katie that it hadn't been me, but she relented when I showed her that I couldn't log in. I googled how to get my Facebook account back and contacted their help center. Thankfully, they were able to get me back into my account. Lots of links to porn sites had been posted all over my page by whoever had jacked my account, so I spent time deleting all of those. I also spent time answering family members who asked about the "strange content" I had been posting. Awkward.

Katie also found out through her feeds that my Twitter and Instagram had been hacked. The accounts were posting hundreds of crude messages and pictures. Those two sites took a little more effort, but eventually I regained control over those too. Fixing my email took a couple of days, but I got access again.

Not wanting to repeat the experience, I made my passwords into really long strings of numbers, letters, and symbols. Each account had a different password. For anyone who has done this, you know how impossible it would be to memorize your passwords. I wrote them down on a sheet of paper and put it in my dresser drawer. I didn't intend to get hacked again.

I'm telling you where I put the paper so you'll know how freaked out I was when Facebook signed me out again the next week. I checked my other accounts. Locked out again. I shot Katie a text to warn her and then called the Facebook help center again. They gave me access back to Facebook and gave me the same warning about making a long password.

When I told them the type of precautions I had taken last time, they suggested checking my computer for viruses in case there was a keylogger collecting all the information I typed.

I called a computer repair center and asked what I needed to do to get my computer scanned. They asked me to bring it down and they'd check it out.

I had a desktop, so 'bringing it down' required a lot of unplugging. When I got down behind the computer to unplug everything, I found a tiny USB stick that I'd never seen before. I frowned and tried to locate its contents on the computer. The computer said no USB was attached.

The computer repair guy confirmed that the USB drive was a keylogger. He asked if my computer had ever been anywhere that anyone could walk up and use it. I told him no and he said he had no idea how it could have gotten there.

He didn't charge me anything, just warned me to keep an eye on my computer.

I changed all my passwords again, going through the motions to get my accounts back.

A few days later, I received three—yes, THREE—credit card bills in the mail. I still had the habit of skimming through the junk mail in case there was ever anything super important. I'm glad I did, because I might never have found out about the credit cards that were registered in my name.

I called the credit card companies to inform them that they were mistaken. I had never signed up for a credit card. My parents had warned me about them so often that I'd been deterred from ever getting one. Before you comment and tell me I need them to build my credit, yes I know that now.

A quick Google search told me what to do next. I called Equifax, which is a company that calculates your credit score and tells creditors that it's okay for you to open a credit account. I placed a ninety-day fraud alert on my credit. They said they would call me if anyone tried to open a credit account in my name.

The dude at Equifax was kind enough to tell me what I needed to do next. He asked me to go online and view my credit report. If I saw any accounts I didn't recognize, I was to write them down and fill out a complaint to the Federal Trade Commission (FTC) explaining the situation. Once I had that submitted, I was to file a copy of it with the police and create a police report. Then I had to take those two reports and call each of the companies that had issued credit cards to my identity and start the dispute process. I instantly felt very discouraged at the amount of effort this would require. It felt utterly insane to be required to follow all these steps just because I was the victim of identity theft. God damn.

Clark was horrified at what had happened and looked at his credit score. He was relieved when it came back clean. I made Katie check hers too just in case. Also clean.

I'll take a minute to tell everyone reading that you are entitled by law to one free credit report per year from each of the three credit bureaus. That means you can and should check your credit three times a year. Clark and I set reminders on our phones to check the scores again in four months. I asked Katie to do the same.

When I first found out about the accounts, I called my parents to ask if they had opened any accounts in my name. If they had, I'd at least know who the culprit was. They told me they hadn't opened any accounts, and I warned them about my problems. They promised to check their credit scores.

Two weeks after I had called them, my dad called. They found fifteen fraudulent accounts between the two of them. What the hell? I told him the steps he needed to take, and he was grateful for my help and warning.

I know this is boring to read, but I want you to realize how insanely painful it was to fix all of this shit. Seriously, watch your credit reports and nip identity theft in the bud before it happens to you.

I had requested detailed bills from the credit card companies that had issued the fraudulent accounts, and they mailed them to me. The bills were full of online purchases. The accounts had been opened almost a year ago, and in that time they thief had spent $62,000 between all the fraudulent accounts. I was pretty upset that in a full year, I had only just found any credit card bills in the mail. I must have been tossing them with the mountains of junk mail. Now I know that the masses of junk mail were deliberate and calculated so the bills would blend in and hopefully get thrown away.

The first few transactions were from stores like Target, Walmart, etc. But the further down I went, the less I recognized. One word stuck out to me: Bitcoin. I had learned a little about it from my Facebook feed as I had some friends from high school who touted it as the next real currency. According to the credit card statements, several thousand dollars had been exchanged into bitcoins.

I started really researching Bitcoin and trying to figure out what it was and why an identity thief would want it. To make the explanation short, Bitcoin allowed my thief to make completely anonymous purchases online. It was as if he'd gone to an ATM and drained all the credit cards into cash. I didn't foresee the credit card companies ever getting their money back.

David now had a hell of a lot of cash he could use to ruin my life. I didn't know it was him at the time, obviously, but now I do.

Guys, identity theft is a serious crime and is very damaging to everyone in the economy. And while the theft had been bad, my life was about to get a whole lot worse.

That's all I have time to write for now. I have to go and get some serious shit taken care of. I'll write again as soon as I can.

My name is Zander, and my best friend is trying to ruin my life.

***

While I was still trying to resolve the credit disputes with those companies, my car's windows started getting smashed. The first time, it was parked on the street in front of my apartment. I woke up one morning to find the driver's window smashed and my car raided. My car was just a crappy Honda Civic, and I didn't ever keep anything expensive in there, but they snatched my stereo, which was shitty anyway, and all the spare change in the car. Desperate much?

I got my window repaired that day and decided to set aside some cash to buy a really nice stereo now that I had an excuse.

The next morning, the same window was smashed again. Again, I had parked it in front of my apartment. I got that repaired reluctantly, and started to park in the underground parking for the apartment complex. See, no one likes the underground parking because the lines are painted too close so it's not uncommon for your car to get scratched up down there. I decided it was better than a smashed window, so I fought for a spot that evening.

I know you're going to ask why I didn't call the police. Mistakes, that's why. We all make them. You have the wisdom that comes with knowing the whole story. I didn't.

Glass was all around my car when I went down the next morning. It wasn't just the driver's window that was damaged. The front windshield and back windshield were deeply cracked. I spent some time looking at every car in the garage. No one else had so much as a scratch on their windows. What the hell? If some random asshole was out breaking windows, he was targeting me.

I noticed the note after I'd gotten into the car. It was a sticky note folded up and slipped into the ignition keyhole. I opened it. "You have to increase your minimum required effort," it said. The phrasing was intentional. David WANTED me to know it was him. And when I saw that phrase, I remembered our conversation.

That. Fucker.

I went into a total rage and drove out of the parking lot, trying my best to drive with the cracked windshield. I still remembered how to get to David's house, and I ran a red light or two to get there.

Parking in front of his house, I slammed the car door shut and marched to the front door. I held the doorbell for much longer than necessary. I tried to breathe and remain calm. David wouldn't help me if I showed up shouting and yelling.

His mom answered after a few minutes. David's parents had held off on having a child until they were much older. As a result, David's mom was already seventy-five even though David was only twenty-three.

"Hello?" she said, opening the door. Then she saw who it was. "Oh, Zander! How nice of you to come over! I haven't seen you in weeks!"

"Yeah, it's been… well it's been almost a year," I sighed. "Mrs. K, is David home?"

"No, sorry dear. He's at work right now."

"Oh, okay I'll go and catch him at the theater," I said, backpedaling toward my car.

"No, no, he doesn't work there anymore."

"He got fired?" I asked.

"No, he quit. Not long after you did. He became a security guard somewhere, he never mentioned where."

"I'll call him then," I said.

"He dropped his phone a few weeks ago and got a new one," she said. "Let me give you the new number." She walked back inside for a minute, and I waited on the porch. She came back with her old flip phone and opened it.

"Do you mind?" she asked. "My arthritis makes it hard to use this phone."

I went to her contacts, found David's number, entered it into mine, and handed the phone back.

"Thanks, Mrs. K," I said. Even if David was being an asshole, I had always liked his mom.

"Any time," she said with a smile and closed the door.

I called David immediately, but only got a voicemail.

"Hi David, it's Zander. I just spoke with your mom and she didn't know where you were so she gave me your number. Please call me, man. I think you know why," I said to his voicemail. I figured that being polite was the best way to get him to fix everything.

In the middle of work that day, my phone buzzed. Hoping it was David, I stepped outside and answered. It was Clark.

"Zander, have you been home today since you left?"

"No, why?"

"We've been robbed!"

"What?"

"Someone broke in and stole a ton of stuff. Your computer is missing, our TV is gone, all kinds of shit."

"Son of a bitch," I said. "Did you call the police?"

"Yes, they're on their way."

"Don't touch anything, okay?" I suggested, remembering all the episodes of CSI that I'd binged on. "We might be able to get fingerprints. I think I know who it is."

"Who?"

"An ex-friend. I'll tell you when I get home. I'm leaving soon."

I told the manager that my apartment had been broken into, and he let me go home. I drove home with my still-broken windshield, praying I didn't get pulled over for it.

When I got to the apartment, the police were already there. I walked to the landing where a cop was interviewing Clark, and another was looking through the apartment.

The cop turned to face me. "Are you one of the roommates?" he asked.

"This is Zander," Clark said.

"My partner is looking through the apartment now. A tech is going to come out and dust for prints. We're going to need you to make an inventory of everything that was stolen and bring it to the station once the tech is done."

"I have a suspect," I said. The cop raised his eyebrows. "His name is David King. He used to be a really good friend of mine, but recently I've suspected that he's doing all kinds of shit to me. I think he's stolen my identity and my parents' identity, damaged my vehicle, and now broken into my house." Clark shot me a questioning look.

"Why do you think he's doing all this?" the officer asked.

"I found this in my car's ignition this morning with the windows smashed," I said, handing him the folded sticky note out of my pocket. He read it.

"Why do you think he wrote this?" he asked.

"We had a conversation about a year ago where we were talking about the minimum requirements for success and how school made our lives easier because it had consequences if we didn't make a minimal effort," I explained. It looked like the idea went right over the cop's head.

"We'll test this for prints too," was all he said, pulling an evidence bag from his belt and putting the note inside. "Come down to the station with your inventory and be ready to make a formal statement about your friend." I agreed to do so.

At that moment, the partner came outside with nothing to report. The tech arrived and started dusting. We waited patiently, eager to see what was missing.

"You really should lock your bedroom doors," the partner said. "Two of your roommates' doors are locked, so I doubt anything was stolen from them. You should make sure they check their rooms for anything that's missing when they get home."

We agreed to ask them, and the tech finished up and told us we'd know in a few days what prints he was able to find.

The house seemed bare. Only the largest couch out of three was left in the living room. The TV, which had been a sixty-five-inch plasma, was gone. Food was missing from the pantry, and even the contents of the fridge were dumped on the floor. Silverware was scattered around the kitchen floor and counters.

"Where the hell is Isaac or Jackson?!" Clark yelled angrily. "They're always home!"

"We should call them," I said.

"I don't have their numbers," Clark replied.

"Well, neither do I," I said, walking to my bedroom. It was stripped bare of anything worthwhile.

My computer, mouse, keyboard, computer chair, boxes of random knick-knacks, and bicycle were all missing. My dresser drawers were lying everywhere, my closet was clearly raided, and my bed covers had been tossed around the room.

I heard bouts of loud cursing from Clark as he inspected his room. "HE TOOK MY GODDAMN XBOX THAT SON OF A BITCH."

Feeling shocked, defeated, and numb, I sat on the bed. I called Katie to tell her what'd happened. No answer. I shot her a text, "My house got robbed," and stared at the wall for a while, thinking.

David King had been in my house. He'd stolen my identity, my public image, and now my things.

It was time to step up my game. No, not my game. My life. Time to stop floating through life and start beating the minimum required effort.

During the rest of that day, we learned a lot about plumbing. David had loosened every pipe he could find in the house. Clark made the discovery when our toilet unleashed a tsunami when he flushed. We spent hours cleaning that up. To fix all the pipes, we had to go out and buy tools because neither of us had any at the house. When my card was declined, Clark stepped in and paid.

My declined card worried me. Clark and I went to the library, and I tried to log in to my online banking site. Locked out. Shit. I didn't even bother retrying my password.

We raced to the bank before they closed, and I breathlessly approached the teller.

"I need... to freeze my... account," I breathed.

"What's your account number?" the teller, apparently named Shauntelle, asked.

I told her my account number from memory. She opened it on her computer.

"Driver's license, please."

I handed her my card. She typed my driver's license number into her computer to verify my identity, then handed it back to me.

"Looks like your account is at zero," she said. "You can only freeze the account if there's money."

"I've been robbed!" I shouted, feeling extremely angry now.

"You moved all of your money to your debit card via our online app, and then withdrew it all in cash from an ATM this afternoon."

"No, it wasn't me!" I said. "I've been hacked!"

"If you'd like to report fraudulent transactions, I can fill that out for you right here."

"Yes. Fine. Do it," I said abruptly. Clark watched me with worry from a chair by the door.

"When did you start to notice the fraudulent activity?" she asked.

"Today, but it could have started any time over the last year," I replied. She raised her eyebrows in a way she thought I couldn't see and started typing.

After a few minutes, she looked up at me.

"Okay, I've filled out the report and submitted it. You should hear back from our fraud department soon."

"What about the ATM cameras?" I said.

"I don't have access to those, you'll have to file a police report," she said.

"Okay, I'll do that." Then Clark and I went back to the car and drove to the apartment. We would have gone to the police department right away, but the apartment was still flooding in places.

We spent a few hours finding leaky pipes and tightening them. It took hours because we looked everything up before we did it to be sure we were doing it right.

Clark inspected the pipes under the kitchen sink while I sat at the table and started my inventory for the police. It was already nine pm, so we were going to take it in the morning. Our local station wasn't open twenty-four hours a day. We had knocked on Jackson and Isaac's doors, but got no answer. Either they weren't home, or they were ignoring us.

"I'm really sorry about all the fraud going on," Clark said as he tightened a pipe. "You said you think you know who it is? Who's David King?"

"David used to be a friend about a year ago," I said. I told him about the dares and the conversation that led up to it.

"You dared each other to ruin each other's lives, and then he took it more than seriously?" Clark asked, incredulous.

"Apparently," I sighed.

"So you're not going to hold up your end of the deal?" Clark said.

"My end?"

"He dared you first, man. And you haven't even tried!"

"Well... no, I guess not."

"Then let's think of something to really destroy his life!" Clark pulled himself out from under the sink and washed the grease off his hands.

"Prison would do it," I suggested. "If I can nail him for identity theft, that'll solve the problem."

"True," Clark said. "But we need to show him that you aren't going to just lie down and take it. I have an idea. It's not going to ruin his life, but it'll make him realize that you're going to fight back."

Clark took me in his car to Home Depot. We bought two cans of black spray paint and Clark paid in cash.

"Okay, where does this dumbass live?" Clark asked when we were back in the car.

"Clark, his mom is great. I don't think I can spray her house," I replied.

"His mom?!" Clark laughed hysterically. "Some guy that still lives with his mom is terrorizing you?!"

"Okay, okay, Jesus," I said. I gave him the address, and he took off.

We drove past the house to see if any lights were on. It was dark. Even the porch lights were off. We parked three blocks away from the house and started walking.

"What's the plan?" I uttered.

"Spray 'THIEF' on the front of the house," Clark whispered with a smile. "That ought to get the neighbors talking."

When we were next to the neighbor's house, we ducked behind a fence and surveyed the neighborhood. All was quiet. No movement, no noise, no people.

We stayed low and silently dashed to the front of the house. I sprayed the "F," Clark sprayed the "T" and we worked toward each other. It barely took three seconds. We stepped back for half a second and examined our handiwork. The letters were three feet tall, easily visible from the road. Perfect.

We turned and started to run toward the car. Then the door to the house opened. I glanced over my shoulder.

David Fucking King.

"Oh shit," I hissed. Clark heard me and we sprinted full-on toward the car. David tore down the sidewalk after us. Clark looked behind as well.

"Oh God, oh God, oh God," Clark chanted with each step. He actually looked worried.

As we approached the car, Clark had a realization.

"Just keep going," he tried to whisper even though he was out of breath. "I locked the door, it'll take too long to unlock. And he'll know my license plate." Clark didn't have automatic locks; he had to use the key manually. I agreed with his logic and we ran past the car as if it were just another vehicle.

I looked back, and David was gaining on us. It was too dark to see his expression. Hell, I didn't even know if he recognized me.

"Split up," I cried, turning right into someone's front yard. Clark kept going straight.

When I reached the white, plastic fence that led along the back of their property, I glanced backward. David had followed me and ignored Clark.

I scrambled up the slippery fence and dropped on the other side. I had landed in someone else's backyard. I started running toward their front yard. A motion-detecting light on the wall went off, blinding me. I looked behind me again to watch David scale the fence in half a second. When the HELL had he learned how to do that?!

I rounded the corner of the house and smashed right into a patio table and chairs. The chairs clattered down and the table tipped over while my body folded around it. My heart was pounding as I untangled myself.

That's when David grabbed the back of my neck and pushed me down, my face against the edge of the table.

***

"Hello Zander," he growled. "Out for a walk?"

"Fuck you," I spat, my cheek jammed against the table edge.

"Why so hostile?"

"You know why, jackass!"

"Not so loud. We're having a nice, quiet conversation."

I struggled to push my head off the table, but he was so much stronger than me.

"Stop struggling and listen. I want to clarify the rules of the game, since you've finally caught on that we're playing."

"This isn't a game! You ruined my credit, stole my money, hacked my accounts, and stole my shit! I'm going to kill you!"

"But I'm not going to kill you. That's the rule. I will not kill you, Zander. That would put an end to your ruined life, and that's not the goal. Now, you haven't put any effort into ruining MY life. Why not?"

"Because I'm not a sick psychopath," I hissed.

"Clearly not," he said coolly. "But this is boring for me. I'm doing all the work making you fight for life, while you're doing nothing to improve me. Not that I haven't learned anything, but it would be more fun if you'd fight back. I'll even let Clark help you. But I think you need motivation."

"You think I need motivation to hurt you? As if."

"Yes, you do need it. Because despite everything that's happened to you, your only attempt to fight back was pathetic. I need you to up your game and fight harder. So, that's where some motivation kicks in."

He reached his left hand into his pants pocket and pulled out a smartphone. He tapped on it a few times before holding it up to his ear.

"It's me," he said when the other line picked up. "Put her on." Then he held the phone to my ear. Someone was crying.

"Say hello," a gruff voice said.

"H-hello?" Katie. Jesus Christ, he'd kidnapped Katie.

"YOU MOTHER FUCKER!" I yelled.

"Easy on the language, Zander," David smiled, talking as if he'd asked me to eat my vegetables.

"Katie, where are you?" I said desperately into the phone. David took the phone away and hung up, sticking it back in his pocket.

"Do you understand the rules now, Zander? Are you motivated?"

"I'm going to kill you, you son of a bitch. You'll burn in Hell!"

"Now, now, this isn't a theological discussion," David tutted. "You and Clark do your best to ruin my life. Do whatever you want. But if you kill me, I kill Katie."

"Can't kill her if you're dead," I growled.

"No, but my friend will. It's amazing the kind of people you can meet online. He's just as excited to play as I am. Do you have any questions before the game really starts?"

"What the hell happened to you?" I asked. "We were best friends!"

"Things change," he said. "I'd been dreaming of this game for years now. You were my only real friend I could do this with. One day I decided to just... go for it."

"You've ruined your own life by trying to ruin mine," I spat. "Once you're convicted of identity theft and kidnapping, your life is over."

"That's part of the game. Can't ruin me if you can't convict me. I've been preparing for years," he grinned. His eyes were dark and menacing.

"Don't you think that's unfair to me? How am I supposed to put in a good effort if you've been preparing for years?"

"I'll consider giving you some advice," he admitted, looking thoughtful. "In the meantime, do your best. And tell Clark to play along because I'll have some motivation for him too."

The sound of scrambling on the back fence alerted us to someone's presence. I shouted for help and David slapped me, but lightly. I tried to see who it was from my limited movement. Clark's face appeared over the fence.

"That's my cue to leave," David said with a smile. "It's been good catching up with you, Zander."

Clark shot across the yard, yelling for David to piss off. David just stood there, looking at me and... waiting. That's when Clark caught up and punched him square in the face. David flew to the ground, releasing my head. I stood up and rubbed my sore face. David started to get up, but Clark kicked him in the side.

"Stay down!" he shouted.

A light went on in the house behind us. We both turned to look. I had the thought to hold David here until the police arrived. When we turned back around, David was halfway down the street. Clark started to take off, but I grabbed his arm.

"Stop, let him go," I said in defeat. "I have something to tell you."

We made a quiet decision to avoid the cops that night. We wanted to file a report with them on our terms, not having to explain what we were doing trespassing in the middle of the night. We jogged back to his car and went home.

We sat on the living room couch as I told Clark about David's conversation. Clark was staring dumbfounded at me.

"I thought you said he used to be a friend?" he said.

"He did."

"And he never acted like this?"

"No, not to me."

"This is insane," Clark said, standing from the couch. "He's kidnapped Katie just so you'll try to ruin his life and follow along with some stupid dare? Is he crazy? He's going to be caught!"

"Let's hope so," I said. "But we should start planning. I'm not taking any chances while he has Katie."

"Okay, man. I want nothing to do with this at all, but I also want to help you. If it was anyone else, I'd nope the fuck out."

"Then let's get started," I said.

I don't know how much detail I want to put here because it'll likely get slow and boring for you. We stayed up all night long mapping out events, people, weaknesses, strengths, everything we could think of. We filled half a notebook with all our notes.

These were the weaknesses we could come up with that we could potentially use against David:

- Boredom with life—we could make the game too boring to continue.

- His mom—if she knew what was going on, she might be able to get him to stop. I know some of you commented that we should kidnap Mrs. K and use her, but we were still very green and had no desire to do the kind of shit David was doing.

- Work—get him fired and make sure no one would hire him

311

again.

• Online accounts—do the same things to him that he'd done to me.

• Police—if we could come up with hard evidence to get him convicted, the problem would be solved.

• Katie—since he had kidnapped Katie, the police would definitely get involved. I could easily report my suspicions about David and they'd search him for the tiniest evidence.

1. Then we looked at his strengths and things to look out for:

• Prepared—he obviously had a timeline he was following and knew what he was doing.

• Time—the junk mail and credit fraud incidents all began long before I felt the effects. This meant that there could be other traps David had set up that would go off like a time bomb sometime in the future.

• Physical body—it was clear from that night that he'd been working out a ton and practicing. Possibly training for his job as a security guard.

• Money—he had a lot of money now from what he stole from me and used fraud to receive.

• Friends—if he'd made a friend who was willing to get involved in a kidnapping, then there were two or possibly more psychopaths to worry about now.

• Knowledge—he knew how to use fraud without being caught (yet) and hack computers, or at least hire someone to do it for him. We had no idea what other dangerous knowledge he might have, so we made a list of things he could know that we should learn how to counter. I won't list it here because it was pretty long.

• Willingness to break the law—it was clear that the law was not part of the rules of the game for him. He was either unafraid to be caught, or confident that he never would be.

3.   2.   After we looked at David, we looked at ourselves. First, our weaknesses:

•   Knowledge—we didn't have nearly the amount of knowledge David had. Not just knowledge about how to do things like fix a pipe, but also knowledge about David: who his friends were, where he worked, who he talked to, etc. We'd have to start learning like crazy to try and catch up.

•   Money—I had no money left. Clark was limited because he'd just spent a ton on that plasma TV that had just been stolen.

•   Home and car—David knew where we lived. We planned to sell our lease ASAP. He also knew our cars, but there was nothing we could do about that until we moved and had some money to buy a junker car we could use when necessary. No matter where we moved, if he could find our car, he could follow us home.

•   Katie—if David decided to change the rules and use Katie as motivation, we might have to rethink everything.

•   Fear—Clark and I knew that deep down David terrified us MORE than he angered us. I would have rather walked away than exact revenge. We were also afraid and unwilling to do a lot of the things David had already done.

4.

5. These were our strengths:

•   Law—the law was on our side so long as we kept things legal.

•   Clark's credit—so far, David hadn't targeted Clark like he'd targeted me, so we could take precautionary measures to protect him.

•   Jobs—we had jobs and could therefore earn more money. Unless David found a way to get us fired from them. We needed to come up with a way to protect our jobs from David.

•   FTC, Police Force, Government—these government bodies, with all their vast resources, were working for us on my identity theft. We thought it was likely that they'd be able to link David to my identity theft.

6.   Looking at all the strengths and weaknesses of both parties side by side, it looked like an even match-up on paper. But just thinking about trying to fight David made us feel like we were up against an impossible enemy.

We sat down to eat breakfast and continued talking over what we would do. Both of us called in sick to work so we could start preparing.

"Alright, I posted our leases up for sale on Craigslist," I said, putting my phone down. Clark was sniffing the air with a confused expression. He leaned over and smelled his cereal.

"Does this smell bad to you?" he asked. I sniffed.

"Smells like cereal to me," I said.

"Huh. Smells bad to me." He dumped the cereal in the sink.

Clark pulled out his phone and called Equifax, letting them know that he wanted a freeze on his credit for ninety days. When those ninety days were up, he would call again and again until this matter was resolved to protect his credit. His credit card with a $3,000 limit was still accessible to us, but no new credit could be applied for.

He then went on every account he had online and changed every password to be random gibberish. He signed up for an online password manager and put his passwords in there. The password manager worked by storing an encrypted file on their server. He would download his encrypted file from the password manager website, read or write to the file, re-encrypt it, and then send it back to the server. The server only held the encrypted file, no passwords. Even if this company got hacked, the hackers would only have a bunch of useless, encrypted files. They could crack the files with time, sure, but it was the best we could do.

The only account he didn't put into the password manager was his bank account information. He wrote down half of the username on one small scrap of paper, and the other half on another. He did the same with the password. He intended to hide them in safe places around town. If David got ahold of

Clark's bank information, we would be dead in the water.

While he did that, I finished both of our inventories. Once the station opened, we were going to head over, hand in our inventories, file a police report for the burglary, and recommend David as a possible suspect. I also planned to point them to my identity theft police report and state that I suspected David to be guilty of that as well.

Once we had the police report, we would go to our landlord and request for the locks to be changed, using the police report as evidence of the break-in. The tech had told us that the door had been opened regularly and not forced. That meant David had somehow made a copy of our key.

As it got close to nine am, we got into Clark's car and drove around town. He got out at four locations and hid his scraps of paper somewhere. He knew it had to be somewhere people didn't touch for months at a time and wouldn't be damaged or moved by sprinklers, storms, etc. I don't know where he hid them, but he assured me they were safe.

After they were hidden, we drove to the police station to file our report.

We waited patiently for an officer to see us. Once we were called over, we took a seat and told him about the break-in and that a police report had been started and we were now turning in an inventory of our stolen things.

"We have a suspect for the burglary," I said at last.

"Okay, who?" he asked.

"His name is David King. He used to be a friend of mine, but not anymore."

"What happened?" he asked, writing the name down.

"Recently, I had my identity stolen," I said. "I suspect he was also behind that, so if he stole my identity, it's likely that he broke in too. He hates me."

"Okay, but what actually happened that made you not be friends anymore?"

I hesitated. I didn't know how to explain the situation. If anyone can think of a better way to explain the situation to a cop, let me know. I only said, "We had a major fight and he threatened to ruin my life."

"When was this fight?"

"About a year ago."

"And you think he's just now stealing your identity and breaking into your home," the cop said dubiously. "Were you friends with him?" he asked, gesturing to Clark.

"No, I'm his roommate," he replied, pointing to me.

"Okay, boys," the officer sighed, scooting forward. "Thank you for the tip and your inventories. We'll investigate this just like any other crime and give it our best effort. Can I get copies of your driver's licenses and phone numbers so I can contact you if I have questions?"

We handed him our licenses and wrote down our phone numbers in the file.

"I'll be right back," he said, taking the licenses to make copies.

We looked at each other for a minute, taking a deep breath.

"He doesn't believe us," I said in resignation.

"We'll find evidence," he encouraged me.

Five minutes passed. Then ten. Then the officer came back, two others at his side.

"Clark Ulysses?" he asked.

"Yes?" Clark said, confused.

"You're under arrest for vandalism and trespassing on private property."

The officers flanked him and pulled him to his feet. I stared at the cops in bewilderment. Clark's eyes were wide.

"When I went to copy your license," the cop said, holding it up, "I checked it against our records. Last night, someone called in a report that you'd been to their home and sprayed 'THIEF' on their house and then attacked him when he came out to stop you."

My mouth dropped open. Son of a bitch.

"David King, the one you just recommended as a suspect, was the one who called it in. Seems to me like you're trying to discredit him before he reported you. Guess he beat you to it. Read him his rights," he said to the other officers.

"Wait," I said, standing up. "Hold on, I was there too, it wasn't just him!"

Clark shook his head at me ever so slightly. No! I wasn't going to let him take the fall for this!

"Mr. King explicitly stated that there was only one vandal and that he watched Mr. Ulysses sneak up to the house and spray it by himself. I know you're trying to protect your friend, but don't throw your life away, kid."

One of the officers started reading Clark his Miranda rights while they cuffed him and walked him toward the door leading to inmate processing.

"Call my mom for bail! I'll be out soon!" Clark shouted behind him. "Don't let him win!"

***

I called Clark's mom right away. I had their home phone number because last Christmas, Clark invited me to his house for Christmas dinner since my parents and I were still fighting pretty harshly. He'd already gone home while I had to work, so he gave me the phone number in case I got lost and he didn't answer his cell.

She was devastated and asked me a million questions. It was very, VERY uncomfortable. She agreed to drive down that day and post bail for him. She lived a few hours away, so she said she'd be there at around five pm. The county we were in didn't allow online payments via credit card: cash only, so she had to physically drive down.

In the middle of the phone call, I missed a call from a number that wasn't in my contacts. I called back, and they answered immediately.

"Hi, I missed a call from this number?"

"Hi, is this Zander?"

"Yeah… who's this?"

"Zander, I'm Katie's mom. Your parents gave me your number."

Shit.

"Hi, can't talk now I'm in a rush and I—"

She cut me off. "Have you heard from Katie? She didn't come home last night. Your mom gave me your number. Please tell me she's with you."

"She's not," I said. "I'm not sure where she is. I have to go—I'll call you back."

I hung up the phone. I didn't want to talk to her about Katie because I was about to file her missing person report.

I walked over to the reception desk.

"I was just talking to an officer, and then he arrested my friend and walked off. I need to talk to the officer on my other case about identity fraud."

"What case number?" the lady asked.

A while later, I was sitting in one of their interrogation rooms after asking for a private meeting. Detective Hernandez sat at the opposite end of a metal table. My two case files were on the table in front of him. He was glancing through them, trying to familiarize himself with the break-in report. A tape recorder sat between us. He pressed a button on the recorder and the tape started rolling.

He stated his name, my name, my case numbers, the date, and the time.

"Alright, go ahead," he said.

"So, I submitted a report for identity theft a while ago and haven't heard anything about it."

"The FTC can take some time to respond," he replied.

"Well, now there's a new report for a break-in at my apartment. I was talking to another officer earlier and told him that I have a suspect for both crimes."

"Yes," the detective said, looking over one of the folders. He had both cases on the table. "One David King, correct? Looks like it was written in your file."

"Yes, David King. He used to be a friend of mine, but now he hates me and has been targeting me."

"Targeting you how?"

"Most recently, he's kidnapped my girlfriend, Katie."

That caught his attention. He pulled a pen from his front pocket.

"When was this?" he asked, setting his pen on a blank page.

"Last night. When we went to go graffiti his house. He chased after us and pinned me to a table. He called someone on the phone and had them put Katie on the phone. I heard her voice and he claimed he'd kidnapped her to motivate me."

"Motivate you to do what?" Hernandez asked.

I told him about the dare conversation. Then about all the junk mail. My online accounts. The credit card fraud. My parents' credit being targeted. My car's windows. The break-in. My bank account being emptied. The graffiti incident. Katie's phone call. Protecting Clark's bank and online accounts. And now Clark's arrest. Hernandez took copious notes.

"It just keeps escalating," I said in defeat. I watched Hernandez carefully, trying to gauge his reaction. I couldn't tell what he believed.

"I need more details about the phone call," he said at last. "What did she say? What did you say? What did you hear on the other end?"

We talked through everything for an hour. Nothing I said was useful for finding Katie, but Hernandez sat back after I finished.

"Zander, I have to be honest. This all sounds very… loose. I don't mean the crimes themselves, I mean the connections linking David to all of these crimes. There's nothing that can be done about the identity theft until the FTC has finished their investigation. The break-in, broken windows, hacked accounts, and emptied bank account will have to produce their own evidence to prove that David committed each one.

"To you, this is all one timeline of events, but to the law, they are separate crimes that have to be treated with no regard for past actions," he said. His tone was reasonable and concerned. "I believe you, but I can't make an arrest without witnesses or hard evidence. Your story is circumstantial at best. But I do believe you when you say they are connected."

Finally. Someone believed me.

"What have the techs said about the break-in?" I asked. "They said they found a few fingerprints?"

"All the fingerprints found belonged to each of you and a few other people who used to live there. According to the file, they've all been confirmed as past residents."

"And what about the ATM camera?"

"Now that's something unfortunate," he said, looking through the folder again. "We got a call from your bank to file a fraud report. It was smart of you to go through the bank to report the fraud. My boss made it a priority and, since it was your same name, it was added to our file on your identity theft. I've been the one personally working on your identity theft case. Once I received the case, I called the convenience store that the ATM was in. They gave me the brand of the ATM so I could request the footage from the company. Problem is: that ATM doesn't have a camera."

"What? How can an ATM not have a camera?"

"Not all brands do. Some ATMs don't have cameras built in, and this was one of them. Someone logged into your online bank account right before the ATM transaction and moved all of your money from savings into your checking account. They also increased your ATM withdrawal limit to $5,000 while online, which was above the $3,500 you had in your account. Normally, you can only withdraw $500 per day."

"What about the store's cameras?!" I practically shouted.

"I asked for them to bring the footage down. They said they'll be in today," he said.

"Where's this store?" I asked. "I want to see this for myself."

"No," he said firmly. "I may have inclination to lean toward your theory, but I will collect the evidence myself and a court will decide. You steer clear."

"Then drive down yourself right now, God damn it!" I yelled. He stood slightly, his hand reaching for his belt automatically.

"Calm down," he said, looking me in the eyes.

"I have no money!" I shouted. "My car windows are smashed and I can't repair them! My rent will be due and I'll have no way to pay! I can't get to work in a car I can't drive! I need my money back!"

Hernandez sighed, sitting back down. I breathed heavily.

"If David is the one who used your information to commit credit card fraud, why would he steal a measly $3,500 from you?" he asked.

"Because he's dead set on ruining my life," I muttered. "That's the dare.

He's taken it too far. Further than any sane person would. He's sick. I just want it to stop." I cried a little, and Hernandez let me sit in silence for a minute with tears rolling down my cheeks.

"What about Katie?" I asked after a while.

"The kidnapping is going to get top priority. That's the one case that has a witness—you. I won't be working on it, but someone in a different section of the department will be. The other detective will want to interview you today and get started."

"Let's do it then," I said, wiping my eyes.

Hernandez stepped out and returned a while later with the detective. Detective White came in and probed me with hundreds of questions. Where did she work? Who were her friends? How long had we been together? When did I last see her? Do her parents know? Questions like that.

When I brought up David and the phone call, he leaned in and asked me the same questions about what I'd heard, what we'd said, and anything I could remember. Again, I didn't remember anything helpful.

"I'll need to bring David in for questioning," Detective White said. "Your testimony is decent, but we'll need more evidence for conviction. I can't arrest him because I need more proof. If we arrest him without enough proof, he'll walk free and can't be tried again."

"You had enough proof to arrest Clark!" I shouted.

"Clark?" Detective White asked.

"I was just talking with an officer who said David called in and told you all that Clark graffitied his house. All he had to do was call, and he got arrested!"

Detective White excused himself to go find out more about what had happened. He came back five minutes later.

"David has more proof on that case," Detective White said. "Photographs of the graffiti, photographs of Clark coming up to the house, his own testimony about recognizing Clark, and a bruised face. Clark's hand is also cut up, which corroborates his story. We noticed it when we booked him. This is the kind of evidence we need to convict in a kidnapping. Right now we have your testimony stating you said 'hello' to Katie on the phone and that David said he'd kidnapped her. We need more evidence to convince a jury."

"But I was with Clark!" I yelled.

"In the pictures you weren't," he said.

"Then they're fakes!"

"An expert will check them and determine that."

I sat back in my chair, feeling defeated. Detective White thanked me for my testimony and left to contact Katie's parents.

Detective Hernandez sat back down, watching me as tears welled up in my eyes again.

"Let me pay for your windows," he said.

"It won't matter, he'll break them again the next day," I said angrily.

"He's broken them more than once?"

"Every time I repair them, they're smashed again the next day."

"I might have an idea," he said, "but I'll need approval from my boss."

If you haven't heard of entrapment in the context of a police investigation, it's a legal defense that's used when evidence can be shown that an officer induces a criminal to commit a crime they wouldn't otherwise commit. When this defense is used, there are two differing views. In some courts, if a defendant uses entrapment as a defense, the prosecution has to prove "beyond a reasonable doubt" that the criminal was not entrapped. In other courts, the defense has to prove that it was entrapped. The state I was in required the prosecution to do the proving.

Hernandez recognized that his plan could be construed as entrapment, and he explained this to me as we walked to his boss's office. He told me that since David had already established a pattern of breaking my windows, Hernandez could set up surveillance on the car and just wait for David to commit the crime he was going to do anyway. Since I had repaired my windows twice, and had kept the receipts, that would serve as good evidence that the crime had been repetitive.

The idea made me hopeful. I sat outside his boss's office while he walked in and presented his idea.

When he walked out, he gave me a thumbs up. David would never know what hit him.

Hernandez drove me to my house where I picked up my car and took it to a repair shop. He followed me over there and paid. We drove to my work in Hernandez's car while they worked on it.

Hernandez ordered us some lunch and I talked to my boss. I told him about my bank account getting hacked and that I needed to cancel direct deposit. Luckily, payroll was next week so they'd be able to change the method of payment by the next paycheck.

I told him about my situation and Hernandez backed me up. He agreed to pay some of my wages in advance out of the store's petty cash until payday came, and I was to pay him back. I thanked him profusely for helping me out and apologized for having to call in sick that day.

I walked out with a full stomach, $335, and a calm mind. With any luck, we'd catch David tonight.

Hernandez took me back to the shop and I picked up my car. I tried to pay from the money I'd received, but he refused, saying I could pay him back after this was all resolved. He told me he'd be at my house later on to start the surveillance and to just park my car on the street. I thanked him again before we parted.

It was about three pm when I got home. I parked my car several blocks away and next to several others for camouflage. I didn't want David to find it and smash the windows before tonight. The walk was hot, and cool air conditioning welcomed me into my house.

"Excuse me?" someone asked timidly as I unlocked my front door. I peeked my head back outside. There was an older woman on the landing, probably in her forties.

"Yes?" I replied.

"You live in that apartment, I'm guessing?" she said.

"Yeah."

"I'm Mrs. Watson. I believe you and my son are roommates."

"Oh. Oh! Hello," I said, extending my hand. "Whose mom are you?"

"Isaac," she replied. "He and I were supposed to be driving out of state to visit family yesterday, but he never showed up."

A chill ran up my spine.

"I've called him a thousand times, but he hasn't answered," she continued. "I've been standing here ringing the doorbell for a while, but no one has been home. Can I go knock on his door?"

I considered asking her to leave or telling her that I wasn't comfortable with her coming in, but I knew that would have been suspicious. I knew what we were going to find.

I told her to come in, and instantly the smell overtook us. She tried to be polite and not offend me, probably thinking we were typical college guys living like pigs. She walked down the hall to Isaac's room.

"Oh God," she muttered. The smell must have been horrific right by the door. I shuddered, but went down the hall toward her.

She knocked. "Isaac?" she called. No answer, as I expected.

"Isaac, it's Mom," she said. I think the smell made her start to panic because she pounded harder on the door.

"Isaac, open up please," she pleaded desperately. I sighed.

Gently, I guided her away from the door and braced myself. I took a running start and slammed into the door. It bent heavily, but the latch didn't break. I tried again. And again. On the fourth try, the door wrenched open and I was inside. The smell, oh God. I don't know how many times I can tell you about it until you understand.

This was one of those moments where I'll remember every detail forever.

Isaac's room was a mess. There were three bookshelves that likely used to have tons of books, but the shelves were torn apart and books were scattered across the room. His computer desk had papers scattered across it and cups knocked over. The window was darkened by a blackout curtain used for gaming. The large gaming computer under the desk hummed and the monitor showed stars moving around for a screensaver.

Isaac was on the bed. His face was pale and patchy with purple lines. His arms and legs were white and also bruised. An extension cord trailed off the bed, the middle being wrapped around his neck several times. Some flies nested on his body, flying to another spot occasionally.

Mrs. Watson entered the room and screamed. I just stood there, staring at Isaac's dilapidated body.

David had jumped to murder.

I called the police and tried to get Mrs. Watson to leave the apartment and preserve the crime scene. She refused and sat sobbing next to Isaac's bed. She was afraid to touch him.

The police came immediately and escorted Mrs. Watson and I out of the apartment. The next few hours were a blur of questions and police. Detective Hernandez showed up and looked inside. Techs were carrying in cameras and briefcases full of equipment.

After a while, they started to carry out some of Isaac's belongings in bags. His gaming computer took two techs to carry out. I sat on the curb nearby, not being allowed to leave by the head officer who was running the scene.

Hernandez sat next to me. "They broke open your other roommate's door. All his belongings are there, but your roommate isn't. Do you know where he is?"

"No," I replied. "I never talked to him much."

"Were you close to Isaac?" he asked.

"No, but it's still…"

"I know," he said. "Do you think David is behind this too?"

"Probably," I replied, feeling numb.

"We'll still carry out the surveillance," he assured me. "Don't worry. They'll analyze Isaac's body and if they find so much as a fleck of skin that we can link to David, we'll nail him. No criminal is perfect."

Hernandez left me alone and I thought over the situation.

Then a car parked nearby and out stepped Clark with his mom. I jumped up and ran over to him.

"Oh my God, Clark, are you okay?" I asked.

"I'm fine," he smiled reassuringly. "Posted bail. It was 350 bucks, so not awful."

"I thought you said you'd be here by five?" I asked Clark's mom. Side note: I don't remember the exact time she got there, but I do remember she was earlier than expected. I was going to meet them both at the station.

"I may have broken a few speed limits," she said in a neutral tone.

"What's happened?" Clark's face suddenly went cold when he saw all the policemen near our door.

"Isaac was found…" I said, "… in his room." I didn't have to specify what state he was in.

"Jesus CHRIST," Clark gasped, putting his hands on his knees. He started hyperventilating, and his mom worriedly put a hand on his back.

"Clark, honey, let's just go for a drive. We can get your stuff later."

"Your stuff?" I asked.

"He's moving out," his mom said sharply. "He told me all about this sick game your friend is playing. I don't think it's very funny."

"It's NOT funny!" I shouted. "It never was! This fucking asshole is trying to ruin my life! IT'S. NOT. A. GAME."

A few of the policemen turned to watch me from the balcony. Her jaw tightened and she guided her hyperventilating son into the car. They drove away, and I was left in the middle of the street, watching my best friend leave me to handle David alone.

***

The police took Isaac out in a body bag. Mrs. Watson left with the body, still sobbing uncontrollably.

I was told that I couldn't go into my apartment until they were completely done with the crime scene. No, they didn't know when that would be. They suggested a hotel room, which I laughed at. I asked if I could grab a blanket and a pillow from my room so I could sleep in my car. They reluctantly brought it to me, and I gagged when I grabbed them. They smelled like death.

Hernandez offered to get me a motel room, or let me stay at his place, or even begged me to call a friend and stay with them. I refused all three.

I walked to my car and ignored Hernandez. I was still too mad about everything and devastated that Clark had left. Besides, we couldn't do surveillance on the car while I slept in it. I marched all the way to my car and slammed the door hard.

I decided I didn't feel safe parking near my house to sleep, so I went to a Walmart parking lot for the night.

It was as if fate had finally begun to root for me. I was walking toward the Walmart entrance from the parking lot to buy some food. When I was only a few cars away, an armored truck pulled up—the ones that carry the money over to the bank, you know what I mean.

And who do you think stepped out of the truck?

David. Fucking. King.

I strafed to my left and got behind a car, using the back tinted windows to observe. He was laughing with his partner, who got out of the passenger side. I was too far away to hear what they were saying, but I definitely didn't recognize the partner as anyone I knew. It was obviously paranoia, but I wondered if he could be the one who had made Katie speak into the phone.

The two of them walked into Walmart, and I took note of the company that owned the truck. And then I had an idea. My first real idea on how I could fight back now that I knew where David was right this second.

I sprinted back to my car.

A little while later, I pulled up to Mrs. K's house. I got out and looked around, making sure David hadn't somehow beaten me here or followed me. I had to hurry. Who knew how much longer his shift would last?

I knocked on the door, and Mrs. K opened it.

"Hello, Zander," she said cheerfully.

"Hi, Mrs. K! Can I come in?"

Five minutes later, I was rifling through David's room. Had to hurry. Had to find something useful, and fast. I'd told Mrs. K that years ago I'd let David borrow a video game and just now remembered and wanted to pick it up. She had happily let me go into his room to find it.

I had booted up his ancient laptop, but it was taking forever to load. Why the hell hadn't he bought a new laptop with all the money he stole? That would have made good evidence.

I glanced at every paper I saw, hoping for something. Written plans. A checklist. A receipt. Anything. Every paper I found was normal, from what I could see. His room was a disaster, which worked in my favor. He may have dropped something incriminating and not known about it.

I stuffed every flash drive I could find into my pockets as I went. He had four of them lying around. They might have incriminating evidence on them.

The laptop finally booted, and I instantly tried to log in. No luck: password protected. I should have known, considering how tech-savvy he'd been in hacking my accounts. In fact, all the incriminating data was probably on the laptop. He wouldn't bother printing anything out.

That gave me an idea. I picked up the laptop and flipped it over. A toolbox laid under the table and I snatched a screwdriver from it. Using the screwdriver, I went to work disassembling the laptop.

When I'd finished, I held his hard drive up in my hand.

"I will ruin you, David King," I whispered.

As I reassembled the laptop, something caught my eye under the bed. A box. Furrowing my eyebrows, I pulled it toward myself. It was a shoe box with dust covering the top. A few spots were less dusty where someone had handled the lid. I opened it slowly and peered inside.

It contained a quarter-inch-thick stack of pages all bound together by a binder clip. The box was too small to let the pad lay flat, so it curled in the box. The pages were old and worn. They'd clearly been handled frequently. I lifted it out and noticed that it looked like a research paper. The front page had a title in the middle of the page and an author at the bottom.

"Psychological Evaluation for: David Edward King." The bottom of the page had the name of the institute and psychologist that had done the study as well as the year. I did the math, and the evaluation must have been done when he was sixteen.

Jack. Pot.

I stuffed it under my shirt as best I could to hide its square form. The laptop was set back in its place as if it had never been moved. David would know something was wrong eventually, but not until he booted it up. I gave a last look around and wondered if there was anything else I should do.

With no decent ideas, I left David's house.

Mrs. K gave me a brownie on my way out.

On the drive back to the Walmart, I tried to come up with a plan. I couldn't take this to the police because it was illegally obtained evidence and wouldn't be admissible in court. I knew that from a bunch of crime shows. I had to get at the evidence myself and somehow get it into the police's hands legally.

When I parked at the Walmart, it still wasn't that late. I walked inside, carrying the flash drives and psychological evaluation with me.

I used the demo computers to look at the contents of the flash drives. Looking back now, I'm amazed they let USB sticks work on the demo machines. The first flash drive had old high school papers on it. Nothing useful there. The second and third drives were bootable drives that could boot Linux.

It was on the fourth flash drive that I had my first breakthrough of evidence. It contained a single text file that had been edited the day before. As I read through it, I realized that it was a conversation. With my current understanding, the flash drive was how David and his kidnapping partner had been communicating. David would write a message and hide the flash drive in a predetermined place. Then the kidnapper would go pick it up and read the message. The process would reverse when the kidnapper had a message to pass along.

A lot of you will probably say, "Why wouldn't they just use encrypted emails? That's so much faster and safer." If they had used any kind of network to communicate, some internet service provider or some cellphone provider like Comcast would have a log entry of the messages being exchanged, even if the data was encrypted. Encrypted data is never 100% secure. If you dedicate enough processing power, you can crack any encryption. It may take thousands of years in some cases, but it could still be cracked. With our current advances in computing power, that could change to be even faster.

David and his partner had reduced their risk of being caught by limiting who had access to the information. If you send an email to me via Reddit, I'm not the only one that "gets" the message. It passes through several servers and routers that all make a note that a message passed through at a specific time. It leaves a trail. Unless you can erase the logs of those servers, you leave a trail no matter how you send your data.

There was certainly risk that someone could find the flash drive, plug it in, and find all of this data like I had, but that could be reduced by choosing decent hiding places. If you plan to pass messages this way, don't leave it lying around your room. Especially don't leave it unencrypted. I still don't know why it wasn't encrypted.

The text file would have a line, then skip a line and add another where the next response was. I don't have the flash drive or a copy of the conversation anymore, so I'll have to paraphrase as accurately as I can remember. I'll use bullet points here to format it more easily for you.

- Payment received?
- Yes.
- Last half of payment comes when this is all over.
- How long?
- Depends on him.
- Good?
- Good. No suspicion. A quiet grab.
- Was she harmed?
- She fought. A couple bruises. Otherwise fine.

There were some extra lines in between, marking the start of a new conversation.

- Any new information?
- A kidnapping report has been filed with the police. Change locations every two days as previously discussed. Are you well supplied?

- We have enough in the truck to keep moving and stay operational.
- Good. With any luck, this will be over soon once he makes an irreversible mistake.

I shuddered as I closed the text file. That was damning evidence. I checked who the owner of the file was. It was blank. Well, that would have been too convenient.

I googled the kind of cable I would need to hook the hard drive up to a computer, and bought a SATA to USB cable. I was thankful that the demo computers were in an aisle out of the view of employees in the tech center. To people who don't know technology, I'm convinced I looked like a hacker.

Let me give you another lesson on technology, since I seem to be giving so many in this series. When you boot your computer, it asks for a password if you've set one. Without that password, you can't access the hard drive unless you do some hacked-up workaround. In some cases, however, you can unplug the hard drive and plug it into another computer instead. The new computer will treat it like a regular external hard drive and voila, you have access.

Unfortunately, David had encrypted his entire hard drive, so it was useless to me at the moment until I had some spare time to either guess the password or find someone who could crack it.

Going to the summer supply section of the store, I took a seat and pulled out the psychological evaluation and looked at the cover page again. "Psychological Evaluation for: David Edward King." I hope you realize that I've removed the institution, author, and date for privacy's sake.

I spent an hour skimming the contents, using the table of contents to navigate. I constantly had to look up lengthy words on my phone, but I was beginning to understand what went on in David's sick little mind.

I won't give you an entire rundown of his whole life, but the report contained transcribed interviews with his parents about incidents, a psychologist's observations while holding David in confinement, and a general list of events that had occurred in David's life that may have traumatized him.

These are the ones I remember:

- David set fire to animals constantly and poked them with various objects. When a snake lunged and bit him once in his backyard, his mother came out to find him whipping the limp body against a tree, guts spraying everywhere. His only explanation was, "it tried to hurt me."

- He was found designing traps for rabbits and other animals that were expertly hidden and designed. He claimed to have never looked at a wilderness guide to make them. His mother later found entire notebooks containing designs for traps. The traps were aimed at getting both animals and humans.

- His father died when he was twelve, which affected him greatly. He became quiet and reserved for years. The first day of high school, however, he changed overnight and became charismatic, energetic, and clever.

- In middle school, one of his teachers had been interviewed after an incident. She had noticed that three boys had begun picking on David, but he quietly took whatever they gave him. One day, she came to class, and all three boys sat ramrod straight and stared straight ahead. They didn't dare look at David, and David was smirking and trying to hide it.

7.   Finally, let me try to summarize what the psychologist wrote about David.

"David seems to have a constant need to harm other living things and cause suffering. Once, in my office, I found him stomping his feet on the floor. I asked what he was doing, and he admitted that he was trying to crush anything microscopic that could be on my floor. I seriously fear that he will not be able to remain in society without serious medication and therapy."

I had no idea that David had any of these problems or experiences. He and I had met when we were both seventeen. He'd been exactly as the report described: charismatic, energetic, and clever. I felt blind for not seeing any red flags, but I knew that he had intentionally hidden them well.

The psychologist made another entry a month later.

"David seems to have performed a complete 180 in his mood, actions, and demeanor. He has been polite and kind every time he has come in, and is very capable of being fully functional."

The sentence struck me as odd. Months of statements about David's instability, and suddenly this comes out?

I googled the professor's name. He'd died in a car crash the same year as the publication date on this evaluation. Son of a bitch. I reread the very last entry. I recognized the words for what they were: a coerced recommendation to reenter society. I could feel the psychologist's words scream through the page.

"Good God, he's going to kill me."

No wonder David was so prepared. No wonder he was always ahead of me. No wonder his expression had spread such an absolute fear through me that night he chased Clark and me. He was insane. He designed traps. He knew what made people and animals tick. He enjoyed inflicting pain on them, and not just that, but watching them suffer.

David was absolutely insane. Insane, but functional. That's what made him dangerous.

I hunkered down in my seat and brought up a Word document in my phone where I could take notes. Then, I started googling. You know what I'm talking about. You're facing a problem, and so you start searching for anything online that could help you fix your problem. The internet was a wonderful tool for me at that moment. Without it, I'd have been dead months ago.

I was kicked out of the Walmart for loitering, but I continued my research in my car. I turned the car on every once in a while to drive around and charge my phone battery.

That night, I learned a lot about hacking, phones, Android, surveillance, police procedure, legal procedure, and all kinds of subjects that related to my situation. I took dutiful notes and outlined areas for further research and learning.

During my research, I found a list of apps that could be used for hacking someone's phone. I checked my installed applications, and can you guess what I found buried in my phone? One of those apps.

David Fucking King had been eavesdropping and tracking me through my phone. Instead of deleting the app, however, I kept it. It could be useful in the future.

I also researched the company David apparently worked for. It was a larger company that served several states, providing "both long and short distance transport of valuable goods." This was good information. If his job was to handle valuable goods, then it could be an easy way to get him fired or even charged if some of it disappeared from his truck. His truck was long gone by then, so I had no current opportunity.

During all hours of the night, Hernandez would call me. So would Katie's mom. I ignored them both. That was a big mistake, I'd later learn.

When the sun rose, I didn't feel tired; I felt empowered.

Finally, I knew more about my situation and enough to be useful. I knew how to get those hard drives to the police legally, but I'd need Clark and Hernandez's help.

I never got to use that plan, though. Reality caught up with me. David moved too quickly.

I was driving to my apartment to see if I could at least brush my teeth and take a shower before work that day when my phone buzzed. It was Hernandez. I answered it reluctantly, prepared to get an earful for ignoring him all night.

"Zander, where are you?" he asked.

"Driving to my apartment," I replied.

"You need to come down to the police station…" he said slowly. "Right away."

"Why? What's up?" I asked.

"It's… bad," he said with a cringe.

Confused, I hung up and turned right, heading toward the police station.

I walked into the police station lobby to find Hernandez waiting for me.

"Did Isaac's body turn up anything?" I asked, looking at his worried expression.

"They're still analyzing it," he said. Then he took a deep breath. "Some… new development has come up."

I gave him a questioning look, and then felt cold metal click around my right wrist. I reacted, but the two cops who had flanked me pulled my arms together. The metal clicked around my other wrist, handcuffing me.

"WHAT THE HELL!" I shouted. The policemen each gripped one of my arms.

"Zander, I know you're upset about everything that's going on," Hernandez said quietly. "But what you did went way too far."

"What the fuck are you talking about?!"

Hernandez held up a bag containing a phone. He used the touch screen through the bag and navigated to the phone's voicemail.

The voicemail was jolty and sounded like whoever had the phone was running. Wind struck the mic, making it hard to hear in places. But the voice was unmistakable. It was mine.

"Fuck you, jackass. You ruined my credit, stole my money, hacked my accounts, and stole my shit! I'm going to kill you! You think I need motivation to hurt you? I'm going to kill you, you son of a bitch. You'll burn in Hell! You'll burn!"

My heart shuddered to a halt. I had said those things. I had literally said those things. The night David chased us and pinned me to the table, I'd said every word. The bastard had been recording the whole thing, and now had edited it into a threatening voicemail.

"David King's home burned down last night," he said slowly, watching me. Gauging me.

"David and his mother were still inside. Firefighters found David alive and were able to pull him out, but his mother was already dead. That voicemail was sent to his phone from yours at around the time firefighters estimate the fire started."

I lost my breath. My eyes watered. The world closed in. I couldn't speak.

Couldn't defend myself. Couldn't explain.

"Zander Jones, you're under arrest."

***

I laid in an empty cell, trying to catch a small nap since I'd been up all night. My mind was racing though, and made it hard to sleep. I kept rehearsing what I was going to say when Hernandez finally came to get me.

They'd emptied my pockets into evidence bags, took my fingerprints, and one cop was heading out to search my car. I wasn't dumb. I knew that the evidence would point the police to three conclusions.

One: that I'd been in David's home recently. After all, the data on those flash drives had been updated just the day before. Even the ones that didn't have the kidnapping transcription on them.

Two: the flash drive containing messages between David and his partner might lead them to believe I had kidnapped Katie.

And three: that I'd stolen David's hard drive, as well as confidential medical information.

I kept trying to play out the conversation with Hernandez. I hoped it would pan out the same way it was running in my head.

I was woken up by a slight knock on the bars. My eyes peeked open to see a man in a suit standing there accompanied by an officer.

"Hello, sorry to disturb you," he said sheepishly. "I'm Terry Jayson, your public defender. May we talk?"

"Yes, of course," I said, sitting up. The officer entered and cuffed me. We were both led to the interrogation room where I'd met Hernandez for the first time.

"I trust you will shut off the cameras," he said to the officer. The cop nodded, removed my handcuffs, and closed the door.

"You can call me Terry," he said, reaching out to shake my hand. We sat down opposite each other with the table between us. "I've heard a little about your case in a brief overview from the chief," he said, pulling folders from a briefcase.

"It's... well it's long," I admitted.

"So I hear," he said. "I'm going to have to apologize in advance. It's likely that you'll have to repeat your story many times during these proceedings. To prevent this as much as possible, you and I are going to sit down and write your version of events down. That way, you can fall back on your statements and ensure that what you say is consistent and accurate. Does that sound good to you?" he said.

It made sense, so I nodded.

"First, I have a contract here for you to sign that says you agree to let me represent you in criminal proceedings." He pushed a paper and pen across the table to me. I skimmed it and signed at the bottom. He pulled it back.

"Would you like me to call you Zander or Mr. Jones?" he asked with an easy smile.

"Zander is fine," I replied.

"Okay, Zander. Let's start writing."

Terry sat patiently with me while I wrote every detail I could think of. I began with my dare conversation with David and continued all the way up to being arrested. It started out as a page with scrambled memories and words to jog my memory. Then it slowly formed into a something that Terry helped me edit into a cohesive, fact-based statement.

"When you are asked about your memories or an event, refer them to this document," he said. We worked for an hour before he spoke again.

"I have to go to another appointment, but I've asked that you be allowed to continue working in your cell. I've scheduled a meeting with the prosecutor and Detective Hernandez tomorrow at noon. Do you think you can have it complete by then?"

"Yes, I think so," I said.

And I did. I spent the rest of my day writing that statement. I slept sporadically, but I was desperate to complete it before noon the next day. So much had happened, and I had so much to say.

I was quite proud of the results.

The next day, at noon, I was back in the interrogation room. Terry sat to my left. Hernandez stood against the wall, facing me with his arms crossed. I couldn't read his expression.

On the other side of the table sat an older man who had introduced himself as Chief Gunderson. Hernandez's boss. Beside him stood a tall, lanky man with slicked back hair. He held his hands behind his back, watching me intently.

The tape recorder between us was running.

"I've been brought up to date on the cases you're involved in," Chief Gunderson said in a gruff voice. "I'm interested to hear everything from your perspective considering the… recent developments."

"You arrested me just to hear my side of the story?" I snipped.

"No, I arrested you because you are suspected of burning down Anne King's house and thereby killing her," Chief Gunderson said. "Hernandez tells me that you might have felt justified in doing so considering all the accusations that you've levied against Mr. King. So, I'd like to hear what has happened from the beginning and hear your side of events."

"Who's he?" I asked, pointing to the lanky man.

"I'm the prosecutor, Adam Leuderman," he answered.

"Oh, so you'll be the one trying to put me in prison," I quipped. Terry put a warning hand on my leg.

"I'll be trying to establish the truth about what happened," he corrected, glaring down at me.

"My client has prepared a statement that he intends to wholly rely on," Terry said, pushing copies of the seventeen handwritten pages across the table. The chief and prosecutor took one. Hernandez stepped forward and grabbed one too. He instantly started reading from his spot in the corner. I tried to catch his eye, but he didn't look at me.

"I trust we can begin the process of discovery today?" Terry asked. "I'll need copies of everything, as well as a copy of the official indictment."

I tuned Terry out and focused on Hernandez. There was something about his demeanor that caught my attention. I couldn't tell what it was. I focused on him for the entire meeting, trying to figure out what my instinct was telling me.

They talked over legal details with Terry and corroborated the process of discovery between the two parties.

A couple days later, Terry was sitting with me in the interrogation room again, talking through what he'd learned from discovery. Discovery is when the two sides of a case share evidence so there are no surprises when they go to trial. Anything not brought up in discovery is not admissible in court.

Before trial, though, would come my arraignment. That's when the formal charges would be laid against me and I would have to plead either guilty or not guilty. Terry was talking through discovery with me so I would be prepared for what they'd say during the hearing and decide whether I'd plead guilty or not guilty.

Here's what I learned.

After I'd been arrested, the police had searched my car and found the hard drive, flash drives, and psychiatric evaluation. And something else that was curious—a half-empty gas canister. That fucker had planted a gas can in my car at some point without me knowing. I'd been in my car all night, so either David knew he was going to burn his house down before I went to Walmart, or he planted it in the few minutes I was in the police station. I told Terry about the gas can being planted, and he wrote down some notes.

The police had searched through the contents of all the flash drives and discovered the conversation between David and his partner. Except, as predicted, they accused me of writing the messages and therefore linked me to a kidnapping. The text file never specified Katie's name, but they claimed Katie's kidnapping was the most likely scenario since I knew about it and was therefore involved.

Despite this evidence, however, the prosecution didn't feel like they could convince a jury without more evidence. So, Katie's kidnapping wasn't planned to be laid against me as a formal charge, but they were searching for evidence.

They had also tried to open the contents of David's hard drive, but found that it was encrypted, just like I had. They'd sent it off to a lab to be analyzed for whatever data could be salvaged.

The medical report was classified as inadmissible because it pertained to an individual who did not consent to the dissemination of its contents. As a citizen of the United States, you get some control over who can look at your medical records. Denying its use in a courtroom is a right in certain situations, including this one. David had decided to exercise that right and deny access.

As a result, the prosecutor could only charge me with possession of someone else's medical records without permission. That was a serious crime, apparently.

Terry had also been informed that the identity theft case was being combined into the charges against me. The credit card companies had done their own investigations and were filing criminal charges against me for fraud. Why would they do that? Because "a technical investigation into the origin of the registration for the fraudulent cards found that the reporter himself, Zander Jones, had indeed filled out and completed the registration forms from his own computing device." In other words, they traced the IP address of whoever had filled out the registration forms for the cards online and found that my computer had been the one to sign up.

Which meant they were accusing me of signing up, spending all the money, and then reporting fraud. Also a major crime.

The emptying of my bank account was also pinned on me. Again, they claimed I was trying to commit fraud by filing a false claim with the bank.

The police had finally gotten the security tapes from the convenience store where the ATM was located. There were three angles. One camera was above the door, one was above the register, and one was in the far corner of the store opposite the ATM.

The tapes showed a man in a dark hoodie walk into the store. The video was grainy as you would expect, but despite that, a large symbol on the back of the hoodie could be recognized. The man in the hoodie walked to the ATM and pulled something from their pocket. The prosecution claimed it was a cellphone since the timestamp on the camera matched the timestamp of the login to my bank account.

The hooded figure looked down at it for a few minutes before typing into the ATM, blocking the screen with their body. The money spat out, he grabbed it, and walked toward the door. The camera on the opposite corner from the ATM was the only one able to catch a glimpse of his face. It was grainy, but the prosecution compared it to pictures from my Facebook profile to claim that it had just enough resemblance to have been me. Comparing to David's pictures, it could have been him too.

I argued that point with the prosecutor pretty fiercely.

When I was done with my outburst, the prosecutor told me that the investigators had also found a hoodie with the same logo in my apartment.

Then they played their trump card. The bank had been logged into from the IP address assigned to my own cellphone during that time period.

Regarding the fire, which was the main accusation against me, they had decent evidence. The gas can was one, and the voicemail was another. But there was even stronger evidence. When I first arrived at Walmart, I parked near the front doors, in view of the cameras hanging off the building. They clearly saw me drive away when I was heading to David's house.

When I came back, though, I had parked in the back of the lot, intending to be away from other cars while I slept. The cameras could barely make out my car parking in the back lot. It was too dark to tell if it was even a vehicle, the prosecutor claimed. So, realistically, I only had my own testimony to support the fact that I got back to Walmart at around six pm.

I should add that it took about fifteen minutes to get to David's house from the Walmart. Just so you can understand the time frame.

Fire crews had received a call at 6:04 pm that David's home was on fire. They had raced over immediately and found the house burning brightly. David had been found trying to lift his mother up from the ground in her bedroom. They'd brought them both out, and it was discovered that Mrs. K was already dead from suffocation. David had been rushed to the hospital with a few minor burns and some smoke inhalation. He had yet to explain his version of events to police.

The firefighters had filed a report stating that the fire had been started from the middle of the living room where a puddle of gasoline had ignited.

The flames had spread throughout the house. Traces of gasoline were found in various rooms, making them believe that the suspect (me) had gone from room to room and splashed gasoline around. Just like in the movies.

They also concluded that the fire had been started some time before it was called in because of how much damage had already occurred by the time they arrived.

I now know that David had set an alert on his phone that was linked to the app he had installed on my phone. When my GPS read that I was at his house, an alert would be sent to his phone as a text message. I can only guess that he'd jumped in his car, left work, and sped all the way home. That's why I think the time was so close.

I'm telling you all of this detail so you can see just how hopeless I felt while I sat in jail. I was there for two whole weeks where it was the same accusations and evidence over and over. I really started to just give up.

During the first few days, I asked Terry about how we could prove that it was David specifically who had committed these crimes. He frowned and told me I should be more concerned about being proven innocent period, not on pinning it to another man.

By the end of two weeks, I was ready to just plead guilty rather than fight.

The arraignment went poorly. No charges were thrown out that had been placed against me. I would list all the crimes I was being charged with, but I don't remember their exact phrases and I know I'll get it wrong. You get the general idea though that I was fucked.

Bail had been set at $5,000, which essentially guaranteed I'd be stuck in jail for a while. I had already contacted my parents out of desperation and they would try to raise money from family members and friends, but couldn't pay immediately.

After three weeks, I was very depressed and not eating much. Terry tried to cheer me up by showing me parts of arguments he was preparing, but nothing could cheer me. I thought about Katie a lot. And Clark and Ivan. And I missed my parents.

I also missed Clark's first hearing in the graffiti case, so I had no idea how that was going, which made me feel guilty that I couldn't support him.

During the time I was in jail, Hernandez only came to visit me once. It was during the third week. I jumped off my bed and ran to the bars.

"Hernandez," I said. "Please tell me you've come to give me good news."

"No," he said. "You're being transferred to the county jail. Your trial will be happening there."

"Why?"

He shrugged. "Just how it works," he said.

"Did they find anything on Isaac?" I asked. I'd been clinging to the hope that Isaac's body would turn up evidence against David. I just wanted to nail him for that one crime. Just one. I wanted it so bad that my hands would shake when I thought about it.

"I'm not allowed to talk about that," he said, avoiding my eyes. "Anyway, I came to tell you that you'll be moved in three days."

"Hernandez," I said as he turned to leave. "I thought you believed me."

"I did," he said. "Until you burned David's house down. Now I'm not so sure who the psychopath really is."

"I didn't do it!" I shouted, but he walked away.

Three days later, as Hernandez had said, they came to move me. After dinner, I was cuffed and led out the doors to a police cruiser that would drive me up to the county jail two hours away.

The two officers who drove were polite to me, but instantly cranked up the radio when we got on the road. I could barely hear myself think, and was starting to get frustrated. I had always hated car trips without my own music. Now I was stuck in a two-hour ride with my hands cuffed behind my back and a radio blasting music I didn't like.

We were about an hour in, and I was ready to scream. I stared out the window, trying to find something interesting to watch and focus my mind on. We were on a two-lane highway with no other cars in sight. It was getting late, so looking back, I figure people were home for the night and that's why it was so dead.

My view of a nice lake was suddenly obstructed by a big gray truck. I tried to find something else to look at, but then noticed it was getting dangerously close to our lane. I looked up at it and saw that it was an armored truck. And it had the same logo as the company David worked for.

The panic was instantaneous. Something gripped my lungs and kept me from vocalizing.

The truck slowly neared the side of the police cruiser before pressing against it. The cops shouted. The cop who was driving slammed on his brakes, and the other cop dropped the radio he was reaching for. The cruiser didn't slow down fast enough, however, and the truck nudged it off the road.

I braced for impact as we rolled down the grassy slope and slammed into a tree.

My seatbelt had held me in place, but my head ached when it rammed against the driver's head rest. The two cops were unconscious, lying at awkward angles. Neither of them had had their seatbelts on.

I started yanking at the handcuffs, trying to reach my seatbelt to undo it. I reached the red button and pressed it. When I turned back around to wriggle out of the loose seatbelt, I saw David Fucking King walking down the slope toward the car.

"Oh shit, oh shit, oh fuck," I cursed, turning to reach for the door handle with my cuffed hands. No such luck. The doors were locked from the outside to prevent prisoners from opening the doors on their own.

David got closer and closer until he was right outside the car. He shot a smirk at me and opened my door. I tried to back away, but he grabbed my arm and tossed me out of the car. I fell to the dirt with a gasp.

I sat up a little and saw that he'd turned his attention back to the police car. I saw one of the cops beginning to stir.

David opened the driver's door and pulled something small from his pocket. With a quick motion, he stabbed the cop in the neck. Blood spurted out, and the cop started screaming and gurgling, grabbing for his neck. I think I screamed too, but I can't remember.

He closed the door and walked around to the other side. I could see that the other cop was moving, but I couldn't tell what he was doing. Apparently he was reaching for his radio, because David yanked it out of his hands and set it on the car's roof. Then he stabbed that cop too.

Both of them were unconscious in seconds.

"Don't get up," he threatened, walking toward me. I didn't bother trying. He walked over to where I sat and went behind me. I tried to face him, but he kicked me lightly. He knelt down and I felt him scratching the metal on my handcuffs. I was confused, but sat absolutely still.

"Nice to see you again, Zander," he said, walking to stand in front of me. I watched him with true fear. His entire demeanor was different from the night we'd graffitied his house. He was changing.

When I didn't answer, he laughed. He was twisting the small object in his gloved hands. I noticed, through the blood, that it was a crudely crafted shiv about the length and width of a finger.

"I told you, I'm not going to kill you, Zander. In fact, for once, I'm here to help you out. Sort of."

"What does that mean?" I asked shakily.

"Remember the night you graffitied my house?"

I nodded.

"I told you I'd consider giving you advice in how to succeed in our game. Well, the time has come. I'm giving you more than advice. See, you're no fun in jail. I've seen the evidence they have on you. You're going away for a long time. I don't want that. So, I'm granting you a second chance to keep playing."

He walked behind me again, and I felt sticky blood on my fingers and hand as he pressed the small shiv against my hand.

"Now, here's how this works," he said, standing back in front of me. "I'm going to leave this knife with your fingerprints on it in the car. They'll think you stabbed the cops and made a run for it. I'm going to remove your handcuffs and let you make a run for it. You'll have a thirty-minute head start before I call in on the radio.

"Oh God, he has a knife! He's stabbed the driver and he's—" David cut off, mimicking the call he'd make. Goosebumps ran up my spine.

"I'll be sitting here and waiting. If you attempt to come back, I'll just take you away in my car and we'll play a different game. Do you understand?"

I nodded, too terrified to speak.

"Get up," he commanded. I struggled to my feet, rolling in the dirt to get to my knees and stand.

"Come here," he said, moving toward the police car. I followed. He opened the police car door and put his hand against the officer's neck. I flinched when he flicked blood at me. It splattered across my jail suit and face. I almost threw up.

"There we go," he purred. He motioned for me to turn around, and I did. He pulled the handcuff keys off the dead cop and unlocked the cuffs. I rubbed my wrists. They were sore and marked from the car crash.

I considered trying to get the shiv from him and attack, but the idea of going with him in his car to play "other games" terrified me.

David had set a backpack next to the car, and now set it in my hands.

"Hernandez says hello," he said with a malicious grin. "I paid him a lot of money to get him to let me track this car. He demanded that I give you half. Of course, I'm not that generous, so here's $2,000, a change of clothes, new shoes, and a map. Nearest town is ten miles west. Better hurry. Remember, in thirty minutes I'm calling it in."

My jaw shook as I put the backpack on and started heading toward the setting sun. The forest looked dark and menacing.

I looked back when I was partway through the trees and there he was. He leaned against the car, drinking from the coffee container one of the cops had brought with him.

Shuddering, in shock, and absolutely terrified, I walked on into the woods.

***

I honestly don't remember most of the night after the car crash. I only have glimpses of memories, and I won't try to coherently express them here.

I got my bearings back after I'd slept off the shock. My higher functions kicked back into gear after I'd gone to a grocery store and bought a small amount of food. The amount of hunger that shock can induce is extreme.

I had rifled through the backpack and found exactly what David had said: clothes, a pair of shoes, $2,000 cash in hundreds and twenties, and a road atlas booklet. I still have that atlas and use it when I'm moving on.

Once I had food, water, and an inventory of my belongings, I could start to plan and work.

I dumped my jail clothes in a dumpster and paid for a haircut to try and alter my appearance. Yes, I washed the blood off my face and hair before going in.

When I looked in the mirror afterward, I still recognized myself so I paid the hairdresser to dye my hair too. I know there are self-dying kits that cost way less, but I had nowhere to do it.

I knew I couldn't stay in that town because David would know exactly where to find me. I had no idea how long this truce would last, so I had no intention of staying there one more night. I bought a bus ticket to an adjacent state and arrived only a few hours later.

The town I chose was larger than the one I had come from. This was intentional so that I could have anonymity and a better selection of services for the homeless. This town had a soup kitchen that I could use to cut down on costs as well as a homeless shelter.

I knew I couldn't live long on the already-dwindling $2,000, so I started going to the library and searching online for odd jobs. I had to find something that wouldn't require a background check, if at all possible, because of the manhunt that was probably going on for me. I'd seen nothing about it in the news yet, but it had only been a day.

After a week of searching, I found a job at a seedy telemarketing place that paid cash under the table. You'd be surprised how many of these there are. I hated the work, but I was out of the sun and making some money.

Before I found a run-down and half-empty apartment complex to live in and pay weekly, I slept in the homeless shelter. I could have just stayed there and saved a lot of money, sure, but I hated going there and avoided it as long as possible when night time came. The money I spent on the apartment was well worth it.

I had some semblance of a life set up and now I could get the real work done.

I had gone to the mall and bought the cheapest prepaid Android phone they had and signed up for a monthly subscription that gave me unlimited data as well as texts and calls. I'd need to find a store to pay cash and top up every month, but it wasn't an expensive plan. And I needed internet when the library was closed.

During the days, I'd spend my time in the library with a cheap notebook I'd bought, doing more research similar to what I had done in the Walmart parking lot. I also spent a lot of time working out and trying to get stronger. Before I had the apartment, I'd paid for a gym membership and showered there instead of at the homeless shelter. I decided to keep the membership and use their machines to get a more effective workout.

The plan at the time had been to stay alive and away from David and the cops. I stayed inside the day the news broke of my escape in the other state. The police finally admitted to needing help in finding me and went public for a request for information. They listed off the crimes I was accused of as well as a request to question me in regards to the two dead policemen. I wrote down every detail of the investigation, though none of it proved useful other than as background knowledge. I kept up with the sporadic news releases so I could stay as far ahead of the cops as possible.

For the next six months, I stayed in that city.

During that time, I learned a lot. Living on a tiny budget, home repairs when the landlord wouldn't fix something, hiding when you suspect you're being followed, and navigating the streets at night all became second nature to me.

I also continued to study computers and networks. I am by no means any kind of licensed professional. I learned by deciding what I wanted to know how to do, and then practicing it over and over.

One day, I was at the library when the news was published online. David Fucking King was suspected of murdering the two cops. I was ecstatic and couldn't believe my luck. David King had finally made a mistake that had cost him. The news story did not specify why the police suspected him, but I didn't care. David was going to get what he deserved.

A month passed with still no news on whether David had been captured or not. I found myself tempted to call Detective Hernandez and ask what he knew. But I didn't. I'd learned a lot of self-control and risk assessment during those seven months. Risk analysis was built into my daily decisions.

After checking for news on David for the third time in a week, I decided that I would no longer be a bystander waiting for David to be caught.

I decided to begin actively hunting David.

Since I knew he was good with computers, the internet was the best place to begin looking for traces of him. I searched hundreds of forums, scouring for a list of keywords that I thought David would either post or look for. I won't include that list here.

In only a couple weeks, I found one of his online accounts on StackExchange. I took notes on everything he commented as well as his account activity. Fortunately, he had kept the same account for several years. Granted, it was under a pseudonym, but he'd kept it. He still uses it today, actually. I just checked. He was logged in seven hours ago when I wrote this.

Once I found the first account, it held clues to many others. He slipped out information accidentally that I could use to locate his other accounts. Posts like, "I've asked this question on this other forum and got no response, so now I am asking it here," would link two accounts and reveal yet another goldmine of data for my study.

I spent weeks gathering pseudonyms, post records, and IP addresses he'd used—anything I could find with the tools I had available. Some pseudonyms he used more than once, and others he created as throwaway names.

The research gave me invaluable insight into the way David thinks, talks, and acts. I got to know him on a level I could never have hoped to understand from just being his friend in high school. It made my hate for him grow, not diminish.

I didn't only check the regular web either. Some people claim the deep web is a terrifying place where you can get killed at every turn, but it isn't if you don't act stupid. I installed Tor and began doing the same data mining in the deep web. The results were fantastic. I found catalogs worth of information. I was able to identity a lot of his false identities online and then map them to the fake social media pages he had created for them when he might need a cover up.

And all of this came because he insisted on using the same usernames over and over again. Why did he do that? Because he wanted people to know who he was when they interacted and respect him.

Weakness.

One day, just for the hell of it, I sent him a message as myself to one of his accounts. I made my email address visible on purpose. He'd need it.

The spam mail started instantly after that. The response was so childish and brash that I was smiling that whole day. I knew that I could get to him.

I also tried calling the psychological institute where David's records should be. If I was lucky, I could get my hands on another copy of his evaluation and study it with new eyes. There was no such luck, however. David had called them and told them not to send copies to anyone because he was the current victim of fraud. How ironic.

I was able to use his accounts that were used the most to track down his location. Sometimes he used a VPN, and sometimes he didn't. Recently—last week, actually—he moved to a nearby city. He seemed to be following his own instructions to his partner to move along after only a couple of days. He was jumping from city to city, but not crossing the entire country every time he moved. He was making a snake-like trail throughout the country.

I went over to the town he'd moved to and walked the streets for hours, hoping for a glimpse of him. It was just my luck that he walked out of a grocery store just as I was walking in. He didn't notice me, but I followed him back to where he was staying. For a couple of days, at least, I knew where he was.

The next few days were spent in surveillance. I watched him day and night, following him everywhere. I saw no sign of Katie being with him, though, which made sense. His partner only came to visit once. He stayed for only ten minutes before leaving in a car I hadn't seen him arrive in. I blew my only opportunity to follow him since I had no car of my own.

When David moved on, I followed him. I slept on the streets again, unwilling to let him leave my sight. I followed him around and learned about him from his routines and habits. I had learned so much about my enemy and my nemesis that I was finally ready to confront him for the last time.

And now, everyone, we come to the crux of the story. This is the focal point that this entire series has led up to.

Hello, David King.

I know you're reading this. I see you check it during your morning coffee routine at Starbucks. It took you a few days to find it, but I knew that if I told the story through to the end, and gained enough popularity, you'd find it. The more people who became interested, the more likely you were to see it.

And now here you are.

I'm sitting here, watching to see your face when you read this part. This has been the build-up of the entire series. I wrote all of this for this one moment.

You've read every comment. I've seen you scrolling through them and opening sub-comments to see what they say. You're very invested in what everyone has to say. And the one thing you can conclude from the comments is this: EVERYONE HERE HATES YOU.

Every. Last. One.

Hundreds of people now hate you. Many of them have offered time, talent, and cunning toward your complete destruction. I have refused their help until now.

I want Katie back.

All my stalking hasn't told me what really matters: where she is. So, I'm using this story to get to you. Either you give Katie back, or I release everything about you to all these people who hate you. I know aliases, addresses, phone numbers, comments admitting to illegal activity, social security numbers, driver's licenses, passports, online account names, everything. The police will have it all too.

I've been tracking you for so long, David.

The first few lines of every post? Where I said, for example, that you'd almost found me? They were lies. I've been watching from afar during the entire publication of these posts.

Right now, as I am about to press submit, you just bought a sandwich at Jimmy John's. The meatball sub. It's currently Saturday, July 2nd, 7:32 pm. There's your proof that I'm nearby.

Convinced yet?

Bring Katie to Welles Park at ten pm tonight and leave your partner behind.

If you don't show, I will release all of the information I have, dedicate the rest of my life to updating that information, and release it to anyone here who wants to do something about it.

I've set up a timed release of the information. It will be automatically posted via private message to everyone who ever commented on these threads. And they will spread it even further.

The timed release will occur at three am tonight unless I'm there to stop it. You need two people to stop it, each one with their own password. No, I won't tell you who the other person is.

For everyone else here on the thread, I will have another post up in at least forty-eight hours. I'm giving myself a time buffer to respond in case David tries anything stupid. If I don't write an update, and the information has been released, you'll know what happened.

You have all asked what you could do to help me. If you receive the information, do what you need to do.

See you soon, David.

***

I put my phone in my pocket and watched David from across the street. He was eating dinner just like I said in my post. His phone clearly went off, because he perked up his head and grabbed his phone from the table. I'd seen his phone go off whenever I'd posted before, so I knew he had set an alert.

I watched his eyes scan the post with interest. Then his eyes slowly widened. I knew when he reached my favorite part, because his gaze shot up and looked around the restaurant. He wrapped up his sandwich and quickly walked out of the restaurant, his eyes scanning the street while stealing glances at his phone to keep reading.

It was a very satisfying scene. It makes me smile just thinking about it.

I didn't follow him home. Instead, I waited for the inevitable email.

Do you want to know why David was so scared of my information release? He was scared because the internet was his safe haven. He was powerful there. When we had our dare conversation, and for so long after that, I was the computer illiterate one and he ruled that domain. And now I had managed to track him in his safe place. Before, I had been weak and an easy target for his games. Now that I had seriously fought back and threatened him, he was worried.

The email came while I could still see him walking away.

"Hello Zander. Bravo, but I'm not going to meet in public," he wrote.

To be honest, I posted Welles Park online because I figured he would want to change the location if it was a public place, and I didn't want to release the real address online. I didn't want anyone crashing the party and getting hurt. Sorry for lying. I'll be apologizing for lying a lot by the end of this post.

I told him that I'd email him the new address fifteen minutes before it was time to meet. He didn't respond. I didn't want him to have the address too early and show up to set any traps. He really should have countered with a location of his own, but he didn't.

I stood up. Time to go to the warehouse and wait.

The location I had chosen used to be a warehouse of some kind. I didn't care what it had been used for, only that it was abandoned and unguarded. If David tried anything stupid, which I thought he was going to, I didn't want any more innocent bystanders in the way.

I took an Uber to a suburban area a few blocks away. When the Uber left,

I walked to the warehouse.

When I arrived, it was already almost nine pm. Not completely dark yet, but getting there. I walked around the perimeter of the warehouse, looking for any sign that David had beaten me here. There wasn't any that I could see.

I approached a side door and pulled a key out of my pocket. I unlocked the chains from the door handle and stored them just inside the door as I entered. The soundscape changed from an ambient evening in the city to a tomb.

The factory had a single floor that was one big, open space. High above it, catwalks ran along the rafters all leading from the warehouse manager's office, which was a metal cube suspended at one end of the warehouse.

Shelf scaffolding that had been abandoned broke up the empty space. Crates and pallets were strewn around here and there, making hiding places. I had previously come and strategically arranged them in case it came down to a fire fight.

That's also when I had put chains on every door. There were four entrances into the warehouse, not including the windows near the ceiling. I had chained them all except the one I entered through. That was my funnel. If you've ever gone hunting for live game, you know what I'm talking about.

There was nothing left to do but wait. I sent him the address at 9:45.

A rattling of the front door alerted me that he was here. He was a half hour late, which was an attempt to unnerve me. The door jolted repeatedly, but the chains held it shut. It was dark now. The only light streamed in the windows from industrial-style streetlights outside.

"How am I supposed to meet you if you won't let me in?" David called from outside. The hair on the back of my neck rose, despite all my preparations. It was time.

David tried all three doors. He skipped over the only one that was unlocked until he absolutely had to. He knew what a funnel was, but he had no choice. The windows were too high and would result in a very high fall once he got in.

The side door silently opened and in walked David Fucking King. I stayed where I was behind a wooden crate stacked with pallets. If he came in shooting, I didn't want to be an easy target.

Slow clapping filled the echoing room.

"Well done," David chanted. I peered through the pallets to see the door shut behind David. He was alone.

"Where is she?" I said just loud enough to be heard.

"I'm so very impressed with you, Zander. Completely unexpected." He pulled his phone out of his pocket, lighting up the wall behind him. He began to read.

"'Fuck you, David.' 'Hashtag, Fuck David King.' 'Zander, you brilliant bastard.' 'Go get your girl!' 'We are coming for you, David.' Thousands of these, almost all saying the same thing! How does it feel to have people rooting for you? Do you feel better equipped to fight me now?"

"Where. Is. She?" I enunciated.

David knocked on the door behind him, and it opened. In shuffled Katie. Her face was red and shimmering with tears. Duct tape had been wrapped around her entire head several times, covering her mouth. Her wrists had been similarly wrapped. A band of tape also tied her ankles together, but had enough slack that she could take small steps. A thick arm was wrapped around her neck as a tall blond man with extremely curly hair guided her into the room.

"I said to leave your partner behind!" I shouted. It echoed.

"If you don't want him here, then come kill him," David said.

I didn't respond. God-fucking-dammit.

"So, Zander, how would you like to proceed? You're running the show here," David called, looking around the warehouse.

"Send Katie forward and leave."

"Sorry, I don't have a guarantee that you won't release all that information anyway. Come on out here and we'll discuss my terms."

"Like hell I am."

David looked to his partner, and his partner used his free arm to punch Katie in the side. She cried out as best she could through the duct tape and faltered, but the blond man held her up by her neck.

"We can do this all night," David smirked.

I stood up. My hiding place was off to David's left, so I walked in a semicircle until I was directly in David's line of sight.

"Come closer," he grinned.

I stepped forward until we were a couple yards apart.

"Look how you've changed," he smirked. "Your hair looks good. You should always dye it darker. You're so stoic now! Confident! Being on the run has changed you! I guess all we had to do to increase the minimum required effort was go on the run, huh? Then maybe we could have avoided this whole mess. Then again, it's all been so fun."

"Let's get this over with," I growled.

"So hostile," David commented. "What's your first term?"

"He leaves," I said, pointing to the blond man.

"Okay," David shrugged. Before I could process what was happening, he pulled a handgun from his jacket pocket and shot the blond man in the head. He collapsed, dragging Katie with him. Katie gave a muffled shriek and untangled herself from his body, dragging herself backward along the floor. She backed into the wall and stayed there, eyes wide.

David looked down at the body before slowly turning his head to me.

"My turn."

Jesus Christ. It finally hit me how in over my head I was. I might understand David King, but I could never, ever match his sickness. It occurred to me that I could die that night, despite David's rules.

"Show me the data," he said. "That's my first term. I want to know exactly what you're going to release so I know it's worth my only bargaining chip."

I tried to hide my shaking hands as I pulled my phone out. I went into my email drafts on a throwaway account where I had saved a copy and emailed it to him.

"I sent it to you," I said. David smiled reassuringly.

Fast as a lizard, he spun around and snatched Katie off the floor. She screamed as he stood her up and held her in front of him.

I pulled my Ruger SR45 handgun out of the concealed carry holster I was wearing and tried to get a clear shot. He was too fast and had caught me by surprise, so she was in front of him before I'd even lined him up in the sight.

"So, you got a gun after all," he said coolly. "Didn't see that part in your posts. Relax, I'm just making sure I can read in peace."

He held the gun to her head with one hand while opening his phone with the other. My mind raced, trying to figure out the next steps. David had waltzed into a hostage negotiation that I had arranged myself and taken over.

He took his time reading through the data dump. His expression changed between surprise and a smirk repeatedly.

"Well now," he said, putting his phone away and slipping his now-free arm around Katie's neck. "I had no idea I was so careless." He sounded anything but careless.

Katie gasped as he suddenly gripped her neck tighter and pressed the muzzle against her temple.

"Let's move somewhere… smaller," he said, looking up at the manager's box. "I don't want you running away when the going gets tough. You first, Zandsand," he said, nodding his head toward the stairs to his right.

The door he had entered from had a set of grated stairs off to the right that led up to the manager's box. They went up toward the back wall, then turned to the left straight into the side of the manager's box. Another set of stairs should have been on the other side, mirroring these, but they had been disassembled and lay in a heap.

I kept my face to David as I walked toward the stairs. I kept my gun pointed in his direction, and he kept his muzzle against Katie's head. Katie was sobbing and watching me.

When I reached the stairs, I slowly backed up them. David followed once I was halfway up.

At the top of the stairs, the door to the office stood. To the left, a grated walkway led out over the floor, spreading into catwalks that sprawled the entire place.

I opened the metal door to the office and backed in. The only furniture in the room were two heavy, wood tables. The rest of the office was bare. A thin slit of a window overlooked the warehouse floor.

David pushed Katie into the room with his arm still around her neck and shut the door behind him. I followed him with my gun, standing against the opposite wall where the second door leading into the office was. The office was big enough that we were still a few yards away from one another.

"Now I don't have to worry about you running off into the dark warehouse. As fun as hide and seek sounds, I don't have the time.

"You know, when I found your posts, I thought I had stumbled across some sort of… therapy story that you were putting up. But it was so much better. You really have surprised me. You've grown and changed to try and beat me." David smiled.

"But you haven't changed enough. I can see it in your face and your trembling hands. You are still you, Zander. You've changed your exterior, but inside you have the same motivations, and weaknesses."

He tightened his grip on Katie again.

"I know your next term is for me to let Katie go, so I'm going to skip your turn. I know you would prefer that she remain in my custody rather than getting shot, so I suggest you put down your gun."

I stood my ground. I wanted to take a shot, but didn't want to risk him being faster than me. I was confident in my aim, but not my speed.

"Put it down," he said again. I stayed.

In an instant, the gun had left her temple, fired a shot into the floor, and returned to her head. She sobbed, and the heat of the barrel on her skin must've hurt.

"I'M NOT FUCKING AROUND, ZANDER!" David shouted.

Slowly, I set the gun on the floor and kicked it in his direction.

"Good choice," he said calmly. "Have you realized why you're here yet?"

My face answered him. What did that even mean? Of course I did!

"You think you're here to save Katie, but you aren't. She's been gone for a year now, and you've only built up memories of her. The Katie you knew is dead. But not even that Katie is the reason you're here right now. No, you gave up on a happily ever after with Katie long ago. This isn't a hero's quest to save the princess. This is a revenge assault on the dragon."

I tightened my jaw. I refused to admit he was right.

"This isn't about saving her. This is about outsmarting me. Keeping Katie safe and sound is just a result," David said, his smile growing.

"So, in that sense, you and I are the same now. It's about outsmarting the other one. You started out simply living life, then progressed to defending yourself, then to protecting your loved ones, and now you've arrived where I wanted you to be all along: trying to ruin me. It took you a couple years, but you made it. At least, most of the way.

"Even if Katie isn't the true reason you're here, she's still a weakness. I'm going to guess that other people in your life are the same way. You still have weaknesses that tie you down. I learned how to get rid of mine."

"Like your own mother?" I snipped.

"She was a liability," he said coldly. "It wasn't personal."

"You're a sick fuck," I said.

The door behind David silently opened. I'd oiled those hinges for hours, making sure they made absolutely no noise.

"I'm about to get a lot sicker," he said.

He'd started to pull the trigger when he was tackled from behind. Katie tumbled out of his grasp as he tried to use both arms to catch himself. His gun went off, but the shot hit the wall.

Katie rolled away from David's reach.

David started to get up, but the assailant was on their feet faster. David, on his hands and knees, looked up at the attacker.

"Remember me, BITCH?!" Clark jeered, and then punched in a downward arc into the side of David's head.

David dropped to the floor, but he was still conscious. He grabbed Clark's legs and tore him to the ground.

I raced forward and pulled Katie out of the scuffle. I dragged her out the door before getting her to her feet and cutting the tape on her hands with my pocket knife. There wasn't time to get the layers off her head. She was wide-eyed.

"Run!" I hissed. "Go outside! The cops will be here soon!" I turned back inside to go help Clark. Not a romantic reunion, I know, but there was still a psychopath in there.

David and Clark were wrestling on the floor, throwing punches and grappling with one another. David was bigger and landed a few hard punches. I looked over my shoulder, making sure Katie was stumbling down the steps.

I dove in, aiming for my gun that was just beside the scuffle.

David saw me and kicked my legs like a tentacle out of the ocean. I tripped and knocked the gun into the corner when I fell. David suddenly shoved Clark off of him, practically tossing him onto one of the tables. I watched as David jumped up and made for his gun.

I writhed on the ground and kicked. My toes barely caught the gun and sent it skittering across the room.

There were two guns in the room, both on opposite sides. Two of us, and only one of him.

Clark rolled off the desk and jumped into David as he ran for the gun. They both slammed into the wall. I crawled for my gun, which was just out of reach by a couple feet. There was another crash behind me.

My fingers wrapped around the gun and I twisted around on the ground, aiming it in their direction. I had turned just in time to see David fire a shot into Clark.

There was no hesitation as I squeezed the trigger. It struck his shoulder. He whirled to face me.

I fired again.

And again.

And again.

And again.

Even after he'd stumbled back against the wall and slid down, I kept firing just to be sure. Just to make sure that the fucker would never get back up again.

My gun clicked to alert me that I had emptied the clip. Ten shots, and every one had hit David Fucking King.

I exhaled and dropped the gun, letting my head fall back to the floor. My heart pounded. My whole body shook. But I couldn't rest yet.

Shakily, I got to my feet and stumbled over to Clark. He was crumpled against the wall, clutching his left shoulder. Blood oozed through his fingers.

"Damn, he shot me," he said, clearly in shock. That's when the police sirens could be heard.

"Get out of here," he said to me.

"No, I'm going to—"

"I'll be FINE! Police will be here any second to help me, just get out! Get back on the run! I'll contact you when it's safe!" Clark yelled. "Go! I'm not letting you get arrested again until they get the facts straight!"

I rushed toward the door, stuffing the Ruger back in my pants as I moved.

I paused at the door.

"Thank you," I said, looking at Clark.

"Go!" he yelled again.

I sprinted down the steps and ran to the door furthest in the back of the building. I unlocked the chains on the door and pulled it open, ducking into the night. I had run this path over and over, making sure it was good enough for an escape in case something went wrong.

I went to my previously established hiding place and hunkered down to stay hidden. I sent a text to the server my script was on and entered the password to cancel the info dump. There never was a second person; that was a bluff. There is no reason to release that information to you now since David is dead. I'm sorry, I really appreciate the level of support to ruin David, but there's no point now. I thought he'd still be alive afterward. The police will get it eventually as evidence, though.

I also tapped out 'I am alive' in the Reddit thread to alert everyone that I had survived. Then, I collapsed into sleep.

This morning, I was thinking clearly again and feeling better. I ate and drank a lot to counter the shock. I have started making plans on where I'll go next. It isn't safe to stay here much longer.

The news hasn't said anything about the incident yet, but I'm sure the story will break eventually. I have stayed glued to the radio app on my phone all day today and am even listening right now, hoping for an update on Katie or Clark.

Thank you, Reddit. You've helped me remain positive these past few days and set this trap. It's finally done. I regret so many things about what I did and how I reacted in the past. I should have fought more forcefully before it came to this. I was too scared, though, and didn't really understand David. But now I do. Only now it doesn't matter because he's gone.

From here, I'll continue to stay on the run. I don't plan to turn myself in until Hernandez says the prosecution is ready to drop all charges.

Hernandez is trying his hardest back at home to mitigate the evidence against me in all of those charges. Clark's testimony about what happened last night should really help reduce the credibility of David's claims. Plus, the GoPros we set up around the warehouse won't hurt. David's confession about his mother was a bonus I hadn't expected.

Originally, we had intended to lock David in the manager's office for the police to find. Clark had called the police just before attacking. Circumstances had changed that plan.

Some of you may wonder, 'well what if David hadn't taken you up into the manager's office?' We had contingency plans; that wasn't the only option.

Regardless, all of our plans involved arresting David, not killing him. It was a last resort option and wasn't built into any plan. I didn't know I was prepared to kill until I had my gun aimed at David King.

I don't think I've fully processed the fact that I've killed someone... I don't know how I'm supposed to feel or act or think or... anything. I feel like I'm acting the wrong way...

Anyway, there's another part that will help persuade the prosecutor to drop the charges against me. I lied before when Hernandez came to visit me in jail. I said he told me he couldn't talk about Isaac's death, but he did tell me. They had found a video file on Isaac's computer from the day he died.

He'd been recording himself playing games for YouTube when there was a crash of silverware in the background. Isaac didn't hit pause on the recording and left the room to investigate.

David came flying back into the room, shoving Isaac into the bookcases. He slammed the door and was on him in seconds. The assault lasted only minutes. David walked out, leaving the door wide open.

The camera watched him come back into the room with my pillow. He held the pillow over Isaac's body and hit it repeatedly. All the dead skin from my pillow fell onto Isaac's body. They found those traces on Isaac's body, but the video proved that I hadn't killed him.

David had walked out and locked the door behind him. He'd made a mistake and hadn't checked what was running on the computer. All he saw was the game.

Hernandez and I had been in contact while I was first on the run. I lied about that too. When I had first contacted him, he started crying on the phone, apologizing repeatedly. He told me that he knew if I stayed in jail, that I would, at the very least, lose a lot of time out of my life while the trial went on, even if David was accused later as more evidence came out.

He had accepted David's deal and demanded that I be given half of the $15,000 he was paid. David, as you know, only gave me $2,000, but Hernandez had hoped it would help me lay low and evade capture until he could successfully contest the evidence. We fully intend to report the bribe to the police.

He told me that after my escape from the car, the police were very suspicious about the circumstances of my escape. There were too many holes in the story, and Hernandez had been sure to point out every last one repeatedly to his boss. A lot of you pointed them out too. Paint from the truck rubbing off, bars separating the front seat from the backseat, GPS in the truck marking his whereabouts, and the location of the crash in relation to the time David sounded the alarm, etc.

David had clearly been desperate to get me out of jail. He risked bribing an official and left a lot of his plan up to chance to get me out. David just didn't want to end the game yet. If I went to jail, it was over. Yet there were still so many ways he could ruin my life.

His need for quick action led to mistakes.

Hernandez also told me when he came to visit that Jackson had turned up. He'd come home a couple days after I was arrested and was brought in for questioning. He had proof and witnesses that he had been staying with his family for a few days.

When asked about the break-in and theft, he told his story.

David had knocked at the door just as Jackson was finishing packing to go on vacation. He told Jackson that he was a friend of mine and was helping me move out. Jackson let him in and finished packing.

He was just walking toward the door with his suitcase when David asked if he would be willing to help carry out the TV. Jackson agreed and carried it out with David. He then grabbed his suitcase and left, asking David to lock up when he was done.

That's when he started stealing everything and trashing our house. That's also when Isaac would have come out and been killed. It solved the riddle of why the door had been locked and not broken when Clark found the apartment stripped bare.

There are still some questions that I don't have answers to. We haven't been able to figure out what he did with all the things he stole from us. We also don't know who the partner is. Hernandez should know that in a few days and let me know.

I also don't know how the keylogger got on my computer, or when the tracking app was installed on my phone, or how David was able to provide my social security number, driver's license number, and all other accurate information to the credit card companies. The same goes for the fraud that was committed against my parents.

I can't help but wonder if David had been in our house before the break-in and done all of that.

As for Clark, his disgraceful exit was a fabrication to throw David off. It was my idea to make him disappear from my life and take the target off of his back. It was both to protect him from David's rage, and so that he could support me in the background. His mom did come and bail him out, but she was much kinder about the situation and worried like all moms do.

When I messaged Clark to tell him my plan in posting this series, he immediately jumped to help me, and without him I'd still be watching David and waiting for a good moment to strike.

It was his idea to plant the information about hiding his bank information on scraps of paper around town. It was placed as a joke and a way to tell if he was reading the series. We wanted to see if David would go hunting for them. He didn't, but that was probably because he was on the run still.

Clark's arraignment didn't go so well. He's still being charged with a misdemeanor for graffitiing David's old house. An expert was called to analyze the photographs and identified them as authentic and undoctored. Either David has someone doing one hell of a Photoshop job, or he took pictures from angles that cut me out naturally. We are still trying to figure out how to resolve his problem.

With Katie, I have yet to see her beyond those brief moments while confronting David. It's been only a few days for all of you throughout this series, but for all of us, she's been missing for a year. I have no idea what David or his partner might have done to her during all that time. I don't know when I'll ever be able to see her again since I'm still on the run until the charges are dropped. *If* the charges are dropped, that is.

I'm scared to see her. I know David did it, but I feel responsible. I wonder if she blames me. I wonder if she hates me. Maybe one day I'll know.

What David said has shaken me. I've spent a lot of time thinking about it today. He told me I was there for him and not for Katie. That I was after the dragon, not the princess. I've realized that he's right. I've read a few of your responses and agree with you: I didn't write all that much about Katie during this series. If it had been about Katie, I would have written more.

The fact that I left her to go back and fight says volumes about why I set this trap.

David was right. It wasn't about Katie. Katie was a result. It makes me feel guilty and dirty to think about it. Maybe it would be best if I never saw her again. She's not likely to want to see me.

Katie, if you're ever reading this, if you can ever handle it, I'm sorry. I'm so sorry.

Once again, thank you, Reddit. You have helped so much with your support, encouragement, and your unknowing aid in making this trap for David. I couldn't have done this without you.

The last two years have been hell. But it's finally over.

We ruined David Fucking King.

Fat Camp

By S.H. Cooper, Reddit User /u/*Pippinacious*

Annual Runner Up—Best Monthly Contest Winner, 2016

Winner—August, 2016

———————

I was an addict. I denied it for a long time, came up with excuses as to why what I was doing was okay, convinced myself that I wasn't hurting anyone, so it didn't really matter, all the typical justifications that are shouted up from the depths of a downward spiral. When Mom noticed, she attributed it to Middle Child Syndrome and said it was a ploy for attention. Dad shrugged it off, figuring there were worse things. My sisters were too busy being perfect to comment.

Dad was right, in a way; it wasn't like I was selling myself on street corners for meth or anything. There were definitely worse things than eating myself sick constantly. What had started as comfort eating to deal with a combination of poor self-esteem and bullying slowly morphed into a need, a craving, an itch I couldn't quite scratch.

I couldn't look at food without feeling the urge to shove it in my mouth in a vain attempt to fill the emptiness that churned in my gut. And when I did give in, there was such a rush and the desire was quieted, even if only temporarily. I felt so guilty, knew I was doing wrong, and that just made me want to do it more. I was caught in a vicious circle of self-hatred perpetuated by the only thing that could make me feel any better: eating.

It got embarrassing fast. I tried to be discreet, eating normal portions in front of others but then gorging myself behind closed doors until I felt like I would vomit. I couldn't look in a mirror without wanting to cry. My face was becoming rounder, my clothes became harder to pull on, tighter, and my sisters started asking if I was "retaining water." That was their idea of tact. Mom was even more blunt.

"You're getting fat," she said over breakfast one morning.

Kelly and Jasmine feigned interest in their cereal, but I could see their amused smirks. I swallowed back tears and shrugged. I'd never been thin, something Mom prioritized, and it was a sore point between us. It didn't matter what she tried, what she made me do, I could just never get down to the same ideal size that she and my sisters were.

"It's disgusting, it's lazy, it's sloppy! Is that what you want people thinking of you? Of your family? You're almost seventeen for God's sake!"

"No," I mumbled.

"Then what are you going to do about it?"

"I've been trying, Mom…"

"Trying to embarrass me? Because you've been doing a good job of that. Cathy Mulrooney saw you at the club pool last week and do you know what she said? She said it looked like you were really enjoying taking the summer off and relaxing. She was so snide! I just wanted to crawl under a rock and *die*, Natalie!"

"Sorry."

"If you're so sorry, then put down the spoon and go for a run."

I did run, all the way up to my room, where I locked myself in and dug out the stash of snacks I kept hidden in the back of my closet. I sat on my floor and tried to drown out Mom's cold, angry words with the loud crunch of chips and candy, but it only made them louder. I caught sight of myself in the mirror hanging on the back of my door and I paused, my hand still in the bag of mini Snickers. Mom was right, I was a pig; gross, unlovable, ugly.

How lucky was I, then, when she told me a few days later that she had a solution?

"If you won't fix it, I will." She had come into my room while I was cleaning and tossed a few pamphlets on my bed.

I picked one up and skimmed the front page. "Fat camp?" I asked, a sickening feeling bubbling up in the back of my throat.

"It's one of the top-rated programs in the country for… girls like you."

"I'll go to the gym! I'll work out every day!"

"Yes, you will. At fat camp."

When I tried to recruit Dad to my side later that night, he sat me down and let me cry against his shoulder. He knew about how strained my relationship was with my mom and he sympathized, but he was a pushover. He couldn't stand up to her any more than I could.

"Maybe it will be good for you, sweetie." He said gently, "You'll get out of the house, meet new people, try new activities. It could be fun."

"She hates me," I said flatly. I had known it for a long time, but never said it out loud before.

"No she doesn't! Your mom loves you, that's why she cares so much about your weight. She wants you to be healthy."

"She wants me to be skinny."

"Natalie…"

"I'm going to bed, Dad. Goodnight."

The morning I left for camp, Mom let me eat whatever I wanted for breakfast. She considered it a last meal of sorts. Despite the queasy knots in my stomach, I managed to scarf down French toast, bacon, sausage, eggs, and a bowl full of strawberries. Mom forced a smile, although I could tell she was repulsed. She gave me a pat on the shoulder as I headed out to the car with Dad.

"Your sisters wanted to say bye, but they went for a jog and aren't back yet. We'll see you in six weeks; good luck."

The drive upstate was long and quiet. Dad made a few attempts at conversation, but I didn't want to talk. I just wanted to get it over with.

The camp was beautiful, I admitted grudgingly to myself as we pulled up.

A lake sparkled invitingly from behind a row of log cabins, neat paths wound off into the trees, and colorful flags and banners had been erected all around, welcoming the newest campers to their home for the next month and a half. As soon as we'd parked, a bright, overly bubbly woman practically pulled me from the car into a hug.

"Hello, I'm Stacey, a counselor! What's your name?"

"Natalie Hunter."

She scanned her clipboard and tapped it twice enthusiastically when she found my name. "Ah! Here you are! You're in cabin three with Ashley. If you want to grab your stuff, I'll take you on over."

Dad gave me a tight hug and whispered, "If it's horrible, call me. I'll come get you."

"Thanks," I said, but I knew he wouldn't.

I was assigned a bunk and given just enough time to unpack before they ushered us into a large dining hall. I was surrounded by other girls, all of whom looked as excited as I was about being there, and I felt the familiar twinge of nerves that set in whenever I was faced with a new situation. I wanted nothing more than to go home, curl up in my favorite pajamas, and eat. My stomach rumbled in agreement.

The counselors introduced themselves and did their best to be upbeat in the face of such a reluctant crowd, which didn't have much effect. Apparently fat camp wasn't anyone's idea of a fun summer getaway. After an awkward skit about making new friends, they served lunch: turkey burgers on whole wheat buns, a garden salad, steamed broccoli, and a popsicle for dessert. I was still ravenous when the meal was over, but they shuffled us out to go through a series of icebreaker activities.

By the time dinner rolled around, I'd become friendly with a couple of girls from my cabin and was starting to think that, maybe, camp wouldn't be so horrible after all. We were given a disappointingly small portion of fish and rice to eat and, halfway through, I noticed that I was unusually sleepy. It *had* been a long, stressful day, so I didn't think much of it and was happy when they gave us permission to return to our cabins. The other girls seemed to be similarly worn out and, sluggishly, we all went back to our bunks and collapsed into bed. I fell asleep the moment my head hit the pillow.

Clink.

"Huh?" I pried open one eye and had to blink the room into focus.

My head felt like it had been stuffed with cotton, making it hard to piece thoughts together. My arms were stretched uncomfortably toward the headboard, but when I tried to move them, cold metal bit into my wrists.

Clink.

I shifted, craning my neck to look up, and it took a long minute of staring to figure out what exactly I was seeing. A pair of handcuffs. Someone had cuffed me to the bed. I blinked dumbly, trying to process what this could mean in a mind still muddied with sleep. Around me, I heard similarly confused murmurs and the curious tugging of handcuffs.

"What's going on?" Gloria—I managed to remember her name from the day before—asked from the bed beside me.

The murmurs became more frantic as reality set in. All six of us were chained by our wrists to our beds, unable to move beyond a pathetic squirm. One of us started to scream and then we all were. The door to our cabin burst open and Ashley, our counselor, rushed in.

"What's the matter?" she asked, looking between us with wide eyes.

"Help us!"

"Someone cuffed us!"

Instead of becoming more concerned at learning our plight, she relaxed, smiling.

"Oh, girls! It's okay! No need to panic. I did that!"

There was a collective demand to know why.

"To start you on your journey to a healthier, happier you! You'll see, girls, it's all part of the plan!"

Somehow, that didn't help. We shouted at her to unlock us, but she just shook her head, her hands on her hips, smiling all the while.

"Aw, listen to all of you! It's only day one and you're complaining already? Tsk tsk!"

It didn't take long for my arms to ache. I tried to sit up to help take some of the pressure off of them, but no position was comfortable. I wondered if the other cabins were experiencing similar treatment. I hadn't seen anyone walk by our window or heard any voices outside, so I assumed that was the case. Ashley walked up and down between the beds, humming, cheerful while she watched us struggle in our restraints.

"I have to go to the bathroom," Morgan said pleadingly.

Ashley paused beside her and crouched. "Okay, hon! Just go!"

"W-what?"

"Go!"

"Ashley, please, it's an emergency!"

"No one's stopping you!"

I couldn't see Morgan from where I was, but I could hear the desperation in her voice as she begged to be released. It went on for another few minutes before she couldn't hold it any longer. She started to cry, humiliated, and Ashley shushed her good-naturedly.

"It's okay, hon!" she said. "You shouldn't be embarrassed! You already live such a sickening lifestyle, why is this any different?" Her tone remained friendly, even sympathetic. "Pigs live in their own filth, Miss Morgan!"

"What's wrong with you?" Gloria asked angrily. "You can't talk to her like that! You can't do this!"

Ashley approached slowly and stood between our beds, smiling down at Gloria. "Oh, hon, I know that being reminded how yucky you are is hard, but we're in this together! Think of me as your shepherd and you, my little flock of fat piggies! I'm just doing what you're too weak to—making sure you stop shoveling food into your mouth long enough to lose some of those rolls!"

"This is kidnapping!"

"No need to be so dramatic, Miss Gloria, your parents signed waivers! Now, I'm going to go grab some breakfast, but I'll be back soon! You girls have fun, okay?"

She left us in a stunned silence. Our parents had signed us up for this, knowing what it would entail? I wanted to cry, to be surprised that my mother would do something like that, but all I felt was numb. Some of the girls tried screaming again, but no one came, and so they cried instead. Tears were replaced by anger and we all swore and made empty threats at the closed door. We tried to comfort one another as best we could, discussed possibilities for escape, but it was only half-hearted and eventually we all went quiet, lost in bitter thought.

Hunger settled hollowly in my stomach, grumbling and groaning for relief. My mouth watered at the thought of everything I wanted and I shook my handcuffs irritably. In the back of my mind, I could hear my mother's voice berating me for being so concerned with food at a time like this and I was immediately flush with guilt and shame. I shut my eyes, praying for any kind of relief.

Ashley didn't come back for many hours, and by then all of us were lying in our own waste. I was so embarrassed that I could barely bring myself to look at the other girls, much less Ashley and her steady, sunny grin.

"Whew, it smells like a sty in here! Who wants a shower?"

I perked up slightly and saw that Gloria had done the same. We'd talked briefly about overpowering Ashley and making a run for it the moment she freed us; maybe this would be our chance! That hope was washed away with the first spray from Ashley's hose, which I hadn't seen tucked discreetly behind her back. I gasped and sputtered under the wave of icy water that was spread liberally around the cabin, soaking all of us equally.

"There, don't we feel better?" Ashley chirped when she was through. "Now, since we're all nice and clean, let's have something to eat!"

My stomach roared in response and she laughed, turning to me. "Well well, Miss Natalie! Your mom warned us about that appetite and now I can see what she meant!" She clapped her hands together. "Okay, piggies, lunch time! Tara, bring it in!"

Another counselor came in wheeling a large garbage bin.

She beamed at us and, as she and Ashley each pulled on a pair of rubber gloves, said, "Hi gals, I'm Tara! I'm part of the kitchen staff here! I just know you guys must be starved, I mean, have any of you had to go this long without eating before?"

Ashley shook her head and laughed like it was one if the greatest jokes she'd ever heard. "Have you seen these fat asses?"

Together, they moved the bin beside Gloria's bed and Ashley reached into it, pulling out a handful of what looked like a combination of yesterday's meals: half-eaten burgers, bits of fish that I could already smell turning, wilted salad bits. Gloria shook her head when Ashley held it up to her lips, her mouth clamped shut.

"Oh, this little piggie isn't hungry!" Tara pouted. "What do you think, Ash? Are any of them?"

"Let's find out!"

One by one, we were offered the food from the garbage and one by one, we refused. I was confident they wouldn't let us starve, they couldn't, and I would not eat garbage! They didn't try to force us, just moved on when it was clear we wouldn't take any. They followed it up with fresh water, which they ladled from a bucket. I slurped greedily until Tara took it away, tsking at me with amused reproach.

"Wow! What a great first day!" Ashley said once they'd finished. "You guys are already learning to listen to your bodies, eating only when you're truly hungry! I'm so proud! Okay, I want you all to really think about how much you accomplished today! Me and Tara are going to take your food back to the kitchen, but don't worry! We'll bring it back tomorrow! Waste not, want not, right?"

They laughed and covered the bin back up before heading toward the cabin door. As she left, Ashley half turned one more time. "Congratulations, ladies, you're all on your way to a healthier, happier you!"

The door shut loudly behind them, leaving us wet, hungry, and, for the first time, more than a little afraid.

***

After the first couple of days, keeping track of time became hard. We were left cuffed to our beds, sprayed down once a day, and offered the increasingly revolting garbage as our only food along with a ladleful of water. I managed to hold out for a little while, but I was weak and I was hungry and, finally, I took a bit of what only barely still passed as a turkey burger.

The smell of rotting meat made my already light head spin and the taste made me gag, lingering on the back of my tongue as further punishment. I choked it down with tears in my eyes and drank the water that followed desperately, like it might help wash the flavor and memory away.

"Aw, so good, hon!" Ashley said. "Isn't it such a great feeling, eating only when you have to? Having that kind of self-control is so important! Proud of you, Miss Natalie!"

Gloria hadn't fared so well. When she tried to swallow the fish, which smelled like a hot dumpster, she retched and then vomited frothy bile over the side of her bed onto the floor between us.

"Oh my goodness, look at what a messy little piggie you are, Miss Gloria! Well, I guess you aren't very hungry after all!"

Gloria groaned and turned her face away from Ashley. She had been so full of fight in the beginning, but the longer we were held there, the more it fizzled out. We no longer discussed escape plans or what we wanted to do to the camp staff once we were free. Talking required energy and we were sorely lacking. Just trying to keep my thoughts coherent was becoming harder.

My arms always ached, alternating between a cold numbness and a burning that made me wince whenever I shifted. I was sticky with old sweat and bodily waste and the damp mattress beneath me stank of both. Insects, attracted by the stench, buzzed all around and every part of me itched beneath the layer of filth. I wanted to shed my skin, crawl out of it and burn it, certain it would never be truly clean again.

We must have passed the first week or so like this, immobile and miserable. I began to think that maybe this would be the entirety of camp and almost resigned myself to a full month and a half of doing nothing but wasting away in my own excrement. *You would be so proud, Mom,* I thought during the night when I couldn't sleep, *I haven't eaten in a while.* I wanted to be angry, but feeling anything beyond the constant, gnawing hunger and hopelessness required too much effort.

"Rise and shine, my little piggies!" Ashley came sweeping into the cabin one morning, clapping her hands and shouting in a sing-song voice, "Who wants to go for a swim?"

When Ashley unlocked the cuffs and they fell away from my wrists, I thought I might have been dreaming. The blood rushing painfully back into my pale hands quickly dispelled that notion. I pushed myself to sit up, stiff and sore, and looked around at the other girls as they also rose. There was an air of hesitancy hanging over the room, as if we were waiting for the punchline to some joke only Ashley would think was funny.

But she just stood in the doorway in her favorite pose with her hands on her hips, smiling. Always smiling.

"You guys sure have a funny way of showing your excitement! Come on, my little piggies, let's go!" When no one moved from their bunks, she sighed and rolled her eyes theatrically. "You guys don't wanna go? I know having to get off your huge asses is a scary thing! I know exerting yourself more than unwrapping a candy bar is hard! But that's why you're here: to learn that being so lazy is unacceptable! Last chance, piggies, let's go!"

Underwhelmed by our continued reluctance, she reached down outside the door and picked something up—a long steel rod with a rubber grip handle. On the opposite end, which she displayed clearly for us to see, were two protruding metal pins.

"Know what this is, girls?" She meandered between the beds, swinging the rod around casually. "No? None of you? Silly piggies, I guess it's better to show than tell!"

She stopped at the foot of Inez's bed and the girl cowered against her headboard. Inez was the largest of us, soft spoken and gentle. I hadn't heard her speak much since the first day we'd arrived, only cry, but now she was babbling about how she'd go, she'd love to swim, she was sorry.

Ashley relaxed, nodded with a soothing smile, and then pressed the rod against the center of Inez's chest. There was a sharp snap of electricity and

Inez yelped and fell back, her hands clutching at her chest.

"Oh, don't be so dramatic, Miss Inez! It's just a low-amp, low-voltage cattle, well, piggie prod! Don't you feel more motivated?"

Inez sniffled and nodded once.

"Good! Then let's get that huge tub-of-lard body of yours out the door and down to the lake! Come on, girls!"

Inez was the first to get unsteadily to her feet and then the rest of us followed suit. I gripped my headboard and pulled myself up, but found my legs shaky, bordering on unreliable. Dizziness threatened to knock me back down, but I was too afraid of Ashley and her "piggie" prod to let that happen. With a great deal of concentration, I forced myself to put one foot in front of the other and fell in line with the others.

We were ushered, stumbling and blinking against the harsh sunlight, down toward the lake. *Could I run for it?* I wondered, looking over to the trees. They seemed so impossibly far and I felt so lethargic. Just walking was proving somewhat of a challenge; I couldn't even imagine how I'd manage to do anything more. Ashley practically skipped along beside us, singing some camp song about having fun and making friends.

At the lake's edge, we were met by two other counselors, Shauna and Megan, who waved enthusiastically and motioned for us to follow them down a long dock and line up in front of them. Ashley poked us along threateningly with her prod if she thought we were going too slow, but mercilessly left it off.

"Hi, ladies!" Shauna beamed at us. "I am just so excited for you guys to be here! Oh my God, we've got such a fun activity planned for you!"

"Yes we do!" Megan jumped in. "It's called Whale Watching! You wanna hear how to play?"

When we didn't answer, Ashley shoved the prod under Morgan's arm and pressed the trigger.

Zap!

Morgan collapsed against me with a cry and we both almost fell backward into the water. Shauna waited until we had regained our balance before continuing.

"Ok, so here's how it works! You guys, the whales, are going to get in the water and tread, tread, tread! We're the watchers! We're going to sit up here on the dock and, you guessed it, watch!"

"But here's the fun part!" Megan said. "The first person that gets tired and needs to be pulled out gets five pokes from Ashley's piggie prod! Every person after will get one less until there's only one of you left in the water! That person won't get the prod; they'll get a nice bowl of fresh salad instead! Doesn't that sound fun?"

The three counselors cheered enthusiastically and directed us to turn and face the water. I remembered thinking how pretty it had been when we first pulled up and how I had been looking forward to going swimming. Now, I was half convinced I was going to drown in it. We were shoved in with shouts of encouragement trailing behind us.

The water was cold and deep and sent a shock through my system. Ashley and the others sat on the edge of the dock, their legs dangling over the side. Occasionally they'd kick up water at us, laughing all the while.

"Don't slow down, Diana! You won't get rid of your blubber by just floating there!"

"You're a whale, not a log, keep kicking!"

"Aw, look at my little piggies! Paddle, paddle, paddle! I'm so proud of you!"

It didn't take long for my lungs to start burning from exertion. My arms and legs felt heavy even submerged and it took every ounce of strength to keep them moving. The fatigue I'd felt before was becoming thicker, a blanket of weariness that threatened to drag me under. Beside me, Gloria's treading started to turn more into flailing and I saw her head bob dangerously low. She went under once, pulled herself back up, but then was down again.

She was gasping for breath, coughing, and her splashing was becoming panicked. I heard her shout for help before going under again. I wanted to go to her, but the warning that a drowning person will pull you under with them echoed loudly in my ears.

"Help her!" Diana shrieked, which had a ripple effect and we all started screaming for them to do something.

After a minute of listening to us call for help, Shauna stood up and lazily sauntered to the pole where the rescue ring was hanging and unhooked it.

"You sure you want this, Gloria? If you give up now, that's five pokes!"

"Someone's gotta be first!" Ashley said, pointing the prod down at Gloria. "Throw her the ring!"

"Alright, then!"

The ring landed with a flat splash beside Gloria. She grabbed at it and pulled it close, clinging to it with desperate fear. The whole time the counselors hauled her in by the ring's rope, she stared back at us, pale and shivering.

After she'd been pulled to shore, Ashley toweled her off and led her down the dock again so that she was standing in front of us.

"Wasn't that pathetic, piggies? Barely thirty minutes and already Gloria's let herself give up! I bet if the prize had been a double cheeseburger she would have lasted longer!"

While the counselors laughed, Gloria's lip trembled. I recognized the shame, borne so nakedly on her face, and I could feel her hurt. While we continued to tread water before them, they berated her and called her names, each one punctuated by the prod. When they were finished, Gloria sank to her knees and buried her face in her hands.

"We aren't doing this because we want to hurt you!" Ashley said, patting Gloria on the back. "We're giving you tough love so that you can be your happiest, healthiest self! Underneath all the rolls and stretch marks, there are beautiful girls just waiting to be set free!"

"We were all like you once!" Megan added sympathetically. "We understand that changing isn't easy! Especially when you've allowed yourself to become such an ugly, unhealthy cow! But we're going to help you, just like we were helped!"

They let Gloria move to the end of the dock, where she could sit alone and cry, while they resumed "whale watching."

Inez was pulled out next, and then Diana, and Morgan. Each time, they were given the same treatment as Gloria and each time, the counselors seemed to delight in it more. The prods were less in number, but longer in duration, and when Morgan's punishment was complete, I was sure I could smell singed flesh.

With only two of us left, Ashley crouched and clapped. "I'm so proud of you, Miss Natalie! You too, Miss Gracie! You sure are showing these other ham beasts how it's done!"

Grace and I exchanged worried glances. The only thing that had kept me going was the threat of that prod, but even that was starting to not be enough. The water felt thick, harder to push through, and my arms especially screamed at me to stop. I could feel the lake trying to suck me down and I knew it wouldn't be long before I couldn't stop it.

The first time my head went under, I managed to resurface quickly, but when I went down again, it was more difficult to find my way back up. I clawed at the water, grabbing at it like I would find something to take hold of. Grace had put some distance between us when she noticed I was starting to struggle, but I could hear her calling to me, telling me to keep going. But I couldn't.

Just as I felt the very last ounce of strength slipping away, the ring landed in front of me. I didn't want to grab it, I didn't want to go back to shore, to Ashley and her piggie prod, but what choice did I have? I slung an exhausted arm around the ring and let them drag me in.

They were chatty while they dried me off, telling me they were amazed that someone so fat could last so long out on the water.

"Must be hippo instead of pig!" Shauna said and they all laughed.

Just as the others had been, I was brought down the dock and made to stand in front of Grace, who was still managing to stay afloat although I could tell it was almost killing her to do so.

"Miss Natalie, you did so good! One hour and twenty-four minutes, I can't believe it! Of course, to a normal person, that's not so long, but for someone like you, wow!" Ashley gushed from over my shoulder. "But, unfortunately, you were only in second place! You know what that means!"

I didn't even have time to shudder. She just stuck the prod against my back and pressed down on the trigger. Every muscle in my body tightened at once and I couldn't move. I was trapped in my own body, locked into place by Ashley and her prod, unable to speak or even really think. She held me there until it started to burn, when she yanked it away and let me sag to the dock.

Grace was helped ashore and dried off and they made a big show of presenting her with a bowl of fresh salad, which had been brought down by Tara. The sight of the round, red cherry tomatoes and crisp lettuce was enough to have my mouth watering. I had never wanted anything so much as I wanted that salad. The others crowded closer, our eyes transfixed and longing. Grace hugged the bowl against her stomach and raised the fork to her mouth.

She got one bite before Ashley knocked it from her hands and kicked it into the lake.

"I want you to savor that bite, Grace! Remember how nice and cool it was! Vegetables should be your favorite food! When you're hungry tonight, think about that salad, how good it was, how much you wanted to finish it! Let yourself crave it! Soon, you won't ever find yourself wanting greasy chips or fatty sweets anymore; you'll want that salad! Great job, ladies, now let's get you back to your bunks for some rest!"

Ashley, Shauna, and Megan herded us back to the cabin, pushing us to go quickly despite how tired we were. If I had thought it hard to run away earlier, it had now become impossible. Every nerve still tingled uncomfortably from the prod, my arms drooped uselessly, my legs barely wanted to carry me. My head buzzed with hunger and thirst and the need for good, solid sleep. None of us argued as we were returned to our beds, the mattresses of which had been flipped over, and handcuffed back into place. We were too exhausted.

Ashley smiled from the door, her hand on the light switch.

"Get your rest, my little piggies! Tomorrow, we learn to let go of dead weight!"

***

After such ominous parting words, I was sure I wouldn't be able to sleep. Let go of dead weight? I pictured dull, rusty knives and Ashley's sugary-sweet voice telling us we only had minutes to cut off as much fat as we could before she sicced a pack of hungry dogs on us to get the rest. Even with images of blood and screaming filling my head, however, the threat of whatever tomorrow might bring wasn't enough to overcome the sheer exhaustion that enveloped me.

I drifted in and out for hours, sometimes waking from the pitiful whine of my stomach, sometimes from the depths of a watery nightmare, sometimes from the pain. Everything hurt; I felt strained, stretched thin, sore. My head throbbed, leaving me clouded and dizzy, and I wondered over and over again how much more I could take.

In a half-dream state, my thoughts wandered to my mother. Had she really known what they were going to do to us? Had she willingly signed away my safety and well-being in the hopes I'd lose weight? Surely no mother would prefer her daughter starving, possibly dying, instead of being fat. Then again, this was the same woman who would only admit I was her child if asked directly; otherwise I was just Natalie the afterthought, only introduced out of necessity. I almost wanted to laugh, or maybe I wanted to cry, I wasn't sure.

Were the other girls from similar homes? We hadn't really had a chance to talk much about our lives outside of camp, much less our relationships with our families, but no sane parent would have sent their daughter here. While I had known there had to be other mothers like mine out there, I'd thought they were few and far between. The number of girls I'd seen at camp that first night —it must have been fifty or sixty—made me rethink that.

I watched the room go from black to gray and then light up with cracks of sunlight that snuck around the drawn curtains and under the door. Grace started to cry when she woke and saw morning had come already. We knew what it meant and it terrified us.

As if drawn by the tears, the cabin door was flung open and Ashley strode in, all pep and good cheer.

"Goooood morning, little piggies!" she sang, stretching her arms over her head and inhaling deeply. "You gals sure know how to stink up a place, don't you? But that's okay! That is okay! We will deal with that later! For now, though, we have other things planned!"

She rubbed her hands together and looked around, excitement shining in her eyes. There was a collective nervous shifting of bed springs and cuffs as she walked down the row of beds, inspecting us, visually dissecting us.

"You little piggies hungry?" she asked once she'd looked each of us over.

We lay in tense silence, unwilling to answer. After the garbage and the trick with the salad, we didn't expect anything from her. At least, not anything good.

"I asked you a question, ladies!" she chirped, her hands on her hips. "I expect an answer! One more time, who's hungry?"

The noncommittal groaning and mumbling she received seemed to have been good enough, because she waved out the cabin door and Tara came in carrying a covered tray.

"Miss Tara whipped up something extra special this morning to help get you prepped and ready for your activity today! Who wants first dibs?" When no one answered, she turned to Inez. "You're the fattest little piggie in here, I bet you're just dying to dive in, huh? Okay, okay, come on, Tara, let's get her some breakfast! But be careful, don't want her gnawing off your hand!"

They tittered together and set the tray on the bed beside Inez. I don't think any of us breathed while we waited to see what fresh torture they'd concocted for us. The lid was removed and Inez's eyes went wide.

Sitting in the very center of the tray, still steaming, was a half-full bowl of plain oatmeal.

Ashley plucked up the spoon that Tara had brought and filled it full of the oatmeal.

"What do you think, Miss Inez, want some yummy food?" Ashley asked, the spoon held tantalizingly close to Inez's lips.

Inez nodded once, her chin quivering. Ravenous hunger burned feverishly bright in her eyes, which never left the spoon. Ashley laughed, delighted, and fed Inez the bite of oatmeal. Tears streamed openly down Inez's round cheeks and she held it in her mouth, savoring the first real food she'd had in over a week. The rest of us had all unconsciously leaned forward, licking and chewing our lips, trying to at least get a whiff of the oatmeal over the rank cabin air.

"Ok, little piggie, before you get too carried away, you need to make a choice!"

There it was: the catch. I had known it was too good to be true, but it still raked like ice down my spine. We all tensed, waiting for Ashley's terms.

"Now, you can have this whole bowl all to yourself! Every. Last. Bite. Or! You can take one more spoonful and pass it down to the next girl!"

The room went silent. Inez's mouth had fallen open and she looked to us. There was a war going on inside of her and we all silently begged that she let the right side win and pass the bowl along. Our empty stomachs rumbled, voicing our hunger for us when we dared not.

"Pass," she said quietly and hung her head.

"Oh my goodness, how generous is she, girls? I mean, wow! That is some impressive self-control there! I am just, wow, so proud!" Ashley said and Tara nodded enthusiastically along in agreement.

They fed Inez one more bite and moved to Diana, who had thin lines of drool dribbling down her chin at the sight of the oatmeal. She opened wide and was given her first bite and then the same choice: keep it all or pass.

Diana didn't hesitate.

"More!" she pleaded. "Give me more!"

"Are you sure?" Ashley asked. "You don't want to share with the other little piggies?"

I wasn't certain Diana had even heard her. She struggled against her restraints, trying to get her hands on that spoon. We shouted at her, no words, just unintelligible, starved anger. She shook her head like it would help block us out and kept shouting, louder and louder, for more.

With every spoonful she got, my resentment deepened. It was only plain oatmeal, something I'd never even *liked*, but watching that bowl become emptier and emptier was like watching a lifeline fade away. I hated Diana in that moment, but there was also some small part of me, a tiny whisper I barely acknowledged, that was grateful. Because of her, I'd never have to find out if I would have been strong enough to share.

"Well, Miss Diana," Ashley said after the oatmeal was finished, "I can't say that I'm not disappointed. Inez, so fat she's barely human-shaped anymore, was able to share, but you were a greedy little piggie, weren't you?"

Diana turned away, her eyes downcast.

"It's okay, though, this was very helpful! Now that all the other little piggies have seen how selfish and disgusting you are, they know what they also look like every time they gorge themselves! It's gross, huh, girls?"

Ashley motioned for Tara to clear away the tray and, once it was gone, she stood in the center of the room.

"Well, now that that's done, on to today's activity!"

As she'd done the day before, she retrieved her piggie prod and uncuffed us so that we could line up and leave the cabin. Diana made sure to stay at the back of the line by Ashley to avoid our reproachful glares, but more than once I looked over my shoulder so that she was forced to see my anger. Ashley told me that no one liked a stink face.

Again, I considered running, but even if I tried, how far would I get? Hungry, tired, in pain from over-exertion, unable to think straight for more than short bursts, and—as Ashley kept pointing out—extremely out of shape. There was no escape. The others must have realized the same thing because we trudged, silent and single file, toward the tree line, where I could see Shauna and another counselor waiting.

"Ladies," Ashley said after we'd stopped in front of them, "I'd like you to meet one of our activity coordinators, Carolyn! She helps think up a lot of the fun things we get to do! Say hi!"

There was a soft murmur of grudging hellos and Carolyn waved with both hands, grinning.

"So, Caro, you want to tell my little piggies what we'll be doing today?"

"I would love to! But first, how'd breakfast go?"

"Well, not so great, actually. Miss Inez, bless her heart, was so quick to share! But theeeen, Miss Diana gobbled all the rest up and left nothing for anyone else!"

"That's not so great at all!" Carolyn agreed. "But that's okay! Mistakes are made and that's how we learn! But, only if there are consequences."

We all looked over at Diana.

"I-I didn't do anything wrong!" she said desperately. "You're starving us! I couldn't help myself, I was so hungry!"

She broke down into heaving sobs that shook her whole body.

"Aw, hon, shh, shh!" Ashley put an arm around Diana's shoulders and gave a squeeze. "It's okay, you're weak, we know! We're working on fixing that!"

"We certainly are!" Carolyn said. "And today's activity was planned with that very goal in mind! Today, our focus is going to be on learning to let go of dead weight! Doesn't that sound fun? Diana, why don't you come here and we will get you kitted out so the others can see what we're going to be doing!"

Diana shook her head and tried to back up, but a poke from the piggie prod had her jumping forward. Carolyn and Shauna grabbed her arms and hauled her front and center.

"Now, girls, today we are going to take a rope," Carolyn held up a length of coarse rope and tied it around Diana's waist, "and tie it around each of you, like so! We are then going to knot the free end to the next girl in line! So, um, you, what's your name?"

"This is Natalie!" Ashley answered for me.

"Ok, Natalie, come here, that's it!"

She wrapped the rope around me like a belt and tightened it uncomfortably before tying me to Diana. Down the line she went, until we were all strung together.

"Ok, now that we're in our little 'chain gang,' we're going to accessorize! Shauna?"

Shauna knelt and picked up a box that I hadn't noticed sitting behind her. She opened the top and held it out so we could see its contents: little black boxes with straps.

"Ankle bracelets!" she said, giving the box a little shake.

"*Tracking* ankle bracelets!" Carolyn corrected her, grabbing one to affix it to Diana's ankle. "You're each going to wear one so we can keep an eye on you! They're waterproof and if you try and remove them, they'll tattle on you and we'll know!"

"Don't need any sneaky piggies in my flock!" Ashley said as Carolyn strapped a bracelet to each of us.

"And now, one more thing just for Diana!" Carolyn rooted around in the box and came up with a pair of wrist weights. "These are each ten pounds; they represent the weight you're no doubt going to gain if you keep eating like the little pig you are! Aren't those heavy? Ugh, fat is such a drag, huh?"

Diana let her weighted arms fall to her sides with a whimper.

"So, who wants to find out what all of this is for?"

"I do, I do!" Ashley cheered.

"Great! It's very simple! All you guys have to do," she paused for dramatic effect, "is run! Not so easy when you're all tied together, huh? Someone's bound to get tired, slow everyone else down, right? Not to worry, just let that dead weight go! You can untie the knot and you'll be free to keep moving! If you don't want to leave the dead weight, we're more than happy to give you a little encouragement!"

"And the girl who's left behind will be picked up by a counselor! There's a few spread out in the woods, so don't worry! She won't be alone for long." Shauna said.

"The last one still running will get a nice bath after and another bowl of oatmeal! Doesn't that sound great?" Carolyn folded her arms over her chest, clearly pleased. "Just make sure you stick to the trails; piggies who wander will be punished! Okay, girls, ready? Set? Run!"

None of us could run. Even if we had the energy, being tied together made it awkward and uncomfortable, so we were forced to shuffle off in a waddling power walk into the woods.

It wasn't long before the huffing and puffing started. Even if we'd wanted to try and plan an escape, we wouldn't have been able to speak through our wheezing. The muscles in my legs cramped and seized, forcing me to slow, but I couldn't stop. I had to ignore the sound of blood rushing in my ears, ignore the weight of fatigue that plagued my every step, ignore the pounding of my head. I could feel the sluggishness of the girls around me pulling at my rope, but I had to keep moving.

When Diana started to lag, I knew it was the beginning of the end.

"Don't leave me," she kept whispering breathlessly, but the rope was taut and she could barely lift her feet anymore. The additional weight had taken its toll.

Morgan made the final decision to untie her, but none of us tried to stop her. I thought I'd feel some kind of vengeful glee at leaving Diana behind, but seeing her crumpled in the middle of the path, calling weakly after us, I only felt pity. We kept marching forward, even after her shrieks started and we were sure the counselors had found her.

Grace fell next, facedown and sobbing, and when we tried to get her back on her feet, a counselor appeared on the edge of the path, a familiar rod in hand. She waved it warningly at us and we were forced to leave Grace behind.

I wanted to be strong. I wanted to prove Ashley wrong, I wanted to walk until my feet fell off just to show her that I could withstand whatever she threw at me. But what I wanted and what I was actually capable of were two very different things. I stumbled and grabbed at Inez, trying to keep myself upright, but she shook me off, unable to bear my weight along with her own.

"Please, help," I begged pathetically.

Instead, Inez undid my knot, freeing the remaining three from me. She looked at me, her expression haunted, and said, "I'm sorry."

I watched their backs as they continued on without me.

"I'm not stopping," I wheezed. "I'm not stopping."

I made it a few, small steps before I was prodded in the back and sent staggering to the ground.

"No, no, little piggie!" It was Carolyn. "You were deemed dead weight and dead weight doesn't get to keep going! Ashley, Shauna, we got another one down!"

Together, they stripped me down to my underwear, leaving the ankle bracelet attached, and dragged me to a thick tree. I was tied tightly to the trunk so that its bark bit painfully into my bare flesh every time I tried to move.

Once I was secure, they each took a turn using the piggie prod on me.

"Since dead weight gets left behind, you get to sleep in the woods tonight!" Ashley crouched in front of me. "I want you to really think about that lazy life of luxury you've been living while you're out here! All that comfort, how easy you've had it, it's made you into the little piggie you are today! You need to learn to toughen up and this exercise will help you do just that!"

She gave me what I might have thought of as an affectionate tweak under my chin if it had come from someone else and stood up.

"Ok, ladies, let's go see if we've got any more dead weight to deal with!"

They linked arms and walked away, leaving me alone, mostly nude and tied to a tree in the middle of the woods.

***

I struggled feebly, uselessly, against the ropes, but all it did was make the tree's bark dig deeper into my naked back. Every time I shifted, I was certain that I could feel my skin thinning, threatening to split. It didn't take long for the insects to find me and feast on my exposed flesh, leaving a trail of angry red welts in their wake. Sometimes, it felt like they were burrowing into my skin, crawling beneath it, eating me from the inside out. Thirst burned in my throat, hunger echoed in my empty stomach, and I itched and I ached and I could find no relief.

Somewhere nearby, up the trail and out of sight, I could hear one of the girls, maybe Gloria, screaming. She was begging for help, for someone to find her, and I almost shouted for her to shut up. No one was coming; I'd already realized that, why hadn't she? I squeezed my eyes shut, trying to block out the noise, and leaned my head back against the tree.

The hours passed slowly. The only way I could be sure time was even moving at all was by the lengthening of the shadows and the eventual darkness that crept into the woods. Usually, I would have been terrified at the idea of being alone outside after nightfall and my imagination would have run wild, turning every bush into some kind of monster just waiting to pounce. But now there was no room for any more fear, no energy to conjure up make-believe beasts. I couldn't even bring myself to cry.

There was no sleep to be had, only a foggy daze, and after Gloria—or whoever it had been—went quiet and silence had blanketed the woods, voices started to ring in my ears; soft at first, but growing louder, angrier. My mother, Ashley, Tara, Carolyn.

"Little piggie!"

"Disgusting!"

"Fat, lazy, weak!"

The chorus went on and on, bouncing through my mind until it was all I heard. I couldn't fight them off, couldn't make them stop. Round and round they went until I was sick and dizzy with grief, guilt, and self-loathing. I was all of those things; I was, I was, I was! If I had been stronger, better, this wouldn't have happened!

I didn't realize I'd started hitting the back of my head against the tree until the voices shattered, broken by the heavy crack of my skull against wood. I forced myself to stop, wrenching my head from side to side and breathing hard.

"I'm losing it," I whispered, and I laughed softly, bitterly, through the few tears that still managed to slip out.

I had thought earlier that I could get through it, that I could prove them all wrong and overcome anything. I knew now how wrong I had been. How many days had it been since I'd eaten real food? How long since I'd really slept or showered or done anything even remotely human? It couldn't have been much longer than a week, a week and a half, but it weighed on me like an eternity.

To keep the voices at bay, I tried to think of a song, any song, but I couldn't make sense of any of the jumbled lyrics that tried to surface. I started to hum tunelessly instead, just a steady stream of noise to fill up the spaces in my head.

"Natalie?"

I looked around sharply, only half sure I'd actually heard my name.

"Natalie!"

There it was again, coming from somewhere just opposite me. I leaned as far forward as the rope allowed, which wasn't much, and narrowed my eyes, trying to see through the darkness. A shadow separated from the tree, short and round, and skittered over to me.

"It's me!" Morgan hissed as she dropped to her knees beside me. "I got away from Ashley on our way back to camp and came back for you. I'll untie you and then we can get out of here!"

I stared at her dumbly.

"Just… just stay quiet. I know they're looking for me." She was working hard on the knot, I could feel her tugging it, and then the rope started to loosen.

She came back around, one loose end in her hands. "Come on," she said anxiously, "we have to go!"

I started to push myself up on legs that had long since fallen asleep, but there was something in the way that she kept looking over her shoulder that made me pause. Somewhere in my prey brain, alarm bells were going off. I froze, a mouse who had caught wind of a cat.

"Come on!" Morgan urged again.

I wanted to believe her, but something in me, some primal, unthinking part that worked only off of instinct, kept me in place. My mind was a mudslide, a mess of half-formed ideas and questions that I couldn't begin to put into words. I wanted to believe her, but I didn't.

"Natalie!" She was almost crying, desperate, and still looking over her shoulder.

"No," was all I managed to say.

She tried pulling on my arms, but I went limp and let myself sink back against the tree. She cursed at me and pulled again, but it was no use. I wasn't going to budge.

"Why? Just come on!"

I shook my head.

"Please, Natalie!"

When it became clear to her that I wasn't moving, she screamed at me, telling me that this was my only chance and I was stupid to just sit there. Insults, cursing, and through it all I remained motionless, my half-lidded gaze on the tree line just behind her. The tirade was allowed to go on for another minute or so before I heard a telling *zap* and Morgan was forced to take a knee.

"What a good, obedient little piggie!" Ashley crooned, her piggie poker slung easily over one shoulder. "I thought for sure you'd be off running—or, you know, waddling—but here you are! I am just so gosh darn proud! You've learned some serious self-control!"

Morgan's shoulders shook with sobs and Ashley pat her on the head. "Miss Morgan here was the winner of today's activity! But the little piggie still hasn't had her oatmeal! We had a surprise part two that she had to complete first and, well, surprise! Wasn't she great?"

It took me a long minute to make sense of her words. A part two? Tricking us into trying to leave? I gaped blankly at them, still trying to fit all the pieces together.

Ashley noticed my struggle and said kindly, "Don't you worry your fat little head about it, Miss Natalie! We'll explain everything back at camp. Now come on, get up, we've got a bit of a walk back."

I stumbled down the path alongside Morgan, the threat of Ashley's prod looming constantly from behind. I didn't feel any sense of betrayal, no anger, no upset with Morgan. I was too numb to feel anything other than exhaustion. We were guided back to the cabin, where all the other girls were already gathered, and re-cuffed to our beds. I had never thought I'd actually feel any measure of joy at being returned to that stinking, stained bunk, but after so many hours spent against that tree, I welcomed it.

Ashley brought me a ladleful of water, which I sucked down greedily, and gave my cheek a little pinch. "Most of you were just such well-behaved little piggies!" she said, waving the now-empty ladle across the room. "Only one of you," her eyes flicked to Grace, who shrank further against her pillow, "was very, very naughty."

She tossed the ladle to the floor and crossed over to Grace.

"I'm sorry!" Grace kept repeating, but Ashley acted like she didn't hear.

"Do you know what will hold you back? Make it impossible for you to be a healthier, happier you?" Ashley asked. "Running away from your problems! You will never learn how to cope without resorting to food if you just keep trying to run away! It's the easy thing to do, and we all know that you fat asses are all about taking the easy way out! But not here, my little piggies, I won't let you!

"Today's activity was about learning to let go of your dead weight and then taking responsibility for your weakness! Miss Morgan did so good, she ran and ran while the rest of you let your fat drag you down! After you had some time to think about aaaall the bad decisions you've made that brought you here, we asked Miss Morgan to go back out there and offer you an easy out, the kind that you've always taken!"

Morgan couldn't meet any of the glances that were shot her way. Shame clouded her expression, made it almost impossible to face us.

"While most of you tried to keep the lessons you've learned close to your overworked little hearts, Miss Gracie here was naughty! Can you believe she tried to run away, after all the help we've given her? Given all of you? I must say, it really disappointed me. But I can forgive you, my little piggie! I can and I will, because we all make mistakes!"

Grace dared to look hopeful. She even tried to smile in return when Ashley gave her shoulder a squeeze.

"But remember," Ashley said sweetly, "in order to earn that forgiveness, you must face the consequences."

Grace's smile faded into confusion and then into a terrified, pleading frown. She tugged at her restraints, begging Ashley to give her a second chance, to let her prove that she was good, just like the rest of us.

Ashley crouched beside her and smoothed Grace's hair away from her face, shushing her gently. "Your whole life has been spent with people going easy on you; that's why you look like you're made of dough! It's time for some tough love, sweetie! Tara! Come on in!"

The cabin door swung open and Tara sauntered in, one of the large metal serving trays in hand. Its cover was in place, hiding its contents. She brought it over to Ashley and, with a dramatic flourish, removed the lid.

"Great! Morgan's bowl of oatmeal is here! Leave the tray with me and bring that on over to our little winner!"

Tara scooped the bowl of oatmeal up and left the tray in Ashley's hands to go and spoon-feed Morgan, who at least tried to act hesitant about accepting. She ate it while we all watched, envious with stomachs growling. With that taken care of, Ashley's attention turned fully to Grace, and when Grace started to scream "No, no!" we tore our eyes from Morgan and followed suit.

Ashley held the tray aloft, panning it slowly around the room so that we could all see the hammer lying upon it. My stomach turned sour and I felt the blood drain from my face.

"Do you know what happens to naughty piggies who try to escape?" Ashley asked conversationally. "They have to be hobbled."

The hammer was in her hand. Grace was shrieking, begging her not to. The rest of us raised our voices as well, all of us screaming and shouting and crying. But it wasn't enough to cover the meaty *thwak* of metal meeting flesh. Or the crunch of bone that followed. When Grace tried to kick Ashley with her free foot, Tara dropped the bowl of oatmeal, spilling it across Morgan, and rushed to hold her down.

Four times Ashley swung the hammer, and each time, Grace became more shrill. Pain contorted her features, bulged her eyes, twisted her hands in their cuffs. I wanted to vomit, but there was nothing in my stomach to purge.

"You see, my little piggies?" Ashley asked, her face flush. "This is what happens when you're naughty! You must be punished! It is the only way you'll learn! You've been coddled your whole lives, allowed to become huge and unhealthy and ugly! The first chance you get, you run right back to what's easy, which just starts the cycle all over! You're never going to improve if this is how you keep living your life!"

Grace was rolling her head back and forth in pain, moaning gutturally. Fat beads of sweat popped up on her forehead and dripped down her face, mingling with her tears. Ashley tweaked her cheek and stood up.

"Ok, girls, I feel like we've made some real progress, but now it's time to rest! So lights out, eyes shut, and try to dream of something other than food!"

On their way to the door, I overheard Tara say, "That always reminds me of the Stephen King book, the one with the author and the crazy lady!"

Ashley giggled. "Where do you think Carolyn got the idea?"

There was no comforting Grace that night, although we tried what little we could. We talked to her in soothing tones, tried to distract her with stories, disjointed and poorly thought out as they were, told her what we'd like to do to Ashley on her behalf. But Grace just kept groaning through it all, absorbed so completely in her pain that I don't think she knew we were even talking.

We gave up after a while, one by one going quiet until the cabin was filled only by the sound of Grace's misery. Her low, animalistic wails lasted through the night and into morning, when Ashley returned to hose us down. She frowned down at Grace from the foot of her bed and gave her an extra spray in the face.

"No need to be such a drama queen, Miss Gracie!" she chastised her lightly. "You deserved this!"

After she'd finished dousing us with the icy water, she coiled up the hose and stood in the door with a sparkling smile. "You girls are going to be so thrilled for our next activity! We have to wait for it to rain, but that should happen any day now! As soon as it does, we are back outside and learning how to really appreciate the hard work that goes into putting food on the table! Until then, enjoy a few days with your feet up! I know that's what my little piggies like best!"

She giggled, wiggled her fingers at us, and let the door slam shut behind her.

***

They took Grace away a few days later. A woman introduced as Nurse Bianca swept in, made a show of examining Grace's swollen, purple ankle, and then had Ashley and Carolyn help her move Grace into the wheelchair they'd brought with them. Grace mewled in pain and was limp in their arms, her eyes rolling and glassy.

"She's going to be just fine," Nurse Bianca assured us on their way out. "A few days in the infirmary and she'll be right back here with all of you!"

But she didn't come back and, the longer she was gone, the more restless the rest of us became. We whispered our theories in the dead of night: that Grace had been left somewhere for someone else to find, that she'd been chained up and left to suffer alone where we couldn't see, that she'd been killed.

"Any of us could be next," Gloria said one night.

After witnessing the depths the counselors were willing to go, something in Gloria had snapped. She was moody, withdrawn, angry, and obsessed with the idea it was only a matter of time before we all shared Grace's fate. Or worse. I didn't disagree.

"But I follow the rules!" Diana squeaked.

"So? They'll change the rules. Don't be stupid, they don't want us to succeed. They want us to break."

Inez started to sob quietly in the dark. She didn't do much else lately. I understood her fear, I shared it, and I wanted to cry too, but it didn't help so I just stayed quiet, sagging against my handcuffs.

"How long have we been here?" Gloria asked.

"Two weeks? A little over?" Morgan said uncertainly. Time was hard to keep track of, harder still when lack of food and sleep made our thoughts slippery and hard to hold on to.

"Not even halfway…" Gloria trailed off and the room settled into an uneasy silence. A month left. A month of "activities" and insults and starvation. A month with a group of psychopaths hell-bent on torturing the fat out of us. I couldn't do it, I knew I couldn't; I was already so weak, in so much pain. The thought of being made to endure more made me tremble.

The day the rain came, all eyes were fixed on the door. The air was tense, stifling, and I felt like a heavy weight was sitting on my chest, making it hard to breathe. Every snap of a twig outside the cabin had my heart racing, every gust of wind that shook the door made me shrink against my stained pillow, certain Ashley had come for us. The longer we had to wait, the more anxious I became.

But it wasn't until the rain had died down and the clouds parted that Ashley and Carolyn appeared, all smiles in their bright yellow slickers and boots.

"Who's ready for our next activity?" Carolyn asked, hands clasped together in anticipation.

Ashley held up a large metal pail, bent and rusted from years of use, in one hand. "Any guesses on what it could be? Anyone?"

I pressed my cracked lips into a thin line to keep my chin from quivering. Whatever they had prepared for us was no doubt degrading and exhausting, and I didn't know where I was going to muster the strength to complete it. My limbs felt like lead; just picking them up was becoming a challenge and any movement sent ripples of sharp pain through my head, blurring my vision and leaving me reeling. If I couldn't do it, if I was too slow or too feeble, what would they do to me?

My gaze slid to their piggie prods, always in hand, and I swallowed hard.

"No one wants to guess?" Carolyn pouted theatrically. "Well, fine, lazy piggies! We're going hunting! For you to really appreciate your dinner, you're going to have to catch it! But don't worry, we know it would be too hard for you to actually catch anything that's capable of walking away, so we're keeping it simple! Worms! Little piggies just love rolling around in the mud, so this should be extra fun, huh?"

"I know my little piggies are looking forward to a big dinner, so I'm sure they'll catch lots! Come on, up, up, up!" The handcuffs fell away and Ashley used the end of her prod to poke me out of bed. I kept waiting for the snap of electricity to vibrate through my body, but it never came, and I fell in line behind Morgan, relieved.

"What's wrong, little piggie?" Carolyn was standing beside Gloria's bed, looking down at the girl.

Gloria had sat up, but she was hunched over, her face buried in her hands.

Miserable sobs wracked her shoulders and she was gasping for air, almost hyperventilating. Carolyn traded an eye roll with Ashley and crouched, resting her free hand on Gloria's knee.

"Okay, okay shhhh, it's okay," she said tenderly. "You can cry all you want, but you know what? That won't make you any less fat. So get your ass up and get in line, okay?"

The bestial roar that followed had us falling back, away from the pair. As soon as the sound had left her lips, Gloria had thrown herself bodily against Carolyn, her hands tearing at the coordinator's face. Her nails, blackened by dirt and grime, raked down pale skin and they both fell back against the wall. Carolyn's piggie prod was dropped in her shock and rolled under the bed. There was a brief scuffle and then they were on the floor, Gloria using her weight to keep Carolyn pinned beneath her.

Carolyn flailed, her hands shoving at Gloria, and she shrieked for Ashley to help her. Ashley shook off her surprise and charged forward, piggie prod raised, pointed at Gloria. I was rooted to the spot, my mouth dry, trembling. They were going to be mad! We were going to be punished! What was Gloria thinking? My mind was a web of terror, catching and encasing all else. I clutched the footboard behind me, shaking my head as if to deny I had any part of this.

Inez lurched forward, her eyes wide, mouth open, bellowing, and she grabbed at Ashley from behind. Ashley brought her elbow back sharply once, twice, and then tried to bring the prod around, but Inez threw her hard against the end of a bed, doubling her over, and yanked her head back by her hair. She pulled hard until Ashley was screeching and her grip on the prod had loosened. She yanked the prod from Ashley's hand and threw it out of her reach.

When Ashley craned her neck around, looking over her shoulder for help, I saw for the first time fear glittering in her eyes.

Carolyn had managed to wiggle halfway out from under Gloria and headbutted her sharply across the nose. Gloria yelped, stunned, and Carolyn, clearly also dazed, flopped on her stomach and started to scramble across the floor, toward the bed her prod was under. She had her hand outstretched, reaching desperately, when Morgan's foot came slamming down on it. Again and again she stomped until Carolyn withdrew it and flung herself backward, her hand cradled against her chest.

Gloria was on her again, one arm wrapped around her throat, her free hand punching wildly at Carolyn's head. Carolyn tried to ward off the blows, but Gloria shook her viciously, compressing her neck. Ashley was crushed beneath the footboard and Inez's girth, her face shoved down into the mattress and its filth. Every time she tried to push herself up, Inez delivered a harsh blow to her side.

Carolyn saw Ashley's prod was close to her and, with a strangled yell, managed to sink her teeth into Gloria's arm. Reflexively, Gloria pulled back just slightly, enough for Carolyn to drive her shoulder into her chest, and then Carolyn was diving forward.

Crack!

Carolyn reared back, her expression belligerent, disbelieving, and pained. Blood had started to fall in a small trickle down the side of her face from the gash left by the piggie prod. Morgan stood over her, her eyes bright and feverish with fury, and swung Ashley's prod again. Carolyn crumpled to the floor.

Diana and I had huddled together, watching with horror, our mouths hanging open. It didn't seem real, it couldn't be real. Gloria hauled herself to her feet, her breathing ragged, and she swayed unsteadily.

"What did you do?" Diana whispered, her gaze fixed on Carolyn's unmoving body.

"I'm getting out," Gloria said. "Come on, help me get her onto the bed."

"Is she dead?" I dared to ask.

"No, unfortunately. I can still see her breathing." Gloria waved impatiently at us. "Morgan, Natalie! Come on!"

I tore myself away from Diana's side and, mechanically, barely aware of what I was doing, I grabbed one of Carolyn's arms and we dragged her over to Gloria's bed.

The handcuffs clicking into place around her wrists was one of the most satisfying sounds I'd ever heard.

"What do we do with Ashley?" Inez asked anxiously. Now that the excitement had died down and the initial rush had worn off, she was starting to struggle with keeping Ashley held down.

Ashley's cheeks were wet with tears when we wrenched her up. She was a babbling, blubbering mess, trying to justify her actions, telling us everything she'd done was for our own good. Gloria put a stop to that by yanking off Ashley's sock and shoving it in her mouth. Diana kept apologizing to her while the rest of us cuffed her wrists around the headboard.

"I followed the rules! I was good! I'm so sorry! They made me!"

"Shut the hell up already, okay?" Gloria snapped.

"They're going to find us, the rest of them! They're going to find us and punish us!"

Gloria reared back and delivered a resounding slap to Diana's face. "Shut up or we're leaving you here."

"Do it! Then they'll know I was good! It wasn't my idea!" Diana, unfazed, leapt eagerly back into bed and looked at the rest of us expectantly, her arms held toward the handcuffs.

"What now?" Morgan asked after we'd locked Diana back in, her face drawn and pale. She looked out the window, across camp grounds that seemed impossibly large, and then back to Gloria.

"We go," she said, but it was clear she hadn't yet thought this far ahead. She sagged against the doorframe, rubbing her temples and wrinkling her brow, trying to collect her thoughts.

"We need a phone," I offered, trying to make up for how little help I'd been. "We need to call the cops."

"The office would have a phone," Inez said.

"Everyone has a phone!" Gloria said suddenly, the slow realization that we'd all come to camp with cells working its way through the weariness.

"Yeah, but they're all locked in the closet with the rest of our stuff."

"What about them?" I nodded to Ashley, who shook her head, trying to mumble her denial around the sock.

Gloria was on her immediately, digging in her pockets.

She came up with a purple rhinestone-covered cell, half charged with a single bar. We all stared at it, almost unable to believe it was real, and more than one of us broke down, weeping, hugging each other like we'd just discovered some long-lost treasure.

And then Gloria dialed 911.

Forty-four girls were found in the camp after the police had finished going through the cabins. Carolyn had to be wheeled out of ours on a stretcher and the small part of me that hadn't gone numb thrilled at the sight of the handcuff linking her to its railing.

The next few hours passed in a blur of red and blue lights, a sea of concerned faces, and a million questions that sailed in one ear and straight out the other. We were allowed to return, one by one, to our bunks to collect our things after they got the closets opened. I grabbed my bag, paused only long enough to stuff one additional souvenir from beneath Gloria's bed under my clothes, and went back out to wait for my parents.

"I thought you'd be… thinner," Mom said as she and Dad, who wasted no time in enveloping me in a crushing hug, walked up later that evening.

I gaped at her, wondering if she was seeing the same scene I was: cops, traumatized children, staff being driven away in the backseats of cruisers. I was filthy, haggard, barely able to stand on my own, and her only concern was my weight. Dad wrapped an arm protectively around my shoulders and scowled at her, but predictably, didn't reproach her. I let him guide me back to the car, Mom's disappointment burning my ears, and I watched the camp fade into the distance as we drove home.

"Huh, did you know they operated out of different locations every few years? Said it was so they could bring the program to different regions and make it more accessible," Dad said over breakfast, the morning paper spread out in front of him. "Cops say rotating kept the complaints against them spread out and made it harder to get evidence. By the time anyone investigated, they'd already cleaned up and cleared out! Doesn't matter though, everyone who worked there is being charged now thanks to what they found."

In the two months since I'd been home, he'd been following the case against the camp very closely and keeping me updated. The only thing I'd cared about was finding that Grace had been taken to a hospital by Nurse Bianca and that's where the cops had found her—underfed, dehydrated, a little delirious, but alive. Beyond that, I didn't want the story, I didn't want to know, I just wanted to put it behind me. I'd tried telling him that, but he insisted on sharing.

"Okay, Dad, I'm going for a walk."

He waved me off, engrossed in the latest article, and I headed upstairs to change.

I'd started working out more since I'd recovered, channeling my attention into slowly improving my health instead of focusing on all the pain I was still working through. Mom continued to berate me, but after dealing with Ashley, I found her extremely easy to block out. The therapist I had begun going to said that was a Big Deal.

Behind the closed door to my bedroom, I dug around in my closet, past my clothes and the stash of untouched junk food, and pulled out the towel-wrapped souvenir I'd kept hidden since my return.

Carolyn's piggie prod weighed heavily in my hands. I pressed the trigger, listening to the hum of electricity flowing through it and remembering its bite. I hadn't known why I'd taken it, it had just been an impulse, but now I knew. It served as a reminder; whenever I felt like I couldn't take that extra step, couldn't resist that last bite, I'd think of the prod, and I knew I could overcome anything.

I still had nightmares, still fought with myself daily over what I could eat, how ugly I was, how much of a little piggie I was, but Dr. Sharp said that was all normal after what I'd been through and, given time, it would fade as I kept looking ahead. I rewrapped the prod and put it back in its place and I pulled out my running shoes.

I was on my way to my healthier, happier self. One tiny, manageable step at a time.

Scariest Story
—2016—

My Grandma Lived Under the House

By Melanie Camus, Reddit User /u/_chewingskin_

Annual Runner Up—Scariest Story, 2016

———————

During the months of June, July, and August, I spent many hot summers of my childhood at my grandmother's house further west on the island of Cape Breton. The forest was plentiful, the plains were a vibrant green, and my grandmother's house was a rickety old two-story that had been built sometime in the '50s and looked like it didn't belong.

Despite its shortcomings, my childhood summers spent here were some of the best I ever had. There were no other children to play with for the next few miles toward town, but I made my own fun running through fields of grass and smelling flowers in my grandma's garden. I can still recall the smell of Nanna's butterscotch muffins wafting through an open window, sweet and heavenly and beckoning me inside. I can still remember the sound of cicadas and a warm breeze brushing my skin. I can still remember my grandma's face watching me from underneath the porch step, smiling with all her teeth and calling me to come inside.

There were a lot of rules at my grandma's house, like no running inside the house with my shoes on and no playing in the garden. Some of them didn't make sense to me, like locking the windows and doors before bed even though we lived miles from society. Turning off the television at eight and being in bed by nine was the worst on a night with no school. There were even unspoken rules, ones that I didn't ask my grandma about, things like not sleeping with our arms and legs off the bed. Things like checking the windows and doors twice. Things like not pulling the shower curtain closed all the way, or hiding under beds and in closets, or pulling the cord to the attic off the nail it was wrapped around.

Though some things were odd, my grandma was a very well-liked woman. She was lithe and her hair was long, shining a bright silver that looked like it reflected the moonlight. While she usually kept her hair up in a tight bun, making the frown lines on her face prominent, when her hair was down she could have been called beautiful. When my grandpa was alive, he would call her a "silver fox," as once she had been young and beautiful and quick tempered, but she was the only one that could say something witty and clever to one of my grandpa's quips. Age made her soften herself, her children made her emotional, my grandpa passing away made her sad and distant, but never once did I question her love for me.

Grandpa spent a lot of time out west so his visits home were rare, but wonderful. My grandma used to say she liked having me around when he was gone during the summertime because it made her feel useful. I guess now that I look back on it, Nanna was lonely.

I will try to detail the events that happened chronologically, but I was little and I blacked out a lot of my childhood there, with good reason. My grandma lived under the house.

I never saw her go to bed once. I never thought too much about it as I was a big kid that could sleep in a bed alone, with my covers tucked around me and my fingers and toes tucked safely away from the edge of the bed. There were quite a few times, though, that she would visit me from the window, standing in her garden bed to whisper things to me from behind the glass.

My grandma's face was pressed up against the window pane, smiling with all of her teeth, her hands cupped around her face to see inside a little better. I never questioned it; why would I? I was just a kid with a silly grandma. There was nothing else to it.

"Sweetie, can you open the door for me? I'm a little chilly out here," she told me once, her lips moving just slightly to sound out the words she spoke from behind the glass. The window was up high enough that I would see just above her collarbone, but I could see that she wasn't wearing anything.

I laughed a childish laugh, and I responded with something like, "That's silly, Grandma! You have a key to get inside! Come in before you get cold!"

My grandma wouldn't respond after this, but her smile would never waver, for not even a second. She was still standing in what would've been Nanna's garden, one of the things my grandma wouldn't let me do.

Though she wouldn't say anything directly to me, every time I turned away from the window I could hear her whisper things to me. I couldn't make it out, and I thought it could've been just nonsense. I didn't turn around to face her. I was uncomfortable with facing her for some reason, and would lie in my bed, listening to her mumble incoherent things until I would fall asleep. It became like a routine—I would listen to her whisper softly until I slept, and by the morning she would be in the kitchen, making breakfast and pretending like nothing had happened.

My grandma would call me silly when I tried to confront her about it, and told me I had a vivid imagination in the way adults would tell kids. I never really brought anything up to her after this. It was like a game between us.

Every couple of nights, my grandma would come to the window and tell me to let her inside. Sometimes she would tell me that I was a good kid, sometimes she would tell me I was a bad child. Once, and only once, did I see her smile drift from her face.

She had been pestering me every night since she had started this game between us. I would ask her, beg her, plead with her to just go away and let me sleep, that I was too tired to play and I didn't want to anymore. It wasn't until I got aggravated enough to yell at her that she left me alone for a few days—but not very long.

"I already told you I don't want to play anymore! Just come inside yourself and go to sleep!"

Her smile turned into a frown, but the look in her eyes made me uncomfortable. She didn't whisper to me that night, but every few moments I would turn around and find her watching me, frowning and glaring. I don't know how I managed to fall asleep, but I do remember waking up to the smell of bacon on the frying pan and the sound of my grandma humming a song.

One night, I decided to purposefully unlock the door.

I waited until Nanna went to bed to creep across the cold floor, unhook the latches from the front door, and run to my room to wait underneath the covers for my grandma to finally give the game up.

She didn't come to the window that night.

She came through my bedroom door.

I could hear her get on all fours. I could hear her shuffle across the floor. I could hear her crawl under my bed, and that night, I heard her whispering from underneath my mattress with my ear pressed up against the bed and the covers pulled over my head.

"I'm hungry, I'm so hungry, I can smell you"

I shifted on the bed with my back facing the wall and the window. I didn't want to play this game anymore.

"I can smell your fucking liver"

The helplessness of knowing there was no one I could call to, to wake me up from this bad dream, was a feeling I'd like to never experience again.

"I'm going to crawl into your insides, you little bag of shit"

I can't tell you what she continued to whisper to me from underneath my mattress. I blocked a lot of it out, curled myself into my blankets and made sure there were no parts sticking out before I slept. I can tell you that when I opened my eyes a crack and peered out from my blankets, I could see my grandma's eyes watching me from the bottom of my bed. I don't know how long I laid there, paralyzed with fear, but I did fall asleep and managed to wake up the next day without Nanna watching me from under the bed.

If she noticed the unlatched door, she didn't say anything. The look she gave me was a curious side-eye as she put eggs on my plate. I can tell I broke her heart a little when I asked to go home.

From that night on, to the next few nights before I went home, I made sure the door was locked—twice.

She visited me repeatedly until I left. I didn't look at the house getting smaller in the rearview window, feeling like if I did I might've seen her watching me back.

I didn't go back to that house over the summertime. My grandma came to visit me quite a few times at my house, but there was nothing out of the ordinary as far as I could tell. The nightly visits were over, and a few years after that, my grandpa was diagnosed with late-stage Alzheimer's.

My grandma and my grandpa were two of the most in-love people that you could've met, without being overly showy. My grandpa's sneaky kisses behind the backs of grandkids and the smile on my grandma's face when he would ask her for coffee was proof. I could see the pain on her face when she would talk about how he forgot her name again that day, or couldn't remember the name of his kids. I watched my grandma suffer through my grandpa's disease as he slipped, slipped, slipped, and finally slipped away.

My grandma died a while after that, hooked up to hospital tubes and being sassy to nurses. Thankfully she never had to experience the deterioration of her mind as Alzheimer's took her away from us. My grandma was spry, beautiful, clever, and a little weird.

It wasn't until we went back to clean her things from her house that I asked my mom about it.

She told me a lot of things that I wouldn't have been told as a child. She told me my grandpa was a war veteran who married a much, much younger girl who worked at a flower shop. They lived in poverty for most of their lives, and when he couldn't afford an engagement ring, he built her a house with his own two hands instead.

I asked her in the middle of this about my childhood. I didn't mention the things I experienced. I felt like she, too, would have given me a flippant wave and a spiel about my imagination as a kid.

"Your grandma was a little superstitious. For a short time, we thought that she might've been getting Alzheimer's herself." My mother sighed as she tucked photographs into a cardboard box.

"There were just little things. Like not remembering where she put her keys, forgetting about doing things in her garden. Just little things."

Suddenly I felt like there was a weight lifted off my chest. That could've very well been the explanation for the oddities and the weirdness. I felt kind of rude saying it out loud myself.

My mother got me to help her pack boxes into the back of her car, ready to start moving out her things from the house and let it become an abandoned shack in the middle of nowhere. When we finished packing, I hopped in the passenger's seat, lit up a smoke, and looked back to give one final farewell to the place where I had spent a lot of time with my favorite grandma in the world.

The only thing is: as we were driving back home, why did I see her watching me from underneath the step with a smile on her face and far too many teeth?

Best Single-Part Story
—2016—

I Trained Crows to Bring Me Quarters

By Leonard Petracci, Reddit User /u/*LeoDuhVinci*

Annual Winner—Best Single-Part Story, 2016

———————

In college, I struggled to make ends meet. Most of my meals consisted nearly entirely of ramen noodles, garnished with a scrambled egg if my finances were stronger than usual, combined with the weekly splurge of a candy bar and soda each Friday. I worked a part-time job, but city rent was expensive, my classes were too tough to work more than twenty hours a week, and my parents had cut me off the year before.

I was desperate, searching for any solution to bring in spare cash. And eventually I found one.

It started as a joke among my friends.

"You know, Tony," said one of my roommates as I poured a sad portion of noodles and half a spice pack into boiling water, "even the pigeons in this city have better meals than you do."

"Meals?" countered another one of my roommates, laughing. "Hell, I bet they even have higher *savings* in their bank accounts than him."

They laughed, and I ate my soup with a frown. But the idea stuck in my head, and that night I lay awake, pondering.

I'd often seen and picked up spare change on the sidewalk on the way to class—nothing huge, a penny here, a dime there, maybe a quarter if I was lucky. But that was just a small portion of the city—from end to end, there was

413

likely a small fortune hidden in the labyrinth, small rewards gleaming from cracks in the sidewalk and among the weeds. I didn't have time to retrieve them, but *someone* did.

And that someone was test subject number one: Jeffrey the crow.

I'd made friends with Jeffrey the year before as he hobbled outside my apartment, pecking for food along the street. His beady eyes had squinted at me as I walked to class, following me as I ate a granola bar for breakfast, a splurge I could justify since I had worked an extra hour that week.

"Caw," he cried, flapping his wings to flutter just past my head to land on the path in front of me. "Caw!"

"Get," I said, clutching the granola bar tight and trying to sidestep him.

His head tilted as he shuffled to stand directly in me and he cawed again. Expectant. Waiting for me to pay the toll to use *his* path.

So I left him a tiny piece of the bar and continued walking. And Jeffrey never forgot my gift.

Every morning he waited for me outside and we developed a relationship, a one-way tribute where I would share a crumb, a noodle, or some other minute piece of food on my way to class. And over time, Jeffrey grew on me — plus, I realized just how smart Jeffrey was for a bird. For instance, after a month he learned that I never left my apartment on weekends, so he stopped showing up outside my door on those days. And after two months, he started giving me trinkets in exchange for the bits of food.

They were always small — a bit of string, a button, maybe a hair tie. But every so often, maybe once every two weeks, Jeffrey would bring me a coin. And now, with the idea fresh in my head, I decided to capitalize on that.

So every morning Jeffrey brought me a coin, I gave him twice as much food, plus a raisin, his favorite treat. For two months, Jeffrey failed to realize the trend, instead complaining on the days where he received his normal portions. Then, on the third month, something clicked. And Jeffrey only brought me coins from that day forward.

At first, it was only amusing. Using my collegiate-level math skills, I calculated that Jeffrey was contributing about sixty cents per week on average to my net worth. Enough to bolster my diet with two to three bananas a week.

But Jeffrey had friend crows, ones that had watched our interactions from the street but never approached. And eventually, they too learned the pattern, until by the time I graduated twelve crows were bringing me presents each morning, a whopping $7.20 a week, equivalent to just over a pound of bacon at the store. It became a running joke among my roommates, but their eyes still widened in awe each morning as the crows queued up bearing gifts.

I was sad to have to end my project when I graduated—it had been fun, but I'd landed a job at a plant six hours north of my college, and that job brought home far more bacon than crows could. So I packed my belongings into my car, feeding Jeffrey one last time as I prepared to move into my new apartment. He squinted his eyes and hopped closer as I started the engine, and I frowned, sad to see him go.

So on a whim, I took Jeffrey with me.

He didn't seem to mind the ride, especially the boiled peanuts I fed him from the gas station at our first stop. And he took a particular interest in the heating vents, fanning his wings out to absorb their warmth.

Civilization drifted away as we drove, fewer and fewer buildings appearing until we were deep in the countryside, forests taking over where I was used to streets. And on arrival I released Jeffrey from my car as I unpacked into my new place, watching him hop after me with each trip until he eventually grew bored and fluttered off.

Each morning he still met me, quickly growing used to my schedule, and still bringing coins in exchange for breakfast. And the other crows in the area were observant to this outsider, watching our exchange, until only ten days in they too started finding coins for me. I smiled—it looked like I wasn't going to leave my project behind after all.

But each day, fewer coins showed up at my doorstep—in the countryside, there were far fewer coins to be found. Jeffrey started bringing other objects again, nudging them toward me for food, until six weeks in there was no spare change left to be found. I felt bad for him, having drawn him away from his home, so I still paid him in full—two peanuts for each item. Now there were twelve crows that showed up at my door, and the number was growing each day.

And then, one day, Jeffrey brought me something different. Standing on the path to my car, he dropped something small and white onto the ground. Something hard that bounced, that made the hair on my neck raise as I recognized it.

A tooth. More precisely, a molar — what looked to be a *human* molar.

"No, Jeffrey," I said, stepping backward and pulling a quarter from my pocket, "you have to bring me quarters. Not... not this."

"Caw," he said, insistent, flapping his wings. He tilted his head as I walked to my car, picking the molar back up and landing on the hood. "Caw."

With a soft *tink* he dropped it on the metal, scratching at it, his eyes narrowed. Swallowing, I reached forward and grabbed it through my mittens, then handed him a peanut out of guilt. I suppose I should have expected him to bring something like this every once in a while, and I put the thought into the back of my head.

But the other crows had been watching the transaction. And by the end of the next week, their numbers had reached two dozen.

Every morning they flocked to me as I waded through them, cawing and flapping, each searching for a reward. And each with something new in their beaks. They dropped them to the ground as I bit my lip, watching the small white objects come to rest on the concrete.

Teeth. Twenty-four of them, one for each crow.

And every day, they brought more. Even after I stopped rewarding them they continued to show up on my doorstep, dropping the teeth in a mound, their eyes angry as I refused to give them payment but instead swept the teeth under my porch. Other crows still picked up on their behavior, and their number still grew larger as more teeth were deposited.

It's been three months since Jeffrey brought the first tooth. I don't know where they find them, or how they can be so plentiful. I don't want to know, because wherever they are getting them from, it must be nearby.

But what I do know is that I now have five pounds of human molars under my porch.

I Found a List in My Handwriting

By J. Laughlin, Reddit User /u/*Jaksim*

Annual Runner Up—Best Single-Part Story, 2016

————————

It all started with an unfamiliar line of dried blood on my cheek. Where did this blood come from? Not from me—I examined my entire body in the bathroom and I couldn't even find a scrape. My head felt… empty. It's not just that I couldn't remember where the blood had come from—I couldn't remember anything.

It all began this morning. I awoke to a ray of sunlight sitting on my eyelids. Groaning, I rotated my neck toward my alarm clock. 11:00 am. I pulled myself out of bed reflexively and walked a few feet to the bathroom. I saw the blood in the mirror and realized that I couldn't remember anything.

What's the word again? *Amnesia*. I found the answer somewhere inside my head. Standing in the empty bedroom, staring at the unmade bed, I realized that the word "amnesia" wasn't quite correct.

Recurring… Recurring Dissociative Amnesia.

Somehow, I knew that was the correct expression. The thought stuck out in my brain like the dried blood on my light complexion. Nothing else would come. My mind was a lockbox and I hadn't yet found the right key. My bedroom was empty. The blinds were drawn. A few feet from the bed stood a new-looking faux-wood desk. On top of it was a laptop. The screen was dark but light emanated from the computer's power switch.

Sleep mode.

I walked out of the bedroom. The hallway outside looked so familiar—its white walls and gray carpet felt very natural to me.

My house.

I meandered past a closed door. As I reached my hand out to turn the knob, an uninvited word came to mind.

Guestroom.

I left the door closed. Somehow, I felt like what I was looking for was somewhere else.

The hallway ended in a carpeted staircase. At the bottom of the stairs was a large wooden door with a glass pane, clearly the front door. An unknown reflex guided me away from the door, toward an open kitchen and dining area. I caught a glimpse of a loveseat and an armchair in a room adjacent to the kitchen, and a glass door beyond that.

Living room. Backyard.

This kitchen was familiar as well, but it was in a particular state of disarray. Dirty dishes filled not just the sink but the surrounding counter area. Cupboards were torn open and a bag of sugar and cans of vegetables lay broken on the floor. The fridge was standing open and the smell of spoiled milk poured out of it. With a hand up to my nose, I closed it. My gaze turned toward the dining room table. In a room of chaos, it was the only thing that was pristine. On it laid a sheet of notebook paper filled with writing.

My list.

Instinctively, somehow, I knew that the contents of this sheet were important to me. As I grasped it, I discerned that all the words filling the page were not just familiar—they were mine. From the first Y on the page to the last N, I could tell it was my handwriting. I had written everything on this sheet. I had no recollection of doing so.

The list was composed of ten items numerically placed from top to bottom. All of the letters near the top—the first five entries—were written in my neatest handwriting (handwriting I somehow knew had been reserved in a past life for filling in tax forms). These entries were all written in black ink with a ballpoint pen. The sixth entry was also written neatly, although it was written in blue ink, presumably at a different point of time.

The seventh entry was written in red ink, a long-handed, messy script—clearly mine, but also clearly demonstrating a lack of concern with its appearance.

The last three entries were written with a fat green marker. They were messy and rambling and took up more than half the page. My eyes scanned the page. None of it made any sense to me at first, like I was reading a foreign language. Obviously I knew what each word meant but it was as though they didn't fit together.

Then, one at a time, the items on the list began to trigger memories in the back of my head. Only then did I remember writing them.

Number One: Your name is Travis Haughy. You live at 756 Camelot Lane in Giliman County with your wife Rebecca.

Rebecca.

Some of the fog was beginning to clear. Rebecca—my wife. She had dark hair and an impossibly light complexion. No… that wasn't right. Her hair was blond… but she had started dying it recently. She liked to do things like that.

How long had we been married? Not too long. A few years maybe, but I'm still having a hard time remembering how many. I knew who she was and I could picture her in my mind, but I had no memories of us together. I could only picture her alone in a never-ending expanse of black. She's wearing a white dress with red roses dancing across it. She's smiling and her hair messily covers part of her face.

Then I read the next entry.

Number Two: You have a steel plate in your head. You sustained acute brain damage during an attempted mugging.

I stumbled over backward like I'd been pushed. My legs barely held me up. Unpleasant images and violent memories were suddenly falling back into place. My hand trembling, I reached up toward the left side of my skull. I tapped with a shaking finger. A metallic noise echoed inside.

The mugging. It had been in January. It was snowing. Rebecca was with me. We were coming back from a movie. No… a play. *You Can't Take It with You*, I believe. Sorry, some of the memories are still coming back. I hadn't enjoyed the play—it wasn't nearly as funny as I had envisioned. Rebecca had loved it—particularly the old man who made fireworks in the basement. We hadn't been able to park close to the theater. We were several blocks away. I recommended we cut through an alleyway. "It's Denver," I told her, "it's perfectly safe."

She was reluctant—she reminded me that there was a serial killer loose in the area who had yet to be identified. I ignored her protests and dragged her through the alleyway.

A man was waiting there. Not a serial killer—just a common thief. He had a gun. His hand was trembling; he must have been nervous. Why should he have been nervous? He was the one mugging us.

"Give me your wallet!"

There was no argument from me, I knew better than that.

"The purse too."

Becca's face looked pale, even framed by her then-blond hair.

"Okay, but just let me get my keys first!"

"No! Now!"

"Please!"

She reached into the purse. The man raised the gun. She really was just reaching for her keys, she would later confide in me, but he must have thought she was searching for a gun of her own. I threw my body in front of her own. Then I heard a deafening bang and everything went dark.

The next thing I remember is the hospital. The bullet shattered part of my skull, but didn't kill me. Part of my skull was lodged in my cerebral cortex.

I set the paper down. The memory had stopped there. There was a part of me that thought I shouldn't read any more, that I shouldn't let any more memories in. Instinctively I knew the rest of the items on the list would upset me—but I couldn't stop.

Number Three: You suffer from Recurring Dissociative Amnesia due to the damage. Dr. Philips instructed you to make a list of important facts to assist in restoring your memory when it's been forgotten. It's critical that you focus on things that you've documented, as false memory creation is a potential concern.

Dr. Philips was my therapist. He was an old, patient man. Rebecca had found him actually — said he had a doctorate from a nearby college that was supposed to be all-that.

"You're going to have these episodes of forgetfulness for a while. Maybe even forever. But visual reminders should cue your hippocampus to retrieve memories that you've buried."

That's what he said. That was the inspiration for this list. How long ago had that been? Days? Weeks? Months? At this point, small memories were coming back in flashes. It's hard to explain — it was like I had short films playing in my head, but certain scenes and clips were missing.

Number Four: Your amnesia is usually triggered by periods of extreme stress. It is important that you relax and keep your head clear.

I looked up from the note to the shambles of the kitchen that surrounded me. A puddle of juice and smashed carrots covered part of the floor. The carrots had gone brown. I still don't know how long I had been asleep. I figured that whatever created this mess must have triggered my amnesia.

Were we robbed?

The funny thing is, I don't remember how the mess was made. I don't remember much of anything before I was in the bathroom. I barely remember waking up — the first thing I can clearly remember is the dried blood on my face. Reading this entry triggered a few brief memories of being told by Dr. Philips and Rebecca that I had blacked out before, but I still had no memory of the most recent blackout that placed me where I was now.

Number Five: You work at the local supermarket. Dr. Philips said it

would be helpful for your mind to receive new stimulation on a daily basis. Rebecca works from home.

I groaned. I had forgotten about work. I briefly considered calling in—but I figured, based on the state of disarray in my home, I probably had bigger fish to fry. I didn't like my job—it was far beneath my level of intelligence—but it was easy for the supermarket to retrain me if the memories of how to do my job disappeared.

This item on the list triggered a whole host of memories. Rebecca is a medical transcriptionist; she types of the audio recordings of doctors' notes so they have a written copy. That's why she worked from home. Before my accident—before I was shot—I used to be an accountant at a big firm. It brought in a lot of money. It bought us this house.

I think before the accident that we were planning on having kids. She always wanted two of them—a little boy and a little girl. They were going to be named after her grandparents, Lincoln and Claire. My mind was filled with images of Rebecca's face stained with tears while she told me not to blame myself. We couldn't have kids now—my memory loss was too big of a liability. I turned back to the paper. The next entry was the first that looked like it had been written at a different point in time than the rest.

Number Six: In August 2016, your cousin Scott moved in with you and Rebecca. He works out of your home as well. Scott.

Scott is my only living family member—the rest died in a car accident when he and I were just kids. We actually hadn't seen each other in years, but he sought me out after the mugging. He's always kind of been a burnout, but the kind of burnout who had insane computer programming skills. That's what he did from home.

Scott was nice enough to offer to help take care of things after my injury, although I always felt like he was just using the opportunity to move into a nicer house. Still, he helped with the chores and he took care of stressful things that the doctor had recommended I stay away from, like paying bills. Rebecca thought it was nice to have someone else bringing money into the house, although she was wary at first because she had never heard about him before. Scott and I were never very close, and like I said, we didn't see each other often.

At this point, it occurred to me exactly how alone I was. There was no movement or creaking throughout the house. Just suffocating silence.

If Rebecca and Scott both work from home, shouldn't they be here?

I stood up from my kitchen table and tiptoed into our living room. It was in shambles as well. The two chairs I had seen previously were in fairly good condition, but the rest of the room was a wreck. A flat screen lay overturned on the floor, dark glass blending in deceivingly with the carpet. In the corner of the room, propped neatly against the stucco wall, was a long piece of wood with a large metal head.

Sledgehammer.

The head of the hammer was a rusty burgundy. The carpet beneath the hammer was distinctively different than the cream color of the surrounding carpet. It was a dried brown-crimson color.

Blood.

Something bad had happened in this house. I looked at the glass door that led to our backyard. Blinds were drawn, blocking the outside. There was dried mud on the floor surrounding the door. The corners of my vision were starting to go gray. My head felt heavy and I had an overwhelming urge to lie down. My own voice started screaming in my head, trying to reason with to me.

No. Don't go to sleep!

But I'm so tired.

It's the stress—it's triggering another blackout. You need to take a breath and relax.

My chest was heaving and my breaths were sharp and irregular.

Hyperventilating.

I took a deep breath. The gray in my vision began to fade. Air filled my lungs and my heart began to beat in a more regular rhythm. After a few minutes I felt normal again. I stood up slowly and returned to the kitchen table. Some part of me knew that I had to finish reading—understanding—the list.

Number Seven: Does Rebecca even still love me?

Tears welled in my eyes. We had been having problems. Visions of Rebecca and I yelling filled my head.

"I'm sorry! I just can't keep it all straight. I'm doing my best!"

"This is your best, Travis? I'm tired of reminding you who I am. I'm tired of getting calls from the police because you've fallen asleep on the side of the road."

"I didn't ask for this! I'm doing my best to provide for us."

"Provide for us? The only one who does anything to provide for us is Scott."

"Fuck Scott!"

Rebecca and I are standing in the kitchen and yelling at one another. There are multiple memories like this. She and I fighting about my amnesia. Some of them I can tell what we're fighting about, some of them I can't. Scott is usually a topic of conflict, but it isn't always clear why.

I kept staring at the list. The next item was the first written in the chaotic green marker. Green bled in the tiny veins on the paper, creating a frantic, unearthly look in my writing.

Number Eight: Rebecca and Scott are getting really close. They're probably fucking while I'm at work I hate myself I hate myself I'll kill us all.

Oh God.

Paranoia. Depression. Both of those things had become notable staples in my recent existence. Rebecca was usually cold to me. Numerous impressions of her ignoring me or treating me like an idiot danced in front of my eyes. I remembered the nervousness in my stomach while I stood bagging groceries, thinking of them alone together.

The pain of how that felt still hurt. I realized that I was crying. All these painful memories were coming to the surface at once.

I'll kill us all.

I had written that. Had I killed my wife and cousin? I couldn't remember. I remember being so upset at the two of them. But I also remember still feeling all the love for Rebecca. I couldn't have killed them, could I?

Then an unfamiliar word fought its way to the surface of the conflicting ideas in my head.

Guestroom.

I practically ran up the stairs. The memories were starting to come back, but I wanted to see it myself before they did. The guestroom door remained perfectly closed. With the blank walls beside it and the immaculately clean floor beneath it, it was a visage of white.

When I threw the door open, my vision filled with red. The bed was smeared in red, the walls were smeared in red, even the fucking ceiling. There was blood blanketing most of the room. It was old, dried blood. All I could smell was the sickening scent of iron. I felt a pressure rise in my chest. I could remember the sound of a hammer hitting something soft and wet. I could remember a scream. A woman's scream.

Rebecca.

I held my hand over my mouth and pulled myself out of the room. I struggled to keep my composure. Gray clouds were already beginning to fill my vision but I was struggling to keep myself calm. If I had killed Rebecca, I wanted to be sure. There was no body in the guestroom. I had no recollection of where I might have hidden it.

It took me almost fifteen minutes to get back to the kitchen. Every few steps I had to stop and calm myself down. The minute details of Rebecca's death kept replaying in my head.

Eventually I made it. I picked up the note, intent on finishing it.

Number Nine: Rebecca is in the garden.

The dirt around the back door. She was buried in our garden. Rebecca loved the garden so much—before my accident we used to spend hours every weekend planting and watering. It was so peaceful out there. She loved planning what we were going to grow every year—tomatoes, strawberries, rhubarb. It made perfect sense to bury her somewhere that she truly loved.

I can see her, in my mind. She's wearing a white dress with red roses dancing across it. The muscles around her mouth have relaxed and fallen into a macabre smile. Her hair is caked with dirt. Shovelfuls of dirt cover her body one by one. I could go outside and look for the body, but it would be pointless. I'm certain that she's there.

By this point it had taken me almost two hours to understand the whole list. It was barely a page, yet reading it felt like I had read a whole book. There was only one item left. I was confident that I had murdered Rebecca—maybe Scott too. I knew that I needed to call the police and confess. But first, I finished the list.

Number Ten: It's not what it looks like. Check the computer.

This item made no sense to me. I remembered the computer in my room, but nothing else. Still, I had to know what it meant. Going back upstairs was difficult. Walking past the open door to the guestroom nearly sent me overboard, but I survived it. I stood in my bedroom—where I had first come to the realization that something was off. Where I had first found the blood on my face that sent me spiraling. The computer was still on. Sleep mode, like I had initially thought.

There was no passcode. When I clicked on the power button, it sprang to life. The desktop was clear except for a single icon—Google Chrome. I clicked on it. It brought me to the generic Google search screen. There were two bookmarks—two different news articles. I dragged the cursor to one and opened it.

A headline blared on the screen.

"Giliman County Crusher Still at Large!"

The story detailed a serial killer in our area. He was famous for breaking into women's homes. He would tie them up, torture them, and then murder them. Police were baffled by him—he had gone months without capture despite the horrific scenes he left in people's homes. His signature was crushing the skulls of his victims with a sledgehammer.

Sledgehammer.

There was a sledgehammer in the living room. I shivered. I couldn't be the Crusher, could I? I had no recollection of doing anything like that. So far, whenever I read something that had meaning to me, it triggered a flood of memories. But I didn't remember killing anyone. I clicked on the other bookmark.

It was an article from fifteen years ago, an obituary detailing an accident.

"Family Dies in Freak Auto Accident"

This article brought back memories by the dozen. Images of my family's van sliding on the ice, crashing through a highway divider, hitting a car going the other direction. Another boy is sitting adjacent to me on the seat. He's my age. The car hit us on his side—his body was crushed. I remember watching him crumple and fold into a knot of gore and metal. I remembered the funeral. Standing with a police officer at my side, tears running lines down my face. I remember burying them all. My mother, my father, my aunts, my uncles—all dead. And the boy on the seat next to me—my cousin, Scott. I was the only survivor.

The article confirms what I've said—it lists the names of the deceased, including Scott Haughy.

How could he have been living with us, then? Who was the person that had moved in with us? I picked up the note again. Again and again I read it, searching for any clue that might explain what happened. My eye caught item three of the list.

It's critical that you focus on things that you've documented, as false memory creation is a potential concern.

False Memory Creation.

It clicked. The person living with us, the person that I had told my wife was a long-lost cousin of mine, the person who spent all day alone with Rebecca while I was at work worrying: he wasn't really my cousin.

But he was convincing. I remember watching him tie Rebecca down to the bed, the stress already causing my vision to go dark. I remember the hammer. I remember her pleading, begging me to stand up and help. I remember tears covering my cheeks and feeling absolutely powerless…

I remember Scott cackling madly as he swung the hammer against her again and again. I remember the sick noise of bones cracking and Rebecca screaming in pain. I remember her shrill, ear-piercing scream… and then it goes black.

I think I've figured out what happened. This serial killer person — he convinced me that he was my long-lost cousin. There are suddenly memories of when I first met him. He came to the hospital right after the accident. No one else was there at the time. He brought flowers — red tulips. We talked about the injury and my family. He came back every week until… until I just assumed he was the same Scott I had known when we were kids.

I had convinced Rebecca of the same. I had no recent memories of him, but I wrote it off as a symptom of my injury. She was under too much stress to really question it. He murdered Rebecca.

I wonder how many times I've woken up and come to this realization and then blacked out from stress. Judging by the state of disarray in my home and the dried blood in the guestroom, this isn't the first time.

I know I should call the police — but my head feels so heavy. Everything is cloudy. My bed looks very, very soft. I'm so tired… I think I'll go back to sleep and call them when I wake up.

Don't worry… I'll remember…

The Price of Sugar

By Caitlin Spice, Reddit User /u/*Cymoril Melnibone*

Annual Runner Up—Best Single-Part Story, 2016

———————

When I was a little girl, if you'd asked me what I wanted to be, 'starving artist' wouldn't have even been on the list.

Most likely I would have told you 'a dinosaur' or 'an astronaut'—and later, when I realized that children couldn't become dinosaurs and brown girls from New Zealand couldn't become astronauts, I would have said 'a teacher' or 'a nurse.'

At school I got progressively worse at every subject but English and Art, but in my teens my aunty got me a part-time job as a cleaner at the local hospital. I thought at the time that the money wasn't too awful, and I was good at it. I enjoyed cleaning, even if sometimes what I was cleaning was explosive diarrhea or blood-laced vomit.

After a while you got used to most of the smells. Well, except for Clostridium difficile—otherwise known as 'C. diff.' But thankfully I rarely had to clean up after one of those patients.

Eventually my minimum wage salary let me quit school and rent a tiny, grimy, one-bedroom place in a block of concrete flats. When I wasn't working or sleeping, I made art to sell down at the markets on Saturday morning.

And so I became a poor, part-time artist.

There are certain staples every poor person needs in their cupboards.

Potatoes and rice were mine; both were dirt cheap and could be made into a variety of dishes. Growing up with equally-poor parents and strictly enforced gender roles meant that mum had taught me early on how to cook dishes that would stretch for several meals.

"Rice is great," she had said. "You can have it sweet for breakfast and you can have it plain for lunch and dinner."

And cabbage. Everything seemed to have cabbage in it.

But I still had my little luxuries in my tiny flat; a jar of peanut butter, some wild manuka honeycomb from my uncle up north, and a big jar of raw sugar for my cups of tea.

You'll understand, then, why I was upset when ants started coming inside.

They were really small things, some of the smallest ants I'd ever seen. When I got up in the morning, they would be swarmed around the tiniest crumb of dropped food, dividing it up and carrying it back to their nest in a steady brown-black pilgrimage of little bodies.

I didn't begrudge them at first—I knew what it was like to be hungry. And I could appreciate more than most people that they were cleaning up my mess, doing me a service.

But when they ate a hole clean through the paper of my spare bag of raw sugar, I decided I'd had enough.

Borax and sugar, I discovered, was a good homemade ant killer.

We had plenty of borax-based cleaning products at work, for clearing drains and dissolving really stubborn filth. So I mixed up a solution as the internet instructed me, then left it in a saucer on the kitchen bench.

It didn't take long for my tiny, unwelcome guests to find it; an hour later, a pair of ants ambled across the clean white formica and found the saucer.

According to my research, they would feed on it, then carry it back to the nest, where others would join the chain until the poison had filled their home. All going well, they would be dead within a week, and I wouldn't have a bug problem anymore.

So when one ant supped at the poison, then settled down on the edge of the saucer beside a companion, I wondered if I'd mixed it too strong and killed the ant outright.

But continued observation showed it was still alive, grooming its antennae and legs, patiently waiting under the apparent supervision of its friend.

Using the opportunity to study a rarely quiescent ant, I took out my sketchbook and started drawing them while I perched on the sole chair in my flat.

By the time I was yawning and craving my bed, the two ants were still sitting patiently on the edge of the saucer.

In the morning, when I emerged for a cup of tea after my shower, the saucer remained untouched—only the body of the poisoned ant remaining, its little legs curled up against its body in strangely fetal death pose.

My attempt to poison the nest had failed.

The next week, they ripped another hole in the sugar bag (which I'd placed inside a plastic bag) and emptied *half* of the contents.

Incensed, I hung the bag from a hook in the laundry roof.

The next morning, the empty bag lay forlornly on the floor, not a single grain of sugar remaining.

Frustrated, I went out and bought some proper ant bait from the supermarket—along with another bag of sugar. When I got home, I placed the bait on the floor of the pantry and the sugar bag in a bowl, which was in turn placed in a larger bowl full of water.

The family of sugar thieves was about to get their comeuppance.

I slept fitfully, the bedroom door wide open, irrationally listening for the sounds of tiny intruders. Some part of me was convinced that they were conspiring against me; I had fragmented dreams of oversized ants crawling through my cupboards, chewing holes through glass and plastic, eating all the food they could find.

Eventually I got up, unable to sleep, and stumbled to the kitchen for a glass of water.

As the light flickered on, I saw *movement*.

The sugar bag had been removed from the bowl and lay sideways on the bench. Ants scattered madly across the counter, scurrying away to any crack or cranny they could find—their mouths no doubt full of my sugar.

Thinking quickly, I grabbed a glass from the sink and placed it over the top of one of the trailing ants, who had just emerged from the nearly empty bag.

I'd caught one of the little thieves.

It was definitely watching me.

Wherever I went, it positioned itself so that it had a clear view of me through the glass. If I came close, if I looked at it, the ant would rear up on its legs and tap the glass with its one good antenna—the other one had been bent by the glass coming down on it.

"I'm not letting you go," I told it. "Not until you stop thieving my sugar."

Tap, tap, tap.

I realized that it was much, much bigger than the ants that had first come into the house. This one was glossy and dark, as though freshly polished with bootblack. The enlarged features lent its face anthropomorphic qualities that made me uncomfortable keeping it in the glass prison.

"I could kill you, you know," I continued, "but I'm not going to. I'll make you a deal: I'll put a little bowl of clean sugar outside the front door at night and you can eat that. Just leave my stuff alone."

The ant stared at me through the glass.

"Okay?"

Tap, tap, tap.

With a sigh, I lifted the glass. The ant's good antenna wiggled furiously for a second, then it industriously trundled away and disappeared into the crack between the stove and the bench.

Whether it had truly understood me, I don't know, but the outside feeding bowl was working.

At night the ants would crowd around the bowl, then chain gang the entire contents back to their nest. As though satisfied with this arrangement, they left my kitchen alone.

I laughed at the whole idea; it was like a tiny, insectoid mafia racket. So long as I gave them their cut of the sugar on the regular, they left me alone.

But even though *I* was happy enough with the deal, someone else wasn't.

My neighbor Charles.

An older gentleman of European heritage, Charles didn't have much time for people like me. If I had my cheap portable stereo up too loud, he would hammer on my door with his walking stick until I turned it down. I couldn't even watch TV at a decent volume, so instead I just watched pirated movies on my crappy phone with headphones in.

The commotion outside definitely included the strident, petulant voice of Charles yelling about something. Opening the door, I found him on my doorstep, a smashed sugar bowl kicked halfway down the concrete path and the squashed bodies of fat ants strewn around my threadbare doormat.

"You stupid *darkie*," he roared at me, "you bloody ignorant savage!"

"Evening, Charles."

"What the *hell* are you doing feeding ants, you stupid woman?"

"Keeps them out of the house," I started explaining, but he cut me off.

"I'll tell the ruddy landlord about this. He'll have your guts for garters—you'll be evicted by the end of the week, you mark my words."

"Goodnight, Charles," I said, smiling tightly and closing the door in his face.

He ranted for a while after that, then fell silent, heading back to his flat.

In the morning, all the bodies of the ants were gone, and a completely repaired sugar bowl sat neatly on my doormat.

I didn't hear anything from the landlord, nor from Charles. I didn't dare feed the ants again, for fear of causing more trouble.

Almost three weeks after the incident, a lone, fat ant wended its way across the kitchen bench and sat beside my cup of tea.

With its one good antenna, it touched the surface of my cup.

Tap, tap, tap.

Then it ambled away, unconcernedly, and disappeared down the crack it had crawled from.

That night I left a bowl of sugar outside, and in the morning there was a surprise for me.

Sitting in the empty bowl was a beautiful creamy-white pendant.

I'd tried my hand at bone carving, but despite my artistic talents, I'd never been very good at it. Whoever had made this piece was a *true* artist; it was a flawless double spiral covered in tiny, intricately etched whorls and patterns, much like the ones worn by my ancestors.

And every morning after that one, a new bone carving appeared, just as beautiful and cunningly crafted as the last.

They sell well at the market, the pendants.

Well enough to keep my little friends in sugar for a lifetime.

The police never found out what happened to Charles. They say that forensics could find nothing—no sign of forced entry, no signs of a struggle. It was as if the old man had simply disappeared.

The new neighbor turned up on Saturday, a sour-faced old woman. On the very first night she bashed on the wall and yelled obscenities when I turned on my TV.

I can't wait to take her to market.

Best Multi-Part Story
—2016—

I Used to Work at a Pill Mill in Florida; I've Seen A Lot of Weirder Stuff than Just Drug Addicts

By Scott Wilson, Reddit User /u/*IEscapedFromALab*

Annual Winner—Best Multi-Part Story, 2016

Runner Up—December, 2016

1

Years ago, I worked in a pill mill in Florida and horrible shit began to happen. I think whatever caused it is coming back.

For those of you lucky enough not to know, a pill mill is a place where doctors pump out prescriptions for absurd amounts of painkillers and Xanax, bolstered by laws in Florida that allow them to do so with no oversight. Before I go into what kind of horrible shit became commonplace there, I'll take a moment to describe this incredible den of narcotics, desperation, and depravity.

Mine was called Executive Medical Solutions, and we gave each and every patient the same prescription, regardless of the "injury" on the x-ray or MRI they brought. one hundred and eighty 30-milligram Roxicodone, forty-five 15-milligram Roxicodone, thirty 2-milligram Xanax and soma, if they wanted it. We saw between five and six hundred people every day as they filed quickly in and out of that disgusting hole in the wall. Rick Scott, Florida's governor, fiercely defended the pill mills, gutting several attempts to stop them. This went on for about seven years, with the drugs mainly going to Appalachia and other states notorious for poor white trash.

"Patients" (or "pill-billies," depending on who you ask) would shamble from their dusky trailer parks into filthy cars covered in plenty of dents and varying amounts of paint. They would cram in as many people as possible and all drive to Florida to pick up their medication, usually with one drug dealer fronting all the money so that they could sell the majority of the pills, often for $30 apiece for the 30s.

Ever since I called that number on Craigslist and went for an interview one hour later without emailing a resume, I have had a pit in my stomach. It was in a horrible part of town, the congested and strangely crowded center of West Palm Beach, in a strip mall that was almost entirely empty except for us, a Jamaican restaurant, and a massage parlor. Yeah, that kind of massage parlor. They actually complained to the cops about our "patients" going in to use the bathroom and passing out with needles in their arms. The normally empty parking lot was filled with junkies by four in the morning, every morning. If it wasn't for the absurd pay and free drugs, I would have noped the fuck out of there on the first day.

The office itself was set up probably within twenty-four hours of the space being rented, and I could imagine the cheap gray paint peeling within an hour of it drying. The furniture was of the cheap institutional variety, with a fabric design from the '90s that was barely visible from the myriad crusted stains the patients contributed every day. The office consisted of one large room that was split between a waiting room and the check-in desk where I worked. The "medicine room" took the bulk of this area. It was locked, filled with massive bank vaults that were filled with amazingly powerful drugs and some blond girl named Jessica who filled the prescriptions while wearing a lab coat. She had previously been a Hooters girl. The manager, Debbie, had previously been a stripper. It was just us and a rotating group of doctors who generally avoided conversation.

At first I thought it was because I knew I was doing something insanely immoral and illegal. While I'm sure that is a part of it, I think I had picked up on something other than Aryan Brotherhood tattoos and a shit ton of money. Did I mention the shit ton of money and free drugs? With my habit I'd be homeless in a week otherwise. I stuck around for a reason.

***

The first day working was the day after my ten-minute interview with a beautiful, but clearly very stressed, former stripper named Deborah. Deborah had dark brown hair and enjoyed wearing expensive, slightly trashy clothing that she would sometimes send me to pick up, courtesy of her gangster boyfriend who ran with the Aryan Brotherhood and owned the clinic as well as five others through various patsies. Debbie opened the place up at five, long after the patients had gathered in the parking lot.

The very first day should have been my last. I walked in at about 5:45 in the morning and was told that we did that because it made life difficult for the cops. I walked in to see Debbie behind the desk, getting wads of cash ready for the registers and someone off to the right at the end of the hallway with the bathroom used by patients. I couldn't see because whoever it was looked like they were halfway in or out of the bathroom. "Hey, I'm Wilks." I waved toward the person in the bathroom and they seemed to shuffle forward.

"I know, I hired you yesterday, remember? Hey do you..." Debbie was about to go on, but suddenly stopped when she realized I was talking to someone in the hallway. Her eyes shot open in terror. She glanced over to her left, but the wall in between her and that hall would have stopped her from seeing the person I had assumed was a coworker. The lights were off in that hallway but I got the distinct impression that whoever was there was wearing a mask, or had something wrong with their face. I saw a distinctly round, pale face.

"Wilks, I need to go, right now, get back to your car and go home for a minute. I'll pay you for this anyways." She was clearly suddenly panicked and

441

rushed through the door with only her keys in her hand. I glanced over at the person moving slowly, almost shyly, down the hall and Debbie almost jumped out of her skin.

"Look at your car, Wilks!" I turned around and looked at my car, hoping a junkie wasn't vandalizing it. No one was near it. Before I could turn around I felt Debbie's hand on my back, pushing me out. "Alright, alright, shouldn't you wait for whoev—" I was about to motion to the person who now seemed to be standing on one leg, fully outside of the bathroom now and in the end of the hall, bending at a ninety-degree angle at the waist toward me with their face still directly aimed at me.

"Let's go! Just go home, someone will tell you when it's cool!"

She had already passed me while I stared. She was ahead of me now but was suddenly dragging me by my arm toward our cars. She never looked back and almost did a burn out on the way out. The junkies lining the parking lot were baffled and before I got out of the lot I saw a line of junkies forming in front of the clinic, watching us. I saw the outline of someone else through the glass too, but I couldn't make that person out.

I thought I would just go ahead and never call Debbie again but in four hours there was a heavy knock at my door. Two gigantic, 'roided-out muscle heads in bright blue and orange Affliction shirts were standing on the other side, looking cramped between the massive lantana bushes that bordered my walkway. I almost didn't open the door but one of them shouted, "It's alright, we're friends with Debbie."

I opened the door and nodded in their general direction, but before I could say good morning one of them shoved two grand in twenties into my hand. One of the muscle heads had thick red hair and the other had a shaved head, one cauliflower ear, and a nose that looked like it had seen quite a bit. Both had an incredible variety of tattoos and excessively tight, ripped, and overly besequined pants. I'm a pretty tall guy at six three, but each of these guys had a couple of inches on me and I wouldn't be shocked if someone told me they were bodybuilders. Both also clearly had open carry permits or something because they were wearing massive guns on the side of those absurd jeans. They almost didn't look real, considering the rest of the outfits.

"Sorry for the inconvenience this morning. One of the patients hid in the bathroom and was probably hoping to rob the place or something. It's all taken care of now. You willing to show up tomorrow, same time?" the redhead asked in a jovial tone, seemingly not expecting me to say yes. This explanation obviously didn't make much sense. The bald guy looked like he'd be just as happy to just punch me in the face. Everything about this screamed "bad idea" but I knew I needed a lot of money.

"Yeah, yeah…" I muttered, stunned as I counted the wad he had just handed me.

"Great!" The redhead seemed genuinely delighted. "Listen, my name is Dave, I'm going to give you my cell, if you ever see that person, or anyone else like them again, give me a call no matter what. Debbie will fill you in on the rest." Debbie definitely didn't seem to want to talk about it, and we never did. After that, creepy became the norm. I got accustomed to the junkies, the drugs, the river of psychic sleaze that powered through Florida and into the rest of the country.

***

Deaths were constant. Patients, or someone with a bottle of their medication, would be found dead all over the country. The cops would call and tell us what number to fax their "medical records" to. Some of them told us what they thought of our little operation but most were professional and probably didn't want to screw up an investigation. Once, I got a call from someone claiming to be a detective but it sounded like a little kid. The kid was giggling the entire time. They said a guy was murdered, horribly, and told me his head was ripped off and his "guts were all eaten" because something thought he sucked. I assumed it was a prank, especially because the guy they were calling about was sitting in the lobby, still quite alive. I hung up.

Two days later and a real detective called and told me the man's remains had been found. The detective this time sounded very genuine and extremely shaken. They didn't normally ask for any information other than the medical files but she asked if anyone knew him or if we could tell her who he normally came in with. After I was finished talking to her I looked on the caller ID for the number that had called a couple of days ago. I don't know why I did this, but I hit dial the second I found the number, probably just out of impulse. I didn't put the phone to my ear, but I heard a horrifying yowling, almost like a cat, ripping from the speaker before I slammed the phone into its holster.

***

After a couple of weeks, Dave stopped by and took me out to breakfast instead of my normal morning routine. We barely talked on the way there but he told me that they were glad that someone stuck through it and that there was a lot of room for advancement in the organization as long as I never pissed off George, Debbie's boyfriend and the head of the network. He also asked if I had seen anyone following me, presumably the police, before getting to the point.

"Listen, some stuff has been happening and I need you to tell me if you've seen anything weird, anything at all, especially in the mornings. Not just people. Anything."

"What do you mean?" At first I thought he meant bugs or other potential listening devices but then I remembered that creepy "patient" on my first day that no one wanted to talk about. He suddenly dropped the joking demeanor and looked as if I had just insulted his mother.

"You need to tell me if you have seen anything *weird*. Anything. A car where there shouldn't have been one, any weird lights on your way to work, people… doing anything… *weird*. And you need to tell me this shit right the fuck now or the split second you see anything. Anything."

I raced through my memories and remembered the creepy kid. I told him about that but even he didn't seem to know what to make of it. He seemed to relax a bit though, knowing that I had made an effort to remember anything helpful.

"Alright, there is something else." His voice cracked slightly and he shifted from intimidating to intimidated in less than a second. "There's been this guy coming around. He's dressed like a Mormon and acts real nice. He wears a bolo tie, one of those pieces of leather that Texans wear sometimes, and has a comb over. If you see this guy, do not say one word to him. Not one fucking word. No matter what he says or does, you say nothing. He's gonna come in, nothing we can do to stop him. But when he does, you help the person behind him in line and avoid looking him in the eyes if you can. Let him talk to one of the other patients, he'll go away after he does, but do not even fucking say 'Hi' to this guy, you got that?"

"Yeah, no problem." I didn't like talking to patients to begin with. I thought maybe this was someone who pissed him off and he didn't want his business anymore, but he seemed almost terrified by the time he was done telling me. We finished our breakfast burritos and headed back.

Sure enough, about four days later the guy came in. He had shocking blue eyes, blond hair in a flawless comb over (although he didn't seem to need it, his hair was thicker than a border collie's) and a white long-sleeved shirt tucked into immaculate blue pants with very thin white stripes down their sides. And a bolo tie with what looked like a piece of turquoise surrounded by ivory. He was smiling ear to ear, and each of his teeth were radiant. He may have been the only person there with a full mouth, other than the doctors. He looked like he was ready for a very nice church. Debbie saw him too, and she looked terrified. She grabbed me by the shoulder before he got to the counter.

"Don't. Just don't," she said urgently. I nodded, despite him being easily the least creepy person in the room by far, including myself. It was at that moment, however, that I noticed that several other people, patients, were also horrified. One old woman with track marks running up both arms turned around and walked straight out when she saw him and the room got quiet quickly.

"Good morning, friend!" He beamed at me. I motioned to the woman behind him, who didn't seem to know who he was. She was happy to check in instead and told me her name so that I could look up her file.

"Excuse me, but could you help me, please?" He seemed just as confused as anyone else would be who had just been rudely ignored in favor of a junkie, except he was suddenly speaking in the direction of the woman. She looked from me to him and then back again, but quietly continued her check in, taking her pack of papers and sitting down, clearly sensing something was wrong.

"I'm having a bit of trouble and I was wondering if anyone might be able to help me…please?" He began to sound worried, but I noticed he was still staring at the area where the woman had previously been standing.

He also looked in my general direction but seemed to look right through me, as if he couldn't quite see me. I motioned for the next person while a fat hick with a Confederate flag tattoo ambled up to the man.

"Might be able to help. Wassup?" The man's speech was slurring and his eyes rheumy, most likely from a solid dose of his medicine or lack thereof. The well-dressed man turned to him sharply and put his hand on his shoulder.

"How do I leave?"

"What?" The patient was wondering whether this was a legitimate question or some kind of weird junkie thing, as is common, and double checked the man's immaculate outfit.

"How do I get out of here? Please, please, there has to be a way out…" The well-dressed man seemed frightened now. Debbie began to pull me away from the counter slowly, and when I looked at her she had her finger over her lips.

"Door's over there man…" At this point the patient had realized that maybe there was a reason no one else had spoken to the man. He pointed the man to the door and the man looked him in the eyes and smiled happily.

"Thank you so much!" He happily bounded out of the office. Everyone else went back to normal, except Debbie, who ran into her back office to do as much of whatever as possible.

The next morning there was a paper envelope in front of the door. Inside was a hand-written note that simply said: **He lied.**

Next to the envelope was a small bit of something like leather with what looked like the Confederate tattoo the patient that tried to help the well-dressed man had. It was perfectly dried and looked like some kind of weird art project. When I looked up from these things, I desperately tried to pretend I didn't notice the well-dressed man, standing in the middle of the road that divided the parking lot, staring at me. I don't think he was smiling anymore.

Debbie told me she would "deal with it," because we sure as fuck didn't need the cops around, but I never heard about it again.

***

We saw junkies doing a lot of fucked-up stuff, but one of the worst things was when people brought their kids into this narco-playland. Once a young redheaded mother and her little boy came in. She looked a little disheveled but not nearly as bad as most patients. We had to get her to pee in a cup, so she asked me to watch her kid while she went to the bathroom. I said sure and just a few seconds later, she came back. But she didn't have the pee cup in hand— she just smirked at me, took the little boy's hand, and walked him out. I had guessed she decided not to do it because there was a line to go to the bathroom, but a few minutes later she came out again and this time she was looking for her little boy. Needless to say, she called the cops, but our security footage just showed the little kid wandering out by himself and the cops blamed the mother. Apparently they found the little boy's ear at the edge of the parking lot, but they kept putting up missing posters for a while. They eventually stopped putting new ones up though.

2

So, needless to say, I didn't exactly react well to the sudden upswing of death. After the thing with the kid's ear and the dude with the bolo tie I started smoking a lot of pot, taking Xanax by the truckload, eating a Roxi whenever I felt like it, drinking and eventually downing Nyquil every day, just to avoid thinking about what was in front of me. The sheer quantity of what I was using was so immense that the idea of leaving was simultaneously enticing and horrifying as there was no way I could afford even a single day without this job.

Living this way can turn anyone into a creep. You don't feel like you are a part of society anymore and the only thing that makes you feel alright is the drugs. I had learned to hate leaving my home with an intense passion, although on the drive to work I usually took the long route, going to Palm Beach Island to watch the amazing cracks of dawn cover the beautiful tropical island with its relatively old architecture that looked as close to European as anything a Floridian junkie was likely to see.

The sour stench of body odor from the patients increased in strength and viscosity until it became a miasma, warmed by the Florida sun and humidity, by about two. After about a month George sent a friend named Aaron to work the front desk so that I could scan medical records and organize the files full time. My new desk was unfortunately facing the wall, which placed my back to the waiting room whenever I sat down. On one side of the main room was a hall with bathrooms and a large storage closet and, opposite that, another hall with four examination rooms where the doctors wrote the prescriptions and a small manager's office where Debbie hid to do drugs. Our own bathroom was between the medication room and the front office.

Aaron was a relatively cool guy for someone who took a fuck ton of steroids and of course always wore brightly colored, extremely tight shirts with a lot of busy tribal designs. I'm a pretty fat guy so I have to admit I always felt insecure next to him, but I got hit on a lot.

This phenomenon had nothing to do with women being attracted to me, at all. I had an absolute fuck ton of drugs and everyone knew it. I managed to bathe regularly, but I pretty much always looked like shit and was wasted 24/7. But gorgeous young women would still manage to smile and twirl their hair at me. Amidst the devastated junkies and constant feeling of hopelessness were stunning young women, often dressed in the short, skimpy clothing Florida tends to encourage. They rarely looked comfortable there and were usually in some varying stage of addiction, but they showed up every day.

"Hey honey! Me and my friends have to go to a school thang, you think you can help me out?" A stunning young redhead with long, cascading hair wearing a short orange skirt and bright turquoise tank top beamed at me from over the counter, hoping to bypass Aaron. He smirked and frequently encouraged this. He would go home with plenty of them.

"Yeah, uhm, sure." I stumbled over to the appointment wall, where we stashed patients' medical files on a first come, first served basis. I was incredibly aware of how awkward and socially stunted I am. I skipped her ahead. She wasn't from the state and they never were, but they frequently tried to act like they were going to school or working down here to cover for that.

"Hey honey, take my number out my file." She leaned over the counter and gave me a look that no girl had ever given me before winking and walking back to the doctor, ahead of the line. I didn't see her again until she left, but she bounced up to me when I was in the doctor's hallway after getting her medication.

"Thanks sweetie!" she said with a thick Appalachian twang. She kissed me on the cheek and pushed a note written on our office stationary into my hand before twirling around and walking out with the group of junkies she came in with. I didn't think anything of it because I was still unattractive and the offers were either never genuine or were just in exchange for drugs. But still, she was painfully beautiful, a redhead with bright blue eyes and a face that faintly reminded me of some celebrity, at least in my head. The group she was with, in contrast, looked like a bunch of frightened hobos, most wearing the traditional camouflage and Walmart garb of the Appalachian people.

I opened the piece of paper as I walked back into the main office and noticed that it simply said: *"Please call me. – Amber"* with her phone number written below it. "Please call me" was written in such a way that the pen had almost punched through the office stationary. The phone number, oddly enough, was a local one. I hated myself for it, but I absolutely had to call her. I told myself maybe she was in trouble. But they were always in trouble and just needed more medication to get out of it. Also they would usually offer to trade for sex, or at least insinuate it. When I got out of work I called her the moment I got home.

"Hello?" a frightened girl's voice asked.

"Hi, this is Ted from the doctor's office. What's up?" I asked casually, expecting her to be more than happy to explain her horrible situation and how easily I could help her. Using a fake name was pretty standard, and "Ted" had already become second nature to me.

"Honey, please, where are you?" her southern twang was thicker than it had been in the office, but it was her. She sounded more frightened than before and I began to become aware of the fact that she may have a more genuinely frightening situation. The kind of people who crammed into those cars were usually broken human beings, easily taken advantage of by the ringleaders who drove them to Florida from Appalachia.

"What's wrong?" I sat up suddenly, my old couch creaking below me.

"I need to, uh, see you." It was absolutely clear she did not mean this in a flirtatious way at all but was trying to phrase it that way.

"Where are you honey?" she asked again, quickly. Praying to God that I wasn't going to regret it and feeling a little disappointed that my deeply creepy fantasy seemed to be going nowhere, I gave her my address.

Eventually I heard an engine revving toward my home on the small street I live on and then revving away from my home. She knocked a moment after that. She was in a different outfit and makeup, a tight and small light blue dress and eye shadow to match, but her dress had been ripped a little at the bottom. She had a deep purple handbag. Through my door's peephole she was staring out at the road she had just come from, as if looking for something. I opened the door and moved aside so she could come in.

"Thanks. Thanks…" she muttered after sweeping herself inside and quickly sitting down on a recliner I had across from my couch, both sitting opposite a TV with a coffee table between them. She was almost shaking and looked like she had been through hell, despite her perfect makeup and nearly perfect dress.

"I need…I'm sorry…" she stammered, looking at the ground and not at me. I sat back on the couch.

"It's alright, you look like you're in some kind of trouble. Do you need help?" I used the most reassuring tone a creep like myself actually had. I doubted she would be able to call the police even if she wanted to. They would probably just arrest her for whatever part she had in her predicament.

"Yeah... I need..." she sighed, looked at me for just a second and then went back to looking at the ground.

"I need help; something happened. One uh my friends is dead. She come with us down here but she ain't got a way home because our ride got pissed at her. So she talk to this guy that looked good, he look clean and she thought maybe he could give her a ride or knew someone who could cuz he looked clean and respectable an all." It poured out of her in broken, stammering Appalachian drawl. She looked around the room desperately while she spoke. The moment she mentioned the guy looking clean, I thought of that dude with the bolo tie. Good holy shit, I did not need that motherfucker again. I began to wonder, just briefly, how exactly Dave had known he was coming to begin with.

"She gone, she gone an went with him..." She breathed in with a deep shudder. Her long, thick red hair moved over her face when she looked at the ground and she made no effort to move it. She sobbed once and the tears began to flow like a river.

"She though he was safe, cuz he seemed clean. She left American Injury with him the day before yesterday and took her part of her meds. She took her meds and went with him, his name Lyle, and they left together but she came back that night when we were in the motel, she pounding at our door screaming at us to let her in. We thought she wanted the meds Brody took to pay for her debt and ride here but before he even open the door she was gone. Her bag was drop, it spilled everywhere, but she was just gone, nowhere in the parking lot, nowhere at all. I call her cellphone an I hear her screamin but it just cut out and she don't pick up at all now!" She was shaking and her makeup was pouring down her face. So she and her friends were going doctor shopping, taking advantage of the fact that Florida did not allow anyone to record how many doctors were prescribing to a single patient. This allowed pill-billies to visit every clinic in the area on the same trip, especially American

Injury Clinic, George's massive flagship and thorn in the side of the DEA.

"And then someone call me from her phone and I just hear laughing and then some kind of screech and now we don't know where she is or who she's with! An everyone else, they just want to leave and pretend they didn't see nothing." That was actually probably the smart thing to do. The police were often just as dangerous as criminals and I was slightly less effective at combat than a Publix sub.

"Do you think you should go to the police?" I asked anyway, more to gauge the severity of her beliefs than anything. She stared at the ground, saddened.

"I mean, maybe... I gotta do something cuz they don't wanna stay, they want me to stay with you a night and get more meds and leave!" It suddenly sank in that all the girls flirting with me didn't really have a choice, or at least didn't perceive it that way. This would give me a chill up my spine every time a pretty girl smiled at me in that clinic from then on. More for Aaron.

"I have plenty of meds, that's not a problem." One way or another I could spare those at least. I reached to the coffee table where a small plastic bag from work contained four large pill bottles. I began to pour a relatively generous amount of Roxicodone, Xanax, Percocet, and soma into a plastic sandwich bag. For just a second I wondered how many plastic sandwich bags were used for drugs and whether manufacturers actually considered this during design. Probably. Her eyes lit up just briefly when she saw the amount of meds she was about to reap. I just wanted her to calm down and they were basically free for me.

"I'll... I'll call my people right... right quick..." she said slowly, still crying but unable to avoid focusing on what was the bottom line for what may have been her friends or family or maybe just some violent criminals she had to hang with. The line between the two was usually pretty thin anyways. She dialed and mumbled into the phone quickly and inaudibly.

"Thank... thanks... I don't know where Stacy gone... I didn't see what kind of car that Lyle was driving. He looked so pleased with hissalf too." I poured some crushed Roxi for her and she got to work, taking in two entire rails. That took the edge off of her, and she was still weeping. As this shit tends to do, it makes you feel more resigned than at peace.

"She ain't even said where he from or going!" I thought to myself that it might not be impossible to look up people named Lyle at American Injury, but that might not be his real name.

"But she said it was cool and she would just call later, so she stormed out after a fight with Brody and told him to go fuck himself. That's why he didn't take her serious when she come back like that!" She said this defensively, and I got the impression she regretted not taking her friend seriously too.

From outside my door I suddenly heard in a deep, white-trash voice: "Samantha, it's me. Come outside."

I was suddenly very aware that I hadn't heard a car pull up. I wondered if they had just dropped off more people, to keep her safe or to rob me. The fact that 'Amber' was actually 'Samantha' didn't bother me, but the fact that he used her real name sent a shock of ice up my spine. That was a bit of a faux pas around people that you didn't know in the pill mills—if it could be avoided, that is. Fake IDs were constant and we didn't have to check particularly hard to dispense medication.

"Brody?" She seemed stunned. She looked to me as if for advice. She hadn't called her friend more than ten minutes earlier, or at least it seemed that way.

"Yes. Come outside, Samantha." His accent sounded as redneck as anyone, but there was something about how he didn't say 'yeah' or really any slang at all, even in those short sentences.

"Just for a moment, Samantha." The voice didn't use a particularly reassuring tone, but it wasn't threatening either. She looked at me and got up. She walked to the door and I felt my innards seize with ice. If it was anyone other than who she thought, or if he had any bad intentions, we were defenseless. I suddenly realized I didn't have a gun. But she opened the door and walked out. I heard her greet someone with a "hey" as she moved away from my house. At this point I really wished I lived in the city, but I lived in a relatively isolated part of West Palm Beach in an area that was more Everglades and less beach. It's a huge county and I didn't mind the drive. I waited a few moments. The moments turned into minutes. The minutes dragged along and I got worried. First for her, then for me.

After about twenty minutes a phone call came in on my cellphone. It was her. I was massively relieved. This meant she had just taken her generous bag of pills and gone home, without having to do anything other than cry, which for her was probably a good deal if her group expected her to get pills from me. It stopped ringing almost instantly, and I suddenly felt the drugs floating in my system as the adrenaline receded. I chuckled and got up to flip the lock on my door. The second I flipped the deadbolt, thinking that that was the end of the night for me, I heard a voice on the other side of the door. Immediately on the other side of the door.

"Wilks, open the door." It was Samantha, and she sounded calm and clear. I turned around, but the sudden and gigantic pit of lead in my stomach compelled me not to bother looking through the peephole I normally made such use of. I wasn't sure what would be worse, seeing her there or seeing something else, but the fact that I never mentioned my name (It's not actually Wilks, but you get the idea) stuck out in my memory like a sore thumb. It was generally a bad idea for us to mention our names, because it made us easier to identify.

"Wilks? Could you open the door? Or come outside. I just want to talk for a second." There was a strange blankness in her questions. The voice from the other side of the door seemed to not know where to aim itself, and each word sounded like it was addressed to a different area of my living room. A thin layer of ice-cold sweat covered my torso and the back of my neck and every second seemed like an hour. I didn't dare answer.

"Wilks, open the door. Or come outside. I just want to talk for a second." It sounded exactly the same as when she had said those words a moment ago, but stitched together differently. For a moment I wondered if a crude recording of some kind was repeating her voice, but I couldn't imagine someone getting a recording of her saying my name to begin with.

Seconds or minutes later, her cellphone called mine again. And again. And again. And then it sent me a picture. I'm pretty grateful that my phone allowed me to delete it without viewing it. I stood next to the door staring at my cellphone, terrified that whoever or whatever was speaking in her voice might hear a step. I kept staring at my phone each time the ringing started again as if expecting my phone to say, "Just kidding bro, she's probably fine."

After a few minutes I heard something rustle away from my door. I never heard another car pull up, or anyone else. I called Dave the next morning.

"Jesus Christ. No, you did the right thing dude. You really did." He almost sounded impressed. He seemed to wave off the hints I was dropping that something other than a person may have been at fault for this.

"Bro, if you get any other phone calls or any of that shit, just ignore it. You know these junkies and their drama, she got you for some pills, just let it slide. You'll see her again in exactly one month, just don't bring it up and be cool about it. Losing some pills is no big deal." He knew damn well that it wasn't the pills I was worried about and I suddenly realized that although there was a chance of the phone call being tapped, he seemed happier to talk about drugs than "weird shit."

The thing is, she never did come back. I pulled the fake ID she used and she never showed for any of her appointment times at my clinic or any of the other clinics George owns. Because I didn't know her real name I had no idea if there was anyone I could report this to that would make a difference. Or at least that's what I tell myself.

***

Things got worse quickly after that. I guess that was creepy enough to convince Dave that I was ready for some new responsibilities and a little more money, because that's what Debbie told me the next morning. I don't recall any other time in my life when a promotion left me filled with dread.

This is how I began to get a much more open understanding of what was going on in the pill mills and Florida in general. Most of the days we left before three because we opened so early, at different times so that no one ever had to work more than nine hours. One time that didn't go as planned.

"Wilks, we have a problem." Debbie didn't even bother looking up when I came in; she was chest deep in junkies trying to check in, but dropped the papers in her hand and motioned for me to go to the medicine room with her. Serious business.

"We're getting an inspection tomorrow." She stated this with such terror that for a second I thought she was hoping for an answer from me. We were technically legal, but only because the authorities had no legal ability to second guess a doctor for prescribing anything they wanted, even if it had nothing to do with their field to begin with. Pharmaceutical companies fiercely defended this sacred right as something that kept our medical professionals functioning at a necessary speed and with necessary flexibility for doctors.

"We have to go through the inventory, we might need to make some deliveries. By we, I do mean you. Sorry about that." She took a deep breath after she said that. I got a bad feeling about this right away. The different pill mills, all controlled by her boyfriend George, had to move fast to make sure each pill was accounted for, even if the accounting was hilariously flimsy. The process was largely written by a pharmaceutical company with no interest in the DEA's goals to begin with. Yale Pharmaceuticals, through an "account representative" named Rhonda, coordinated with us on exactly how to pass this. They also made sure the representative they were required to send only came after store hours, so they wouldn't have any reason to report the army of junkies in the parking lot. There were a ton of tricky little things like that at every step of the process to buying as many painkillers as you needed, just as long as you did it in bulk.

"We need at least 15,700 Mallies, a lot of Fentanyl, Xanax, you know, shipped to the American Injury Clinic. We have to make the books right too. We're two and a half ahead."

Being $250,000 ahead in cash was a serious problem for this kind of business. Mallinckrodt was a particular brand of Roxicodone that was well known for their easy breakdown and comfortable inhalation. It was entirely possible for pharmaceutical companies to make additives that would make injection a lot less likely, but you see how it is. The American Injury Clinic was a massive building—a former school—that dealt exclusively in painkillers and was the heart of George's empire. It pumped a vast river of narcotics into Ohio, East Virginia, West Virginia, Tennessee, Kentucky, Alabama, Georgia, Louisiana, Mississippi, and everywhere else that had a lot of Confederate flags and not many jobs.

"I'm going to need you to grab at least two trips…" She said it as both an order and a question, wondering if I would go through with it and clearly watching my reaction. I needed about 160 milligrams of Roxicodone and six milligrams of Xanax every day just to feel normal at this point. To put this in market terms, it would be what non-junkies refer to as "insanely fucking expensive."

"No problem." I stared her straight in the eyes, so that we both knew I wouldn't be putting up the bill for my own habit any time soon, at the expense of God knows how many others. She nodded and left, and I went back to my desk, grateful that this meant a couple more hours of me getting to face my wall. This was toward the middle of November, so the days were getting short. I had never worked past 3:30 or so in the afternoon and usually started before seven, almost always before sunrise.

"The bags will be ready; I have the doctors' powers of attorneys." Getting a physician to give a criminal power of attorney over their affairs was a critical part of the business plan that allowed them to store massive amounts of medication on hand. I decided to never ask how they got that. If anyone knew I was making the drive I could be guaranteed to be robbed and killed. Also, as far as they knew, I might just try and drive off with a few million in merchandise and cash. The cash, legally speaking, did not exist, which made it a particular point of anxiety. The pills, legally speaking, had been resting in their destination the entire time and if the authorities knew that we had to play an insane balancing game we'd be toast. Knowing that my mother could be killed, I could get sent to prison, and I could run out of drugs right away—and that I'd get extra pay if I did the job—was a solid way to keep me honest, though.

"Alright, just let me know when I go to the clinic."

"You're not going to their clinic, you're doing a dead drop on the island. Drop it at the golf course in front of the schoolhouse and go." In addition to the possibility of being robbed, now the possibility that the dead drop could simply be taken by a group of teenagers existed. The "island" in question didn't need any introduction to anyone in South Florida. Since the Kennedys reigned, Palm Beach Island had been host to a crowd of wealthy, aging, and disconnected white people. The golf course had a small schoolhouse on it, left over from the days when Henry Flagler built the first railroad into the area.

He also had a small village built for his black workers, right on the island. And when he didn't need them to build a railroad anymore he invited them to a party and while they were gone he had men burn their homes down and kill anyone who had a problem with it. Then he built a tiny little schoolhouse right on that spot, while the poor black people were forcibly moved to an area called Riviera Beach and central West Palm Beach, where they were never heard from again. Suffice to say that schoolhouse is now in what is generally considered the more expensive part of town, a wealthy enclave with nicer, older architecture.

"Alright." I pretended I didn't have a huge problem with this.

"Good luck." Her voice wavered at that. She didn't seem happy with this either, but she wouldn't turn away from the counter to tell me about it to my face and I wasn't going to force her to. I went about my day and waited for the bags of cash and drugs to be prepared by George's henchmen—different guys this time, same amount of muscle and brightly colored Affliction shirts. They didn't say a word and were gone in minutes, leaving three large and two small duffel bags. I quietly drove around the back of the building where Debbie and I loaded the bags as quickly as possible. It was a small alley between two buildings so it was relatively assured that no one could see us.

"Wilks, if you see anything… anything at all, you need to call Dave." The redheaded hulk had appeared more than once as a representative of George, sometimes giving Debbie orders, and was usually very easy to like once you forgot that he probably had hurt people for money before.

"Are they worried about me getting robbed? Because dead drops are generally a bad way to go with that." She smirked, so I guessed that a robbery genuinely wasn't on her mind because otherwise she would have gotten serious.

"Just let him know what you see." Now she was being serious. I was suddenly deeply worried. I had already seen plenty and this could have been a really convenient way to get rid of a liability that was no longer needed. But I was at the end of a long stretch without a pill and I knew in the back of my head that I didn't really have a choice unless I wanted to be shitting myself in a hospital bed in no time.

I nodded and got in the car. She banged on the trunk when it was loaded and I drove off. The sun was going down, turning Florida's sky into an explosion of pinks, oranges, purples, and blues that defied the imagination. I drove through West Palm Beach, grateful that the rivers of SUVs and economy sedans were moving in the opposite direction, toward the residential areas of the county. I headed down a massive bridge in between relatively large towers and a small, absurdly expensive private Christian college across the Intercostal Waterway from Palm Beach Island named Palm Beach Atlantic University. Creepy little place. The sky over the ocean was jet black by five thirty, making it look like the city was on fire with some kind of incredible burst of neon turquoise and angry fuchsia. These colors reflected on every single pane of glass and ivory surface in the small, beautiful island town.

I drove down the jet black coast until I reached the curve in the single road on the island that let me know the golf course was coming up. I slowed down and briefly checked behind me for any other cars, but the curving road and thick vegetation made that futile. By the time I got to the golf course I had made my peace with the fact that if I had been followed I was too unaware of it to do anything about it. The parking lot was empty, but there was a slight indigo glow coming from the beach that I assumed was from high school students getting drunk or high. Sure enough, I heard laughter, some music, and talking from that direction after I put the first bag down where I was told. After the second I noticed that the talking seemed to be coming closer to me and I looked up.

They kind of looked like kids. They were small, at least they looked that way from a distance. Two of them were wearing what looked like shabby brown pieces of loose clothing while the third I couldn't really make out, but seemed to be dressed in white. There were three of them that I could see on the hill that buffered the beach from the rest of the island. I kept my head away from them in case the cops asked them what I looked like and moved the bags into a crevice between the pavement of the parking lot and school as fast as possible.

By the end of the bags I realized that I no longer heard any music, talking, or laughing. If the sound of footsteps creeping up on you is bad, the sudden lack of sound from someone you know to be there while you're committing a felony is a thousand times worse. I looked around expecting to see someone, but the kids were gone. I dropped the last bag and slung my fat ass into the driver's seat. I spun the wheels just a little accidentally trying to get out of there quickly and prayed to God that a cop hadn't heard it. As I pulled out of the parking lot I noticed in my rearview mirror one of the kids staring at me.

It was the one in white, and he was standing on top of the schoolhouse I had just pulled away from. The only light was a parking lot light in between us so it was difficult to see, but I know it was staring at me. The "kid" was standing on one leg, his entire torso bent at the waist and his face turned up at me, just like the person in the bathroom on my first day. I saw a bright, pale, oval face but couldn't make out any of the features, turned up at me at an unnatural angle like something out of Cirque du Soleil. I didn't give a shit about the cops anymore and hit the gas a little.

Never hit the gas when you're not looking through the front windshield. Basic rule of driving.

Almost right away I heard a terrible thud and something got pulled underneath my 1986 Monte Carlo. A blast of what looked like brown cloth or feathers went everywhere. A sickening snap underneath my car let me know that I may have just crossed a serious line in life. The adrenaline was so much that I had no idea what to do. I drove. I swerved to my left, almost off the parking lot, to get away from whatever was underneath me. I furiously threw the wheel in the other direction to aim myself back at the exit again and hit the gas again just as I heard something smack the roof of my car.

A brown blur struck the window right behind my head and blew out the glass. I heard something that sounded like either an old church organ horribly misfiring or several people wailing at the same time from the beach. I was out of the parking lot by the time I heard it though and I had no interest in whatever was making it. Despite having potentially just killed a kid, I felt very strongly as if I was the one who was going to be a victim tonight. I sped like crazy until I was off the island.

The whole sky was jet black then, with just the lights from the towers looming over West Palm Beach. Then I drove at exactly the speed limit, as if the shattered glass wasn't even there. I didn't even turn on the radio or air conditioning during the ride. There were oily-looking feathers in my front grill when I got home. The roof had deep grooves scratched into the metal right behind where my head was. There was a smell coming from the car that reminded me of the smell of dead fish on an overused and under-cleaned pier.

When I got home I called Dave right away and told him everything in one very long sentence. He didn't seem surprised at all.

"How many of them were there?" he calmly asked.

"Three? I dunno? Two other than the one I hit." He chuckled at that.

"I don't know what happened to the bag." I was horrified at the prospect that my employers might take such a loss personally, but if the bags hadn't been picked up he gave no indication.

"Listen, I'm not going to stop over there and neither is anyone else." I breathed a sigh of relief. I took this to mean that he wasn't going to hold me accountable, at least not right now, for the loss.

"So if you hear me outside of your house, or Debbie or anyone else you're not expecting, do not leave your house. Even if you hear me telling you that it's alright and that we need your help, you do not set foot outside of your house unless we call you on your cell. Don't worry about the bags or the cops, you did good. Don't worry about coming in for a while, just relax. How much water do you have at your place?" I checked quickly. I had ten gallons in two large five-gallon containers.

"I got ten gallons."

"Alright, sit tight for a couple of days at least, don't go out and I'll be by on Tuesday to drop off more water and let you know what's going on. Don't trust the tap water. For now, you did good though. Oh, if you happen to look outside a lot try not to do it from night time to the early morning, especially not the morning." He cleared his throat loudly while I wished I could make myself believe he was talking about the cops. I wondered how much of what was happening he understood and from where.

"So remember, never go out in the morning. The morning worms are for the birds." He hung up.

That last statement ended up scaring the shit out of me until I had enough Xanax in me to kill a donkey, but he hung up right after saying it, leaving me wondering whether I was in danger if I did leave the house and from what. About a minute after he hung up I heard a scraping sound coming from my roof, brief but clear. Six days later when I was given the all clear I found horrible-smelling, greasy white feathers in the gutter right over my door.

After that Dave seemed to gain some trust in me. Possibly because I was shit terrified, taking drugs to hide it and not asking questions. In retrospect, I was for the first time in my life what an employer would consider a model employee. I got a huge raise, a call girl sent to my place as a gift, and a ton of drugs. This soon became apparent because I was clearly the organization's go-to guy for extremely weird shit. Christmas was just around the corner, and apparently Santa decided it was time for me to pay up for years of missed coal opportunities.

At that moment though, the only thing on my mind was getting Dave to talk in person so I could learn whatever he knew about this shit, because he at least seemed to know when and where these things would be.

3

* * *

I was mainly stunned for about a week after that. Once and again, a gigantic, mute bruiser in nuclear green and purple handed me a bag with money and drugs and said to let them know when I felt good to come back. Dave did not respond to my texts during this time and Debbie just told me to rest up and to tell her when I could come in because she didn't want to talk about it over the phone. I began to rack my mind for experiences of situations that I could at least google. It was difficult to tell which parts were Floridian junkie mythologies and which came from people reacting to something genuinely weird, whether they had their facts straight or not.

Everyone used to say that the area that is now Bryant Park and the expanse of Lake Worth was deeply haunted. Bryant Park is an increasingly beautiful suburban park on the Intercostal Waterway. It borders Lake Worth, a formerly poor neighborhood that still has really bad parts and rough roads, but has been increasing in value thanks to the older homes which are frequently easy to renovate thanks to concrete block construction. It's a beautiful old neighborhood with a distinct style formed out of the blocky homes and frequent use of pastel colors. It used to be a great place for the homeless to crash, as Lake Worth used to be a lot cheaper. It still is, but not as much.

If you were out at the park at night, you had to be careful, because things that looked like people would occasionally come out of the water in the summer (and for some reason only the summer), turn and face the seawall that lined the walkway with their backs to the park, and wait for people to get close to them. When someone did, they would see something that looked almost human but with giant mouths filled with large blunt teeth, oddly shaped eyes, stringy wet hair, and slimy pale skin. There had been plenty of missing homeless from that area, and every now and then the area underneath the Lake Worth Bridge, which crosses the Gulfstream Hotel and goes over the park, was sealed off by police, who had presumably found something there.

It was absolutely agreed upon that the Gulfstream Hotel had a man living in it, despite being boarded up for who knows how long. He would stare angrily down at passersby and if you tried to get his attention or willingly made eye contact with him he would motion for you to come up to him. I've never met anyone who went past the first flight of stairs though, as that creepy old building was built with the old Floridian rule of air conditioning: make it as drafty as possible and preferably out of wood even in places it shouldn't be. This made it creaky and therefore creepy. This meant the wind screamed throughout the building, but I remember one guy named Andy — who is now a physician — who told us that it sounded like a person whistling something.

I remembered a girl I had gone to John I. Leonard (and later dropped out) with, Meghan Water, an adorable long-haired brunette who was into Radiohead and who I used to score weed from. She started dating some older guy on the island. I remember this because the cops came around asking the people on her phone and text history if anyone knew his name or what he looked like. The top part of her head, missing the bottom jaw, had been found hanging from her hair from a streetlight near Datura, which was a largely desolate street at the time near Clematis Boulevard. Clematis was a tiny, pathetic strip of ever-changing clubs and restaurants across the water from the island. They've made it a hell of a lot nicer these days.

I'd heard Meghan had tried to break up with her older creep boyfriend and was really afraid because he wasn't who he said he was. One of the worse rumors was that he demanded that she marry him so that they could move away together and when she said no something began stalking her. Her friends said she was really afraid in the days before her death.

I also remembered John Parks, a stupid junkie who was into theatre and a lot of drama. I never liked him so I never paid attention to the fact that he was killed in a hit and run near the Breakers, but they found pieces of him in Manalapan, which was down the way by a normally beautiful twenty-five minute drive. They found the pieces months after he was killed.

Some of the stories about how they died were pretty horrific, and I thought they were just cruel high school bullshit at the time. I remember hearing that John had been seen screaming and trying to get someone's help the night he died, waving to people from across the Royal Palm Way, from the path that leads to the Flagler Museum. But when they caught up with him, it was someone else who claimed they hadn't seen a thing.

Some of the stories didn't even need a death for an origin. It was widely understood when I was growing up that the schoolhouse I would now be avoiding for the rest of my life was, in some way, haunted. I had never really paid attention to that, but I remember Stimpy, a kid from High School who was an idiot, a basket case, and obsessed with occult stuff (in that order, unfortunately). He had insisted that not only was that place deeply haunted, but that Hobe Sound had even worse things. Weird ghosts who wore insanely colored masks and hunted humans, or made bargains with them.

I can't remember all of what he said but I've been googling it and can only find bits and traces. I remember him telling us about people made out of sand who would try to imitate humans and a demon that haunted the Wellington Green Mall. As I said, it's pretty difficult to tell which parts had any genuine inspiration because most were bullshit.

There were urban legends about Native American spirits that still haunted the land, dead slaves and other victims of Flagler who kept looking for revenge or solace, and other, stranger spirits that had less clear definitions. Jessica, the blonde who had been hired by Dave to run our medication room, mentioned something about reading up on that stuff. She came from Hobe Sound and had become interested in missing persons reports after a girl in her high school went missing. A lot of people were contacted by a girl who went to school in Hobe Sound and who had apparently spent her last moments trying to contact someone to get help. They claimed she said she was horribly wounded by something that came out of the sky and was afraid that it was hunting her. I'm still looking for any bits left on the internet about that. Her friends posted something on Facebook because they felt like the cops ignored what they told them about the girl's last phone call and decided that she had probably just run away.

Still, I had no idea which of these stories was even based on truth and even then I really doubted their accuracy. The people I hang around couldn't be expected to report what color the sky is accurately. Aside from the deaths, I wasn't sure there was any truth at all, but I did want to avoid the Lake Worth area from now on.

After about four days I took my car to the shop and googled my own name to see if I had a warrant for running over a kid. Nope, not a single thing. I almost hoped I would get stopped by a cop just to see if anything came up. The suspense made it hard to focus.

***

After I got my car window fixed and the vehicle detailed I started to pay a lot more attention to the patients and the weird stories they always told. I had previously, sadly, assumed these things to be bullshit, but there was no chance that my employers hadn't heard the same stories. Had Dave or Debbie or George known what they were sending me into? I knew I had to confront Dave—who seemed higher on the totem pole than Debbie—about what exactly he knew.

I wanted to gather more information; it seemed like everyone around me knew of a vast system of weird shit that I had only yet seen the edges of. Debbie knew to get the fuck away from that bird thing, Dave knew that creep with the bolo tie (whose name I really hoped *was* Lyle because at least that would consolidate the sources of creepiness) was coming and not to talk to him, and I was willing to bet there was plenty more. Dave still hadn't returned my text about talking to him one on one, but now that I was back at work I was certain he would come around soon and I needed more to ask him about.

Most of them wanted nothing to do with anyone, since they were quietly but openly committing a felony. But some of the miscreants who came in smaller, less-regular groups that were cut off from the herd were chattier. They were always more than happy to talk, especially since I worked for the people who handed them pills. The amount of people involved in moving these pills up what was called "The Blue Highway" was absolutely staggering. Tens of thousands of people were directly involved in driving from Appalachian states to Florida in order to procure drugs to resell at home. Middle-level dealers recruited low-level junkies of all stripes to go down to Florida and many of these people were impoverished, uneducated, frequently mentally ill "white trash." The "runners" usually came from trailers that were little more than thin tin shacks for homes, or dilapidated homes left over from an era when people in that area could afford to build them. At home, it wasn't rare for them to go without electricity and sometimes even running water, but they always managed to get their pills. Some of them went missing from time to time.

I heard dozens of weird stories pretty much right away. The most consistent definitely involved the man wearing the bolo tie. I asked some regulars, a fat old couple from Ohio with more track marks than arm skin, about him. The balding old man was in camouflage and his wife, I shit you not, came in wearing a bright orange muumuu with brilliant flowers. Henry and Louise Thompkins. You could smell either from about ten feet away.

"Hey, that guy with the nice getup and the Texas tie, he ever say anything different?"

The old man put down his gigantic soda and looked at his wife in consultation. She nodded sagely to him, keeping her eyes fixed on me from behind her big red glasses. He leaned over to me even though we were the only ones there.

"Nah, hear from someone else that he came up on some people in Jacksonville at Josh Rhoade's clinic. Kept botherin them bout how to leave and where are they and whatnot. Weird fucker."

He shot his wife another look, this one far more dire, and the obese old woman nodded one more time, this time only slightly.

"Heard he got couple of em. Can't talk to him. Can't say nuthin, don't know what he lookin for. Always dress the same."

I heard more or less the same thing from a couple of people. One person told me it happened in a motel and that no one saw how he got there. Another said they were waiting in a pharmacy but that no one said anything and he just passed by, confused and talking to himself. They said they watched, with their own eyes, as he ignored a person of the non-junkie variety when that Good Samaritan tried to help him at the pharmacy.

Of course, plenty more of the stories were clearly bullshit. Sometimes stuff they probably heard through the junkie grapevine, like him being a cop or member of some organized crime group or another. Sometimes they were just junkies talking in the moment and didn't mean anything. But there were other stories too.

People were prone to going missing and it's hard to tell which stories were just explanations for overdoses and which ones were genuinely weird shit.

I kept hearing that we should all stay away from the beaches and the parks, especially in the mornings. A lot of people who try to sleep there overnight on the trip down to Florida simply don't make it. Even the large groups, who occasionally had their own armed hicks for security, were prone to avoiding the living shit out of the coast and driving inland, even though it was covered in police.

The Everglades is a place no one would cross, and the fact that there were almost no junkie outlets in areas along the more rural southern part of the West Coast, or at least fewer of them, was taken as proof that all junkies should avoid it. This made me worry since I live on the edge of an area called Loxahatchee, all the way across the county from the Grand Island and pretty much bordering the massive wetlands covering Florida.

Miami was loudly and openly known as its opposite, and it was known for being absolutely safe for even the most absurd behavior. I kept hearing relatively consistent stories about "strange people" who would warn junkies about police and in at least one seemingly less-batshit story, even distracting the police. They wore weird clothes and smiled great big smiles, even though I kept hearing that they didn't look happy. Despite being helpful, people were generally scared shitless of them and they kept repeating that stuff about the mirthless smiles.

One of the most infamous legends was to avoid the tourist traps and fields along the lines of the Blue Highway (I-95, for the uninitiated). Over and over I would hear about how people would pull off the main highway into largely uninhabited areas that compose the majority of Florida and seem relatively safe. Over and over I heard about people going missing that way. I remembered hearing about this from other junkies before, but how many times? I never paid attention to these urban legends, but now they were suddenly becoming crucial in my mind. I wondered how many of them were true or even just half truths.

The most frequently repeated junkie legends involved people or things coming out of the woods and leaving very little of whoever they found. It was always a friend who disappeared as part of a larger group or something else distant. I noticed that people hated talking about it more than anything. I also noticed that there were no stories of single people being killed or going missing. It was always entire groups and some exits were worse than others.

A guy named Damon (pretty sure he picked that name for his fake license) had been coming around for as long as I knew and was pretty friendly with Debbie and Dave, and had name-dropped George on more than one occasion. He came in just after Samantha disappeared, wearing a normal Stone Temple Pilots shirt and black denim jeans, but seemingly almost impressive for his relative level of hygiene and the quality of the clothing and car he owned. After he checked in and was waiting in the doctor's hall I decided to start a conversation.

"Good morning, Mr. Damon. Would you mind if I asked you a question?"

"It's a free country, ain't it?" He smiled kindly from behind unreflective aviator sunglasses.

"If I were driving along I-95 and I needed to stop and rest, say off of Yeehaw Junction [an area about thirty miles away from bum-fuck nowhere], where could I stop at?"

He stopped smiling.

"I'd say skip an exit or two and forget whatever you thought you needed at Yeehaw Junction. Even when we go to Lake Wales we drive around the long way."

Lake Wales was a major crystal meth production center at the time, and it was close to rural spots like Winterhaven and Eustice, attracting its own narco-sphere of interconnected supply workers and distributors quickly. He meant driving down the other coast, an entirely different group of operations I had no knowledge of. For so many scumbags to avoid such an obvious shortcut wasn't just unusual, it was borderline impossible. I had driven through there and slept in parking lots as a teenager all the time, with nothing to worry about.

"Why do that?"

He looked exasperated. "Less heartache." He clapped his hands to his knees and shrugged to show his lack of enthusiasm for the subject. I nodded and moved on.

Eventually Debbie asked me why I had bothered Damon about it. She was gorgeous, with dark brown hair, a kind of Native American look, and a dislike for being hit on or being told to smile. She often dressed in the frumpier version of her wardrobe and didn't care what the patients or I thought about her appearance. When she wanted to look great it was easy, but right now, with slightly smeared eye makeup, she looked angrier than she was.

"Wilks, I need you to tell me what you were talking to Damon about. George texted me about it."

This was actually a big deal, since George was the real power and despite Debbie sleeping in the same bed as him we almost never heard about his wishes.

"I wanted to ask him about places to sleep along I-95."

She stared at me with a hint of accusation. "Why?"

"I keep hearing patients talk about this spot I used to camp in when I was younger like there is something wrong with it."

She sighed and thought about it for a second. I stared at her, knowing that she had some idea as to what the fuck was going on, or at least what the scale of this shit was. She glanced at the ground before meeting my eyes again.

"You need to stop asking people about it. It scares them and they might start to think bad stuff if they think you've been going there."

She stared at me defiantly, and I was suddenly in no mood to concretely find out what she knew. What she knew was that the place was clearly dangerous. I took this to mean that it was widely known enough to just stay away from. Looking back on all of this, I probably should have stayed away too.

That afternoon before I left, a little girl who came in with what appeared to be her mother and father bounded up to me. She was wearing a little blue shirt and white pants and seemed delighted to talk to someone after having to stay quiet to avoid the junkies for so many hours.

"Hello! Me and my mommy and my daddy were coming down here and we tried to sleep off of Yeehaw Junction but a man in a blue alligator mask ran up to us and yelled at us twice and bit the front of our car. You shouldn't go there."

I was more than a bit stunned, and she just happily bounded away. We were standing outside the clinic and she ran to her dad, an old man with a stained trucker hat and a gray t-shirt, who didn't look like he enjoyed the people who normally came to our clinic. He nodded to me and walked off to their car, which was missing the front bumper and had a spare tire. Jesus Fucking Christ. So, if this was entirely caused by supernatural shit there is no way I was the only one who noticed. I stared at their car as it limped away, for once hoping they got good money for their meds.

***

Patients overdosing became so common that the phone calls from police demanding information on the amount of medication prescribed to the deceased stopped registering pretty quickly. It wasn't long until someone that I genuinely knew ended up being the reason for one of those calls.

"Corey Franks was found today in a ditch off of Southern well past 441, dead from an overdose. We're going to need all of the information you have on him."

The detective was blunt, fully aware that she was talking to one of the people who had helped to expedite this young man's death. He was a twenty-two year old surfer local—locals were rare—and a friend of a friend. He was definitely an idiot, one of those people who listened to a lot of Sublime and talked about how it "resonated" with him whenever he got high. He hung out with me a couple of times, especially if I had weed, and was usually full of shit and only hung out with people who were generally pretty awful even by white-trash standards. A lot of his friends genuinely thought Insane Clown Posse and roleplaying games where you dressed up as a vampire in public and really acted it out were entirely acceptable.

"Whoever he was with may have been the one who left the poor kid's body in a canal near the Loxahatchee Glades. Didn't even take the medication, it was all there. We're trying to find any information on any close relatives or anyone that won't hang up if we call about him."

She was saying a lot more than they normally did, I wondered if she knew that I knew Corey or if she just sensed that she could strike a chord with me. A sudden feeling of terror ripped through me, turning me cold as ice. I didn't so much think about what prison would be like as much as feel it, as if it were waiting around a corner for me.

"I don't know…" I stammered while looking at his file on my computer. The cheap plastic desk suddenly felt ice cold and I was all too aware that the DEA was probably watching my every move. This phone call could very well end up in my trial. The feeling of eyes on my back made my skin crawl.

"I talked to him a few times, but he didn't list any contacts and he mentioned that his dad kicked him out a year ago."

I knew he had been staying with a bunch of junkies from South Carolina who took him with them to pick up and sell their medication at a profit, and I began to search my mind for the words to use to summarize this.

"He was staying in a motel for an extended period of time and we have the license plates and names of the people he seemed to be staying with, would you mind checking if they are patients too?"

I already knew that at least one or two of the names would show up. The ringleaders who owned the cars and fronted everyone else the cash for their visits rarely stayed as patients themselves. I had no interest in exerting any energy in protecting them and happily faxed her all of the relevant files without telling anyone.

The rest of the day went by quickly thanks to a lot of pipe hits in the bathroom and doxylamine. I said goodnight to Debbie and Jessica as the doctors filed out to their luxury cars. The moment I opened the deeply tinted glass storefront door the feeling of eyes watching me was almost physically palpable. The sun was down and the parking lot empty aside from some homeless gathering in front of some empty storefronts. I whipped around and in the dark I saw a beaten-to-hell '90s Buick Roadmaster station wagon. I remember it clearly because it was the one Corey used to drive. He thought it was the coolest thing in the world because he read on a website that station wagons were cool and it had a V8.

The headlights weren't on, despite the sun being only a dark orange slit. It seemed to be moving toward me, but if it was it was much slower than I could easily gauge, especially in the dark. I didn't hear the threatening burble of the engine. But I got the impression it was moving toward me. I had no idea why Corey's junkie friends would swing by this place after he died and I didn't want to find out. I avoided making eye contact with the vehicle's front windshield and opened my car door without bothering to see if the movement I saw in the reflection on the windshield was something actually behind me.

By the time I got back to my shitty one-bedroom house in the middle of Loxahatchee it was pitch dark and the swamp was emitting its usual deep, guttural sounds. I put on some romantic comedy that had made me feel good once. I tried to envision myself as one of the characters of the movie, happy and normal, but at this point I was just trying to remember the last time I had successfully escaped to that degree. That night I got more fucked up than usual. I desperately chugged the remainder of a 750 of dirt-cheap vodka. I remembered buying the expensive stuff and telling myself that I'd make it last but I had stopped telling myself excuses a while ago. I followed this with some Xanax and a little Nyquil. I put on some headphones and tried to either get into the music or the movie, but no amount of weed could let me escape reality. I went to sleep with the TV on mute, in a desperate attempt to let some of the positive emotions from that saccharine movie soak into me.

I woke covered in cold sweat, gasping for air. It was still dark out and colder than usual for Florida thanks to some exceptional December winds. Despite the money I was bringing in, the only pieces of furniture in my room were a mattress on a box spring on the floor and a desk and chair for my PC. I was desperately craving the sweet burn of booze, despite feeling deeply nauseous. If I had to guess, I was probably still drunk.

I got up in a start and saw something move in the dark near my door. I squinted in the dark and suddenly I heard my front door open. I ran out of my room in my underwear only to see my front door wide open and the beaten Buick on the road that ran perpendicular to my small driveway. It was facing me as if it was about to drive directly into my front door, sitting across the road attached to my house.

My home, like most in rural Florida, was hemmed in by plant life. This combined with the flat land ensured that you usually only see a wall of green or a shitty strip mall when you drive anywhere in the state. The car was sitting on the road, facing my house directly, blocking the road entirely. It was the only object in my field of vision other than woods and road. The lights still weren't on and once again I got the impression the car was moving. I could feel something watching me and a sudden feeling of terror froze my spine, this time entirely without any connotations of the FBI or jail. Whatever was inside of that car was watching me. I saw something move in the air in between the car and me, but couldn't make out what it was. I flipped on the light switch nearest to me and didn't bother looking to see if it revealed anything. I slammed the door shut and ran through the tiny concrete shack I called a home, flipping on every light and turning on the TV to full blast, as if the sound of people in the movie laughing and falling in love would somehow ward anything off.

I didn't dare look directly at any window, instead catching them from the corner of my sight to make sure the blinds were already pulled shut. I staggered into the kitchen, still fucked up apparently, and pulled a Red Bull from my fridge. The sharp taste did refresh me for a brief second. I wanted to get out of there, but I would not dare go near the door in case something wanted to come back inside. I sat down on my couch with my back to the concrete wall. My cellphone had a missed call from my friend Carl at 1:30. It was 3:37 at that point. I called him, praying to God he wanted drugs badly enough to drive to my place right away. He didn't, but I offered some free Xanax and I could hear him putting on clothes before he ended the sixteen-second phone call in a confused tone.

I didn't move until the doorbell rang, when I just said loudly, "Come in."

I was terrified it wasn't going to be Carl. Carl looked exhausted, even for a junkie, but smiled weakly with an interested look in his eyes. I was more than happy to open my private stock, hoping to God he would try and strike up a conversation in an effort to get more drugs. I showed him the giant bottle of soma pills I had pilfered and he brightened right up.

"That does sound good! I get horrible back spasms and, like… yeah…"

I was already pouring some out for him before he finished the excuse for his addiction and he seemed too happy to question it.

"Hey, do you have some new neighbors or something?" he asked absentmindedly as he popped a few of the soma."

I blinked hard and tried to shake off the fear that was still with me, or at least keep it from showing.

"No, no. Why, did you see someone?" I tried and failed, and he seemed to notice but kept going.

"Yeah, when I drove up here there was someone standing in the road, staring at your house? It looked like their car had broken down because they were standing outside of it. I tried to talk to them but they just drove off." 'Them' wasn't the word I wanted to hear about right now. He seemed to think maybe my new neighbor was just nuts, because he was smirking.

"Are they gone?" I was pretty openly fucking terrified at this point and Carl seemed to become concerned.

"Yeah, I only saw one person for a split second and I'm pretty sure there was someone else inside, they must have run off. Do you think it was the cops or someone following you? You could crash at my place, my mom wouldn't care." He tapered as he was speaking and I guessed that maybe he was just offering concern as thanks for the free drugs, but I had to take it.

"Yeah, that would be cool; I could sneak out before she woke up anyways." Carl's mom was sixty-seven and suffering from a laundry list of medical issues. She took care of Carl as if he was a perpetually wounded bird, no matter how many times he stole from her. She was barely hanging on to a job where she had been quietly demoted repeatedly and offered various severance packages to retire, but she had no savings thanks to Carl and couldn't dream of it. She was perpetually nervous and drank a lot of wine and I hated seeing her because of the guilt I felt for giving this asshole drugs. I swallowed this and followed Carl out to his car, massively relieved to not see the Buick out there. I slept like a baby on his couch for almost three hours, before whatever was in me wore off and I woke up and drove to my place for a shower.

Work went by, but not easily. I told Debbie that the car had been following me, and that it had belonged to a friend of mine who had overdosed. She listened intently and when I left her office I heard her speaking into her cellphone with a concerned tone. Aside from the typical junkie business, it was a normal day, with the normal amount of terrible shit. Not a single human being wanted to be there and most were disgusted with themselves for showing up. People spat chewing tobacco into bottles of Mountain Dew and left them there. They got into fistfights over drugs in the parking lot and a couple of girls who looked like they were ready to kill themselves waited outside near the parking lot in outfits of varying degree of skimpiness, willing to turn tricks for pills. Eventually I decided to finally stop procrastinating and confront Debbie. She was in her office and told me to come in when I knocked. She had an array of drugs in front of her and a laptop with a spreadsheet open.

"Hey, I have to talk to you. Some shit happened on the Island at that drop. And some other shit."

She sighed and shut her laptop. She had clearly hoped I would dump this one someone else's plate.

"I know, shit went bad." She turned around to face me and motioned for me to sit in a chair across from her desk. "Listen, we got the bags, alright? You did good. Someone was trying to fuck with you."

"I haven't even said what happened yet and I'm pretty sure it was not people who have been fucking with me."

I sank into the chair and stared at my knees while I prepared for either bullshit or something worse. I don't know what was more amazing, that she thought this was just weird people or that they sent someone to pick up the bags later. I'd been worried the bags were just filled with newspaper and that they didn't plan on me coming back.

"A lot of weird people are involved in this shit. They do anything to get more. We had to make the drop there but we thought it wasn't likely for anyone to notice you since you're kind of new. It usually takes people a while before the weirdos notice you."

This opened up a lot of questions and no answers. I was already frustrated. "Why did you have to make the drop there? That doesn't make sense, and why were there 'weirdos,' and by the way that is not what they were, there?"

I found myself deeply unwilling to state that rotting bird demons may have been at fault, as if saying it out loud would make all the weird shit true. As long as there was the possibility that I was mistaken, there was the possibility that it was just junkies and thieves the whole time.

"There is some shit going on around here that belongs on *The X-Files* and I have the bird feathers to prove it."

She had a deeply unsettled look, and she stared down at her desk as if reading something for a moment. "We had to make the drop there. We didn't have a choice. Look, I'm going to talk to Dave… when he gets back… do you want to crash at me and George's place, for the time being? If you don't feel safe, that is."

She sounded sincere. And a little guilty. This was good, but the idea of sleeping in the same house as her mobster boyfriend with swastika tattoos just didn't seem as reassuring as a shitty motel room or a friend in City Place, the tiny cluster of expensive restaurants in the middle of what had once been a massive ghetto. I did not want her to extend that offer any more than she already did, as the thought of being in her home was more than a little disturbing.

"I'm alright… for right now… I'm going to crash at a room at Simon's or a motel."

I muttered a thanks and goodbye and went back to work. It was less than a week to Christmas and the patients were as demanding as ever. My friend Simon wasn't excited about putting me up so I said no worries and decided to head to a La Quinta nearby that thankfully had a filled parking lot. Without being in my home, and not giving a shit even if there was a car outside or a bird on the roof because there were cameras and other people and somehow I didn't think any of that weird shit would be too courageous, I finally slept deeply and without too many drugs. Aside from some dream where I was looking for a mask in an old station wagon, I slept like a baby.

4

The following days were right before Christmas and I really had no interest in going back to my place, even for clothes. I called Debbie and let her know I'd be a little late and then texted Carl to see if he could check up on my place. Both said something along the lines of "no problem" and I went shopping for clothes at the nearest Marshalls.

I had forgotten that when you're not locked in a dungeon that would make Charlie Sheen feel uncomfortable due to the amount of substance abuse, West Palm Beach is actually a genuinely nice place to live. During the winter the humidity and temperature both drop and it becomes increasingly difficult not to enjoy the brisker weather. I took advantage of this and the extra time and decided to get a few relatively nice things from the discount bin of the biggest Marshalls in town before heading back to the motel room to shower and get changed. I wanted to do something other than wonder to what degree the bird monsters and whatever had been driving that car were related to the other creepy shit.

It was probably the first day I hadn't tried to push it with the Xanax because I can remember it clearly without going to my journal. I didn't want to think about the drug dealers, hooking, the smell of urine, feces, and human rot that pervaded the clinic, or the constant look of misery on every single person's face. I stood outside of the motel as the sun was just finishing its rise, despite the pit in my stomach that remained from Dave telling me it was the worst time of day to go outside. I kept an eye out for birds. The sky was an explosion of turquoise, with ribbons of violent pink and orange and reflective clouds that looked impossibly bright. This is a pretty typical Florida morning, especially in winter. It looked like a Trapper Keeper from the '90s. Three hours later, the way the cashier at Marshall's had smiled with genuine-looking happiness before going back to a conversation with a coworker shook me to the bone, like a cold shower after a bender.

At about nine in the morning, the sky was bright blue but still shot through with a handful of scintillating neon tangerine bolts left over from sunrise. One of the upsides to living in a flat place that rarely gives a hint that anything beyond tree level could exist is that riding over different parts of town could be an absolute thrill, especially with your windows rolled down or if you were lucky enough to own a convertible or motorcycle, enjoying the full throttle of the elements.

Dave had sent a single text, asking me to meet him at Dubois Park in Jupiter. I didn't feel great about this since it was along the water, but the thought that he at least knew something of what was going on—and the fact that it was at 12:30, when families would be there—was reassuring.

I stopped at the Paris Café near Clematis Street and treated myself to a chocolate brioche something or another.

A library was at the end of this street during the time, facing the waterfront with a massive glass window that was relatively gorgeous as far as public buildings in Florida go. At night time the area is usually a slow, stunning show of neon pinks, oranges, blues, and purples set amid a sea of jet black, from the signs of bars and other night-time establishments. At daytime it's a classy affair with small trees planted every now and then in between the beige to light pastel buildings with wealthy white people walking their dogs in between. No more than twenty minutes of walking the nice streets, or five minutes of driving, and you would arrive at a place right past the City Place outdoor mall that would redefine how you viewed the words "poor" and "destitute." After a few minutes of driving over the only (man-made) hills in Palm Beach County I turned around to the nearby Okeechobee Boulevard, which bookended the nicer part of City Place, and drove to Military Trail where I then drove north through suburbia for about an hour, skipping I-95 to enjoy the long way through South Florida.

By the time I got to Dubois, it was 12:30 and I was right on time. Dave was waiting in a salmon pink Cuban-style linen shirt and black pants outside of the parking lot nearest the beach. There was a more secluded one inland near a massive brackish river, but I wasn't going to argue with having families playing in sight. He stood beside a matte black Mercedes AMG something or another with his arms crossed, smiling toward the sea. He almost looked like a particularly peaceful supervillain. He motioned to a nearby picnic table within view of both the families and a massive rock seawall that allowed a powerful man-made river that ran the sea to inland water sources.

The park itself was a historical one that was built on a midden used by the Jaega people who lived here before the Seminole or the whites who came after. Aside from some old homes built over 100 years ago, there were a variety of archeological sites of interest to anyone who wanted to look at rocks some Natives used. Apparently due to the lack of load-bearing animals they had a tendency to live near large bodies of water even when the water wasn't fresh, as it made travel and carrying baskets filled with goods easier. Traces of buildings they made before being enslaved by Spaniards and taken to Cuba had been found at some point during the '80s.

It was a popular and beautiful park, hillier than you expect Florida to be. The sight of other people and the thought that he probably wouldn't be friends with whatever I had seen before reassured me enough to take a seat next to where he had a few joints and a sandwich and coffee from Havana's, Palm Beach's most popular Cuban restaurant.

He smiled slightly, unapologetic.

"So let's clear the air."

He clasped his massive hands together in a V over his breakfast.

"First, I'm going to need you to hand me your cellphone."

This was a common but mildly threatening practice. I'm not sure what good it would have done had the cops actually been watching. I handed both cellphones I owned to him, and he took them and put them in the trunk of his car for the time being. I know, I have no idea what possible good that would do even if I was an informant, but I assumed it was mainly for the show. These guys weren't bright. When he sat back down, he looked particularly relaxed as he motioned for me to speak while he dug into what looked like a medianoche, a pressed ham sandwich on an egg bread similar to challah.

"Listen, I've had a rough time with this. No one told me what was waiting for me at the drop and they haven't exactly left me alone. I need to know what's going on here."

I said this in an apologetic tone that surprised me, but the size of the muscles on this guy as well as his gun reminded me to be polite. Also, the fact that I would run out of pills within a week put more than a little pressure on me. He lit up a joint before replying, and took a long drag before exhaling and placing the joint on the table next to his sandwich.

"You've done great. We're all really surprised, you took this really well. I'm going to tell you what we know of this shit, but first let me just say that we had to make the drop there because the police wouldn't go near it either and it was the only place we could have gotten away with it. We thought you would have an easier time getting in and out, but I'm glad you made it out safe and we'll know better than to throw you out like that next time."

Despite his absolutely reassuring tone, I could not have been more horrified. He knew something was there *and the cops were prone to avoiding it as well.* I had to wonder if the well-dressed man would be able to interact with police the same way he did with junkies. Were there old ladies who just called the police three times a week about the bird demons terrorizing their teacup Yorkie without getting a response? Did the Young Men's Choir at Palm Beach Atlantic just learn to schedule their beachside concerts around possible swooping attacks?

"What were those fucking things?" This time I spoke without any reluctance; now that he had acknowledged the frightening part of this I didn't hold back.

"We don't know. That's the honest truth of it, man. The people who told us about them used to be with the "Cocaine Cowboys" of the '70s, who would drop packages of blow in the Everglades by prop plane. Apparently they ran into a lot of problems."

"What about the car?"

This time he looked at me as if I might not be serious.

"A little while ago a friend of mine died. Now his car has been showing up, without the engine on, stalking me."

"Wilks… you need to listen to me… we've never heard anyone complain about a car. We've heard a lot of spooky shit, and keep in mind to not ask anyone about traveling near Yeehaw Junction again, but driverless cars just haven't been on the list. Maybe one of your friend's ring-mates have the car and just put quieter mufflers on it? Are you sure it wasn't a junkie? I hate to break it to you, but they might start wondering what you're keeping at home. You should consider buying a gun, one way or the other."

It seemed a bit absurd that he thought I was being ridiculous for worrying about the car after being attacked by bird creatures. A slight hint of a Boston accent came out when he pronounced 'car' as 'cahhr.' I was instantly relieved that at least that seemed, to him, to not be supernatural and desperately wanted to believe that it was just a B&E from some guy while I was wasted. After having it confirmed that it may, in fact, have been something non-human attacking my car, it would be nice to have a human source of fear again. He put his sandwich down, finished a chew and followed up with the coffee you could smell from a block away.

"Why don't you tell me what files to pull that came with your friend and I'll find out if one of them has been seen driving the car?"

I described the Buick while he texted the information to some unknown colorful wad of muscle. He resumed talking while he did it.

"So, we've heard about the other shit though. Bird people, right? We heard them called Stickaninny or something before, at least that's one some pill-billies call them, but we don't know what they are. We just know to avoid them, just like anything else weird we encounter. We're drug dealers, not whatever bureau gets assigned to shit like this. What I can tell you is simple:

stay away from beaches during the morning. If something takes an interest in you, avoid anyone else and stay indoors for as long as you can. We've heard of people getting tricked by things using other people's voices, but never during broad daylight, always at night or in the early morning, but usually the morning."

He said this seriously, but with the attention someone would give a list they had read out loud too many times before.

"What about that guy with the stupid tie? He left something at the clinic after he came…"

He nodded solemnly at me.

"I know, Wilks. And you're doing damn good by keeping quiet through all of this. We don't know who or what that guy is, but he's showed up at other clinics before and he's been known to go through clinics in an area. Whenever he shows up at one he'll be nearby later, maybe at a motel where groups are staying or something like that, but he always moves from area to area. I told you as soon as I could after he left the American Injury Clinic. It may take a while, but he always comes around. Other than that, I've only heard stories, but those stories come from as far away as Oregon, where the European Kindred were apparently looking for him."

The European Kindred are a group of racists, loosely connected to the Aryan Brotherhood, known for haunting the poorer and more ignorant parts of northern California to Washington and Idaho. They were just as frequently known for violence and if I remember correctly they were prominently featured in a horror movie recently, something they are probably proud of. The distance that guy seemed to be able to cover was something to be worried about, and if a group connected to the AB couldn't put a bounty on the guy it probably wasn't much use trying to get to the bottom of him myself.

"Does he have a name? Lloyd, or maybe Lyle or something?"

He gave me a look of patience being expended. "If someone asks him his name, they're probably so fucked it's not worth worrying about. At least that's what I've been lead to believe. You're better off having a conversation with the DEA as far as getting dead goes."

He happily went back to his sandwich. I didn't know what else to ask without accusing him of lying and knowing more than he was claiming. He seemed to enjoy the silence while I sat and thought about this.

"I can't tell you how much of this is junkie talk and how much of it is real, like those fucking bird things. What I can tell you is that if a bunch of organized crime groups and drug dealers all start avoiding something, you should too. I've heard tons of crap that turned out to be just crap. These people are loaded most of the time anyways. But it's not like anyone has ever taken the time to explain this shit to us, we're just hearing about it while we try to make money, you know?"

This didn't answer why I had to make that drop and I became increasingly aware of the fact that he sent me out knowing there was danger and wasn't telling me why that place was necessary. Once he resorted to the old "they're just junkies who don't know what they're talking about" bit, I knew he was done talking. Honestly, at least. I kept repeating the word 'Stickaninny' in my head, over and over. I was hoping it meant something and wasn't just typical hick slang.

I took a few bites of the croissant from my favorite café and pretended that I was put at ease by his comfort with the supernatural. I took a joint and lit up myself, and sure enough it was a good one. I took a moment to fantasize that if I ever got arrested, it would be worth it for me to snitch just to ask what the cops knew during the proffer (the meeting with the prosecuting attorney where you trade knowledge of other people's crimes for your own freedom). For the time being, I desperately tried to play it cool.

"Ok, well, cool."

There was a high-pitched squeak somewhere in there that made him smirk and raise an eyebrow, but other than that he seemed to ignore it and nod happily before wolfing down his sandwich. For a moment I wondered if they would have rolled over on it had I been ripped apart by said bird things. If the cops already knew but didn't put a patrol car out with a guy and some birdshot it probably wouldn't do any good to do anything else.

We made some small chat where I told him a story about an old lady pretending to be crippled to get more meds and then dropping her crutches and running like hell when someone got too close to her bag that was left in the waiting room. He had a great one about a guy with swastikas tattooed everywhere complaining that the black doctor was racist against him for not prescribing more than normal despite a clearly badly cut finger.

Then, of course, he asked me if we were 'cool.' I couldn't say no to more drugs, and I mean that in a very literal way. It wasn't really an option. This made me hate him even more. He reminded me of the clinic and I'd rather emasculate myself with broken glass than have an extended conversation with him, but you do a lot of weird, horrible shit for drugs. I got out of there and texted Debbie that I'd need the rest of the day, which she didn't object to. Carl had tried to call me twice.

***

I began heading back to my shack after listening to the message Carl left saying that my door had been flung open and many of my possessions were lying out in my front lawn. He also said that he had just gotten out of the hospital for a "little thing" and that he had taken too many pills. I wondered, briefly, how much stress this put on his poor mother. It was his third overdose this year, and it was right before Christmas. It was a miracle he kept surviving them.

If I had neighbors who had to drive by my place, this may have even been a problem. When I got there, my hackles began to rise immediately. I took a few moments after the long fifty-five minute drive from Jupiter to my place to stretch and carefully look up and down my road for any sign of a sneaking Buick or bird feathers. I didn't see them on the road or the way to my front door, but noticed the telltale signs of junkies after that. A crushed Mountain Dew can was lying on my pathway. Someone had pissed and shat all over my bed and there was chewing tobacco on my couch. My TV had been stolen; anything else was scattered or destroyed, including three windows. I couldn't be happier.

If this meant that Dave was right and that had just been a breaking and entering I experienced while wasted, that may have been the greatest news of my life. I cleaned up to the best of my ability, threw away my bed, and got high as fuck on my reclining chair, which had only had a couple cigarettes put out on it. I had taken my drugs with me and they probably weren't happy at leaving empty-handed. I snickered at the thought of Dave's goons figuring out who they were and fucking them up and mildly regretted not being able to call the police. Still, the drugs were worth more than everything in the house and they hadn't touched them. As the pills I ate were slowly absorbed, I googled Florida's gun-buying process on my phone and texted Carl back that everything was under control and that I wouldn't mind hooking him up later. I rarely went for the quick high and preferred the slow-moving lurch of the pills when they were taken orally, and Roxicodone and Xanax both had excellent oral bioavailability rates.

First, I got a relatively cheap new computer. It was nice to see a normal retail store and I enjoyed wasting the associate's time, watching the high school kid try to upsell me eventually to something that could play a video game or two. I didn't have the heart to tell him why I didn't want to open a credit account and needed to pay for it in cash.

Then I went to a shooting range and got the small booklet I needed on gun safety and gun laws before heading home for some googling. I absentmindedly left a message for my landlord about the broken windows, knowing that he would certainly force me to pay for it anyway and that I should probably call a glass place. After arriving at my now much more drafty and urine-scented home, I plugged my new 'rig' in and started the long boot process. Instead of looking up glass though, I decided to find out what a 'Stickaninny' is.

Needless to say, "Stickaninny" didn't bring anything up, and neither did a combination of that and "Bird" or "monster." When you google things like this you usually end up wading through websites made by new-agers who seemed to compensate for their lack of knowledge with enthusiasm and shitty backgrounds, but eventually you might get the rough edges of an idea. It didn't take me long, however, to find out that many Seminole believed in sorcerers called "Stigini" that often took the shape of an owl. Apparently they were believed to be shapeshifters with the ability to take on an owl-like form that they then used to hunt humans. Unfortunately, I only found a single webpage that seemed legitimate. It covers Native American legends. I couldn't find any information on how to kill one, just in case, nor any hint of why they might take an interest in drug addicts. I quickly wrote a couple of emails to the website and to another group on Facebook that apparently focuses on Native American stories from Florida specifically, but tried to make it seem like I wasn't fishing for information on how to deal with them in real life. Then I called my landlord and got yelled at for a few minutes over the windows, which I claimed were in perfectly good shape when I left my home for work one day, before securing a cheap new bed to be delivered via Craigslist. The word Stigini kept repeating in my mind, like a catchy tune I couldn't get out of my head. After the bed came and I found a lamp post that looked like it could vaguely defend me against an unarmed hobo, I got ready for an early night of drug use and romantic comedies blaring at high volume.

I didn't want to sleep there and was suddenly more aware than ever that the drug dealers who tore my place apart would be more than willing to beat the shit out of me or kill me for drugs, but we don't always get to choose. It occurred to me that in light of recent information it was very likely that Corey had been given a 'hot dose,' a small but deadly amount of fentanyl or something mixed with his normal junk. It was a common way of getting rid of unwanted junkies when a dealer needed things to calm down and there was no telling how many overdoses were actually murders. The police never investigated anyway. Hours later, before nodding off, I wondered if Corey Franks had told them something that would make me seem like a particularly good target before either they or his own prescription killed him.

***

The next day went by with the usual amount of urine and fighting. Debbie called me into her office toward eleven to let me know I could go home early and pass on a message.

"George wants me to tell you something important," she said in a calm but severe manner. As the head of the operation, I had never been in the same room as him. It was important to make sure only certain people interacted with us so that the FBI didn't have photographs of the entire group working together, because that would make a RICO case a cakewalk. Getting a text or phone call from him would be unheard of. Being asked to meet him in person was like getting to meet a celebrity you never wanted to meet and being expected to pretend to be interested in everything they say. George had an incredible level of control over me simply because I didn't want him to think he needed to correspond with me any further.

"Alrighty…"

"You need to think about whether or not someone has gotten angry with you lately…"

"Is this about the car?" I cut her off almost right away. For a moment I hoped this was related to the car whose occupants may or may not have just been junkies who broke into my place.

"No, Wilks, you need to think. Who or whatever attacked you has a reason for it. We don't know why they pick people, but it's not always random, we think. This is serious. Sometimes they come back, but we don't know what they can or can't do."

She said this in a tone that was almost angry. I'd heard her use it before when she needed me to do something serious, usually involving instructions on avoiding law enforcement.

"Dave is looking into that car you told him about… you should have mentioned something sooner. Whoever is doing that may be behind everything else. He thinks it might be someone named Teddy Rance, the guy who used to ringlead for your friend's group. There's a good chance he's at the Castle Inn near Palm Beach Lakes tonight, his friends just stopped by American Injury…"

She began to rattle off details of the group that traveled with Corey Franks. The group was now probably being closely watched by authorities thanks to my giving them all of the information possible on them and essentially fingering them in his death.

"You need to crash at my place tonight. You'll be as safe as it gets there."

Sleeping in the house of a notorious crime boss normally doesn't sound like a good idea and I hustled fast for a way out of it. I couldn't find one.

At about five thirty, I ended up meeting Debbie at her place. One of the doctors had me stay later than normal to help organize some Roxicodone he had to sign over to another doctor to hide the fact that we were missing thousands of pills. It was located in Wellington, a relatively wealthy area known for cookie-cutter McMansions in gated communities. The gate, as well as the cameras, drastically increased my confidence that this may have actually been a good idea. The memory of the sheer amount of firepower kept in the house also helped.

The house itself was two floors and looked much like the other massive homes in the neighborhood, with a massive pool and lagoon in the backyard. It had massive, sharp angles for a roof. A single second-floor window looked out over the front door, almost looking like a cyclops. Debbie's BMW M6 sat in the driveway, dwarfed by George's outrageous Ford pickup truck, which appeared to me to be the approximate size of a semi-truck, outside of a five-car garage that I knew was filled with a variety of vehicles. The home had cathedral ceilings and marble floors that made the entrance foyer look bigger than my home. It may have been. The furniture was all black leather, with dark walnut wood for cabinets, but mostly black and steel. It looked like the interior of a sports car, but endless, with a huge room that drifted between spaces used for a kitchen and what could have been five living rooms, all overlooking the beautiful lagoon.

George himself sat on the sofa; it would be impossible to miss him. He was wearing black sweatpants and a black tank top that revealed his Winstrol-enhanced muscles and his gigantic swastika tattoo on his arm. He had a flat top that made him look like a slightly graying (he was in his early thirties, but had a couple streaks and didn't hide them) criminal version of a marine. Two skinheads with tattoos on their faces, who I would later discover were Steve and Kyle, flanked him silently. One had only a small line of teardrops, while the other had his neck and arms entirely covered in addition to teardrops, a swastika between his eyes, and a quote along the line of his ear. This was Kyle, and I had heard about him before. Both wore an almost uniform-like pair of black Dickies shorts and white t-shirts that I had seen on some Floridian skinheads before. George nodded to me when I came in and, without saying anything, motioned for me to sit on his couch with Debbie and him as they watched *Duck Dynasty*. In between commercials, he bounced off of his couch to me, smiled charmingly and shook my hand.

"George."

"Wilks"

We introduced ourselves with our names alone, but he warmed up after *Duck Dynasty* was over.

"So, what happened?" He asked this casually while preparing a meal that he seemed to be focused on controlling down to the calorie. "And are you hungry?"

I told him I was and filled him in on what happened at the dead drop. He listened silently while I rambled on about Corey Franks, the birds, the guy in the bolo tie, everything. Debbie stared at us with a concerned and interested face. When I was done explaining it all the first time, so was the meal. Dinner was a single skinless, boneless chicken breast with a lot of greens and exactly a tablespoon and a half of dark brown rice. The fat man in me was horrified and I planned on eating two Publix subs to compensate for this. As I finished explaining the Samantha thing for the second time, he sighed and motioned for me to let him speak.

"I'm sorry you've had a rough run of it. They're something we've seen once, or twice, but never as frequently as you're describing. We've only heard about them from people who had isolated encounters with them… you've seen them at least twice and the first time was on your first day. I'm really hoping they aren't interested in you specifically. Aside from what Dave told you, I'm afraid I don't really know anything else. We focus on police movements; things that cause junkies to disappear are a dime a dozen and never get genuinely investigated, so aside from your situation nothing like this seems to have ever focused on us before. But yeah, we do know about them. We were hoping they would ignore you because you're new, and that seems to make a difference."

He said this in the most erudite tone you could ever imagine, polite and with excellent pronunciation. As he finished the painfully small meal, he nodded to Kyle, who began to count out a myriad of small pills for himself for dessert.

He was taking "scoops," or GHB, which bodybuilders sometimes took for sleep and everyone else took to get fucked up. I was grateful that he had managed to somehow make me feel safe in this disaster and wasn't quite up for question and answer time, so I popped a few of the ones he had out, as well as my normal regimen of a shit ton of Xanax and just a little bit of soma and Roxicodone.

We went to the couch again, and we all placed our feet on the massive coffee table that stood in front of the couch, with little spots especially for comfortable feet holsters. For a moment I imagined any European at all being offended at this custom design, but then I drifted into a rerun of *The Walking Dead*. I guess George and I didn't agree on what made for pleasant sleeping entertainment. I suppose taking it light for a few days had done more good than I normally assumed it would, because I went right to sleep after that. I woke to the sound of their grand doorbell ringing.

"No… nurgh…"

I grunted at Debbie, but she was up and moving the moment the doorbell rang. She opened the door and smiled to whoever was outside of it before I heard a woman's voice beg for help and begin to vomit uncontrollably. Whoever was there had managed to get Debbie to open the door without anyone else by her. I heard a feeble female voice begging her again. Then I heard a sickening wet splash hit the concrete in front of her door. Debbie screamed.

"Oh shit!"

At the sound of her raising her voice, whatever was left of the adrenaline in my body kicked into action. I tried to get off of the oversized couch and look around, but everything was black and someone had thrown a blanket over me. I fell to the ground instantly and hit my head on the enormous coffee table.

"Shit! Help!"

Debbie screamed to both me and George as I heard the front door fly open. I could see her turned, facing me while I heard George in the cavernous bedroom on the opposite side of the living room, a great distance away. It sounded like he was moving fast, whatever he was doing.

She rushed out to help whoever it was while I was still stunned. Ahead of her, from the doorway, I saw very little light, but a ribbon of red ran from the ground in front of the door to the area where the light from outside could not reach.

"No! No, Debbie, NO!"

I screamed at her while I got off of the ground and got to the door as quickly as possible. Every step seemed to take an eternity and I heard sobbing and retching while I ran.

And there was Carl's mother, Cynthia. The delicate old woman was wearing a pair of sweatpants and an old t-shirt and not her normal semi-formal attire, but I could recognize her. She was almost doubled over, but I could see her face clearly. It was craned upward to the door. Blood and long ropes of viscera were pouring out of her mouth and onto the ground endlessly.

Debbie was trying in vain to help her, placing her hand on her back and telling to me come help, or call an ambulance or something. She took a second look at Cynthia when she noticed the horrified look on my face. I don't remember what she was saying, only the look on Cynthia's blood-covered face as she looked up at me and smiled. A long rope of gore was attached to some kind of roundish object that had just made its way out of her mouth. Her entire body was impossibly thin, except for her arms which seemed to be bigger. He face had gotten wider, her skin paler than cocaine, and her skull and hair seemed to rise in two sharp ridges above her eyes, which were now bloodshot and seemingly stretched. Debbie began to back away slowly, and then shouted for George, before a horrible sound erupted from Cynthia's throat.

"You're... killing... my... son..."

The voice was twisted, warbling, and growling at the same time. It was both extremely high- and extremely low-pitched. Cynthia retched more, and it seemed like the last of a pile of her intestines and other innards had collected at her feet. She stood up, suddenly strangely graceful, despite being covered in blood. Her eyes had grown massively wide, and her mouth was beginning to take an angular shape, almost like the "duckface" but horribly out of proportion, making her mouth look terribly sharp and the skin suddenly very hard. We all stood silently for just a moment, Debbie in shock, as Cynthia surveyed us and the area above us carefully. The skin of the old woman was pure white, but strangely mottled. These changes made Debbie decide that this was clearly a threat. A tiny pistol appeared out of nowhere and I fell to the side.

"George! Trouble!"

I had already known George was coming the first time she called him, but now I got an idea as to why it had taken him a moment when he knew there was an issue.

I began to hear heavy footsteps making their way to us from some bedroom off to the side. A metallic clink followed, followed by two quick blasts from Debbie's small handgun. An incredible splatter occurred, like hitting a water balloon with a baseball bat. Cynthia's face blew inward and her tiny body staggered back, but she was still moving. It felt like it took entire minutes to get back up and start running into the house. Debbie was right behind me, and I heard another quick blast before she shut the front door.

A horrific sound came from outside the door, an animal wail of rage and pain. It slowly grew in volume and pitch until it became a terrifying shriek that echoed throughout the area. The thought of the police, for once, seemed to be on no one's mind. I remember going around a corner to the kitchen area to hide as I saw George walk out with a furious look on his face and a massive shotgun in his hands. I peered around the corner to see the massive giant point it wildly after opening the door, only to see nothing there. A strange sound seemed to move directly over us and then back near the door.

We heard what sounded like cackling. From the backyard we suddenly heard someone cry out and a single shot go off. I looked and can only assume they did too, but I didn't see anything out the back, which was entirely visible through the wall of glass that allowed the previously beautiful view. Within a few seconds, we heard a quick scream in front of the house and a splat.

As I slowly crept up on the area to see what that was, I noticed a massive red stain on the concrete where Cynthia had shown up. She had taken her entrails with her for some reason. Behind the stain, in the road, was a crumpled body, on which I could make out a lot of red and what appeared to be a pair of Dickies shorts.

George stared down at the ground in the same area before slamming the door and calling a few friends as well as the police. I couldn't quite hear that call. He then went to a small panel about ten feet from the front door in the foyer and began flipping switches on it. Floodlights turned on all around the house, and shutters dropped in front of every window. Also, a horrible wet sound came from directly above the front door. Apparently we had interrupted Cynthia with whatever she was doing, because the next thing I saw was George sticking his head out of his door, firing two quick shots into the sky before going back behind the door frame. Debbie motioned for me to get back and kept her gun up, but not pointed at the door area where her boyfriend was.

Suddenly, in a disgusting surprise, the seemingly loose pile of innards that had violently erupted from the old woman hit the ground directly under the perch above the door. Spooked, George accidentally fired a shot into the disgusting wet and black pile before aiming upward at our unseen assailant again. Instantly, a horrible sound rang out. The scream that came from above was beyond horrible. In the road in front of the massive house we suddenly saw a small white and red body fall to the ground about seventy feet away from either Steve or Kyle's corpse with a wet *thwack*. George looked down at the pile of guts he had just shot with surprise and then to the now-lifeless body in the middle of the road. In the distance, we could hear sirens.

We got our stories straight after a moment of trying to figure out how shooting its intestines had killed it. That native mythology group told me later that apparently salt works on their guts too. We told the police we hadn't seen how Cynthia died. Apparently Kyle had decided to stay over and we would later find that his body had been crushed from an incredible impact, such as by falling or getting hit by a car. We decided to say that we hadn't seen it, and since the neighborhood surveillance came up with nothing, we were only suspects. That's pretty good, by our standards. We heard plenty of saber-rattling about it later and it was in the news, but it was assumed that someone had tried to rob George and failed. The cops seemed to want nothing to do with it.

Cynthia's body was never identified and we were in no rush to help with that.

I was told that someone would be by my place with cash, but to lay low until they figured shit out and waited to see where the cards fell with the cops.

I was mainly worried that Carl had more family I needed to be aware of. He would never see his mother again and would never find out why. Four days later, right after Christmas, he overdosed—for good this time, and with the pills I gave him. I think about that a lot and generally drink a lot on Christmas. I wonder if Cynthia had done whatever she had done to protect Carl. I wonder if she'd ever had a bad bone in her body, or if I had driven her to a new extreme by slowly murdering her son, pill by pill. I used to tell myself that he was just a guy who made shitty decisions, but I can see the reality now. If it weren't for me, they and too many others would still be alive.

I hope I get the chance to update this further… as to what happened in the years later.

5

One would think that anyone in their right mind would have had enough at this point, but there were two issues in my life. Number one: I needed a fuck ton of drugs. Six milligrams of Xanax a day, which came out to three pills that would be five dollars apiece on the street. Ninety milligrams of Roxi, at one dollar per milligram. And that was just to maintain, not to get high. After what I had seen, I absolutely **needed** to get high. I had no other way of handling stress, and that was a lot of stress.

Number two: I still had no idea what Carl's mother had turned into or how. She never showed up anywhere, and what was left of the crumpled pile that used to be her body was never identified by the police. I assumed, at the moment, that the thing puking its guts out on George's doorstep had been her. From the part where it vomited her organs out, I was starting to wonder if there were any other Native American legends that I should be aware of before narcing out in the future. Everything seemed relatively close to what the internet described as a Stigini, kind of like a vampire or witch. What the reality of Cynthia's ability to fly around after vomiting out her intestines was I had no idea, but I at least had the notion that we weren't the first people to tangle with them.

I was still too stunned by a direct assault from something clearly supernatural to worry about poor Carl, who never learned what exactly happened, or the fact that the police seemed to want absolutely nothing to do with the multiple human beings turned to red goo in an expensive residential neighborhood. They said George's friend looked like he had been hit by a car, but that was bullshit. Both bodies had been splattered across the pavement. The cops didn't seem disinterested. They seemed like they were worried. Two of them stood away from the bodies, watching the two roads that curved around the development. I noticed them both staring into the sky a lot. The police barely mumbled at me, but George talked at great length with one of them.

They were smiling a few times, and during the week that followed I learned that old George was close with a lot of police officers. Being a Good ol' Boy sure had its benefits, and as long as their relatives were kept in good supply of drugs, they were more than happy to ignore George. One of them stood off to the side, not speaking to anyone, just smiling. He was the only person who looked relaxed that night. He had jet black hair that looked like it had been slicked back with vegetable oil it was so shiny. He was paler than most white Floridians. He wore a long-sleeved button-down white shirt with old-fashioned suspenders running up along either side from a black pair of pants, and a badge kept inside of a large black wallet. I tried not to pay attention to him; it looked like the other police felt the same way.

Somewhere in all of that thinking I remembered that I had seen three of them at the beach, not just one.

So I ended up crashing with Debbie for a while. It was a pretty nice pad anyway. She was in no mood for work either so George ended up sending in goons to cover for both of us. George seemed strangely happy after the incident, even more relaxed than when I had met him. He didn't exactly open up about what he knew, but I told him what I thought it was and I noticed a look of recognition on his face when I said it was a Stigini. He smirked and said that he was glad there was a way to get rid of them, but that he had only heard fleeting rumors about their existence. I didn't feel safe asking him about any other "weird" things. I was getting the impression he was never going to tell me anything he didn't think I already knew to begin with.

I had the impression that he was lying, but he casually dropped that he didn't mind me staying over as long as I needed, seeing as he "always had protection." Great, now two reasons this asshole owned me.

I spent a week "recovering" by narcing out on a colossal supply of pretty much every abusable substance known to man, from shrooms to propofol. Three days into the process, Dave dropped off a handgun for me. Someone had gone through all the loopholes for me, he said, and sure enough the papers that came with it had my picture and said my name. I daydreamed about taking the small gray nine-millimeter gun to a range before remembering that I didn't actually know anything about guns and put the thing in one of my bags. I hoped I would never need it.

Then I lurched toward a computer to see if I could find any more information on Native American legends that might be more than legends. Before going back to work for the first time in about eight days, I thought about stopping at my small one-bedroom hut. It didn't sound like a great idea, and I doubted something like whatever Cynthia had been would just leave me alone. I eventually called my landlord and told him I didn't feel safe at my apartment anymore and that I was giving my notice. I hadn't bothered looking for a new place yet, but I never wanted to see that one or Debbie's place again. I booked a room in the brightly lit, expensive part of Palm Beach before going back one last time to pick up my drugs and anything else I might need. I looked forward to shopping at Marshalls for new clothes.

I took an extra buttload of drugs my first day back, to brace myself. No one seemed to give a shit, and Dave had kept an additional guy in the office, Steve, to hold down the fort while Debbie took some time to think about shit and recover.

***

The next day at work was a typical day pumping tons of narcotics into the ignorant arms of people with southern accents. It was jarring to be around the smell and to see the stained light pour through the heavily tinted windows instead of enjoying the fresh air and bright blue sky that I had relished the day before.

About halfway through the day, at around ten or eleven, a beautiful old lady with long, flowing white hair and a blue Fleetwood Mac t-shirt came in with a group I was familiar with. She had piercing blue eyes you could practically see from across the street. She was new and filled out her patient packet while listening to music on an old cassette player. When she was finished she bounded up to her group's ringleader, the junkie who fronted them the money and took a serious amount of their pills, and he sighed before handing her what looked like a baggy filled with pills. She took them and barely hid them behind her cassette player before heading straight to the bathroom, presumably to cook and inject before her doctor's appointment.

No more than two minutes later, a drop-dead-gorgeous young girl with bright strawberry-blond hair, shocking blue eyes, a face full of freckles, and the same Fleetwood Mac shirt came out, dancing slightly as she walked. She was radiantly beautiful. I was numb to the fact that something weird was going on. Besides, she seemed pretty high but in a good mood. I watched her, noticing that the shirt looked like it was brand new. She bounded up to the small stretch of the window that wasn't covered in tinting and plopped down in an empty seat. She stared out happily while sitting next to a group of confused addicts.

After just a moment, the beautiful blond girl suddenly went stiff, as if shocked by electricity, her mouth open and slack with her eyes wide, staring in the direction she had come from, the bathroom. She made a sudden gesture to the bathroom, something that looked like desperation, and then went still. A scream shot out of the bathroom the patients use. I looked toward the bathroom but when I looked back to the window the young girl was gone. The old lady with the bright blue eyes and matching Fleetwood Mac shirt had overdosed. Everyone in her group ran before the EMTs even came to get her corpse off the toilet.

I wondered if anyone would be at her funeral.

I didn't bother saying anything to Debbie.

***

I spoke to Jessica, the girl who used to work in our medicine room, doling out medication into pill bottles for the doctors to sign off on so that we didn't have to hire a legitimate pharmacist. Jessica had been hired under an absurd legal loophole that allowed doctors to let regular staff dispense medication under insanely flimsy protocol, which we took advantage of so that we didn't need to hire anyone who might know what they fuck they were doing.

Because of that, one of George's friends had taken the liberty of hiring a beautiful, surprisingly healthy-looking blonde whose only previous work experience had been working at Hooters and other fine Floridian establishments. She used an incredible array of machines that automatically sorted the pills by weight, measuring them out perfectly every time—I mean, as far as we knew. The doctors then had to "check" the bottle and sign off on it and that was enough to replace a professional with an advanced degree who might be interested in not letting those drugs hit the street. She had the largest room to herself, with several massive vaults containing enormous stockpiles of medication that the doctors ordered in their own names so that they could "self-dispense."

We never talked, aside from coming and going. She didn't make much of an effort to hide her disgust for us drug addicts and never left the medication room unless absolutely necessary and we didn't blame her at all. I remembered her saying that when she went to high school in Hobe Sound that she had heard of a girl who was attacked by something from the air. I remember a note of disgust in her voice when I talked to her, the sound of a girl who was grossed out by me but trying to be polite.

"Hello?"

"Hi, I need to ask you a question… it's kind of important."

She sighed into the phone and sounded instantly disappointed.

"Alright, what is it?"

"I need to ask about that girl who disappeared in Hobe Sound…"

"She didn't disappear, she was killed! Some of my friends got a phone call from her the night she didn't come home and said that she told them something came out of the sky and attacked her. She said she couldn't move her arm. The cops wouldn't even listen to them!"

She sounded instantly angry, as if I had challenged her belief that it was anything other than a legitimate concern. I was massively relieved to hear something other than "we don't know."

"Her name was Claire Alyssa Redding and her friend was Janette, they never found either body, but I was there when Claire called us. She said something attacked her and she needed to get to a hospital, but she couldn't get through to 911."

She said this as if it were the most important bit of information available.

"Did you remember them saying she said anything else? Anything at all… someone I know may have gotten attacked by something near downtown Lake Worth and they don't want to go to the police about it."

"She said she was digging for something when it attacked her. Grace, our friend, said she was doing a project for school. She had camped out on the beach and she said her car was torn up or something… they never found her car either… only windshield glass and parts of the door. One of her friends went missing at the same time and they thought it was just as stunt because they both had been arrested a couple of times."

For a quick moment the mental image of the sorrowful father driving away in a critically wounded old Ford popped into my mind.

"Did she describe what was attacking her, at all? Was there anyone who had any guesses?"

At this, she turned around away from her desk and narcotic-counting equipment. She spoke with a conspiratorial tone in her voice.

"The cops said it looked like she ran away and that they couldn't find anything, but that was bullshit. My friends and I went back to the place she was digging when she called us. She was doing an assignment for class on pottery shards in Hobe Sound. There are tons of Native American things buried up there, a whole city used to be there before the Seminole even came to Florida. We found blood, some ripped pieces of her clothes, and some of her stuff in a tree. The cops said that they searched the crime scene and found nothing and wouldn't even talk to us after that. She had friends though, and they thought something jumped on her car roof and attacked her. That might be why she thought something came out of the sky. A lot of shattered glass was in the parking lot and a piece from a car door. "

The realization that this girl was doing anything involved with Native Americans did not sit well with me. My stomach lurched.

"I'm sorry to hear that. It sounds like the cops just ignored it all."

I said this in the most sincere tone I could summon, purely to remind her that I was on her side.

She straightened up at that.

"I wish. One of them kept coming around to my friend Grace. He was one of the guys who was there when we called them the first time, who told us that she had probably gone missing. He kept bothering her and trying to get her to go clubbing with him. She was like sixteen and he knew that, but he kept calling Grace. When it got too much and Grace called the police to file a report about it, they said they had never heard of the guy, and that only two cops went to talk to us, which is bullshit."

Creepy dudes weren't exactly rare in south Florida, and this kind of thing was hardly unheard of. She seemed shocked by it, but I had heard a thousand stories of cops trying to get laid with more attractive perps and they really stuck together. You could count on them to cover for each other before they even knew what they were covering for.

"Listen, I need to ask you something else. What kind of a person was she? Was she like us, did she party at all? Maybe there is a chance someone me or Debbie knows might have known her back in the day?"

Asking her whether or not her dead friend was a junkie wasn't easy.

"Yeah, maybe, why?"

"It might help if I knew if she was clean or not… this thing may have attacked my friend because of it…"

"She… probably wasn't… she did hang out with Grace, who used to do stuff whenever she got the chance. They had gone down to Miami together a bunch of times. The week before she died they all went down to party at South Beach with fake IDs but had to leave early. Her friends, Grace and Chris, are still trying to look into it. Do you want their numbers? If you know of something similar, they might want to hear it…"

I wondered if she had guessed that maybe something not entirely natural had taken her friend, because she had a strange look on her face but seemed excited about connecting me to her friends. I said 'Yes' and wondered if perhaps we were just sharing a hallucination before remembering the bloodstains in front of George's place. I wondered if the police had the same nervous look to them, like they wanted nothing to do with the case.

***

After the latest bird-watching incident I was suddenly more aware of every death, every creepy story a patient muttered. One patient got pissed and started screaming when he realized the cocaine his piss test was showing as positive for would delay him getting his medication until he watched a stupid tape on the dangers of mixing drugs—about twenty minutes. Patience was never their strong suite.

It was what looked like a college kid, except a hell of a lot grungier, with greasy brown hair that was matted to his head from a trucker hat he took off but kept in his hands. Aside from the wear and tear from heavy narcotics use, I didn't think he looked old enough to drink. He was wearing oil- and paint-stained blue jeans and a black and neon blue shirt that was torn under the arms and his habit made him look worn down. He looked malnourished, with hollow cheeks and bones poking at the back of his skin. Like most patients he looked like he'd never had any luck to run out of to begin with.

Keeping Aaron from turning him into a fine red paste wouldn't be easy, and the patient just did not seem to realize that it was time to get polite, not curse the giant multi-colored muscle guy out. I was feeling generous so I told him I would handle it and pushed the kid through to his appointment. I remembered how bitchy I got when I was out. People act weird when they need drugs. At about noon the eighteen-year-old kid had finished his appointment and was overdosing big time in the middle of the parking lot. His friends brought him in and a doctor rushed out to meet them with Naloxone. Every junkie in the waiting room clapped when they realized he was going to be alright.

Four hours later I got a phone call from a sheriff. The kid had overdosed again, this time for good. His friends were actually much more responsible than normal and tried to go to an ER, even stayed there after they realized he was dead.

After his system was clean from the Naloxone the cravings kicked into high gear again. He must have been as sober as a judge after the stuff, because he apparently went through a huge part of his pills and overdosed. This happens more frequently than anyone would like to admit. At the time I was mainly concerned with whether or not the police would be in the clinic again, but they decided not to. I googled the name though. According to his friends' Facebook posts, he had just gotten back from the army and had gotten hooked from a genuine back injury while on duty and couldn't live with the pain, or get better with anything the VA was willing to do.

I pulled the file, but didn't feel the need to let Debbie know.

***

After work that day I decided I didn't want to be around anyone. I called the small hotel I was booked at, the Hotel Flagler off of Evernia Street, to double-check my booking. Leaving George's place was a nerve-racking relief. He had at least five goons there, all in brightly colored shirts with elaborate tribal or floral designs. I was both uncomfortable sleeping in the same house as them and very comfortable, knowing that they doubled their numbers in the face of something that would scare the shit out of most people. The Aryan Brotherhood is less than scum, but holy shit does it understand violence. Debbie hadn't shown up to work for half a month at that point, and had taken to not getting dressed in the morning to begin with. After work I went to George's place and began to gather the stuff that I had been using as a bug out bag, including my new gun, which was in a case in my duffel bag.

The Hotel Flagler was located just west of the Intercostal Waterway that separates Palm Beach proper from the much larger and more heavily populated "West Palm Beach" where us poor folk live. Built in the 1920s, it was cheap and used to be used for free housing for the poor until it was repaired and turned into a luxury boutique hotel much later. It was just inland, right near Clematis and City Place, the two party destinations of the area. I wouldn't have armed criminals guarding me, but the amount of people in the area was reassuring. Before checking in, I went to the seawall that separates the land from the waterway. I decided to call Grace and Chris, Jessica's friends from high school whose numbers she had given to me. A tired-sounding man with a slight Spanish accent answered the phone.

"Hello?"

It sounded more like "Aloo", and the lack of Appalachian twang in his voice was strangely reassuring.

"Hi, I'm sorry to bother you, but my name is Wilks. I'm a coworker of Jessica Grover. I need to ask you about two friends of yours that…

disappeared… during high school."

I left some space around the word "disappeared," hoping he would notice that I didn't think she disappeared either.

"Alyssa and Janette." The voice had a matter-of-fact tone to it, but was still listening.

"Yes… something happened recently…we think it may have been the same thing. I was wondering if maybe we could meet some time and talk about it, maybe with Grace?"

"You need to listen to me. And make sure to tell Jessica too: Grace is dead."

He sounded very stern.

"I… I am so sorry, I had no idea. I'm sorry, I didn't mean to upset you…"

He cut me off right away.

"She died months ago. So if you see her, or if she contacts you, you need to run. Don't say a word to her. Not a single word. To her or that cop."

I listened as he told me a place we could meet the following day, between where he lived in Miami and West Palm, a pier in Fort Lauderdale. He told me not to call him again and asked me to tell Jessica the same before hanging up.

6

The next day at work, I felt almost invigorated. I actually felt like going for a jog for the first time since middle school, but it was early and I was worried about being eviscerated. The conversation with Chris had been both better and worse than I expected. I guess I couldn't really expect the guy to tell me 'Don't worry, it's just a junkie prank.' The pier where he asked to meet me was located at the Fort Lauderdale Beach Park, an area about forty minutes south of my location on I-95. It was a nice area to live, but it bordered Sunrise and Hialeah, which are extremely low-income "diverse" neighborhoods. When people are being polite they call them 'colorful,' which is technically as well as figuratively accurate, as the homes and businesses in the area tend to be painted a shocking variety of colors, all muted by the grime of South Florida.

Part of me was actually looking forward to it. The meeting spot was in Fort Lauderdale at the beach park there, but I was looking forward to getting mofongo for dinner in Hialeah because of the proximity to a particularly incredible restaurant, El Rinconcito De Santa Barbara.

The other part of me was also focusing on the mofongo, just so that I wouldn't have to think about what the meeting was about. Since Christmas, I had spent my time listening to every single neurotic patient story I possibly could. Ninety-nine percent of them were about some other junkie who stole from them or performed some kind of miracle of getting drugs or money.

Every once in a while, however, I would hear mumbling about someone disappearing or the cops acting strange, and I wondered if it was just the hazard of the trade or something else, something horribly wrong.

***

Because I had been getting paid to sit around at George's and do drugs, I was placed at the front desk when I got back. My job was essentially pointless anyway, so I didn't argue with Dave when he called and told me. That morning a couple of junkies brought in a kid again. It wasn't every day this happened, but it did happen, and even the drug dealers were usually disgusted. Or at least they acted that way—scum like us usually get uppity at child abuse so that we can tell ourselves, "Well, at least we're not like those animals."

The woman could have been anywhere between her mid-thirties to late fifties. She had bleached blond hair that looked like it had been scorched by chemicals one too many times; it had an orange tinge that matched the cheetah-print-lined jacket she was wearing along with a fuchsia and black tropical-print shirt, which must have been the most colorful thing at her local Walmart, and black skin-tight leggings. Her skin looked like leather and I instantly felt horrible for her. She looked more miserable than most patients. Her boyfriend and/or pimp walked next to her, chewing tobacco and wearing a black trucker hat to match his badly receding oily black hair. His age was also ambiguous, but the fact that he walked in with a can of Bud Light that he was drinking after putting his cigarette out on the door told me that he was typical Appalachian white trash. The act of drinking beer and chewing tobacco at the same time was horrific alone. He wore a wife-beater that had been stained horrifically in the pits and jeans that looked like they had more mass from pure body odor than denim. Both had track marks running up their arms that looked like river maps. There was clearly a pack of beer or malt liquor in her purse.

All of this was absolutely normal, everyday stuff. We served people like that all day, giving them absurd amounts of painkillers to go home with. But this case was special because the little girl who stood between them looked like an image from a movie. She couldn't have been more than six or seven, and was wearing a bright pink shirt with a cartoon character on it and bright blue jeans, which were framed by her long, tangled blond hair. Aside from the fact that she had clearly been crying, with puffy red eyes, she looked like she had all the health her parents clearly didn't.

"Mah'need my pointment," the shit head muttered angrily, in a dialect of hick that sounded almost like Boomhauer. He sounded as if he was pissed off that I didn't greet him by name.

"I'm sorry, sir?" I responded in my best English, and planned on continuing to ask him to repronounce the sentence endlessly until I could ask Aaron and his goon friend to remove them.

"My name is Melissa Rogers, and this is Cliff Rogers." The tired woman motioned to her husband. "We came in last month on the same day; we have an appointment in an hour. We'd like to check in, please."

She was clearly accustomed to both Cliff's douchebaggery and the douchebaggery that I was prepared to respond with. I was mildly disappointed, but confident that Old Cliffy would give me another opportunity, so I beamed a smile at her and got their charts.

When I came back, I heard the girl sobbing and saw her little hand reaching up as if attempting to drag her mother down.

"What if he comes back?" she asked the air above her.

"Shut the fuck up," Cliff responded flatly.

I was going to be keeping this guy's file. I wasn't sure what I was going to do with it, but I instinctively hated him enough for it to involve law enforcement. Also, that little girl needed out of there. In my head, my drug-besotted memory strained for anything related to Child Protective Services.

They got their papers and sat in the waiting room, the little girl sitting next to a giant fat man in tattered camouflage clothes drinking a Big Gulp. The giant fat man barely came out of his opiate-induced trance when she began to cry quietly again, while staring at her feet. Neither of her parents looked over or made a noise until forty minutes later when they were called into the hallway that served as a second waiting room right before the patients went to see the doctor.

The charts were set up so that the doctor they went to see was random if the one they saw last time wasn't there, but they usually saw the same doctor, as if continuity of care mattered. We just put the folders into slots next to the door and the doctor would take whichever folder came next, call the patient and ask them to describe their symptoms while writing their names into prescriptions that were pre-stamped with what they were getting, regardless of who they were. I decided Cliff could skip ahead of a gentleman who had been slumped into one of the chairs, eyelids shut and drool flowing, for well over an hour. Aaron met some attractive young ladies and they ended up skipping him in line as well just before the Rogers family showed up. Cliff was called into the office of Dr. Beshers almost right away. I decided to be as close to direct as I possibly could, without getting another phone call from George.

"I hate to bother you, ma'am, but I overheard your daughter saying something about someone bothering you. Would it happen to be a… strange… man? We've had a lot of problems with someone who just isn't normal."

I said it with the same tone and inflection that a customer service agent would use, as if I was just performing a professional courtesy. She moved her daughter just slightly closer and gave both of us a concerned look before glancing at the door her husband had walked through. I made it look like I was looking for a specific file, so that I didn't seem too interested in her response.

She coughed a loose piece of phlegm into her tallboy before speaking.

"We drive down here…" she gulped hard, "…an he wanna stay at this motel with his friends an all, but they pissed at him an we couldn afford it. They wasn't having any of it when he asked the clerk if we could sleep in the parking lot so we went to the beach to sleep there, because we never had a problem with that in Hilton Head or driving down through Georgia when we came."

She pronounced Georgia 'jaw-jah' and it almost sounded pretty. She stared down at her feet and then over to her little girl, who was watching her closely with concern.

"When we started to sleep, there was a man there, he knocked on the window and told us to leave. But he wasn't no cop or nothing, He look real funny, he was jus a kid an dressed like a hippie or something, so Cliff tole him to go fuck himself an that he'd beat his ass if he came around again."

She clearly sounded very proud of the fucking idiot. She stared at her feet before swallowing deeply again and continuing, this time looking at her little girl while talking.

"That kid said we needed to leave her there, or else. He said that we wodn't have no trouble if we just left her there and went on our way. He smiling like it was no different than saying how do you do. He started creeping me out so I tole Cliff to jus go, an we would find some other place. But when we try to leave that man start to holler, an his mouth…"

She turned from her little girl and leaned in closely to me. She glanced around quickly, as if someone could have entered the small crypt-like hallway without her knowing.

"His mouth got real big, an his jaw popped down!" she whispered with intensity.

"What do you mean, popped down?"

"Well, we used to have this snake an all, and when it ate, its jaw would pop down so it could fit a whole rat or whatever in there. His jaw popped down! When he start yelling, it did the same thing and just popped down, an even when we turning away in a big truck, he start running up at us. And we look out the mirror, an we saw more people coming, so we thought maybe someone call the police, but they was running too! I heard glass break behind us an saw some kid behind us! I tole Cliff to go, but he just kept lookin at this man and this man face just start to open up an I slapped him, cuz I was scared an then he finally hit the gas an get the fuck out of there. We heard screamin so loud an it didn't even sound like people, it sound like cats in heat but angrier."

It all rushed out in what sounded like a single breath, a massive run-on sentence that took me a moment to decipher. She looked exasperated now, and it was clear that she had been more stressed than usual from this particular run.

"We pull in a police station, even Cliff was scared and he ain't never scared! An officer talk to us real quick an said we could sleep the night there, Cliff told him we was going to relatives tomorrow and couldn't afford a hotel. We look and there was scratch marks on the back of the car an something sharp was dug all the way into the trunk! It a hooked thing, look like a cat's claw but without the cat. Whatever the fuck it was, it broke our brake light, an the cop said we'd have to get that fixed."

She said this as if the car repair was the worst part of the story and it took me a moment to restrain a chuckle. To most of these people, a small car hiccup could mean the difference between having a roof over their heads and having to desperately call relatives and friends for a bedroom.

"I don wanna come down here no more." The little girl said this matter-of-factly as her mother ran her fingers through her hair. Her mother looked at me pleadingly.

"You ever hear uh that shit before?" she asked with genuine fear.

"Yeah. Don't sleep near the beaches, or near tourist traps. Only sleep in places people go, especially if they're going to clinics, even if it's a bad neighborhood. Go straight up I-95 and don't pull off of any exits you don't hear about other people going down."

They seemed like shitty parents, but they were probably better than whatever the fuck that thing was. The woman wiped a bit of moisture from her eye.

"We stopped at the motel the next day an Cliff apologize an stuff, but when we stayed the night… she kept tryin to leave… she won't tell me why…"

She gripped her child fiercely and looked at me with pleading and concern, and I could see the abscessed veins spreading from her fingers. Even there, she had injected heavily. I felt emotionally uncomfortable, and had no way to reconcile my loathing and sympathy both for her and for myself for giving her the drugs that were about to fuck up that little girl's life even more. I ended the conversation politely and told her she should be alright, then went to the bathroom and googled the Child Protective Services process before calling them and letting them know Cliff had some issues to work out.

Sometime later I would get a phone call from a sheriff in Eustice, a small town relatively close to Orlando. The parents never made it home. A quick Google search revealed that Cliff had been found near an abandoned tourist trap and that authorities were desperately searching for the remains of his wife but were still holding out hope for the child, whose name I only then learned was Daisy Rogers. I would sit and wonder for a moment how they knew the wife was dead but were still searching, before deciding to get very drunk on that particular night.

***

The rest of that particular day, however, went smoother than usual. There was a junkie fight, an old lady pretended to be crippled and got up and started screaming at the doctor when she found out she wouldn't get more meds, and someone covered the bathroom in feces and urine. There were plenty of offers from patients to clean it, all of them excited at the disgusting possibility of earning up to $100, which Aaron decided to award to a yokel in a Nascar cap who was deeply grateful. Toward the end of the day, I started to move amongst the patients while pretending to clean the impossibly disgusting sitting room once there was no one left to check in.

I overheard usual junkie chatter, mainly complaints about doctors in other clinics they were getting drugs from, or people asking how much their ringleader was letting each other keep, to see if they were getting a fair deal. A fat guy in a wrestling t-shirt and a thoroughly disgusted young girl wearing purple shorts and a green tank top were negotiating how much Dilaudid she would get for a blowjob. Someone else was talking about a dead friend, but sure enough it was just another overdose.

Two young guys were talking about some place in Miami, though, and it got my attention in case I needed to remember it later. A kid with dusky blond hair in a heavy metal band t-shirt with blue lightning everywhere sat against the wall next to a nearly destroyed drink vending machine that had chewing tobacco spat across what was left of its plastic facade near the hall that led to the bathroom. He was chatting with a shorter kid with black hair and glasses that had been taped together, who was wearing blue jeans and a camouflage t-shirt with the logo and address of a local hunting gear company in Ohio.

"Dude, it was fucking incredible, and he got like six bags of it for free!" the blond kid practically yelped at his black-haired friend. "And he said they had plenty more! We could get jobs and move to Miami!"

Blondie seemed thrilled, but his friend had a look of concern on his face.

"I ain't never heard of 'ephemera.' If it was so good, and it's free, why ain't it everywhere?"

He pronounced the name of the drug "effamara," with some derision. I had heard some mention of ephemera before and was under the impression that it was a cocktail of hallucinogens. I had initially written it off because of the amount of people messing with those in Miami.

"An he ain't answering his phone no more, or on Facebook, we don't know what he up to or where he is. He coulda got played, easy, been a patsy for somebody. We don't know no body down there anyhow. "

He seemed concerned and they both were becoming aware that I was listening to them, so I decided to enter the conversation.

"Excuse me, gentlemen. I couldn't help but overhear your story and I had a friend who liked that 'ephemera' stuff a lot as well, but he just fell off the face off the earth after inviting me to party with him. Do you know anything about where to get the stuff?"

With anyone else they probably wouldn't have said shit, but I was a thoroughly respected connoisseur of narcotics and indeed, all things junk. They looked at each other and the kid with the glasses nodded to me as if he knew me and thought I was cool. It was kind of weird being a sort of micro-celebrity, but only with people I hated deeply. The blond kid was excited for an opportunity to share his enthusiasm for the drug.

"Well, our friend from school, Kyle, he tole us bout this place in Miami, it's a club like."

He grinned and nodded at the word 'club' and I nodded back. He had probably only seen real nightclubs in movies, and even those weren't as packed full of beautiful people and loud music as some of the ones in Miami.

"An they have this 'ephemera' stuff an it's just like free, an it's everywhere! I tried some an tripped balls for a whole day! I saw some weird shit man, for real!"

He was using his hands to express every word; this was clearly a thrilling prospect for him. His friend looked sourer, however.

"I ain't never heard of this shit before, an I hear of everything. An Kyle, he stopped calling and deleted his Facebook, even his mom and them getting worried. An his mom know every dealer in Florida and ain't never heard of no 'ephemera' before, but Cassie, his cousin's baby momma, she said her friend went looking for it and when Cassie tried to talk to her she just kept smiling like and tried to get her to stay down here for it…"

The family networks these people had were as absurd as the people in them. He began to look legitimately concerned and stared down at his feet.

"She said her friend wouldn't stop smiling, ear to ear she said. She wasn't acting right and had a bunch of friends try and give her more of the stuff. Who the fuck gives out free drugs? Not like they usually need a lot of advertising, especially if they in a nice club an shit. An why they only got it at one club all specific like? It jus don't make no sense…"

I nodded to the kid with the broken glasses and slowly walked away. I think they got the impression that I thought he was right to be cautious because they looked at each other and the kid with the glasses gave blondie an "I told you so" look.

***

The drive out of work was confusing, for a moment I thought I was going to my old home, but I forced myself to continue on I-95 past the boundaries of my normal daily existence. I was heading to the Fort Lauderdale Beach Park, a large sprawl of water-based family fun near Hialeah, where I remembered my favorite restaurant was.

Like much of Florida, the urban sprawl is composed of small homes and occasional apartment complexes. Homes built in the 1920s aren't as rare as you think, and they litter the area near the waterfront in various stages of repair. They're just slightly taller than modern single-floor buildings and in Florida sometimes still have a "shotgun" layout, with a large center hall dividing groups of rooms. Their windows always have at least one example of a series of horizontal stripes of glass that can be opened and separated to allow air to flow through. They usually sport pastel or tropical colors, and are terrible to live in.

In wealthier areas they renovate them and sell them for absurd sums, in poorer areas like Fort Lauderdale—and especially Hialeah—they usually show their age, and in Sunrise most of them looked like they might fall down. It looked like they were fighting amid the cheaper, blander constructions of the 1980s through '90s and somehow winning, with the newer facades that tended to be fixed and concrete block homes coming apart here and there in more obvious ways, like peeling fake wood. Every now and then a mission-style home or building used as a church dotted the landscape, strange bits of Spanish design that somehow never looked out of place next to the old homes. The sunset was an explosion of dark reds and burned oranges alight with flickers of turquoise, purple, and soft white clouds, an incredible scene that lurked over and behind every building, turning most of them into dark pastel silhouettes.

I pulled into the park about ten minutes past the time I was supposed to be there and saw only a tall, well-dressed black guy facing the one of the piers, away from the parking lot. I briefly remembered an urban legend about things that wait for people near waterways with their backs to the land, but shook it off and approached the man. He was wearing a light blue linen shirt, spotless white linen pants, and a black belt and matching shoes, both with blue accents. His hair was somewhere between dark blue and indigo on one side and faded seamlessly into a perfectly bleached white color. It was the first time I had seen anyone take that much care of their appearance in a long time and I was taken aback for just a moment, even more so than when I spoke to police or other people who might arrest me. The motherfucker looked like he just walked out of a music video.

I was very impressed with his Floridian-ness.

"Excuse me… Chris?"

He turned around and smiled wearily. He wore thick-framed black glasses that made him look gracefully pretentious.

"I'd say it's a pleasure to meet you, but I'd rather it be under any different circumstances."

By the look on his face, probably not at all. I occasionally forgot that I was a disgusting-looking junkie that rarely shaved and probably smelled like shit, but this guy's appearance really made me a lot more aware.

"Yeah, I think we have some experiences in common." I looked around the park again, to make sure no one else was there. I couldn't see anyone and he walked closer to me.

"Did you tell whoever you work for where you were going?" He had a look of deep concern. The question startled me.

"No… I…"

"But they do know what's going on, don't they?" he asked, cutting me off. I had no idea what to say.

"They sent me to make a drop, near the beach. There was something there. One of them killed one when it came to his house, so they can't not know. But I don't know what they do know… or how much of this shit is connected…"

As I was speaking I was slowly becoming more aware of the fact that I didn't know this guy at all but that we were jumping into a pretty fucking weird conversation. His face didn't look surprised at all though, so I guessed that we were both talking about the same thing. The other thing I started to realize was that I had no idea how many of the urban legends and weird stories were based on truth and out of those, which ones were connected or the same things.

"I looked online, I think they're called Stigini… by Indians and stuff…"

I realized that I now sounded as desperate and ignorant as the junkies I had previously listened to. I wondered how many of them edited out the crazier parts of their stories.

"I think you might be right. At the very least, something got three of my friends and most of what it did fit the description of a monster from pre-Seminole Florida, the Ishkitini or Stigini…"

He was about to go on, but I had to cut him off.

"How did you know I worked for someone?" I asked pointedly.

"Grace, Alyssa, they both ran drugs for money. Cops don't arrest a lot of cute girls. I think whoever they were working for got them killed and I think they did it on purpose."

I felt the ground go loose beneath me and my legs buckle just a little. A cold shock went up my spine, even though I should not have been surprised. We walked to the bench where I described in detail what I had seen, and then decided that we should get dinner (or rather I should, he had apparently eaten, which somehow stopped him from eating more) and continue the conversation.

7

After the ground felt a lot more settled, my absurdly costumed acquaintance and I both seemed to want to get out of there. The Fort Lauderdale Beach Park was pretty nice during the day, but the small wooden fortress used by children as the fuel for imaginative battles looked larger and more ominous against the dark water behind it. The entire park was in the nicer area of town, right after a field of avenue-like waterways that bordered several groups of man-made islands. During sunrise the area is infamously beautiful and the people living there have gotten used to the strange early morning traffic through their tiny domain. Twenty minutes west, my favorite restaurant for mofongo was no longer keeping me distracted from what Chris had just told me, and I didn't want to stick around anyways but for the moment I didn't feel entirely alright with what I had just pieced together.

After gushing out the vague details of the dead drop and George's misfire that killed whatever Cynthia had turned into, I felt one part exhausted and two parts wary that this guy was either some kind of trap or someone who would think I was crazy. For simplicity, I decided to leave out any crap that I saw in the day-to-day pill mill activity because I had no idea how this guy was going to react. As I was going over my story, I noticed how insane and junk-fueled it must have seemed, but the strange man just kept nodding and listening as I went on. Toward the end of the story I was feeling antsy to leave; I just didn't feel safe so close to the water. With a fancy blue linen shirt and white linen pants and hair that slowly faded from pure white to dark blue, he was going to stand out pretty badly anywhere he went, including my favorite mofongo restaurant, but I didn't care.

"Are there any other employees that seem to know what's going on?" he asked almost pleadingly. I briefly thought of Aaron and Jessica, but Jessica seemed to be willingly unaware of whatever was going on outside of her office and Aaron seemed to be "in good" with George.

"Probably, but most of the people in the mills owned by George are close friends of his."

He nodded with a defeated look on his face. "Yeah, people with tight lips and close friends are a running theme."

"Loose lips sink ships." I muttered the phrase that was repeated with urgency in one form or another by anyone who has driven over state lines with something illegal. The more people involved, the higher the risk that someone would spill the beans. Except a lot of people seemed to have had run-ins with various weird shit, and no one was making a sound.

My mind began to reel at the thought of how many people may have experienced some of this shit but were unable to say anything because they were runners on the Blue Highway, moving meds from Florida to Ohio, the Virginias, the Carolinas, Tennessee, and especially Kentucky. I tried to stop thinking about that by focusing on the much more immediate threat at hand.

The idea that I was being used as some sort of patsy had occurred to me, but for some reason I simply couldn't force myself to think about that fact that my employer seemed to have sent me on a trip specifically to have me killed. It was absolutely normal for junkies to get a hot dose. The overwhelming narcotic could kill even a veteran junk fiend if said junk fiend knew too much, even if there wasn't reason to expect a threat. No one likes loose ends.

While I didn't know for sure, the thought that Chris's friends had possibly been killed by their employer, or that their deaths were related to the junkie business, unsettled me to the core. I mentioned George's cool reaction to the insanity at his own home and the death of one of his goons. As I sat on the bench looking out at the fortress and the water behind it, Chris seemed to get the situation.

"So you think the dead drop may have been planned?" He sat next to me very slowly, and sounded genuinely concerned.

"I don't know," I answered truthfully. "What happened to your friends that make you think their bosses were involved?"

"Grace worked as a shot girl in some hellhole near Las Olas. She loved partying too much." At the mention of Fort Lauderdale's favorite drinking region he seemed to relax into the bench before expounding. I was glad, because in addition to his outfit being a little outside of normal I had no idea who the guy was.

"She got hooked on blow, then everything else. She started running packages from Miami up to Orlando and back again, mainly money from one end and molly to the other to make money back from her habit. But that's not where it starts. Before Grace, Claire Alyssa—we just called her Alyssa most of the time—and her friend Janette both went missing. We hung out a lot in high school and Claire wanted to do some school project showing how to dig up pottery correctly. We were supposed to meet up at the Starbucks near our high school, but she never showed."

He sat forward and seemed to focus on the now-invisible horizon lurking over the ink-black ocean. He was clearly watching me out of the corner of his eye, but now that he knew I had been attacked by bird people he showed some signs of being more comfortable.

"We got this call. About an hour after we were supposed to meet with her. She said she was still in the Seabranch Preserve State Park and she needed help. She was crying and we could barely understand her, but she said something about her arm. She said her phone wasn't working until then and that something came out of the sky and attacked her. We heard some kind of a weird sound and she cut out."

He breathed in and out deeply and finally looked directly at me, scrutinizing my reaction.

"We called the cops right away; they said they'd send people. But the next day, they showed up at our doorstep and practically called us liars. They said there was no way to prove that Alyssa actually said that stuff. They said they didn't find anything, but when we went to the parking lot she always used two days later, we found broken glass and broken pieces of door. Up a tree we saw what looked like blood. They told Grace that they checked and that it wasn't human blood, but we didn't believe that for a second. Grace was pissed. She made a Facebook group and tried to tell everyone the cops were ignoring us. I didn't want to tell her that our story sounded crazy, with the police saying that it wasn't blood or a door part from Alyssa's car, but Grace didn't believe they had checked to begin with."

He sighed and clenched his fists briefly.

"Except one cop, they all ignored us. Grace said one guy believed her. He kept talking to her and eventually they started 'hanging out.' She stopped returning my calls, all that new guy stuff. Except for the fact that she was like seventeen and he looked like he was in his forties. I didn't trust him to begin with, because the other cops didn't seem surprised that our friend had called us at all. They didn't look like they didn't believe us, they just didn't want to hear it. It went on for a couple of months or so. I eventually moved down here with family and assumed that it was just a natural falling off the face of the earth thing. Things didn't go well and she broke it off when he asked her to run away with him, whatever the fuck that means. She cleaned up, and stopped returning his calls, but he kept at it. After a couple months she showed up at my place asking if she could crash and saying that she was going to the cops the next day."

He took his glasses off of his face and briefly rubbed them with a small piece of cloth he produced from the front of his shirt. I noticed they were slightly misted inside.

"My mom hated it, but she ended up staying for a while. The cops said that they never had an officer by that description and that they had no idea what we were talking about. She didn't have any pictures of him and said that they always met in public places or the hotel he stayed at on the island. She kept saying that he was different at first and that it felt perfectly fine but that he changed and wanted her to go away with him. I never got a clear answer as to what she meant. I think she was afraid to tell me all of the details."

He sounded miserable. I could imagine him thinking he could have done more to help his friend, but I doubt that was actually true.

"She started using all the damn time, anything she could. I had to lie to my mom to explain why all the NyQuil was gone when she went through that too. She said she thought she saw him moving through the cars at a parking lot near her work and she just got even worse. My mom tried to talk to me about it every day, but I couldn't tell her something supernatural had happened. The guy never came to my place, and eventually Grace and I went out to the Sunrise Flea Market to help clear her head, get out for once, stop scaring the hell out of my mom."

The Sunrise Flea Market was a spectacular spectacle of poverty. A massive, sprawling parking lot filled with various buildings—some just tents and some genuine concrete—called home by vendors of everything from stolen goods to crappy clothes. It was a powerful reminder that south Florida was and always had been closer to being part of the Caribbean than part of the "American South." A massive open-air market for fruits, vegetables, fish, and occasionally meats existed, with hawkers offering chilled coconuts with straws and other tropical favorites to drink. Almost anything filthy and Floridian could be found there.

"He was at the entrance."

I assumed he meant the massive gate that separated the lot where people parked from the lot where people sold junk and nodded for him to go ahead. He looked like he needed some confirmation that it was alright to continue.

"Grace saw him first, she walked ahead of me a ways while I parked the car. She thought it would be safe in public. The place was packed, it was the middle of the fucking day. There were four security guards in sight, but he didn't care. He looked pissed. He started walking up to Grace and he took out this big hammer, it looked like fucking farming equipment, but I wasn't about to take his shit. Before he got to us, I called over one of the security guards who know my cousin to have the asshole removed."

I noticed that the man's right fist was now clenched and shaking.

"I stood there pointing at the man while he just walked up to Grace with a hammer… Desmond, the guard, he just looked at her helplessly with a confused look. That man walked right up to Grace with that fucking thing and almost managed to grab her hand before she realized something was wrong and started to run. No one gave a shit that the guy pulled a weapon in public, and there was a crowd with well over a hundred people right there. She screamed for help and people were looking around… they didn't pay any attention to the man with the hammer."

He took a deep breath out and looked at me. I nodded again to indicate that I believed him—and I did.

"What did he look like?"

"He was wearing suspenders and a white shirt. Creepy fucker, pretty good looking but still. I have no idea what Grace was thinking."

I saw this coming from a thousand miles away, but it hit me like a ten-ton hammer.

"She was running to me, but he was right behind her with that hammer. The car was fifteen feet away and I didn't know whether I should run to it and get it moving or try and help fight him off. I just knew I'd get killed if he got to me. I ran to the car and Grace screamed so loud I can still feel my ears ringing. I managed to get in and get it running and threw the passenger door open while still dodging families and shit crossing the way. She caught up with me and got in the car but that creep had hit her in the shoulder, and it was already jet black and bleeding badly. She was almost in when he caught up with her. She raised her hand to block him and tried to fall in, but he hit her so hard that it looked like part of her hand was just going to fall off. I floored it and we got out of there, but the security guards flagged my car. Blood was spraying everywhere in broad daylight and people were just standing around, confused."

He shook his head sadly.

"We only realized later that we were the only ones who could see him. Whatever that thing was, it got Grace. It wanted her, but I could see it too. I only saw him one other time, but I know it got her. When we got out of there the cops were practically on us, but they just took me to some station while she was in the hospital, and let me go with an apology when she told them it was someone else."

"What did you mean when you said that I should avoid her?"

At this question I heard what sounded like a cough, but when I looked over I saw him dabbing his eyes with the same piece of cloth he used for his glasses.

"About two weeks later, she got a call. She had to do a drop, for her boss. She was using a lot to cope with all this shit and the bill ran up fast. She had been staying at my place for a while at that point, and stayed indoors more and more often. She was afraid to leave because she was afraid he would be there, but her boss said her line of credit was up and either someone would come to my place to collect or she would make the trip. I told her I would get the money, about four grand, but she was worried about not getting more coke. I got her to agree not to do it, but I went out to the grocery store for my mom and she was gone when I came back.

"A couple hours later I got a phone call. She was crying and I could barely understand what she was saying, but she was asking for help and saying she was sorry. I know I heard something about a bird, but she was babbling wildly.

She screamed and the phone cut out. She mentioned earlier that the drop was at Bryant Park, so I called PBSO and told them I was nearby and heard gunshots from over there."

He took a deep breath in. Now that he was in the weird, he was firing the words out so quickly he barely had a chance to breathe. His cheeks were damp at that point from the buildup of occasional tears.

"I started driving as fast as I could. I just took off, didn't even put away the groceries. By the time I was on I-95 for about ten minutes she called again. She sounded fine this time. But she asked me how I was doing, as if the other phone call had never happened. Then she asked me why I wasn't home. This was no more than twenty minutes after I got the first phone call. Even if she was fine, she couldn't have made it there. It wasn't her."

He pounded his fist into his leg and was shaking with some volatile mix of fear and anger.

"I had to go home." He said this with an incredible resolution. I remember being absolutely stunned.

"What?! What?!" I had no idea what else to say. He looked at me with a firm look, despite openly weeping at that point.

"Whatever had called me was at my house and it wasn't Grace. I had to get home. I hung up and got on an off-ramp. I went as fast as I thought I could without getting pulled over. When I got there, my mom and some of her friends were just leaving the house. I didn't see anyone else. I called Grace's phone back… I had to know for sure… but I just heard someone breathing in really heavily, right before they screamed into the receiver. I couldn't tell if there was something wrong with the line, but it like nails on a chalkboard in Hell."

He resumed staring aimlessly at the waterway and cleaned his face before continuing.

"The next few weeks, the cops came in and out of my house every time Grace's family felt like it was a good idea to ask them how the search for their daughter was going. Her boss was questioned, I got brought in three times but they decided to remove me from the suspect list because the drug-dealing piece of shit was a way more obvious suspect. He even threatened me once, but nothing came of it. Her family still thinks I had something to do with it, at the very least that I knew something that I wasn't saying. I wish I could say they were wrong."

He shook his head; I knew the feeling. At the moment, however, I was pretty selfishly worried, seeing as Grace and I had way too much in common.

"What was her boss's name? Just out of curiosity, you know…"

"John Hulpert, creepy dude, sold a lot of coke."

I involuntarily breathed a sigh of relief. I had heard of the guy, but he wasn't a direct associate of George. He clearly noticed, but didn't say anything.

"There were others who went missing too. Grace, Alyssa, Janette, but also this kid named Pablo who also worked for Hulpert. I can't tell if it's all connected, but it's a lot of people, you know?"

I didn't want to tell him how much worse it was at the pill mill, but I nodded. My stomach gurgled angrily. It had been promised mofongo, and so far we hadn't even gotten into our cars yet.

"And it all has something to do with Stigini, or whatever. God I wish there was just a burial ground we peed on or something. So, would you like to finish this conversation somewhere less creepy?"

He chuckled and nodded. I could almost smell the fried plantains and broth. "Yes. Yeah, I really do."

We both stood up, a little staggered from sitting on an uncomfortable bench long enough for us to air out our experiences. We drove away from the massive, beautiful homes and avenues of water, with rich, old white people walking their dogs or jogging and in no time we were both adrift in the sprawl of old mission homes, crappy apartments, and wooden homes that looked older than any hurricane would forgive.

We got to the mofongo restaurant—El Rinconcito De Santa Barbara, a nice-sized restaurant in a cheap-looking strip mall. Their mofongo was a legendary thing, even among people who viewed Hispanic food as boring and commonplace. We ended up trading the information that we shared on the Stigini and he expressed how thrilled he was that one had been killed by what was, in retrospect, a pretty bad mistake on the part of Cynthia. He had a textbook he had brought which explained that the native myths weren't really clear if the Stigini was a monster, or if it was a person who somehow learned to do horrible magic. Native American magic was something neither of us knew about, but he worked in a library under work-study and had already borrowed and read every book he possibly could imagine pertaining to it. The problem was, the Ais and Jaega—where the myth seemed to be closest to what we were seeing, specifically being able to attack someone while unseen by people around them—were ancient. They predated the Seminole and almost nothing was recorded of their beliefs, which were apparently as robust as any religion.

My voice was becoming a little raw from talking more than I'm used to, so I let him go on about what he had read, including information about vampires and similar monsters elsewhere, until the food came.

When the mofongo came, it seemed his appetite had returned, because we focused mainly on eating after that. I felt massively better, and not just because I was eating mofongo. I got the impression this guy wasn't the kind of scum I was used to talking to. The belief that this Chris guy was genuinely alright, at least on some level, was the most reassuring thing in my world at that moment other than drugs and mofongo. When we parted ways and I headed home, he let me borrow several of the books he had brought with him and we added each other on Facebook. I drove back up to Okeechobee Boulevard in West Palm Beach, almost an hour away, and slept well in my shitty, ancient hotel.

8

I felt even better when I woke up in the morning. The tiny, dingy hotel room seemed like a small palace with its ancient tile floors and high ceiling. It somehow felt better, clearer, to know that George was, in fact, my enemy. I wondered if I could survive as an informant. Considering the fact that I was very worried that my boss might want me tied up to avoid loose ends, it might not be a horrible idea at all. Besides, the good times were killing me. I felt pretty anxious, and for once it had little to do with supernatural threats. I was about to spend the day working with someone who wanted me dead in the middle of a room filled with people willing to do it for nothing. The patients were wretches who were easy to laugh at, but even the most pathetic person alive can pull a trigger.

They weren't the only ones with a certain nihilistic strength though. I wondered why Chris hadn't been exposed to anything "weird" even after the close encounter with something trying to kill his friend. I was guessing, at the time, that it was almost certainly the lack of narcotics in his system, something I had not even yet confirmed but felt confident of, especially by his reaction to Grace's use. I was presuming some things I should have asked him, but I still felt more confident and less insane than I had in months, despite knowing my boss would probably like me to die.

The hotel I was staying at was just off of Evernia Street, a massive building for its time (it was built in 1921) with doors that looked almost medieval. Henry Flagler was so smitten with Villa Zorayda in Saint Augustine that a powerful Moorish influence began to pervade much of his favorite architecture and then slowly, but surely, architecture that he had nothing to do with. South Florida is filled with "mission-style" architecture largely because of this lasting influence. Even Flagler's home is strangely Hispanic-looking considering the Anglo-American origin of its builders. It was abundant in the 1920s hotel, with massive dark brown tiles, stucco and stone everywhere, nearly floor-to-ceiling windows, creaking floors, and very little electrical lighting or plumbing. My bathroom was small and had a claw-foot bathtub and a washbasin that looked like it may have been original. It reminded me of the kind of apartments they have in New York City, especially with a higher view of the semi-urban sprawl.

I put myself together and thought what a nice place to do drugs it was, but decided to keep it slim. I decided to take a good bit less Xanax that morning, coming down to just two milligrams. That is still enough to knock a normal human being unconscious with more ease than Benadryl could muster, but I knew that every minute of the day was going to go by with incredible anxiety that would make every second seem like an hour.

The lobby of the hotel was massive, with huge pillars on the corners of the room. Almost everything was a shade of brown, taupe, or beige, giving me the impression that the room was in sepia. The cracking stucco and massive stone floor made it look far more ancient than it was. It was barely lit, with small light bulbs here and there and nearly makeshift fluorescents fixed to the ceiling, which was up to thirty feet high in some places. The darkness was thorough despite the small windows, making it appear as if it were nearly night time. If there was a private eye smoking in a button-leather chair it would look like a noir movie. This was in contrast to the explosion of turquoise and louvers of violent pink clouds that loomed outside.

Chris and I were planning on meeting at the end of the week, and I had to make a fast decision about whether I would continue working there and try and uncover the mystery, or if I should prepare for some truly brutal withdrawals and a proffer from the FBI (where the FBI offers one protection from prosecution in exchange for information on one's employers or dealer or whatever). I decided to take a walk from the hotel to the seawall, about a twenty minute walk each way, despite the fact that the bright turquoise and pink sky indicated it was still early morning. Somehow I felt bold, possibly by the thought of fucking over George, possibly because I felt more secure knowing that Chris was a potential ally.

The area just north of the tightly packed new buildings featuring "luxury lofts" and obnoxious bars and boutiques known as City Place was filled with older buildings. They often had wood floors and sported either utilitarian box shapes or were grand structures, with nuanced details in every alcove and column. The people were similar enough, either pointlessly wealthy or outrageously poor, and at night they either panhandled or moved between clubs and stores. I've heard it's gotten a little nicer, but there are still a lot of homeless. The entire expanded area of "Downtown West Palm Beach" had far more high-rise buildings, and it ran along a stretch of seawall that was always a great place for a walk.

I made my way away from the hotel and toward Makebs, a small bagel restaurant near the well-bubbled Christian University that lurked off of Okeechobee Boulevard. There were plenty of people out that morning, business people going to work at the many law firms near the massive semi-arch-shaped courthouse that loomed over the district, or just walking their dogs or begging for change. A kid bumped into me after just about two blocks while riding his skateboard. Aside from that no one interacted with me at all. He didn't turn around or say anything and from the way people looked at me I was guessing perhaps I could have shaved or done something better with my hair this morning. I reached Makebs and thoroughly enjoyed an egg and salami sandwich to go, on the seawall it was close to.

This was a practice enjoyed, in some way or another, by almost everyone living in the area. The waterfront view was amazing, and the architecture of some of the old churches and other elderly buildings interrupting the skyline once every other block or so made it feel like the modern era had somehow only invaded West Palm Beach. Art deco, Spanish influences, and high-rise condominiums and offices were wrapped in light turquoise and pink from the reflections of the sky they offered and framed with the dark green of ubiquitous palm trees. Some people went to the seawall, some people had views from their desks, and some people just enjoyed the brief drive from Okeechobee that happened to touch the water, but it was hard not to take a relaxing, deep breath in whenever one saw the water.

I felt much better. Almost like a normal human being. I was walking up a massive artificial hill near an amphitheater about the size of a football field when I even began to smile and say good morning to passersby. Some of them even responded in the positive. I was greeting a particularly delighted Lhasa Apso that was being walked by a beautiful young woman in yoga pants when I felt a sharp smack on my back. The sound of wheels on the sidewalk pointed me to the kid who had hit me earlier while riding his skateboard, who was catching up with a few friends who had skated ahead. He was wearing a backward baseball cap with a UM logo on it and carrying what looked like a bright blue and yellow hat in his hand. He didn't bother apologizing again as he sped up to join his friends, who had found a concrete staircase perfect for mischief. The woman and her dog continued on, obviously weirded out.

I turned up Clematis Street, where restaurants, clubs, and boutiques entirely different than the ones that had existed the month prior had confidently sprung up and workers were preparing the outside eating areas for a brunch crowd that wasn't deterred by weekdays. I wondered what it would feel like to go to the gym in the mornings or something. It was feeling like an incredible day when I suddenly realized I was going to be low on opiates soon, and therefore at risk of God knows what. I reached into my pocket to grope for my stash when I suddenly felt a shocking pain in my back and the strange sensation of falling on my face. I hit a small rise in the cement outside a shop hard, and my vision filled with stars. I could tell from the sharp pain and taste of pennies flooding my mouth that I had bitten down on my tongue.

The kid whirled past me, his wheels making a low, almost innocuous growl on the sidewalk. This time he whipped his board around to face me. There was nothing weird about him at all. A small teenager with a crisp-looking plaid shirt and hipster jeans, he had a mop of brown hair under his UM cap and light blue eyes. He picked up his board and held it under one arm, while holding what was apparently not a hat, but a bright blue and yellow striped mask in his other hand. The shape of its face was clearly that of an ibis or wood stork, and what I had previously thought was a bill tapered off into a thin but brightly colored beak. It looked like slick stone, almost as if it had the scintillating appearance of some strange kind of opal. The small group of skateboarders waited on the man-made hill that separated Clematis from the street that ran through City Place. He had a smug grin on his face.

I got up as fast as I could, shambling back and into some railing, surprising a waiter. I heard a few of the kids snicker. I walked away from them at an incredible pace, turning ninety degrees right away and pretending I had somehow not seen them at all. I managed to get back to the safety of the other junkies in the hotel in record time, keeping my head down and not looking behind me whenever I heard wheels on the sidewalk. I didn't see them after I rounded the next block and finally made it to the street with my hotel in view. A pixie-like young girl with dyed gray-blue hair wearing a bright orange tank top and dark blue and turquoise paisley swimming trunks sat on a bench opposite the hotel, next to a homeless man who smiled at her happily. She had a large dark red and seafoam green mask on her lap, and even from that distance I recognized the fat diamond shape of a gator's head. I stayed indoors another couple of hours and called in late. I hurried to my car and tried not to check if anyone was following me.

***

As I began to wait for another week to end, I hoped to avoid my coworkers and patients while I obsessively read the books on Native American myths Chris had given me. Debbie was standing behind the desk talking to Aaron when I came in. She turned and smiled at me, but Aaron had a much less happy face as he sank behind his check-in counter.

"Good morning! It's great to see you again!"

I muttered some kind of greeting, but her saccharine attitude and Aaron's obvious displeasure was making the FBI seem like a great idea already.

"Good morning…" I smiled weakly and nodded to Aaron quickly to avoid prolonged eye contact.

"Could I ask you a question really quick?" She turned and walked back to her office, not bothering to wait for a response. Aaron nodded back to me, but seemed more distracted by a small pull in his bright fuchsia, skin-tight shirt. Or maybe he was looking for an excuse to show his abs to the young girls at the front of the incoming group of patients. I waddled to Debbie's office, hoping this was going to be something not creepy.

"Dave wanted to talk to you, when is good for you?"

Mondays are inherently fucking terrible. "How about later this week, maybe Friday?"

If I could bring him to my next meeting with Chris, maybe we could share some insight into whether or not they were trying to kill me again.

"Sounds great! Also, I hate to ask, but could you help work the desk today? I'm feeling under the weather."

This made me quietly furious, as I had planned to hide from the patients and smoke pot whenever possible that day. The lack of Xanax was making me feel deeply stressed. After nodding dutifully I marched back to the front.

Within minutes patients had already filled the disgusting lobby. I was about to get to work filing patients into the computer system when I noticed a young lady who looked like she had been crying much more than usual. Her ringleader was an alpha-douche, short with a thick Tom Sellick-style mustache, tall black cowboy boots, stained black trucker hat, tight black denim pants, and a camouflage tank top to show off Confederate flags and eagles on wiry-looking arms. He was chewing tobacco and motioned for his friends to stand back before he leaned the upper half of his body over the counter and motioned for me to talk to him.

"Bro, I got fifty bucks if you can help me get outta here a little quicker."

While it was common to offer money or anything else to get ahead, it was rare for someone to assume that fifty bucks would make me happy to see him. He was about five foot six, but had the confidence of a man who was both taller and less inbred. I nodded, not wanting to say anything because I hated the man already and didn't want it to become obvious. I moved his file ahead in the doctors' waiting area and tried to put the two feminine names in the back so that I could talk to the girl who seemed distraught. She had frumpy brown hair tumbling over a powder blue tank top and blue jeans and it looked like she had cried the entire ride down. I couldn't see her eyes because she was staring at the ground the whole time, but she wouldn't leave this little creep's side.

"Byron James."

I called the little twerp into the second waiting room, where he slipped me a small greasy wad of money that I would bet anything didn't add up to fifty. He marched happily into his appointment and left the crying girl in the waiting room, as well as a six-and-a-half foot muscular skinhead that was apparently named "Ashley." The look on my face when he confirmed this must have been priceless because both everyone in the main lobby cracked up when I called him in. I made sure Ashley had his appointment first, leaving the weeping girl sobbing quietly in the corner. I took care of something in the office to give her a couple of minutes before approaching her to make sure at least someone asked her if she was in immediate danger.

I made it look like I was inspecting files when I suddenly noticed that there were no more files left for her group. That could mean that she was just a tagalong, but I wasn't feeling great about my odds. Thoroughly creeped out, I backed away. As I moved away from the files and the girl, I noticed that she was no longer crying and I felt confident that if I turned around, I would see her staring at me. I turned to go back to the office, but heard her first move, then get out of the chair at a cautious pace. When I reached the office door, I could see her standing out of my peripheral vision, facing me away from the doctors' doors in the hallway. I was starting to get a little creeped out, so I decided not to ask her any questions and shut the door behind me. I sat at my desk until I noticed them leaving ten minutes later.

"Thanks for the help, bro!"

Byron James was clearly thrilled as he held up his prescriptions and threw me a peace sign before handing the prescriptions to Aaron to be filled. His crew shuffled out behind him, one at a time. I couldn't help but watch them. After Ashley lumbered out of the door I still expected the girl to file behind them. The spring attached to the door quietly but promptly moved it shut after Ashley passed. Aaron got up and walked through the second waiting room to get to the counter where the doctors placed bottles of medication and their completed paperwork. The second waiting room was empty too.

Byron got his medication quickly, and began chatting up a pretty blonde while he waited for his lackeys to get their medications and sort out their agreed trades with other junkies in the parking lot and bathroom line. I went back to work in earnest, scanning files and trying not to notice how many had their records shipped to this and that place because the Narcan didn't come soon enough.

"Pst, hey bro…"

I could hear the sleaze dripping from his voice. Without turning around, I knew Byron was leaning over the counter again, taking advantage of Aaron's brief absence to be even more of a douche than necessary. The problem with taking money from junkies was that they assumed that either you were cool or that you needed money enough to get favors from. Either invited further conversation.

"I got some good friends and shit and I was thinking, maybe you could like, help them get through faster? I love coming here an' all but these lines, you know?"

He paused his bullshit to gauge my reaction and to take a long sip from a tallboy of Chelada, a surprisingly refreshing mix of Clamato, beer, spices, and lime juice. As I turned from my desk I saw the girl again. She was sitting in the lobby now, directly next to the pretty blonde Byron had attempted to fraternize with. Sheila Mae Cassidy was her name, according to her file. She was staring at Sheila with a wide-eyed expression of shock and rage. Her cheeks were still wet, and her pale, oval-shaped face was starkly beautiful. Framed by tangles of brown hair that looked incredibly frizzy and as if they hadn't seen a brush in years, her weeping made her blue-green eyes look particularly vivid. From the angle she was sitting I noticed that she had a dark red, wet stain on her crotch.

"Gyuh… gyuh… sure… whatever…"

I felt like I had been punched in the stomach. I turned away from Byron, who looked triumphant despite my failing to meet his high five. I had almost talked to her. No one else seemed to notice her except for a fat old biker who had put down his Mountain Dew and was now moving cautiously toward the door.

I sank down into a brown folding metal chair and lit up a joint, despite being barely obscured. Later on that day, I would get a call asking for Sheila's file and any information about her. It was PBSO this time, not a distant sheriff. Some officers came by to ask us about her too, but were tight-lipped about why. According to the news, they found the lower half of her body outside of a La Quinta. I found a couple of tiny tufts of blond hair in the waiting rooms and outside the next day.

I didn't want to take anymore Xanax so I decided to drink some NyQuil, just to be on the safe side. I got away from my desk, went to the back door that met the alley behind our junkietarium, and told Aaron that I needed a quick break for a joint, prompting him to nod and put out his cigarette.

***

After smoking a couple of joints and drinking a little more NyQuil, I staggered out of my folding metal chair. I wanted to simply feel nothing. I went into Debbie's office to see if maybe she had some shrooms or something, but her office was empty. The door to the second waiting room was closed and I noticed her car keys were missing, so I assumed she had run out. Her office had a single small fluorescent light that she ignored in favor of a tidy-looking desk lamp. It was the only thing tidy about the office, with papers everywhere and the walls covered in stupid posters and framed pictures of her and her friends. After rummaging around in her desk for a few minutes I found a few shrooms, a small bag of pills, some coke, and a lot of half-finished paperwork. Since I was already shamelessly rifling through her shit on the pretense of being in the back for an innocent narco-break, I decided to look through it.

Behind some unfinished attempts at lying to the DEA about diversion practices, there were some pictures that she had developed. They were from work and her house and seemed to be from the same group as the ones on the wall. I even saw one of me, looking wasted at her house. That was when I noticed the one of her drinking a beer at the Gold Ring pub with a friend. Her friend was a young man wearing a blue t-shirt and smiling awkwardly into the camera as Debbie flaunted her massive silicon valley in a black tank top. The young man was the young man who I had seen dressed nicely, with a bolo tie, asking for help. In some of the pictures, he was helping out with paperwork at American Injury Clinic, the behemoth narco-factory that was George's flagship. I wondered if I had been his replacement. For the first time in years, withdrawal seemed like a better option that continuing the many seemingly intertwined risks. When I got to my desk I began to google news investigations to see if I could find the names of the prosecutors or agents specifically involved.

***

I went back to work a lazy half hour later. Longer than usual, but not enough to raise eyebrows. Debbie came back an hour later, with slightly darker skin than she left with and a Frappuccino. I felt a twinge of disgust when she smiled at me and the blunt trauma of betrayal made it difficult to focus on anything else. I began to scan files again, now keeping an eye out for names; anything that seemed familiar I tried to file away. The lack of Xanax was helping quite a bit. I wondered what a proffer from the FBI would actually look like.

"Wilks, could I talk to you for a second?" Jessica's voice came from her medication room, directed at no particular direction. I happily shambled back to the only consistently clean room in the clinic.

"Grace and I were talking and she mentioned that she never heard from you…" She trailed off, expecting an answer, but I didn't have one. After calling the first number, Chris's, I had happily been under the impression that Grace was something to avoid.

"Uhn… when did you talk to her?" The pit was already forming in my stomach before I had begun to ask the question. I quickly hoped that she had called her and that there was a strange story behind it to confirm that something had happened to Grace.

"We went out shopping the other day. She works at the Neiman Marcus on the island and gets a killer discount. I guess she hasn't heard from Chris in a while, did you manage to get a hold of him?"

I shook my head, not knowing what to say. I felt like the room was suddenly thirty degrees colder.

"No… no… I will call Grace though… some stuff happened I just… I need some time to chew on things."

Jessica looked dead serious and nodded at the ground, seemingly genuinely sympathetic.

"You look like you've lost weight and cleaned up a bit lately…"

"Thanks." I had actually gained weight. I'm a stress eater and wasn't taking the lack of Xanax and opiates well, although my bowel movements were a lot better, but I was wearing clean clothes and didn't smell, so I took it as a genuine compliment. I awkwardly shuffled away from the beautiful girl. I wondered why whatever Chris was would give me books and talk to me instead of eating or killing me. I wondered what relation he had to the other things I had seen. I wondered if maybe Jessica had gone shopping with the still-moving corpse of something that used to be Grace. I couldn't think clearly enough to even imagine a scenario that might tie it together.

***

The next day, I wasn't taking the decrease in Xanax or creepy kids outside my hotel very well. I hadn't seen them again, but I also hadn't ventured outside during the night or morning, and I'd kept the blinds shut. Sure enough, by the time the next morning started in earnest I felt as if I'd had four cups of coffee and was ready to scream every time anyone made even the slightest traffic error. When I got to the clinic the parking lot was half filled with beaten-down vehicles that were packed like clown cars filled with junk aficionados, many with towels or blankets over the windows to keep light out while the occupants slept. Some of them stood in circles, forming small narcotic stock markets as middle dealers debated how many of which pills would be best to trade off with others. Many people would get killed over deals made in that parking lot. Entire fortunes came and went every day, usually in cars worth less than three thousand dollars. The strip mall with the pill mill faced another strip mall on the other side of the parking lot, which looked like a flea market for narcotics.

I tried not to pay attention to their stares as they whispered angry speculations as to when they could expect to finally get in and get their medications. Before I made it to the door, I suddenly recognized an increase in volume from the back of the lot, and finally the telltale yelps of hicks shouting. I took my cellphone out of my pocket and ran toward it, texting Debbie to send Aaron out as I went. When I got to the noise I saw a ring of filthy human backs, with heads pointed toward whatever was in the center of that ring. If they were fighting, especially over drugs, a lot of people could easily be going to jail if the cops had to come to break it up. The wall of backs was too densely packed to see around.

"Come the fuck on, people!" I yelled, hoping that someone would want medication badly enough to have some interest in helping get the two combatants apart. They ignored me, other than a few frightened faces turning to glance at me before focusing again on whatever was in the center of the circle. They did this while backing away. I could hear a gurgling and cracking noise over their frightened yelps and calls to relatives nearby.

I pushed my way between an obese biker with Confederate and American flags on his black leather vest and a skinny man with thin black hair who looked like he'd had more junk than food lately. The skinny man looked horrified and was shaking violently; he recognized me and pointed to the center of the action before backing away with a frightened babble. There in the center of the human filth I saw him. An old, tall, and very fat man, his face turned away from me, struggled to get up with the help of his cane. His bright yellow long-sleeved shirt and khakis were covered in blood. I looked around and couldn't see anyone near him, much less an obvious assailant. I saw Aaron picking up the pace from a slow jog to a quick sprint toward us so I cautiously broke through the ring wall.

"Alright everyone, calm down, we're going to get this man medical attention… sir… do you need help walking?" I asked as calmly as I could and hoped he didn't. It looked like a lot of blood. I heard a strange gurgle and more cracking and the people facing the man as he finally got to his feet cringed and backed away. When he turned around, I could see why. It was a fat old man named Ted, who was the ringleader for a particularly scummy group. He regularly tried to get as many young girls as possible hooked and turning tricks. Red gore dripped down from his chin and everything around his mouth was smeared with red. Gleaming white shards poked from the red flow of blood from his mouth. He appeared to be grinding his teeth, using every ounce of force the muscles in his jaw could allow to force what was left of his mouth to grind together, shattering and uprooting several teeth in the process. He stared at me with a glazed-over, peaceful look.

"Plish… elp… meee…"

Each word came with a small spray of blood and shattered teeth fragments. Veins bulged on the sides of his head, but he had a calm, almost serene look in his eyes. He swung his cane forward and began to walk toward me, with his hand outstretched for help. What was left in his mouth was so broken down it resembled shattered bits of porcelain draped in his own gore. He lurched toward me to take my hand, while I slowly walked to him until I felt two strong arms on my shoulders yanking me back.

"Let's go!" Aaron shouted directly into my ear and practically threw me in the other direction. I walked, slowly at first, toward the clinic door until Aaron gave me another shove and jogged past me. I saw the junkies shamble quickly to their cars or the front doors of the clinics. I heard a deep gurgle some yards behind me and picked up the pace when a scream rang out. The skinny man with the black hair had been cornered by the fat bleeding man after he ran into an alcove in the strip mall across the way. He hadn't realized it was a dead end, with a small concrete-block corner that was frequently used by junkies for sleeping, shooting up, and turning tricks. When I reached the strip mall columns I saw him in the tinted reflection. He had tried to move around the fat man, who fell down in an attempt to grab him. I could see that the front of the skinny man's shirt was covered in blood from the fat man's spraying.

As I got to the door, I forced myself not to turn my head to look at the kid with something brightly colored in their hands, standing at the end of the strip mall walkway, staring at me.

An hour or so later, when the police one of our neighbors had called finally showed up, they found the fat man, crumpled in the windowless cement corner. I saw them dragging a bag out but we heard later on that the police were asking people if anyone had hit him, because apparently most of the bones in his body had been broken. The tall, skinny man never got to the front door, but someone he was with was asking if anyone knew where he had gone to. Apparently he told them happily not to worry about him and strolled right out of the parking lot instead of getting his meds and going back to Kentucky where his family was waiting.

***

The next day I almost felt like praying for peace and quiet. The small hotel room was beginning to feel less unique and cool and more threatening, and I checked every kid with a skateboard to see if they had a mask as well. I waited until there wasn't a hint of the nuclear colors of dawn that cover Florida and began to get ready in the small, ancient bathroom, where I shaved using a razor I had bought at Publix instead of my shitty old electric for the first time in years. I wasn't used to the sight of my face without stubble left over. I drove quickly to the clinic, wanting to get the day over with. In the clinic someone had put *Stranger than Fiction* on instead of the action movies the patients typically enjoyed, and some deeply sad song was playing while Will Ferrell had a pensive, frustrated look on his face. I walked into the front office and saw Debbie waiting for me in front of the door where the second waiting room linked the front office to everywhere else.

"Dave wanted to know if he could meet you tonight instead of later," Debbie confronted me out of the blue, before I was even able to sit down, speaking matter-of-factly.

"Uhm, I kind of have something, it's actually really important. Could we do it tomorrow?" I needed at least a little while to chew on things.

"He actually needs to see you tonight." She smiled pleasantly and spoke in a soft but slightly happy voice. I wondered if it was just another meeting, which wouldn't be atypical, or if I was about to die. Or maybe Chris would kill me before I even got there. I nodded and sat down at my desk without a word. She went to chat with Aaron about some guy who hit on her while she was on a gambling boat with George. Patients began to pour in when Aaron finally flipped the lock and I was safely filing useless paper.

It occurred to me that it might be possible to discreetly contact authorities and maybe get some help. I remembered the name of the detective who I had read was investigating a pill mill they managed to close down south. After an hour or so I googled the name on my phone and brought up a number. While sitting on the toilet, pretending to be horrifically constipated due to opiates like normal, I texted a Detective Juan Roa that I was working for George and needed to talk to him discreetly. I got a text back asking what time and place I would feel comfortable with and responded that tonight would be great and that I would get back to him on the location. He agreed and I flushed the empty toilet.

Before I could reach the doorknob, my phone rang. It was Chris. I stared at it, disbelieving. It continued to ring, and I muted it and sat back down on the closed toilet seat. It went to voicemail and instantly began to ring again. This was clearly happening one way or the other.

"Hel—"

"Tell them to meet you at Bryant Park, after sundown," Chris's sharp voice cut me off before I could even finish the word 'hello.' It was followed by the screen on my phone telling me the call had ended. I stood up, my knees shaking, and almost instantly fell down. I got back up, feeling weak and nauseous. A combination of a lack of drugs and too much supernatural shit was getting to me.

After finally getting up, I threw cold water in my face repeatedly and texted Dave that I was going to be at Bryant Park (where I decided to lie and say I was staying near) after dark. He asked if I could do it earlier and I told him I had promised my mother something. He agreed and I went back to the office, moving slowly and carefully. My shoulder and back ached horribly after two bad falls in a short period of time. In the front office, Aaron and Debbie stopped talking when I entered the room and looked at each other. Aaron smirked a little while Debbie looked depressed, staring down at the floor and leaving the room instead of making eye contact with me. At the end of the day, I felt weak from having been sitting terrified all day, wondering what was going to happen to me. I took a long look at the clinic before heading out to the park to wait for sunset.

9

* * *

I sat near an outdoor auditorium that bordered a small dock. There were rows of old rotted wood making benches for the crappy reggae bands that sometimes played on the weekends. Normally, the homeless used the covered stage as a home for a particularly large group that congregated during the nights. As the boats began to pull into the docks to be towed away by SUVs and trucks, the hobos began to appear, cautiously at first, as if worried the sight of people with money might bring some kind of threat. Slowly but surely a small group of seven began to move to the auditorium, with most laying on the ground and two men watching the seawall and coast carefully, as if waiting to see something. After some time, a pair of headlights and a deep burble alerted me to a Dodge Challenger, a dark purple car I had seen Dave drive at least once before. He pulled into the small parking lot, looked at the homeless and motioned for me to come to him. I began walking to him and felt one of my legs shake a little, but he had a pleasant and relaxed smile on his face. He was wearing a light green shirt and dark sunglasses with orange plaid shorts. As I got closer, two massive men got out of the car. One wore a lavender-colored shirt with dark black letters spelling the name of some brand, the other just a white tank top and black denim shorts, assumedly to show as many tattoos as possible. Both were covered in tattoos, many such as an 88 on the forehead of one and the letters HH and shamrock on the neck of the other, which would let anyone aware of the crime world know that they were ranking members of the Aryan Brotherhood.

"Let me see your cellphone really quick." I thanked God that I had already deleted all of my previous texts and calls other than to him and one to my mother. I handed him the phone, and he removed the battery and handed it to one of his associates, who put it in the trunk of the car. It began to occur to me that even with two possible sources of backup or new problems on the way, a gunshot to the head would only take a second that I probably didn't have. Dave motioned for me to walk with him and we began to walk away from the amphitheater parking lot and to a large concrete outcropping that jutted from the park on the other side of the dock. It was a small cross-shaped fishing pier, with two side abutments that were often used by the elderly to enjoy the view of the water. Right before the top of this cross, after the four sections met, was a pavilion that used to be used as housing by the homeless. But tonight the entire area, and the shuffleboard court in front of it, was empty. Dave and the men were completely silent as we walked toward what felt an awful lot like my doom.

"So how is everything going at American?" I tried to make small talk, my voice cracking, as we got to the shuffleboard court in front of the pier.

"Relax, we'll talk in a second." He had a friendly ring in his voice, but there was a curtness behind it that confirmed my suspicions. We walked past the shuffleboard, with the two men suddenly much closer, behind me on either side. I knew I had no way to run. We turned the corner and in front of the pavilion where the homeless used to sleep, between two badly dimmed lights, Chris sat on the ground, watching us.

He wore a white shirt with white pants, but I couldn't see the details in the dark. Something dark spread around his neck and the front of his shirt. A pair of shoes was just off to his right. What I could see was the brightly colored mask in his hands. He slowly moved the mask to his face, where it stayed seemingly without anything to hang over his ears or the back of his head to keep it there. What looked like a pile of smeared gore sat on top of the pavilion, hanging just slightly in view from behind a roof turret. He stood up in a single fluid movement, and I felt a hand on my shoulder from one of the men, stopping me from moving back. Chris began to walk, slowly but confidently, toward us with what appeared to be a beautiful translucent light green mask that seemed to be some kind of bird. I could still see the features of his face through it, but I noticed he looked absurdly slender after he stood up. His clothes hung off of him like a sail. He was walking toward us steadily, his bare feet not moving slower or faster than a casual walk.

"Hey, we're going to need you to head out, buddy. Sorry, but we're going to need the area."

Dave said this quickly and turned around to face me and his friends. He scowled angrily. I doubted he liked being seen with me at the time, but before he could turn around to say something else, he noticed the odd look on his friend's face as Chris moved closer.

"Let's just go to the other pier," the skinhead in the tank top growled to Dave.

"Shit… yeah." The other skinhead sounded disappointed. Dave looked at me with deep consideration.

"The fuck is he doing, anyways?"

Dave turned around to see what the two were staring at, only to see Chris within about ten yards. What looked like a mask seemed to be melting into his skin. I could hear a faint ripping sound coming from him. At first I thought it was from his mask, but he doubled over, involuntarily, and it became clear that Chris's entire body was making horrible cracking and gurgling noises. Blood poured down his neck as the edges of the mask seemed to eat into his skin. All at once a hundred small changes seemed to work together, starting and finishing in slightly more than the blink of an eye.

His jet black skin was becoming mottled, like a plucked chicken, but stayed its dark hue. Tears in his skin were visible here and there as it stretched to cover what seemed like much longer arms, showing bones and viscera. The mouth of the mask seemed to invade his own, the beak suddenly moving, first crudely like an animatronic. His eyes were still visible, but the skin around them was stretched and moving. His eyes were larger than they should have been, massive orbs that seemed to move slightly away from each other. His knees snapped and popped with a horrific sound, bending backward. The flesh underneath his mask where his nose had been emitted a sickening wet crack. The beak began to move more gracefully. The three men were stunned; the skinhead in the lavender shirt staring slack-jawed until Chris's beak opened wide at us, revealing a long rotted tongue before shrieking. It sounded like metal tearing metal, or a fax machine gone horribly wrong. He began to move faster, walking more like a stork, and I could see that his fingers had giant black hooks at their ends. Taking advantage of the lack of a hand on my shoulder, I jumped to the side, into a small buildup of sand on the fake peninsula.

"Fuck!" Dave screamed, taking a small silenced 9mm from a discreet holster on his side and taking aim. An angry snapping sound came from the gun, but what had once been Chris leapt at Dave with an enraged chortling sound before his friends could take out their firearms. Its legs flung the thing at Dave at an incredible speed, and all I saw was a bright blur and a sickening, solid-sounding smack as both Dave and Chris hit the ground right where I had been standing, between his friends. Before getting up and running I saw Dave's two friends bring out their weapons a split second after the long beak that was once a mask landed on and poked through Dave's chest as easily as a syringe through the arm. It crouched over him, tearing its beak out of Dave's chest a split second after landing, bringing a spray of red gore with it. In less than a second, as his friends attempted to save their own lives, I heard a loud bang, or rather felt it. Two blinding flashes of light came from the scene and I looked away. Suddenly I could only hear ringing and my ears hurt like hell.

I got up and in what felt like an eternity, I began to run like hell away from the scene and toward the streetlights of the main road that seemed so far away. A splash of some warm liquid landed on my back and I decided I didn't need to know what it was. I ran as fast as a fat man can possibly run. Out of the corner of my eye, I saw something move insanely fast toward the fight and prayed whatever it was would delay any surviving skinheads or Chris. My whole torso hurt, but my lungs fought to suck air in and burned worse than any bong hit. I managed to get past the shuffle court and into the parking lot lights in front of the boat ramp, but couldn't see a soul there. I couldn't hear anything other than ringing, but a single bright flash of light behind me let me know it wasn't safe to slow down. I pushed myself as hard as I could, and I began to run past the auditorium, thinking the homeless were probably going to do anything they could not to get involved. As I reached the edge of the auditorium, I suddenly hit a hole in the ground and fell.

My mouth filled with warm, viscous blood and I let it simply fall out of my mouth rather than truly spitting. From the parking lot lights, I saw something make a silhouette on the ground coming from behind me and I struggled to do a push-up for the first time in years to get off the ground and start moving again. Before I could even get all the way up, two pairs of bright lights pulled up with an angry roar from a side street connected to the park and I saw someone get out of the car and point a gun at me. I put my hands up, on my knees. My brain couldn't even process what I thought was going to be my death. Instead, there was nothing. I just waited, with two headlights and then a flashlight aimed directly at me. The man with a gun was a police officer.

"Haaahhlelp." I could not hear my voice, but I felt the word falling out of my mouth along with more blood.

Later on, I would find out the sound of gunshots had caused an officer who was just getting home from his shift to drive over someone's front lawn and through the wrong way of an alley to get to the sound within seconds. From the blood pouring out of my mouth, he assumed I had something to do with it and called backup.

Detective Juan Roa managed to get there for our appointment just a few minutes later. A tall, dark-haired man with pale olive skin and a youthful mustache who wore a PBSO white polo with dark green pants, he had a surprisingly uncop-like voice. He was so delighted to hear that I wanted to wear a wire and have constant police surveillance that they completely forgot to do the whole "bad cop" routine. They brought me to the station, got a doctor to come to us and checked me out, and ordered some medianoche sandwiches when the doctor told them I had only broken two teeth on one side and could still eat if I avoided that side. I told an officer what I normally text like with George and Debbie, and he told them that Dave and company never made it to the drop. They were both horrified, but the police can't just arrest someone without anyone finding out and they had only found a few strings of gore, a bit of bone, and some shell casing where the fight happened, so they were eventually just filed as missing since I declined to mention the stuff about a bird demon. They assumed a fight had broken out among them, since I told them I had seen Dave raise a gun to his friend and ran away instead of walking over.

The next week felt great. My employers suspected a robbery, since they were apparently carrying enough to make it worthwhile. They asked me plenty of questions and at times seemed worried, but eventually decided a witch hunt for whoever had robbed them was in order. Debbie and George never really did figure out why I was suddenly less wasted, more focused, and always willing to chat about business until it was too late.

I went out in the morning again a couple of weeks after I had a doctor give me enough benzos to sleep through the opiate withdrawals. My tolerance was pretty weak by then. There weren't any kids standing guard by my hotel, but I saw the kid with brown hair near the Publix that separated City Place from Clematis after a short walk. He stared at me inquisitively, but after a few moments seemed to lose interest. He and his friends began to move in a pod toward the Dreyfoos School of the Arts, a selective high school. After that I started taking morning walks, slowly, but then more regularly. Plenty of weird shit happened in the clinic, and I usually just kept my head down, but nothing ever bothered me directly again—at least none of those bird things.

Some legal changes have occurred in Florida and at the time I'm writing this, there is a significant chance the pill mills may return in full force. They seem to think a lot of the horrible shit that became common back then might be coming back.

Did Anyone Else Answer This Ad On Reddit?

By SnollyGolly, Reddit User /u/*sharpermatt*

Annual Runner Up—Best Multi-Part Story, 2016

Annual Runner Up—Most Immersive, 2016

———————

1

My name is Matt. I haven't been sleeping much lately. It all started a month or two ago when I lost my job.

It was a factory job, and a pretty sweet one at that. I got paid to pick aluminum siding up off one line, check it for defects, and move it to another line. I did that for ten hours a day, and did a pretty good job.

The company got bought out, and they told us that robots could do our jobs just as well, and that was that. The company I'd worked at for ten years just up and laid me off. I got a few weeks' worth of pay as severance, so I guess that was okay. Unfortunately, I didn't really have any skills. Siding was the only thing I had ever done, and I wasn't really sure what I would do next. I got on with the job hunt and really tried hard. I thought for sure something would fall into my lap, but it just didn't. I started burning through my meager savings, and pretty soon, I was selling possessions to make ends meet.

Luckily, I just recently found a new job. It's even in my field of siding! I go out and install it on people's houses. It's really not that bad, just kind of rough in the summer. The crew I work with are really great guys, so shooting the shit with them makes up for the not-so-great pay and really demanding work. That's how I found out about Reddit. Tony and I were talking during a break a few weeks ago and he told me all about it.

"Yeah man, it's got all kinds of shit on there. Funny shit, sad shit, interesting shit, it's got all of it. Even naked ladies!"

Tony isn't a man of many words, but I could see his entire face light up when he talked about it. I figured anything that made Tony light up couldn't be all bad, so I signed up.

Reddit is really overwhelming. There's content everywhere. Baby pandas rolling down hills, candlelight vigils that make you tear up, and something called a "poop sock?" I don't know what that is, and I'm not sure I want to; Reddit is kind of weird sometimes.

Soon after I signed up, every spare minute was filled with Reddit, and I loved it. Well, until I saw that link. It was at the top of the page, and it said, "Volunteers wanted! You'll be compensated fairly. Be your own person."

My paychecks hadn't arrived yet. I was barely scraping by, and after two weeks of eating nothing but ramen, I was sick of it. If there was even a slight chance I could make some extra money, I wanted to take it. The link went to a research group called "Gray and Dean Research." There's not a lot of information on their site, but from what I could find, they do some sort of behavior research. I looked around the site for a little bit to try and get a better idea of what it was they did, but the huge "sign up" button called me to it like a moth toward a flame. They said I could be compensated for participating in their research study, and I didn't even need to leave the house. They were vague on the compensation, but I just didn't care. I think the sodium from all that ramen had started to affect my judgment, and I just took the leap and went for it.

They didn't even want that much information from me. They wanted my email address, and for me to answer a few questions.

"Do you consent to Gray and Dean Research monitoring you throughout the duration of the experiment?"

"Do you understand that Gray and Dean Research may withhold compensation until a time where the experiment's criteria is met?"

"Do you believe that you are your own person, and that your actions are your own?"

Kind of weird questions, I know. You know, in retrospect, I probably wouldn't have agreed to them on any other day. I was just so hungry, and poor, and tired of being poor. I thought participating in some harmless experiments from home would be worth it if I could change my situation. I also... well, this sounds crazy, so please just hear me out. I felt compelled to. I don't know that I can explain it, I just went to the site, and I felt like I needed to do it. Weirder yet, I didn't even really remember submitting it. I just woke up the next day with an email in my inbox:

Subject,

We're pleased to inform you that you've been accepted into our research study. A username and password has been created for you. Please log in at the following address to start the experiment. We look forward to your participation.

Gray and Dean Research | Department of Acquisitions

~LINK~

Like I said, I don't really remember submitting the form, but I was a little out of it. I clearly had. Flashing through my mind were images of me in a hot tub with models, on a private yacht somewhere drinking champagne, never wanting for anything else in life. These little daydreams were a welcome escape from my actual life, and with the money I'd get from this study, maybe I could at least drink beer at a lake.

I clicked the link provided at the end of the email, entered my username and password, and I was in the site. I'm not really sure what I expected, but

549

this definitely wasn't it. I was instructed to focus intently on a movie that they would be playing in my browser. I was to watch it for a minute, and then answer a series of questions.

I read the instructions, and proceeded to the next step. I'm not sure what kind of video this was, but it wasn't like anything I had seen on Reddit before. It was red in the middle with a bunch of static around it. Something about it though, it made me feel different. As I'm writing this, I'm trying to find the words to explain how it made me feel, or why it felt slightly off, but I just can't. All I know is that the video wasn't right, and it made me feel disjointed and like I wasn't myself.

Even though every fiber of my being was saying this video was wrong, I watched the whole thing. I needed the money. After a minute, I was directed to the questionnaire, and that's really where things got weird. It wasn't that long, although I don't remember the exact length. Most of it was fairly mundane:

"Do you consider yourself a good person?"

Well, yeah. I think so. I clicked "Yes."

"Are good people capable of bad things?"

Um, I guess so. I clicked "Yes."

"Are you capable of bad things?"

I started to get a little uncomfortable. I had never really thought about what I was capable of. Come to think of it, most of my life had been spent sort of just drifting and being on autopilot. When I really started thinking though, I supposed I was capable of bad things, but I had no desire to act on them. I clicked "Yes."

"Would you hurt someone?"

This question seemed fairly vague. What did they mean? I played a little bit of football in high school, and I had given out my share of hard hits. It wasn't mean-spirited though, it was just part of the game. I guessed I could hurt someone though. I clicked "Yes."

"Would you kill someone?"

This strange little questionnaire was making me do more soul searching than I had done in my entire life. I was perfectly content not thinking about how far I'd go in unfortunate or desperate situations. I had to answer though, and when I really thought about it, I clicked "Yes."

"Would you kill someone?"

I just answered that! I was starting to get a little bit freaked out now. I clicked "No."

"You are your own person."

That's not even a question. Of course I'm my own person. The strange thing about this one was that there weren't multiple choices, just a "Yes" box, so that's what I clicked.

After I had completed all the questions, I glanced up at the clock and realized two hours had passed. Man, it was already eleven pm! *Where did the time go? I could have sworn that I started just ten or fifteen minutes ago. Also, when did I get such a splitting headache?* I decided to take a nice hot shower and retire for the evening to get some much-needed sleep.

Honestly, though, I don't think I slept at all that night. I just lay awake in bed and tried to let my exhausted body rest. My mind wasn't having it. A constant stream of intrusive thoughts kept me awake.

Would I kill someone? Do I want to kill someone? Am I my own person?

The disjointed thoughts kept racing through my head. I desperately wanted them to stop, but they just wouldn't. So I did something drastic. Something I try not to do; something bad.

I smoked some weed.

I know what you're saying: *Matt, you're working at a construction job and using tools that could hurt people, why are you doing drugs the night before you have to work?*

Well, I used weed pretty heavily when I was younger, and besides giving me a terminal case of the munchies, it typically helped my headaches and always helped lull me to sleep. I figured half a joint might do the trick.

I had just lit it and taken a big puff when my cellphone lit up the night and startled me with its tinny rendition of Biz Markie's "Just a Friend."

I picked up. "Hello?"

I waited for a few moments, but there was nothing but the faint whispers of static on the other end, and then a robotic voice saying words I didn't understand the meaning of.

Then nothing.

Just like that part of my life had been erased, and I was here in the present.

I was suddenly in my living room during the day. My phone was nowhere to be seen. The light was pouring in from my window and illuminating my entire apartment. My mind started racing with anxious thoughts and panic. *Oh god, when did the sun come out? What time is it? I'm late to work! Why does my head hurt so much? Where is my phone? Oh god, I'm really* late to work.

Waking up late is the worst feeling in the world, but today, the splitting pain in my head was giving it a good run for its money. I trudged to the bedroom with squinting eyes, trying to block out the sunlight coming in from the windows to give my head some relief from the pain. My phone was lying on the floor and it said I had missed seven calls.

"Shit."

I texted my boss and told him that I had been up all night sick, and lost track of time. I told him I'd stay home today, and be in tomorrow. He seemed to accept that, and I felt the smallest bit of my anxiety abated.

I sat down on the bed and put the phone on the nightstand. My head was still splitting, and I just wanted it to stop. I put my head in my hands and felt my eyes welling up with tears of frustration and pain, and that's when I noticed it.

Dirt. On my palms, and under my fingernails. Where had it come from? I had taken a shower before bed, and it definitely wasn't there last night. I didn't remember weed doing this to me before. *Maybe it's gotten stronger?* You know they talk about that on the news all the time.

I pushed my confusion out of my thoughts for the time being. My brain couldn't handle it. I was confused and scared, but the pain center was overriding all logical thought. All I could do was lie down and try to sleep. I don't feel like I actually went to sleep, but then again, I don't really remember. I think I must have though; I remember dreaming about running through a field, chasing something, maybe someone. I don't know why I'm chasing it, or why it's running from me. I just know I need to catch it. Somehow during the chase, it falls, and I fall on top of it. There's a struggle. I hit it. I feel nothing.

So that's where I am now. The headache is starting to subside, but I still feel a bit out of sorts. I really just want to get back to sleeping regularly and feeling like myself again, but I'm not sure how. I don't like how I feel. I don't feel like I'm my own person.

2

It's been an interesting couple of days. I wanted to clear up a few things that I saw while skimming what I've written so far:

• I don't work for Gray and Dean Research, and I don't think they are selling my information. I haven't gotten any other spam emails or phone calls, so I think it's safe to rule that out.

• I haven't gotten paid yet, but I hope that's coming soon.

Things have been going pretty well here; I can't complain too much. Although even as I write that, I realize it's a lie. It's just something people say, even when things aren't going well.

Let me try that again. Things aren't going well for me, and I think they're getting worse.

Things were looking up for a little while. My headache started to fade into a dull roar, and I was back at work bullshitting with Tony the next day.

"Hey Matt, what do you make of all this monkey talk on Reddit? People keep talking about taking their dicks out for that monkey that got shot at the zoo, but I don't see how that's gonna help fuck all," Tony said.

Listening to Tony talk about "that monkey" from the zoo made for a welcome distraction from all that weirdness last week. I tried my best to concentrate on doing a good job at work, and hopefully get paid soon. Unfortunately, when I talked to the boss about getting paid, he told me that the first check always took a little while, and I was probably at least two weeks away from seeing a dime. I left work kind of dejected, and the research study entered into my mind on the way home. I knew they had mentioned compensation, but I hadn't seen a dime from that, either. I figured I'd follow up on it later and see if maybe they forgot to send the check.

That evening, when I was back at my apartment enjoying another excellent cup of ramen while wishing it was Chipotle, my phone chirped. I had a new email:

Subject,

We'd first like to thank you for participating in our research study. Your experience and input will be immeasurably helpful. We'd like to remind you that in order for you to be eligible for compensation, you must complete both experiments on our secure subject portal. Failure to complete both may result in disqualification.

Gray and Dean Research | Department of Acquisitions

~LINK~

Honestly, I didn't even really debate internally on whether I should drop out or not. After all that weirdness last time with the headache and the missing time, I was certainly more than a little sketched out. The truth of the matter was though: I *needed* that money. I clicked the link in the email, and right away I was back at the secure subject portal.

I don't know if any of you have signed up, but there's something weird about that video. I dismissed it before, but after I watched it the second time, I was sure that there's something more to it. *How do they get it to look like sparks are coming out of the screen?* That's a really strange effect.

After the video, it was back to the weird questions.

"Have you ever been scared?"

Well of course. Doesn't everyone get scared? I clicked "Yes."

"Have you ever been really scared?"

I thought about it for a second and my mind went back to being a kid and playing around with my friend, Todd, in the ditch behind my house. I was sure he would make that jump, but when he didn't, I was scared. When he was lying at the bottom of the ditch and not moving, I was really scared. He turned out fine, just a couple of broken bones, but the memory stayed with me. I clicked "Yes."

"Are you scared right now?"

It's the oddest thing: I wasn't until I read the question. Every fiber of my being was suddenly screaming at me. Yelling at me to jump to action, yelling at me to do something to get myself out of the situation. I have struggled with anxiety throughout my life, and that's the thing with it. Your body tells you that you're scared, and tells you to run, but you don't know why you're running. I pushed the feeling down and clicked "No." Machismo, I guess.

"You should be."

Every single hair on my body stood up at once, and those voices telling me to run got even harder to push down. *What kind of joke was this?* Was this some bored scientist's way of being funny? I might have found humor in it before, but sitting alone in my apartment at night had me more freaked out than chuckling. I submitted the form and closed the laptop lid. I didn't want to deal with it anymore.

My head had started to hurt again, so I made my way to the bedroom to try once more to get some sleep. I guess I haven't mentioned it yet, but I've still been having a really hard time sleeping. I lie in bed and close my eyes, but I don't feel like I'm sleeping. Stranger yet, I feel like I'm dreaming. "How can you dream if you're not sleeping?" you might be asking yourself. I don't know, but it's the same dream every night.

I'm somewhere foreign—no idea of how I got there. Someone is whispering in my ear, but there's no one there. I don't even bother looking to see where the voice is coming from because I don't care. I can't hear the words, but I understand what they want. They want me to get "it." I don't even know what "it" is, but I start running at full speed trying to catch "it." It's pitch dark, and I can't see anything except silhouettes moving in the dark. I hear nothing except the labored breath of "it" as I gain ground. As I get close, I lunge at "it" and tackle "it" to the ground. My target lets out a groan as I make impact with "it." I hit "it" over and over, but feel nothing.

I gasp and open my eyes to find that it's morning, but I don't feel like I've slept even a minute. Rubbing my eyes, I try to get the will to get out of bed and get dressed. Thank god for Monster Energy; I don't think I'd be able to go to work without it. It doesn't really help the headaches, but then again, nothing really does. As I go about my morning routine, I catch my reflection in the mirror. *Man, I look like shit these days.*

Once I get to work, I can kind of get in the zone. It's really not that different from my other job. Pick up this piece, put it over here. Ironically enough, even though it's physically difficult, it calms my mind and makes me forget about the problems in my life.

My phone started playing the familiar rendition of "Just a Friend," and I started walking away from the job site so I could hear the other person. I answered it and said, "Hello?"

"Hello, this is a message from Gray and Dean Research. If you're expecting this call, please stay on the line; otherwise hang up."

I debated whether I should hang up the phone right then. I was at work after all, and if I thought money was tight before, it would be a lot tighter without a job. I figured it wouldn't be that long though, so I stayed on the line. It was the same weird static and robotic voice, I think. I mean, I don't really remember. I think it was spelling something out? Or asking me a question of some sort.

That brings us to today. I'm in a motel about 150 miles away, and I have no idea how I got here. My truck is outside, but I sure don't remember driving here. I've got twenty-four missed calls on my phone and seven voicemails. I haven't listened to them yet, but I doubt they're good. I'm starting to get really scared now; it's not like me to lose track of time like this. I'm wondering if maybe I hit my head or something. Would that explain the missing time?

Maybe it's carbon monoxide poisoning. I remember Tony telling me about a story like that not too long ago. "Yeah man, dude was leaving notes for himself when he was all fucked up on that carbon monoxide gas. Shit was wild, man."

I guess either of those would explain the headaches and the missing time. What I'm really having a hard time with though is the clothes. I'm wearing new ones and mine are in the bathtub. It's not that my clothes are in the bathtub that worries me, it's that they are covered in blood. I know I can't remember what happened to me these last few days, but I checked myself, and I hope with all my heart it's not so, but I don't think it's my blood.

I don't know what's going on, but I'm terrified. I've never felt less like my own person.

3

It's been a crazy couple of days. When I woke up in the hotel room, I was really freaked. I'm still freaked, but I think I'm starting to understand what's going on. Unfortunately I sound like I'm crazy, and I'm even more scared than I was.

I went to the bathtub to look at the clothes again, just to make sure I had seen what I thought I had. They were definitely my clothes, and that was definitely blood. I've had chronic bloody noses since I was a kid, and I've ruined more than a few pillowcases in the night. There wasn't a doubt in my mind what this was. I'm sure you're thinking, "Matt, if you bleed in the night, is it so crazy that you ruined some clothes and put them in the bathtub?" No, it's really not that crazy in theory. The problem is how much blood there was. It seemed like all my clothes were covered. I filled the bathtub with cold water—a trick my mother had taught me—and let my clothes soak while I dealt with my phone.

Twenty-four missed calls and seven voicemails.

"Hey, Matt, this is Tony from work. You were acting all kinds of strange yesterday when you left. Did I do something to piss you the fuck off? Be easy brother, let me know you're okay."

I pressed delete.

"Matt, this is Bobby from work, you left mid-shift yesterday, and you're late for your shift today. I know you've been sick, but you gotta come to work, man."

"Shit," I said out loud in response to the message. Bobby was a great boss, and when I lost time and didn't show up the first time, he was understanding, but I suspected his patience had its limits. I pressed delete.

"Matt, you know I hate to do it, but I gotta let you go, man. If you get your shit together, give me a call and we'll talk about coming back."

Great, not only was I God knows where, but I was jobless and had blood-soaked clothes in the tub. If this wasn't me, I'd think it was hilarious, but in that very moment I felt the weight of the world crushing my chest, and it felt like my head was competing to see who could give me the most pain. I wasn't sure who was winning.

I skimmed through the rest of the voicemails and missed calls, and deleted them all. It just didn't seem to matter. I figured I'd at least call back Tony and see if I could piece together what had happened. I scrolled through my recent calls and tapped his name to dial him.

"Jesus fuck, dude, you're alive," he said, sounding relieved.

"Yeah, man, at least for now," I replied, cringing from the effort that talking on the phone required. "Hey, this is going to sound weird, but what happened yesterday?"

"Man, you don't remember? We were working and you picked up your phone to answer it. You walked away a little bit to take the call and then after a few seconds, you turned around, and started walking straight to your truck. You had this fucking deer-in-the-headlights look about you. When I asked what was up, you shoulder checked me hard enough to knock me down. That's not cool dude."

I did all that? I'd never hit Tony. For one, he was the closest thing I had to a real friend, and secondly, he's a big dude. Now he's telling me I knocked *him* down?

"Tony, I'm so sorry, I haven't been myself lately. Ever since that research study I signed up for online, I've been feeling less and less like my own person."

"You gotta get some help, man, losing time like this ain't healthy. I don't think I'd blame some weird website on it either, man. I signed up for that site you were talking about the other day, and it was weird, but it didn't make me into some kind of disappearing weirdo. Just get your shit together and call me if you need anything," he said.

"I will, Tony," I said and then hung up the phone. What the hell was going on here? I was in pain and confused, but I tried to push that out of my mind because it was time to get some answers. I collected myself for a minute and put together a game plan. First, deal with those fucking clothes. Second, head home and get some rest. Third, figure out what the hell was going on with me.

I went back into the bathroom, wrung out the somewhat-less-bloody clothes, and wrapped them in a hotel towel. "People steal these things all the time, I'm sure they won't miss one," I said out loud. Partially to alleviate the guilt my uncharacteristic petty theft made me feel, and probably also to put out of my mind that I was trying to get rid of bloody clothes. I couldn't think about that right now. I needed to get home and figure out what was going on.

I took my soggy bundle of clothes to my truck and hopped in. I opened up Google Maps and saw that I was a little over two hours away from my apartment. I turned on the truck and started to drive. Now, I don't know if it's just me or not, but I've always felt at peace on the open road. Something about it calms and centers me. I started to think about my predicament. *Everything was going pretty well until this research study, but how does a website make me lose time?* It didn't make any sense. I didn't even spend that much time on the site. I just watched the weird video, answered some questions, gave them my phone number and got the… call. *The calls.*

That was it! Both times it had been directly after that weird phone call. What did it even say? It spelled something out, and asked me if I was open? No, that can't be right.

Time had slipped away from me a little bit, because before I knew it, I was pulling into my apartment's parking lot. By habit alone, I got out of my truck, locked the doors, and walked to my mailbox to check it. Bills, bills, bills, spam, bills, a postcard, spam, bills.

The postcard was odd. I looked at it and saw that it was from Gray and Dean Research. *Did I even give them my address?* Jeez, I must have. With all the missing time, I definitely couldn't rule that out. I looked at it closer. It was fairly plain on the front except for a picture of two smiling older men in lab coats. On the back, it said the following:

Gray and Dean want to congratulate you for your performance in phase two of our research study. Not everyone is cut out for the type of research we do, but you're one of the special chosen few. We will be making contact with you in the next couple of days. It's vitally important to keep this postcard on your person AT ALL TIMES. You will not be eligible for compensation if you do not. Thank you, we'll see you soon.

I felt a small weight lifted as I realized I'd finally be getting compensated. I couldn't say that all the hassle and headaches had been worth it, but at least I was almost done. I folded the card in half and put it in my back pocket.

I walked up the stairs with the last bit of energy I had left, went straight to my bed, and fell down into it. It was comfortable, but every time I tried to clear my mind, my brain kept me awake with questions:

"What have you been doing with the lost time?"

"Where did all that blood come from?"

"Am I my own person?"

After realizing that sleep wasn't going to come for me, I opened my eyes and resolved to find answers. That's when I booted up the computer, went to Reddit, and searched around to get a clear picture of what had happened so far.

That brings me to now. Have you ever googled "Gray and Dean Research?" I'm sure some of you have, but I hadn't until right now. Nothing comes up. I mean sure, there are people named Gray or Dean, but none of them have a research institute together. I went back to their website to look to see if I missed anything the first time around. They claim to be based in New Mexico, but they don't list an address. *Maybe the phone number has some clues?* I decided to call it and see if anyone answered.

"Gray and Dean Research is not accepting calls at this time, thank you."

Whoa, talk about timing, I just got an email from them. Here's what it says:

Subject,

Your compensation is on its way! As a reminder, if you don't have your postcard on you, you won't be eligible for compensation. You've come this far, make sure you get what you have coming to you.

Gray and Dean Research | Department of Acquisitions

Well at least that's good. Although I still don't know why I need a postcard to get a check in the mail. Does that seem strange?

***

Hey, matt here again, i figured something out. Explanations for what's been going on! Last time i wrote, some weird stuff was going on. Probably had everyone really scared. Man that's nice of you guys to care. Except that it's really not that big of a deal. Got put on meds a few months back which effect my memory. Didn't remember to mention it until now. Real silly, matt! Entire time, it was just the drugs messing with my head and making me think silly things that aren't true. So my doctors have decided i should keep taking the medicine, but in a more controlled place. Except i need to go away somewhere so they can watch me. A nice place with lots of nice doctors. Really will be good to have so many people helping me. Caring people always make me feel better. Have a good time, and be your own person. i know i will!

• matt

Best Under-500 Upvotes
—2016—

The Basement Door

By Tristan Lince, Reddit User /u/*Discord and Dine*

Annual Runner Up—Best Under-500 Upvotes, 2016

———————

Mommy always tells me to never open the basement door. She always says that if I open the basement door, I'll see something that I was never meant to see. I never understood what she meant by that, but I never opened the basement door anyway, so I didn't worry that much about it.

The one time I did ask what was behind the basement door it was dinnertime. My little brother Nolan was upstairs reading a book. He had already eaten his dinner. It was just me and Mommy. The moment I asked the question, Mommy frowned. She looked angry. I regretted asking her at once. "Hannah, I thought we said you wouldn't ask what was behind the basement door. You promised me."

I just hung my head and said, "I'm sorry, Mommy."

She shook her head. "Now you don't get any dessert. I'm very disappointed in you."

We ate the rest of dinner in silence.

I ask Mommy sometimes why I can't go to school. After all, I'm eight and Nolan is six. He gets to go. Every afternoon he comes home from school, comes into my room, and tells these amazing stories of learning and making cool friends. I'm always sad when he tells me the stories. Why can't I go to school?

Whenever I ask Mommy, she just sits down beside me on my bed and says, "Hannah, honey, you can't go to school because you're sick. We don't want you getting the other children sick. You wouldn't like that, would you?"

"No," I always say.

The funny thing is: I don't feel sick. Mommy says I am, but I don't think I am. I feel fine. But what Mommy says is right is right, so I don't go to school.

Sometimes I hear creepy noises coming from behind the basement door. One time I woke up in the middle of the night and heard laughing and footsteps. I left my room and snuck to the basement door, putting my ear up to it. There was more laughter and then the sudden sound of breaking glass. I heard a yell of shock, then silence. It scared me, so I went back to my room and hid under my covers. I cried out for Mommy, but she must have been busy, because she didn't come. I didn't fall asleep all night.

Every morning, Mommy comes into my room to put lotion on my face. She takes out a mirror so I can see my face. I have this great big cranberry-red birthmark that goes across my face from my left ear to the right side of my chin.

"See, Hannah?" Mommy says as she puts the foul-smelling lotion on my face. "If I put this stuff on your birthmark, it won't get any worse than it already is." I always ask her if she has anything that will make it go away completely, but she always changes the subject or doesn't respond.

I keep hearing strange noises coming from behind the basement door. Just last week, I heard the most awful sound of all. It was loud, aggressive noise. The thing that made the noise sounded angry or threatened. It scared me. So I went back to my room and sat on my bed, trying to ignore the sounds. But they just kept going on and on. Then, something howled. I screamed and yelled for Mommy, but she didn't come. Shortly following the howl came more laughter and someone clapping their hands.

At dinner that night, I asked Nolan if he knew anything about the strange noises coming from behind the basement door. He laughed and started to say something, but Mommy cut him off. "No, Hannah, Nolan doesn't know anything about the basement door. Right?"

Nolan looked at Mommy strangely, but he said, "I guess not. Sorry, Hannah."

The noises keep coming. I hear heavy footfalls and a strange jangling noise almost every few minutes. Then the loud, scary noise comes again. Someone behind the door laughs and then everything is quiet again.

I asked Mommy one morning if she thinks my face is getting better. After all, I don't feel that sick. It's just my face. She just shook her head, slapping on more of the smelly lotion. "I'm sorry, Hannah. I don't think your face is getting better. Give it more time. You might even be able to go to school soon." This made me feel better, but I was still bummed out about not being able to go.

That night, I heard the most awful noises yet. I was woken up by a loud sound of breaking glass. I got out of bed again and went to the basement door, putting my ear up to it again. There were heavy footsteps, much heavier than the ones I'd heard before. Suddenly, the loud, angry noise came again. I heard a very loud scream and the footsteps fading away. There was another sound of breaking glass, followed by the loud, angry noise five times in a row. Someone laughed and then everything was silent again.

I need to know what's behind the basement door. If Mommy or Nolan won't tell me, then I'll find out myself.

I wait a few days. We eat dinner. Mommy puts lotion on my face. Nolan tells me about school. Then, one morning, I wait until I'm sure Mommy has left for work and Nolan has left for school. I slip out of bed, put on my slippers, and go to the basement door. I put my hand on the knob, take a deep breath, and turn it.

The door creaks open. I'm shivering and scared, but I need to know what's making all the strange noises. Once the door is open all the way, I see a strange room. It's a long, thin room. Counters run along the right and left walls. Cabinets hang above the counters. A huge, humming white machine is to the right of me.

Is this what's behind the basement door? Just some strange room full of machines? I take my first step in. Nothing happens. I don't see any causes of the scary noises. Where did they come from?

I walk through the long, thin room, expecting something to jump out at me, but nothing does. I reach the door at the end of the room and pull it open. It's a hallway. Hanging on the walls are pictures in frames. There's a few of Mommy, a few of Nolan, and few of them together, but there's none of me. That makes me sad, but I look down the hallway anyway. Off to the right are three closed doors. Off to the left is a huge room full of couches. A large black machine with a wide screen hangs on the wall. I turn left down the hallway toward the strange machine.

Then, I hear a growling behind me. I don't want to turn around, but I do. I scream out loud at what I see. Standing in the middle of the hallway is a horrible creature. It's on four legs and covered in shaggy fur. Its mouth and nose protrude out of its face. I just stand there, too scared to even move. It peers at me with its huge yellow eyes and then growls.

I can't take it anymore. I scream and run back toward the door to the long, thin room. The creature behind me howls and begins running after me. I scream for Mommy, for Nolan, for anybody as I reach the basement door. I pull it open and look behind me, just in time for the creature to open its mouth and bite my slipper with its fangs. I scream and kick it in the face. It whines and tumbles off the left. I run through the basement door, closing it behind me, without my slipper.

I don't leave my room for the rest of the day. I just sit under my covers, shivering, wondering if the awful creature knows how to open the basement door.

That afternoon, I hear a scream from behind the basement door. But then, for the first time, someone says something. I recognize it as Mommy's voice. "NO!" she cries. "Bad Sparky! BAD DOG!" she yells. I'm confused. What's a 'dog'?

The basement door creaks open and Mommy walks down the stairs. She's holding my slipper in one hand. She looks very angry. "Hannah Ann Smith," she says, her face screwed up. "Did you leave the basement?"

I hang my head in shame and say, "Yes, Mommy."

She sighs and hangs her head in her hands. Then, she walks over to my bed and sits down. "Hannah, I thought we agreed, no leaving the basement. You don't want to embarrass Mommy in front of her friends with your face, do you?" she asks.

"No, Mommy," I answer.

She shakes her head. "I just want you to know I'm very disappointed in you. You won't get any supper tonight." I nod meekly and watch as Mommy goes back up the basement stairs. I think about asking her about the creature, but I decide not to. Right before she closes the basement door, she says, "I love you."

"I love you too, Mommy," I say.

Then she closes the door, plunging my cot, my basket of clothes, the table, the three chairs, and the grimy toilet in the corner into darkness.

I don't think I'll open the basement door again.

Most Immersive
—2016—

Playing the Game of Seven Doors

By Katie Leute, Reddit User /u/*shortCakeSlayer*

Annual Winner—Most Immersive, 2016

———————

1

I'm not sure how we started, or who had the idea first, but when I was in middle school I had a group of friends who would all go into the woods together past the race track and play a game we called "Seven Doors." This game involved one girl laying her head on the lap of another; the second girl would cup her hands over the eyes of the first girl to block as much light as possible from shining through their eyelids. We would all circle around them, seated on the forest floor, and chant softly, "Seven doors, seven doors, seven doors…"

The girl whose hands were cupped over the first girl's eyes would ask her questions after we chanted for a few minutes. What do you see? Where are you? Do you smell or hear anything? All leading sensory questions that would paint a picture of a location in the mind's eye. The girl lying on the ground would begin telling us what she saw, describing what she was doing, even where she was walking. Usually every "session" like this started in a forest similar to the one we played in, except that the girl who was "traveling" would be alone.

Within the woods were seven doors, each one a different color: red, blue, green, yellow, orange, purple, and white. They were scattered, and usually the goal of each session was to find a door, open it, catalogue what was inside of it, and get back "safely" to the "entry point," or the clearing in the woods that all of us originally arrived in when it was our turn to travel.

We only had forty-five minutes for lunch at school, so we would usually only have time for one person to go under per day. Originally, it was just for fun; we would giggle and chant and listen with rapt excitement and attention at the visual story the girl who was traveling that day would spin for us, finding all manner of animals and plants in the "forest." We respected the hunt for the doors; no one was eager to slip a discovery into their story until it felt right or made sense. Thus it took us two weeks to find three of the doors and explore a little bit of what was beyond each.

The Blue Door was found first, and it led to a deep valley lake, with short white houses cut into the cliffsides around the lakeshore. We hadn't delved deep enough yet to know if the small cliffside villages were occupied or not.

The Red Door led to a huge city, built from gold, terracotta-type material, with towering buildings that connected and reconnected through complex bridges. Again, we had yet to encounter any sort of dwellers or people there. A few strange birds followed our progress through the city any time one of us ventured into the Red Door.

The Green Door led underground, into a dank, glowing grotto filled with soft, phosphorescent fungus that wove across the ceiling like a webwork of fine, jeweled thread. There was a single fire pit with a crackling fire lit at the water's edge, and a small tent suitable for one or two people at the furthest place within in the darkness.

We were slowly moving beyond the point where it was a game. In the beginning, perhaps we had tapped into the effectiveness of soft repetitive noise and some sensory deprivation by blocking the light from the eyes, and achieved some very mild meditative states. It may have helped with our intuition, our ability to get lost in our world that we all created together. Like a creativity exercise done to stimulate those more-abstract portions of the brain that we are so plugged into as younger kids, and lose access to as we get older.

Maybe we were just at that right age: not quite children anymore, not quite grown, but in between. A gray state of being; transitional creatures each with a foot in two different worlds.

Maybe this is what made us susceptible. Who knows?

I remember going under on a Wednesday, when my turn came around. My friend, Jay, had her fingers cupped loosely against my cheeks. She had been taking guitar lessons, and I remember how calloused her finger pads were against my twelve-year-old skin. It made it harder for me to concentrate for a while, to sink into that soft, fuzzy, half-awake state that made it easier to immerse myself. A flash of irritation shot through me but I quenched it, squeezed my eyes shut, and tried to concentrate. The anticipation in the circle around us had changed in the last week. No giggles or smiles; we used to make faces at each other across the circle to try and get one another to crack the chanting with a laugh, but the last few days everyone had intently stared at whoever was on the forest floor, focused. Resolved. There was a mystery there and we were going to figure it all out.

Hindsight is 20/20. Isn't that what they say? If I could stop my twelve-year-old self somehow, I would.

Finally, the chanting stopped, and Jay asked me, "What do you see?"

The clearing was around me, as it always had been. I looked down and could see myself, wearing the flared Dickies and blue-striped, cap-sleeved shirt I had put on that morning. I circled around the clearing, getting my bearings. Our friend, Shina, had found the Green Door the day before, and she had turned twice before heading off into the forest. I was really curious about the grotto. I hoped I could find the Green Door again and spend a little more time exploring. I turned steadily, making a second complete circle, before walking out of the clearing into the woods.

It was midday; sun shafts broke through high canopies of thickly layered pine trees. Dead needles and rocks crunched under my shoes as I walked, threading in between tree trunks and larger ferns. I described the landscape around me in colorful detail, until I was stopped short when Jay asked, "Do you hear anything?"

Huh. Besides my own footsteps, I hadn't thought about sounds. I paused, finally tuning in to the forest around me. There was a stillness, a heaviness to the forest that seemed to dampen all noise as if the sounds were trapped beneath a blanket. I waited, but besides me there was no sound. Not even one of the creatures my previous friends had identified in earlier explorations. My mind was a total blank.

"I don't hear anything," I whispered, and somehow saying it out loud filled me with a sudden, blood-chilling dread.

Ice in my veins, I slowly turned in a circle right where I was standing, peering sharply into the woods around me. This was… strange. Something was off. I didn't see anything out of the ordinary, but this weird, suffocating stillness seemed much different from the soft, breezy forest we had come to know. I don't know why I was stupid enough to do this, but I called out, "Hello?"

A pause.

Then, in the distance, a sound. Leaves rustling?

The snap of a branch, so singularly loud in the stillness that it might as well have been a gunshot.

My heart cracked and fire surged through my limbs. I whipped around and began running back to the entry point, the clearing where we all entered and exited from.

Fuck. What was I thinking? I should have realized something was wrong right when I arrived but nothing had ever happened before, so why should it now?

My breathing came fast and hard as I dodged tree trunks and leapt over exposed roots. Jay later told me that I had called out, "Hello?" and then started almost hyperventilating. She had been tempted to wake me up, but we had a rule about waiting until a person had returned back to the entry point before coming back. Something about exiting the same way we had entered, in order to keep everything structured and ensure that we had really "woken up."

I was mostly looking down at the path as I ran, to ensure that I didn't trip on a root or large rock. So when I looked up briefly, and saw a dark, hulking shape ahead of me in the woods, my heart nearly stopped right then and there.

"Shit!" I veered suddenly, dodging behind a pine tree, clutching the rough bark in my hands as I pressed myself against the trunk. I stuffed my hand in my mouth, stifling my gasping breaths, ears craning desperately for any sound. What was that? Were my eyes playing tricks on me? *What in the actual fuck was going on?*

I waited, hearing nothing but the thick silence and my own blood pounding in my ears. After a few moments, I cautiously peered around the edge of the trunk.

It was closer to me now. I hadn't heard anything, but there, in the direction of the dark hulking thing I had seen earlier, I could make out the distinct, rectangular shape of a door.

"What is it? What do you see?" Jay's voice squeaked a little higher than normal.

"There's a door ahead of me," I whispered. I stared at it, fingers white-knuckled and stinging with sharp pain as the rough bark of the tree dug into them.

"A door?" A pause, then Jay spoke, her voice calmer, colored with curiosity. "What color is it? Is it green?"

I swallowed hard. "It's black."

It stood alone in the woods about fifty yards ahead of me. A dark, solid stain on which the light of the sun seemed not to touch. I couldn't see much else from my distance outside of a faint embossed pattern covering the center of the door.

There was a long pause. Then, another voice, from the circle of our friends around us. "I thought there were only seven doors?"

"Elia, shhh!"

"Well she's changing the game! We haven't even found all the doors we decided to have yet and she's making more doors?"

I couldn't be sure, but somehow the door was getting closer to me through the woods.

"I'm running around it," I said, and began moving through the trees, circling around the door to the left. It didn't seem to move while I was looking at it, yet every now and then I realized that even though I was moving around and away from it, it somehow was closing the distance between us. When I realized that in the time it took for me to circle around it, it managed to halve the distance between us, I couldn't take it anymore. I broke my gaze, turned, and ran full sprint.

I was nearly at the clearing. *Just make it to the clearing and get out of here; it's a door, it's not like it's going to chase me—*

The trees broke up ahead of me, opening up into the clearing and my way out. I gasped in shaky relief, and slowed for a moment, peeking over my shoulder to see if the door was still following me. There was nothing behind me but trees and forest and I almost laughed.

"Guys! I think I lost—"

I turned, and screamed as I nearly ran right into it. It was three feet in front of me, and I barely avoided slamming right into it, throwing myself off to the side into the brush.

"Fuck, you guys," I cried. "Fuck, *fuck!* Jay, get me out, get me out!"

"Are you in the clearing?" Her voice was sharp.

I scrambled to my feet, and threw myself around the door, taking off into a hard run. The moment my toes passed the edge of the forest into the grass, I said, "Yes! Yes, get me out, now!"

"Five, four, three, two, one, and… open your eyes!" Sunlight nearly blinded me as Jay's hands lifted from my face and I scrambled up, frantically brushing off dead needles that had collected on my backside. I was panting. Jay's face looked pinched as she watched me. No one else said anything for a long time before Elia finally spoke up. "I can't believe you didn't open it."

"Are you shitting me? A creepy Black Door?" Remembering the sight of it chilled me and I shivered unconsciously. "No."

The bell rang, signaling five minutes until the end of our lunch time. "We'll try again tomorrow," Jay said quietly, and without another word, we got up and trudged back toward the school, a strange sobriety having fallen over everyone.

I almost didn't go to school the next day. Looking back, I should have stayed home and faked being sick.

2

When we met out in the woods the next day for our lunchtime adventure, everyone was a little quieter than usual, but most of the girls had regained their good humor. I, however, had not. I had slept poorly the night before, waking multiple times throughout the night, drenched in sweat despite the dreary, forever-fifty-degrees Pacific Northwest weather. I had no recollection of my dreams, but it was hard to peel myself out of bed that morning. Needless to say, I almost didn't go to school, because I knew they were going to try again, and maybe even actively look for the Black Door. We were a curious bunch, and no one had seen it or experienced it besides me.

I was silent the entire way out into the forest, even when Elia shoved up next to me as we walked, digging an elbow playfully into my rib.

"Did the Black Door follow you home?" she mock-whispered.

"Elia, the day you take something seriously is the day I die of shock." Aubrey had come up behind us and swatted at Elia's backside. Elia shrieked and leapt forward, skipping ahead of us while laughing.

"Should we call it eight doors now, since Kat found a new door?" This came from Emory, walking a little off to our left.

"No," I said quietly. "I don't even really know what the hell I saw, but… let's keep it at seven." Somehow, acknowledging the Black Door's existence seemed like it would make things worse.

I wanted to pretend it had never happened at all.

Emory fell into step beside me. "Did you see anything on it? You know, besides that it was black."

I shook my head. "Honestly, I wasn't looking super close. I think there were designs in the center, but of what, I don't know."

When we got to our spot in the woods, Jay and the other girls were already there. We formed our circle, with a girl named Lauranne taking the honored position of the traveler this time. Jay did most of the question-asking when it wasn't her turn to travel, so she knelt on the carpet of dead pine needles before Lauranne situated her head on Jay's lap.

"You ready?" Jay asked.

Lauranne nodded and shut her eyes. Jay cupped her hands and placed them over Lauranne's face. She took a deep breath, shut her own eyes for a moment, and then nodded briefly. The circle of girls began chanting.

Seven doors, seven doors, seven doors…

After a few minutes, Lauranne's breathing became slow and heavy, as if she were sleeping; we could see her belly rising and falling beneath her baggy Soundgarden shirt. Her hands fell open and slack at her sides, her feet splayed gently outward. She looked deflated against the forest floor, as if she were a discarded doll with all the stuffing ripped out. Jay's voice cut through our chanting and all our voices fell silent. "What do you see?"

Lauranne let out a slow breath. Her voice sounded tiny as she said, "I'm in the woods. In the clearing." A pause, and then, "I don't see any doors. I'm going to start walking west."

"Do you hear anything?"

Pause. "There's a breeze; really slight. I can hear the leaves rustling. But nothing else."

"Do you see the Black Door?"

This came from Emory, and Jay looked sharply across the circle at where Emory was sitting. It was against the rules for anyone besides the question-asker to say anything or ask questions, to prevent any confusion when trying to "pull" someone back out of the imaginary woods. Lauranne's face furrowed slightly beneath Jay's hands, and Jay quickly repeated Emory's question to get everything back on track. "Do you see the Black Door?"

Lauranne seemed to wait for a moment before answering, and my heart began to pound.

"No. I don't see anything like a Black Door anywhere around me."

Lauranne continued to wander the woods for a while. She spotted a previously identified creature, a white stag, in the distance. It looked like a normal four-pointed stag when we first saw it weeks ago, only it had a third horn spiraling straight from the center of its head, in between the two arching antlers. It always ran away if we walked directly toward it. It occasionally shadowed us, following off to the side as we made our way through the woods. Lauranne didn't even bother walking toward the stag when she saw it, and changed direction to continue walking. She noted that it began following her off to the side as it had done to many of us in previous journeys.

After a few minutes of this, Lauranne came to the edge of a previously undiscovered ravine. A small, narrow trickle of water cut through the forest floor below her, and after a moment, she announced that she was climbing down to the water.

"Is the stag still there?"

A pause as Lauranne looked around. "No," she said. "I don't see him anymore."

The ravine was dark and narrow, shallow enough to jump down, although once Lauranne was next to the river she noted that it was much darker than up on the forest floor. She began following the water south, describing roots and trailing moss sticking out of the sides of the ravine as she walked, overhanging branches and fallen tree trunks crossing over either side above her. After a few minutes, she said in a little whisper, "I've stopped walking. I think it's getting darker."

It was silent for a moment. Even the woods around those of us in the circle seemed to have become still, the cries and noises of the lunchtime chaos back on the school's grounds seeming to get further and further away.

"You mean the sun is blocked out from where you're standing?" asked Jay.

"No," replied Lauranne. "Like… like the sun is going down or something. Like it's getting later in the afternoon."

This hadn't happened before. Every time we journeyed, the sun was always at midday, bright and cheerful. Our gazes met nervously around the circle. "Do you want to continue, or head back?" asked Jay.

A long pause. We all held our breath. Then, "I'll continue for a little bit," said Lauranne. "But I'm going to start heading back toward the clearing."

Lauranne described walking a little further down the ravine, looking for a good place to climb back up. She said she found some knobby roots hanging out of the mud wall that looked like they would work well for handholds, when suddenly her breath caught.

"What is it?" asked Jay sharply.

"I think I see a door."

Alarm pierced through me, but moments later, Lauranne said, "It looks like yellow wood. Like a bunch of bleached, yellowing tree roots knotted together and woven into a door in the side of the ravine wall, across the river from me." Before Jay could respond, Lauranne added, "I'm going to try to swim across the river and get to it."

"I thought she was coming back?" I whispered to Emory next to me. Jay gave me a warning glare. We were supposed to be silent. Lauranne went from being carefully cautious to suddenly diving into strange waters alone in an astral forest, ready to open a new door we'd never found before.

Lauranne described herself walking into the river water. The current wasn't terribly strong, and she waded out to the center, carefully stepping on submerged boulders scattered along the base of the river. She got out to almost her chest, when suddenly her relaxed, deflated body stiffened in a spasm, and she let out a choking gasp.

"What is it?" Jay asked quickly.

"It's *in* the river!" Lauranne's voice was a squeak. "Holy shit, there's a Black Door in the river! It's right underneath me! I almost stepped on it. Oh my god!" Her fingers were clenching and unclenching against the forest floor. "Oh fuck, I'm coming back right now. Shit! It's right there, how the—"

"Come back, Lauranne," Jay said sharply. "Hurry! Just get to the clearing."

Lauranne described herself turning and splashing inelegantly back to the shore, launching herself out of the water and climbing the roots up the side of the ravine. Her breath began coming in short, sharp gasps, feet twitching and hands scrabbling slightly against the ground. She said that she had gotten to the top of the ravine, had crawled away from the river on hands and knees and had turned around once, only to see that the Black Door was now at the edge of the ravine where she had just climbed up, towering against the backdrop of trees and sky and completely shadowing her from the sun.

"No, no, no," she began muttering to herself. "I'm running. Fuck, it's right behind me guys. What the fuck?" She began panting again, her chest heaving against the ground. I felt a cold sweat against the back of my neck, watching her. A few of us had grabbed each other's hands. We sat there, waiting; white knuckled in our circle.

After a few moments, Jay asked, "Is it still behind you?"

A short gasp from Lauranne. "Yes," she said. "Every time I look back it's —" A few more gasping breaths. "It's maybe ten feet from me." We waited as she panted against the forest floor, her body wriggling and writhing in distress. Then she let out a sharp cry.

"Lauranne?" Jay's voice was alarmed. "What is it?"

"It's starting to appear next to me. Off to the side. Just not there one minute and there again the next. Oh fuck, you guys." Then she suddenly inhaled deeply. "I see the clearing!"

"Hurry," Jay muttered. "Just let me know once you're there."

Lauranne described looking over her shoulder and off into the woods on either side a few times. As she neared the clearing, she said she lost sight of the Black Door. She checked the woods one more time as her feet crossed the threshold, before saying, "Jay, I'm here, get me—" her voice cut off with a horridly loud scream, loud enough that every girl in the circle jumped.

"It's in the middle of the clearing! Jay. Jay, it's opening."

"Five, four, three, two, one. Open your eyes!" Jay ripped her hands back off of Lauranne's face. Lauranne's eyes snapped open and she sat bolt upright, one hand clutching at her throat.

"Oh, Jesus," she said, gasping. "Oh, holy shit."

We all closed in around her, asking a million questions. *What did the door look like? Why was it following her? How was it opening, quickly or slowly? Did she get a glimpse of anything behind it?*

Once Lauranne caught her breath and calmed down a little, she said that it had begun slowly swinging outward as she stepped into the clearing, so she didn't get a good look at what might have been behind the door. She noticed a pattern on the door, especially the few times that it had gotten close to her, and with a shaky hand, she took a stick and drew a long horizontal line, with three shorter lines beneath it, two that were right next to each other and the third one centered and a little below it. Around the lines she drew a circle. "That's all I can remember," she said. "There was more but these were the biggest designs." She drew a shaky breath. "I know we're here to explore and learn, but you guys. I just. I didn't want to get near that thing." She shivered visibly. "There's something wrong with it."

The bell rang across the forest, and we all stood up, brushed dead needles from our clothes and began the slow walk back to the school. Lauranne was unusually pale, and she kept rubbing at her eyes. "Are you okay?" I asked.

"Honestly? Not really." She pinched the bridge of her nose as we walked. "I have a splitting headache. I kind of thought you were making up that whole 'Black Door' yesterday. You know, to make your session interesting." Her tone was slightly apologetic.

"I'm going tomorrow." Elia's voice cut across the air as she fell into step next to us. "I don't know why you didn't just open it and see what was inside."

"Yeah, you don't know, Elia," Lauranne retorted sharply. "The door felt. I don't know. It felt menacing. Like it was threatening me."

"I felt the same," I offered. "Like it was stalking me or something. It seems like it was a lot more aggressive with you."

Lauranne didn't answer, but the pinched look on her face spoke volumes.

"All the doors move," Elia quipped. "No door is ever in the same exact place twice. Maybe this one just moves a lot more than the others. We won't know anything about it until we open it, and not knowing just makes us more afraid." She squared her shoulders as we trudged back into the main building. "I'm looking for it tomorrow, and if I see it, I'm opening it up. I want to know for sure what's behind this Black Door."

3

I slept badly again that night. I kept hearing a faint knocking sound in my sleep, but whenever I woke up it would cease, and I could only hear the soft sounds of my parents and brothers sleeping in the rooms around me. At three am I even got up, walked down to the landing and checked the front door, but no one was there.

My mom woke me up at 6:45 am. My alarm had been blaring for the past five minutes, and I hadn't even heard it. She said she had to shake me a few times to get me up. I felt like my head was stuffed with sandpaper; at the time I didn't know what a hangover felt like, but looking back, I definitely peeled out of bed as if I'd participated in an all-night rager.

It was dumping rain that day. When we met at lunch at one of the corner cafeteria tables, everyone immediately started talking about how we'd squeeze our next session in. The woods were completely out; it was raining hard enough that the ground would be muddy swampland for the next few days. It was Friday, and if Elia didn't take her turn that day it would mean waiting until Monday to find out what was behind the Black Door, if the weather cooperated. Frankly, I was kind of in favor of stopping the game altogether, but when I said as much, I got quite a bit of backlash.

"Kat, we know it's scary but we don't know anything about it. Maybe Elia's right and we're just scared of it because it's… you know, unknown." Emory softened her words with a peace offering of jo-jos from her plate, which I reluctantly accepted.

"I don't know, you guys. It's not just that we don't know what's behind it. We don't know what's behind at least four of the doors and even the doors we've opened are still a little bit of a mystery. It just feels so invasive. Like it's doing everything it can to get us to open it, almost leaving us no choice but to open it. It's not a door that we previously knew was going to be in the forest. And it showed up inside our clearing! I thought the clearing was supposed to be like a safe zone, where we pop in and out?" I stuffed a piping hot jo-jo in my mouth. When the world crashes onto your head, let the starchy warmth of spiced middle school cafeteria fries be your comfort.

"I brought that up to Jay last night on the phone," Lauranne said quietly. "She said technically we never decided to set the clearing as a safe zone, or whatever. Some of us just assumed it would be safe because nothing's ever followed us into it before."

Elia sat down next to me, slapping her lunch tray on the linoleum cafeteria table. "I just called my mom from the payphone in the hall," she announced. "If you guys want, she's cool with having everyone over for a sleepover tonight." Elia rubbed her hands together, silent-picture-villainesque. "She's working a night shift so we won't even have to keep the screaming down." She winked at Lauranne, who coolly flipped her off.

A few had to check with their parents, including me. Shina said that she had plans already and couldn't make it.

Jay joined us halfway through lunch, apparently caught in a long lecture by one her teachers, and said she would definitely be at Elia's house later.

"Are you sure you want to do this in your house?" Aubrey asked. "I mean, we've always done it in the woods." She seemed about to say something else, but changed her mind at the last minute, and began stabbing at the steamed vegetables on her plate listlessly.

Elia shrugged. "Not my first choice, but I don't want to wait three days to find out what's behind the door. I'm worried if we wait too long it won't be there when we get back." She smiled wickedly. "Besides, if something follows me back to my house, maybe it'll eat my sister first."

***

Elia lived with her mom and older sister on the lower south side of my home town; not the wealthiest of neighborhoods, but still clean, respectable, and only a little run down. Her mom was a nurse who had been pulling late night/early morning shifts for the past two years, so she was on her way out once we were all situated, sleeping bags strewn over the tiny living room, with three ordered pizzas and a massive box of Diet Cokes on the counter. After repeatedly telling us to call her if we needed her for anything, she left. The moment her little Toyota pulled out of the gravel drive and disappeared down the road, everyone turned in silent unison and looked at Jay.

Jay scowled. "Can I finish my pizza first, you assholes?"

I was nervous, but strangely less afraid than I had been for the past few days. Somehow in the slumber-party setting it actually felt more like a game again; my friends were all laughing and shoving each other as we all moved the furniture around to accommodate a circle of seven girls in the middle of the room, with Jay and Elia getting situated in the middle.

"Shina's going to be pissed that she missed this," someone said.

"Okay, everyone chill for five seconds. Should we light some candles?"

"Very 'light as a feather, stiff as a board,' Jay." I got up and helped Emory pull a few emergency tapers from the kitchen, setting them up around the outside of our circle seating area. Then we shut off the lights, and a rapt stillness fell over everyone as Elia settled her head in Jay's lap and shut her eyes.

We began chanting. *Seven doors, seven doors, seven doors…*

Elia sank quickly, her entire body melting like pudding against the carpeted living room floor. It was warm still, the light soft and hazy, and in the past few weeks we had all gotten extremely good at chanting together, at the same tone and volume, creating a rippling wave of soft noise that fell into the background and grabbed your focus all at once. Elia was "out" almost immediately, but Jay waited for a bit before signaling us to silence and asking, softly, "What do you see?"

It was strange to hear Elia's normally brash, mischievous voice so tiny, so childlike and far away. "I'm in the clearing. Jay, it's really weird. The grass." She paused for what seemed like forever.

"What about the grass, Elia?"

"The grass is brown. Dead, dry, straw-brown, like what happens to our lawn at the end of summer." Elia described herself touching the ground around her feet, and then walking to the edge of the clearing. She said that some of the leaves on the bushes right at the edge of the forest looked black, as if they had been burned.

"I'm going to walk south," she said. Elia made her way slowly, describing in elaborate detail everything she saw that might be noteworthy. Her intense personality was offset by a deep obsession with detail and a keen perceptive eye, and I had to admit that her journeys were some of my favorites, as she painted such a vivid picture for the rest of us.

The first ten minutes of Elia's journey were relatively uneventful. Here and there, she would see tiny patches of black underbrush, similar to the state of some of the plants at the edge of our clearing. Other parts of the woods were just as lush as ever, and she said she could hear birds, though she couldn't see any. She caught sight of what we had decided to call the green monkey a few weeks prior: a little primate-like creature with a long tail and peacock-green fur that shone iridescent in the light of the sun, like the wing of a raven or crow. She called to it a few times, but it seemed content to peer down at her, head cocked from one side to the other as she whistled and coaxed. Eventually Elia grew tired of this little game and kept walking. The monkey didn't follow.

She claimed that the woods were beginning to get darker the longer she walked through them, similar to Lauranne's experience of time passing as she explored the forest in our previous session. We were so rapt in her descriptions that when she abruptly said, "I think I see a building," there were more than a few soft gasps from the circle. We'd found buildings through some of the doors, but we'd never found any sort of nonorganic structure in our woods before. Elia described what looked to be a large farmhouse or barn, settled in a part of the woods that was less densely populated by foliage than the rest. There seemed to be smaller trees arranged in neat rows to the east of the building, planted in a bare open plot of earth edged by the pine trees we were used to seeing in the forest. The dark wooden structure loomed three stories high, with windows looking out at each level, and a high pointed roof with rotting shingles covered in trailing green moss. There was one door at ground level.

It was entirely black.

"By black, you mean…" Jay looked uncertain.

"It's totally, solid black. It looks like there's writing or carvings on the front of it." Elia's voice quickened with excitement, and nerves. "It may be the same door Lauranne and Kat saw."

Everyone was silent for a moment. I could tell that Jay was searching for something to ask, when Elia said, "I'm walking toward it."

Aubrey grabbed my left hand and squeezed it.

"I'm walking slowly. I'm about thirty feet away. Now twenty." She paused. "The forest is really quiet again. I don't hear the birds anymore." A longer pause, followed by, "Okay, I'm going to keep walking. I'm about ten feet away. Now, I'm almost up to it—" Elia's voice cut off in a small little choking noise.

"What?" demanded Jay. "What? What is it?"

Elia let out a slow, unsteady breath. I'd known her for years, and despite all her bluster and bravado, I could tell that she was shaken by whatever she was looking at. "There's a bunch of symbols and carvings on the door. I see the pattern that Lauranne described. Lots of smaller shapes, lines intersecting making stars and weird holes, sort of like those illusion tunnels we drew with a protractor in art class. And... jesus... okay. So." Elia took a deeper breath. "So, there's also... a bunch of names."

"What names?" Jay was staring so intently down at Elia's face I don't think she even remembered the rest of us were there.

"It's. It's our names." A pause. "Our names are all over the door."

I'll never be able to fully describe the sudden, gut-puckering, hot and cold dread that sank from my head to my feet in that moment. It felt like someone had poured live ants down the inside of my back. Aubrey was nearly breaking my hand with her grip, and I let her. My painful, squished knuckles were the only part of my body that wasn't crawling.

Elia described the location of each name; hers was right above the circle. My name was to the left of it, Lauranne's to the right, Jay's below. The other girls' names flared at different points in between, creating a star of letters around a central symbol.

"I'll draw what symbols I can remember when I get back," Elia said quietly. She took a shaky breath. "But I'm going to open it."

"Elia, don't!" Emory squeaked. Jay didn't even reprimand her. It was pointless. Her attention was solely on Elia's face, as were all of ours.

Elia described grabbing the black, round doorknob and turning it slowly.

She said it felt warm against her palm, as if she were taking a person's hand. The door was silent as it opened, barely a whisper as Elia stepped back to pull it wide. Past the threshold, she could see what looked like the inside of a barn. Straw littered a dirt floor, and it was horribly dark, beams and support poles scattered around the wide open space in front of her.

"What else do you see?" Jay asked, breathless.

"Not much," Elia responded. After a few moments, she said resolutely, "I'm going inside."

"Elia, stop it! Just come back, we saw what was inside and now it's over. You did what you said you'd do." I spoke without really meaning to, but again, Jay didn't reprimand me.

"I'm already inside. It smells like… well, a barn. Like horses and dirt and hay." Elia's voice grew a little stronger as the moment passed. "It's dark but there's still some light coming in through the windows. It looks like there's some stalls, and stairs leading up to a second floor. Everything is really…" She paused, as if considering her next words carefully. "Everything is gray. Even the forest outside the windows looks gray, like an old black-and-white movie." A pause, and Elia lifted her hand off the ground where she lay in her own living room. Then, "I'm looking at my arm and even my skin is white. Like, blanched white; there's no color anywhere."

She described herself walking toward the stairs at the back of the barn, looking around for a lantern or flashlight or something to help her see. After a few minutes, she stopped and said uneasily, "I just noticed it now, but it's been happening since I walked in here. There's a weird sound going on in the background. I don't know how else to describe it. It's super quiet, but kind of low and choppy, with a kind of light rumbling beneath it." Her voice became distant for a moment. "Like I'm hearing a helicopter in an earthquake, but on the other side of the world."

Jay wasn't even asking leading questions anymore. We all just listened, silent, rapt, as Elia described reaching the stairs and taking a hold of the railing. As her hand touched the banister, she let out a sudden shriek.

"The door! Fuck, the door just slammed shut behind me. Jesus fuck, that scared me!"

"Elia, you need to come back, right now," Jay said forcefully.

"It's fine, it's fine... nothing else happened, I'm just. God, that fucking sound. It's still going. It's making my head hurt. It's like once I noticed it I can't stop hearing it." Elia took a shaky breath, and then reached for the banister again. She climbed the stairs, eyes straining up through the darkness. It looked like the stairs wrapped around and led up to a third level, but as Elia climbed she casually glanced out the windows in the stairwell, looking out over the orchard.

Her breathing stopped for a moment. Jay gave her head a little shake. "Elia!"

She let out a huge breath and began breathing a little faster. "There's something coming through the orchard. Toward the barn. Like the shadow of a person, but not a person. Tall. Like almost as tall as the orchard trees." A pause, and then, "Okay, I'm getting the fuck out."

Elia turned and ran back down the way she came. She said she raced for the Black Door at the entrance to the barn, grabbed the knob, and flung it open only to see the same gray landscape stretching out ahead of her that she could see through the windows. The lush, colorful, green forest she had trekked through to get here was gone.

"Shit." Elia said she tried shutting and reopening the Black Door a few times, willing the green forest back into existence. Every time, it reopened to the colorless world, and when she glanced over her shoulder, she said the tall shadow was almost to the barn. "You guys! What the fuck do I do? Do I just walk through and try to come back the way I came? It's not the same forest." She gasped sharply, suddenly, and then almost squealed out, "It's here. It's looking in the window at me!"

"Jay," I said in a panic. "Jay, we have to pull her out now!"

"The rules," she said, distressed. "I don't know what that's going to do! We're supposed to bring her back the right way or else something could go wrong."

"Do it, Jay," Elia said. "Oh god, please do it. Get me out. Fuck the rules.

Just get me out now."

Jay sucked in a deep breath, and then, with a despairing look on her face, said, "Five, four, three, two, one, open your eyes!"

She pulled her hands back off of Elia's face as if they burned her. Elia's eyes snapped open, and she immediately sat up, hair disheveled and face pale.

We all stared at one another, a sick feeling of dread falling over us.

"Are you okay?" I finally asked.

"Yeah." She was quiet; she absently rubbed the side of her head. "Yeah, I'm fine. I'm… fine."

After we all calmed down a little, Elia drew what symbols she could remember from the door. To be honest, none of it made sense to us at all. Looking back now, some of it looked like sacred geometry that anyone might recognize, like mandalas and the tree of life.

Some of it was and still is gibberish to me. At that point, Jay suggested that we watch a movie to try and relax. Elia put in *The Cable Guy* and the mood lightened somewhat. Someone made popcorn but it mostly went uneaten. Three quarters of the way into the movie, almost everyone was in their sleeping bags and we all decided to go to bed at that point. But even though the lights were out and everyone was trying to lie still with their eyes shut, I could tell that hardly any of us was really sleeping. I kept lifting my head to peek over at Elia's sleeping bag, watching her breath rise and fall beneath the thick synthetic fabric. I couldn't shake the feeling that we had just really, seriously messed up somehow.

4

The weekend was a mess of anxiety and apprehension. I called Elia once on Saturday and on Sunday to check in on her and make sure she was okay; by the time I got her on the phone Sunday afternoon, she sounded pissed. "Look, it's sweet that you're all worried, but everyone's been calling me all day, all weekend. I'm fucking fine. I'll see you tomorrow." She hung up abruptly.

Jay was off hiking with her parents all day. I got a few of the others on the phone, but there were no solid theories on what we might have stumbled into. Elia wasn't talking much to any of us. It was 1996, so there wasn't much information on the internet, or even much of an internet at all; still, I got a call at six pm Sunday night from Shina, who hadn't been at the sleepover on Friday but had been filled in on what happened.

"You got a sec?" she said when I took the phone from my mom.

"Yeah, we just finished eating. What's up?"

"Okay, so I've been keeping track of all the symbols that we've seen on the door. This afternoon I slipped into a chatroom on AOL called Esoterica. Usually it's just a lot of Wiccan fluff and throwback New Age stuff from the '70s, but sometimes a few hardcore occultists float through and spew nonsense for a while before being booted by a mod. I decided to scan in photos of that big symbol that Lauranne first saw in the middle of the door, and the other symbols that Elia remembered, and post them all to the room, just to see if anyone recognized anything or knew what it might be." I heard the shuffling of papers on the other end of the line. "Most of the conjecture didn't seem to go anywhere, but one guy, uh, user EnochLives77. He said some stuff that kind of made sense."

"EnochLives77?"

"Yeah." Shina sounded embarrassed. "This chat room was pretty intense. Like, people believing that they're vampires and stuff. That was definitely not the weirdest username I saw."

I sighed. "Okay, well what did Mister 77 have to say?"

"He said he recognized one of the symbols at the top of the door, the one that looked like spokes on a wheel; he said it was an old Sumerian sign called 'dingir.'" She pronounced it like "danger." "And that it meant, like… 'god,' or 'deity.' He said that if archeologists usually find it on plaques or carvings or whatever, and it comes before someone's name, then that means that person is some sort of deity or higher being."

"Sumerian?"

"Uh, like the oldest civilization. Remember in history class, we did that whole Mesopotamia thing, and we read Gilgamesh for two weeks?" Shina paused, adding, "Jay almost failed our final because she kept slipping her headphones in during the class readings? It was when she finally got *Frogstomp*, and she could barely function unless she listened to it at least twice a day."

"Oh, yeah. Jesus." I glanced over my shoulder to check and make sure my mom was still in the living room, and slipped into the hallway, dragging the phone cord with me. "How would anyone in a chat room know that?"

"They apparently geek out hard over this stuff."

"Okay, so one of the marks on the door means deity. Special super-powered person. Did they say anything else?"

"Well, once we got on the Sumerian track, he mentioned that another symbol right below it could be one called…" More shuffling of papers in the background, and then Shina's voice butchering the pronunciation, "…Usbalkit. He said that some people are still arguing about the meaning of some of these words. This one sometimes means 'rebel' or 'revolt,' but it can also mean to, like, turn something upside down, or reverse it. He said he wasn't sure, but that the second meaning would make more sense in this case."

"So, what, the top of the door reads, 'god, reverse?'"

"No. No, it would be more like, 'god, upside down,' or 'the upside-down god,' I guess."

Silence hung over the line. The quiet static of landline dead air hissed faintly in my eardrums as my heart pounded. Finally, I spoke up. "But this is just from some dude in a chat room, right?"

"Yeah." Shina sounded uncertain. "Honestly, Kat, none of us know what the fuck we're really doing here. I think it was fun when we started but now I just feel like, I don't know, like we're way out of our depth. Even if what this guy is saying is totally whacko, what you guys described that happened on Friday night. I just don't think we should play anymore."

"I don't either." I unwound the phone cord from around my finger; it was wound so tight that the tip of my index finger was starting to turn blue. "Okay, I have to go; I'll see you tomorrow. We'll talk about what you found out then with the others."

"Sweet dreams, Kit Kat."

"Ha! Bye Shina."

***

I was late to school. My alarm once again failed to wake me and my mom was pissed; she told me she wouldn't let me stay over at anyone's house anymore if it kept throwing off my sleep schedule. I told her that I had been sleeping badly; she blamed the computer, and too much TV, and whatever else she could muster up before telling me that I had to lay off the pop from now on. I kissed her cheek and slid out of the car without a word, heading toward my second period class.

By lunch time, I was dragging. My stomach was queasy, so I didn't even get food, but I bought a huge sixteen-ounce Jolt Cola before finding the table my friends usually sat at.

Elia wasn't there.

"She's at home sick," Aubrey reported, gravely. "Something about her stomach; her mom said she puked twice this morning."

We all stared at one another for a moment.

"Guys, this is getting really fucked up." I listlessly twisted and untwisted the cap on my plastic cola bottle.

"Yeah," Lauranne slipped a hand on my shoulder briefly. "I feel like we need to stop playing, but I also feel like we need to undo whatever the hell it is we just did, first." She absently rubbed her forehead. "I haven't been feeling well, either. Like, kind of sick. And I sleep like shit."

Surprisingly, everyone else started piping in; apparently no one in our group had gotten a solid night of shuteye in the past week.

"Well, if you'd like to sleep even worse, then pay close attention." Shina then related what she had told me the previous evening. She had pulled out her copies of the symbols Lauranne and Elia had drawn and spread them out over the table, pointing to the ones she was referring to.

After she was done, everyone was pensive. "We have to help Elia. There's no way she's just conveniently sick after going through the Black Door."

Aubrey was staring down at the symbols, brow furrowed.

"So what do we do, exactly, to fix it?"

Everyone looked at Jay. She was chewing pensively on her lower lip, eyes thoughtful. "When we pulled her out, she was behind a door, and she couldn't see a way to get back to the clearing. Maybe we should try to send someone in and get back to the correct entry point. Maybe doing it the right way will set everything back to normal?"

Everyone thought about that for a moment. "And what if it doesn't?" Lauranne asked pointedly.

"Well, we don't have a better plan; we can't leave things the way they are. We broke the rules and I don't see how going back in could make it any worse at this point. But maybe we can make it better." Jay stabbed at the cafeteria spaghetti on her plate with her fork. "Anyone else have a better idea?"

Silence.

"Great. Then we're doing it."

Shina piped up. "So who's going to go in next?"

Everyone took that moment to study their lunch trays closely, avoiding eye contact with anyone else around the table.

"For fuck's sake," I said, exasperated. "I'll go in. We'll plan on tomorrow?"

Jay nodded. "Tomorrow, then."

***

That night I fell asleep over my homework twice; each time, faintly, I swear I could hear a low, far-off rumbling, just at the edge of my hearing, with a slightly louder *whop whop whop whop* layered over it. I'd wake up maybe ten minutes after drifting off, my head splitting and my face crumpled forward against my textbook. The second time, when I awoke, I found I had drawn a small symbol in the corner of my spiral notebook paper: a single circle, with a long horizontal line across the top, and three smaller lines below.

The same symbol Lauranne had seen on the Black Door.

I felt that we were all spiraling; that Elia's current state would befall all of us if we just left things the way they were. I knew that if someone didn't do something, my own situation—and everyone else's—was only going to deteriorate.

Maybe there was no way out, really. But I decided that night, as I settled in for a fitful round of sleep, that if this was my last time entering whatever realm we'd tapped into, then I'd try to make it count.

5

"Are you ready?"

My head rested against Jay's crossed ankles, eyes staring up at the sky beyond her head. It was a gorgeous day; crystal-blue skies and wisps of white cotton clouds danced past the tops of the trees straight above me. It was actually warm for the first time in a long time; everyone around me in the circle seemed lit in soft fire as the afternoon sunlight broke through the pine trees and scattered like liquid gold to the forest floor beneath.

I took it all in for a second, and then sucked in a breath, shutting my eyes. "Ready."

Seven doors, seven doors, seven doors...

I was nervous. I had no idea how I was ever going to relax enough to slip into the altered state I had become so familiar with at this point, but suddenly it was happening; I sank, my vision receded into darkness, and the voices of the girls seemed to come from far away, as if I had dropped underwater. I shivered, and when I faintly heard Jay ask, "What do you see?" I opened my eyes.

I was in a huge, expansive field. The sky, the tall grass that brushed against my jeans, the few small birds in the sky, all were gray, like I had stepped into an old black-and-white movie. All color leached from everything, including, as I looked down at myself, me. And when I raised my eyes, I nearly jumped; a sharp gasp escaped my lips, and from very, very far away, I could hear Jay's voice: "What is it?"

"I'm surrounded," I whispered. "They're all around me."

They stood on four legs, soft, sable fur glimmering in the dull gray light. Bristling antlers towered toward the sky, ending in wickedly sharp points, tipped dark with some unknown glimmering liquid. They looked like elk, but larger; in the center of each velvety forehead opened a third eye, unblinking and staring.

They surrounded me in a circle, and they were staring at me.

"Jay," I whispered. "Jay, what do I do?"

"Just move very slowly. And don't piss them off, please. We've got enough shit to worry about right now without adding to it."

I took a few hesitant steps toward one edge of the circle. The elk seemed disinclined to move, but as I approached, almost touching one of them, it shifted to the side slowly to allow me to pass. The circle closed behind me, and I could feel the weight of their enormous bodies, antlers clicking as they tapped against one another, moving in unison. Ahead, in the distance, I could see the tree line of a forest, and before that tree line, a huge building towered. Rows of smaller trees laid out across its front lawn like a small orchard. It reminded me of those plantation houses in the south, elaborate and impressive in its physicality, but also wilting, with crumbling shingles and dark moss claiming the corners of ceilings and the base of columns.

In the background, I started hearing a low, almost imperceptible noise; the low rumbling of a far-off earthquake, and a softer chopping noise layered over the top.

I described it all to Jay as I began walking forward through the tall grass, the mansion looming up ahead of me. The low, rumbling sound encroached on the edge of my hearing; it was always there, subversive and barely loud enough to pick up, but for some reason the hairs had been standing up on my arms the moment I opened my eyes in the field. As I finished describing the scene for the others, I heard a faint sound coming from the building ahead of me. It sounded like a phrase. Like someone was repeating something over and over, but at the end of the jumble of words I could distinctly make out one syllable.

"Kat," it repeated with a jumble of words.

Fuck.

"Guys," I whispered. "I think I hear Elia's voice."

I took off in a light jog, booking it through high grass that slapped against my legs as I ran. Surprisingly, the herd of elk followed; they kept a medium distance behind me, but they moved like a silent tide over the field, spreading out behind me in a wall of antlers and muscle. As I approached the house, they fell back, marking a line about fifty feet from the front entrance with their bodies. They fell still, silently watching me as I approached the huge front porch.

The windows were dark; I couldn't see anything beyond the faded, cracked panes of glass. No sign or indication of what lay inside, waiting for me. The voice was a little stronger, yet I still struggled to make out the entire phrase. I simply heard a jumble of words, followed by "Kat," repeated over and over in discordant sing-song melody. Now that I was closer, I was even more certain that it sounded like Elia.

"There's nothing on the porch," I whispered. "It's bare; no furniture, nothing." As I approached the door, I balked: the front door loomed dark and heavy against the white wooden building, and I knew immediately that it was the at-once familiar and dreaded Black Door. Yet something about it had changed. I swallowed and stepped forward cautiously, the porch creaking softly under my weight.

The large symbol in the middle of the door was different from what Lauranne and Elia had described. There were still a circle, a long horizontal line, and two lines beneath it, but where the third and lowest line had cut across the bottom of the circle was now a long outline of an ovoid shape, with a solid circle in the center of that shape. And as I looked, something dark stained the white wood wall next to the door. Maybe I was seeing things or recognizing a pattern where there wasn't any, but it looked like there was a handprint against the door frame; a dark central palm with long, ragged-looking fingers stretching out, reaching in toward the doorknob.

My eyes took it in, and that keening, rumbling noise at the edge of my hearing seemed to intensify, filling my eardrums. I found my right hand lifting, slowly reaching out toward that handprint. My limbs were shaking; my whole body shook. My organs and my heart and my lungs, rumbling and quivering and becoming that noise, until I heard nothing else and saw nothing else as I reached, palm desperately wanting to press into the blackness of its hand.

Pain exploded on the side of my body and I was launched sideways, sprawling over the porch, wrists and head slapping against the wood like a rag doll. One of the members of the elk herd had climbed the porch and stood towering over me, antlers shadowed against the gray sky behind it. It stared down at me as I gasped for breath on the ground, ice in my lungs, my head bursting with pain and my ribs bruised.

Jay's voice seemed to whisper from far away. "What happened?"

"I. Fuck, nothing. I just need to get out of here fast." The elk snorted at me, and I perceived a contemptuous note in its heavy breath before it backed off the porch and stood in the grass in front of the mansion, watching me impassively.

I scrambled to my feet, and approached the door, keeping my eyes off the grotesque handprint and reaching for the doorknob. I noticed with trepidation the names of all my friends carved into the wood, and at the top of the circle, where Elia had claimed her name had been, I now saw the name "Katherine."

I opened the door.

The mansion expanded around me, massive. The ceiling was as high as a cathedral, with arching points and angled apexes; nothing at all like what it might have looked from the outside. Everything was pale white, but there was an insidious darkness that hung heavy, coalescing in every nook and cranny and settling, as if it were waiting for me to do something.

Because of the unique architecture, there were corners everywhere, not just in the walls but on the ceiling as it sloped and dipped, arched and folded and met itself again in high peaks pointed up toward the sky and beyond. The massive space was decorated with strange furniture unidentifiable to me, and again, there seemed to be extra edges to things, as if I were looking at one of those Magic Eye pictures where illusions pop out of flat spaces. I developed a headache as my eyes tried to make sense of it all and couldn't.

There were two staircases lining the walls, leading up to a second-floor balcony and dark hallways beyond. Ahead of me at the far end of the large entryway seemed to be a huge, looming structure. A structure that I felt an immediate aversion to—a sick, gut-deep revulsion shook through me every time my eyes tried to focus on it. It seemed a tangled mess of angles and shapes that moved with slow undulating purpose out of the corner of my eye, yet when I grew close to looking at it it went still, an indecipherable statue in an indecipherable room.

At its base, hunched over in a curled ball, was someone that looked like Elia.

"Jay! I see Elia. Jesus. She's still in here." I kept my eyes on her form, refusing to look at the large structure she was huddled in front of any longer. "I'm moving toward her; maybe if I get her out of here, this whole thing will be over."

A garbled whisper hissed in my ear. It sounded like Jay, but it was as if she were talking over a malfunctioning walkie-talkie and I could only make out every other word. "Careful," I heard through the static.

"Elia," I whispered sharply as I got closer. "Elia! It's Kat."

She was muttering to herself, unintelligible words interspersed with what sounded like my name. I inched closer toward her, fingers reaching out to grasp her shoulder. *If I could just get her out of here, get back to the clearing, have Jay pull us out.*

My fingers touched her shoulder just as her muttered words finally unjumbled and became clear.

"Curiosity killed the Kat."

She uncurled then, and turned to look back at me. It was Elia's face, but her eyes were fathomless, completely black, not empty, filled with a vastness and an unending void so deep that it terrified me. It felt like looking at a moonless night sky. Instead of standing grounded on my backyard patio, I had stepped out beyond the sky, beyond the stars and planets, as if everything recognizable and warm was behind me and I was right on the edge where only the blackness remained. I stared at the vastness and it stared right back.

I snatched my hand back as if I'd been burned, and Elia slowly stood up to face me. She kept repeating the phrase, "curiosity killed the Kat," and as she straightened onto her feet she cocked her head to the side, as if listening to something far off. Then, her head continued in that direction, bending further and further to the side until I was sure her neck would snap, and it still kept going, turning around in a horrifying slow-motion circle, those eyes staring at me, until her head had turned all the way around and her chin pointed up toward the ceiling while her long hair dangled down the front of her body.

Her mouth opened wide, the sentient vastness of the abyss beyond the cavern of her mouth, and she screamed, multiple voices crying in an agony and rage that rocked me to my core.

I ran.

I have never felt such blinding terror before, or since. There was no reason, no plan, no strategy to where I was going. I simply threw myself forward into any available empty space that would take me, feet pounding against white wooden floorboards. I sprinted toward the front of the building. The Black Door slammed shut as I reached it, and I let out a strangled, helpless cry, trying the knob once before letting go, accepting that the door refused to budge. I turned and ran for the stairs, and Elia's twisted, shuddering shape made its way toward me in a stuttering half-step.

I ran up the stairs, two steps at a time, legs and lungs burning, eyes watering, vision blurred. I heard a horrible *crunch* as I reached the top of the stairs, and I turned to look behind me. Elia's form had reached the bottom step and she had fallen forward, catching herself on her arms, limbs lengthening in horrible proportions as she began crawling up each step with unearthly speed. Her horribly turned head wobbled back and forth in grotesque fashion. Her mouth was still wide open, still screaming wordlessly. I turned and sprinted down the dark hallway.

The ceiling was high, shadows stretching above me into nothingness. I threw myself around the corner at the end of the hall, only to find another stretch of hallway in front of me. With Elia close behind, I ran further into the darkness, Elia's enraged screams echoing around me. The rumbling background sound had grown more intense, pulsating through me and vibrating my bones as I bounced off walls and skidded around corners, gasping for breath. No matter how many bursts of speed I put on, how many times I thought I'd lose her, she was soon on my trail again, crawling like some unearthly animal, long legs and arms stretching, snapping forward.

I glanced behind me, terror rising anew as I saw her skid around the corner I'd just cleared, and as my head turned, from the corner of my eye, I saw a glimpse of color.

A flash of deep red in the darkness.

To my right, down a side hallway, was the Red Door.

I should have questioned it, but there was no time. I hurtled toward it, Elia grabbing at my heels, and reached out for the doorknob, turning it in an instant and shoving it open. Light poured through the door, illuminating the hallway, and as I turned to slam the door shut I caught a final glimpse of Elia. She was crawling on the ceiling, hands and feet gripping the darkened wood as her face, now right-side up because of the angle, hung down almost level with my own; her mouth split into a wicked grin.

"Curiosity killed the—"

I slammed the door shut, leaning against it hard.

THUMP! The door shook violently, rattling against my back. I squeezed my eyes shut and pressed harder against it, lips clamped together to stifle my own cries.

Thump thump THUMP!

Go away, go away, go away…

After a few moments, the door finally fell still. All sound from the other side ceased. I stood, drenched in sweat and gasping for breath, in the golden, gilt courtyard we'd always entered when we'd stepped through the Red Door in the past. Impossibly tall buildings rose high above me, glittering in the light of a deep crimson sunset. The air was cooling, but the sparkling bricks and walls around me radiated the ambient heat of a long, hot day coming to a close.

"Jay," I said hoarsely. "Jay, can you hear me?"

"Yes! God, finally, are you okay? What's happening? You've been babbling nonsense and hyperventilating for the past five minutes. I was about to send someone to call 911."

"Jay. Elia… she's…"

A rush of hot wind tousled my hair, caressing my face. A shadow passed over the courtyard and I quailed, looking up as a dark shape suddenly dropped down from the air onto the cobbled pavement in front of me. An owl, huge, almost as tall as me, scrabbled its talons against the gilt stonework. It cocked its head at me once, twice, and then seemed to shiver, shake out its feathers, twitching uncomfortably.

Then a woman's head unfurled, standing tall, much taller than me, the feathers of the owl settling and draping over her body like a fine gown. She folded a pair of wings against her back; her eyes were impossibly large, nearly filled with luminescent red irises shot with gold, huge unchanging black pupils swallowing the middle.

"Kat… Kat, what is it? What do you see?"

The woman's crimson lips curled in a smile. Her voice was… otherworldly; intense. So uncanny that it raised the hairs on the back of my neck the moment she spoke.

"I've been waiting for you."

6

"Kat," Jay's voice whispered. "Kat, what do you see?"

"Give me a second," I whispered back. The woman paced in front of me; she seemed to have a hard time sitting completely still. While her eyes remained rapt and focused on me, her head shifted this way and that at every noise, tilting almost imperceptibly against the breeze. Her wings shifted and ruffled constantly, giving the impression of tireless energy and intense power held at bay.

"You are younger than I expected," she said after a moment. "Not yet a woman. But the smell of your blood is much older."

Oh Jesus Christ, the smell of my blood???

My knees nearly liquefied; her presence was crushing, as if I was standing in front of every leader of every nation of Earth. I was still pressed hard against the Red Door and refused to move forward into her wingspan. "I…" I swallowed, clearing the sudden lump in my throat. "I apologize, um… but I don't know what that means."

She seemed to find that funny. "You are truly a youngling. And yet you and the others wander through these expanses with such relative ease. We have watched you ever since you stepped through that door." Her gaze snapped to the Red Door behind my back, and then back down to my face, obvious interest unveiled on her features. "You have something that would be very valuable to many here."

I didn't know what to say to that. I opened my mouth to ask what she meant, but she suddenly cocked her head sharply to the side, pupils contracting to tiny pinpoints of black in a sea of red and gold. "It encroaches. Whatever you've done to disturb It, It now presses It's influence between the expanses." Her gaze flicked back to me. "You are here to clean up your missteps, yes?"

"I… um. Yes. That's the goal." I felt like I had forgotten something extremely important when talking to her, as if she were in on an inside joke and she expected me to join in, and yet I didn't know what it was.

"It's coming closer." She shook her head, feathers ruffling around her face for a moment, and her wings expanded. "It may know that you are here. I tire of holding this form, but I will give you this: that It's door and It's Self are intrinsically connected. It is a being of gateways, of passages, of in-betweens and not-places. What you do to It's gateway, you do to It's Self."

She shuddered before I could get a word out, shivered and hunched forward, and in an undulating ripple of feathers the woman was gone and the owl blinked at me, wickedly hooked beak flashing in the eternal sunset. It flapped its wings in a powerful downbeat and lifted off the ground, rising higher overhead before clearing the skyline of buildings and disappearing, taking off into the twilight.

"Jay," I said quietly when she was gone. "I think I have an idea."

"What happened?"

"I'll tell you, I promise, but just bear with me. I may not be able to talk much."

I took off in a light run, keeping my eyes peeled for anything that would seem out of place in the red-gold world. Every few moments, a shadow would fall across me as a dark shape would fly overhead between buildings; like every time before when we had explored the world behind the Red Door, I was watched from a distance. I wondered if it was only the owl woman watching, or if there were more like her far above me in the sky.

And then, as I reached a wide, open marketplace empty of stalls or beings, I heard it.

A low rumbling, with a choppier sound layered over the top.

Fuck.

"It's here, Jay. I don't have much time." I walked out to the center of the empty marketplace, turning in a slow circle, watching the nearby buildings and doors. "When I say so, I need everyone in the circle, including you, to picture the Green Door in your minds. Try not to think of anything else, but just the Green Door. You got it?"

"Okay, we can do that. What are you doing?"

"Right now? I'm waiting."

The noise grew. Not louder, but intensified—sending low vibrations throughout my body. The gilt cobblestone beneath my feet seemed to shiver through the bottoms of my shoes, and I kept turning, barely blinking, staring hard into the surrounding architecture. On my third turn in this manner, I saw it.

The Black Door.

"All right," I said quietly. "If I die, or go crazy, you guys had better come in and fix this."

"No promises," Jay said wryly; I could sense her attempt at humor, but underneath her voice, there was a slight tremble. She was scared.

That makes two of us.

I walked slowly toward the door. It looked the same as it had before, but larger, looming against the backdrop of a glittering, golden wall set on the far end of the marketplace. I was a tall girl, and the doorknob was almost as high as my eye level, making me feel like a child again. I turned it, and purposefully pulled the door open.

The inside of a barn greeted me, heavily obscured in shadows, dead straw and dirt scattering into the darkness ahead of me.

I took a deep breath and stepped through. The moment I crossed the threshold, I was once again in the gray world, color gone and that distant noise thrumming through my bones.

But this time, I turned and immediately shut the door behind me. "Jay," I whispered. "Now. Now, now, now, do it, the Green Door."

"Come on you guys," I heard Jay say; her voice was muffled and far away, but I heard her, and with that I pushed the Black Door back open. The red world was gone, and in front of me were the blanched, gray woods, so similar and yet so different from the woods we had created ourselves.

I stepped back outside, heading purposefully into the forest.

I had taken a few steps when I heard a deep, heavy thrumming, and glanced over my shoulder back toward the barn.

It stood there, in front of the Black Door. It was tall, much taller than the threshold of the door, and roughly humanoid shaped, but dark, like a hole had opened up in the world and had taken on sentient form. The edges of It's shape seemed to bend and warp the atmosphere immediately around it. As I stared, the darkness seemed to deepen, and I thought I began catching glimpses of something else. Far behind in the blackness, there began to appear the hints of a shape, or shapes. Shapes with extra edges, with lines and dips and points in places that made no sense, undulating in unsettling movement when my eyes looked elsewhere. My stomach churned in repulsion, my eyes desperately wanting to reject what I was seeing.

I felt a trickle of wetness slide down my cheek as I stared and I reached up to wipe my eyes, my fingers coming away stained with blood. My head was pounding. My very thoughts squeezing under It's heavy weight, and as I stepped back, It seemed to take a step toward me.

And then another.

Fuck no. I turned and ran, hurtling into the trees.

"Jay!" I cried. "Come on you guys! I need that Green Door!"

She didn't answer. The forest around me kept flickering, shifting in a cacophony of buzzing noises and that deep rumbling sound. Trees were to my left or right in one moment and then suddenly in front of me in the next, and I had to keep changing my direction; a few times I slammed into tree trunks, scrabbling in a panic against the ground as I regained my footing. I glanced behind me a few times, and always, the shadow followed, seeming to never lose ground, but always gaining a little, following steadily behind me, long limbs moving in disquieting non-synchronicity, with the patience and dark purpose of something that has all the time in the world.

I felt myself weakening. It was different from getting tired in the physical world. I suddenly felt less, as if I were a canister of water that had cracked, and was slowly spilling my contents out onto the ground around me. My vision began blurring, tunneling at the edges. Nausea overtook me, and I was panting heavily, sweat and a darker liquid sliding down the sides of my face and into my eyes. It's thrumming, deep, bone-cracking sound sunk into my body and I could feel it squeezing, pressing, emptying.

"Jay," I whispered weakly, and tripped over a tree root that had suddenly appeared in my path. I hit the ground hard, breath escaping my lungs in a heavy grunt, and I turned onto my back as the shadow closed in on me, reaching ever taller in the sky, It's edges rippling like the surface of a puddle that had begun to spread.

"Jay!" I scrabbled backward, and then my hands touched something underneath me, something that felt wholly alien compared to the pine needle-covered ground.

Smooth, solid wood and the shape of a doorknob.

I glanced down. The Green Door had appeared directly underneath my body, lying on the ground. I didn't hesitate, but gripped the knob hard and turned it, allowing the door to fall open beneath my body. I flew downward, my brain spinning at the shift in orientation, and I landed heavily on the sandy shore of the grotto, sprawling with the Green Door open in the cave wall in front of me.

I could see the gray sky through the door as I scrambled to my feet. The dark shadow bent down over the door, blocking out the sky, filling the opening as It tried to reach through. I swiftly leapt forward, grabbed the edge of the door, and slammed it shut in It's face.

I held it closed for a moment, panting. "If you want me, asshole," I whispered, "you'll have to come in here the hard way."

I turned and faced the grotto. It was exactly as we had left it: gorgeous. Luminescent algae made the water glow, while threads of fungus wove a tapestry of green, blue, and purple across the rock walls. The far edge of the underground cavern opened up into landscape and sky far above, but what I focused on now was the little camp that had always been at the edge of the water, the tent and the campfire blazing merrily away in a fire pit dug in the sand.

I moved quickly. I knew It would have an easier time pressing into the expanse this time, and I swiftly knocked over the tent, stepping hard on the fabric and pulling up with all my strength, ripping it open. I removed one of the tent poles, and snapped it in a similar way, using my weight to bend and break the flexible wood. I quickly bound the shattered pieces together with the shredded tent canvas and repeated this a few times, until I had at least four bundles of wood bound in cloth.

A deep rumbling filled the air. *Whop whop whop whop…*

I turned to face the far cavern wall. There was smooth rock wall, and in the space of a blink the Black Door was there, ominous in its height, a black stain in this beautiful place. I moved fast, my heart pounding; no time to question or quail.

I grabbed one end of one of the bundles and passed the other end through the campfire; it took a few tries, but soon the thick wood and bundled fabric caught fire. I looked up as I straightened, and noticed that this time It wasn't waiting for me; the door had begun slowly swinging outward on its own.

I approached it quickly, and as it swung open, there It was, standing in a far-off field of gray grass, a stark black wound against the sky, tall and impossible. It began walking toward me. I held my breath, swung my arms back with all my strength, and tossed the flaming bundle through the door.

The last thing I saw through the door was an eruption of white, colorless flame as the bundle landed in that dry sea of dead grass and immediately caught fire.

My eardrums nearly burst as the explosion of sound that reverberated from that fathomless thing filled the air with sound. I gripped the edge of the Black Door and shoved it closed with all my strength.

I wasn't done yet. Two more bundles went against the base of the door, and I lit a third bundle on fire just as I had done the first bundle. With my flaming prize in hand, I stalked toward the Black Door.

THUMP!

It rattled and shook. The knob turned furiously back and forth.

I carefully bent down and placed the flaming bundle against the others, propping it up so that the fire would have a stable base.

THUNK!

I lunged back. The door bowed outward, an unearthly rumbling filling the cavern for a moment, wood screeching in protest, and then the fire caught and blazed stronger and stronger, finding purchase in the kindling I had provided, and began to steadily work its way up the surface of the Black Door.

A horrible keening ripped through the grotto, and I slammed my hands over my ears, falling to my knees. Rock cracked and split, dust and pebbles falling to the sandy grotto floor, and I curled down into a ball, eyes squeezed shut, waiting for the worst.

And then the rumbling slowly went silent.

I looked up. I was a lone girl kneeling in a grotto, watching a slowly growing fire blaze merrily away.

I moved and sat at the far end, pressing myself against the cave wall next to the Green Door, and watched it burn all the way down, wanting to make sure. While I sat, I related to Jay and the others what had occurred in the red world, and how I had used the campfire in the grotto to hopefully destroy the Black Door. I waited, ready to run if my plan didn't seem to work, but as I watched, the flames seemed to burn brighter and brighter until the door finally crumbled in a heaping pile of ash and coals, leaving nothing but a smooth rock wall behind it.

I stood, turned to the Green Door, and cautiously opened it.

Lush, green woods greeted me. I stepped through, closing the door behind me. I could feel my weariness digging through my mind as I trekked back through the forest, heading in the direction of our all-too-familiar clearing. On the way, I spotted some movement far off between the trees; as I glanced to my left, a beast very similar to an elk, but larger, with dark-tipped horns and a large, staring eye in the middle of its sable forehead, caught my gaze. It inclined its head to the side for a moment, before turning and disappearing into the forest.

When I reached the clearing, Elia was there, waiting.

I stopped, eyeing her cautiously. She looked like her normal self, wearing the pajamas she had worn Friday night.

"Are you actually you?" I asked.

She snorted at me. "Do you have any idea what I just went through? Don't be a dick."

Well, it definitely sounds like Elia.

I walked into the clearing, eyeing her warily. She was not a demonstrative person, but she smiled at me as I approached. "Not bad," she said. "Thanks for coming back." She took my hand.

It would have been easy in that moment to mistrust everything I had been seeing, but a part of me needed to believe that we had fixed whatever it was that we had broken.

"Jay," I said, "bring us back." I squeezed Elia's hand and closed my eyes.

"Five, four, three, two, one… open your eyes!"

***

Elia was back in school the next day. She seemed pale, and still a little weak, but mostly herself. She said she didn't remember much while she was sick, and was constantly in and out of consciousness with a bad fever. She didn't remember anything about the part of herself that was lost in the shadow land's gray world, or coming back with me, but didn't seem overly concerned about it. I think she was just relieved that she wasn't sick anymore, and was eager to put it all behind her. All of us were.

We never went out into the woods again, and once high school came around, we all seemed to drift and go our separate ways. I've lost touch with most of my old friends through the years. Some I've found again on Facebook, and a few I saw at my high school reunion a few years ago. Everyone seems to be well adjusted in their adulthood, but no one has ever tried anything like Seven Doors again.

No one seems to have any contact with Elia, or know where she is.

I've mostly stayed away from any sort of astral projection, lucid dreaming exercises, or journeying-type meditations. While I tend toward being agnostic and skeptical, I also collect various religious paraphernalia, including blessed Saint Benedictine amulets. One I keep in the house, the other in my car. I also have a few statues of other saints and Vedic deities. Ganesha guards the hallway upstairs in my house.

We have little Jizo statues on the front porch, and sometimes I surreptitiously hide little bowls of salt in the corners of the house. My husband thinks it's quirky that I am constantly questioning everything and demanding proof, but then secretly filling the house with protective charms and statues.

Last year, I became pregnant with my first child. I found that I was having increasingly vivid dreams, which is common during pregnancy, but something strange about them made me question what I was really dreaming and made me think back on this childhood experience. A couple of times, I would dream that I was walking through beautifully sunlit woods, relaxed and comfortable, and though he didn't show up physically as himself, I could feel the presence of my child with me, floating over my shoulder like a tiny ball of warmth. We would walk for what seemed like hours, taking in the woods. Sometimes never speaking, but feeling each other deeply in a way that I can't really describe. If you've ever carried or given birth to children, you may know what I mean.

During one of these dreams, I remember sitting at the edge of a pond, looking out across the expanse of water, the little presence of my son hovering softly next to me. For some reason, I looked down into the water below me, admiring the reflection of the woods in the still, smooth surface. I saw something strange on the far end of the pond, reflected back in the water. Puzzled, I glanced up.

Ahead of me, across the water, a large gray barn stood on the shoreline. The barn was on fire.

Alarm and a sudden shock of terror shot through me, and I gasped awake, shaking. My husband woke up, asked me if I was alright, and did his best to settle me down before falling back asleep.

I don't knowingly enter any sort of meditation that may take me elsewhere. After that experience, I know better. Maybe we stopped It for a little while; made It's connection to whatever plane we were exploring a little weaker. But I know that what we did won't last, that I am not forgotten, and that I am still, twenty years later, being watched. Maybe, someday, I'll find a way of severing It's connection to me for good.

Be safe, travelers.

And for fuck's sake, if you see it, please never open a Black Door.

MoonyBites

By Thaddeus James, Reddit User /u/*hartijay*

Annual Runner Up—Most Immersive, 2016

———————

I'm not sure exactly when, but within the next few months there will be a mass release of a sugary junk-food product called MoonyBites. You'll probably start to see the ads sometime in late November, early December, but it's possible that they may be released quietly at an earlier date—after all, Halloween is right around the corner, and what better holiday is there to serve candy?

I am employed by the marketing firm that was hired to help advertise this product. We're not a large firm by any means, and the company that hired us did so because they want to keep this on the down-low. This company that is producing MoonyBites is not well known at all, but they're incredibly well funded and the execs I've talked with are all very confident in what they're doing.

The snack is fudge chocolate with a white chocolate coating. It's made to resemble lunar rocks. Everything about this product is fucking evil. The company producing it—MoonyFood—doesn't have a single friendly person in its staff. They seem to hardly want to speak about anything except for MoonyBites—if the name merely comes up, they get super excited and will talk your ear off about how great it's going to be. Any other topic of conversation they couldn't possibly give a shit about; sometimes, they won't even respond to anything but their stupid junk food. They are complete assholes with disregard for anyone who isn't them.

So, at the risk of my own job and possibly safety, I'm coming forward to blow up their spot: MoonyBites are not just bad for you in the conventional sense, they are **potentially lethal** and I don't think they're made with ingredients from this planet.

Why do I think this? Well, let me tell you about Josh Morris. Some of you may already know of him, but to those who don't: Josh was the creator and star of the YouTube channel *JoshMorrisEats*, which no longer exists thanks to MoonyFood and their fucking MoonyBites. The channel was basically made up of humorous videos featuring Josh eating different snacks and "reviewing" them, mostly newer or weirder products for entertainment value. It wasn't a particularly popular channel, but it did have a few dozen-thousand subscribers.

MoonyFood thought that exposing their oh-so-perfect product to the internet would be a fantastic idea, and asked our firm to get into contact with Morris for them. They would send him a sample, and he'd try it and review it positively on his channel in exchange for compensation.

Morris was pretty thrilled when we contacted him and immediately accepted the offer, so MoonyFood sent him the sample for review. The review went up a few days later with Josh eating the entire bag of the snacks and praising it up and down. The video got quite a few thousand views, general interest in the comments section; everyone was happy.

The next day, we get a call from Josh. He was freaking out, asking what was wrong with the MoonyBites, telling us they were making him super sick. So my supervisor gave him the contact info for MoonyFood. Josh swore to us that he was going to make a new video badmouthing the ever-loving shit out of the snack.

We kept checking the guy's YouTube page while trying to contact the MoonyFood execs about what had transpired. No video went up and the company didn't speak to us for the next few days.

One of my coworkers noticed that the *JoshMorrisEats* channel was not just closed, but completely nonexistent. Like it had never been created. We never spoke with Josh again.

A couple weeks went by, and our association with MoonyFood dwindled quite a bit. They were mad at us for our "failed" viral marketing attempt, but whenever they visited our firm, they would never answer our questions about what exactly about it had failed.

My supervisor was getting pretty pissed at their attitude and eventually sent them an email saying that our firm was going to have to pass on any future business relations with their company. MoonyFood did not reply to the email. What they did instead was send our entire staff a "complimentary" bag of MoonyBites.

The other day, my coworker Bill came up to me, looking scared shitless. Sweating. Telling me that one of the MoonyFood guys left a briefcase at his desk after coming in to transfer some files.

The MoonyFood reps were always so weird and off-putting that I honestly didn't blame Bill for doing what he did. The suitcase had a flash drive in it, which Bill plugged into his computer to look through. Bill was so rattled by what he had seen that he couldn't even tell me what it was.

"Just come look and see," he said.

So I went to his computer, and I saw the flash drive folder open on his desktop. Bill had opened a sub-folder on it that its owner had thought was appropriate to call "Funny!"

It was four or five photos—probably taken on a cellphone—of Josh Morris, dead. He was lying on what looked like some sort of medical table. There was a substance I did not recognize leaking out of his eyes, nose, and mouth. His face was a grayish-blue color. It looked like he had just been suffocated to death by whatever was coming out of his face.

It was absolutely horrible. I could barely look at it.

But Bill told me there was more.

Not photos this time. Saved emails. I can't recall them all exactly, but there was some bizarre shit that this company's staff was sending throughout its organization. I can think of some specific examples: all sorts of shit about how what they're doing is "absolutely legal" and any sign of "Phase 2" (whatever the fuck that means) happening won't be brought into the "public eye" anytime soon; one email, which looked like a newsletter, kept referring to the MoonyBites release date as "the Start;" another email containing the photos of Josh was sent to a handful of people, again titled "Funny!" One of the last ones I remember looked like a list of articles and essays about natural satellites.

We told our supervisor about all this and he immediately left to bring the suitcase to the police. The authorities took everything and instructed us to not contact MoonyFood again.

I'll admit, I'm an investigative person at heart. Something as juicy as this was too good to pass up looking into.

I stole something from the case before it was taken away by my supervisor and given to the police.

It's a small Ziploc bag containing about an ounce of a white, watery substance. I immediately recognized it as the liquid that was coming out of Josh's face in those horrible photos. Someone must have taken a sample to hang on to.

It smells just as gross as it looks. I have it sitting on a shelf a good five feet away from me right now and I can smell it as if my face was in the bag with it. Reeks like burned rubber. Once in a while, the liquid splashes by itself, as if someone was shaking the bag. I've been trying and failing to capture it on film, it only does it when I'm looking away or doing something else. It's like the shit's fucking with me.

The bile also makes noise when it's recorded. Not in the sense that it starts going off when I start filming it, though—the playback has always has a sound that the liquid seems to be emitting.

I have not tried my complimentary bag of MoonyBites. I refuse to eat them and I insisted my coworkers do the same. When that Josh kid ate his sample, this disgusting fluid built up inside him and asphyxiated him as a result. I'm going to take it one step further and say that I personally believe that creating this bile is what the product was made for in the first place. Like I said, everything about it is fucking evil, including the sick fucks behind it. If anyone from MoonyFood is reading this, please feel free to go fuck yourself.

Consider all of this a PSA if you'd like. On Halloween, keep an eye on what your kids are eating to make sure none of this horrific shit happens to them. And, for the love of God, when MoonyBites get released, don't buy them. That's exactly what these creeps want, and even I don't want to find out why.

***

UPDATE: The bile is gone. It's fucking gone. The bag is right where I left it, but it's completely empty save for a few stains. It could be anywhere now.

Don't buy this junk food, guys. I'm serious. It's not from here.

Best Original Monster
—2016—

The Prisoner of Griffin Drive

By Lily T., Reddit User /u/_draegunfly_

Annual Winner—Best Original Monster, 2016

———————

1

200 years ago, a young and foolish priest held an exorcism in the gray house on Griffin Drive. He did it without the approval of the church and with little to no experience. He went about the house blessing the walls, so that no evil could hide there. The floor, so that no evil could tread there. The windows, so that no evil could climb through. And the thresholds, so that no evil could pass through ever again. With every blessing, he used a combination of white sage, pepper, clove, and holy anointing oils to mark a small and ancient script known to some as the language of the Nephilim. Where he found those symbols, or why he used those instead of Latin or Hebrew, I'll never know. After all, that damned priest was a fool.

It was my ghost-hunting Uncle Roar's favorite story to tell me when I was small. He told me how after the house was blessed, the priest performed an exorcism on the very possessed master of the house. It took three whole days to get the demon to name himself. Apollyon, the Destroyer, king of an army of locusts. He cast him from the man, but something went wrong. After the exorcism, the family was plagued by a nightmarish haunting. Eventually they gave up and moved away.

Under the safety of our blanket fort, with the ever-present protection of our story light, he regaled me with the curiously mysterious tale of the haunted gray house of Griffin Drive. He was my best friend and my solace from my mother's tumultuous relationships. I loved my Uncle Roar. He passed away in a freak accident right before my sixteenth birthday and left me everything he owned. Rory, his namesake, was born two days later. With the chaos that followed the death of my beloved uncle and the birth of my sweet brother, his estate was quickly forgotten.

Right before little Rory turned one, our mother chose to end her life. The doctors said it was severe postpartum depression; I was sure it was my abusive stepfather, John. Rory and I lived in hell for a year until John came into my room one night. We left the next morning before the sun was up.

I sold Uncle Roar's beloved car that he left me; we needed the money to escape John. In the process of cleaning out old ghost-hunting equipment, I found a worn, old notebook titled "Griffin Drive" and a manila folder with my name on it. The long and short of it? Uncle Roar had purchased the house on Griffin Drive to protect people from the nasty spirit inside. He had spent my childhood quietly preparing me for when I would be entrusted with the burden. My Uncle Roarke had also spent my childhood lying to me.

In 1823 a family of five moved into the house. Only two survived. The father beat the mother nearly to death; the mother's last action was to bash in the skull of their middle child while his siblings watched. The house then remained mostly vacant for many years. Rumors of blood-curdling screams and missing people chased away any potential buyers for over a century and a half, until in the early 2000s a house flipper bought the house. They reported no hauntings or nefarious acts during the entirety of the renovation, until the night the last of the repairs were completed. One woman was found with a giant gaping wound. The police reports said it resembled a giant bite, as if a massive cow-sized dog had grabbed the woman between the legs and bit down. She was nearly halved and bled out within seconds. One man's head was severed. The head was nowhere to be found. Another appeared to have gutted himself with a butter knife, and then wrapped his own intestines around another's throat and strangled the man to death. The bits and pieces of offal found throughout were all that was left of the other members of the house.

A handful of years later, my Uncle Roar and his paranormal group held a session in the house. Only my uncle left alive. The house on Griffin Drive haunted him until his dying day. And now, armed with his book of notes on the cursed gray house, I was willingly and knowingly moving my sweet little brother and myself into that house. We had nowhere else to go.

You may think me crazy; mostly I'm just desperate. I'd rather face the evilest of paranormal beings than stay with the monster that calls himself my stepfather.

***

The once-gray siding was faded and peeling from the house when we arrived. I imagine the centuries of screams are what curdled the paint. It loomed above us as we approached. A dark sense of foreboding welled in the pit of my stomach when I stepped into the shadow of the wraparound porch, everything we had in a duffel on my shoulder, Rory on my hip.

I raised my fist and shakily knocked on the door. Of course there was no reply. It was just a house. A murderous house with a lineage of death. The key glided into the lock, freeing the bolt with a metallic click. The door moaned as it slowly swung inward and an old piece of police tape fluttered free from its prison in the jamb.

"Hello?" My words reverberated through the house. "I know you're here. I'm sorry to intrude, but we have nowhere else to go."

I shifted Rory on my hip, giving him a little bounce while he sucked on his fingers, and peered into the house. He was getting big and heavy fast. Hopefully he was too young to remember the horrors we survived at John's hands. I choked on my fear and swallowed the bile that rose in my throat. The swelling in my eye had gone down, leaving an ugly purple and green bruise. The place between my legs was still sore and tender. I tried not to think about it and stepped into the house.

"Please? He won't look for us here," my voice broke. "We won't be any trouble."

Nothing but silence. The house was strangely clean. I had expected to spend the day airing the place and dusting. It should have given me pause—who would come here to clean? Who else had keys to the house? But all I really thought was that it was one less thing to worry about. Rory, spittle dripping down his chin, stared at the ceiling.

"Hello?"

Since I got no reply, I decided to take it as permission. I tossed our bag by the door and set Rory gently onto the floor. After closing and locking the door, I leaned against it. Sliding down I pulled my knees to my chest and buried my face in my arms. *Don't cry, don't cry, don't cry.* I could feel a sob trying its best to force its way out of me. Wiping my face on my sleeves, I caught movement out of the corner of my eye. Rory, peering upward, was holding both of his chubby little baby hands up toward the ceiling and bouncing on his diapered butt, like he did when he wanted to be picked up.

"Chaa-wee!" he shouted in excitement and burst into a fit of giggles, his eyes never leaving the spot on the ceiling.

The sweet sound of his laughter significantly lightened the shadow on my heart. I had to stay strong for him. The money we had gotten for the car would last us a few months if we used it sparingly. Hopefully, I could find a job before we ran out.

The next few days passed mostly uneventfully. I was still on edge, waiting for the being to make its presence known. Rory mostly kept himself busy by baby talking to "Chaa-wee," aka the ceiling. His babbles and happy giggles did wonders for my soul. The house was minimally furnished. Whether the pieces were left over from the flippers, or from Uncle Roar and his unfortunate team's sessions, I didn't know or care. The strange markings around the house creeped me out. According to the notebook, they were the supposed Nephilim characters left by the priest all those years ago. I tried scrubbing at them, but they would just reappear moments after. In some places, I scrubbed so hard the paint came off and still the markings would leach back onto the surface.

The morning of our second week, I woke to find Rory standing over me. He just stared down at me, a level of intelligence and curiosity beyond his two years shining from his deep brown eyes. "Hungry?" He smiled a toothy grin at me.

Since we had no booster seat, we'd been eating on the floor. This particular morning, little Rory toddled to the small table in the kitchen and struggled to pull out a chair. "Oh? Wanna sit at the big boy table today?" He nodded. It should have struck me as odd that my two-year-old little brother was no longer constantly sucking on his fingers and suddenly wanted to sit at a table he'd barely be able to see above, let alone eat at. Nonetheless, I sat his bowl of dry cheerios in front of him and made sure his sippy cup of milk was within his reach. He looked frustrated.

While I made my own bowl, he let out the biggest sigh I'd ever heard. Before I could even say anything, he had wiggled from his seat and walked up to me in the kitchen. He stared impatiently before scrunching up his face and sighed again. "What is it, buddy?" Rory placed one hand on my hip and gave a small shove. Curious as to what this was all about, I took a step back. He stood on his tiptoes and opened the drawer I had previously been in front of. His little fingers grasped about the silverware drawer while he teetered precariously.

"Rory! You're gonna hurt yourself!"

If toddlers can give dirty looks, this one was just plain filthy. He ran back into the little dining area as I watched him from over the island. He began to tug on a chair, as if he was trying to bring it over to the drawer, but lost his grip and fell on his butt. I could have sworn I heard him mumble, "Damn it."

"Rory? Sweetheart, what do you want?"

"Spoon."

I stared in disbelief. He still ate with his fingers, and he was asking for a spoon? And he knew where they were in the kitchen? He was more observant of his surroundings than I thought. I got out a spoon and handed it to him. He climbed up into his chair and fussed with his sippy cup, finally opening it and dumping the milk into his bowl. Now content, he began to eat his cereal as if all this was normal. With. A. Spoon.

I could feel the hair raise on the back of my neck. "Rory, what's my name?"

He looked at me, annoyed that I had interrupted his cheerio feast. "Moima." Milk dribbled down his chubby chin.

After breakfast we sat in the empty living room. Rory sat patiently by the front door, his toys untouched. "Buddy, whatcha doin' over there?"

He turned and looked at me. "Waiding on coppany." There was a loud knock on the door to the tune of "Shave and a Haircut." Rory excitedly threw open the door. The most beautiful man I had ever seen stared in surprise at us. His blond, sun-kissed hair fluttered in the soft breeze that now blew through the house. His bright emerald-green eyes widened as they went from Rory to me and back again.

Rory was the first to speak, "Heywo Wook."

The blond Adonis let out a snort. "What the fuck is this?"

2

Little Rory grinned at the blond man. "What do you fink?" He did a little pirouette and nearly toppled over.

The man, with chin in hand, eyed my small brother. "Seriously, what ARE you doing?"

I recovered from my momentary shock and rushed to the door, pushing Rory behind me. "Who are you? What do you want?" I asked of the man.

He smirked. "I could ask you the same." His voice was soft and deep, like velvet dipped in seduction. He stared at me for a moment longer and then gave a deep bow, one arm flung into the air behind him. "You may call me Luke, and just what, may I ask, are you doing in this house?"

Rory struggled away from my grasp. "Dey asked to stay. I tot it would be fun," Rory explained.

"I can't take it anymore." The beautiful man's face crinkled into the kind of smile that made legs turn to jello and hearts into a quivering mess. "Please, that little voice doesn't suit you. Show yourself."

Rory gave me a sidelong glance and then shrugged his shoulders. A shadow rose from his little body like a plume of smoke, rising up until it formed a puddle on the ceiling. It was like looking up at the night sky on a clear night, darker than your mind can grasp with tiny flecks of light shimmering softly on the surface.

"Come now, become something they can fathom," Luke demanded from the door. The darkness on the ceiling stretched and took the form of a man. If Luke was the sun, or the brightest morning star, the figure above me was the moon.

"Chaa-wee! Again! Again!"

I'm ashamed to say, but I fainted.

When I came to, the world was blurry and spinning. I could hear little Rory crying and another voice shushing him. "Moima. Moima hurt?" he sobbed.

"There, there, little one, she's just taking a nap. You're getting snot all over me." My eyes finally focused as I struggled to understand what was happening around me.

"I think she's coming to," a gravelly voice said from above me. Above me? Recollection shot through me like lightning. There was a man looking down at me. From the ceiling. He was just lying there, hands behind his head, ankles crossed. Pale skin, eyes black as night, and a wicked grin. I bolted up and nearly puked as the world swam around me. "Careful girl, you fell pretty hard."

Rory pushed himself from Luke's lap on the porch and ran to me. As I clutched him to myself, little Rory pointed up at the ceiling. "Moima see Chaa-wee?"

Luke sighed from the door. "Excuse me for being blunt, but while you try to comprehend what's going on, he," he gestured to the being above me, "and I have business to attend to. Private business. So if you could find yourself in another room, that would be great."

I didn't know what to do, so I took Rory to the kitchen. Maybe it was shock, or the concussion, but I found myself making four servings of lunch. Meanwhile, I could barely hear the two men talking back and forth. The only words I could discern where Penemue and Amezarak. I only knew those words because I had seen them in my uncle's notebook. They were Nephilim.

According to legend, Amezarak taught spells and herb magicks. Penemue taught man the art of writing with ink and paper. Who was Luke and why was he talking to the being on the ceiling?

***

I knocked on the wall of the living room and announced myself before entering with three plates laden with sandwiches. Both men shot annoyed glances my way, Luke sitting crisscross applesauce just outside the front door, the dark one just inside the door and mirroring Luke's stance from his perch above.

"Uh… I made lunch… it's not much, but…" I shrugged as I handed one plate to the wide-eyed Luke and lifted one up to the resident monster. I stared at him. "Do… do you eat?" Luke took the plate and peered inside the sandwich, his mouth dropping open in astonishment. I felt the plate I held aloft lifted from my hands and suddenly the room was filled with a deep rumbling laughter. I looked from one to the other, nervous I had made an egregious error. Luke's eyelids fluttered, the corners of his mouth twitching.

"YOU," boomed the one above, "you…" He chortled some more. "You would serve us peanut butter and jelly?"

"Well, I'm sorry, I was fresh out of the blood of my enemies!" I yelled back, instantly both embarrassed and afraid. "It's all we have. Unless you want more cheerios?"

"Chaa-wee, funny?" Rory already had peanut butter and sticky jelly all over his face.

"It's," Luke wiped a tear from the corner of his eye, suppressing his laughter, "it's fine. It's really fine."

"You can come in the house you know," I said shyly.

"Hmmm. While it would be more convenient, I can no more enter the house than he can leave it."

That stopped me in my tracks. I found my eyes drifting to the markings on the threshold and walls.

"Yes, those."

Suddenly, my offer of peanut butter and jelly seemed ludicrous. Those markings, the ones placed there so long ago to keep evil from entering the house were keeping the beautiful man on my porch from crossing the threshold. That meant that he was like the terrible thing on the ceiling. The thing that had possessed little Rory just that morning. And I had served them both fat PB&Js.

"So," the dark one said around a mouthful of thick peanut butter, "your name is Moima?"

"Moira," I corrected.

Luke cleared his throat. "The little one is Rory?"

"Yes."

"What does 'chaa-wee' mean?" asked the black-eyed man.

"Oh. I think he's calling you Charlie."

"Charlie? Well, that's a new one."

"Chaa-wee, Chaa-wee!" Rory butt bounced, reaching for Charlie.

"My turn." Even though I was determined not to show these demons my fear, my voice shook. "What are you? What are you doing here? Why don't you leave? What have you done to Rory? Please don't hurt us."

"Woah woah woah." Luke held up his palm, stopping my barrage of anxious word vomit.

Charlie cleared his throat and held the plate down to me, clean of any crumbs, though I imagine they had probably fallen off and were sprinkled over me and the floor. "I could answer those, but you won't like it nor would you be capable of understanding."

"Try me."

"You could just show her." Luke held his plate up, but just outside the door.

"What happens if you try to cross?" I took back the plate. Both monsters had demolished their sandwiches.

"It hurts," Luke answered curtly.

Charlie flashed a malice-filled grin in my direction. "Would you like to see?"

Before I could answer, he stood, making him face to face with me. It's terrifying looking a monster directly in the mouth. He leaned forward, his body dripping down from the ceiling, drenching me with himself. My chest constricted and my vision began to swim. The world went dark around the edges like I was about to pass out. I saw my hand come up and wave in front of my face, but I had not moved it.

You taste exquisite. Charlie's voice echoed through my head. *Such fear, so ripe for the picking.* I felt my body inhale deeply as my soul shivered. We looked toward the door. Luke was leaning back on his elbows, Rory in his lap once again. *Prepare yourself, Moira.* I watched as my hand raised and ever so slowly pushed against an invisible wall where the doorway should be. Burning, searing pain shot up my arm. It felt like every bone had been instantly crushed, every nerve pinched beyond endurance. Someone was screaming; was that me?

Rory watched, wide-eyed. "CHAA-WEE! BAD! NO CHAA-WEE!" He shook his spit- and peanut butter-covered finger at us. His brown eyes were alive with a fury only a two-year-old can feel.

Charlie relented, pulling my hand back. Pain aside, it had been like pushing against a concrete wall. *So no evil can pass through.* He left me then and I collapsed to the floor, gasping for breath and clutching my arm to my chest. Rory rushed me and patted my back. "S'okay Moima. S'okay."

***

After I had put down Rory to bed that evening, I went in search of Charlie. "I know who you really are," I said, trying on my biggest adult-sounding voice.

"Oh?" He was still languishing on the ceiling.

"Why don't you come down from there? Looking up at you all the time hurts my neck."

"No evil may tread there."

I looked down at the floor and noticed the symbols there for the first time.

"So tell me Moira, who am I?"

I mustered up the remainder of my courage. Sassing a monster demon took a lot of energy. "Apollyon."

He raised one perfectly shaped eyebrow and snorted at me. "No child. I am not Apollyon, though I gave that name many years ago. I might add, Polly was greatly amused by that prank." He stood and walked a few steps away. It's strange holding a conversation with an upside-down man. "I was bored with the priest's unrelenting drivel. I thought the idiot priest would go away if I gave him a random name. The King of the Locusts was the first name to enter my head that day. If you insist on calling me by a name, Charlie will do." He turned and looked at me thoughtfully. In the blink of an eye he was but a few inches from me. He reached out and stroked my hair, gathering it in his fingers and pressing it to his face. He inhaled deeply.

"Give me your fears. Let me taste your darkest hate. Indulge me and I shall leave you unharmed. The little one too." I couldn't stop my body from trembling. I couldn't stop the tears from rolling down my cheeks. He leaned in and licked one from my face; his nostrils flared and his breathing became heavy.

"Do you promise?"

"You would trust me?"

"Do I have a choice?"

He chuckled, my hair sliding out of his grasp, "You have my word, strange human. Show me why you sought refuge in my prison."

So I did. I felt myself go static as his presence filled me. I should have asked how this worked before I agreed. *Think on the things that make you quake. Your darkest moments.* My mind instantly flashed to the night John came to my room. *What sort of monster do you take me for? I don't wish to taste that. It is foul and rancid.* I felt a small twinge of relief that I could tuck that raw memory away for when I could deal with it. Instead I thought of the beatings and all the yelling John had doled out since Mother's death. *NO, silly girl. That is not fear, that is rage.* I thought for a moment, trying to think of a time I felt true fear. The thought of John finding us sent bile boiling up my throat. *Yes. Yes. This is it. More.*

For whatever reason, I still blame my not-quite-clear thoughts (due to the concussion I gave myself), but I could think of no more. Charlie became angry. I felt like I was burning from the inside out. *Then I shall show you fear.* My body felt heavy and liquid, like I was being pulled down through the floor. The house shifted about me. Suddenly there was furniture and people. I could hear laughter and echoes of conversations.

Perhaps you've heard of the people that purchased this house to modernize it? Let me show you the truth of it. I left them alone when they came because they planned to renovate. I had never heard this word before them. You see, when I take you, I have access to all your thoughts and memories. In an instant I can learn your darkest secrets and fears. I peek into blackest parts of your hearts to find the hard knots of hate you hide there. Usually, I use this to discover ways to break you. This time I learned that you can buy a decrepit house and make it new with state-of-the-art repairs and turn a profit. You humans and your greed, it will always be your undoing. However, they planned to pull down walls, replace windows and doors. They were unknowingly planning my escape. I left them be. They tore out the kitchen and replaced it with shiny new appliances. They opened up the walls and upgraded the electric and plumbing. The new windows let in more light, shining upon the freshly refinished floors. Judging by the groaning of the walls, they redid the siding and roof. The night the renovations were complete, they held a small gathering to celebrate. The doors were left open to the night. While they clinked glasses and joked about the supposed hauntings of the house, I drifted to the floor. It had been so long since I stood upright in the world. There was only pain though.

He made me watch his past.

"What's that?" a voice called. A small group of people all gathered around a spot on the new linen-colored wall. I watched, filled with his disdain, as the Nephilim script appeared like a dark oil stain on the fresh paint. One by one, each dastardly character seeped to the surface.

Amezarak and Penemue had taught the ancient humans well. These new humans would taste my wrath. He didn't bother possessing any of them. Instead, he endured the pain that racked both our bodies and showed himself. He took the forms of their greatest fears. He caught one woman in his great jaws and snapped her in half, her blood splattering the new ceiling fan. The doors and windows slammed shut. *If I couldn't leave, neither would they.* He sunk massive claws into a man's soft eyes and flung him across the room. The long talons tore another's abdomen open with a flick, sending viscera over their makeshift table. The others clambered and screamed. They beat upon the walls and doors. One woman's hair tangled against his rough palm; he ripped it from her head slowly.

He forced me to watch as he tore the party to shreds, each in a different vicious way. *Not even the finest of your doctors were able to piece them back together again. How I wish I could have attended their mass funeral to taste the agony I had wrought.*

He sluggishly pulled himself from my body. I dropped to the floor and sobbed. I had also pissed myself. "You will live, girl. I have hungered so long for a fix." He ran his fingers through his messy hair and vanished from my sight.

I was left in a puddle on the floor, shivering from the trauma. My only thought: when would he need more?

3

I woke that morning to Rory delightedly screeching, "Again! Again!"

Wandering out from the room we'd been sleeping in, I found pure baby chaos. Rory was stark naked and hanging from Charlie's black, mercurial being, swinging back and forth. His little bare bottom would tap the ceiling and Charlie would swing him down in an arc, his little toes grazing the floor, and back up so that his button nose almost touched the ceiling on the other side. Rory would then push off the ceiling with his feet. Down and up, back and forth, only slowing down just enough so his small body wouldn't collide in a crash with the ceiling.

"WHAT THE—CHARLIE! PUT HIM DOWN!"

"I wasn't hurting him," his smoky voice sulked.

I gave him the stink eye. "Rory, where's your diaper?" Rory gave me his most mischievous giggle and pointed out the wide-open front door at his dirty diaper and a small mound of dirty wipes that must have been haphazardly tossed through the door. I looked to Charlie. "Did you try to change him?"

"As you know, I cannot leave this place. For that matter, I cannot enter any room with a threshold. I am bound to wander this room, the hallway, the room you sleep in, and that place you eat in for an eternity. The small one was stinking the place up and for the first time EVER, I have wished for death. We could not reach his fresh diapers."

"And you were swinging him, why?"

"We were airing his foul-smelling bottom."

I did my best not to laugh at the hysterical image of this dark, ancient being attempting to wipe Rory's butt. I let the rest of what he said sink in. So he could traverse through only part of the house. I had chosen the room we slept in, which was probably a formal dining room or den, because it was closest to the door. It had also contained the only mattress. Perhaps I should consider lugging the old, ratty mattress into one of the actual bedrooms that had a threshold.

After a quick breakfast, Rory stripped off his clothes again and ran through the house, giggling. I wanted to walk to town to get groceries so I didn't have time for his nudist proclivities. I guesstimated that it would take at least an hour to walk to the nearest store. Rory continued to streak through the house; Charlie was still sulking on the ceiling in his blob form. "STOP HIM!"

"Charlie, he's just a kid—"

"No," he morphed into his human form and pointed, "stop him!"

Rory was at the end of the hall struggling with a closet door I had been unable to open. I figured the old house had shifted, warping the door frame, permanently shutting the door. "He can't get it open, it's just a closet—"

The door swung open with a creaking, screeching moan, revealing a set of stairs which Rory quickly crawled up, giggling and laughing. I took off toward Charlie, who was scowling and stomping across the ceiling toward the door, mumbling to himself. My curiosity outweighed my fear as I ran beneath him.

On each stair was a long line of inscribed Nephilim script. Looking up from the bottom of the stairs, I could see sunshine spilling through a window set in a soft cream colored wall. "That's where they hid from me," Charlie grumbled.

It was a room. A beautiful sunshine-filled room with a huge closet and a massive bath. The flippers must have set this space up as a master suite. I had figured those windows had led to an attic so I'd never gone searching. If the living room housed a demon, I hadn't wanted to know what lived above. Around the topmost part of the wall, the outermost edge of the floor, and on all the rafters ran strings of the archaic script. I caught my naked baby brother and brought him back down the stairs. Charlie eyed us suspiciously. "It's just a room, Charlie. I thought Rory was going to get hurt." He harrumphed at me and went back to sulking. I would definitely be dragging the mattress and our stuff up there that night.

***

It took us two hours to get into town. Rory, deciding he wanted to be ornery because he couldn't stay at home with Charlie, made what should have been a quick trek into an arduous journey. People stared at us with wide eyes full of fear and concern. When I bought a little red wagon at the local toy store, no one would look me in the eye, though I could hear them all whispering behind my back.

The entire time we were in the small grocery people would deliberately go down different aisles or turn around and back out if we appeared. It didn't look like we'd be making any friends here any time soon. When we got to the checkout, it seemed like all but one cashier and bagger had decided to go on break.

While the older lady rang out our purchases I watched her gaze shift from me to Rory and back again.

"Oh dang it!" she exclaimed, "I can't take it anymore! You see, Earl said he saw Cliff driving y'all to that damned house—"

"Judy! Shhhhhh," mumbled the bagger.

"No, I will not shush, they're just kids! And look at her, the circles under her eyes are darker than a new moon night. I'll be damned if I let that house —"

"Ma'am," I interrupted, "it's really okay. I know about the house."

"What the hell you want to live there for?!" the bagger shouted more loudly than he meant to, judging by the red hue his cheeks took.

"We don't have anywhere else to go. And that house is safer than the one with my stepfather in it."

There was a mass intake of breath in gasp form from all the hidden eavesdroppers. Judy, the kind-hearted cashier with eyes full of tears, grasped at my hand.

"Oh, darling," she stuttered.

"It's okay. We're alright. And we're safe for the most part."

A giant hand clamped onto my shoulder and I was roughly spun around by a grizzly of a man.

"No ye ain't safe, the devil's in that house!"

As I stared into the eyes of the man I tried to decide which would be easier, to tell him that Charlie and I had come to an arrangement, or to lie. The cross Judy was now fingering around her neck made the choice easier. I lied.

"Sir, I prayed and prayed for help with my stepfather, and God told me He cleansed the house and sent us there. He said we'd be safe. It's just a creepy old house now."

Judy put one hand in the air, looked toward the sky and uttered a soft "hallelujah."

"How'd did you'ins even know about that place?"

"My Uncle Roarke left it to me."

"So crazy Roarke bit it, did he?"

I was surprised; did this man know Uncle Roar? He must have noticed my surprise because the hard look in his eyes softened.

"Everyone knew OF him." He took off his ball cap and scratched at his thinning hair before replacing it. "He was the last person to leave that accursed place alive. Then he went and bought up the whole street. Darlin' you own all of Griffin Drive, why don't you and the sprout live in one of the other houses?"

"Damn," Bagger Boy looked excited, "if the devil's really out of the house, you could have a seriously wicked haunted house party for Halloween this weekend!" Judy promptly ended his excitement with a slap up the backside of his head.

***

The whole walk home I contemplated this new knowledge. I COULD just move us. It's not like we owed Charlie anything. But I had made a deal, and just because Charlie couldn't leave to come after us, didn't mean he wouldn't send Luke. I was startled out of my reverie by Rory suddenly shouting, "Wook!"

I had never actually stood so close to him before. Out in the bright sun, his beauty was even more breathtaking.

"Luke! Where in the hell did you come from?"

"Wook, Wook, Wooooooook! Up!" Rory stretched his arms up to him. Luke pointedly ignored him as he stared at my face.

"Hmmm. Where in Hell? Some say a well-fortified cell, others the throne." He shrugged and then eyed me. "You let him taste your fear," he said flatly.

"He said he wouldn't hurt us and we could stay if I did."

"You realize this is not a one-time thing right?"

"WooooooooooOOOoooook!"

"What do you care?"

"Look," he said, stopping and turning toward me. The little wagon slammed into my ankles. "Do NOT mistake this as concern for you or the small one. You humans are nothing to me. But... Charlie," he cleared his throat, "is my... friend..." He chewed on his words before he spat them in my face. The word 'friend' must have tasted strange in his mouth. "He is an addict. He hasn't tasted human emotions in years. He's so close to being clean. I can't have you peddling to him for favors."

"Wook?"

"Fine! You persistent little bug!" He leaned down and grabbed a grinning Rory. He tossed him high into the air, caught him, and placed him on his shoulders. Seeing Rory grinning madly, his little fists filled with Luke's golden locks while perched safely on his broad shoulders, warmed my bruised soul just a bit.

"I don't understand. Addict?"

He sighed and looked down at me. "His kind was born long before any one god claimed ownership over creation. They were there for the first murder. The first rape. The first genocide. They were watchers, and felt nothing for human plights. Then someone got the bright idea to take one of your kind out for a spin. For the first time in their history, they felt something. To him, feeling your happiness is like taking a lukewarm shower. Feeling your pain and misery though, is like the highest high one can possibly feel. It invigorates him. And so violent possessions were born."

I stared at him. I'm quite certain that my mouth was gaping open. "So… when they do this, what happens to our souls? If he takes me too much, will my soul disappear?"

He chuckled. "You watch too many movies. They don't want or need your souls, though some collect them as trophies. Little sparkly trinkets to show off and brag about, and when they're feeling in the mood, they can poke and prod them and get tiny whiffs of the delightful highs you once gave them. My kind, on the other hand, does take souls. But that's another conversation."

Rory had been sitting silently upon Luke's shoulders watching us both, but now his patience had run dry, "Giggy up Wook! Giggy up!" He tugged on the golden locks.

"Not so hard, Bug."

***

Charlie eyed us suspiciously when the three of us returned. Luke stopped and put Rory down at the door. "What are you three doing together?"

"Have you been sulking all day?" I asked him.

"No. I've been brooding." Luke rolled his eyes from the porch. I pulled the groceries into the kitchen and began putting them away. I had been unsure if Charlie and Luke needed or wanted to eat with Rory and me, but I had bought extra just in case. I set out some steaks and eggs and began making lunch. I figured I needed to make up for the peanut butter and jelly I had offered them before.

I was trying to sift through all the information I had learned that day when an idea came to me. I knew from previous experience that Charlie could go into the little nook where the table was, and just past the table were two French doors leading onto the back porch. I threw both doors open and set one chair outside before shoving and scooting the table halfway out the door. When I was done, the table could now be the bridge between the two men; they could both sit and talk to each other. We could have our meal as a nice, happy…. I didn't finish that thought.

When the food was ready I made them all sit at the table, Charlie on one end facing Luke on the other. Rory and I sat side by side. Charlie and Luke stared at each other for a long quiet minute. "I haven't seen you right-side up in… 200-odd years?" Luke asked of Charlie.

Charlie shrugged and looked down at his steak. "Why are you being nice? I thought you were mad at me."

I cleared my throat to answer, but he suddenly looked up in a rage. He glared down at Luke and his hand whipped out and touched my face. I felt his fingers melt into me; before I could pull myself away he ripped his hand back.

"HOW DARE YOU! I am NOT an ADDICT! If I could reach through the damn barrier, I would—"

"She should know. If you're going to feed your ADDICTION using her, she had a right—"

Charlie gripped the edge of the table, his knuckles going white, and looked at me. "You may have heard of him," he finger-jabbed toward Luke, "his REAL name is Lucifer! And His Majesty plays a fucking saxophone in a fucking band in New Orleans."

Luke just sighed and put his face in his hand. I neatly filed away this new information to freak out about later. Right then, I had to stop the impending storm before the yelling upset Rory further. His little lip was already popped out and quivering, crocodile tears forming in his eyes as he looked from one man to the other. I said the first thing that came to mind: "The people in town think we should have a haunted house for Halloween."

They both stared blankly at me and in unison said, "What?"

"The people in town think we should have a haunted house for Halloween. I told them that God had cleansed the house and there wasn't a demon here anymore."

They blinked several times.

"Is this steak rare?" Charlie asked.

"A haunted house could be a lot of fun," Luke said as both men began tearing at the still slightly bloody meat on their plates.

4

"You could help, you know," I grunted at Charlie while trying to move the mattress.

He crossed his arms and scoffed from the table. "Luke and I are figuring out your stupid haunted house."

I sighed and went back to tugging it out of the room and toward the stairs. I really hadn't expected them to be so for throwing a haunted house. Luke was on the bandwagon until he realized Charlie would have access to whoever set foot in the house. With people all riled up and excited for a scare, there was no way Charlie wouldn't taste their fears. With much grumbling about "not being an addict" Charlie finally promised that IF he took people, he wouldn't do any lasting damage, and that this would be his last hurrah in the fear industry. I didn't believe him for a second, but Luke seemed satisfied. I wondered what would go down if Charlie broke his deal with the devil.

By the time I got the mattress up the stairs, I was worn out. Rory was downstairs happily babbling away at Luke and Charlie while they argued over "scary decor." I shoved the bed to the middle of the room and flopped down. The sheets could wait a minute. Luke had asked if he could call in some help. I had said sure, but was now having second thoughts. Who or what would arrive to "help"? With the windows open, the breeze felt amazing. I could feel my body lulling into a restful state. I rolled over and the floor let out a creak of all creaks and startled me into a sitting position. I wiggled my butt back and forth on the mattress. Creeeeeeaaak, clunk, creeeeeeeak, clunk. Well that would most certainly NOT be pleasant to sleep with. Getting up, I pushed the mattress over. I used my weight on each floorboard until I found the culprits. If the boards hadn't made such a racket, I never would have noticed. There, smack dab in the middle of the room, was a small section, deliberately made to be invisible, that lifted up on a hinge.

The small space below was dark and filled with cobwebs. It made me uneasy. The rest of the house was spotless. But this hole was dank and dusty. I reached in slowly, imagining all sorts of creepy crawlies would be on me in seconds. Probing around gently with my fingertips, a chill ran its fingers down my spine. I didn't like this. I was about to yank my hand out of the black hole and slam the little door closed, when my fingers grazed a lump. *Great.* It was wrapped in a thin cloth that had been ravaged by time. *I wonder how the flippers missed this?* Maybe they hadn't. Maybe it was something bad and they had put it back in the hole and forgotten about it? My heart was racing; I was dripping in sweat. It would drive me nuts if I didn't take at least a peek.

It was a book.

There was a loud crash followed by yelling. I sighed and set the book on the floor and closed the small hatch. I'd finish checking the book later. My supernatural idiots were up to something.

***

Splayed out on the front porch was a young man holding his bleeding nose. Both Luke and Charlie were laughing. Rory was peering out from behind Luke's leg. Luke leaned down an offered the man his hand.

"Did you forget?" he asked the bleeding man.

"No. Yes. I don't know." He stood up and gingerly raised his fingers to the barrier. It shimmered and gave a zap. "Damn it!"

"Ummmmm... who's this?" I asked. The three men turned toward me. Charlie was sitting backward on a chair, his feet tucked up on its legs so they didn't touch the floor, Luke was leaning on the porch railing, and the third just stood there with blood running down his face.

Rory ran to me, giggling, and pointed at our new guest, "Boo boo!"

"My name is not Booboo."

Rory looked at him like his was an imbecile, then rushed to the kitchen. He returned with paper towels trailing after him and offered them to the bleeding man.

"For boo boo!"

"I'm NOT Booboo!" He stared down at Rory's confused face.

"It's for your nose," I explained. "You're bleeding. A booboo is an injury... you know... like an owie?"

"Hmmph." He wiped at his face. "Well, we're here. Do you want us to start setting up?"

I looked out to the front yard. There were at least thirty men standing there looking excited.

***

In the next few days Griffin Drive was crawling with the supernatural. I wasn't sure if they were demons or not, but I wasn't going to ask. Right then, they all looked human. I had been back and forth to town buying up every candle and pumpkin I could find with money Luke had forced on me. At least five of the "men" were with me at all time. They bought candies and gift cards and passed out papers inviting the townsfolk to "Walk the haunted Griffin Drive." Everyone seemed ecstatic.

The night of Halloween, after the sun had gone to bed and the moon claimed her rightful place, Griffin Drive came alight with the glow of hundreds of candles. Creepy carved jack-o-lanterns lined the whole of the road. In each abandoned house, scary—sometimes gruesome—scenes took place behind foggy and warped windows. The "men" had dropped their facade and now wandered as they truly were.

Luke was in the backyard, sitting beside an absolute treasure trove of candies and goodies.

"What's this?"

He flashed a smile at me, showing teeth that were much too sharp. "Halloween is one of the few times we can show ourselves and people just write it off as fancy costumes and expensive makeup. It has been soooo long since I've shown anyone the way I was made."

His body was enveloped in a bright light that nearly blinded me. I covered my face with my hands.

"Oh, sorry. Like I said, it's been a while. You can look now." His voice was deeper and had a musical quality to it. I almost shrieked at the sight before me.

His body was now that of a lion, rippling with the hard and lean muscles of a predator. Four giant wings erupted between his shoulder blades. They stretched and flexed; the tips spanned twice as long as his body. A long serpentine tail thumped softly on the dead grass. His beautiful face shared its space with the face of a hawk and a bear. Six pairs of eyes blinked at me, almost in unison. My heart was in my throat as I backed away and tripped, landing in the ginormous pile of candy.

"Luke?" I gasped.

He sighed in return. "I'm quite positive no one actually reads the Bible." His body shivered. The four wings became two, the three heads morphed together, leaving only the face I had come to know.

"Better?"

"What ARE you?"

"Right now, a Sphinx."

"I thought the Sphinx was a woman."

He laughed, the pitch of his voice rising until it sounded like the soft ringing of a bell. His hair darkened to the shade of spun gold and grew long, covering the plump breasts that had sprouted from his chest like ripe fruit. His chiseled features had softened—t—and he became she. All of the world would fall to their knees to worship such beauty.

"How's this?" Her voice was like honey.

I could only stare.

"Good. It makes the riddles harder to answer when you can't find your tongue."

"Riddles?"

"Yes. If they correctly answer, they get to take some treasure." One massive, clawed paw gestured to the pile I was sprawled in.

"If they don't?"

She grinned, leaned in close to my face, and growled, "I shall eat them."

"Woooook! Wook? Boobies!" Rory tumbled down the stairs in his goblin costume, got up, and rushed to Luke. He buried his little face in the soft downy fur below her breasts and giggled, "Kee kee!"

"This child..." Luke sighed.

"You're not really going to..."

"No, I won't eat anyone," she laughed as she set him atop the mountain of sweets. The sound reminded me of wind chimes and silver bells.

***

The night went off without a hitch; the whole of the town showed up. Charlie and Luke had picked a long, flowing—if not slightly revealing—black gown for me to wear. I sat on a red velvet chaise on the porch, welcoming the guests. The townspeople gaped at the houses filled with horrors and screams. They took pictures of my dozens of jack-o-lanterns. Right as they were lulled into a false sense of security, the league of terrifying demons chased them down the road to me.

"Welcome to my house of horrors." I gestured to the door. "You may enter in groups of five—if, that is, you wish to leave alive." Everyone would cling to each other, giggling nervously. You could see them silently counting out their groups, looking to see who would be left out. One of Luke's men was stationed across from me, dressed in a butler's uniform but with the massive head of a raven. He would push the door open and let five unlucky souls in. The door would slam shut behind them with the help of the fishing line he had tied to the handle.

When they entered, they would find a roaring fire, and a single red velvet wing-back chair beside it. Except I had no fireplace. Once they entered, they were in Charlie's web. They would hear their names whispered by the voices of loved ones long dead. The fire would go out, leaving only a single candle burning on the imaginary mantelpiece. As their eyes would adjust to the waning light, their heartbeats would rise, they'd hear a childlike giggle, then hot moist breath on the backs of their necks. Charlie would take them then. He would show them a planned-out horror. We had to be careful that everyone would see the same thing.

After he would release them, they'd see light through the French doors, leading them to Luke. As soon as their fingers touched the doorknob, Charlie would softly call out, "In the garden you will find, a monster that is as old as time. She loves to riddle, but it 'tis no jest, beware for the wrong answer will lead to death."

Just outside the door a ram-headed demon in a suit was waiting to give them the jump scare of their lives. Afterward, they'd meet the Sphinx.

So many screams rang out that night. The street echoed with them. They were all followed by laughter as the groups came out of the garden and found a large bonfire with hot dogs, hamburgers, and a bar tended by Medusa herself (well, there was a massive resemblance, but you could actually look at this one).

The whole town had gone through and it was now time to join the fun. As I started around the side of the house, my mind momentarily drifted to the prisoner trapped inside. Poor Charlie couldn't leave to join the festivities now that he had done his job. I told Raven Head I'd catch up and ran into the house. Charlie was on me in a second; I felt my body go static as he took my mind.

I was standing in the living room, surrounded by cameras and men with strange beeping boxes pointed at me.

"If there's anyone here, can you tell us your name?" The voices sounded hazy, like

long-forgotten whispers.

"Can you make a sound for us?" The house moaned a response. I turned; the man behind me held what looked like an infrared camera nearly in my face.

"I think we got something. Nope, it's gone." The voices were getting clearer.

"If there's anyone here,"—that voice, was it familiar?—*"we mean you no harm, can you make yourself known?"* I tried to answer but found I had no mouth. My fingers clawed at the smooth spot where my lips had once been.

"Maybe we should try something else? You know, 'cause it isn't responding?"

"I don't think we should anger it." That voice I knew. I spun around; it WAS my Uncle Roar. What was going on? My mind was fuzzy. The one that had thrust the camera in my face was lighting something. Smoke filled the room. It was burning my nose. My lungs were filling with fire. I tried desperately to scream, but the spot where my mouth once was stayed firmly taut. My skin felt as though it was blistering, or millions of fire ants were biting me. Tears ran down my face. Suddenly, the man holding the smoldering sage was bleeding on the floor. Half his face torn open, one eye rolled out of its socket and plopped on the floor. The woman with all the questions was dangling in the air by her throat, choking and gurgling. She slammed into the wall with such force her head exploded and it rained coppery-smelling brain matter across the floor. I turned and saw my beloved Uncle Roar in the monster's clutches.

Rage filled me. I felt the skin rip apart on my face as my lips pulled into a feral snarl. "NO!" I charged forward and tripped on my skirt. I blinked a few times and looked around. I was in the living room still, but there was nothing in it except a red chair. Charlie was squatting in the chair, looking at me curiously. I don't know what came over me, but I charged him. I wrapped my fingers around his throat as he just stared at me, mildly amused if not a little surprised. I squeezed with all my might; he grabbed both my wrists and easily pulled me off of him.

"Why?" he asked calmly. His eyes were glassy. He was high as fuck, the bastard.

"That was my Uncle Roar," I spat out through gritted teeth and tried to slap at him. He held my wrists firmly. The faint sounds of laughter filtered in through the open windows.

"Charlie," Luke purred from the door, still female but no longer a Sphinx, bouncing a half-asleep Rory on her hip. "What the FUCK are you doing?"

Charlie looked toward Luke, then back at me. "I didn't know." As soon as he let me go I snatched Rory from Luke and ran up the stairs to our protected haven. I curled around Rory protectively and cried myself to sleep.

***

I woke up puffy-eyed and congested. Rory was sitting on the floor, flipping through the forgotten book. It was full of the same Nephilim script that was all over the house.

I threw off my wrinkled costume and changed quickly. Grabbing my half-naked brother, and the book, I rushed down the stairs and shoved past Luke on the porch.

"We need to talk." He was a man again, his voice velvet and lust once more.

I glared at him and stomped down the stairs.

"A rather bear of a man left this for you." He waved a piece of paper at me. I stomped back up and snatched the paper from him.

Moira, I saw the symbols in the house. You still have a problem. Call this number, they may help, for a price.

I stuffed the note in my pocket and headed to town.

When I got there I headed straight to Judy's grocery. I set a grumpy Rory on her counter and begged to use the phone. In my rush to leave John's house, I had left my cell. He would have probably been able to track me with its GPS anyways.

"Sure honey, but is something wrong?" She handed me the phone. Tears threatened to leak from my face as I took a few deep breaths, shook my head no, and dialed the number.

The phone was answered before the first ring was finished by a warm and sunny voice. "Mr. Lore's Antiquities, Betty speaking."

* * *

5

What was I doing? I hadn't even shown Charlie or Luke the book I found. I couldn't take it anymore though. Charlie had crossed a line by taking me without permission. This couldn't go on. "Hello?" Her voice really was like audible sunshine.

I sucked in a deep breath. "I was given this number. They said you might be able to help me. There are curses all over my house." I glanced at Judy who was playing with Rory, cupped my hand around the mouthpiece of the phone and dropped my voice to a whisper. "The runes are keeping a monster trapped inside. But I found a book in my bedroom floor and it's filled with the same writing. I don't know what to do."

There was momentary silence on the other end. "Do you know what kind of writing it is?"

"Nephilim."

There was a quick intake of breath. "Are you sure?"

"Positive. The book is completely written in Nephilim as well."

"Well, we can certainly take a look! I'm sure Mr. Lore would love to see that book. I can send someone by to pick it up, if that's okay?"

"That… that would be amazing. I don't have much money, but if you can help me get rid of the monster, you can keep the book. It's at least 200 years old, it's got to be worth something." I gave her my address and mentioned that it would be best not to enter the house unless I answered the door. She informed me it would probably be a few days before anyone showed up, but not to worry—someone would definitely be around.

***

I felt sick as I walked through town, Rory on my hip. He chattered happily away and waved at everyone we passed. I thought Charlie had known about my uncle. The first time he had taken me I had felt him search through my thoughts and memories, looking for something to frighten me. I thought that was why he had chosen to show me what he had. Because I had thought I knew how the flippers ended. Memories of the laughter and scares I shared with my uncle in our blanket fort filled me and my tears threatened to spill down my cheeks.

Rory patted my face. "Moima sad?"

"I'm okay, baby. I'm okay."

When we arrived at Griffin Drive I took the time to stop and check the forlorn and abandoned houses that lined the street. Time had ravaged each one in its own way. Only my house stood untouched by time, partially because of the renovations, mostly because of the curse. I sighed to myself. None of the houses were livable without a lot of work. We'd be stuck in the gray house a while longer.

Luke was still reclining in the chaise on the porch when I dragged my feet up the walkway. His brows furrowed at me as I did my best to ignore him.

"Moira, I know you're mad, but we need to talk."

"I need to feed and change Rory."

Charlie blocked my way into the house. "It's important." He wouldn't meet my eyes.

"Whatever it is, it can wait," I gruffed at them. Twin sighs escaped them.

I purposefully took my time with Rory. After he was clean and fed I put him down for a nap in our little haven above. Charlie's voice boomed through the house, "MOIRA DON'T YOU HIDE UP THERE!" I wondered how long he'd yell if I didn't show myself. I kissed Rory and went to face whatever hell they had planned below.

Luke started first. "Charlie wasn't trying to upset you—"

"Oh really? He did a damn good job of it." I crossed my arms and turned to Charlie. He was seated, staring at me curiously, in the plush red chair.

"I was… I was not thinking. The human fear had swallowed up my sensibilities, I wanted to tell you about your uncle and thought it would be easier to just show you… but… and then…"

"What he's trying to say is… well when he took you…"

"When he took me, what? You can't just possess me whenever you want! You need to ask! I'll cut you off, I'll cut one of those symbols into my flesh and you'll never be able to—"

"You're pregnant," Charlie said flatly.

I had to swallow my heart to keep it from coming out with the geyser of vomit that left my mouth. "What the fuck Charlie?" I gasped. "That's not even funny." I found my knees had turned to jelly and my world went black.

When I came to, Charlie had cleaned the vomit and Rory was curled up beside me, tears fresh on his little face. I sat up and pulled him into my lap and took a deep breath. I begged them to tell me it was an awful joke, but both shook their heads no. I sobbed into Rory's hair; he didn't understand what was happening so he just cried with me. What would I do? John had not only stolen my first time and defiled my body, but he had left a part of himself there. Bile rose up in my throat.

"I can end it," Charlie stated, as if we were talking about something small and trivial and not an innocent life. I only cried harder. It would be so easy to tell him to do it. But that wasn't a decision to make at a flip of a hat. If I kept the child, Rory would become an uncle and a big brother all at once. It was just fucked. I was only eighteen. Did I really think that I could provide for Rory, myself, and another? The money I had from the car would only last so long. I had an inheritance from both my mother and my uncle in the bank, but if I used it, John might be able to find us. That bastard John. If I did keep it, would I despise the child? Could I truly love the product of my rape?

"You're a good girl, Moira, if you want to end it, no one could blame you. No one even has to know. But," Luke said quietly from the door, "there is another option."

"Have the baby and put it up for adoption?" I asked, snot running down my face. When I got no response I raised my eyes. Luke's green ones were staring at me intently. He looked hesitant to say anymore. Charlie reached down and scooped up Rory, shushing him softly.

Luke crossed his arms and paced across the porch for a minute. He seemed to be working something out in his head. "Okay, hear me out. This could work." He paced some more. "We could make the child mine." Charlie dropped Rory, but quickly caught him. We all just stared at Luke.

"How? What do you mean?" A million questions ran through my head. Charlie looked as amused as I was confused.

Luke looked toward Charlie. "You could do it, right?"

Charlie nodded yes. A mischievous grin spread across his face. "You do realize what you're saying, right?"

Luke just grinned at him. "Do you think it could work?" Charlie's grin stretched into a wicked smile and both men aimed their ferocious gaze at me.

"I don't understand." I suddenly felt small and afraid.

"If we make the child mine, it would be Nephilim. I am, after all, at my very core an angel, a son of God; and you, a daughter of man. But I'm not just any angel; my Father gave me all his wisdom when he created me. The child would be the most powerful Nephilim to walk the Earth. It could be capable of removing the script that keeps Charlie contained."

It took a few minutes for me to comprehend what was happening. I realized that they wished to use me and the unborn child in my womb. I knew it, but all I could think about was that the child could have a different father. It wouldn't erase what had happened to me, but I could forget it. I could box the trauma up and put it back safely into the dark corners of my mind. I wouldn't risk feeling a lifelong guilt either. Luke was beautiful too.

"Do it." The words were out of my mouth before I could stop myself. Things happened quickly after that. Charlie set Rory down; Luke cut himself deeply. Where had he gotten that knife? Said knife was tossed through the barrier. Charlie licked the blood off the blade, and slid inside me like melty chocolate. *You'll be okay Moira.* Warmth spread through my belly. As Charlie slipped out of me, I heard a soft, whispered *I'm sorry about before.*

"That's it?"

Luke chuckled. "Well the kid was still just primordial goo with a heartbeat at the moment."

"Switching out parts isn't difficult," Charlie responded.

The hair rose on my arms, and a soft, prickly sensation ran up and down my body. There was a deafening CRACK and a blinding flash of light.

"WHAT HAVE YOU DONE, LUCIFER?" Two men had appeared in my living room. The metallic smell of ozone accompanied them. Rory screamed. I tried to go to him, but one man caught my arm and yanked me back.

"Hello brothers, be kind to Moira," Luke's voice threatened.

"Do you know how many armies we had to raise to rid the world of those ABOMINATIONS the FIRST TIME? The CITIES we had to BURN?"

Luke rolled his eyes. "And the millions of innocents you killed for Father?"

"HOW DARE YOU MOCK HIM! How dare YOU make a MOCKERY of HIM by making another NEPHILIM!" He spat out the last word like it was the most disgusting thing to have ever come from his mouth. Charlie had moved back to his chair and was watching the drama unfold with rapt attention.

I'd never seen Luke angry before. His presence became almost oppressive as his two brothers' beautiful bright white wings fluffed and stiffened like a dog with its hackles raised. Rory sat in the middle of the floor, his little hand frozen halfway to his mouth, a string of drool attached to his fingers, tears rolling unabashedly down his face. His eyes were wide with fear and his breath came in short, quick gasps.

"Father will smite this disgrace!"

The world seemed to slow as white-hot light filled the room. Everything looked like an overexposed picture, too much light. A high-pitched ringing felt like it would surely rupture my eardrums. The air was hot and felt alive with electricity. Rory wailed. The two angels moved away from me. My limbs felt like they were weighed down by all the failures of the world. I felt my body moving of its own accord toward Rory, wrapping tightly around him. God wished to end the tiny life in my womb; I would pay the highest price for my lapse in judgement. I couldn't let Rory die with me.

"LUKE!" I screamed, heaving Rory's tiny body with all my might. I just hoped he'd make it through the barrier. Luke leaned forward, arms outstretched, and collided into the invisible wall of pain. He cried out in agony, Rory tumbled through the air, slamming into Luke's chest. The air sizzled; the smell of burning wood and hair filled my nostrils. Luke stepped back and unfurled his majestic, golden, scorched wings, curling them tightly around himself and my screaming brother, his eyes full of sorrow as he ducked his head into his feathers. At least Rory would be safe. There was a boom like a cannon going off, and the house shook and screamed in protest. It was time to bend over and kiss my ass goodbye.

Nothing happened. The light receded to a soft glow. I blinked and slowly looked up. Charlie stood above me in all his cosmic glory. One hand—if it could be called a hand—was raised up in the air, his fist full of God's wrath. He squeezed and extinguished the light. Ash from the disintegrated upper half of the house floated down around us like snowfall. Charlie's body was as black as the places between the stars. If you looked close enough you could see the cosmos; little specks of light moved slowly through him and winked out in his center. It was as though the entirety of his body was a black hole. The angels gaped at him, slack-jawed. Charlie's inhuman presence became suffocating.

"What ARE you?!" cried one, some of his feathers falling from his wings. The twin angels quivered with fear. Charlie's deep chuckle filled the house before he vanished. The second angel slowly turned his head toward the first. His eyes were now jet black.

"I am that that was, before your beginning," Charlie's deep, reedy, and very angry voice came from the angel's mouth. "I am that that watched as you were created. GET. OUT. OF. MY. HOUSE."

He exploded out of the angel and took his human form. "Tell Yahweh, Zeus, Odin, whichever miserable god you serve, that he is not needed nor welcome here."

The trembling angels tripped over themselves trying to get out of the house; the one whom Charlie had possessed mumbled something and pointed at the Nephilim script on the threshold as they passed and nearly collided with Luke at the bottom of the stairs. All four of his wings were spread, a devilish grin across his face as he took in the ruins of the house. Rory kept his face buried in Luke's neck.

"AS IT WAS!" shouted the molting angels in unison as they took to the sky and disappeared in another flash of light and crack of thunder.

The house above me groaned and creak as it shifted back to 'as it was.' Now whole once more, the house would continue to contain Charlie with its simple magic. He roared in anger and disappeared into the shadow. I threw up all over the place... again.

***

It was dark when I awoke to an empty-feeling house.

"Charlie?"

Nothing.

I searched the upstairs and down; both Rory and Charlie were gone. Rushing from the house, I skidded to a stop. It looked like an atomic bomb had gone off. Wasteland as far as I could see. Burned bodies littered the ground. The air smelled of ash and death. The clouds, an angry gray, stained the blood-hued sky.

"Luke? RORY?!" My voice only echoed back.

Hot, putrid breath came from a voice close to my ear. "This is what you have wrought, oh foolish mother of the abomination." Fingers wrapped tightly around my neck and squeezed.

I woke up again, this time screaming. Charlie slapped me hard. "Stop with all the racket, girl!" It was just a nightmare; Charlie was much too irritable to have been attempting to sneak some fear out of my unconscious form.

Spotting Luke and Rory lying in the yard, I ran to Rory and held him close. He smiled and nuzzled into me. Luke got up on his knees and put his ear to my belly and smiled.

"Hello, little one," he whispered.

What the fuck had I done?

6

* * *

I had spent days in and out of the library with the book. I could find nothing online—or in any of the many mythology and religious texts I combed through —on deciphering the scripts. I was at a loss. I could only hope that Mr. Lore and his associates would have better luck. Rory had spent his time playing with Ms. Judy's grandkids. She had been my saving grace. Her daughter was a stay-at-home mom and had been delighted to take my mischievous brother for a few hours a day. It had done worlds of wonder for little Rory. He was talking more than ever now. He had rarely spoken when we lived with John.

Luke had been strangely absent since the incident with his brothers. Charlie said Luke's presence had actually been more unusual because he only visited him a few times a year. I could only wonder what he was up to.

At night I found myself staring at my stomach and wondering about the life hidden inside. The nightmares that plagued my sleep should have made me fear the growing child, instead I felt a lack of any emotion at all. I couldn't avoid the situation for too long, my belly would begin to swell eventually and I would have many questions to answer. What would I give birth to?

It was probably three weeks after the fateful day that Charlie saved my world when I heard a deep, rumbling roar come up Griffin Drive. Despite the fantastic turnout for Halloween, we still never received any visitors. I was up to my elbows in chicken and breading—I did have to eat better now, didn't I? Cereal and PB&Js aren't exactly the best fetus-growing foods. Charlie was coloring with Rory at the kitchen table when there was a knock at the door.

"Are we expecting anyone?"

"I get it!" Rory took off toward the door, Charlie following closely. I still find it hard to believe that I had gotten used to a man walking on my ceiling like it was normal for every family to have an upside-down, all-powerful being trapped in their home.

I heard Rory fumble with the doorknob and the subsequent creak as the door swung open.

"Hi!" his bright voice chirped as I washed off my hands and dried them.

"SONOFA—" came a woman's surprised voice.

I came around the corner to find Rory staring suspiciously at our visitor. She held one hand protectively to her chest as the other rubbed it. Tentatively, she reached out and received a zap to her fingers. She couldn't cross the threshold. I came up behind Rory and pulled him to me. Charlie had once again pulled his disappearing act, or so I thought.

"Can I help you?" I asked.

"Are you Moira?" the woman questioned back. She looked a little rough around the edges, but maybe that was the fauxhawk and the sleek black muscle car I could see parked in the driveway.

"Yes. And you are?"

"Faust. Betty sent me."

My eyes must have widened, or maybe they narrowed, either way the look on my face elicited a smirk from Faust. She looked exhausted and maybe a little pissed as she eyed my doorway.

"I'd invite you in, but I see you can't pass the script." I pointed down at the accursed lettering on the frame.

"She's hooman. Missin' hur sowl." Charlie said with Rory's mouth. Faust looked down in surprise and back up at me.

"Charlie. Stop it." Like an idiot, I slapped the back of Rory's head. I meant it for Charlie, but forgot my poor brother would feel it. Tears welled up in his big eyes as he rubbed his head and looked at me like had I betrayed him. Cursing inwardly, I knelt down and kissed his forehead and apologized. Charlie appeared, in his human form, beside me. Hanging from the ceiling of course.

Faust's eyes only widened a little bit, to her credit.

"Faust, this is Charlie. My resident… ummm…" I turned to Charlie who was leaning closer to the barrier, sniffing at Faust.

"Who is Betty, and why has she sent one who smells like a Harbinger?" he asked me.

"A what?"

"He means Gumdrop. My dog." She glared at him.

"Oh… okay. Umm, one second." I bolted up the stairs and grabbed the book from its hiding spot in the floor. Charlie was waiting for me in the hallway when I came back down.

"Who is Betty? What's going on? Moira, don't make me—"

"Charlie, I'll explain later." I squeezed past him and ran through the rest of the house. I knew running from Charlie wouldn't do me any good if he really wanted to catch me, but if I could get outside before he realized I was actively hiding something from him… well… it'd be for the best. Practically flying into the living room, I grabbed Rory and nearly slammed into Faust trying to get out the door.

"Hey Charlie? Put the chicken away, will you?" I yelled, closing the door behind me. I was answered by a muffled and miffed, "I CAN'T GO INTO THE KITCHEN!"

"Coffee?" I asked Faust.

***

We got our coffee to go at a little diner in town and then walked to a park where Rory could play. I found myself telling Faust almost everything. I left out the part about my pregnancy; I wasn't ready to say any of that out loud yet. When I was done, she looked down at her coffee in thought. *Great. She doesn't believe me, but who would?* I'm sure she thinks I'm an absolute lunatic. She cleared her throat.

"My soul is missing, my dog is a harbinger of death, a plant tried to eat me…" She lifted her twinkling eyes to mine, a crooked smile on her lips.

"I fed a cosmic being and Lucifer himself peanut butter and jelly sandwiches."

"My guns never run out of ammo."

"I think God tried to smite me."

"Which one?"

We dissolved into a fit of giggles. It felt amazing to tell someone the truth. Someone who would believe me. I pulled the book out of my purse and slid it across the table to her.

"I don't know what's in this. I don't know if it has anything to do with the writing in my house other than the fact it's written in the same language. But please, please, if you guys can figure a way to get Charlie out, promise you'll let me know?"

She nodded her head and smiled. "Promise. I've got an idea," she said and flashed me a wicked grin.

***

Charlie was probably quite curious when Faust and I arrived back at the house, both of us exiting her car with sledgehammers slung over our shoulders and plenty of spunk in our step. We'd run into Ms. Judy's daughter while purchasing the sledgehammers. She seemed pleased to see me with a friend and insisted on keeping Rory for the night—which worked out perfectly for us.

We picked a spot on the exterior living room wall and pulled down the siding. Maybe we'd had too much caffeine, or maybe neither of us had been getting enough sleep and were slightly delirious, but we went at that wall like a couple of maniacs. Splinters of wood, insulation, and bits of plaster flew everywhere. We high fived each other when we broke through and saw a wide-eyed Charlie through the hole. As soon as our hands met, the wall became whole again.

"What the fuck!" we said in unison.

I don't know how many times we put holes in the walls. Every time we'd break through, the house would instantly repair itself. Over and over we bashed in those walls, until our arms could no longer pick up the hammers. Covered in plaster dust and splinters, we surrendered ourselves to the lawn and stared up at the sky.

"Welp, I guess that book is my only hope."

"Don't worry kiddo, we'll figure something out."

***

The next day—with Faust gone and Rory home—was calmer than I expected.

Charlie had yet to ask any more about Faust and Luke was still MIA. I was still sore and tired from my adventure with the sledgehammer, so when it was time for Rory's afternoon nap I decided to join him.

Again my slumber was disturbed with macabre visions. I walked through war-torn fields filled with the dead. The acrid stench of gunpowder and the sickly sweet scent of death filled my nostrils. Ash drifted from the sky and hung in the air with the dense fog that surrounded me. Whispers echoed and hinted at the destruction wrought by the wrath of my child.

Look what we've become, sang the corpses at my feet as their mangled bodies writhed in pain. *Your foolishness stole our endings. There is no Heaven or Hell anymore. We must drag ourselves through this desolate place for eternity. Oh Mother of Ruin, why did you give life to Death?*

I woke covered in slick, cold sweat and sick to my stomach. After I purged my angst along with my lunch, I went in search of Charlie. I wanted him to look, to see if the child was as truly evil as my dreams prophesied. He was waiting for me in the crimson chair.

He listened quietly to my request. "And if it is?"

"End it," I choked out.

He tucked one leg underneath himself and drew the other up to his chest, the fingers of one hand softly tapping the arm of the chair. He sat staring intently at me for a few moments, I couldn't read his face no matter how much I wished to know his thoughts. He sighed.

"Well then, come here." His fingers grazed my hand and in that second he filled me with his being. The static that I had become used to feeling calmed me. *I had hoped to taste your fear, Moira. Why is it there is only sorrow?*

"I think I've made a huge mistake, Charlie."

You don't have to speak aloud. I can hear your thoughts, feel your doubts.

As a soft warmness filled my womb, I showed Charlie my truth. I didn't know how to feel. I had wanted to be a mother at some point. I wanted to honor my mom by passing all the good I learned from her onto future generations. I wanted to build blanket forts with children of my own, and pass on the memories of my beloved Uncle Roar. I didn't think I could take the precious life from the one inside me, no matter how he or she came to be. I worried that had Luke not offered up the choice he had, that I would have resented or even hated the child because of the sins of its father. Would I, even now, be capable of looking into its innocent little face and love it? Or would I only be able to think of how it came to be? The warmth I felt from my little one radiated upward and touched my heart. *Do you feel that, Moira? That is the love this little being feels for its mother. This life is too small to know hate or evil. It only knows you.*

Charlie appeared in the chair before me again, a small, shy smile on his face.

"That child will become what you make it. He is half you, you know. Do you doubt yourself?"

I could only duck my head in response. Did I doubt myself? Don't we all?

"No matter, my strange little human. I took the liberty of taking a precaution. As much as I don't wish to say it, you need fear no more."

"What did you do?"

"Just a little thing. It will be fascinating to watch the outcome. I am, after all, a watcher at heart. Now tell me of this book you gave to the one called Faust."

I felt the color drain from my face.

"What's going on in here?" Luke asked from door. I hadn't heard him open it.

"Moira was just about to tell me about a book she found hidden upstairs." Charlie's voice hardened a little. "One that she kept hidden from us."

7

"What book?" Luke raised his eyebrow at me.

I cleared my throat. "I found a book hidden upstairs. It was written in the same language as the markings through the house."

"And you didn't tell us—why?" Charlie was angry. The black of his irises expanded until the whole of his eye was pitch black. "What if that was the key?!"

I found myself stuttering as I backed away from him. His body was slowly changing. The soft, pale flesh of his hands turned black as the darkness crept up his arms. The long black locks that usually hung messily from his head rose up, no longer bound by gravity. Swirls of smoke-colored ink covered his face. He no longer looked like anything he had ever shown me before. Ebony claws dug into the arms of the chair where his fingers once were.

"Charlie, will you at least let her explain herself?"

Charlie let out a feral growl as saliva dripped off his razor-sharp fangs. "I have been stuck here for CENTURIES!" He sprung from his seat and pounced me, one clawed hand wrapping around my throat, lifting me dangling into the air. His body crackled and shivered with rage and the pain that radiated up his body from his feet, which were firmly planted on the floor.

"A few measly hundred years should be nothing to you. Put her down!"

Charlie glared into my eyes as I grasped his wrist, struggling to breathe. His fangs receded into his maw, his angry sneer pulling down into a pain-filled frown. He leaned into me, his nose pressed into my cheek as his hot words hit my ear.

"Know my pain."

The room spun around me. I could hear Luke shouting at Charlie; they'd wake up Rory if this continued. I didn't wish Rory to see his beloved Charlie like this. The familiar and once-comforting static filled me. I felt as though I was floating. Luke was screaming now. I saw nothing but darkness; I felt nothing.

I lay suspended in void for what seemed like an eternity. Small lights like fireflies sparked into being and danced around me. I reached my hand out and touched one. The tiny light floated above my palm. "Grow," I whispered. I watched as the light in my palms and those around me grew and spread into the cosmos. Beautiful rainbow-colored nebulae swirled and tumbled in the air; some of the lights collided, causing explosions of stars. It was the most beautiful thing I had ever seen.

I was not alone. I stood back to back in a small, tight circle with four others. We watched in awe how the beautiful lights danced. One raised his arm and pointed at a small cluster of light. Floating toward the small universe, I recognized it as my own. As life began, another of the beings flicked his fingers and the gods were born. We watched as they molded man, some from clay, others their own flesh. Man grew and bowed to their gods. We watched, fascinated. Always watching, never touching, until one bloody day we walked among you. We ate of your food, smelled your air, touched your hearts. Tasted your fear.

We never stayed anywhere long; when people saw us for what we were, they either ran screaming or tried to kill us. Though we lusted after your emotions, we... we? I shook myself. *What is happening?*

Watch.

I saw the worlds through Charlie's eyes. Humans were like playthings to them. One of his siblings tore the limbs from one tiny human to see what would happen. He seemed surprised that the human died, but became excited over the fear of the others. Death, it seemed, was our greatest fear. So they played on it. Watching, watching, watching, rarely interfering. Taking from us little bits here and there. As the world changed, the gods abandoned us, wars were fought, times forgotten, Charlie and his kin sat back curiously, waiting to see what we would do.

Then Charlie took the man in the gray house on Griffin Drive. Suddenly he was stuck, and like a lost child he felt his own fear for the first time. So used to watching everything at once, he was now limited to the view outside the three little windows he could see through. All he had now was time, and it passed slowly. His anger and rage was directed at his siblings, who watched his plight and did nothing. What would happen to a Nameless One that lived amongst the humans for too long? Would he ever ascend to the heavens again? Or would he continue to slowly change into a being trapped between worlds?

Tears ran down my face. *Why do you cry? I need not your pity.* I reached my hand out in the darkness and found his face.

"Charlie, this feeling you have, this is called loneliness," my voice echoed around us as my fingers ran down his neck and chest, stopping at the spot where a human heart would be. "This is heartbreak."

No. I don't feel silly emotions like a wretched human.

"You aren't alone anymore, Charlie."

Light returned to me then. Luke was still screaming at Charlie. Had only a fraction of a second passed? Charlie set me down gently, though he still glared.

"Moira! Come here, get away from him!" Luke was positively rabid.

"Since when do you care so much?" I spat at Luke. I didn't mean it to come out as angry as it had, but I was currently filled with both Charlie's and my own emotions. I might as well have slapped Luke judging by the look he gave me now.

"That's my child too," he scowled at me.

Oh. Right. I vomited everywhere, for the millionth time.

***

I spent the next few hours explaining myself to both Charlie and Luke. I told them about the library searches, and finally about Faust and Mr. Lore. When I mentioned Mr. Lore, I noticed the men exchange a quick glance at each other. Apparently, they had heard of him.

Rory had gotten fed up with the lack of attention paid him at that point and begged for PB&Js. We pulled our little table half out of the house again and ate at it like a family. I laughed so hard at that thought I choked on the sandwich. Two humans, just babies compared to the Nameless One at the head of the table and The Devil at the foot.

Luke did not like being called The Devil. I got a long and lengthy lecture on how The Devil and Satan are titles in Hell. Luke had broken free of his chains a millennia ago, and no longer held either title.

"I also am not the cause of everyone's problems and I DON'T MAKE ANYONE DO ANYTHING." Luke was a little red in the face. "I MAY plant seeds of thought into a person's head. Like seeing something from a different perspective, or a different way to go about doing something. But it's up to them to fertilize the seed and let it grow, or pluck out the thought. I never force anyone to do a damn thing!"

Charlie grinned. "Seeds, you say. Like the time you crossed America planting apple seeds?"

Luke balked and blushed. "So I was feeling a little spiteful at the moment. Humans tend to believe the forbidden fruit was an apple, so I thought I'd give my Father the finger by planting a shit ton of His 'Tree of Knowledge.'" Luke smirked. "It didn't quite go over like I thought it would. And, by the way, I was NOT the one to tempt Eve with the damn forbidden fruit. Even the Bible says it was a serpent. Why does everyone always blame me for that shit?"

"Of course it wasn't you," Charlie snickered, "one of my brothers took the serpent that day." His snickering grew to laughter. "We wondered what would happen if they ate of the fruit."

Luke stared slack-jawed at Charlie while he chortled.

"It was more amusing than we thought. You should have seen what happened when another brother took one of Odin's children for a spin."

Luke slammed his fists on the table; Rory jumped and let out a squeal of fright.

"Wook, you scare me! Don't wike it."

***

That night as I sang Rory to sleep, I wondered how much human life had been altered by the meddling of the curious Nameless Ones. I dreaded going to sleep. What horrors would haunt me tonight? Instead I dreamt of a beautiful garden and apples. The craving grew so strong, I woke from my slumber.

As I padded downstairs and into the kitchen, I overheard Luke and Charlie whispering at the door. Pressing myself against the wall, I inched closer to eavesdrop.

"Let me take them," Luke was whispering.

"No. There'll be a bigger chance someone else will see them. You could make it worse."

"And what happens when he finally finds out?"

"I haven't eaten anyone in a long time."

"Charlie, that could implicate— Moira?"

I swallowed hard and stepped out of the shadows. "Sorry. I couldn't help myself."

"What are you sneaking around the house for?" Luke crossed his arms.

"I'm hungry. I kept dreaming about apples."

Charlie laughed as Luke rolled his eyes.

"What are you guys talking about?"

They both went tight-lipped. Putting my hands on my hips, I raised an eyebrow at them. Still they remained silent. Charlie looked thoughtful for a moment and pursed his lips.

"John is looking for you."

"Charlie! I thought we agreed!" Luke tried to slap at Charlie, only to be met with a zap from the barrier. I felt faint and nauseous. No, no, no, no, no. He couldn't find us. He could take Rory away, he could have me arrested for kidnapping, he could notice I was pregnant. He could kill us both. I turned from the men and went upstairs. I would just move us again. I didn't know where, but I could just pack up and go—except I didn't have a car this time and taking a bus was too risky. Anything that I had to show for our identification was out. John would know the minute I bought a ticket. John was a cop, after all.

It's not that I thought all cops were bad. Most of them are amazing people, putting their lives on the line to keep complete strangers safe. No, the problem was: if I told anyone about what happened, or what I feared really happened with my mom, well, who would they believe? A teenage runaway that technically kidnapped her baby brother or a trusted and seasoned detective? Who knew what he had told people had really gone down. He may have beat me and raped me, but I didn't go quietly. As much as I'd love to have heard how he explained the scratch marks down his face, or the bite marks on his arm, I'd rather just not see him ever again.

"Moira!" Charlie called quietly up the stairs, "Moira, come down here." If I didn't go down, Charlie would just get louder and wake up Rory. So I acquiesced to his request.

"I've got to pack, Charlie, I don't have time to talk," I was feeling sick again. He walked with me back to the door Luke stood at.

"You aren't going anywhere," said Luke. "Charlie was right. The more people that see you, the higher the risk. I can't have him mistaking my child for his."

Of course that's what Luke was worried about. He promised he'd have some of his men run around the country dropping off false leads. I only hoped that would keep John busy until he just gave up.

***

Do you ever say to yourself, "it can't get any worse," and then instantly the universe starts laughing? It was probably two weeks later, just before Rory's third birthday, when I heard back from Faust. We'd played the most insane game of phone tag using the grocery store's phone when Ms. Judy thrust a prepaid phone in my hand.

"Sweetheart, for heaven's sake, use this phone. Besides, if me or Missy need to get a hold of you, it'll be a lot easier with a phone! Now, I paid the first month, you just got to pay the rest. I gave your friend the number, so she'll call it now." Her eyes drifted down to my belly, which was just starting to swell the tiniest bit.

"Ms. Judy, thank you so much. I'll pay you back for the phone, how much was it?"

"Don't you worry about it. Moira?" Her eyes stayed fixed to my stomach.

"Yes?"

"Oh never mind me. You bring Rory by my house again soon and have yourself some downtime."

The phone rang in my hand on my walk home.

"Hello?"

"Moira?"

"Faust?"

"We've got a problem."

8

"What sort of problem?" I asked Faust

"The book is disintegrating. It's just falling apart and turning to ash. A friend was able to read some, and Moira, it's even worse. According to what we were able to read before the book started vaporizing, the script is permanent." She was talking fast, and I could hear slight panic in her voice.

"What do you mean? Faust, I don't understand? The book... it was fine... I took it to the library and everything."

"I know. I am so sorry Moira. All we can figure is the script you said was all over the room, it must have been protecting the book too. I just... fuck, Moira... I am so sorry. I could bring it back, but I don't think I'd make it in time."

"It's permanent?"

"In order for the script to act as it has, the priest must have followed a ritual that was outlined in the book. It said something like it would last for an eternity."

"How..." I could feel my breath catching in my throat and the world started to spin. I sat down on the curb I had stopped at to answer the phone. Rory watched curiously. "How do I get Charlie out?"

"I don't know. I'm worried if we handle the book more, it'll be a pile of dust. Half the book is gone now, but we put it in a box to try to preserve the rest. I'm sorry Moira, I really am."

"It's not your fault, Faust. If you ever find a way to read the rest—"

"I'll call you."

With that we ended the call. My chest tightened and squeezed my lungs. The world was closing in on me.

"Moima sick?" Rory tugged my sleeve. I couldn't answer. My breathing hitched and I began to wail. Charlie was going to kill me. He'd be stuck in that house forever because I moved the book. Even if Faust was right and there was no way to remove the script, Charlie would never forgive me. I put my head between my knees and sobbed. Rory climbed from his wagon, hugged my arm, and patted my head.

My hysteria was beginning to calm a little when I heard a car pull up and the sound of a window roll down.

"Moira? Everything alright?" It was the giant man from the grocery, probably the same "bear of a man" that left the note with Mr. Lore's number on it in the first place. He pulled his lifted Jeep to the side of the road and climbed out. The body of the car rose a significant amount once it was free of the massive man it had contained. He sat beside us on the curb.

"What's wrong, child?"

I don't know why, but I told him everything. Every last dirty little detail—from the last night at John's all the way to the phone call with Faust—poured from my mouth as that giant of a man rubbed my back. When I was done spewing out my dark secrets, I finally raised my eyes to his face. His long dark hair was pulled back into a low ponytail, a few loose strands dangling in his face, brushing his snub nose. Dense stubble covered his awkwardly wide and square jawline. Ancient smile crinkles surrounded his almond-shaped eyes. He reminded me of a kindly, cuddly boar, though I imagined he'd be terrifying when angry.

He looked out at the empty lots across from us in a still, thoughtful manner. Taking a deep breath, he turned to me. "You are a good girl, Moira. Though your heart is heavy, it remains pure. You could have easily left your brother behind and disappeared. Instead, you chose to take him from a bad situation, even though you knew you would struggle more. You could have ended the life in your womb with a single word. Again, you choose the hard path and decided to save a life, nearly dying in the process. You befriended a fallen angel and a Nameless One with your kind heart and a peanut butter and jelly sandwich. You've been in my town a few short months, but already you are loved by all. Because of all this, I will help you. But you must promise to never lie to me again."

My eyes widened, and I stuttered out, "What lie?"

"The first time we met you told me the demon was gone from your house."

"The grocery store."

"Yes."

"How can you help me?"

A large smile and a faraway look crossed his face. "Before I tell you that, first I must tell you a story. One you must promise to never tell another soul. Or even those without souls."

"I promise."

"A long time ago, when my people first came to the new world, they brought with them their old gods. As it is with most things, with time the old ways were lost. So just as many of my people abandoned their gods, their gods abandoned them and went home, leaving my kind behind and forgotten. I am Otoroshi, but you may call me Mamoru. We were the guardians of the shrines. Our jobs were to keep the wicked and imprudent from our holy places. You see, the wicked have a certain smell which makes them easy to tell from the pure. Evil smells like chocolate. You laugh, but it's true. What is more tempting than chocolate?"

"What do the pure smell like?"

"Hmmmm. I'd have to liken it to lilac and incense. Now don't interrupt. After I was abandoned by my god, I wandered. I met a Nameless One, long before I knew of your Charlie. They smell of neither chocolate nor lilac. Their smell is different. It's like the smell of fresh snow on an early winter morning, just as the sun begins to rise. Your Charlie no longer smells like that. He has forgotten himself. Forgotten who he is because of his lust for fear. You must remind him of this. Nameless Ones are neither evil nor good; they are the only truly neutral beings I have ever met. Help Charlie overcome his addiction and I am sure he will walk free from that house."

I could only stare in awe at him. He squeezed my shoulder. "You and the little ones will be okay, sweet child. As for your stepfather," his voice came out in a growl, "I shall keep my eyes out for that wicked soul." He licked his lips greedily.

As he climbed back into his towering Jeep, he turned and looked at us. "Aren't you going to ask?"

I stared at him dumbly for a minute; there were a million things I wanted to ask but I was still trying to wrap my brain around what I had just learned.

He laughed. "You and Rory smell of moonlit lilacs and whiffs of my favorite incense. The tiny one you carry though, his scent is unique to him alone. It's the deep aroma of woodsy amber touched with ice. I look forward to meeting the tiny one."

***

I took Rory to Missy's house before I headed home. I offered her $100 to keep him for the rest of the week. She refused the money and willingly took in Rory. I made the excuse that there were some things I wanted to do at the house, like paint, but I didn't want Rory around the fumes.

I bought some paint on the way home because I felt guilty for lying. No one asked why my eyes were swollen and puffy or why my face was tear stained. It was a small mercy.

"I should have asked Mamoru for a ride," I grumbled to myself.

I arrived home to find Luke and Charlie proudly displaying a crib. Judging from the size of the old box shoved to the side, I'd say they had spent the few hours I was gone building it. It was beautiful and definitely an antique.

"Guys, it's beautiful!"

Luke picked up and examined the paint can. "Sage green, huh? Is this for the baby's room?" He narrowed his twinkling eyes at me. "Or is this some kind of dig at us because you don't want us near the baby?"

"What do you mean? And yes it'll be for the nursery." I fidgeted. It was going to be a lot harder to break the news to Charlie than I thought.

"Sage?"

"Oh, that. No, I just liked the color. Just because it's called sage doesn't mean it'll work like sage." I found myself getting annoyed. *Just say it, Moira! Spit it out! Like ripping off a Band-Aid.* That's when I made the second of two very critical mistakes. The first was that I hadn't been paying that much attention to Charlie while Luke teased me about the paint. He had been silently watching me the whole time. The second mistake I made was stepping a foot into that house. The second I was across the threshold Charlie pulled me to the middle of the room. It wasn't a pull like a normal person would do, it was more like one second I had just walked through the door and the next I was in the middle of the room squaring off with Charlie.

"What's wrong, Moira?" He had a hand on each shoulder, but there was no static.

"What's going on?" Luke called from the door.

Just rip it off, just like a Band-Aid. Like a Band-Aid, like a Band-Aid, likeaBand-Aid LIKE A BAND-AID. JUST SPIT IT OUT!

"THE BOOK IS GONE! I'm so sorry Charlie, but as soon as they started reading it, it turned to dust." His fingers dug into my shoulders, his eyes went black. "I didn't know. Andtheysaidthescriptispermanent. But it's okay! Charlie, I think I know what to do!" Charlie grew to twice his normal size. All claws and fangs, Charlie dripped with anger. The tips of his talons pierced the flesh of my shoulders; warm blood dripped and pooled under the cloth of my shirt.

"CHARLIE! LET HER GO!" cried Luke from the door.

He snatched his hands from my shoulders and backhanded me. I slid across the room while Charlie boiled with rage. Luke went feral at the door, wings out, smashing against the barrier. Blood dripped from my busted lip and I could feel my eye swelling.

"You stupid STUPID WRETCHED HUMAN!" Charlie towered over me.

Luke screamed threats and profanities from the door. Part of his wings charred from the force of trying to push himself through the barrier. "That's my child, Charlie. They belong to ME; if you hurt them—"

I raised my hand to Charlie. "You are a Nameless One! It's the human fear you feed on that keeps you here!" Charlie raised one clawed hand high into the air—this strike would rend my body. "Charlie! Charlie PLEASE! LISTEN TO ME!"

As his clawed wrath whistled through the air at me, there was a loud explosion and wood chips flew through the room. Luke screamed, "Fuck!" The world became encased in shadow. I looked up slowly. It really was a shadow.

The claws of the massive blue paw beside me dug into the wood floors, gouging out a grip. I followed the paw up. Crouched protectively above me was a massive beast. Coarse blue hair covered his body, long wild black hair hung from his head, huge tusks protruded from his snarling mouth. Charlie's dagger-sharp talons had pierced the beast deep in its shoulder.

The plumes of hot breath came from the beast's wide nostrils. One colossal paw was wrapped around Charlie's face, holding him steadily in place.

"Know thy self, Nameless One. Remember who you really are!" the deep voiced boomed from the beast above me.

"Mamoru?" I whimpered.

9

"Go back to your shrine, Guardian," growled Charlie through Mamoru's paw.

"My shrine?" he scoffed in response. "You are a fool, Nameless One. This house has been anointed with the blessings of the most powerful gods that ever walked this earth. I was made to protect holy places. What do you think this house has become?"

"The Nephilim weren't gods, beast." Luke glared from the door. "Put him down if you know what's good for you."

Mamoru's blood dripped down from the wound on his shoulder, splattering the floor beside me. Charlie yanked his claws out, ripping wider the gash.

Mamoru only chuckled. "Of course they were gods. They were gods the same way mothers are to their children. They could have ended humanity, but they chose instead to educate and nurture. They were the only gods with the blessed gift of mortality. They cherished their time and used it wisely." His massive head turned to Luke. "If your Father hadn't feared them so, and wiped them from the earth, imagine how humanity could have been." He released

Charlie's face and quickly grabbed his throat; Charlie struggled in his grip.

"If this is a holy place, where is your god?" Charlie's black, oppressive form thrashed futility.

"What are gods even? They are creators, supreme beings, a moral compass and a divine protector. Moira has life in her womb. She has only wished to protect—even at the risk of her own life, even for you. She offered you what little peace she had in exchange for the trauma you bequeathed. You have forgotten yourself. You were here before even time, and yet you've only wrought fear and destruction. She is more a god now, as a soft and frail human, than you are with all your omnipotence. Has she not been through enough? Release her from your chaos!"

Charlie went still and returned to his human form. His shame-filled eyes drifted down to me, still cowering under Mamoru's massive blue body. Slowly Mamoru let go of Charlie. "Will you be calm now?"

"Yes."

"Will you apologize?"

"Yes. Moira…" He looked at me with such sadness. I didn't hear the rest of whatever he said because pain became all I knew. The world went dark at the edges as agony gripped my belly. Hell was burning me from the inside out and trying to climb it's way forcefully from my uterus. I grabbed at the life and begged it to stay. I could hear shouting but it was muffled.

Someone scooped me up. "Moira …… 'kay …… breathe …… hospital." I could only guess they were taking me to the ER. I couldn't afford that kind of doctor visit, but before I could say anything, I succumbed to oblivion.

When I awoke, it was to the steady beeping of a heart monitor. Someone was holding my hand. It took my eyes a minute to adjust to the white of the hospital room.

"Moima? Wake up!" Rory chirped from somewhere nearby.

"Oh thank god! Moira, sweetheart, you gave us all a scare!" Ms. Judy stood at the foot of my bed; Rory struggled in her arms, reaching for me.

"Where's Mamoru?" I croaked, my throat burned with the fury of a thousand suns.

"Oh, don't worry about that old bear," Ms. Judy chuckled. "He got all stitched up and went back to your house to clean up. It's a good thing he was driving by when that dog got in!"

"Dog?"

The hand clasping mine shifted. Luke cleared his throat from the seat beside me. "Yeah, the feral dog that got in the house. The one that attacked you…" He lifted an eyebrow and gave me a knowing look.

"Oh. The dog." Why did my throat ache so?

A buxom nurse and gray-haired doctor sauntered into my room and fidgeted with the monitors and IV bags attached to my sore body.

"Try not to talk too much, young lady," the nurse chided. "You were screaming in your sleep for quite a while. I imagine your throat is raw." She poured a glass of water from the tan plastic pitcher nearby and handed it to me. "Drink up."

While I sucked down the icy water to soothe the burning desert that was currently ravaging my throat, the doctor pushed up his glasses and cleared his voice. He explained that while I had been dangerously close to losing my child from the amount of stress I had been placing on myself, we would both be fine. I breathed a great sigh of relief. I guess I finally had my answer. No matter how the child came to be, or who he grew into, I desperately loved the tiny life. I was to stay in the hospital for the rest of the night, to ensure that everything was back to normal, and could go home the next morning. He informed me I needed to improve my diet, lower my stress, and be on bed rest for the next month.

"A month?!" I gaped at him.

"Yes. A full month, then I want you back here and we'll decide if you need to continue bed rest or not."

He and the nurse both nodded and marched from the room. I felt hot tears well up in my eyes. "I don't have time for a month of bed rest. I have to take care of Rory, and I have to find a job. I can't afford however much the bill for all this will be…" As I began to hyperventilate, Luke scoffed next to me.

"A job?" He snorted. Ms. Judy gave him a disapproving glare as she set

Rory on my bed. Finally free, Rory threw himself into my arms and nuzzled up against me.

"I'll run out of money eventually. There is going to be another mouth to feed and I can barely afford to feed us—"

"You have no need for a job. Ask for anything, and it is yours. Do you really think I would let the mother of my child wither away and rot?"

"You have done enough, Luke; I can't ask for any more."

"You could start by furnishing that house of hers," Ms. Judy snidely told Luke. "There was nothing but a few chairs when we were all there for Halloween."

"Done." Luke nodded his head.

"You could get her a car so she's not walking everywhere. That probably didn't—"

"Ms. Judy! I don't need anything from him. I can get a job and take care of myself!"

"You will do no such thing," Luke said curtly. "You don't like accepting help, but you'd offer the shirt off your back if you saw someone in need. You won't get your way. Let someone take care of YOU for a change. It's really nothing." He shrugged. His arrogance pissed me off. I didn't need some fallen angel telling me what to do. We had been just fine before he came around. Hadn't we?

I thought to the first time we had met. How many times had he rescued me from Charlie? At the same time, it was his fault I was nearly smited. But that had also been my choice as well. It was so frustrating. Ms. Judy sat on the edge of my bed and stroked my hair.

"You can't just let a man knock you up and turn him away when he tries to take care of you, sweetheart." Bile rose in my throat as horrible flashes of That Night bubbled to the surface of my thoughts. If only it *had* been Luke…

***

I arrived home the next day to find my home a mess of intriguing workers.

Mamoru, with his arm bandaged and in a sling, was shouting orders at the strange creatures in my yard. Tiny little beings the size of toddlers, all wearing kabuki masks, ran here and there. Some carried items of furniture more than twice their size as though it weighed nothing. A large moving truck sat in the driveway, several human-looking men bringing boxes and furniture out and onto the lawn. One tiny being, adorned with a fox mask, spotted us and let out a shrill cry.

"She's back!" The tiny ones scattered and disappeared. Mamoru turned and smiled as he walked toward us. Luke helped me out of his SUV and began to unbuckle Rory from his car seat in the back.

"You're a little earlier than I expected; we're almost done too." I looked at him suspiciously. "Some of it's from Luke, some is from the town. Ms. Judy went out last night and did a small collection for you. It may be a small town, but we take care of our own."

Charlie was nowhere to be seen when we entered the house. I stopped and stared in disbelief. Tears flooded my eyes and I may have gotten a little choked up. Rugs on the floor, a couch and TV, and an overflowing toy box now accompanied my crimson chair. They had turned my house into a home. Each room was now furnished and the house felt warm and inviting for the first time. The fridge was filled to the brim with casseroles and lasagnas. Little cards wishing me well covered the countertops. Human kindness can truly overcome even the direst of circumstances.

Luke stayed by the truck talking to the men as they finished unloading a bed frame. I recognized one of the men as the raven-headed demon butler from Halloween. He waved and smiled.

"I have something special for you," said Mamoru while offering me a beautiful lacquered box. He smiled nervously as he lifted the lid. Carefully stacked inside were delicate papers, the width of a dollar, with kanji written down them.

"These are ofuda. They are to help you with Charlie. When he's at his worst, these will protect you and the little ones. I..." The large man blushed. "I made them myself."

"Thank you, Mamoru." I carefully hugged him, doing my best to avoid his injury. He laughed and gently squeezed me back.

After all the work was done, I pulled out several casseroles and was quickly made to go sit down.

"Mamoru, will you push the table half out the door?" He gave me a curious look.

"Luke and his men can't come inside the house. I wanted to thank them by feeding them. If we push the table out, we can all eat together. You too." He stared at me for a minute, threw his head back and let loose with a jovial laugh.

"You, my dear, never cease to amaze me. You do know we don't actually need to eat human food, right? I will accept nonetheless."

"What about the little ones?" I asked. "Won't they join us?" I heard soft excited giggles come from every corner of the room. One by one, the tiny beings appeared. Rory let out a shriek of delight and yelled, "Found you!" and grasped at one, who in turn stuck its tongue out and hid behind the couch. Round and round Rory chased him.

"Those are shrine spirits. Similar to myself. When I wandered the new world, after my god left me, I found many that were also abandoned. They wished to also help the kind mother of Griffin Drive."

A small voice beside me spoke up, "It is always those with so little that give the most. You have given much. We have been watching you, sweet Moira." Furry ears twitched behind the mask, and a foxlike tail thumped the floor behind it. "Until you are well, we shall help out around the house. It will be good to be of use again."

That night there was much laughter and merrymaking at the dinner table. Charlie remained absent.

***

The weeks went by in a blur. The doctor released me from bed rest and my small celestial helpers returned to their home in the forest with Mamoru.

Under his watchful eye, they had managed the house and exhausted a playful Rory. Charlie had yet to show his face, though I sometimes felt him in the dark corner of the living room.

The quiet house felt strange. Under Luke's insistence, Rory had been placed in preschool during the day, leaving me to myself for the first time in weeks.

"Charlie, come out please. Chaaaaaarlieeeee, come out, come out where ever you are!" I sang.

"No," came his melancholy voice from the direction of his favorite chair.

"There you are!" I waddled over to him, my swollen belly now obvious in its nature.

"Leave me be, Moira."

"We should talk. Show yourself."

He grumpily smoked into existence. His eyes were dark and lined with heavy purple bags. His hands gripped the arms of the chair as if he feared floating away. His face was sallow and puckered. Perspiration lined his knitted brow.

"Are you okay?"

"Do I look okay?" he snarked through gritted teeth.

"What's wrong?!"

"Do you have one of those talismans on you?"

"The ofuda? Yes." I held up the cream paper. He snarled and grimaced away from me. "Is it hurting you?"

"Not yet. Go upstairs, Moira." Eyes filled with malevolent need, his words came out in heavy pants. "GO! I can't control it anymore!"

As I ran from him, the house began to shake and groan. I slammed the door to the stairs and leaned against it. Loud crashes and banging went on on the other side of the door. He screamed in agony and the house swallowed his cries. He thrashed in pain somewhere down the hall; glass shattered and tinkled to the floor.

"MOI-RA give mee your feeeeeeear." Charlie's voice seeped up from the crack at the bottom of the door. The door sizzled as he bucked against it.

"Give it to me. Make the pain stop. Please Moira! It hurts so much," he begged.

I slowly opened the door and came face to face with the monster that was once Charlie. His eyes were black, bottomless pits accented by the bruise-like rings around them. His mouth was partially opened and his breath stank of sulfur. Long, too-sharp teeth jutted from his gums haphazardly like broken glass. Yellowish putrid saliva dripped from them, running up his face and splattering the floor. He turned his head 180 degrees so his face was righted while his body still hung suspended from the ceiling. I wet myself, although it could have had something to do with the growing child pressing against my bladder.

"You smell delightful. Give it to me! Give yourself to—"

I calmly placed the ofuda against his forehead. He screeched like a dying animal and flew back from me.

"Remember, Charlie! Remember who you are!" I yelled and slammed the door. I cried as I listened to him wail in pain and betrayal. Mamoru had told me it would be hard to not succumb to Charlie's withdrawals. It broke my heart to hear him sob. Maybe if I just gave him a little to help with the pain, so he wasn't going completely cold turkey.

Again, I creaked the door open.

"No! No Moira, go back! I've lasted this long. The temptation is too strong now that we are alone," he whimpered, his head in his hands, black tears leaking from between his fingers. I stayed in the stairway and sang softly to him. It helped Rory when he was sick or in pain, maybe it could help my supernatural addict.

***

Charlie was shivering, curled up in his chair, when Luke arrived with Rory. Little Rory ran to Charlie consumed with worry.

"Chawee sick? Moima! Chawee hurting!"

Time stopped for me then. I heard Luke scream for Rory to get back as I

675

pushed my ballooning body from the bottom step and tried to run to him. My legs felt like lead and jelly. I watched helplessly as Charlie's eyes widened and he reached for my brother, his clawed hand latching into Rory's downy curls.

Horror filled Charlie's blackened sockets. He couldn't help himself as he yanked Rory to him.

"No." Rory flicked Charlie's forehead with his chubby baby fingers. "Don't like it," he said calmly as he put both little hands on either side of Charlie's face. "Bad Chawee." I've never been so proud of my little brother as I watched as he head-butted Charlie in the nose.

Charlie burst out in a strange cacophony of laughter and hugged Rory to him. "Yes, my strange tiny friend, Chawee was bad. Thank you for waking me up."

Rory patted Charlie softly.

***

I was almost to my third trimester the day Charlie tentatively stood at the front door, his feet firmly and painlessly planted to the ground for the first time in centuries. He looked nervously to Luke, grinning outside. I had kept Rory home from preschool that day. Mamoru and the spirits waited with welcoming smiles in the yard.

"Like dis Chawee," Rory reached up and grabbed Charlie's hand and put one small foot over the threshold.

We all let out a collective breath after he stepped through safely. He took a deep breath of the fresh cold air of the perfect winter morning and turned to me slowly.

"Moira, I don't know how to thank you," he turned to those gathered there for him, "all of you." He turned back and pulled me through the door, held me close for a minute and then kissed my cheek. "I will never, for the rest of eternity, forget your kindness."

"Will you come visit?" I asked and the boy in my womb kicked at Charlie's hand. He looked at me and then at the house.

"I never want to see this fucking house ever again. But you can visit me." He smiled the first of what I hoped would be many carefree smiles.

In a flash of smoke and a rustle of wings, both Charlie and Luke disappeared from the porch. Mamoru and his rowdy family left a little while later. For the first time in just over six months, Rory and I found ourselves truly alone.

The next few days were filled with occasional bouts of tears from both myself and Rory. I had never figured I'd miss Charlie's sometimes overbearing presence. My new phone chirped frequently with messages from Luke of the two powerful men's adventures into the modern world. My favorite was the message from Charlie professing his newfound love of bubble tea.

One night, as I put Rory to bed in his very own big boy room, I heard the front door announce the arrival of a visitor with its loud creak.

"Hello? Mamoru?" I was met with a deafening silence.

I penguin-waddled down the hallway, hoping perhaps the wind had blown open the door. I was knocked to the floor by a painful blow to my jaw.

"Hello you little whore. Long time no see."

John had found us.

10

Every part of me screamed to run. Rory was in his room; if I ran to him we'd be trapped. If I escaped the house, that meant leaving Rory behind. That was something I refused to do. I attempted to get up, but received a boot to the chest. John's eyes widened when he saw my belly.

"You little fucking whore. How far along are you?" His boot pushed at me with every syllable. "That mine?"

I refused to look at him. How would I get out of this? Charlie and Luke were both gone. My phone sat on the little end table behind John. If I could just reach it.

"Answer me bitch!"

I slapped at his foot and the moment he became unbalanced I tried to lunge for my phone. He snatched it from the table and waved it in my face.

"This what you lookin' for?" he sneered. "Gonna call your boyfriends to come rescue you? Do you have any idea how long I had to wait to get you alone?" He threw it to the ground and smashed it with the heel of his scuffed work boot. "You and your cunt of a mother. She tried to leave me too you know. Your fucking uncle had her alllll worked up. Sayin' I was dangerous and shit." He ran his fingers over his buzz cut and paced the room. "You ruined my life."

The soft sound of padded feet pitter-pattered close by. A small hand touched my shoulder. "Mistress," a gentle voice whispered in my ear, "I shall send the others for Mamoru. You are not alone."

"No," I hissed quietly under my breath, keeping an eye on John as he became a little more frantic in his pacing. "Get Rory out of here. Hide him."

John spun around and angrily pointed at me. His rage was palpable. "I did my job and reported you for kidnapping my son." He paused and looked around for a minute. "Of course I wasn't allowed on the case. Everything was going well, then they found your goddamn diary. You fuckin bitch, what did you write?!" Spittle flew from his fury-filled words. "They opened up an investigation into your cunt mother's death. It was easy enough to drug her and get her in the bathtub; I don't even remember her scratching me while I cut open her wrists. They found my skin under her nails. They wanted to charge ME with MURDER." He was rambling now, punctuating every other word with a death glare.

"I shall not leave you, Mistress." I felt warmth from the tiny body. More tiny paws scuffled down the hallway and into Rory's room; the door shut quickly and quietly while my little guardian squeezed my shoulder in comfort.

The door didn't shut quietly enough. John's head whipped around to look down the hallway. He gave me one more suspicious glare and began to stomp in the direction of Rory. I moved quickly for a skinny eighteen-year-old with a six-plus-month swell. My child was going to be a big one, if the size of his current room was any indication. I beat John to the door and did my best to block his entry. He pulled his fist back and slammed it into my womb.

"This world doesn't need another stupid bitch whore anyways," he growled. I crumpled to the floor as he pulled his foot back and swung it toward my face.

CRACK! My little guardian became visible. She had caught John's boot to her mask. It cracked in half and shattered to the floor. Her fox tail fluffed, hackles raised along her neck.

"You shall hurt my mistress no more!" Blue flames appeared above the little white paws.

"WHAT THE FUCK IS THAT?" John pulled a gun from his waistband and aimed it at her as the door behind us swung open. Rory stood there. Click. John pulled back the slide. The spirits in the room, who had been opening the bedroom window, turned in unison and ran toward Rory.

"KIT!" he yelled and barreled toward her, eyes full of fear.

Several things happened at once. The little fox spun and threw her flames toward Rory, the blue light encapsulated him and he slammed into the wall, out of harm's way. As she spun, her body crackled and grew. Her soft fluffy tail split into nine and her gentle features turned feral. She let out a roar and charged at John. The gun went off with a deafening boom and the house shook with the terrifying screams sounding outside the windows. Rory fell limply into my lap, unconscious.

Kit, the sweet fox spirit, caught the bullet between her eyes and crashed to the floor, taking John down with her.

"NO!" a chorus of voices cried.

"GO! Get Mamoru!" I shouted.

All hell broke loose outside the house. The floor vibrated with the violence of the beings trying to get in; the house groaned in pain.

Rory was still breathing. He had a goose egg forming on his head, but he was alive. Kit didn't move as John roughly shoved her off of him. He was on me in seconds. His harsh fingers tangled in my hair and he pulled me down the hallway. The more I struggled, the harder he yanked. Some of my hair was ripped from my scalp as I clawed at his hands.

As we passed into the living room, I caught a glimpse of a flock of ravens pummeling the house with their black bodies. They cawed and screamed in effort. Kit's body glowed softly with her blue flame. Little blue embers floated up from her prone form and flickered out of existence.

"Do you know how hard it is to crack a steering rack so it looks natural?" John leaned down and spat in my face. I swung at him as hard as I could but he blocked it and slapped me in return. He pulled my head back roughly with my hair. "Or how hard it is to puncture a brake line? I knew your stupid uncle would come running if I told him you were hurt. I knew he'd speed through the curvy mountain roads."

"What?" No, it wasn't possible.

"He had it coming." He grabbed my mouth with his calloused hand. "He tried to get your mother to leave me."

Tears streamed down my face. Suddenly, John was thrown off of me by another small spirit. This one wore a bunny mask. A third tended to Rory as it sobbed over Kit. The bunny pounced John and slapped an ofuda to his face. Nothing happened. The brave spirit gripped John's collar firmly and punched at him with the talisman as John flailed. The masked face turned toward me, black eyes filled with fear.

"It's not working!"

"That monster," I pushed myself to my feet, "is human."

John threw the bunny off of him and charged at me again. He hadn't noticed yet, but the gun was between us. The house shuddered with the efforts of my raven-headed friend outside. I planted my feet and lowered my shoulder, John's abdomen collided into me. Wrapping my arms around his waist and locking my wrists together, I thrust upward and back. We crashed to the floor, John's face slamming into the hardwood. He rolled over and kicked my belly, the child inside danced to the side, painfully squishing my kidney. He rose and sat on my chest and ravaged my face with his fists.

"CHARWEE!" screamed Rory so loud it drowned out the cacophony of noises outside. The front door splintered into oblivion as Mamoru crashed through, blue body seething in rage. Kit growled above us, bloody foam dripping off her snarling muzzle. The world went black and I was surrounded in warmth.

"My sweet Moira," said a soft, nearly forgotten voice. Strong and gentle, golden glowing arms scooped me up and held me close. John screamed somewhere in the dark. "I'm sorry I left you all alone. I thought your mother was stronger." The ghostly apparition of my beloved Uncle Roar carried me through the house, past the violently swirling lights surrounding John. Everything moved slowly. Mamoru was suspended in the air, mid-pounce, tusked mouth opened wide, snapping at John. Charlie was a whirl of furious galaxies wrapped tightly around John, pinning his arms to his side. Uncle Roar sidestepped the overturned couch and pulverized door and took me out into the night outside the house.

"I promised him I'd get him out." Uncle Roar pushed my blood-soaked hair from my face. Luke was in full fallen angel form, singed wings spread wide, casting bright light throughout the dark night. Ravens flew above him, battering the eaves of the house. Shrine spirits peppered the yard, hands stretched out toward the house, raw power flowing from them.

"Thank you, little Moe, for keeping my promise." Uncle Roar set me down, kissed my forehead and smiled as he disappeared in a burst of sparkling light. The world caught up to me as Bunny crashed through a window, Rory riding his back. The house screamed under the barrage.

Charlie's baritone boomed from the quivering house, "You would dare harm the friend of both the Heavens and Hell?!" He cackled demonically. "Let me show you true fear."

John's screams pierced through the chaos as blue flashing lights and sirens flew up Griffin Drive.

***

The Gray House of Griffin Drive had fallen and crumbled to dust in the aftermath of the war that had taken place inside. The police were able to dig John out of the rubble and promptly sent him to a prison psych ward. He kept screaming about monsters and demons pulling his limbs off and beating him with them.

Clearly, he's insane.

Luke and Charlie built a huge white house with a sage green roof at the end of the road. It has plenty of room for guests. It's also free of Nephilim script.

I asked Charlie how he had known we were in trouble. He looked at me in surprise.

"Rory summoned me."

Turns out, if you know the true name of a Nameless One, the name they keep secreted away in their heart of hearts, they can be summoned. Charlie had never had a name before Rory gave him one. He said he wanted to be the being little Rory thought he was. And so, he became Charlie, the Watcher of Griffin Drive. Protector and best friend to a small and feisty human boy.

I was put on bed rest for the remainder of my pregnancy. My face healed quickly with a single touch from Charlie's gentle hand.

We asked the police about the charges of kidnapping against me and the warrant for my arrest.

"Eh? As far as we see it, you ran away with your little brother in fear for your lives. Then some shit happened." He shrugged. "Far as I know, Moira Shepherd and Roarke 'Rory' Kincade are still in the wind." He winked. "If you ever see 'em, let us know. We probably ought to give her some kinda award for ridding the department of a bad egg."

***

A few quick months later, I gave birth to a beautiful baby boy with hair the color of sunshine, my nose and mouth, and beautiful jet-black eyes that you could see the endless expanse of the universe in.

Luke charged out of my delivery room screaming, "CHARRRRLIE! WHAT THE FUCK?!"

My sweet son is something this world has never seen.

Do Not Add Bryan B. Westbay on Facebook

By Thaddeus James, Reddit User /u/*hartijay*

Annual Runner Up—Best Original Monster, 2016

For the past year now I have been dedicating my free time to researching something incredibly strange and incredibly interesting. It's a topic that I was desperate to find information about, but I may have gone too far in my search for answers. I am here to warn you not to do the same.

Some of you might already know the "legend" of Bryan B. Westbay, a Facebook account that is reported by many to have unusual properties. Sometimes the Westbay account will friend request other users on a whim, but most of the time it remains quiet. Those who have added the account as a friend have told stories about strange messages they've received from the account. Everyone gets weirdos added on Facebook from time to time, but this is something different.

Bryan Westbay is not a person. I don't know EXACTLY what "he" is, but it's nothing human. I have added him, I have spoken to him, and he has spoken back. He never told me what he is, and I'm not entirely sure HE knows what he is. All I can do is assume one little theory is correct.

I believe—as do many others—that Bryan Westbay is a sentient Facebook account.

There are stories about how the Westbay account came to be, but two are the most popular in circles who talk about this sort of freaky shit. The first is that it was created by some sort of shady branch of the government to be used for surveillance—a sort of social-media-grounded AI that was built with the desire to make as many friends as possible and to keep tabs on all of the people that added it. Something went haywire, a fuck-up in the system, and it failed to provide any results so it was subsequently abandoned, left to exist alone in cyberspace forever.

The second story is a spookier one. It tells that Westbay was once a regular guy, just like you and me, but was completely obsessed with social media. Constantly using it, constantly posting on it, from the moment he woke up to the moment he went to sleep.

One night, drunk as a skunk, he takes an embarrassing video of himself and posts it onto Facebook—it goes viral, and he becomes humiliated. SO humiliated that he unfriends everyone, deletes his account, and eventually commits suicide by jumping off his apartment building's roof—**SPLAT**. As the story goes, the account is now Westbay's "ghostly remains," the only "part" of him that wasn't turned into a sidewalk mess.

Those are the two most popular explanations. A rather rational one (considering the circumstances), and a supernatural one. What do *I* think? I think it falls somewhere between both. I don't know if I believe in ghosts, but I *really* think that if there *are* ghosts, they wouldn't operate Facebook pages.

But there is something unnatural about the page that defies explanation, and it can affect you in a terrible way. I'll get to that in just a moment.

After quite a bit of research surrounding Westbay, I decided to take a crack at adding and private messaging him. His profile, for the most part, was blank—no profile picture, no cover photos, no statuses. My request was accepted after a few minutes, and my message was replied to. It was mostly nonsensical gibberish, but one sentence was completely coherent:

"i am happy to be your friend"

Everything I wrote after was replied to with one repeating sentence:

"we are friends"

No other response besides that. I tried saying a vast number of things to him but only one solicited a different response (something I had said slightly out of frustration):

"Can we speak?"

Suddenly, an audio file was sent to my Facebook inbox. It was rather disturbing—quite a lot of noise and unintelligible whispering. Then, at right about the end of the sound clip, something spoke:

"Hello, friend."

This honestly frightened me terribly. I don't know what came over me, but I suddenly felt the need to be very firm and hostile:

"We aren't friends."

Westbay sent back a few "frowny" emoticons and went silent. Not long after, his profile picture suddenly changed into a photo of a dark, distorted, grimacing face. I looked at it for a brief moment, but felt sort of… drawn to it. It was hypnotic. I started to get a little freaked out so I closed our conversation, unfriended him, and shut my computer down.

That night, when I turned out the lights in my bedroom to go to sleep, I saw Westbay's face. Not on my computer, but staring at me in the darkness. It was out of the corner of my eye and only for a split second, but I was sure it was there. *He* was there.

Days went by and I would see Westbay out of the corner of my eye almost everywhere I'd go, especially at night and in darker places. As time went on, I saw him more. I initially talked to him over a month ago, and there hasn't been a day that I haven't seen him. Sometimes he'll be there when I wake up in the middle of the night, inches away from my face, grimacing down at me.

Like I told you all before, I don't know if I believe in ghosts. But *something* is following me because of that Facebook account, and while I'm not sure what it is, I know that it's very insecure and jealous. It craves friendship. I've been too afraid to go out and see any of my own friends, simply because it's entirely possible this thing might latch onto them.

At times, I want to throw myself off a roof just to get rid of him.

Bryan Westbay is ruining my life. And I can't blame anyone for it but myself and my stupid curiosity.

So, I'm here to do you all a favor. In this sentence is a link to Westbay's

Facebook account. Right-click it, "inspect" it, copy the URL and put it in anything that can keep your browser from going onto it.

If there are any of you who are dumb enough to go onto that page to get a look at this thing, I have to ask you to reconsider. At the very least, do not spend too much time staring at the profile picture.

Because, whether you like it or not, Bryan B. Westbay wants to be your "friend."

And, so far, it's looking like he's a friend you can't get rid of.

I Had a Friend Who Lived in the Air Vents

By M.J. Pack, Reddit User /u/_mjpack_

Annual Runner Up—Best Original Monster, 2016

———————

When you're a little kid, you do some strange stuff to get attention. Especially when you're an only child and then _poof_, you're not; you're getting the "little brother or sister" pep talk from Mom and Dad and everything changes. You're used to being the center of their world, being told you're the most special little girl, but as Mom's belly gets bigger and bigger and Dad's patience with you gets smaller and smaller you realize it's not going to go back the way it was. Not ever.

That's what happened to _me_ when I was seven, anyway. I was the kind of kid that needs a lot of attention. I hadn't had to try hard for seven years; I'd been coasting on my parents' single-minded doting. But pretty soon I noticed some small differences; they were less interested in what I'd done in school that day, more interested in getting ready for my new little brother or sister.

I was like an alcoholic without a bottle. You feel fine at first but soon the tremors set in and you realize you just _need_ it, you know? You _need_ their eyes on you, loving you, reminding you that you're the most special little girl in the whole wide world, maybe the _only_ special little girl.

So in the last month or so before the baby came, I got creative.

"I made a new friend!" I told them one night at dinner.

"At school, sweetheart?" Mom asked.

"No!" I was fidgety, excited, twitching in my seat when they both looked at me with rapt attention from across the table. Time to launch my plan into action. "He lives in the air vents! His name is Marty and he's MAGIC."

"Oh," said my Dad, and he smiled a little. "That's fun. Eat your peas, Rosie."

And that was it. That was IT! I'd just told them that Magic Marty lived in our air vents and all I got was 'that's fun?' And what's worse, they went back to talking about the BABY—I always heard that word with an ominous sort of importance—and whether they thought the nursery could be painted over the weekend or not.

I stewed and pushed peas around my plate. I knew I was going to think of something better. Something to make them ask me questions about Marty, about me, like they used to.

Stupid BABY. I didn't care if it was a brother or a sister. It was a pain before it even got here.

Over time, I came up with new tidbits about Magic Marty and how amazing he was. He only ate jelly beans! He could move things with his mind! He had a cat named Baseball and he was my VERY best friend!

Mom and Dad didn't care all that much. I mean sure, they smiled and nodded and gave me the barest hint of recognition. They had their minds on other things.

I upped the ante and started talking to the air vents in rooms all over the house, loud enough so that my parents could hear me in the den.

"Marty!" I'd cry excitedly. "You moved my coloring book when I was at school! Did you do that with your mind?!"

"Marty!" I'd shout with glee. "I wish I could eat jelly beans for dinner!"

"Marty!" I'd exclaim. "Have you let Baseball out? Kitty cats need exercise!"

Nothing. The dumb old BABY got everything. I started wondering if I was really so special after all.

After one particularly hard day when I'd brought home a gold-star paper and Mom left it on the counter—didn't even bother to put it up on the fridge with one of my favorite fruit-shaped magnets—I crawled under my bed. I'd hidden under there before during games of hide and seek with my best friend Britney and that day I didn't even want attention anymore, I just wanted to hide away from the world and think about how things used to be.

I lay there glumly on my stomach with the dust bunnies, chin on my hands, trying to decide whether or not I had it in me to even cry when I noticed it: the air vent.

A slotted metal rectangle set in the carpet hidden by my bed. Mom sometimes yelled at Dad for rearranging the furniture—he covered the vents up and then they had an argument about whether the air conditioning could even cool the room properly with some huge couch covering it. I guess she'd never noticed the vent under my bed because there'd never been a fight about that one.

I don't know why, but I started talking to it. For real.

Up until then, it had all been stories and playing for show but that day I decided if I wasn't going to be the most special little girl anymore I may as well have a friend, even if he was a made-up one.

I told Magic Marty I thought Baseball was a very good name for a cat. I said moving stuff with his mind must be hard but it was a neat trick to have. I confessed that it was really cool he only ate jelly beans. I liked the red ones best. Which color was his favorite?

And the air vent said, "The pink ones."

A pause, and then: "They taste like cotton candy."

I stared at the vent. I had a hell of an imagination, sure, but even at seven I knew that voices weren't *really* supposed to come out of the air vents.

"Oh," I said, lifting my chin from my hands. I didn't really know what to say, you know?

"You're a very nice little girl, Rosie." The voice was a man's voice, pleasant and lilting, almost like a song. It was, if I'm being honest, exactly as I thought Magic Marty *should* sound. "You're a very nice little girl for talking to me, telling such wonderful stories about my life to your parents. You're a very *special* little girl."

"Wow, thanks," I said, surprised. It felt like the first nice thing someone had said to me in a long time. And I mean, if someone as great as Magic Marty thought *I* was special—maybe it was true!

Wait.

"But I made you up, Marty."

There was a long pause, then in a tone that almost held a chuckle in it, "Are you sure, Rosie?"

Suddenly, no. I wasn't sure at all.

"Rosie, my special little girl, how could you make up all of my magical adventures? You're special, yes, but you're not *magic!*" Now Marty did laugh, a wonderful musical sound that made me giggle a little too. "How could you make up good ol' Baseball here?"

A pleasant meow floated through the metal slots of the air vent.

Marty had a point. I mean, all those crazy things that he could do, and a cat—a real life cat that meowed and everything!—I couldn't have made it up, not on my own. It only made sense that I'd been talking to him all this time for *real* and just been so distracted by—

The BABY.

"Magic Marty," I said, lying back down again. "I don't want a little brother or sister. I miss when Mom and Dad liked just me."

Baseball meowed again, and this time it sounded sad.

"Of course you don't!" Magic Marty said sympathetically. "Of course not. What good are babies anyway? Garbage. Noisy little stinkers. They can't even do a cartwheel!" He let this sink in before prodding slyly, "I bet *you* can do a cartwheel."

"I can! I can!" I cried out, eager to scramble out from under the bed to show him, but he shushed me right away.

"Quiet now, Rosie. If your parents find out we're friends, well, they may not like that I live in the air vents so much. They may decide to make me *go.*"

The idea struck me with such cold horror that I scooched even closer to the vent, nearly pressing my face against its smooth metal.

"No, Marty, no!" I'd only just found my new friend, how could my parents make him go so soon?! "They're going to have their stupid baby, why can't I have *you* for my friend?" There was a small, hard lump in my throat that I couldn't swallow down for some reason; I was on the verge of tears.

"Don't cry, Rosie," said Magic Marty in a voice as sweet and smooth as honey. "I will think of something."

***

For the next month, Marty and I talked about everything. Every day after school I would crawl under my bed, push my face close to the air vent, and tell him all about my day. I told him when Arthur traded me his plastic snake for my slide whistle, I told him how we only needed three more gold stars to get a class pizza party, I told him that Marissa S. was the best hop-scotch player I'd ever seen. Marty oohed and ahhed and asked questions, asked for more. He also asked when he thought I'd be getting a new brother or sister. I told him I didn't know.

One day I came home and Teresa, my teenage neighbor one house over, was sitting on the couch instead of my heavily pregnant mother.

"Hey, Rosie girl," she said as I walked in and dropped my backpack. "Your mom and dad are at the hospital! You're going to have a new little brother or sister soon!"

"Neat," I said, but I didn't think it was neat at all. "I'm going to my room."

Under my bed, I moped and played with my plastic snake. When you held it by its tail, the segmented pieces slithered back and forth like a real snake. My plastic snake was neat—the baby was garbage, like Marty said.

"It's coming, isn't it, Rosie?" Magic Marty's voice asked me from the vent.

"Yeah." I wiggled the snake back and forth, back and forth. "Maybe tomorrow, or a few days, I don't know. I don't care."

"Do you think it will be bad when it gets here?" For the first time there was something else in Marty's voice—not laughter, not honey. Something… else. "Do you think it will be very bad? For you, Rosie? Do you think your parents will even look at you ever again once that stinky little thing is here? Do you think it will be *even worse?*"

I hadn't even considered it. I knew the new normal, sure, but it never crossed my mind that things could get *worse*. Baseball let out a plaintive mewl.

"What do you think, Marty?" I asked, worried.

"I think," he said after a very long moment, "that I promised you I would think of something, and I am so very pleased to tell you that I *have*."

A glimmer of hope. I glanced left, making sure Teresa couldn't hear us, then looked back at the vent.

"Really? You can fix everything? You can make it so the baby doesn't ruin it?"

"Oh, Rosie girl." Marty let the words draw out like stretching a wad of chewing gum. "I'm *magic*. I can do *anything*."

Magic Marty told me to wait. He told me he would fix everything.

He was my friend, so I believed him.

***

Mom, Dad, and stupid baby Sophie came home a few days later. She was a pink bundle of squished-up skin and soft little tufts of hair.

I had to admit, she was sort of pretty. And it was kind of neat how small she was. I didn't like how she sounded when she cried, though, and that first night she was screaming *loud*. So loud I got under my bed and put a pillow over my head, hoping that if I couldn't block out her cries long enough to sleep that maybe Marty would be around and we could talk about his secret plan.

"Marty?" I whispered, but no one answered.

"Baseball?" I tried instead. Nothing.

After a while, the muffled sounds of Sophie's shrieks finally stopped and I fell asleep under the bed, hoping that Mom and Dad hadn't found out about Marty before he could fix everything.

When I woke up, my room was full of light but dark at the same time. Strobes of red and blue streaked the walls like fireworks on the Fourth of July. I was waking up because someone was pulling at me, trying to get me out from under the bed.

For half of a sleepy second I was sure it was Marty—he was pulling me out because he didn't have to live in the vents anymore! He'd talked to Mom and Dad and they'd decided he could live *with* us in the house—but then I saw a police officer with a serious stern face and I knew something was wrong.

Police officers were only around when there was something bad. They were around when people needed to be saved.

Did I need to be saved?

Turns out I did. A neighbor, Teresa's mom I think, had heard screaming and called the police but it was too late.

My parents were found in their bed, shredded into bloody meat. Stab wounds, a lot of them, the autopsy reports said. More than likely a robbery gone wrong. Or, more accurately, an abduction gone wrong.

Because little three-day-old Sophie was gone, her brand new crib empty.

The police told me I was lucky. Whatever monster had hurt my family probably hadn't found me because I'd been "hiding" under the bed.

Pretty lucky, right?

***

I made it out okay. I stayed with relatives, in foster homes, got lots of therapy. I was treated all right. None of the horror stories most unfortunate orphans have to survive.

In therapy I realized that I had made up Magic Marty as a coping mechanism. He'd become more real to me than my parents had because I so desperately needed to think that someone found me special. I'd never really heard anything and my coping mechanism, as it turns out, probably saved my life.

Against the odds I grew up well-adjusted (well, well-adjusted *enough*). Did all those things you're supposed to do—graduate high school, meet a guy, get married. And, eight months ago, got pregnant.

I've been so excited. So long without a real family of my own, and now all that was going to change.

But yesterday I was setting up my daughter's nursery and I dropped one of her little blankets on the ground. My husband wasn't home so after a few clumsy attempts, I managed to get down to a knee and pick it up.

It was covering an air vent.

I felt a cold chill slither through me for no reason at all but I told myself the same old mantra—Magic Marty wasn't real. Magic Marty was a coping mechanism. Magic Marty was something I made up.

And then, a voice as syrupy sweet as dripping honey said:

"It's coming, isn't it, Rosie?"

It was like all the strength had gone out of my legs. I wobbled backward and landed on my ass.

Not real. I made him up.

"Is it a little girl, Rosie?" Magic Marty said, because there was no one else that voice belonged to, no one else it *could* belong to. "I hope it is. Oh, I *so* hope it's a little girl. Do you know why, Rosie girl?"

"You're not real," I said, but I didn't believe it, and I suddenly realized I'd never believed it.

"Because I *fixed it.*" He started laughing then, and somewhere in the laughter I thought I could hear the yowl of a feral cat. "I *fixed it* just like you asked and *you don't even know the best part.*"

I'd just wanted to feel special.

"The best part," Magic Marty chuckled, "was how she tasted."

The last thing I heard before I scrambled to my feet and fled screaming from the house was this:

"The pink ones taste like cotton candy."

Best Title
—2016—

My Sister Was Murdered and She Won't Shut Up About It

By E.Z. Morgan, Reddit User /u/*EZmisery*

Annual Winner—Best Title, 2016

As kids, my sister Cassie and I didn't know we were different. How could we? We spent all of our time in the house. Our parents never let us play outside. They said this was for our own protection. I remember clearly our father outlining all of the horrors of the world beyond our front door. "Vicious animals, dangerous men, deathly illnesses." Every day brought a new reason why we couldn't venture outside the walls of the house. I realized the truth much later: they were embarrassed of us.

Cassie and I were close, literally and metaphorically. We spent every moment together. I've read that twins are often this way, but we were more than that. We woke up at the same time, closed our eyes for bed at the same time. We would often dream the exact same dream. We read books together (she'd read the left page, I'd read the right). Our parents said we were unnaturally close. This didn't make sense to us at the time.

When we played we would stick two toys together at the head, gummy see-through tape obscuring their faces. We would walk the one-headed doll in staccato movements—Cassie moving the left leg, me moving the right. Soon all of our toys were paired up. The stuffed pig was taped to the alligator. The china doll was matched up with the plastic dinosaur. Cassie and I even went so far as to glue our pillows together. "So they'd never be lonely," I told our outraged mother.

Despite our bond, Cassie and I were very different. I was perfectly fine obeying all of our parent's rules, although they were plentiful. Cassie, on the other hand, hated the rules. Even the small ones like brushing our teeth at night would send her into a fit. I liked the dresses Mother would make for me, but Cassie ripped at them with her teeth. Cassie was also non-verbal. It wasn't her fault. She just couldn't get her mouth to move the way the rest of ours did. This didn't mean we couldn't communicate. In fact, Cassie and I spoke constantly. Always in our mind.

Yuck I hate bananas, she'd tell me in the morning as our mother served us breakfast.

Shut up, Cassie. I turned and smiled at Mother. "Thanks for breakfast!"

Cassie growled under her breath. *You're such a suck up. We're prisoners here and you treat them like angels.*

They're our parents! Mother could see we were arguing in our head. She never commented on it though. I don't think she wanted to know what was going on between us.

When we were younger, I noticed that Cassie and I didn't look like the kids in the picture books. These kids were alone. But Cassie and I were always together. I asked father about it and he told us we had a condition. "You're sick," he said sternly. "But the doctors can't separate you. It would kill her."

He would like me to die, Cassie whispered in our head.

Of course he wouldn't! He loves you!

But he didn't. I knew this secretly. Our parents didn't do much to hide the fact that they favored me. They viewed Cassie as dead weight. And as we got older, I have to admit that I started to understand their opinion. She was difficult. She was always upset over something. Plus she was the reason I wasn't allowed outside or able to have any friends.

Around the age of twelve our parents started letting us use the computer. It was only supposed to be for our studies, but when were alone we tried to google ourselves. "Twins who share a brain." The first article was about twins who eat each other in the womb. This clearly wasn't relevant. The second was about Siamese twins. We skipped this one because we were from America. Then we got to the third one, which had a picture—two grown women who shared a head. One woman was large and the other was small. It looked a little like Cassie and me. The article called them "conjoined twins." It said that although the women wished they could be separated, the doctors ruled that it was too dangerous.

That's us, I said to Cassie.

Why would anyone want to be separated? she responded.

Maybe so they could look like normal people.

I would much rather be with you than be normal.

I paused before saying, *Me too, Cassie.*

But that was all before Cassie was killed.

She died of suffocation. We were fourteen. I knew the second she stopped breathing. I could feel a shiver in my entire body as if something was crawling down my nerves. I started screaming. I didn't intend to, but the reaction was involuntary. Maybe it was Cassie screaming through me. My mother appeared in our bedroom as if she had already been inside. My father was close behind.

They rushed us—me—to the hospital. It was the first time I felt night air on my face. Any fear about being outside evaporated. It was freedom. I saw men and women of all different races. They crowded around me, staring at me like a wild animal. I didn't care. It was bliss. I even forgot about the corpse of my sister hanging off of me.

No one tried to resuscitate Cassie. Even though I knew she was dead, there was not a single attempt to save her life. The only thing the doctors did was prep me for surgery. Mother and Father stroked my hair. They told me they loved me. That soon this would all be over. That the doctors would remove the tumor.

The tumor that was my dead sister.

I woke up some time later with the oddest sensation of weightlessness. My eyes were barely open but I could see my parents asleep on a nearby couch. I was hooked up to a number of machines. I looked over and realized I was alone. The normal feeling of Cassie's body next to mine was gone. I was in a twin-sized bed. Logically I knew what had happened. Cassie died, and so they removed her from me. But the shock of the lack of her made my heart race. This thing I had secretly wanted, quietly yearned for, was terrifying.

I lay back and moved my head around. It was so strange to be able to move freely. There was no extra body to hinder me. Fleetingly I wondered where her corpse was. Was it lonely? Was I lonely? I lifted my hand hesitantly and felt the flesh that had once connected me to Cassie. In its place was a large scar and raised stitches. All that was left of my sister was empty air.

It didn't feel real. I had only been conscious a few minutes and already panic was setting in. This was a mistake. What happened to Cassie? Where was she? I needed her. Desperately, I whispered, "Cassie? Are you there?"

A minute ticked by. Silence.

Then a massive wave of screams filled my brain. It was Cassie's voice, igniting my mind with a thousand horrified shrieks. My eyes stuck wide open. Cassie's voice began to speak through the screaming: *They killed me! They killed me! They killed me!*

"Shut up!" I yelled. My parents rose from sleep. I realized I had said this out loud. They came to me, trying to soothe my fears. But all the while Cassie was tormenting me. *They murdered me!*

I tried not responding to the voice. But it didn't matter. Cassie didn't care if I spoke back. For days she just kept lamenting her death. As the doctors tried to teach me how to stand and walk without Cassie, she made herself known in my head. I pretended to be fine but the voice tore through my sanity. I couldn't sleep. Every time I closed my eyes she'd start up again. *It was them. Our filthy parents. They put a pillow over my mouth and killed me.*

I didn't tell anyone about the voice. Who would understand? Soon I was cleared to go home by the doctors. My parents made arrangements for me to start attending school. They bought me a wig to cover up the disfiguring scar. The doors were all unlocked now. There was no more hiding. It should have felt like heaven, but instead the voice of my sister haunted my mind. *Dead. I'm dead. They killed me.*

Months passed with the same agonizing existence. I lost weight. I barely slept. Nothing could bring me any happiness. Cassie was slowly driving me insane. I didn't know if this was my imagination or if Cassie was really alive somewhere in my brain, but one day I'd had enough. I couldn't do it any longer.

They killed me. Our parents murdered me, Cassie was sobbing against my eardrums.

I took a deep breath and said, "Cassie, you have to stop." I put a hand over my mouth in surprise. I hadn't spoken in my brain. Only out loud. I tried again. "Stop it, Cassie." Desperately I shoved my fist in my mouth to stop myself from talking. But nothing came out. The ability to speak through my mind had died with my sister.

I crawled into a corner of the bedroom, arms over my head. I started to sob. Waves of horror and sorrow careened across my body. Cassie just kept screaming and screaming. *Our parents are filthy monsters. They murdered me so they could have a normal daughter. They smothered me with a pillow. They*—

"THEY DIDN'T KILL YOU, I DID!" I shrieked. Cassie's voice suddenly stopped. My tears kept coming. In a whisper, I continued, "I couldn't live like that anymore. I wanted to be normal." I could still feel the weight of the pillow as I shoved it onto Cassie's face. I remembered the moans for help. I could still feel her clawing at my arms.

Then something changed. I felt woozy and looked down at my body. It seemed like I was floating away from it. My being shrank. I felt myself pull out of my arms and legs, up into my torso, finally lodging into the back of my brain. I was a tiny ball of myself hidden somewhere deep. My arm raised slowly. My arm? Her arm?

My voice spoke out loud, but it wasn't me talking. "Finally, you admit it."

Terrified, I tried to call out, *What is going on?* But it was just in my head. Our head?

"Just because you killed the body doesn't mean we don't still share the brain." My voice came out crackled. "I was waiting for you to do it. I knew you would. You are just like our parents. Filthy, disgusting monsters. But I've always been stronger and smarter than you. You killed the body, but I still control the brain."

Cassie stood up in my body, shaking out my limbs. I desperately tried to control anything but she was right—she was stronger than me. "It's strange being able to talk," she said out loud. "I like it more than I thought I would."

What are you going to do?

"I am going to become you. The prettier one, the one our parents wanted. Then I'll kill them. Maybe I'll staple their skulls together. Remember how they hated when we did that to our toys? And the best part is, I'll still have you, stuck there in the back of our brain." She laughed. "I always said we'd never be separated."

This was seven years ago. Our parents are long dead now. She never went through with her promise to staple their heads together. Instead she used our glued-together pillow to suffocate both at once. I had to watch, completely helpless. It was my hands over their mouths, just like I had done to Cassie.

You might wonder why she let me write this. This is supposed to be my confession. One of the ways she can torment me. She allows me to control the body for minutes at a time, giving me a taste of freedom before snatching it back.

I should have known I couldn't ever get rid of her. She is a part of me. And now, I am stuck here. Forever.

I wish I had never murdered my sister. But she sure seems happy that I did.

The Pancake Family

By AA Peterson, Reddit User /u/*aapeterson*

Annual Runner Up—Best Title, 2016

That pale, huh? Jesus, I bet I look like a ghost. I feel like I've bled out two gallons.

What? No. Not a scratch.

Sorry to ramble. It's just that I'm… what's the word for it?

Detached.

Strange feeling. Seen it enough times in the field. Sort of figured if I was ever going to experience it myself then I would have experienced it by now. Hell of a thing. I feel like I'm floating outside of my body. Just cut the cord and I'd float away.

Did you see the crime scene?

Don't.

Don't look at the pictures. Don't even touch the file. You'll thank me.

I can't get my knees to stop rattling. Is that why you're holding onto your coffee like that? I'm shaking the table, aren't I? Hold on a second, let me back up my chair. There, that's better.

INTERVIEWER: We've got to go official now, Hob. Can you confirm for the record that you're waiving your right to an attorney?

No, I'm still not interested in an attorney.

I mean, yes, I'm waiving my rights.

Sorry.

And I'm as sound of mind as I'll ever be.

INTERVIEWER: Are you sure?

Yes.

INTERVIEWER: Let the record show that Detective Hobson Milgate, retired, has waived his right to an attorney.

I won't need a lawyer after the DA stops puking and considers taking it public.

They're not showing that to a jury.

INTERVIEWER: Are you ready to begin?

No, but I'll talk anyway.

INTERVIEWER: What led you to the crime scene on the night in question?

Would you believe I was planning a fishing trip before this started?

Never mind.

Hold on, I'm thinking.

Hard to organize it.

Never been on this side of the interrogation table before.

I guess it started with the reporter. Name of Bamer. She contacted me a week ago by email and claimed she had new information on the Driscoll murders. I was the lead investigator. The case had gone unsolved for twenty years. Cold as ice.

Frankly, I thought it was all bullshit at first.

You know how that can be. Most of the time it's not even on purpose. Everyone thinks they know something that will crack a case wide open. Theories are easy when you don't have to check them against evidence. The Driscoll murders were a big story around these parts. Lots of interest. Lots of press. Over the years, I must've gotten a couple hundred shit theories.

When I retired, I handed the investigation over to Detective Caroll, but I didn't want him to be bothered. I know he's busy with the recent gang activity. I figured I'd check it out as a courtesy. I wasn't expecting it to go anywhere.

I met her for lunch at Puryear's Cafe. Good-looking blond gal, professional, so she didn't fit the typical profile of a hoaxer or conspiracy theorist. Not that I put too much faith in profiles. She also might have been one of those creepy gals that gets off on death. God knows I've dealt with those, too.

I still thought she might be pulling my leg, or maybe she had been fooled too, but she had a file with her. Looked legit. It contained what appeared to be a confession by the Driscoll... well, he wasn't a murderer was he?

I really do wish he had been, you know.

It would have been so much better for everyone.

INTERVIEWER: Can you please fill us in on the relevant details of the Driscoll case?

Let's see, it would have been twenty years ago now. Thinking of all those years... I mean, twenty goddamn years. That's a long time to be...

INTERVIEWER: Take your time, Hob.

Thanks.

[Throat Clearing]

The Driscolls were a family of six out in the suburbs. Upper middle class. Father was an attorney, mother ran her own business selling pottery out of the house. Four children, all high school age and below. Good kids. Honor roll. No criminal records to speak of. The oldest son was caught smoking dope at his high school once, but nothing much besides that. Just the typical stuff you find when you look at people too closely.

They disappeared October 13th, 1994. No trace was found of the bodies. The mystery and seeing as how it was right around Halloween is probably why the press went so crazy. You still see it show up on some of those unsolved mystery shows. A whole family disappeared and no one saw a thing. No one knew where they went.

A neighbor lodged a sound complaint, which is how we got involved. There was an alarm going off and they figured it might be an intruder or something. We dispatched a vehicle. When no one answered the door, the patrolman went in to investigate.

There were obvious signs of a struggle in the youngest daughter's bedroom. The bed had been flipped over and the sheets were torn. The alarm was a carbon monoxide detector. We found elevated concentrations of carbon monoxide in the fabric of all the bedspreads except the youngest daughter's. We wouldn't have known to look without the alarm.

The neighbor indicated the alarm had been sounding for over a day, and he'd been unable to get anyone to answer the door during that time. We also found several aluminum canisters and some hoses in a dumpster a few blocks away. At the time, we assumed the Driscolls had been gassed and disposed of at a different location. Except the daughter who woke up and put up a struggle.

The investigation gave no leads.

Of course, our first thought was that the father did it. We checked it out but he didn't have motive. No leads to follow up on. Same with the mother. Surviving family checked out clean, too. The father had a few clients who might have had motive, but the means weren't there. He was a divorce lawyer, but not for anybody who could have taken out an entire family without leaving evidence. There was a chemistry teacher who lived three blocks away and we investigated him for a bit because of the canisters but he alibied out. Same with a dentist who lived nearby. The wife had an online flirtation with some kid out in England but nothing adulterous and he wasn't even in the country at the time of the murder.

We settled, unhappily, on the idea of a random killing. Hardest pieces of shit to catch when there's no pattern like that. We must have sunk tens of thousands of man hours into this case, chasing down leads. Nothing ever came of any of it.

We did track down the canisters. They were stolen from a laboratory ten miles away. There was no security footage. We couldn't find any leads on the thief. After six months with no repeat attacks the investigation went cold.

The Driscolls had been knocked out and abducted. Like I said, no one ever found the bodies. Who was to say they hadn't just run off?

Until, well, I'd rather only talk about that once.

INTERVIEWER: What can you tell us about how the confession wound up with Miss Bamer?

She'd been following the case for some years, both personally and as a reporter. Like I said, it captured the imagination of a lot of people. Even seemingly normal folks thought it could have been aliens, ghosts or demons. Miss Bamer published a retrospective on the murders given the twenty-year anniversary. It caused a renewed interest, which happened from time to time. As usual, I declined to comment citing lack of new evidence. I remembered her asking for my quote though, which is why I accepted the lunch meeting.

After publication of the article, Miss Bamer claimed that she had been sent a file. She wished to have me authenticate. The most pertinent part of the file was a confession. I assured Miss Bamer that such false documents are not uncommon, especially on older cases like this, and that I'd personally heard two dozen confessions of the Driscoll murders. She was insistent. Once I felt she wasn't trying to pull off a hoax or getting off on the idea of talking about a murder, I agreed to the meeting.

She stated the confession had been mailed to her in the same envelope she showed to me when we met for lunch.

INTERVIEWER: *Can you describe its contents?*

Old newspaper clippings outlining the progress of my investigation. They seemed appropriately yellowed, so I'd guess they were from the trophy book of the perpetrator. There were also six photos alleging to be of the individual members of the Driscoll family, as well as several other photos of the… facility where they had been taken.

Look at that.

My hands won't stop shaking, see? I'm trying as hard as I can and I just can't make it happen. I'll have to ask the paramedic for a sedative when I'm done with the statement. I don't think I'll be able to sleep otherwise.

No, I'm fine for now. I don't want anything to interfere with my recollection for your recording.

Just carrying it around in my head is like… sorry, I'll stay focused.

The photos were of the Driscoll family, of course. At the time I didn't know that. The photos had aged poorly and they could have been of anyone. It was very hard to distinguish features. However, given the elaborate nature of the file I figured it did warrant a further look.

As to the confession letter, well, it was brief. It gave an address. That's the first thing I noticed. I couldn't locate the address online, which meant it had to be old. The confession letter said, 'Stop printing lies. I never killed anyone. It just took a while to get them ready for breakfast.' There was no signature.

I just remembered something.

God dammit.

We got sent a breakfast menu a month after the disappearance! Someone had drawn a red circle around a picture of pancakes. The letter said 'They're not dead, they're getting ready for breakfast!' We put it in the junk lead file.

Oh God.

INTERVIEW: Detective Milgate, do you need a moment?

Oh God.

I… how could I have known?

We tried to track down that menu. We could never find out where it had come from. It wasn't any place local. The identifying information had been cut out.

I don't know what else we could have done.

I just… dear God.

INTERVIEWER: Why did you decide to personally investigate the location mentioned in the letter?

Sorry.

I wanted to make sure it wasn't a hoax. Part of me still wasn't convinced. I've had twenty years of people sending me fake evidence. I guess maybe the case captured my imagination, too. I always figured one day I'd think of something I'd overlooked and solve the whole thing. Felt unbelievable to have someone dump the answer in my lap. I needed to see with my own two eyes.

Miss Bamer had pinpointed the location with city records, but neither of us was sure if it was still there. It was an abandoned industrial building. The last time it had a valid mailing address was fifty years ago. It might have caved in for all we knew.

I think I also wanted to be the one to crack it. Whether or not it was dumped in my lap. That case has hung over my head for twenty years.

Miss Bamer and I agreed to meet there the following morning.

INTERVIEWER: Can you describe the crime scene?

Yes.

It was an industrial building, as I stated. Approximately one hundred twenty feet long by maybe forty-five feet wide. It was a wooden structure and at first the condition seemed to match the neighboring buildings, however I noticed the facade had been recently patched in a few locations. Further investigation also revealed that the entrance had been chained and locked. My understanding was that it used to be a sheet metal shop. At least... excuse me, is there a garbage can?

I might vomit.

Thank you.

We—

[Gagging]

Sorry.

I thought I was empty.

No, I want to get this done with. Then I'm going to want that sedative.

I could smell something from inside the building. Very faintly. I figured that would count as probable cause, not that I need it as a civilian, but you never forget the way a corpse smells.

They were... bad enough they had that same smell.

I hadn't forgotten how to pick a lock, so I let myself inside.

You know, I really do wish they had been corpses. I really do wish he had been a serial killer. I really do.

Please say you believe me.

INTERVIEWER: I do. Can you describe the interior of the building?

I'm trying to focus through this. I really am. I'm sorry, it's just that I'd like to go to sleep after this for a very long time.

Is the paramedic here? Is the sedative ready?

Thank goodness.

The warehouse had not been as abandoned as we were previously led to believe. The interior had a hallway with six rooms. The construction was old but visibly newer than the rest of the building. The walls between each room had been soundproofed. There were no windows to the outside or doorways between the rooms themselves. The only access was through the hallway.

I tried to make Miss Bamer leave at that point.

You see... the smell was stronger inside.

You could feel it. The smell. Like a grit getting stuck in your nose. Like bits of sand all over your skin.

The rooms, uh, the rooms contained presses. Hydraulic presses. Four foot by eight foot custom presses. I couldn't figure out what they were at first, because they were hovering over what looked like hospital beds. There were IV bags in each room as well as other medical equipment.

That's how he kept them alive for so long, of course.

I think I might be seeing black spots.

INTERVIEWER: *Do you need to take a break?*

The idea of having to start this again is worse than the idea of finishing it.

INTERVIEWER: *Then please describe your next course of action.*

The building was obviously an active crime scene. I had no doubt at this point. I was in the lair of what I believed to be a serial killer.

I tried to tell Miss Bamer to leave several times. She refused on the grounds that it would not be right to leave me on my own. There wasn't much time to make an issue out of it. My opinion of her was that she was a bit nosy but basically alright and I didn't think she'd be a liability if she stayed out of my way. I had to make a judgment call as to whether or not I should proceed on my own in case the family was somehow, impossibly, still alive and perhaps in danger or if I should leave and call for backup.

I had told my wife where I was going previously so I knew my absence would be noted and reported if the worst happened. Neither of us could get cellphone reception.

Sorry, I'm rambling.

It was then that I heard... not even a gasp. It was like a gasp, but not really. I don't want to describe it any more than that.

There was a sound. It drew my attention further on. I had to act. That's all the matters.

There were some stairs at the very far end of the warehouse descending into a basement. I told Miss Bamer to remain behind and pulled my service revolver. I had a flashlight on my person as well, and turned it on as I descended into the basement.

The basement had been hand dug. Maybe even over the course of the entire twenty-year disappearance. I don't know. The floor was dirt and there was a tunnel that retreated back far enough that it had to be supported with struts at regular intervals. When my flashlight first illuminated the... stack...

I wish they'd been dead.

I wish he'd been a serial killer.

INTERVIEWER: Please take a moment.

After I... after I recovered my first thought was 'Thank God, they are all dead.'

[Gagging]

I'm sixty-four years old for Christ's sake. I'm not a young man who can forget things anymore. When you're young you have this sense that you're invincible and that you're never going to die. I don't have that to protect me anymore.

Look at me whining, when they had that done to them.

It's my fault. I should have found them. Saved them, somehow.

INTERVIEWER: I'm sorry, Hob, I've got to ask. Can you describe the scene?

Yeah—

[Gagging]

I can.

I didn't know what I was looking at, at first. Hell, I still don't. It was... well, it was a stack. Maybe two feet thick. From the stink and coloring it was obviously made of flesh. I thought maybe he'd hacked them up and stacked them up in pieces. That would have been bad enough. The first thing that alerted me to the truth was the eyeball. On the top of the stack was a perfectly round eyeball in the middle of a socket that had been distorted to the size of a saucer. That's when I realized what I was looking at was...

Twenty goddamn years of torture, basically.

He had the entire Driscoll family under those presses for twenty years, keeping them alive on an IV drip, increasing the pressure on them so very slowly that their bodies had time to adapt, until they'd been flatted like... well, like pancakes. He squished them by about a quarter inch every year for twenty years. Then he'd pulled them out when they were too broken and wretched to move, without any chance of recovery and stacked them on top of each other. I've got no idea what for. I don't want to know.

And I was still thinking 'Thank God they're all dead' when the one on top started gasping again.

INTERVIEWER: *What did they say?*

Nothing at first. It couldn't speak without help. I think... it would have been Avery Driscoll. Not that I could tell much about the gender or the age. But the hair was blond where there was hair. The head was a mess of scars. I think the son of a bitch who did this must have removed parts of their skulls. I've got no idea how he got their heads so flat, otherwise. Not as flat as the rest of the bodies but flat. Who the hell knows how their brains handled that. Their lips were punctured by teeth everywhere, after the presses had flattened out their noses, I guess.

Avery was fourteen when he disappeared.

I've stopped shaking.

Goddamn weird the way our bodies work, isn't it?

What else?

There was a machine. A sort of pump. I followed a hose with my flashlight and realized everyone in the stack was hooked up to the pump. I don't think they could breathe on their own, you see. Not after a while. There simply wasn't enough volume for their lungs to inflate. There was some sort of opening cut right into each of their chests. There was a switch on the pump. I don't know why I pressed it. I was in a panic. I wanted to do something. Maybe some stupid part of me thought that if I switched it on they would inflate and be okay.

I switched it. It increased the volume of air to the topmost hose. I could hear the pump working harder.

Which is when Avery Driscoll started to scream.

He begged me to kill him. He said other things too. He didn't make much sense. Kept yelling 'Bane of Error' over and over again. Something about 'the Family' too. Didn't understand it. He was in pain and I would hope he had gone insane several years previously.

INTERVIEWER: Oh my God.

My thoughts exactly.

I didn't know what to do. He wouldn't stop screaming. I believe he was convinced I was his torturer. A closer look at his eye revealed that it was mostly a mess of white scar tissue. He was as blind as a bat.

You know, I spoke with some burn victims once. They told me that they managed to find meaning and purpose again after a while. I don't know how anyone in the Driscoll family could have done that.

I stated my name. I told him I was a detective. I told him I was there to help. I repeated it over and over again, knowing of course there was nothing that anyone anywhere could do to help.

Miss Bamer arrived, drawn by the sound. Before she saw the stack she told me that I had screamed and she had come to help, but I do not remember having done so. Nevertheless she arrived. Then she saw the stack and screamed but I was intent on Avery Driscoll. He was able to hear. He became lucid for a few moments. It was a strain to understand what he said, but I will never be able to forget it.

"Please kill me. It hurts. I don't want to be a monster. Please kill me and tell my family I died a long time ago. I don't know if they're still looking for me. Don't let them know what happened to me. Please kill me."

He could still cry and he did, although his tear ducts were too deformed for it to be noticeable.

I should have forced Miss Bamer to leave. That is the only action in the matter which I regret more than failing to solve the case twenty years ago. Not just for her own sake, but for what she did next. I don't think she could have wounded them anymore deeply if she'd tried. She took away the last comfort any of them in that stack had.

You see, they had not been able to speak to one another for twenty years.

She said, "That's all of them isn't it? That's the entire Driscoll family. They're all alive in there. The whole family."

For twenty years, each member of the Driscoll family had been unaware their fellow inmates were the other members of their family. They'd all been holding out hope their family was okay. All of them dreaming someone out there loved them and was free from suffering.

Do you know what the screams of six people tortured over two decades, smashed down to a width of four inches, sounds like when they're all stacked on top of one another?

It sounds like the gates of Hell swinging open.

INTERVIEWER: *I think that is enough, Detective Milgate.*

Not yet.

It was my mistake. I should have tried harder. Tracked down that lead. Maybe that's what they meant, screaming that. It was my error so it was my responsibility.

I shot them. Mercy is hard, but I owed it to them. I am the one that failed to save them.

It only took one bullet to go all the way through. I emptied my revolver, though. To make sure they didn't linger. To give them that final peace.

It was the only kindness I had to give them.

We left and called for backup after that. Neither Miss Bamer nor I wished to remain with the bodies. I elected not to follow the crime scene investigators back into the basement. I asked if I could make my statement and leave and after one of them saw what I had seen they agreed.

May I have my sedative now?

INTERVIEWER: *Yes… yes, of course.*

Thank you.

Please show in the paramedic. I'll roll up my sleeve. My wife has diabetes so I'm well aware of the routine. Oh, and please make sure you have the same courtesy available for Miss Bamer. She seemed to have it worse than me, after. Poor woman couldn't even throw up or cry.

INTERVIEWER: *Of course. Do you know where she is now? She told the lead at the crime scene she was going home but we haven't been able to reach her.*

Did you try the paper?

INTERVIEWER: *Which paper?*

The *Daily World*.

INTERVIEWER: *Are you sure? There is no one by the last name of Bamer on staff with the Daily World.*

About The Authors

K. Oresnik, Reddit User /u/_TheLovelyFreja_

K. Oresnik is a perfectly average woman with an intense interest in the paranormal. She lives with her husband as well as her dog, Freja, and cat, Leto. She has a strong interest in charity, especially those whose primary focuses are on human rights.

Henry Galley, Reddit User /u/_DoubleDoorBastard_

Henry Galley was born in the sleepy town of March, Cambridgeshire, where he attended primary and secondary school. He's loved telling stories for as long as he could remember, and found only a few years ago that he seemed to have a knack for horror. He's always wanted to be able to tell his stories professionally. He currently studies Psychology at the University of East Anglia in Norwich, UK. He spends the weekends with his family.

Jared Roberts, Reddit User /u/_nazisharks_

Jared Roberts is a Canadian man who lives in Oklahoma with his wife. He's just a normal guy who likes being creepy, big boobs, and horror movies. He tried combining these interests as a stockbroker, but it didn't pan out. So he took to writing.

Links: Come visit me on Goodreads https://www.goodreads.com/author/show/6242909.Jared_Roberts.

Marshall Banana, Reddit User /u/*demons_dance_alone*

Marshall Banana has been writing from an early age. Favorite authors are H.P Lovecraft, Joe Hill, and Kim Newman. Lurks around nosleep on the weekends, mostly.

Visit https://www.amazon.com/Carol-Stories-Marshall-Banana-ebook/dp/B01MYBI14Q/ref=tmm_kin_swatch_0?_encoding=UTF8&qid=1490548959&sr=1-1 to read more of Marshall's work.

M.J. Pack, Reddit User /u/*mjpack*

M.J. Pack, a horror fiction writer, has been obsessed with all things scary since she was a little girl growing up in the Midwest. She spends her days producing creepy content for the horror-loving masses, from short fiction to serials to true crime coverage. Pack is the author of "Certain Dark Things," "Ravenous: Small Stories With Big Appetites," and "Highville State Asylum."

Visit Facebook (http://facebook.com/MJPackAuthor), Twitter (http://twitter.com/megslice), Website (http://themjpack.com) for more information about M.J. Pack.

Howard Moxley, Reddit User /u/*IamHowardMoxley*

Howard Moxley is an independent government inspector and unpublished poet. Much of his professional work has been translated into the arena known as the The Secret Expo. He shamefully holds a degree of statistical finance with distinction and has worked with Federal bodies and private parties to create solutions to disastrous problems. Moxley has been rumored to donate wealth under anonymous names and to be a collector of artifacts. He cannot substantiate either.

Visit https://www.reddit.com/r/TheSecretExpo/ for more information about Moxley.

Felix Blackwell, Reddit User /u/*Blue_Keycard*

Felix Blackwell emerged from the bowels of reddit during a botched summoning ritual. He is best known for his popular short horror series colloquially referred to as "Romantic Cabin Getaway," for which he won the NoSleep writing contest. He writes novels and short stories in the horror, thriller, and fantasy genres.

Visit www.felixblackwell.com or www.facebook.com/felixblackwellbooks to get to know Felix. He also posts stories under his other user name: /u/ thecoldpeople.

Paul Ross, Reddit User /u/*pross40745*

Paul posts stories on Reddit under the /u/pross40745 handle.

Harrison Prince, Reddit User /u/*Zandsand90*

Harrison is just another 24 year old married guy who writes for fun. He enjoys bands such as Brand X Music, Audiomachine, and Two Steps From Hell because they give him inspiration for scenes to write. Also, Harrison is the one writing this, so he isn't sure why he is referring to himself in the third person. Yikes.

/r/HarrisonPrince and Twitter @harrison3790 and YouTube Harrison Prince.

S.H. Cooper, Reddit User /u/*Pippinacious*

An aspiring author with a penchant for horror, S.H. Cooper began publicizing her works on Reddit's NoSleep community before publishing her first book, a collection of short horror stories, through Amazon in December 2016. In addition to writing, she is an avid PC gamer, reader, and crazy-dog-lady-in-training.

* * *

pippinacious.tumblr.com, https://facebook.com/authorshcooper, https://www.amazon.com/Corpse-Garden-Collection-Horror-Stories/dp/1520186509.

Melanie Camus, Reddit User /u/*chewingskin*

Melanie Camus was raised in a rural area on the eastern side of Cape Breton, Nova Scotia. While most of her stories revolve around this area being the focal point of nightmares, she lives a relatively quiet life as a self-proclaimed hermit with close friends to keep her company. The love of her life continues to be animals, but with horror coming in as a close second, she hopes to devote her life to one of the two aspects.

Leonard Petracci, Reddit User /u/*LeoDuhVinci*

Leonard Petracci is a recent graduate of Georgia Institute of Technology currently living in the Northeast United States. In his spare time you can find him hiking, at the beach, or generally enjoying the outdoors. Leonard is working on three series which can be found on his blog or Amazon. The first book of each of these are: In Horror, Eden's Eye. In Fantasy, Life Magic. In Science Fiction, The Bridge. To contact him, reach out to LeonardPetracci@gmail.com.

If you enjoy his work, the best way to compliment him is to share it.

* * *

Visit Facebook.com/leoduhvinci or http://Leonardpetracci.com

Leo's Free Ebook of 12 Terrifying Stories: https://www.amazon.com/Tales-Sinister-Twelve-Terrifying-Stories-ebook/dp/B01MS26HGK.

J. Laughlin, Reddit User /u/*Jaksim*

J. Laughlin is a horror writer from the midwest. For Mr. Laughlin, writing horror is a process with two main steps - finding a way to scare the reader and finding a way to make them think. As a result, Mr. Laughlin's stories often deal with difficult questions and situations that make one question what they believe. He finds himself in a niche genre of "sad-horror". When not writing, he enjoys studying, public speaking, and listening to podcasts.

Visit https://www.facebook.com/Jlaughlinhorror for more information about J. Laughlin.

Caitlin Spice, Reddit User /u/*Cymoril Melnibone*

Caitlin Spice is a Wellingtonian author with a complicated relationship with writing. Primarily a short story enthusiast, she has some 300+ original works posted online on various Reddit writing forums, but has also recently published a collection of thematic works in a book titled 'The Silver Path', which also features artwork from some talented local and international artists.

Visit https://www.reddit.com/r/HallowdineLibrary/ or https://

www.facebook.com/CMScandreth/ for more information about Caitlin.

Scott Wilson, Reddit User /u/*IEscapedFromALab*

Scott Wilson is a Floridian who lives in West Palm Beach. He is an amateur historian in the area and spends much of his free time looking for historical artifacts in the greater South Florida area.

Visit https://scottwilsonsemail.wixsite.com/mysite.

SnollyGolly, Reddit User /u/*sharpermatt*

SnollyGolly is a writer who pushes the boundaries of genres and is never limited to a single platform.

If you enjoyed his story, you can dive deeper down his rabbit hole by visiting this post: evilmousestudios.com/immersive-horror-through-web-technologies/.

Tristan Lince, Reddit User /u/*Discord and Dine*

* * *

I live in Washington state and I'm in the 11th grade. I'm heavily involved in his school's drama department and love writing stories for Nosleep every once in a while between rehearsals.

Katie Irvin Leute, Reddit User /u/*shortCakeSlayer*

Katie is a yoga and dance instructor, studio owner, metal smith and designer. She's spent her life on the lookout for magic amulets, childlike empresses, acorns that turn things to stone, puppy-faced luck dragons, haunted swords, iocane powder, and enchanted roses under every bell jar. While looking for real magic in the world, she makes things that could be magic with her own hands and some respectfully borrowed stardust.

Her work can be seen at alchemieadornment.com.

Thaddeus James, Reddit User /u/*hartijay*

Thaddeus James is a writer and entertainer whose stories mostly include various props, soundclips, and videos in an attempt to make them more immersive.

Visit www.technohorror.com for more information about Thaddeus.

Lily T., Reddit User /u/*draegunfly*

I live in a little house, on a little farm, on top a quiet mountain. Since childhood, I've enjoyed attempting to scare people with stories of my inner demons and dreams.

E.Z. Morgan, Reddit User /u/*EZmisery*

E.Z. Morgan (EZmisery) looks like an adorable librarian but writes stories that will keep you up at night. She likes the sound of cracking knuckles and rain. She gets 8+ hours of sleep a night. Her writing has been shared on numerous podcasts, online forums, and probably some horror-themed knitting circles. Don't tell her to smile. She lives in a snow-filled wasteland with her two cat daughters, one dog son, and The Boy.

Visit www.facebook.com/EZmisery, http://ezmisery.tumblr.com/, https://www.reddit.com/r/EZmisery/, https://twitter.com/EZmisery.

AA Peterson, Reddit User /u/*aapeterson*

AA Peterson is some guy who lives in Idaho.

* * *

Visit aapeterson.com or Facebook.com/TheDorkKnightReturns for more information about AA Peterson.

23515058R00432

Printed in Poland
by Amazon Fulfillment
Poland Sp. z o.o., Wrocław